Good luck, Gotham Games!

Kurt Sanderfeld

Bottom Dog Press

Jack's Memoirs

Off the Road

A Novel

by Kurt Landefeld

"Myths are made for the imagination
to put life into them."
-Albert Camus

Harmony Fiction Series
Bottom Dog Press
Huron, Ohio

978-1-933964-91-1

Bottom Dog Press, Inc.
P.O. Box 425 /Huron, Ohio 44839
http://smithdocs.net

Credits:
General Editor: Larry Smith
Cover Design: Susanna Sharp-Schwacke
Cover Art: Loren Kantor

Acknowledgments:

Many people helped make this book possible. I met Jack Kerouac formally in the middle '70s at Bucknell University when we read *On the Road*. Then in an American poetry class I discovered Charles Olson and the extraordinary cast of characters who built Black Mountain College. For that I have my professors Dennis Baumwoll and Jack Wheatcroft to thank. Part of my writing experience I've shared with Vanita Oelschlager and Jamie Barlow. I thank both of them for inspiration and patience.

I shared progress with an extraordinary group of writers at the Firelands Writing Center. Their feedback was helpful and supportive. In particular, I'd like to thank Dr. Joel Rudinger, Nancy Dunham and Patrick O'Keeffe for their close reading of the first draft. There are a few friends who've traveled many stretches of miles with me. They are David Alquist, Peter Balakian, Stu Cubbon, Steve Hartwell, and Laura Yanne.

Finally, I'd like to thank my publisher Larry Smith for his vision and his editing skills and the crew of Susanna Sharp-Schwacke and Devlin Geroski for their support.

* * * * *

This book is dedicated to my wife, Carol, without whose love and support even contemplating this journey would not have been possible.

A Prologue for Off The Road

January 1, 2002

These are words from an old man. A really beat old man. Many of you will think they're written by someone else—a much younger man. Because that's how you remember me. Or want to remember.

Some of you will remember me as I was when last I made the headlines. Dying in 1970. 48 years old. Alcoholic. Broken. Angry. And rejecting the same young generation that loved me for what I wrote when I was their age.

All that's true. Except the dying part. I needed to get away. Do something to shake off all the crap of being me. So I died. Or so I made everyone think. Everyone except Memere and Stella and Allen. Had to let them in on it. Now they're all dead too.

They were kind of sore I did it this way. Eventually they understood. But they knew then that, even though I didn't die, I was going away. I had to go away. For a long time. So it was almost as though I really did die.

It was the last time I saw them, Memere and Stella, there in St. Pete. Well, almost the last time. I slipped back in to see them about a year before Memere died. That was 1973. But I missed Stella's dying in 1990 and I'm sorry about that.

I saw Allen twice. Once in 1975. He came down to Mexico where I was living at the time. We did a lot of talking. A LOT. Of course Neal was dead. Froze to death in Mexico in '68. And I was too. Kind of. So all that San Francisco stuff had kind of fallen to Allen.

The other time I saw him he was performing in Cleveland with Phil Glass. I think it was

1991. He didn't know I was there. I happened to be passing through on another of my trips across the country. Saw they were doing something at this auditorium east of downtown. I snuck in the back right before they started.

Allen looked old. But so was I. Almost 70. I left before the lights came up. Maybe I should've stayed. But it would've caused too much commotion. The last thing I wanted then was commotion.

Now I'm 80. It's time to get it all out. Put everything down I can still remember. I didn't stop writing in 1969. But I had to do it under another name. Now I want to bury that name and tell you what's been going on the last thirty-three years.

I had a daughter, Jan. She's dead too. Would've been fifty now. I only saw her a couple of times. We hardly spoke. But what could I have said to her? I was an awful dad. Just awful. She had to hurt all over. I didn't do a damn thing for her. Joan, her mom, had to chase me for years just to get some support. Now Joan's dead too.

It's been a hell of a life. Everyone's dead. Well, almost everyone. Maybe I should've come back twenty years ago when lots of us were still around. But I wasn't ready. I liked it quiet. Liked it under-ground. Still do.

Chances are by the time this gets out, I'll really be gone. And I won't have to worry about people hounding me for interviews and those speeches and those damned explanations about everything we did and why we did it.

So why write this now?

Because I still have things on my mind. I've been to hell and back. Seen a lot of beautiful things too. So I want to leave that for anyone who's still interested in old Jack Kerouac. Old, beat up Jack Kerouac.

But do not, I repeat, do *not* think I'm giving you the history of the Beat Generation or anything like that. That's one of the things I hated. People falling over me because they thought I invented the Beat Generation. Or that I *was* the Beat Generation. It was all crap. Just crap.

It was good it all ended for the first Jack Kerouac in St. Petersburg. Saint Pete for the Beat Saint. And, man, I *was* beat. But I was no saint, that's for sure. I'm just a writer. That's all I ever wanted to be. Looking for *satori*. Trying to find my truth. I didn't want to be a spokesman for anything or anybody. I just wanted to walk my path.

So that's what I'm writing down now. My truth. My path.

Fortunately, it's not just memories coming out of my head. As I just said, I've been writing all this time. I have my journals, my notes. And you'll read some of them here.

I also have some things to say about my times with Neal Cassady and Allen Ginsberg. And also about some of the others you've heard about: Greg Corso, Gary Snyder, Lawrence Ferlinghetti, Robert Creeley, Robert Duncan, Charles Olson. And the others too. Jo. Lissa. Anne. God bless them, too.

So that's about it. Just stay with me. Remember I'm an old man. But don't think of me as I was. Don't idolize me or the guys of my time.

Try to see my path.
Try to see theirs.
Then make your own.

Chapter 1 — Visions of Gerard Redux

1969 sucked. There's just no other way to put it. Still, I guess it's the only place to start.

Anybody who'd seen me those last few years knew I was a slow-moving train wreck just waiting to happen. It was all Stella and Memere could do just to keep me going, keep me alive. Besides, the question you probably have on your mind is "What happened?" As in, what in the hell happened to me when I decided to "die," then disappear? Fair enough. Here's what happened...

In the spring of 1970, I "died" in St. Petersburg, according to the newspapers, with Stella and Memere at my side. In truth, I almost died the fall before. I drank way too much back then. Had for years and years and years. Almost drank myself to death.

To tell you the truth, I think that's what I wanted to do. Go off and die in the desert like Neal. Except I never made it that far. Why? Who knows?

Well, I *do* know. And that's a big reason why I'm writing this now. Because there were things going on then that I wanted to get away from. Things from a long time ago. Things that wouldn't let go.

But you know what? That getting away from it all—it's all cliché. Bullshit. I was running from myself. Deep down I knew it. Even if I didn't say anything to anybody. Snyder knows this about me better than anybody. And Gerard, my lost older brother.

I was running away from my failures. As a husband, a father, a son, a friend. I could never settle down and live a normal life. I was always on the move. Especially from all those who saw me as something special and my not wanting to be anything special. All I ever wanted to be was a writer. A seeker. Just trying to get at the truth.

So when I had that attack in St. Petersburg October of '69, it was bad. Real bad. Blood everywhere. Because I was rotting out my insides from all that cheap wine. Pills too. Uppers. Downers. What have you.

And I can remember thinking at the time, *OK, here it comes. Here it comes. That last mile. That last mile...to where? Heaven? Nirvana? Face-to-face with God? My...Siddhartha?*

I stared into that goddamn bloody toilet bowl and I...didn't have a clue. I was scared shitless. I just wanted to curl up and close my eyes and never open them again. But Stella found me and called the ambulance and they got me to the hospital. Just in time, according to my doc. If I'd lost much more blood, there would've been nothing they could've done for me. Still, I was there for almost a month. Not just to fix the hemorrhaging. The booze too. Doc said he wouldn't do anything for me if I didn't give up the booze.

To be honest, I don't know what was harder. Getting my insides healed up? Or getting the booze out of my body? Sometimes I shook so bad and wanted a drink so bad, I cursed Stella for even bringing me there. But she came every day to see me. *Every day.*

Once in a while Stella would bring Memere too. But it was hard for her to come. Not only because of her own health. But because she'd already buried one child almost 40 years before, my brother Gerard. And another, my sister Nin, just a few years before I almost checked out for good. A husband too. Now she might have to bury her last one.

How does a mother face Death taking her family away that many times? Losing one child to a disease that comes out of nowhere, or a husband broken down by life itself? Or a daughter to a broken heart? Or losing her man-child because of all the dumbshit things he's done chasing people and things even he's not sure about.

I felt pretty bad about all that. So I tried to get better so she'd feel better. But it took a while. And it sure as hell wasn't easy. On me. Or her. Or Stella.

One night Gerard came to visit too.

I was feeling pretty low. I wanted a drink. My insides still felt like someone had stuck a pitchfork in them and left it there. I tried to sleep. But I couldn't. And I couldn't move around. Why hadn't Stella just left me there at the house curled around the toilet and let this godforsaken mess of a life I'd lived just seep away? I cried silent, unholy tears.

Then I opened my eyes. Gerard was sitting on the bed looking at me. I guess I should've been surprised to see him, but I wasn't. He still looked like the boy I remembered when he died. But he spoke to me like he was the man and I was the child. Always the older brother.

I wrote what happened that night.

October 31, 1969
Visions of Gerard Redux

"Ti Jean...Ti Jean, why are you here?"

He asked the question just dripping with disappointment. Over and over.

He looked at me with his big dark eyes searching mine for an answer. He uses my childhood name which made me feel even smaller than I was.

"I don't know, Gerard. Stella decided my life was worth saving. Otherwise I might be looking for you." We talked like we hadn't missed a beat since 1922 when he died and I stared at his lifeless little body and I lost any sense of God's mercy.

"Ti Jean, you give up too easily. You always did. Papa and Memere could never understand. You were given lots, Ti Jean. You had the brains. The looks. The way with people. But you get into a little trouble, then you run away. You ran away from your studies. You ran away from your football. Then...you ran away from

everything. And you broke Papa's heart. Memere's too, Ti Jean.

"Look here at me, Ti Jean. Yes, I was oldest. But then the fever came and...Poof! I was gone. I never had a chance to do anything. Even Sammy got a chance to fight before he died."

I stared at him and different tears came to my eyes.

He was right. How could I argue with him here and now? How could I explain all the things I'd done? But had I really run away? Look at all the books I'd written. Look at the poetry. Look at how people loved me.

"Gerard, I wish you hadn't died. You would've really been something."

"But I did, Ti Jean. And there's nothing I can do about it. But you, Ti Jean, you can still do something. I think maybe Death is a little afraid of you, Ti Jean. Like you are a holy or something. How you got across all those miles and in all those towns with all those people—some of them weren't very nice, Ti Jean—how you got there and didn't get sick or killed... that is really something.

"You've gone places and seen things and written about a lot of them. And now? Now what? You want to run away again? Run away one last time? To where, Ti Jean? Where do you want to go?"

"Can't I go with you, Gerard? Can't I go with you now? Memere would be sad. And Stella. But they would get over it. Then you could come for them and we can all be together again."

"Yes, of course, Ti Jean. You can come with me. You can come right now. But you are being given a second chance. Isn't there more you want to do? Isn't there more you want to write?

"I tell you, Ti Jean, I would trade places with you right now. Because I never had one chance to test my gifts. I never had one chance to feel the love of a woman. Or climb a mountain. Or even cross a river,

let alone an ocean. My path was short and brutal, Ti Jean. Yours could be much longer."

He stared at me with something like anger and sadness mixed. I just stared back. What could I say?

"If you really want to go, then I'll come back for you. But Ti Jean, be sure. Because you still can choose. That, too, is a gift."

"Gerard, Gerard! It's so hard. Help me, Gerard. Help me."

I closed my eyes and sobbed into the night. When I opened them again, Gerard was gone. Sad black night was giving way to sad gray dawn.

Had he really been there? Yeah, I think he was. I'd seen him before, years and years ago when I wasn't so sick yet I missed him just as much.

When they visited later that day I never told Stella or Memere about Gerard. It was something I had to think about. Something had changed. My guts still hurt like hell. But when I looked at my journal, I could see my writing looked better. Stella said I smiled for the first time in months.

Chapter 2 — Salvation

When I got out of the hospital, I went back to the house. To what, I wasn't sure. But I hadn't asked Gerard to come get me. Not yet.

The day I left, the night shift nurse who'd been taking care of me came in to say goodbye. I'd been sleeping a lot better the last week so I hadn't seen her much.

She was about my age, maybe a little younger. She struck me as one of those women born to nursing. Quick. Efficient. Probably knew a helluva lot more about taking care of people than the docs she worked for. She was pretty too. Brown hair and eyes. Trim. All business. Probably used to having men patients fall in love with her and having none of that. Didn't wear a ring though. That made me wonder.

She also had a good from-the-heart smile. Nothing like the nurse in Ken Kesey's book. She was the real deal. On her badge was "Amanda Hauser, Registered Nurse." I believed every word.

The morning she came in, I was hungry. Thought maybe I was getting an early breakfast. I was sitting up making some idle notes and thinking about getting out of there at last. She had a paperback book with her clipboard. Break time reading, I guessed.

"Good morning, Mr. Kerouac. Nice to see you awake. I understand you are leaving us today."

She had that native Florida accent. Not quite full southern, like their South Carolina, Georgia, and Alabama neighbors. But soft nonetheless. A pleasure to listen to.

"Yes, I am. Doc says there's nothing more he can do for me here."

"I'm sure he's right. You know we almost lost you. Doctor Sam said you were lucky to make it."

"Yes, I was lucky I guess. Have my wife to thank for that. And Doctor Sam. And you, Nurse Hauser," I said smiling a bit. "I feel a lot better now."

"Well, I'm happy to hear that. You're too young and good-lookin' a man to let that Devil Alcohol take you away."

I thought I was going to get another lecture about the booze. Everyone'd been talking to me about that. Made me mad at first. I hated when people would go holy-roller on me and try to tell me about all the evils of alcohol as though I wasn't already quite familiar with them. Else why'd I be there? Then I kinda got used to it. I'd make up my own mind when I got out.

She looked over her shoulder and took a step closer. When she looked back, her eyes had softened and her lips turned up into a small smile. It was genuine and warm and nervous. "Mr. Kerouac, why didn't you tell us you were a famous writer?"

She fiddled with the book. It was a copy of *On the Road*. I waited. Then it all came spilling out.

"My son, he's taking classes over at the university. And he had this book lying on the sofa. I picked it up and there you were! I said, 'James, I think he's one of my patients!' And his eyes got real big. He said, 'Mom, are you sure?' And I said yes. And he said you are one of his biggest heroes. He said he didn't know you were still alive. But he wants to do what you wrote about in this book. Travel all over the country and see and do all kinds of things."

She caught her breath, then asked the question that mothers worried about their babies all over the country have asked me at book signings and what have you, "Do you think he should do that, Mister Kerouac?"

I could hear in her voice wonder and admiration and ignorance and anxiety all rolled into one. A month ago I would've gotten pissed. I would've hated being asked the kind of Dear Abby question I had no answer to anymore.

Instead, I said, "It's a big, big country, Amanda. I've seen a lot of it. But I haven't seen all of it. There's a lot of beauty out there. Lot of ugliness too. I don't know what to tell your boy. I just tried to tell what happened to me. He's got to make up his own mind."

I thought that would maybe end it. But she went on, almost as though she was talking to him instead of me.

"I just want him to stay in school and get his education. Stay in school and stay away from that Vietnam. If he quits his school and goes wanderin' all over and gettin' into God knows what kind of trouble, the Army'll find him and send him to war for sure."

I didn't want to get in a political discussion right then.

"Well, make sure he keeps his grades up then. I got started and never finished. Maybe things would've been different if I had. But maybe I wouldn't have become a writer either. And then we wouldn't be talking about any of this, now would we?" I smiled as I said that. She smiled back, still uncertain.

"Mr. Kerouac, I have to check the rest of my patients before I get off. But, could I ask you for a favor?"

I really didn't want to, but what choice did I have? "Of course."

She thrust the book at me.

"Could you maybe write something for James? Something that would maybe make him think twice before he gets all googoo-eyed about hitchhiking to California and what not?"

I took the book. It was used, second edition Penguin. I looked at the photo of me staring back. I didn't want to write anything. This had happened so many times before. People wanting me to write something. Something *for them*. Like I was the goddamned Oracle at Delphi or something. What could I say to someone I didn't know, wouldn't ever know, and maybe wouldn't care to ever know?

I looked at Amanda, hoping I could maybe just wait her out and she'd have to grab the book back and finish her rounds and then she'd be gone. And I'd be gone. But she looked back at me with all her reserve melted. Now she was just another mother. Scared that her son was going to do her what I'd done to Memere. Or worse and get drafted into that craziness overseas.

I opened the book to the end of Chapter 11 in Part 1. And I scribbled, "To James, if you get to this place, get there your own way. Don't go because I went. Don't go expecting to see what I saw. That's gone. Make your own path. Then tell others what you've seen. Maybe that will make a difference. Jack."

I handed the book back. Amanda read what I wrote. I could see she was trying to understand. A tear started in her right eye and stopped.

She leaned and placed a kiss on my forehead.

"Thank you, Mr. Kerouac. Thank you. And God bless you."

Then she was gone.

Chapter 3 — Home

So Stella came and took me home. Funny calling that place "home." It's where we lived. But it wasn't home. Not really. Lowell was home. But we didn't live there anymore.

After I left Lowell for New York and Columbia, it seemed like I never had a place I really called home. I stayed lots of places. Wrote my books in lots of places. This last twenty years it's been a little place here in Frisco. After Lowell, I've loved San Francisco most of all. So maybe, finally, this *is* home.

But in 1969 home was St. Pete. We were there because of Memere. Eastern winters were too cold for her anymore. After her stroke, she couldn't get around easily. So I understood. Still, I could feel it almost as soon as we walked in the door. The itch. That damn itch to get on the road. A sure sign that I was feeling better. Of course I couldn't say anything about it. At least not right away.

Stella wanted to hover. Memere too. Make sure I was all right. Both said I looked better than I had in years. That was probably true. I could see in the bathroom mirror that my face wasn't bloated. Eyes weren't bloodshot. I did feel better.

I didn't even have to ask to know they'd gotten rid of all the booze. I was even smart enough not to ask. And truth to tell, I didn't feel the pull as badly as I expected to. Maybe I had really dried out in the hospital.

Of course, the doc had given me the scared-straight talk. Told me if I got into the booze again, my insides would rip up and then maybe there'd be no saving me. I half believed him too. Stella had been there when he said all that. Held my hand. But she didn't say anything, for which I was grateful.

It took me about a week, maybe ten days, but I got the stir-crazies bad enough I had to get out. Told Stella and Memere I was going for a drive. I remember seeing the fear in their eyes, but I didn't care. I had to get out. It was Thanksgiving weekend.

I told them I'd be back. I know they didn't believe me. Or thought I'd come back drunk as a skunk. They were afraid that all the care and cure would all come to ruin in a few hours or a few days. They'd seen it before.

Before I landed in the hospital I just sat around. I would watch TV. Listen to records. And drink. Sometimes call faraway friends like Lucien Carr. Or Allen, if I could find him. And talk. For hours. At least that's what Stella and Memere said. I don't really remember. Like I said, I was a train wreck in slow motion, jumping the track, spilling my guts and everything else all over hell's half acre.

Now I just wanted to get out. I headed down to Gulf Boulevard. I didn't want a bar. Which kind of surprised me. I wanted the ocean. Wanted to smell it. Wanted to feel the wind.

I drove out to Long Key, then headed up to Treasure Island. Drove it slow with the windows down. Finally stopped and got out to walk.

Always loved walking. Even today. My 80-year-old legs can still handle these San Francisco hills. Maybe not as good as fifty years ago, but I get around all right. Got me a new knee.

It was out there on Treasure Island I started to put my plans together. My plans to "die" and then hit the road. I didn't think of it that way at first. I still wanted to write. I still wanted to see America. Maybe not from the back of a flatbed like I did once. Or from a boxcar. Or even from the back seat of a brand spankin' new Hudson.

I wanted to do it in a quiet way. Kind of like how Snyder and I did it up in Yosemite and, later on, when I had the watchtower job.

Maybe I'd drop in on Allen. Or Burroughs. But then maybe they'd blow my cover. And that would ruin it. I didn't need anybody chasing me all over the country. And I didn't want to chase anyone either.

Leaving Stella and Memere would be tough. I couldn't do it right away. I decided to head out the first of the year. New decade. New start. A second chance. Maybe Gerard would come with me.

In the past I always wanted to head west. Get to the great big skies of Colorado. And the crazy streets and people of Frisco. But this time I remembered a place Creeley and Duncan told me about. A little college in North Carolina. It didn't exist anymore. Folded in the Fifties about the time *On the Road* got published. Called Black Mountain.

The last guy to run the place was from Marblehead, Mass. Pretty close to Lowell. Snyder said he was huge. More than six and half feet tall. Almost as big around. Olson was his name. Charles Olson. Wrote an essay in the early fifties called "Projective Verse." And a book, *Call Me Ishmael.* And some pretty crazy poetry. Allen told me we'd met. But I don't remember.

I had a couple of Olson's books, including *Ishmael*, in my stack of stuff at the house. I started reading it, then put it down. I resolved to read it again. I wanted to hit the road. Again. By myself. Go to Black Mountain. Then try to find this guy Olson. Snyder said he was camped out in Gloucester now.

I wondered if I could pull all this off. Dying. Driving. Meeting people who might recognize me. I didn't know. It sounded like a plan. Kind of. But it was something I had to do. Just *had* to. Been like that all my life.

I got back in the car and drove home.

Stella and Memere were relieved to see me when I pulled in the drive. I was glad I didn't disappoint them. But I was also excited I had the beginnings of a plan. A plan to stake out the next section of my life's road. That felt good. Really good.

Chapter 4 — North

I didn't leave St. Pete until April, 1970. It took me that long to get things taken care of. Explain my plan to Stella and Memere. Get them used to me taking off again. It wasn't easy. For them. Or me.

They tried talking me out of it. Where was I going? Who was going with me? What was I going to do for money? What did it mean that I "died"?

They were good. Almost had me second-guessing myself. But every drive down to the beach and the Gulf stirred me up. I wanted to get out. There were places I'd never been that I wanted to see. There were places I'd been that I wanted to see again. This time I wanted to travel alone. That wasn't going to be hard to do. Stella had to stay with Memere, even if she wanted to go, which she didn't.

Neal was dead. All the others scattered. Or dying. Or both. I was used to being on my own. Even when I was with Neal and Allen and Holmes and I guess with Lucien and Burroughs and the women and all the rest, I felt like I was separated somehow. Watching. Taking notes. Trying to take it all in and figure it all out. So taking off by myself seemed natural. Knew I'd meet people along the way and looked forward to it. And then I'd write what I saw and felt.

We rehearsed my story: that I died of hemorrhage, was cremated and they spread my ashes in the Gulf. They'd go back to Lowell a few months after I left for North Carolina and have a memorial service so everybody could say goodbye. Even have a little headstone made up for me and put in the family plot. I also got things tidied up with my estate and publisher so my money would come to them.

I don't think they really knew why I had to do this. After all I'd put them through maybe I didn't either, but I knew that I had to go. I was practically dead anyway.

If I stayed, I'd shrivel and die. But, just as I was to that nurse, I was still "Jack Kerouac, Famous Writer" to the rest of the world. I knew if I went on trying to be that, then I might as well be dead.

Here's what I wrote in my journal:

January 1, 1970

New year. New decade. Been out of the hospital about six weeks now. Feeling better and better. Memere and Stella say I look it too.

Thinking more and more about my road trip. Not sure how far I'm going or how long it'll take. But going by myself. I'll take a slower pace than our crazy mad dashes twenty years ago. Want to see more. Hear more. Experience more. Write more.

Writing is the only thing I really know. The only thing that really makes me ME. I know I haven't written a damn thing worth reading for years. Going to change that.

Looking at North Carolina for the first leg. Then Massachusetts (slipping in undetected). After that...open road. Maybe Quebec and family roots. I know I'll feel the Frisco pull. But don't want to get there too soon. Can't be discovered. Staying underground.

Memere and Stella will be taken care of. At least what I've written so far is good for something. Leave them with more than the sorrow and pain that have been my "gifts" to them for too long. But I do believe a weary soul can be made new. And I'm going to try. Have to.

Before I left, I did make them feel good about one thing: kicking the booze. Not that it was easy. It wasn't. But the doc gave me a good report in February. Said I was healing up and asked if I was staying off the booze. Said I was. Could see he believed me. Felt good about that.

Got to where I was driving down to the beaches almost every day and walking myself into decent shape. I even tricked myself into thinking I still had my football legs and made mad little dashes across the sand, dodging tacklers with the cuts that made me a star in Lowell.

The Gulf beaches made me long for Marin and Stinson. Even Big Sur. Gulf beaches are tame. The Pacific beaches are wild. The ocean's wild. The water's wild and deadly cold. Those beaches and that water, they dare you. And will kill you if you're not careful. For me, they were irresistible. I would go back to them again and again. Surf pounding so loud you can't talk. Just listen. Satori. For now, though, I mapped my way north.

I started by writing my obit for Stella and Memere to send in to the paper. Here it is:

"John Kerouac, Writer. Born 1922, Lowell, MA. Died 1970, St. Petersburg, FL. Son of Leo (deceased). Brother of Nin (deceased), Gerard (deceased). Survived by mother, Gabrielle, and wife, Stella (Sampos).

"Author of The Town and the City, On the Road, The Dharma Bums, Visions of Gerard, *a dozen others.*

"Cremation has taken place. Family will host a memorial service in Lowell on a date to be announced."

Short. Sweet.

Maybe when I really go, somebody else will write something more. Or maybe nothing at all. Maybe all was said back then by Allen and the others. Even when I saw him again, he was good to his word. Didn't let on to Greg or anyone else I was still around. Allen did say that seeing me was enough to turn him into a Christian. But he was joking. And I'm getting ahead of myself.

I pulled the maps out and showed Stella and Memere how I'd be traveling. Georgia. North Carolina. Black Mountain. Then Virginia. Maryland. Pennsylvania. New York (staying out of the city). Then Massachusetts. The Cape. Marblehead, but not Lowell. On to Maine and maybe into Canada.

Memere showed me a couple towns in Quebec where our people were. Or once were, and I told her I'd visit. But I couldn't tell anyone who I was. Or wasn't. She understood.

When they asked "After Canada, what?" I knew they were hoping to hear I'd be back. Maybe in two or three months' time. I said I didn't know, but I'd write. And I didn't tell them about San Francisco, knowing they'd give up all hope on me then.

But I felt good. I'd dropped forty pounds, cut my hair short, and grew a short beard. Just in case I ran into someone else carrying a copy of *On the Road* and was tempted to ask if I was the guy on the back cover.

I'd bought a '66 Ford wagon. Yellow. Nine-seater. Big and dependable. I didn't pack a lot. Clothes. Camping gear. Some maps. Books. My note-books. Bit of food. And money. About a thousand dollars, if I remember right. Had to make that last a long ways because I wasn't sure where or when the next bunch of money was coming from. No more bailouts from Memere, that's for sure.

All this took a little while to get settled. But when it was time to go, it was time to go.

I said my goodbyes. Said I'd see them again. I don't think they believed me. They cried. I cried. Then I was gone. It was April 1. "The Beat Saint is now The April Fool," I thought to myself.

I headed north on US 19, looking forward to a quiet, lazy drive up western Florida. I stopped in Tarpon Springs for lunch. The main road leads right down to the docks where boats go out for fish and sponges. It's a working town, the kind I like. Men wore those short-billed sailor caps like the one I had in Tangiers.

I decided on a little Greek restaurant, one of two across from each other in the few blocks before you got to the docks. I'd missed the lunch crowd, so it was quiet. I think I was the only person in the place.

I also remember the waitress. Early 20s. Young enough to be my daughter. Clear olive skin. Shiny black hair and dark eyes. "Sophie." For some reason she took an interest in me. When I was about finished, and she, for the tenth time, asked if I wanted more coffee, she sat down opposite me in the booth.

"You're not from around here, are you?"

"No. St. Pete."

"Oh that's not far! My mama and I go shopping there sometimes. She makes me go because she doesn't speak English very well. Papa neither."

Clearly, she thought talking to me might help her afternoon go a little faster. "Are you Greek?" she asked.

"No. My people are French Canadian."

"I didn't think so. You have blue eyes. But you kind of looked Greek so that's why I asked."

"Are you?"

"Oh yes! Papa and Mama came over after World War Two. My uncle Teddy was already here. They're from Rhodes. Do you know where that is?"

"Big island near Turkey?"

"Yes! How did you know that? Have you been there?"

"No. Closest I got was Tangiers. You know where that is?" I asked smiling back.

"Of course! Were you there during the war?"

"No. After."

"Did you fight?"

"Not really. I joined the Merchant Marine and sailed on some ships in the North Atlantic. I had a bum knee and the Army wouldn't take me." This was kind of a lie, but I didn't feel like getting into all of it.

"My dad wasn't in the army either. Said he fought the Germans underground. They come from a little village. Reni. South of the city. He had a restaurant there. Just like here. Have you heard of it?"

"No." I failed this part of her geography quiz.

"That's OK. Nobody who visits here does. I'm surprised you even knew where Rhodes was!" She paused, looking in the direction of the kitchen.

"I have to go in a second. You don't look like most of the tourists we get in here. They're old. Are you just visiting, or..."

"I'm starting a trip."

"Oh! That sounds like fun! Wish I could go on a trip! We have cousins in California. Have you ever been there?"

"Many times. Where are your cousins?"

"Near San Francisco. Monterrey. Do you know where it is?"

"Yes. Beautiful spot. On a big bay. Another town nearby called Carmel. You should go there sometime."

She looked back with sad eyes now too. And then talked even faster. "I want to! But this restaurant! We have to work all the time. I'm an only child. I had a brother, but he died when he was young. Sometimes I just want to walk out of here and hitchhike all the way to the West Coast. There's so much going on out there...but then Mama and Papa would be all alone."

I pulled a paper napkin out of its holder and wrote down

John Steinbeck
Cannery Row
Travels With Charley

I passed it to her.

"He's a good writer. The first book is about Monterrey and the fishermen there. The second is about a trip he took around the country with his dog. Maybe they'll help you figure out how to get where you want to be."

She looked at me like she wanted to talk more. But I knew it was just time to go.

"Sophie!"

"Coming Mama! Are you leaving? I mean, thank you for this. But you seem like the kind of man who's easy to talk to. You know things. Like this... Steinbeck."

"Sophie!!"

We both stood.

"It's nice meeting you, Mr...."

"Jack. Just Jack."

"Well, Mr. Jack, enjoy your journey. Maybe you'll stop back and tell me about it sometime."

"Maybe I will. And maybe you'll tell me what Mr. Steinbeck had to say to you." I walked out into the bright afternoon light. It felt like a dream. A good start.

After a couple more hours on Rt. 19, I could feel the ground rising slowly until I got to where Florida jutted west. I was curious to curve on around and see Tallahassee and the Panhandle. But maybe I knew I might get tempted into something and I really wanted to put some miles on. So I kept the Ford headed north, straight and true.

I spent that first night just inside Georgia. Near Thomasville. Here's what I wrote:

April 1, 1970

Beat Saint. April Fool.
First night on the road.
Good weather today. Warm.
Hard leaving Memere and Stella.
Memere's last words: "I pray for Papa and Gerard and Nin. They watch out for you. They bring you home."

Memere, I know they will.

Once I got St. Pete behind me, the road opened up, and I started getting that old feeling back.

Freedom. Windows down. Salt air. Clackety-clack of tires on concrete. Easy beat of the road. My soul soared!

I don't remember a whole lot of that drive, to tell you the truth. What the drive *felt* like was a slow trip through the real old South. I do remember the soil, how it changed from Florida sand to Georgia clay, from brown to red. Real red. How the soil dominated the landscape in between all the small towns that had been settled a hundred and fifty years before and hadn't changed a whole lot since. Meigs. Camila. Albany. Zebulon. Georgia was different from Florida. Older. More withdrawn. Unchanged from all the other drives I'd made through it and other southern states. And it stayed that way until I got to Atlanta.

That was one time I wished Neal had been with me. If he'd been driving, we'd been on the other side of Atlanta in a third of the time it took me. He probably would've talked his way out of a traffic ticket too. Neal was fearless. Or crazy. Or both.

But then I was through the city and climbing through more small towns. Alphareth. Coal Mountain. Dahlonga. Slow, steady climbing. And in a couple hours I'd crossed the border into the toe of North Carolina. I didn't make it to Asheville or Black Mountain that day. But I camped near the Smokies, close to the Cherokee reservation. I was glad I did. It felt good to be back in the mountains. Hardly anyone around as I remember. It was spring cool, almost chilly. I built the first of many campfires and settled in.

Chapter 5 — Black Mountain

Waking from my second night out felt good, the morning came crisp and sunny. And quiet. Nobody else in the campground that I could see. I decided to hike a bit before finding my way to Black Mountain. There was a trail that led off the site down to a small river already full and cold from winter melt.

These were old woods. I've always loved old woods. This was the first one I'd been in for some time. Old hardwoods. Oak and beech, maple and birch and shag hickory. A few hemlocks grabbed hold close to the water. Forest reminded me a little of Muir and Yosemite and the ancient redwoods north and south of San Francisco. And the massive pine and fir forests I'd watched from my fire tower on Desolation Peak. Tree leaves weren't out yet, but some were starting to bud. A few early flowers, too. The earth was warming back to life.

In Florida the earth never died. Everything was always growing. And I guess these old bones can appreciate being someplace where it's always at least warm. I know now why Memere wanted to leave the Northeast for the South.

But dying helps me live. Seeing leaves fall, plants pulling back into the earth, snow falling. These are good things too. A rest for the earth. A rest for old souls too. The stillness and freshness of that morning has stayed clear in my mind ever since.

Maybe because it was the second morning of my trip. Maybe because the silence felt holy. Maybe because I felt the first great rush of energy to get out and start trying to gather my past with my present and hopefully my future. Maybe I was simply grateful Stella and Memere and the doc and Nurse Amanda—and Gerard too—gave me a second chance at life.

The trail I was on was wide and worn. As it curved closer to the river, then moved away and up, I wondered if Indians had been the first ones to walk this path. Or maybe herds of deer or elk with Indians following. Now it was marked so campers and hikers could navigate easily and not get lost.

I climbed to a rock outcropping that looked back down on the river and opened out to mountains north and west. Clingman's Dome was out there somewhere up in the Smokies. I closed my eyes and listened. I could feel a kind of rising up inside when the world is silent and you are open to the sky. It felt good to me.

Turning and opening my eyes, the sun was still fairly low in the east. Asheville might've been on the horizon. Beyond it, somewhere, Black Mountain. Time to get there. I was ready.

I suppose I should write something about Asheville, but I don't have much to say. My mind was on getting through town and over to Black Mountain. It was easier when Neal was driving and I was riding next to him or in the back seat. Or when I was on those long bus rides. Or even when I was catching rides from strangers. Then I could see the details of the land. Faces. The desperation in a young man's eyes. The curves of a woman's body. Buildings. Lights. Color of the dawn sky. How bright stars looked in the dark West. I'd have the time to take it all in and feel it. But driving, I had to pay attention and not get on the wrong road.

Neal was a much better driver than I ever was. He blew down roads he'd never seen like he'd been driving them all his life. Neal *felt* the road. I think he would've done it eyes closed if I'd dared him to, which I didn't. He was honest-to-God happiest behind the wheel headed to parts known and unknown. He and the car and the road were one. A force blowing across an infinite land that was all his.

To this day I don't know how he did it. Driving and talking a hundred miles an hour. Spinning out great big ideas of where to go, what to do, who to see and why. And maybe making some girl at the same time. I've read some people who say it was the drugs, but I don't think so. Yeah there were drugs. Mainly bennies to keep us awake when we were driving all day and all night trying to make the West Coast or the East Coast in three or four days. But I think Neal could've done it all without anything except maybe some coffee. His energy was his own. His high was the road. We were there for the ride. I just did my part by telling people what happened to us along the way.

I didn't know what to expect as I drove into Black Mountain. Guess from all I'd heard I thought the college would be sitting there squat in the middle of town. But nothing jumped out at me and yelled "Black Mountain College." The town itself was nice. Old. But not the kind of place that could've held the likes of Duncan and Creeley and Olson. It was just another small town in a long line of small towns I'd passed through the last few days.

I drove around a bit looking for something that might have been a campus once. But there was nothing. Just a downtown with some buildings and a couple stoplights. Then streets branching off to houses for a few blocks. Getting frustrated, I was about to give up and just skip the whole thing when I saw the one place that might have some idea where this Camelot was or had been—the library. More specifically, the Buncombe County Library.

The woman behind the desk smiled as soon as I'd made my way through the double glass doors, like she'd seen me coming a mile away.

"Good mornin'! Can I help you?" She spoke with a clear, soft Carolina accent that's about the sweetest sound in the world. The frustrations of driving lost melted away.

"Hi. Yes. I'm trying to find the college. But maybe I'm in the wrong place."

"The college?" She asked sympathetically and with a drawl that made it sound like 'cawl-ledge.' "Do you mean the university? That's in Asheville, the next town over. About fifteen, twenty minutes."

She looked to be in her early 30s. Attractive. Tall with golden brown skin and high cheekbones. White teeth and a broad, friendly smile. Dark eyes. Black shiny hair. Straight. Parted in the middle to well below her shoulders. Maybe Cherokee blood somewhere in her past? She wore a black turtleneck and a short plaid skirt.

"No. I meant Black Mountain. The college. Someone said there used to be one here."

At this she brightened some more. I got the sense I had already made her morning far more interesting than she was expecting.

"Why, yes! We don't get many people in here asking about Black Mountain College because it's been closed for so long now."

"I know. Couple friends of mine went there. Said if I was ever passing by I should stop and take a look."

While I was talking she was eyeing me up, probably trying to figure out what to make of this stranger who'd dropped into her quiet library world. Then she looked right past me and said in a louder-than-you're-supposed-to-be-in-a-library voice, "Bye-bye now, Miz Parker!"

An old woman walked steadily, if slowly, to the doors. She stopped to wave and smile.

"We'll see you again on Saturday! Remember Book Club meets at ten a.m."

The woman nodded and pushed herself into the door. I was about to step over and help when the door seemed to give way through sheer force of her determination. Then the second gave way too and she was outside and down the walk and gone.

We looked back at each other. My librarian started talking again as though called on in class to give a report on a famous person.

"Miz Parker is the smartest, sweetest woman in the world. She was a school teacher for a while. Taught both my daddy and my mama tenth grade English. But she was already retired when I got to high school. Never married. I heard she had TONS of boys chasin' her when she was younger. But maybe she was just too smart for'em. Some boys just don't like a girl smarter than they are."

Then she focused again on me and why I was there.

"I'm sorry! Prattlin' on like that and all. And you just wantin' some directions."

"No, that's alright. She sounds like an interesting person."

"Oh, she is! And nobody fools with Miz Parker. With her daddy's money she could buy up half this town and not miss a dime. But after she came home from New York, I guess all she wanted to do was teach English. And I heard she helped quite a few go to college. Not Black Mountain. But State. And Wake Forest. Even Duke. Quietly. She didn't want anyone to know."

Then she shifted gears. "Now which way did you come into town? From over by Statesville?"

"No. Asheville."

"Oh! Then you drove right by the turnoff. Lake Eden Road. Go back out the way you came on State Street and follow the sign for Old 70 off to the right. Take that just past the quarry, and Lake Eden is on your right. Just follow it up out of town until you see the lake on your left. Main building is just across it. It's a summer camp now. Camp Rockmont. For boys. Camp Hollymont's just past it. That's for the girls. Not ten minutes from here. You can't miss it."

She kept her gaze and smile on me.

"Thanks a lot." Then, wanting to talk a little longer, I asked, "Is there anything to see up there?"

"Well, I'm not really sure anymore. It's been with the Bible folks for a long time now. Maybe you'll see James Thomas, he's the caretaker. He might be able to tell you more. You said you had a friend who went there?"

"Yes. Actually a couple. They were teachers. Writers. Poets."

Now her eyes widened with studied interest. "Poets? Are they famous? I have read Mr. Dickey's poems. And Mr. Frost's. But I would have to claim Miss Plath as my favorite even though she died so young. Almost the same age I am now. And a mother with young ones too. What are their names?"

"Well, one is Duncan. Robert Duncan. He lives in California."

She frowned. "I'm sorry. I haven't heard of him. And who is the other?"

"Another Robert. Creeley. I think he's maybe in New Hampshire now. Haven't seen him in years."

"Sorry. I don't know him either." Her face darkened with disappointment as though she was not used to being stumped.

Then she brightened again leaning forward across the counter. "Are you a writer too? Are *you* famous?" She dazzled with her smile and with her questions. I almost blew it.

"I've written a few things. But, no, I'm not famous."

"When I saw you comin' up the walk I could tell right away you weren't from around here. And it's too early for the tourists. But sometimes we get famous people sneakin' through tryin' not to be recognized. Are you *sure* you're not famous?"

"Yeah. Pretty sure." And now I laughed.

"Okay, then." She stood back up as though ready to dismiss me. "But I'm pretty good about people and I think you are holdin' somethin' back. I think you might be famous and you just don't want me to know it!" she said continuing her smile. "Well, you get on up to the camp and then stop back and tell me what you found."

"Thank you. Maybe I will. Eden Lake Road. "I smiled and turned to walk out.

"Lake *Eden* Road. And what did you say your name was?"

I turned back and she was still smiling. She extended her arm. I reached out and shook her hand. It felt warm and strong.

"I didn't. But it's Jack."

"Just Jack?"

"Just Jack. For now." I smiled back at her.

"Well, Mr. Jack, I'm Jo. Short for Jolene. Harris. At least *I* am polite enough to give you my full name. If not I'm not here when you stop back, just ask for Mrs. Stam. She's head librarian. I'll let her know where I can be found. And you can tell me what you found up there!"

"Thanks. Thanks a lot. You've been very helpful ...Jo."

I thanked my lucky stars when I got to the car. What was going on here? Maybe it was just my middle-aged imagination, but I could've sworn two younger and very pretty women had come on to me in ways that hadn't happened in years. It was time to get up to the "cawl-ledge." Then get out of town, before I blew it totally and almost got sidetracked just two days into my journey.

I found Lake Eden Road barely wide enough for two lanes that started up slowly out of the valley, and sure enough ten minutes later I was parked on the road staring across this small lake at a large low-slung, flat-roofed building that looked far more contemporary than I expected. It jutted out towards the small lake made by damming up a stream that came down from the hills above.

I almost turned around. It just didn't look like the kind of place that would interest me. But then I thought, what the hell, nothing to lose and nowhere to get to. I turned in the long drive and drove right up to the front where the drive widened with parking places for a couple dozen cars. Getting out, I turned around and had to admit it was a pretty spot. High up. Mountains distant. Fields and woods below. Peaceful.

Later, I read a book that quoted Henry Miller's *The Air-Conditioned Nightmare*: "from the steps of Black Mountain College in North Carolina one has a view of mountains and forests which makes one dream of Asia." I've never been to Asia. But I've been to his workshop and museum in Big Sur and have to say he must've been mightily impressed to compare this piece of North Carolina to Asia.

Miller visited in the late thirties on his own trip across the country. He also wrote this: "The most interesting college I visited was Black Mountain College in North Carolina; it was the students who were interesting, not the professors."

I walked up to the building. It was long and angular, two stories high. It looked like it belonged to something else with the other parts missing. It wasn't in the best of shape. It was set on large concrete pillars. I climbed the stairs up to where I imagined the classrooms would be and peered in the windows. Nobody around. Not a sign the college was ever here. I knocked on a door, tried the knob. Locked.

Then I about jumped out of my skin when a thin, high voice asked from below, "Can I help you?"

Turning around and looking down there was a small wiry man with that North Carolina tan. White hair. Guessing sixty. Overalls. Flannel shirt. Denim jacket. He was standing at the foot of the stairs looking up at me. Friendly face. Used to strangers. But hardened into not being taken advantage of by them.

"Uh, sorry. Is this the college? Or what used to be the college? I had a friend who taught here. Said I should stop by and take a look if I was ever passing through." I quickly came down to show I didn't mean anything by trespassing.

"Yessuh. If you mean Black Mountain, it is. Or was. College's been closed now a'most fifteen years. It's a summer camp now. For the boys."

"Are you the caretaker? James...Thomas? The young woman at the library said you might be around if I stopped."

"Yessuh, I am. Have been off-and-on for twenty years."

"So you worked here while it was still the college?"

"Yessuh, I did."

"If you don't mind my asking, what was it like?"

"Well, it always seemed kind a hand-to-mouth like. Had this great big feller runnin' the place. An'...an'...well, it just was never like no school I'd ever been 'round."

"So I've heard."

"And who are you? Friend of the big feller? You kind of sound like him."

"No. I don't know him. But we both come from Massachusetts. Actually I hope to maybe meet him in a week or so."

He stood there looking at me some more. I was on his "land," and it was clear he wanted more of an explanation about who I was and why I was here. I knew whatever I said probably would get to Jolene before I even got back to town.

"My friend taught here about that time. He lives in California now. His name was Duncan. Robert Duncan. Ever hear of him?"

"No. Cain't say I remember that name. What'd you say yours was?"

"Jack. Jack Moriarty. I drove up from Florida couple days ago. Stopped here on my way back up to Massachusetts."

That seemed to satisfy James Thomas. At least temporarily. He relaxed a bit and smiled.

"Well, y'all welcome to look 'round a bit. Not much to see tho'. This used to be what they called the Studies Hall. Now it's camp administration. Most of the college stuff got packed up and hauled 'way someplace else. Asheville I think. What was left behind got burnt or buried. Seems like them Bible folks what made this the boys camp had no use fo' what them professors was preachin' anyway! Hee-hee!"

"It's a beautiful spot." Looking around the lake, I could see another large building at the southern end and a few smaller ones surrounding. A couple docks looked like they were made for jumping off of.

"It sure is. Lot o' work when the boys are here. Quiet when they're not. Like now. That'll change in a few weeks when the others show up for summer."

"What do you do here?"

"Oh, jus' 'bout ev'rything. Jus' like I did then! Some carpentry. Some plumbin'. Back then I even kept the cars runnin', what few they had. Even helped with the farmin' and butcherin'. Don't do that now. But I didn't do no cookin'. Lipseys took *good* care of that. Always ate real well."

"There was a farm here?"

"Oh, yass! Needed it to feed the people. Then things got tight an' first they rented, then had to sell the land. It was kinda sad watchin' it go downhill. Them kids wuz nice. Po-lite. Jus' seemed like that big feller and the others couldn't make a go of it. Like they kinda gave up at the end. You know that feller's name?"

"Was it Olson?"

"That was it! Hee-hee! Lord, I'd never seen a man that big! Big as ol' Black Mountain hisself. Olson. Charles, right?"

"That's right. Charles Olson. He got to be a pretty big writer too."

I was enjoying James Thomas' company. He reminded me of the many working men I'd met on my trips back and forth across the country. He also reminded me of some of my dad's friends back in Lowell.

"My friend Duncan knows him. He's said the same thing."

"He was a wild man, for sure. He'd run around here tryin' to do this an' that, pokin' into everything. Then you wouldn't see him for weeks. Holed up in his room. Or maybe off someplace else. It was like one minute he wanted to be here. Then he didn't. I think all that back and forth jus' did this place no good. But...he was a wild man."

James was clearly delighting in the memory. We'd walked around back to a bare space of ground and a view up to the mountains.

"Now here is where what they called the pottin' barn used to be. Them kids, girls mostly, used to set here for hours and hours just spinnin' them pots 'round and 'round. Then they'd stick'em in the kiln used to be here and bake'em to just right. Took'em a long time to figure that out. I cleaned up lots of broken ones. I got a couple good ones back at my house."

"Why'd they take it down?"

"They? Oh you mean the college people? Naw, they didn't take it down. It was the church people. Didn't see no use for it. To be honest, think they wanted to get rid of anything that reminded them of what used to go on here."

"Why'd they do that?"

"Well, I'm not fit to rightly say. But maybe the things that were taught here weren't what the church people wanted for a Bible type camp." He pointed to the other large building. "Kept the Dinin' Hall, of course. Even church people like to eat, hee-hee!"

"Mind if I take a look?"

"No, sir. Glad to have some company up here today."

We walked along the lake a couple hundred yards down to the Dining Hall and then back around where some of the smaller buildings were. He was right, not much to see. Looking back across the lake, I tried to imagine this place full of students and teachers—and radical ideas. But it wasn't hitting me that way. Then we were back at the drive and looking at the back side of the Studies Building. I was feeling both disappointed and wanting to know more.

"Is there anything to see…inside?"

"Naw…not really. But if you want a look, I can unlock it fer ya."

"You don't mind?"

"Me? Naw. I got things to do. But they can wait. Nobody to bother me up here now. Church people won't be comin' round 'til almost Dec'ration Day."

We climbed back up the stairs where I'd been. It was very modern, very utilitarian, but shabby from lack of use and I'm guessing money for upkeep. "Yep. This was quite a place back in them days. Always somethin' goin' on. Even if 'twas just them kids and their teachers talkin' and whatever. But they had concerts and plays and ev'rythin' here. People come from all over the country. Famous people too."

James paused while I walked around trying to imagine Duncan and Creeley and Olson and the others here.

"Lot quieter now. Even with the Bible folk 'round. They's not much for singin' unless it's a Jesus song."

I nodded, "Duncan always said nice things about this place. He's kind of a spiritual guy himself. But maybe not in the Bible way of the people who own this now."

"Yessuh. Well, I always liked bein' 'round them young people. They was quite a mix. Lotsa times folks in town didn't know quite what to make of 'em. Or their teachers neither. Of course, they always liked the business they got from the college. Always liked that college money.

"Some called 'em communists. But, shoot, I'd never seen anythin' like that. Free spirits, what I called them. An' some of them girls was really pretty, too, hee-hee!"

I thought of Jolene Harris. "Did any of them stay around? Or are they all gone now?"

"Oh, they's all gone. Just memories now. Been fifteen years almost."

We walked out and James stopped before the stairs. "There's one gal in town might remember. She snuck up here away from her mammy on school days so she could learn some of that pottery makin' I was talkin' about. The college people let her sit in even tho' she couldn't afford to pay. They was nice that ways."

"What does she do now?" I thought for sure this was my librarian.

"Oh, she's got her own little pottery shop. Can't think of its name now. On Hemlock. About two blocks north off Main Street. Her name's Lissa. Tawney."

"OK. I might look her up. Librarian asked me to stop back and tell her what I found up here."

He gave me a quizzical look.

"Ol' Miz Stam wants you to tell her about the college?"

I laughed.

"No. Sorry. Jolene. Harris, I think her name is."

He brightened at that. "Jo asked you to stop back? Hee-hee!! She must have thought somethin' 'bout you! Hee-hee! Jolene Harris don' seem to have time for no fellers 'round here."

"She was very helpful. I was about to leave town without having even seen the place. She gave me directions."

"What kinda work do you do, Mr. Moriarty?"

"I'm a writer."

"I knowed it! I knowed it! That Jolene she's a looker. Smart as a whip too. Well, you just tell her James Thomas said hello."

"I will. Thanks."

We walked down the stairs and to my car. "Mr. Thomas. James. Thanks for your time and the walk around. I hope to see Olson in about a week. And Duncan maybe later on this summer. Anything else I can tell them about Black Mountain?"

"Just tell 'em I'm doin' my best to keep it up like they left it. Maybe don't tell' em about the buildings that got tore down. They might be sorry 'bout that. The church people have different priorities I guess.

"And you can tell that Olson fella I hope he got his women troubles worked out. I wasn't supposed to know about those. But word gets 'round. Felt sorry for him. Big fella like that, think he'd have no trouble keepin' his women in place. Seemed like they weighed him down as much as the money troubles did."

He and I looked at each other with the knowing look of men who've had our own share of "women troubles." Nothing more needed saying. It was time to go.

We shook hands and, just before I got in the car, I asked, "What was that woman's name again? The potter?"

"Lissa. Tawney. Red-haired gal. Real spitfire from what I hear."

"OK. Thanks. Who knows? Maybe I'll run into her before I leave."

"Good enough. Enjoy your stay, now, hear?"

I drove away from James Thomas and Lake Eden with a wave.

Chapter 6 — Women Troubles

I didn't drive straight back into town. Even though the afternoon was getting on and I had to think about where I was going to spend the night, I felt like exploring a bit more. My original plan was to drive here, see Black Mountain for a couple hours, then make my way east and north.

Even though there really wasn't much of the old campus to see, at least from a college point of view, I could tell from the way Jo and James talked about it that it had been something special at one time. Duncan had talked about it that way too. But not in the way old guys do about their college years. It was like something had clicked for him here. Like Henry Miller looking out across these North Carolina mountains and seeing Asia.

I took the turnoff to Black Mountain, the mountain, and started climbing the road to its peak. I wanted to see what was up there and what I could see from there. Actually I felt a little foolish doing it this way. Snyder would've told me you can't see the top of the mountain with your eyes. You can only see it with your feet. Feet that have to start at the bottom and see their way all the way to the top. That's the only way you ever know any mountain. And the only way that you can see the world the way the mountain sees the world.

Here's something he said when we did our hike into the Sierras: "The secret of this kind of climbing is like Zen. Don't think. Just dance along. It's the easiest thing in the world. Actually easier than walking on flat ground."

I would do that kind of climbing again. For now, I'd have to be content with driving this old Ford.

I stopped at the top near a little pullout and took in the view. It was long and gentle. I looked back down into the valley. I could make out the campus and the lake standing apart from town. I tried to find the library, but couldn't. Beyond, the country took over again. Smaller hills and greening valleys, though I couldn't see China. Then again I wasn't Henry Miller either. But this quiet, graceful place lent itself to bursting ideas and the kinds of exploration I loved as a young man. If I ever saw Snyder and Duncan again, we'd certainly have a few things to say about this place. But the private way I was traveling now, that couldn't happen, unless by accident and then things would really have to change.

The afternoon was getting on and I was getting hungry. And I needed to find a place to pitch my tent for the night. I thought about driving back to Nantahala, but decided I wanted to keep moving forward. So I headed into town. I thought about stopping back at the library, but held off. If Jolene Harris was still as interesting tomorrow morning as she had been today, there'd be plenty of time to tell her what I'd seen and pass along greetings from James Thomas. Truth is I was a little worried about getting mixed up and detoured. As it turned out she became the least of my "women troubles."

I found a little campground a few miles east of town. Family-owned. Because it was still early in the season, it was empty except for me. But it did have hot water for a shower. Which I hit right after pitching my tent. Even trimmed up the beard a little.

I settled in for my third night on the road. The day had started cool, then warmed up nicely. But now it was cooling down again, and I was glad for the fire ring and its bundle of wood. I hadn't traveled far in miles. But I'd gotten a look at Black Mountain and the buildings that used to house the college. And I'd met a couple of interesting people.

Here's what I wrote:

April 3

Black Mountain
Made it!
Not a college town. Not hick town either.
Quiet. But alive.
Almost left because no sign of college anywhere.

Jolene Harris. Librarian. Gave me directions.
Likes Dickey shared roots
Likes Plath shared dreams/nightmares(?)

Black Mountain College
Studies Building long, modern facing Lake Eden
Dining Hall other end of lake, looks like the real focus of college action

James Thomas caretaker
Remembers Olson
Not much to see now
Bible camp different priorities

Drove up mountain
(Snyder would be disappointed I didn't walk it)
Didn't see China (Miller said it reminded)

Tired, but getting old road feeling back
Not the Neal road feeling running one end of continent to other
Thumbs out feeling
Taking miles and people as they come
Like when I saw that big Cheyenne sky the first time
Wonder what's next

'What's next' came the next morning and didn't even know it.

I was kind of curious to see Jolene Harris. Then again, if I blew my cover not three days out of Florida the whole rest of the trip, maybe the rest of my life, *my underground life*, was ruined. She was curious enough—and smart enough—to maybe figure me out.

I thought about just packing everything up and making my way to New York. But I worried if I could even go into the city and come out without being recognized. Even with the short hair and the beard, I still looked like me. A sober, un-bloated me.

Already this life of playing dead was proving harder than I ever imagined.

And, hey, Black Mountain deserved a little more of my time than I gave it yesterday. Maybe I wanted to be able to say more in case I ever ran into Creeley or Duncan or Olson—or Snyder!—again. Of course, I couldn't do that and stay on my path. But another day here couldn't hurt. Plus, it was warm and I knew heading north meant plenty of cold nights for another month at least. I kept my tent pitched, paid for another night and headed back into town for some breakfast.

The main street was busy with Saturday traffic and people on the sidewalks. I angled the car into a space in front of a W.T. Grant five-and-dime. After walking a block I stopped in at a restaurant—The Candy Kitchen—wedged between the bank and Jump's Clothing Store. It was nearly full, even the counter.

The waitress showed me to a two-seat table in the back. I could feel people looking. To be expected, I guess. If Jolene was right, I was an early stranger in a town more or less used to them. The head-turning didn't feel like Jimmy's small-eyed wariness. A more gentle curiosity. Maybe like wondering if I might be someone "famous." This is something you get used to on the road. Going into towns and always the stranger.

I filled my belly with hot coffee, eggs, toast, grits. Ate quietly. Listened to the chatter of a restaurant at breakfast time. I smiled and appreciated the refills on the coffee and was about to leave when I heard a quiet, genteel, but determined voice ask, "May I sit down?"

I looked up and was startled to see the old woman from the library—Mrs. Parker—standing on the other side of the table. I stared for a moment and she smiled.

"Oh yeah, of course," trying not to show my surprise.

I don't know who was more shocked. Me. Or the rest of the restaurant who were now craning their necks to get a better look at this man their leading citizen had just walked up to and was now sitting with.

She extended her hand. "I know we haven't met. I'm Ruth Parker."

I took hers and replied, "Yes, I…uh…know. Jo...I mean Miss Harris...talked about you yesterday at the library after you left. I'm Jack. Jack Moriarty."

"Pleased to meet you, Mr. Moriarty. Sounds like Jo likes to talk about both of us," she said good-naturedly. I guessed she'd been back to the library, and so singled me out of a crowd?

The waitress hurried over with coffee. She accepted. I took my fifth refill.

"Will you be having breakfast, Mrs. Parker?"

"No, dear. Well, wait. Maybe some toast. Rye. With a little butter."

"Yes, ma'am."

"It looks like you've already had your breakfast, Mr. Moriarty," she said pleasantly.

"Yes. And it's Jack. Mrs…."

"Ruth. Please."

She paused, taking a determined sip.

"I do apologize for interrupting your morning, Mr.…Jack."

There was an obvious keen intelligence in her eyes and smile, as well as her manner of speaking. Her accent wasn't as pronounced as Jolene's or

Thomas' or the waitress', as though she had been somewhere else for a long period time and was just now adapting to the speech of rural North Carolina.

"No. No. That's all right. I guess you recognized me from the library."

"I did. I do believe that's the most excited I've seen Jo in quite some time. When I saw you sitting back here, I decided I ought to find out why."

And now I looked more carefully at her face. Her skin was smooth and lightly tanned. Her hair was pure white, the kind that almost glows. It was pulled tight into a bun. She wore a pair of earrings, silver with small stones that looked like turquoise and ruby. My sense was that she was older than she looked. She reminded me of Georgia O'Keeffe.

"Did you find what you were looking for at Black Mountain?" Again, a smile as she lifted her cup.

Her directness surprised me. I knew she was asking about the college, not the town.

"Well, yes and no. I wasn't sure what I'd find exactly. I had a couple friends who always spoke highly of the place. Said I should stop and see it if I was ever in the neighborhood. But with it being closed and all, there wasn't much to see, to tell you the truth."

"Did you see James?"

I was about to answer when the waitress brought her toast and offered a refill.

"Thank you, dear!"

The young woman seemed anxious to please.

Ruth returned her gaze to me. Clearly she was going to pump all the information out of me that she could. I worried that she'd be an even better interrogator than Jo.

"Yes I did. Nice guy. He showed me around. Seemed almost apologetic about how some of the buildings have been taken down. I guess the current owners have other priorities." I smiled at Ruth, trying not to sound judgmental.

"Yes, there's not much left now. Except the memories and the seeds they scattered to the wind. Of which there are many, thank goodness."

Ruth paused, then bore in again. "Jack, your accent is unmistakable, if you will pardon my forwardness. Boston, yes?"

I nodded. If I'd said Lowell that would cut things too close for comfort.

"Would one of your Black Mountain friends happen to be Charles Olson? I believe he is also from Massachusetts."

I had to be careful here. I didn't really know Olson even though I'd met him once. But Ruth was sharp. And obviously she knew a lot about Black Mountain. I believed her curiosity about me was sincere.

"No, I'm not friends with him. I know about him through my other friends. And I know his writing." I held up on telling her about the book I'd packed. "But I'm headed back up that way and hope maybe I can stop by and see him."

Oops. That was a mistake. More information than I intended to share.

"Well, if you do, please extend my warm regards to Charles."

"I will. I guess you know him, then."

"Oh yes! I gave him some money to keep the college going...there at the end. But then even I could see they weren't going to make it. Charles is many things, but a good businessman he is not. Of course, it wasn't all his fault. The place was always a fish out of water down here. After the war, I think things moved on. It just became harder and harder to keep a faculty together and bring enough students to make it all work. The last years were an unhappy time. Like a marriage breaking up. Which one or two of his did, I believe."

She surprised me with all this information, which had me wondering why she was sharing it. "Did you know the college when times were good?"

Ruth's eyes brightened as the question sparked distant memories. "Oh, yes! That I did." Here she paused, looking into her cup for a minute. When she looked up it was almost as though she was looking at someone else.

"John Rice. Now *he* was a man! All that energy. And ideas. Standing up for what he believed in and getting himself fired from a good college job in the middle of the De*press*ion! Then coming here and starting this college."

She paused for a sip. "As my daddy used to say, 'That took *guts*.'" The way Ruth said that, lowering her voice to echo her father's deep drawl, made me laugh. I relaxed a little seeing that she wanted to talk about Black Mountain, and not just be my Grand Inquisitor.

"I don't think I know the man."

"John Rice? Oh, he was the one who started it all. Came up from Rollins College after he got fired for having too radical ideas about what a college education should be. Brought along a couple others from that faculty and got Black Mountain going in the early thirties. 1933 to be exact."

"Were you here then?"

Now it was her turn to size me up. I think she was used to asking the questions and here I was turning the tables on her. But she read my interest as genuine, and so continued.

"I was living in New York. But I came home for the holidays, and Daddy said someone had started a college at the Robert E. Lee. So I was curious enough to drive over there and see who was who. That's where I met John and his wife, Nell, and a few others."

I wasn't sure what she meant by the Robert E. Lee. I didn't remember James Thomas calling the big building I saw or the one down at the other end of the lake that name, but I assumed she meant the Studies Building.

"That is one big building. But looks like James keeps it in good repair," I added, "He seems to miss the college days."

"Oh, well, who wouldn't? When it was going well that place was special. I mean here it was *the worst* of the Depression and almost like a little candle out of the darkness comes this flickering idea of what a real college should be like. *Here.* In little ol' Black Mountain, North Carolina. Unbelievable!"

Clearly Ruth Parker had sought me out because she wanted to discover how much I knew about Black Mountain. She also wanted to talk about the college and her many memories of it. Apparently Ruth Parker was a lot more than the grown-old daughter of the town banker.

"Who are your friends who taught here? I got to know some of the faculty and a student or two over the years."

"Oh, I don't think you'd know who they are."

Ruth looked straight at me and smiled, "Why don't you try me?"

"Couple of poets. Robert Duncan. And Robert Creeley. Ever hear of 'em?"

"Mr. Duncan? No, I don't think so. But Mr... Creeley? Now that name sounds familiar. You say he was on the faculty? It has been a while, and I only went up there now and then when I was home visiting. I moved back for good in 1959 when Daddy grew ill. When he died the college had been gone for a few years. Are they good friends of yours?"

"Used to be, I guess. It's been a few years since I've seen them."

"They must have found their time here worthwhile if they suggested you stop even when there's not much to see."

This was falling into a much more interesting conversation than I'd ever thought possible with the woman I saw shuffling out the library door yesterday. I really had to be careful though, because if she got me talking about New York or Frisco, she'd figure me out for sure. Or so I thought. And it didn't look like she was in any big hurry to end this and get on with her day, even though others had thinned out of the restaurant to get to jobs or shopping, or whatever else goes on in Black Mountain on a Saturday.

"Yeah, I guess a lot was happening here. A lot of big ideas getting tossed around."

"Oh, there certainly were!" she interrupted, laughing as she did so. "Rice and Albers. They were the drivers. There were others too, like Charles. But John Rice, he was the one who got it all started. Big ideas. Lots of energy. And it was all right here."

"What do you think made it so special?"

"Oh, they were nonconformists! Almost every single one. They came here because they knew they couldn't fit in on most campuses. They were looking for something different. They wanted to try new ways. In almost everything! Painting. Sculpture. Weaving. Writing. Architecture. Music! Theater! Even the sciences. Mix it all up. See what comes out.

"This place encouraged you to be different. Of course, maybe there are a lot of colleges like that nowadays. But back then, not so. The thirties were a very stirred up time. It took a lot of courage for John Rice and the others to set up what they did here and try to see it through. A lot of courage, Jack."

Here Ruth Parker paused. I took a deep sip on my coffee even though my bladder felt like bursting. Then I took a step even though my brain said "Don't!" I felt like I could maybe trust this woman a bit.

"When I was in California, Duncan talked about Black Mountain almost like it was a holy place. A Shangri-La." Ruth studied me closely now.

I stumbled ahead. "I think as writers we are always trying to experience things as they are. Sometimes it means getting into the moment so deep you lose yourself. Like a jazz riff that just invites you inside and holds you there. Sometimes it means losing yourself in the immensity of nature where silence is the loudest sound there is. And somehow when you go through all that, you come out on the other side of the experience understanding the world a bit better. And sometimes understanding yourself a little better too.

"It was certainly peaceful up there at the lake. And with all these mountains around, I could start to feel what maybe Duncan and Creeley felt here too. It was something I think I felt when I hiked the Sierras with another friend of mine."

Ruth kept looking at me, her cup at her lips. I was enjoying her a lot. She seemed to almost invite me to tell my whole story, spill the beans, lay it all out. But, of course, I couldn't.

"Well, Mr. Jack, I do believe you might be the most interesting man I have laid eyes on since the Great Charles himself. Jo said as much even before you walked into her library. She said she could tell by the way you *walked* that you had the ways of the world about you. She's very good about people that way. She can read them like a book!"

I about jumped out of my seat when Ruth said this. Maybe Jo knows! Maybe Ruth knows! Maybe the whole town knows!

"She said sometimes people come through town and stop by the library and she can tell they are running from something."

My blood started to run cold here.

"But frankly she said you looked as though you were running *to* something, Mr. Jack." Ruth smiled warmly as she said this. "Would she be correct in her assessment?"

How to answer this kind of question? I took another long sip. Then the waitress reappeared with the ever-present coffee pot.

"Would you like a last refill? You're welcome to stay as long as y'all like. But I'm goin' off shift in ten minutes and..."

I smiled and said, "If you'll give me both checks, that'll be fine."

The waitress looked uncertainly at Ruth who smiled and said, "If our gentleman would like to pay for my coffee and toast, I will accept his gift most kindly." Relieved, the waitress hurried away to do her math.

"So, Jack, what did you say your plans were?"

"Well, I didn't in so many words. But I'm headed east to New York and out to the Cape to see Olson. Then when it warms a bit, I plan to run up to Canada and then start heading west."

This was already more than I should have said.

"So your stay in Black Mountain is going to be a short one?" Ruth finished this question with a tone of disappointment.

The waitress came back with the two bills. $3.75. I handed her a five, thanking her for keeping our cups filled.

"Well, bye-bye Mrs. Parker," said the waitress, adding, "It was nice to see you again! And...it was nice to meet yew! Come back now!"

Even as the waitress hurried back around the counter, undoing her apron, ready to end her shift, Ruth Parker seemed content to finish her coffee and see what more she could drag out of me.

"Ruth, would you excuse me for a minute? I can't hold my coffee like I used to!"

When I got back, Ruth was writing something on her napkin. She didn't reveal it to me as I sat down.

"So, Mr. Jack, are you going to turn me into a prying old lady?" This was spoken with such good humor that I couldn't help smiling.

"I'm sorry, Ruth, what more would you like to know? I'm a writer. A travel writer. I'm just passing through and kind of know generally where I'm headed next. But I am not in a rush to get to the next place.

No one is waiting there for me, if that's what you're getting at."

"So you are on a journey? But you don't know where it ends? Only that it has many stops along the way? Why, Mr. Jack...that sounds a lot like life itself!"

I did smile again as she said this, making my trip sound both profound and mundane. Important and silly.

"Maybe it is, Ruth. I just know that I'm not cut out for some nine-to-five job stuck at some desk waiting for my gold watch when I retire and then die."

Then I went on, blurting out the rest, almost not knowing what I was saying.

"I almost died once. And I had a brother who did. And a sister. I probably should have too. But the doctors saved me. And ever since then, I've known Death will come for me again and maybe I won't be so lucky. So I want to get out and see what else there is in this wide world. See what else I can learn about it. And maybe write some of it down. And maybe someday someone will read what I wrote and maybe they'll learn something too. And then they'll pass on what they learned to someone else who isn't even born yet."

She looked into me as I went on. "And that's how the world goes on, each of us passing along a little something we learned so the next one won't have to make the same stupid mistakes we did. Even though they'll make their own and maybe they'll die before they even have a chance to bring anything to the world. You see, that will be their own type of suffering. But I want to do more. Learn more. Write more. And leave a part of me for someone else to get to know somewhere down the road."

Ruth's eyes were wide now. It was clear we had moved beyond the little cat-and-mouse chitchat. And I remember thinking that maybe this was the kind of talk she heard at Black Mountain in the thirties and forties.

"Sorry, Ruth, I didn't mean to impose on you like that with a big speech and all..."

"Jack, you do not have to apologize for speaking your mind. And, Lordy, you did put me in a mind of John Rice right then."

I drained the last of my coffee. It was time to go. Somewhere. I probably should've jumped in the car, headed back to my camp spot, folded up my tent, and gotten the hell out of Black Mountain.

"So, you're leaving us now?" Her voice tinged with disappointment.

"Yes, I guess so. But not this very minute. I mean, I kind of wanted to walk around the town a bit. Is there anyone else here I should talk to about the college?"

"Have you been over to the Robert E. Lee?"

"You mean the Studies Building...where I was yesterday?"

We looked puzzled at each other.

"Why, no! I mean the *Robert E. Lee*...where the college got started! You mean you haven't been over there?"

I shook my head.

"Oh, Lord! Well, Jack you cannot leave this town until you have seen the Robert E. Lee. That, my friend, is the original Black Mountain College. It's the Blue Ridge Assembly now. A Bible studies camp. But from 1933 until 1941 that is where the college got its start under John Rice. Might have been its finest years."

Things were starting to get a little clearer.

"It's just a few miles south of here." Ruth continued animatedly, as though she'd gotten a new mission in life herself. "Take the light out here and go down to the next road that bears off to the right. Follow that for a couple miles at most. And then you'll see the signs for Blue Ridge Assembly. The Robert E. Lee is the big hall that's right there. At the end of a long drive. You can't miss it. I'm not all sure who's there right now. But if you ask nice, maybe they'll let you walk around a bit.

"Now where are you staying again?"

I told her about the campground east of town.

"Well, before you leave, I cannot imagine anything resembling Southern hospitality if I did not have a friend of Charles Olson's over for a fried chicken and mashed potato supper!"

It did sound tempting. We were both standing now. I helped Ruth on with her coat.

"Are you accepting my invitation, Mr. Jack Moriarty of Boston, Massachusetts?"

I laughed at her mock formality.

"Why, Mrs. Ruth Parker of Black Mountain, North Carolina, I do believe I am!"

"You will come to 123 Sumter Street promptly at six p.m. You may dress as you are, although if you have something a bit...tidier...that would be acceptable as well."

"123 Sumter Street. Six p.m."

"Now, Sumter Street is three blocks north of here. Mine is the large white house with the veranda. It's where I grew up. And it's where I am going to die! But not anytime soon, Lord willing."

We walked through the now-empty restaurant and out the door into bright late morning sunshine.

"If you will walk me to my car, I would appreciate that very much." She leaned lightly on my arm and walked a half dozen parking spaces over.

We stopped in front of a white 1959 Cadillac in mint condition. I thanked my lucky stars Neal wasn't here. He'd have been inside that thing and had it halfway to Texas before poor old Miss Parker knew what hit her.

"This was my Daddy's last car. It'll be my last one too."

"It's a beauty."

"Thank you, Mr. Moriarty. And I'll see you at six p.m. I appreciate promptness."

"Yes, ma'am. Thank you very much. 123 Sumter Street."

And away she went. Whew!

Chapter 7 — Lissa

I knew I'd have to stop by the other campus and see this Robert E. Lee building before showing up at Miss Parker's for supper. But I didn't feel like going over there just then. As long as I'd committed myself to another night in Black Mountain, I thought I'd have a look around. My curiosity level had gone way up on account of my extended breakfast with her. The little town was bustling. All parking spaces along Main Street were taken, with more cars spilling onto side streets. The Post Office and the bank looked busiest with a steady stream of people moving in and out. Here and there people stopped on the sidewalks talking.

I crossed over to the Post Office and bought half a dozen postcards. It was time to send something back to Stella and Memere. Then I headed east up Main Street. A couple blocks later I turned north. The businesses petered out after a block or so, and now there were just small, comfortable houses with small, getting-ready-for-spring yards and gardens. I crossed an alleyway and was about to move on to the next block when a small, colorful sign caught my eye. It hung just above a picket fence and read like this:

Black Mountain Ceramics
Lissa Tawney, Artist

The letters framed two hands cupping a bowl on a wheel. I looked down the alley and saw another larger sign like it hanging from an old barn or garage. I couldn't resist.

I've always loved old, unpaved alleys. That deep smell of oil and dirt just draws me. It didn't matter where...Lowell...the Village...Denver...San Francisco...Mexico City. I was never afraid and ended up having some of the wildest times of my life in them. I didn't expect this little alley to live up to those, but I had to have a look.

I followed a hedge down to what I guessed was the entryway of Black Mountain Ceramics, which was just a garage door. It was swung up, opening half of the wall facing the alley. I stood outside for a minute, wondering if anyone was around. I couldn't see past the darkness inside. I stepped into the shadow and let my eyes adjust. A radio was on loudly playing some country music station.

"Hello?"

I still wasn't sure anyone was here and was about to turn around and head back out when I heard another sound…a whirring. There, deep in the corner of the shop, a woman sat bent to a pottery wheel. As my eyes finally adjusted, I could see she was working clay into what looked like a tall vase. She was so intent on her work that she either didn't see or hear me, or chose to ignore me in favor of the work in front of her.

As my eyes adjusted, I watched her hands move up and down the vase, shaping it from a wide base along a long, narrow neck and up to a wider opening. It seemed her hands moved confidently outside and in commanding the clay to a shape in her mind's eye. Her work rhythm seemed to harmonize with the wheel. The radio wailed a woman's song of heartbreak.

I glanced around the studio, trying not to move or make a sound. I didn't want to disturb what seemed to be a particularly delicate part of her work.

The cement floor was cracked and pitted. A couple of long shelves and a table beneath held a variety of her creations: bowls, vases, mugs, plates, dishes. All looked very functional as opposed to decorative art work. I've always liked things you can use instead of just look at.

There was a metal desk with large sheets of paper and a couple pencils on it. There was also something that looked like a cash box. Above the desk was a larger photo, framed, that hung from a barely finished wall. An old propane heater next to the desk looked like the only source of heat. The garage had a loft accessed by a ladder set in the middle. The rafters had been covered with some old plywood and were now used for storage.

My eyes returned to the woman. It was hard to tell her age even from the short distance. But sunlight sheered through a crack in one of the back wall boards, illuminating long red hair held back by a comb. She wore a flannel shirt with the sleeves rolled past her elbows. Her jeans were worn, a bit of knee showing through.

Her hands stayed with the vase skillfully. In her right hand she now used a metal pick to add decorative swirls at the neck. With her left, she steadied the vase as though caressing it. Her fingers and palms were caked with the dark brown mud. I thought I heard her singing along softly with the woman on the radio.

She reminded me of Indian women I'd seen in New Mexico and Arizona doing the same thing on their reservations. Bending and shaping mud into everyday things that then took on lives and meanings all their own.

The song ended and some announcer came on starting his list of commercials. The wheel kept spinning. The woman was making subtle movements against the mud, slipping fingers inside, caressing its neck, finishing a design. Then her foot moved over the treadle and the wheel slowed to a stop. She kept her hands on the vase.

"Hello?"

She let out a small scream and jumped up.

"Oh my gosh, I'm sorry! I didn't see you there!" She started wiping hands across her jeans.

"No, no. I'm sorry. Didn't mean to scare you."

She squinted at me. I realized all she could see was my outline against the alley sunlight. So I took a step into the garage.

"Are you...open?"

"Well kinda, I guess. I was just finishing this. Now I need to let it dry."

"I can...uh...come back later."

"No, that's alright. You wanted to look around the shop? I don't have a lot for sale, but you're welcome to whatever catches your eye."

She wiped her hands one more time, then extended her right.

"I'm Lissa Tawney. But I guess you kind of guessed that."

I smiled and took hold of her strong grip.

"I'm Jack. Moriarty. And, yes, I did."

She wiped a smudge off her cheek. "Are you a buyer? Usually I don't see you guys for another month or so. I'm just starting on some new designs for summer. I have some sketches I can show you."

"No. No, I'm not. I'm just passing through and saw your sign. That's all."

She looked disappointed, but also maybe a little relieved.

"Oh, OK. Well, look around. Everything's for sale. Except that pitcher. Already spoken for. I need to wash up a bit. Back in a minute."

With that, she disappeared out the back door and to her house.

Then it hit me. The name. Red hair. Potter. This was the woman James Thomas talked about yesterday. The one who maybe knew something about the college. Now I was *really* interested. I looked at the pieces she had on display. I don't know a lot about pottery, but it looked to me like a mix of some contemporary designs with some things that had kind of a "mountain" look. I picked up a mug. Big. Heavy. A mix of grays and blues. Something good for the trip.

"See anything ya like?" Now it was my turn to jump. Almost dropped the mug too.

Lissa had slipped back in without me hearing. I turned back to her holding up the mug.

"I kinda like this."

She frowned. "Not my best. Made the handle too large. But maybe it's a good one for a man with big hands. Sixteen ounces. Biggest mug I've thrown. Have some other twelve ouncers, same design, if ya'd prefer."

"No...I like this one just fine." I smiled back at her. "You have a nice shop here."

"Thanks. It's not much. Things are always slow in the winter saleswise. But I try to get my inventory built up. Be ready when the buyers and tourists start coming through. You sure you're not a buyer? I mean I know you're not from around here."

I was about to say the same. She didn't sound at all like Jo Harris or James Thomas or Ruth Parker or any of the other locals I'd met the last couple days. Maybe I had the wrong woman from the one James talked about.

"No. Sorry. I'm really not a buyer. Stopped in town yesterday on the recommendations of a couple friends of mine who taught at the college back in the fifties."

Lissa's eyes got wide as I said this.

"You mean Black Mountain?"

"Yep."

"Who're your friends? You said they taught there?"

"Yep. Writers. Both Roberts. Robert Duncan. And Robert Creeley."

"Oh my god! I remember them!" Lissa interrupted. "I mean not well. But...I took classes up there. When I was in high school. They let me sit in on some art and ceramics classes. Robert C. he just looked different with that one eye. And Robert D., he was a cutie, even with his crossed eye."

Then she looked at me closely again. "Are you a writer too? I mean, you know, a famous one? I guess I should know, but your name doesn't sound familiar. And you're here to see what's left of the college? If you've been up there you know it's not much. I mean from what it used to be."

"Yeah, I guess so. Spent a little time up there yesterday. James Thomas showed me around."

"Oh, you got to see James! How is he? I haven't seen him in a while."

"Yeah...said to say hello if we met. He said you were someone to see about the place."

"He did? Is that why you stopped?"

"Actually, no. I just saw your sign out by the street and it looked interesting. It wasn't until you went back in to wash up that I put two and two together."

We paused for a second.

I looked at her broad face. The Indian-high cheekbones again. Freckles. Perfect teeth with a broad, friendly smile. And her eyes, brown, that seemed to smile with her lips and teeth. Someone who looked used to laughing. And the beautiful red hair falling easily to her strong shoulders.

I guessed she was about the same age as Jo...early thirties. Maybe they knew each other. A reminder to be careful of what I said.

"Mind if I smoke?" she asked. I shook my head, thinking it odd that she'd ask me in her place. I kind of wanted one myself, but somehow said no when she offered.

"So you're here to learn all you can about Black Mountain? Doing a book?" She smiled, exhaling ringlets with her question. We both leaned against her display bench.

I laughed a little. "Not really. I mean, yeah, it's something I've wanted to see for a while just because of the Roberts. But I'm not doing a book. Headed out tomorrow."

"Where ya goin'?"

"No place in particular, I guess. Headed back to Massachusetts. Maybe out to the Cape. Might stop in and check on someone I know."

"Who's that?"

"Another Black Mountain guy! Charles Olson. Maybe you've heard of him too."

Lissa started laughing and coughed a bit. "Of course I know Charles Olson! I mean not *know* know him. But when he was on campus you couldn't miss him. I was just a kid, but he was the biggest man I've ever seen. And loud. I didn't see him all that much. But when he was around you knew it!"

"Yeah, I don't know him well either. But we have some friends in common, and since I stopped here thought might as well check in and see how he's doing."

She took another drag, looking closer at me.

"You sound like him. You from Boston too?"

"Yeah. But I've been gone a long time."

"And you know the two Roberts. From Boston?"

"Nope. Met 'em when I was out on the West Coast. Been a few years. We had a little group that kind of hung out together."

"Only been to the West Coast once. Ten years ago. Vacation with one of my sisters. We went to Disneyland. Walked the pier in Santa Monica. Drove up the coast to San Francisco. What a drive! You ever do that?"

"Yeah I have actually. Couple times."

"What's that town south of San Francisco? On a bay...arty place..."

"You mean Carmel?"

"That's it! Loved Carmel! Thought if I ever made enough money off this place maybe I could move out there and set up a shop."

"Yeah, that's real pretty." I thought for a second about Big Sur. How that was pretty, too, but bad memories. "Did you like San Francisco?"

"Oh, yeah! It was such a cool town. I guess it's kind of all hippies now and everything. But back then it was beatniks. I felt like such a hick!"

I smiled, "Can't imagine that..."

"Oh, I did! I remember we just walked into this bookstore and there was a poetry reading going on. In the middle of the afternoon! We just kind of sat down and listened. Don't think I understood a word, but it just felt so....*cool*!"

I almost asked her if it was City Lights, but decided I better not.

Lissa stubbed out her cigarette in an ash tray which I'm guessing she'd made. There were two other butts in it. She wanted to talk some more.

"What part of San Francisco did you like best?"

The question caught me a little off guard. Not sure I could talk about all the little jazz joints and bars I'd been in with Neal and Allen and the others. Or the other crazy places with LuAnne and Carolyn. I played it safe.

"The Wharf is always a lot of fun. And the cable cars. And Chinatown."

She looked a little disappointed.

"That's funny. You don't strike me as a touristy kind of guy. I mean you look like some of the people in that bookstore."

I rose to the bait.

"Well, for a time I lived across the Golden Gate in a little house that was tucked in a valley surrounded by big woods. From there I could walk down to the beach. Or up this mountain—the one you can see from the city—where you could see for miles and miles up and down the coast."

I had her attention again.

"See, that's the kind of place I'd love to have! We didn't have enough time to even drive across the Bridge."

"That's too bad. You ought to try walking across it some time."

"Walk across! I don't know about that! My knees get shaky three steps up on a ladder. Have you walked it?"

"Yeah. A few times actually. Can't beat the view!"

Lissa looked at me with increasing interest. "When was the last time you were there?"

"Seven, eight years now I guess."

"Wow. Almost as long as me. Are you going back out there?"

"Yeah, I guess so. Eventually. But I'll spend a little time in the East. Then head north to Canada. Then probably head West."

"So you're not in any big hurry?"

"Not really. But I'll have to stop when the money runs out. Then make some more."

"What kind of writer are you?" She kind of leaned my way as she asked.

My heart jumped at this. If I told her fiction, I'd be giving away more than I wanted to.

"Mostly travel," I lied. "Articles for the travel magazines. Sometimes some freelance for a newspaper or the wire services."

This seemed to deflate her.

"Oh! I thought you were going to tell me you were a big famous fiction writer like Hemingway or that guy who wrote *Love Story*. What's his name?"

I cringed. "Ummm...maybe Erich Segal?"

"That's him! I just finished it. So sad. I cried and cried the last twenty pages."

"That's too bad."

"No! Even though it's sad, sometimes crying feels good. Know what I mean?"

I nodded. I knew exactly what she meant. "Yeah..."

We looked at each other wondering what to say next.

"You want a cup of coffee?"

Even though I'd drunk about a gallon at the restaurant, I said yes. I wanted to talk with her some more.

"Can I bring the mug? I'd like to buy it."

She laughed. "You really want that big ol' thing? It's gonna cost ya five bucks."

I fished out a five and handed it to her.

"My first sale of the day! Probably my last too! Come on then."

I followed Lissa out the door, then up a little walk to the house. Up a few steps to a screened-in porch, then into her kitchen.

"It's not big, but it's home."

"Looks nice." Her kitchen was as organized as her shop was. Small, but tidy. And colorful. I could look through a doorway to a small dining room beyond.

"Have a seat."

I sat down at her small table and watched while she poured water into the pot, then spooned coffee into the basket. She lit the small gas stove and put the pot on to percolate. Then she sat across from me.

"So. You're a writer travelling around the country and maybe writing some travel stories about the places you visit, but you're not going to write about Black Mountain? Not even for your West Coast friends?" Her eyes and lips teased as she said this.

I smiled back and fingered my empty mug. "Did I say that?"

"Are you?"

"I might."

"What would you write about?"

"Well...after almost fifteen years I can faithfully report that Black Mountain College is still closed."

Lissa laughed. "I'm sure that'll grab your readers!"

"What would you write about?" I shot back.

She kept smiling and gave me a studied look. Then glanced at the pot. Then back at me.

"Well, let's see. You could write about all the Black Mountain people who are still around, tucked into little spaces around town, up in the hills, over in Asheville."

"Are there a lot?"

"More than you might think. You've already met James Thomas."

"Does he count?" I asked, being a smart ass.

I saw right away I'd made a mistake. Lissa's eyes went from smiling to flashing in a heartbeat.

"Why wouldn't he! If it hadn't been for James and some of the others, those people would've either froze to death or starved to death and nobody'd cared which was which!"

On cue, the pot gave up its last gurgle, letting us know coffee was ready. Lissa stood up and grabbed it, turned and started pouring.

"How do you like yours?"

"Black's fine, thanks."

She poured hers, then added some milk.

When she sat back down, she looked at me evenly. She took a long sip. I did the same. When she spoke, she'd calmed down. Some.

"See, the smart asses who come here from New York and Boston or maybe San Francisco, all they think about the college is the way out ones, the crazies. Like Olson!

"But there were a lot of just ordinary people here too. They were the ones who made sure things got done that needed to get done. Teachers. Students. The help, like James. They all pitched in together. And they made it last a whole lot longer than if it'd just been the artsy-fartsy ones trying to make it go.

"So, if I was writing a story about Black Mountain I'd try and go find some of those people and listen to them and let them tell you what it was really like here." She paused for a second. "Then you could really write something strong about how the spirit of Black Mountain lives on."

I nodded and looked at her intently.

"So you think the spirit of Black Mountain is still alive even though it's been gone almost fifteen years?"

"Yes I do! I mean why would people like you come sniffing around so much if it wasn't?"

Ouch. I wasn't sure if I should tell her about Jo Harris or Ruth Parker, so I didn't.

"Fair question. So let me ask, what do you think is the spirit of Black Mountain?"

She could see I was serious, so she returned in kind, her lips lingering at the cup while she thought up an answer.

"I don't know. Black Mountain for me was always more than a place. It was this great big...*idea.* It was what getting an education should be about. Sounds hokey, I know."

Lissa paused again, looking past me to the porch door.

"I mean, for me, they let me come up there and just kind of hang around and learn as I could. I was in high school and I was bored to tears with the stupid stuff they were ramming down our throats. But up there they let me work with my hands. Painting. Weaving. Sculpting. Ceramics. Everything. And I just, well...came alive!"

She looked back at me now, eyes full with memories, brimming.

"Sorry! I don't even know you, and here I am babbling and crying and everything."

"That's all right. Sorry about the crack about James. I really did like meeting him."

I smiled sympathetically, our eyes meeting. Lissa started in again, this time more slowly, pulling up deeper memories and showing them to me.

"You see, I'm not from here. My family's originally from up around Statesville. Then we moved to Cleveland, Ohio, because my dad could get work in the auto plants. That's where I started school. During the war. Then he was killed in an accident when I was twelve. Got caught in a press..."

She paused again. More brimming. I waited.

"There was nothing to keep us in Cleveland then, so Mom, me and my sister moved back down here. She didn't want to move back to Statesville, so we moved to Asheville. Then she got talked into buying a little card and gift shop here in Black Mountain with the insurance money. It was a good business six months out of the year. But we like to have starved the other six months!

"That's how I got to thinking maybe I could help out making things to put in the shop. And I'd heard about the college. Then one day Karen Karnes came into the store and we started talking. She taught ceramics in the summer. Guess I showed some interest, so she invited me to come up and sit in on her classes."

She lit another cigarette, offering to me again. I declined.

"What did you learn?"

"That I wasn't stupid!" she shot back. "Just because I wasn't good at remembering body parts or the exact date the Roman Empire fell didn't mean I didn't know anything."

I sympathized with her on that part.

She exhaled deeply, blowing smoke towards the porch door.

"I mean Karen and some of the others showed me I could *make* things, you know? Make things that were pretty, had good design, that people liked. And used."

"Like my mug?" I smiled.

"Like I said, not my best effort. But if you want it, why not?"

"So that's how you got started, huh?"

"Yeah. I think they kinda treated me like a mascot or something. I got to know a lot of the teachers, some of the students. And I tried to help out with some of the chores. Sometimes Mama got a little POed that I was spending too much time up there. But then I'd bring her some bowls or cups to sell. By the time I graduated, we were doin' OK with the extra I was bringin' in."

"Graduated? From college?"

"Then? No. High school."

"You go to Black Mountain then? For college?"

"No. First, no way we could afford college. Second, I could see the place was kinda falling apart. Karen'd left. I was going to get a job in Asheville for the summer, save up enough to buy my own kiln..."

"Something happened?"

Lissa's eyes brimmed again.

"Yeah...something happened. Mama and my sister were up with family in Statesville for July Fourth. I stayed behind to mind the store. Plus I was seein' somebody...and...and Mama she just had a heart attack and died right there at the picnic. Laughing one minute and gone the next..."

I looked at her. So strong and so vulnerable at the same time. I was tempted to say something about my dad or Gerard or Nin. But I knew this wasn't place or time.

"I'm sorry. That's gotta be tough. Losing your mom and dad so young."

She looked straight at me. Then stubbed out the cigarette. She fingered the pack like she was going to pull another, then laid it down.

"Yeah it was. When you're eighteen that's not how you're thinking about your world getting turned upside down."

"So that ended any thoughts of college for good, then?"

"Actually, no!" She laughed a little. "But we had to give up the store. And my sister, she's three years younger than me, she went to live with my aunt and uncle in Statesville. And someone paid for me to go to State."

"Who was that?"

"I don't know! I just got this letter one day from Admissions saying my transcripts were good and I'd been accepted and all the money details were taken care of. I hadn't even applied!"

"And you don't know who it was? Or how it happened or anything?"

"It had to be somebody up at the college. Black Mountain, I mean. But anybody I talked to up there played dumb."

"That's pretty amazing..."

"You're telling me!"

"So you just went off to college?"

"Yeah. I thought what the hell, I'll give it try. My sister and I split the little bit of money from selling the shop inventory and what was left over from the insurance money after we buried Mama. Then I gave her some of mine to buy out her share of the house. Then I rented it out while I was away to cover the mortgage and taxes."

I smiled in appreciation. "Sounds like you grew up in a hurry."

"I had to! If I was going to make it to State in time for the fall, we had to get things taken care of. Fast."

She finished her coffee. I finished mine as well.

"You want some more? I think there's a little left."

"No thanks. But that was good coffee." I meant it.

"Thanks."

"Could I ask...why didn't you sell the house too?"

"Yeah, I got asked that a lot at the time. I don't know. We'd moved around a lot. And maybe Black Mountain was where I was starting to feel at home. It's a nice enough town. But, to be honest, I wanted someplace to fall back on in case college didn't work out. I didn't want to have to move in with my aunt and uncle too."

I thought about all the moving I'd done in my life. And here I was on the move again. But I could feel the attraction of putting down roots. Somewhere.

"Did you like college?" I was surprising myself at all the digging into this woman's life I was doing. But she didn't seem to mind.

"It was alright."

"What did you study?"

"More ceramics. It's funny, but I think sometimes I already knew more than my professors. I was already pretty good. But I got better."

"Anything else you liked?"

"Yeah! I took some art classes. But you want to know my favorite?"

I laughed a little. "Yeah, I do!"

"Accounting."

"What?"

She laughed. "I know!"

"Accounting?"

"Sounds crazy, doesn't it? But, turns out I'm pretty good with numbers. Maybe from those years helping Mama with the shop. Took two classes. Accounting I and II. Full of these uptight guys in ties and everything. I'm like one of two chicks in it. And I kind of looked like an arty and beatnik type. But I aced 'em."

"Not bad for a girl from Black Mountain."

"After the second class, my professor came up to me kinda embarrassed and asked if I'd think about going on for a degree in business administration. I told him, no thanks. I got what I needed. I think he'd gotten a crush on me," she laughed.

"So you got your degree in art?"

"No. Actually I only got three years in. After my junior year, the college closed for good. I was up there kind of hanging around wondering what was going to happen. Olson was there and remembered me. Asked what I was doing. Told him I was studying ceramics at State. He asked if I wanted a kiln. I said sure. He gave me Karen's kiln! It was probably the most I'd ever talked to him. But he seemed relieved to get it off his hands.

"So I brought it down here and set it up in the back. And started throwing some bowls that had kind of a Cherokee look to them. I put them in on consignment at the old store. Some New York people were in town, I think to say goodbye to the college, and saw my stuff. They bought it all. Then they gave me two big orders for their Christmas season that I'd need all summer and most of the fall to fill. And that was that. No more college. Time to start a business."

I was fascinated. When I saw Olson, I'd make sure to tell him their Black Mountain mascot was doing just fine. But I was thinking about the time it would take to get back to my tent and clean up a little before supper at Ruth Parker's.

"Well, look, I should be going. I'm sure you've got plenty of stuff to do."

"Yeah, I suppose. But it's nice talking to you. Sorry I got all blubbery there."

"No apologies needed. You're every bit as interesting the two Roberts told me Black Mountain would be."

"Even though I'm just a townie...like James Thomas?" She laughed as she got one more dig in.

"Yeah. Point taken."

Lissa took off her mitts and walked over to where I was standing by the garage door.

"So, you're leavin' tomorrow?"

"Yeah, guess so."

"Got all you need for your article?"

"Hardly!"

"Then why're ya leavin'?"

"Well, I gotta get up to Boston. Get out to the Cape. Tell Olson you're doing just fine."

She smiled at the reference to Olson. "What're you goin' to write about?"

"I think you asked me that before."

"Well?"

"Well..." I was stalling for time. "Maybe I'll make Lissa Tawney Ceramics the focus of the piece. Something about how the spirit of Black Mountain College lives on. Research a couple of graduates and where a few of the faculty have gone. But then kind of bring it back home and talk about how a girl who hung out at the college during her high school years is now a world famous ceramist right here in town."

Lissa laughed and blushed. "Believe me, I'm not world famous!" she protested.

"OK. Then nationally famous."

"I'm not even that," she replied, less emphatically.

Another pause.

She took one more step and looked at me closely.

"Jack, you remind me of someone so much, but I can't put my finger on who it is. I mean you say you're a travel writer, and I believe you. But something tells me there's a lot more to you than what I've seen so far."

"Well, if you remember, why don't you give me a call?"

She punched my arm.

"Ouch!"

"Now how am I going to do that? You walked in here an hour ago out of nowhere and now you're going to leave the same way you came!"

I rubbed my shoulder.

"I'm sorry. Did I hurt you?"

"No. Just surprised me a little, that's all."

"Sorry. I shouldn't have done that."

"That's alright. But, hey, wish I could stay longer."

"Will you be coming back this way?"

"I might. I really just don't know. Like I said, all I know for sure is I'm headed up to Boston. Then I thought I'd go on up to Canada. Then was going to head west. San Francisco's kind of where I hoped to end up by the fall."

"Ohhhh...that doesn't sound close to Black Mountain."

"No. But my trips have taken stranger turns before. Maybe I could stop back on my way out there."

She looked at me hopefully, but then could see it was just talk. She turned away.

"I guess you better get going then."

"Yeah..." I held out my hand. "It was really cool meeting you, Lissa."

She took it and we shook.

"Nice meeting you, too, Jack. Moriarty."

I turned and started heading out the door.

"Oh wait! Jack! Your mug! It's in the kitchen. I'll get it."

"Okay."

I watched her nice hips scamper through the door. She was back in a minute.

"Here ya go."

"Thanks. It's a great mug."

"Here. Take this too."

She handed me a business card.

"I...I...wrote down my phone number on the other side. If you think you might come back this way and want to...you know...know more about the college..."

"Thanks a lot." I tucked the card in my shirt pocket. "Maybe I will."

We stood awkwardly for a second. Then she kind of threw her arms around me and gave me a quick hug.

"Okay. Bye."

"Thanks for everything. Hope to see you again."

Then I turned and headed out the garage door.

"Tell Charles I said hello!"

I turned and waved. "I'll do that!" Then I headed back down the alley to the street and her sign.

Soon I was back at the car. It was after two. I sat for a few minutes and thought about what had just happened. Lissa was a looker and a spitfire, just like James Thomas had said. She was also a real artist and a smart businesswoman too.

As I watched a few people walk out of Jump's, I thought how this town was turning out to be a whole lot less about Charles Olson and Robert Creeley, and a whole lot more about Jolene Harris and Lissa Tawney. Good thing I was leaving tomorrow.

The Robert E. Lee! I'd forgotten all about it. I had to at least see the place from the road or Ruth Parker would be disappointed for sure. I started up the car and tried to remember Ruth's directions. To the light, turn right. Follow another road off to the right. Look for Blue Ridge something or other.

Somehow I managed to find the road. Then saw the sign "Blue Ridge Assembly." Turned again. And there it was. A really magnificent antebellum structure. Huge. Three stories. Half a dozen pillars. Terrific porch. I drove by slowly, then turned in the drive and stopped. But after hours of talking to Ruth and Lissa, I really didn't want to get into another hour long conversation with anyone. Besides, I had to get back to camp and get cleaned up for this evening. Six p.m. *Sharp.* I backed out and gunned it heading into town, then east to the campground.

Chapter 8 — An Evening at Ruth Parker's

I wasn't the only one at the campground when I got back. A couple of others had pitched tents, maybe coming out to enjoy the early warm weather. We waved in that way campers do, acknowledging each other, but not wanting to get too close.

I had a little over two hours before I was supposed to be at Ruth's. Between Lissa and her, I felt all talked out. But I knew there'd be a full evening of talking ahead. So I did the best thing I could to get ready: I took a nap. When I woke up a little after five I went over to the little shower/washroom. Then I changed into something "tidier," a pair of khakis and a little better quality flannel shirt.

"Goin' to town on a Saturday night!" I laughed to myself. I thought about some of the other Saturday nights I'd gone to town in New York, Denver, San Francisco, New Orleans and dozens of other wild places. Saturday nights that became Sunday mornings...and Sunday nights...and Monday mornings and...oblivion.

Then I got a chill that ran straight to my gut. What if Ruth offered me a drink? Could I say no? Would I want to? I didn't believe that AA bullshit about one drink leading to another, then another and another until you're passed out in the gutter again. But I did kind of believe what the doc told me about how beat up my insides were and how I might wreck myself once and for all if I tried drinking again.

I remembered the knifing pains of drying out. And I remembered what Gerard said: *You can choose Ti Jean. That is a gift.* When I was with Neal, I could never say no. Maybe with Ruth it'd be easier. Only one way to find out...get my ass in gear. The way she said "Six o'clock" told me you weren't late for dinner at Ruth Parker's.

The house at 123 Sumter was a white mansion set way back from the street. Victorian. With a pair of rising steeples, it dominated the rest of the homes. When I pulled in, I followed the sweeping circular drive to the front steps. I figured this was where I was supposed to park, even if my old Ford didn't quite match the grandeur of this house. A separate drive led to the back, where I could see a carriage house. That's where the Caddy was, no doubt, although I saw the rear corner of another car that might've been a Chevy.

A huge covered front porch surrounded the house and seemed to double the size of the structure itself. A swing, chairs and a couple of small tables suggested that it was used often. Pots for flowers were already hanging, but nothing was blooming yet. Before I started up the steps, I stopped to look at some ancient, well-pruned azaleas that formed the front landscape. Their purple-pink buds were just bursting. Oh how much I loved spring growing up in Lowell. After months of grays and browns, snow and ice, to see those first little crocuses gave my young heart great joy.

I remember Gerard coming home from school with one he'd picked for me. "*Pour mon petit frère* Ti Jean," he cooed at me. I twirled the little purple and white flower endlessly until the petals frayed. The next spring Gerard was gone.

"Mistah Moriarty?"

A booming voice of some authority pulled me out of my memory. I looked up and saw a handsome, large-boned black woman of middle age standing a step out onto the porch. She wore a dress and an apron.

"Yes!" I bounded up the steps. "Sorry, I was admiring the azaleas."

"Yes, they're just a little early this year. We should have their full color any day now. I'm Bessie McPherson, Miss Parker's housekeeper. You're right on time."

"Thanks. Is it OK for me to park there?" suddenly self-conscious about the old Ford.

"Why, yes, of course! You're company!"

I extended my hand. With a slight hesitation, Bessie extended hers and we shook.

"Won't you come in? Miss Parker is waitin' for you in the library." She stepped back and I stepped into the foyer. Then I followed her down the hall to a room on the right. I could smell something good cooking. My stomach growled. For the right reasons, I thought to myself with some satisfaction.

"Miss Parker! Mr. Moriarty is here."

Ruth was sitting with a large book in her lap. She had changed into a dark evening dress. Her hair was swept up into a fashionable bun. She wore a brooch with some serious stones on it. It looked like she'd put a little rouge and lipstick on. Even though I'd "tidied up," I felt like a bum next to her.

Ruth closed the book and stood up. "Mr. Moriarty! I'm so delighted you came!"

"Excuse me, ma'am, that pie'll burn to a crisp if I don't get it out of the oven right now!" With that Bessie disappeared down the hall.

I walked over and we shook hands. She covered both of ours with her left for a moment. I wondered if I was supposed to kiss her cheek or something. I didn't.

"Thanks for inviting me, Ruth. It's great to have a chance at some home cooking."

"Bessie is the best. You will leave this evening thinking you need not eat for another week!"

I chuckled.

"Won't you have a seat?" She directed me to a chair opposite hers.

"So what have you done with yourself today since we almost got swept out of the Candy Kitchen?"

"Well, I had walked around town. Stopped at the Post Office and got some postcards. I was tempted to look at the sale at Jump's, but figured where I'm headed, probably wasn't much there I could use." I didn't see any need to tell her about Lissa.

I tugged at my khakis, again feeling self-conscious at not being dressed up enough for a Ruth Parker dinner.

"And where are you off to again? Boston?"

"Yes, ma'am. Eventually. I may go to D.C. first. Or cross that new bridge over the Chesapeake and go up the Delmarva. And from there maybe to New York, then Boston."

"Your time is your own, then?"

"Yeah, I guess it is. But there are quite a few things I want to see before I get settled down again. Or the money runs out."

Ruth looked at me intently.

"So Boston is not your final destination?"

"Don't think so. As I said, I'd like to get up to Canada and then back out West. But I'll take it as it comes."

"Charles used to spend a lot of time in D.C. He was a New Dealer before he was a poet and the rector here. Did you know that?"

I guessed she was referring to Olson. "No, I didn't. Funny, hard to imagine him as a politician."

"Oh, no! Charles was *all* politician! I'm not saying he was a *good* politician, necessarily. But he was always scheming at something. Not in a bad way. But he was at his most energetic when he was trying to get people to do something for him. Or for the college. I think it was politics that caused the final split with his personal hero."

"Who was that?"

"Ezra Pound."

I knew Pound by name and reputation, but that was about it. Honestly, I didn't think much of the guy because he was with the Fascists during the war. And then locked up in a looney bin after.

"Are you familiar with his work?"

"Pound's? Not really. I think I made a stab at his *Cantos*. But that was a long time ago."

"I guess I am not surprised. He and Mr. Eliot were the giants when I was a girl and growing up. But Ezra had his own flirtations—with Mussolini—and fell into disfavor with many folks here and in Europe. I think at the end that was the case with Charles, too. He used to visit him at St. Elizabeth's after the war. Then that stopped."

Ruth spoke so familiarly of Pound I wondered if she'd met him and been friends too.

"Yeah, normally I don't care all that much about politics, but have to admit with Pound he went off the deep end. Ended up nuts, didn't he?"

"You are premature putting him in the past tense," Ruth corrected me. "I believe he is still among the living in Italy. As for his sanity, I cannot say. But many men after forty are not nearly who they were before." I didn't want to argue with her.

Suddenly she stood and started walking to a cabinet on the far side of the room. "I believe I would like a glass of sherry. Would you care to join me in one, Jack? Or perhaps you would prefer something stronger?"

I heard the familiar sound of bottles and glasses tinkling. "I think there is a very respectable bourbon here. And an equally disreputable whiskey. If you would like some ice, I can call for Bessie."

I got up and followed her halfway.

She turned and waited for an answer.

I wanted that whiskey. Bad. My stomach rippled in anticipation. Somehow I managed to decline her invitation.

"I'm sorry, Ruth. But I...don't...drink. Anymore. Hurts my insides."

Her eyes got wide for a second. Then she poured for herself from an expensive-looking decanter. I felt a shake coming on. Then it slipped away. I exhaled.

"Oh! Well, I can respect a man for knowing when he must keep his alcohol beyond temptation. My daddy never touched the stuff and he lived until halfway through his eighty-sixth year. Of course, his daddy drank himself to death at forty-three. Almost took the whole family down with him. So there you are."

She walked back to me.

"Surely I can offer you a glass of Bessie's lemonade? I believe she has a pitcher made up for supper."

"Yes! That would be great, thanks."

Damn! I shivered once more while Ruth had her back to me. Then I relaxed. For the time being. I'd passed the first real test. But barely.

"Bessie!" Ruth called down the hall. "Would you be so kind as to bring Mr. Moriarty a glass of your lemonade?"

"Yes ma'am!" was the echo from the kitchen.

"There we are. Now Jack, come over here. I want to show you something." I followed her to a large desk. A worn album was opened to a set of black and white photos. They looked to be from the thirties and maybe forties.

"These are some photos from Black Mountain's early days. By the way, did you get over to the Robert E. Lee?"

"Yes I did."

"Then I'm sure some of these will look a little familiar to you."

Bessie came in with my lemonade. "Here you are, sir." I took a large glass filled with lemonade and ice cubes.

"Thank you, Bessie."

"Miss Parker, we will be ready to sit down at seven o'clock."

"Thank you, Bessie. Our other guest should be arriving shortly."

"Yes, ma'am."

Other guest? Ruth Parker was turning out to be one surprise after another. Wonder who this was going to be. Wouldn't be shocked if it were Olson himself.

"Now, look here. This was taken in the summer of thirty-four. You recognize the porch?"

I nodded.

"That's John Rice, the man I told you about this morning. And his wife Nell. And Ted Dreier, he came with John from Rollins. And his wife Barbara."

"Who's that on the other side of Rice?"

"Why, Jack, that's *me*! I guess my vanity allows a little disappointment that you did not make the connection between the woman in the photo and the one before you now."

I thought maybe she was teasing, but didn't want to take any chances.

"My apologies, Ruth! I should've looked closer. Your smile is dazzling. And your clothes look a lot nicer than the others'."

"Well, that's because I was just home on vacation from New York. And an actress is expected to dress a certain way."

"You were an actress?"

"Why, yes! Does that surprise you? Didn't I tell you that at the restaurant?"

"No."

"This was at the very end of my career. Not much work for a woman in her thirties. Still isn't. But...it was fun while it lasted." She paused with the memory.

She turned back to the album. "Now these pictures were taken the same summer. This is inside. Did you get inside?"

"No. Didn't see anybody around."

"Pity. Although really there's even less there now that would suggest the college had ever existed than over at Eden Lake. Thirty years already! The time...

"Anyway, they were always having concerts and putting on plays and whatnot. This was a play. O'Neill. *Morning Becomes Electra*. They needed someone to fill a small role. That's me off to the side. I don't think we did a very good job with it."

She turned to me. "Do you like O'Neill?"

"Yeah. I do. His work was very breakthrough. He took on some tough stuff."

"Do you have a favorite?"

"I guess it'd be easy to say *Long Day's Journey Into Night*. But *Morning* is also excellent. Even if you think you didn't do a very good job with it that night."

I smiled as I said this.

"Yes. I like *Morning* very much also. Daddy was never much of a theater-goer. Whenever I'd come home and tell him the latest plays I'd seen or been in, he'd just roll his eyes and say things like 'I don't know why people waste hard-earned money on foolish fantasies.' He was a banker through and through. But his heart was good."

"What about your mother?"

Ruth paused for a moment, taking a sip of her sherry. Her voice lost its lilt, slipping into a sad memory. "We lost her in the Influenza Epidemic. Nine-teen eighteen. My first fall away at college."

"I'm sorry to hear that. Must have been tough."

I thought about Lissa, losing her mother at the same age, her father even earlier. Then I thought about my dad. And Gerard. And Nin. And Neal. And almost me. How life can be long and rewarding for some. Short and awful for others. Who decides who gets what kind of life? And if yours ends badly, do you get another crack at it?

"...wouldn't you agree, Jack?"

"Ruth, sorry, didn't catch that."

"I...was...*saying*," she sounded a little annoyed. This was a woman used to being paid attention to. "How tragic it was that Europe lost tens of millions in that wasted war. And then lost millions more with the epidemic. It's no wonder people went into revolt against the stupidities and incompetence of their governments. Wouldn't you agree?"

I assumed she meant World War I, which I didn't know a whole lot about to be honest.

"Yeah. We got off pretty easy by comparison."

"Yes we did, Jack. Yes we did. I lost one of my high school classmates over there, but that was nothing compared to what families in Europe suffered. Then they did it all over again twenty years later, only worse. And since then it seems like the only thing we've learned is how to blow up the whole world with missiles instead of bombs."

She surprised me with the intensity of her feelings.

Ruth paused, then looked at me and asked, "Did you serve in the last war, Jack?"

"Not really." Ruth's eyes widened at this unexpected answer.

"I tried to sign up, but the Army didn't want me because of my bum knee. Something I hurt playing football in college. Then I got into the Merchant Marine and did some runs across the Atlantic. But never ran into any of the really bad stuff, thank God."

"Daddy never served either. But that didn't stop him from being the biggest cheerleader for going to war—any war—when the time came. I always thought he'd have been a little less enthusiastic if maybe he had served at some point. Of course, after Pearl Harbor we didn't have much choice."

"No, we didn't. I lost one of my high school buddies in Italy. One of the greatest guys I've ever known. He'd have been a doctor if he'd made it back."

Now Ruth was thumbing mindlessly through the album. I saw more photos of her with others at the Robert E. Lee, including one with John Rice wrapping an arm tightly around her waist. Both had big, shiteating grins. She *was* vivacious, no doubt about it. Like she could be the life of the party when she wanted to be.

"I wish we'd had a better doctor here for Mama," Ruth continued. "It was hard losing her. Daddy depended on her for so much. But after she miscarried—I was eleven then—her health was never the same. Daddy did his best. But when the influenza came, it took her away so fast I didn't even have time to come home to say goodbye. Now she and Daddy are together again. But it took him forty years to finally lie down beside her."

I stood close, letting her relive those memories in silence. If I'd had the whiskey, I'd have slugged in down as a salute to their memories. I sipped lemonade instead.

"Did you quit college and stay home after that?"

I seemed to shake Ruth out of *her* memory.

"What? No. I offered to. But Daddy wanted me to get my education. So back to Vassar I went."

"You went to Vassar?" I asked with more than a little astonishment.

"Yes, does that—"

The doorbell went off with a loud ringing. I heard Bessie hurrying down the hall.

"Well, I believe the third of our dinner party has arrived, Jack. Maybe we'll have an opportunity to look at more of these photos later."

"I'd like that, Ruth. And, I gotta say, sounds like you've had a pretty interesting life!"

I could hear a muffled "Come in" at the door.

Ruth lightened up at this and tittered, "I have! I have! So far! And you don't know a *tenth* of it, Mr. Moriarty!" She squeezed my hand.

Footsteps. Bessie announced, "Miss Parker, Miss Harris is here."

We turned and there was Jo. My jaw dropped. She looked stunning.

"Why Jolene, you are punctual, as usual! I believe you have met Mr. Moriarty already."

Silence.

"Miss Parker, supper'll be ready in about fifteen minutes."

"Thank you, Bessie! Just call us."

We all stepped towards each other, Ruth and Jo embracing familiarly with a quick kiss on the cheek. Then Jo smiled at me and extended her hand.

"Why, yes. Mr. Moriarty, it is nice to see you again."

"Yes, good to see you again...Jo. Uh...sorry I didn't get a chance to stop back at the library. It was too late when I got back into town."

"I take it you found your way to the college? Or what used to be the college?"

Ruth stood to the side. Now she was beaming.

"Yes, I did. And James Thomas was there. And he was kind enough to show me around. And he said to say hello if I saw you again."

I tried hard not to stare at Jo. She was nearly as tall as I am. Her long, black hair was parted in the middle and flowed almost to the middle of her back. It glistened and was held back by a thin beaded headband. From what I could tell, she'd added a little makeup that made her eyes look larger, her cheekbones even more prominent, her smile...dazzling.

She wore a long, flowing dress with some kind of floral pattern on it. It nearly touched the floor. I could see her feet in sandals peeking out from under. The neck scooped low. She wore a silver and turquoise necklace that commanded attention at her breastbone. And when she moved, I was positive she wasn't wearing a bra. She looked like some kind of Indian maiden fantasy come to flesh.

"And did you find what you came looking for?"

"Well, kinda. I mean it's hard because, you know, there's not much there to remind you the college'd ever been there. The Studies Building and Dining Hall, they're pretty impressive. Wish I'd had more time to talk with James."

Ruth interjected. "I have been trying to accelerate Mr. Moriarty's education today. But I think you and I will have to work even harder this evening ...before he leaves us. Possibly forever."

Ruth smiled broadly at me as she said this. I was getting the feeling these two had cooked something up long before Bessie put her pie in the oven.

Jo said, "Well if you weren't in such a surefire hurry to leave us, I'm sure James would be happy to tell you more. And he isn't the only one with stories about Black Mountain. Or even the best ones." With this, she smiled back at Ruth. And both laughed.

"Yes," Jo continued. "Jack, I hope before you leave that you will have a much deeper appreciation of what your friends experienced when they were here. And what Black Mountain means to those of us who are left behind."

"I guess I'm glad I had the sense to stop at your library yesterday. I was getting frustrated that there didn't seem to be any signs of the college anywhere and I was just about ready to head on out of town. But this has turned out to be a real interesting stop."

"I'm glad you have found it so, Jack. It is a rare treat to have someone visit who has a connection with some of our Black Mountain folks now scattered to the four corners."

Ruth gestured back to the table. "Jo, I was showing Jack some of my photos from the early days."

Jo looked at Ruth, then me. "I love those! Isn't she ravishing?"

Ruth laughed, "So 'ravishing' that Jack didn't recognize me!"

Bessie appeared at the doorway. "Miss Parker! Supper's ready!"

"Thank you, Bessie! We'll be right there."

Ruth turned back to the liquor cabinet. "I believe I'll freshen my sherry for supper. Jo, would you like a glass as well?"

"Ruth, I would prefer a glass of that Spanish wine I had the last time. It was delicious! Is there any left?"

My mouth watered.

"I believe there is. Please help yourself to a glass."

Jo and I followed her over to the cabinet. I could see now that there was an impressive collection of various liquors along with several bottles of wine. Jo picked up one with some kind of bright yellow label. She shook it. "Ruth, I believe this is almost empty. May I open another?"

As Ruth filled her sherry glass, she pointed below. "Of course. There should be some more there," pointing to a table covered with a richly wooded wine rack that was recessed enough to be almost hidden from view.

I watched as Jo bent over and found another bottle of the same vintage. Then she straightened up and looked at my glass. "Is that just lemonade, Jack? Or are you hiding something stronger?"

Ruth answered. "Jack told me that he and Mr. Alcohol are no longer acquaintances. But he does not begrudge our occasional familiarities."

"Is that so, Jack?" Jo sounded both slightly disappointed and mildly intrigued.

"Yeah, afraid so. Wish I could join you. But had a pretty rough go of it last year. Doc said no more. Or I'd be wrecked for good."

Jo opened the bottle expertly and poured a full glass. "I am sorry to hear that. But I'm impressed you are able to be strong when we know how much easier it is to be weak."

"Thanks. It's not easy, believe me." I smiled at Jo. "But don't let my lemonade get in the way of your chianti. Used to love the stuff."

"And where was that?"

"Oh, all over I guess. Denver. San Francisco. Mexico. Tangiers."

"Tangiers!" Ruth exclaimed. "Why, Jack, you *are* a man of the world!"

I laughed at that one. "Not really, Ruth. I've seen some. Hope to yet see a lot more."

Jo added, "Did Ruth tell you she's been to Europe several times?"

"Miss Parker!" The voice boomed from down the hall, commanding our attention.

"Coming Bessie!" Ruth started for the door. "Come on now, you two. She'll start fussing if we linger any more while her chicken is cooling!"

I followed Ruth and Jo out across the hall, through an expansive living room and into a large dining room that looked out over a deep yard ringed with more azaleas, rhododendrons and dogwoods. The beds were neat and full of spring flowers. Several oak trees towered over all.

Sure enough, a large platter of fried chicken sat steaming at one end of the table. My stomach growled again, this time in earnest.

"Bessie, I apologize for our tardiness. We tarried a bit so that I might refill my sherry."

"Oh, that's alright, Miss Parker! Everythin' is ready jus' how you like it! I jus' didn't want it to get cold on you."

Ruth assumed her place at the head of a dining room table ready for ten. More, if needed.

"Now, Jack, you will sit here. And Jo, you will sit there." I sat to her right, Jo to her left.

Bessie went back into the kitchen and, seconds later, emerged with a huge bowl of mashed potatoes.

"Jack, I hope you brought a determined appetite this evening. Bessie is disappointed if she has to scoop up leftovers."

I laughed. "I'll do my best, Ruth. I haven't eaten since breakfast."

Bessie reappeared with a large bowl of green beans with bits of bacon layered over and another with spears of broccoli covered in some kind of cheese sauce. Then she brought out a loaf of homemade bread, sliced, with a slab of butter. Then a large bowl of gravy. Lastly, the pitcher of lemonade. There was enough food to feed that table of ten if Ruth had made the invitations.

"There y'all go. Enjoy!" Bessie announced proudly.

"Looks great!" I said.

"Bessie, you know this is why I can only come every couple months," Jo cried. "If I came any more often, I'd be as big as..."

Ruth jumped in. "Charles Olson?" The women howled at the joke and I smiled trying to remember how big that man was.

Ruth then asked, "Bessie, would you be so kind as to retrieve my sherry and Jo's wine from the library?" They already had their glasses; the women wanted their bottles too.

"Yes'm."

Something told me this was going to be a long night. After Bessie had returned with the bottles and retreated into the kitchen, we took turns passing around the chicken and vegetables and bread until our plates were overflowing. Both Ruth and Jo surprised me, matching the fill of my plate with theirs.

Before we started digging in, Ruth proposed a toast.

We held our glasses together as she said, "To wonderful friends, old and new; and to Black Mountain College and its people who live on still and are responsible for the uniqueness of our company this evening!"

Our glasses clinked. I stole a glance at Jo, who looked at me as if anticipating a reply.

"To Black Mountain, the college *and* the town," I rejoined.

"To Black Mountain past, present and *future*!" Jo chimed.

As we started, I could sense Ruth getting ready to pounce with questions. I didn't have to wait long.

"Now, Jack, why don't you tell us a little bit about yourself? What do you do? For a living, I mean."

"I'm a writer. A travel writer." I surprised myself at how easily I used the same fiction I'd told Lissa earlier.

"And for whom do you write?"

"Magazines mostly. Sometimes I'll freelance for a newspaper."

"Do you enjoy it?"

"Yeah, most of the time I do. Gets me out. Lets me tell people about places maybe they'd like to go. Which is what sells magazines after all."

"Will we be seeing anything of yours in upcoming publications?"

"Nothing right away. I'm sure I'll kick out a few articles from this trip."

"Something about Black Mountain, perhaps?"

"Sure! If I can find something that maybe hasn't been covered before."

"Like the college?"

"Yeah. Maybe."

Looking from Ruth to Jo and back, I said, "Guess I could say I've found less than I expected. And more."

Jo reached over to my hand and said, "That would make an intriguing start to an article. 'If you come to Black Mountain, North Carolina, looking for the college of the same name you will not find it. But, then again, you might find more than what you came looking for.'"

"That's an excellent lead!" I said. "You won't mind if I just steal that, will you?"

"Certainly not! I believe we could stand to have another tourist or two come here in search of our poor, lost college. Ruth, wouldn't you agree?"

"I do! In fact, I believe our little town is going to see more and more of the summer trade. But, Jack, I have to ask: do you aspire to something more?"

"More?"

"More as in something longer? A more lasting contribution. A book perhaps?"

"Yeah, as a matter of fact I do. It's been on my mind."

"I wondered because at the restaurant this morning you did not strike me as a...*journalist.*" She said that so drippingly I actually winced.

"Well, I gotta make a living. But, like I said, my goals are a little different this time around."

"Yes, I think making a mecca to Black Mountain to investigate a long-forgotten college would seem to indicate that. It has been my experience that many say they *want* to write. Some actually do. But only a few write anything of consequence. And it is the rare one who is remembered, even loved, for what they leave behind."

Ruth looked at me with all seriousness as she said this. "Have you decided what kind of writer you want to be, Jack?"

I was tempted to blow it all right then and tell her about *On the Road* and everything else I'd written. But her question really went deeper than defending my ego. It went right at what I was after with this trip, with what came on the trip after that, and the ones after that.

It's why I let Stella save me. Why I listened to the doc and Nurse Hauser. And why Gerard reminded me I had choices he never had. Why I didn't take that whiskey, as bad I wanted it.

"Ruth, I'd have to say that's not quite the right way to put it. I'm not sure I can decide what kind of writer I want to be. I mean I *could* say, 'I'm going to be the greatest writer since...Olson.'"

The women now laughed at my tease back at Jo. I think Ruth knew, too, what I'd heard about Charles...about an ego reported to be as large as the man himself.

Then I got serious. "All I can do is go out and take the world as it comes to me. Then write about it as clearly and truthfully as I know how. Whether it's an article for a magazine, or a book about being on the road for a long time, it shouldn't make a difference. I know it does. But it shouldn't.

"I think maybe the difference in writers is how deep they experience the world. Or how deep they *want* to experience the world. The only way I know how is to plunge in. And maybe this is where Olson and I have some things in common.

"He got onto Melville because Melville rode life out to the very edge. Quite literally. He wanted to see if he could stand up to the biggest, darkest forces this world can throw at a man. Then come back to tell the tale. As a result, we have *Moby-Dick*. Melville grabbed that whale out of the depths of the Pacific and gave him to us. Moby-Dick, the whale, is now part of who we are.

"I'm not going to jump on a whaling ship and try to do what Melville did. But there are other spaces, other darknesses, waiting to be explored. If I'm good enough, maybe I'll find one or two. And maybe I'll live to tell the tale. There's no way for me to control if what I write is remembered or loved, Ruth. All I can do is tell the tale."

We all looked at each other for a minute. I'm not used to making speeches, but I felt like I'd said enough to not disappoint Ruth Parker in her invitation, nor Jo Harris in her decision to join us.

"Jack, I believe you would have been most welcomed at the college. And I am beginning to understand better why your friends insisted you come to Black Mountain."

Then Ruth changed the direction of our conversation and asked me something I hadn't expected. "Are you married?"

I was stunned by her directness. Maybe I shouldn't have been. Then I did something I wasn't proud of. I lied. "No. Used to be."

As I answered Ruth, I could see Jo still listening carefully. Ruth seemed to take my answer in stride, returning to her chicken with a careful bite, as though she were a semi-bored district attorney. "And do you have children?" Another bite.

"Yes. A daughter."

"Do you see her often?" Another.

"No. Only a couple of times. She's twenty now. Her mother and I split before she was born."

"Are you sorry for that fact?" Another bite, but now a studied look at me. I put my fork down, wiped my mouth and looked back.

"I am. Very much. I've done a lot of stupid things. But fathering a child I've never been a father to is probably the stupidest. And I'm sorry her mother had to hound me for support. I don't know if I'd've made a very good father, but it was irresponsible of me not to have even tried. So, yeah, I'm real sorry about that."

"Do you know where she is?"

"No. Not for certain. I met her mother in New York. But then she moved back to Albany and her family to have the baby." I dove into the mashed potatoes and beans.

"Well, I, for one, am not one to judge you, Jack. Certainly in my years I have seen all kinds of families and all kinds of parents. Good and bad. Just because you wear a ring doesn't mean you are going to be a good parent or raise a good child. Just because you don't doesn't mean you are a bad parent or will raise a delinquent. You may still have the opportunity to be a good father to her. Or, if that is now forever denied, perhaps to another."

"That's kind of you to say, Ruth. Her mother is, or was, a good person. A little bit wild when I knew her. But then, so was I."

I paused for a second, then closed this part of the conversation.

"I just hope my daughter's grown up to be half as beautiful as her mother and twice as responsible as her father."

The women smiled at this. I felt relieved. In a strange way I started to feel comfortable talking about my life, disguised as I could make it. Although I was letting out many details that, if they'd put them together with other things written about me, might have been enough to blow my cover.

I also felt the ache that often hit when I least expected it. Not knowing my daughter. Having run from Joan and being too poor and too screwed up to even send her some money now and then. Until her lawyer tracked me down and shook some out of my sorry ass. I doubt Joan and I would've made it. But that didn't excuse me from trying to be the father our daughter deserved.

Jo asked, "Jack, I saw that your car has Florida license plates. Is that your home now?"

Jo's voice brought me back to the dinner table. I was glad for the change in subjects.

"Yeah, kinda. Actually, the house belongs to my mother. I've stayed with her the last couple years. St. Petersburg area."

"Have you been on the road very long then?"

"No. Left just a couple days ago. Stayed in Georgia the first night. In the Nantahala park night before last. Over at Harrison's campground last night. And tonight."

"Have some more chicken, Jack."

This started another round of food. The women picked at their seconds, but looked at me expectantly. I obliged them with taking on a full plate.

"Your mother is well enough for her son to leave her and go gallivantin' around the country?" Jo asked teasingly. The question stung a little, but I smiled back at her.

"Yeah, I guess so. She has the old age aches and pains, but she'll take Florida and the heat now over Boston and the cold. My dad's been gone quite a few years now. But she has someone to look in on her."

Ruth jumped in, "I believe our Black Mountain climate is just about the nicest in these United States. I, for one, enjoy our change of seasons. Not too cold in the winter, although we do get our snows higher up and even down here from time to time. And not too awful hot in the summer. We get our share of city folk coming up here looking for some relief come June, July and August."

Jo added, "I have not seen nearly as much of the world as you, Ruth, but I would have to agree. I have noticed more and more summer people comin' from all over. You may remember last year, we had a couple come in to the library all the way from New Mexico! They were lookin' for information about the college, too, Jack."

Ruth said, "That four lane highway has made it easier for people to get everywhere. Daddy was one of the first in this part of the state to have an automobile. But he couldn't go very far because there were hardly any paved roads! Now this...what do they call it?"

"Interstate?" I offered.

"Yes! These interstate freeways will take you anywhere and not a stop light or a town to slow you from start to finish!"

"Did you come here by interstate, Jack?" Jo continued her smiling as she reached for the bottle to refill her glass.

"Just a little. I took Route 19 up from St. Pete. Got onto a stretch of four lane around Atlanta. But then it was 19 to Asheville and the turnoff to Black Mountain."

"I hear Atlanta's about to burst at the seams. Did you see anything like that?"

"Yeah, seemed awful busy down there. Had to really watch the road signs so I didn't miss the turnoff for Asheville."

The women had finished their meals, but I continued eating and talking. This seemed to suit them just fine. I was the evening's entertainment after all.

"I know what you're saying about interstates and all, Ruth, but I've always liked traveling the two lanes and the back roads. Even did a share of hitchhiking in my younger days. I think you get to see a whole lot more of this great big country. On the four lanes you get in too big a hurry and miss things. You miss meeting people."

Ruth and Jo were all ears. And eyes.

Jo put her head on her hands and leaned into her request like a kid at a campfire, "Tell us a hitchhiking story!"

I thought back. The miserable hike that was supposed to be cross country and got aborted at Bear Mountain, New York. Then the bus trip. One of many. I settled on the one I liked the best.

"On my first trip west I hitched a ride on the back of an open flatbed truck with a bunch of other guys. Got picked up in Nebraska by a pair of brothers headed to Montana. Way those two drove, it's a wonder we all didn't fall off.

"But, man, what a ride! First time I'd seen those big open spaces. And at night all those stars. For a young guy like me from the East it was a whole new world. Not just the land. The people too. On that flatbed ten of us from all over the country going different places for different reasons.

"Here we were, all piled together hanging on for our lives, passing a bottle around for warmth. Not saying much. But hoping these two crazy brothers would get us to our destinations, our hoped-for salvations whatever and wherever those were."

Ruth asked a little sardonically, "Your highway angels delivered you safe and sound, I presume?"

"Yeah. I got off in Cheyenne. They were having a round-up and the place was crazy full of all kinds of other of people. I caught a ride the next day to Denver which is where I was headed."

"Why Denver?" Jo asked.

"I had friends waiting for me there. Some guys I'd met back East."

"Oh, so you weren't chasing a girl out there?" she teased again.

"No. But really what I wanted was to get out and taste the world a little. Meet different kinds of people. Listen to their stories. Try to figure out what makes sense and what doesn't.

"I had a friend who all he wanted to do was drive, drive, drive! He was from Denver. And I went with him across the country a couple times. This was way before the interstates, but I tell you he drove the two lane highways like they had four lanes and sometimes more! It was like he lived for the road.

"He was happiest when he was behind the wheel. Didn't matter where he was headed as long as it was fast. And, boy, we saw a lot of country because of him."

"Obviously, you enjoyed his company, Jack?"

I could see that Ruth and Jo were still trying to figure out exactly what kind of animal they had caged here in Ruth's dining room. I looked from one to the other.

"Yeah, I did. He was one wild cat, that's for sure!"

"Was?" Ruth asked.

"Yeah, he's dead now." I paused. "Died in Mexico a couple years ago."

"Were you with him?" Wow. Ruth really knew how to bore in.

"No. No I wasn't. In fact, I hadn't seen him for many years. Then I heard he was dead. Sad, really. He was four years younger than me."

"Did he meet up with some...*desperados*?"

I laughed, although that wasn't out of the question with Neal. We'd certainly met our share of "desperados" over the years.

"No, I don't think so. I heard he wandered out of the town where he was staying one night, got lost in the desert and died from exposure. Hard to imagine if you haven't been there, but it can get cold in Mexico up in the mountains. Probably been drinking."

"I am sorry to hear that. It sounds as if his demise was untimely. You mentioned that you've been to Mexico. Did you like it, Jack?"

"Yes I did, Ruth. Wonderful country. Wonderful people. Have you been?"

"No, I have not. It has not drawn my attention as it has others'. But our mutual friend, Mr. Olson, has. Perhaps you know that."

I vaguely remembered Allen, or somebody, saying something about that. But it was so long ago I couldn't even begin to remember why or how.

"Ruth, to tell you the truth, I don't. I think I remember another friend of ours saying something about Charles going to Mexico, but I have no idea what that was about."

"I understand he headed to the Yucatan to look at Mayan ruins. I believe he was one of the first to start interpreting some of the figures he saw there. He was always searching for...primal meaning. The origins of things. Would that coincide with your knowledge of him, Jack?"

Bessie came through the swinging door.

"Is ev'rybody finished?"

Ruth looked at me. "Jack?"

I scooped up one more glob of potatoes with one last bite of bread, swooped them into my mouth and pronounced myself finished.

The women beamed with that curious satisfaction they get from seeing a man well fed.

We—really I—had devoured nearly all the food she'd brought out a half hour before.

"Bessie, thank you," I said. "This was a memorable meal. I have not tasted fried chicken like that *ever*. Ruth was right. I don't think I'll eat another thing until I get to Boston."

The women laughed as Bessie started clearing dishes.

"Thank you, Mr. Moriarty. I do take that as a compliment. But I hope you saved some room for a slice of my strawberry rhubarb pie."

Even though I was filled to bursting, to say no would've been a grave insult. Plus, strawberry rhubarb was a favorite of mine.

"Bessie, I love strawberry rhubarb. Been years since I've had homemade."

Jo seemed fixated. Whether it was me or the wine, I couldn't tell.

As Bessie disappeared back into the kitchen, Ruth turned to me again. "Are you looking for primal meaning in the same way as Charles? Is that what has put you on the road now from Florida to Boston and possibly places beyond?"

Geez! Another shot right between the eyes! How was I going to answer that between fried chicken and strawberry rhubarb pie? But it was clear she wanted to be sure I was worthy of her Black Mountain friends and memories.

I tried to parry. "Ruth, that's a tough one. 'Primal meaning.' Those're pretty heavy words."

I paused. I didn't want to insult Ruth by suggesting her word choice was more suited for dried up academics than the streets where life is lived.

"I think Olson and I are looking for the same things. But maybe in different places. Maybe he went off to the Yucatan like Melville went to the Pacific. Trying to get at the primal forces that push us all along, but maybe disguised by all the crap of modern life."

I stopped again, trying to figure if what I said made any sense or was just bullshit. Then added, "I did bring along his book on Melville and Moby-Dick."

"I know it." Ruth smiled in recognition. "*Call Me Ishmael*, is it not?"

"That's right. I've read it a couple times. Thought maybe it'd be a good companion for the road."

"Did it get you any closer to understanding him? Or the Great Whale itself?"

Ruth's eyes bored in with deep curiosity. I felt she was searching as intensely as I was. She may have looked like a party girl in her earlier years, but Ruth was no lightweight.

Bessie returned with a tray and three slices of pie. One was bigger than the others. "Would y'all like some coffee? Or some tea?"

"Bessie, I do not care for either. Jo? Jack?"

"I believe I will nurse this glass of wine, thank you, Bessie."

"No thanks, Bessie. Your lemonade is just fine."

"That's good. Y'all just holler if you need anythin' else."

I dug into the pie like I'd gone after the chicken. This was some of the best home cooking I could ever remember. Jimmy may have bragged on his Susie back in Americus. But I doubt she could've outdone what Bessie laid before us this evening.

"So Jack..." Here came Ruth at me again. She may have been in her seventies, but she was as relentless as a prosecutor half her age. "...what do you think of *Ishamel*? Caused quite a stir in some circles when it came out."

Even though Jo was kind of a bystander through this conversation, she was listening closely. Like Ruth, she was no dummy. I was feeling the pressure to measure up to both. Ruth's question was an invitation.

But, at the same time, I wasn't up for empty intellectualizing. And I don't think Ruth was, either. Or Jo for that matter. If they wanted to get after it,

I'd give them the best this old "travel writer" could give. And I'd have to do it stone cold sober.

"You know, it's been a few years since I cracked those pages. But I could never forget that big opening: 'I take space to be the central fact to man born in America, from Folsom cave to now.' And—Ruth you may remember this—he wrote 'space' in all capital letters to really drive it home."

She nodded in acknowledgment.

"When I first read that I was pretty excited. That was what? Twenty years ago? Olson reintroducing Melville to America exactly a hundred years after *Moby-Dick*. But he wasn't giving us some bit of desiccated prose. And he wasn't reminding us that *Moby-Dick* was just a great sea story for all growing boys to read—like *Treasure Island*."

The women smiled at that.

Jo teased, "Why, Jack, I have to say that *Moby-Dick* is still popular among our younger readers. Our younger *boy* readers."

"Yeah, well, girls should read it, too. And women also."

Ruth said, "I have. Although I confess it was at Charles' insistence, after his *Ishmael* came out. I will say I think the female reader does have a different appreciation of it from the adolescent male."

"Ruth, I can't argue with you on that one. But Olson was after something big when he started chasing Melville. Because Melville was chasing something big too. And that line—'I take space to be the central fact'—really was a kind of new sound, a kind of literary be-bop. He's saying our geography defines who we are. Growing up in this great big land of ours shapes how we see things. Not God. Not our forbearers. Not even our individual circumstances... tenement or mansion. It was being born into America. 'From Folsom cave to now.'

"We are a big people because we are born into a big land. And it doesn't matter if you come into the world on the East Coast or the West Coast or somewhere in that great wide open Middle. We share that common root."

Jo jumped in, "You made me think of Mr. Frost and one of my favorite poems of his that begins 'The land was ours before we were the land's.' Do you know it, Jack?"

"Think so. Isn't it called 'The Gift' or something like that?"

"I believe the full title is 'The Gift Outright.'"

"Jo, I am not familiar with that particular poem. But I do have a collection of Mr. Frost's in the library," Ruth said. "Would you be so kind as to pull it down for us? I believe you will find it on the far wall on the third or fourth shelf up from the bottom."

Jo jumped up and I watched her glide into the living room.

"She is lovely, isn't she?" Ruth said following my gaze.

"Yeah. She was a real help yesterday. I might've been in Boston by now if I hadn't stopped and talked to her."

"Well, she was very impressed with you, Jack. Like I said, she could see you're pushing *towards* something. That's not a quality she sees in many men. At least around here."

"Why does she stay?"

"She came back when her father took ill. Then he died. And she didn't want her mother alone managing that farm. She loves that farm, Jack. But she's also a woman and I do believe she worries about the years hurrying along and wondering if maybe a husband and children are not to be part of her future. Not that she couldn't have had both a long time ago. But...she is *particular*. A quality that I admire."

Bessie came back in to get our dessert plates. "Miss Parker, I'll wash these up and then it'll be time for me to get on home."

Ruth reached out for Bessie's left hand, both of hers looking even smaller and whiter against the other woman's.

"Bessie, I want to thank you so much for making sure our guest will not soon forget Black Mountain, North Carolina."

Jo returned with a book and sat down. I tried not to look at her breasts moving beneath her dress, but, in truth, I did. Then I tried to give Bessie my full attention.

"Yes. Bessie, thank you. I haven't had pie like that since I was a boy," I said, reaching for her right hand.

The woman smiled broadly. "I'm glad y'all liked it. Miss Parker, if it's all right, I'd like to take Henry a couple pieces of chicken and a slice of pie."

"Of course! I was going to suggest you do that anyway." Then she lowered her voice to ask more seriously, "How is he doing now?"

"He's still pretty laid up. His back hurts him awful bad. But the company doctor says he's well enough to come back to the mill. Light duty. Doc Badgeley thinks he's slipped a disc. If he hurts it anymore, could put him in a wheelchair rest of his life."

"Well, I'd trust Doc Badgeley a whole lot more than some company doctor any day. Do you want him to see a specialist? I will make the arrangements..."

"I think he should, Miss Parker! But you know how men are! Apologies to you, Mr. Moriarty. He jus' thinks another day or two of rest and he'll be fine. But it's been almost a month now. And he ain't makin' no money lyin' on the bed. 'Course, all the company's worried about is him claimin' disability."

"Bessie, if you want me to come over and talk some sense into his thick male skull, I will!"

"I 'preciate that, Miss Parker. Let's see how he is next week. I already tol' him he's too old to be workin' at that mill. 'Course he says he does the work of two and where else can a black man make money that good 'round here?"

"Unfortunately, he does have a point. Well, you get on home and tell him we are concerned for his well-being. Then Monday, you and I will put our heads together and see if we can't come up with a plan to get him well and maybe doing something that won't turn him into a cripple."

Now it was the black woman's hands covering white woman's completely. "Thank you, Miss Parker. I do 'preciate you wantin' to help. Now, let me get these..."

"Oh, don't you mind! I can take care of them later. You have done more than enough. I will see you Monday morning."

"Okay then. Jo, it was awful nice seein' you again. And Mr. Moriarty it was a pleasure meetin' you. I hope the rest of yo' trip, or whatever it is, goes well."

"Thanks. I can tell you it's gonna be hard leaving Black Mountain!"

"Nobody says you *have* to leave, Mr. Moriarty!"

Everyone laughed at that one, me a little more nervously.

"I know....I know..."

"Well, good night now. God bless."

Bessie slipped back into the kitchen, and we looked at each other wondering where to pick up our conversation. Rising, Ruth said, "I believe I would like to retire to the living room, where the seating is a bit more comfortable. I see you found Mr. Frost, Jo!"

We got up and followed her. Ruth settled into one end of a long, plush sofa. Jo the other end. I almost thought they wanted me between them, but I opted for a deep Queen Anne's chair at Jo's end facing Ruth.

I noticed the large fireplace and the large portrait of the young Ruth over it. She was stunning, no doubt about it. More so because it looked as though the artist might have painted her nude, then added a wisp of clothing almost as an afterthought.

Ruth noticed my staring. "Do you like it, Jack? I had it done in 1925. A New York painter. I was afraid Daddy might think it a bit risqué for Black Mountain. But he had it hung right there and there I've stayed."

"Yeah, it's...you're...beautiful, Ruth. You could've been a model!"

"Well, who is to say that I didn't do a little of that to supplement my meager income from the theater?" Ruth asked mischievously. Jo laughed.

"And this is your father?" I pointed to an equally large portrait over the sofa. Father and daughter stared at each other across the room.

"Yes. We had that done in twenty-seven. An exceptional year for the bank, as I recall."

Ruth was ready to move on. "Now, Jo, have you found the poem of Mr. Frost's that you wanted to recite for us?"

"Let's see. Yes! Here it is! 'The Gift Outright.' May I read it? It's not long at all."

We both nodded our heads. I loved the opportunity to take in all of her loveliness.
Jo cleared her throat and began.

"The land was ours before we were the land's.
She was our land more than a hundred years
Before we were her people. She was ours
In Massachusetts, in Virginia,
But we were England's, still colonials,
Possessing what we still were unpossessed by,
Possessed by what we now no more possessed.
Something we were withholding made us weak
Until we found out it was ourselves
We were withholding from our land of living,
And forthwith found salvation in surrender.
Such as were we gave ourselves outright
(The deed of gift was many deeds of war)
To the land vaguely realizing westward,
But still unstoried, artless, unenhanced,
Such as she was, such as she would become."

Jo stopped and looked for reactions.

Ruth said, "Jo, that *is* lovely! I am surprised I was not familiar with it before now."

I said, "I didn't know it either. I like that line 'The land was ours before we were the land's.' I see now why Olson's opening made you think of Frost."

Jo said, "I've always enjoyed Mr. Frost's poetry. Even though he was just an old *Yankee*, I've enjoyed his knowledge of country livin'. I can feel his melancholy moments too." She paused, collecting another thought. "But this poem seems to be speakin' to the bigness of our land getting into our blood. Kind of in the way that Mr. Olson—and Mr. Moriarty—have been tryin' to do."

Ruth chortled at Jo's "Yankee." I sensed she knew too well that, a century removed from the end of the Civil War, Southern passions still ran deep among many, even among those who believed the South had to change or be permanently left behind in an America changing racially and culturally.

"Jo, we should remember we have another 'Yankee' in our midst! We should be careful of speaking pejoratively lest he call down the ghost of General Sherman himself upon our poor Southern heads!"

"Oh, I'm sure Mister Moriarty doesn't take any offense, do you, Jack?"

"None at all, Jo. Though I'll tell you coming up through Georgia I felt more like a 'Yankee' than just about anyplace else I've been in the South. At least until I got to Atlanta. One place I stopped for gas, a guy my age was nice enough about me being from the North until I mentioned I was a writer too. Then he couldn't wait for me to get out of town."

"Why do you think that was, Jack?" Ruth asked, sincerely curious.

"When I said 'writer' I think he assumed I was a reporter. And to him I became someone sent to write about race relations down here. He seemed pretty touchy about that."

"Yes, I can imagine. Last ten years have been hard ones in many ways."

Jo jumped in, "Ruth, you are so right. I really thought the country was goin' to come apart again couple years ago after Doctor King and then Bobby Kennedy got shot. It was like everyone had just gone plumb crazy or somethin'.

"When they started those sit-ins down in Wilmington and Greensboro, you could just feel somethin' startin' to build. Then you see all those marches on the television and then those dogs and the fire hoses. Then the President gets shot. And you just wonder what is the world comin' to?"

Ruth took another sip of her sherry and then continued this thread of the conversation.

"And this damnable war is tearing at the country just as badly. I really don't know what to make of it. Jack, you are a well-traveled man. Perhaps you have a perspective that would be of help to these two small town Southern women."

I dreaded these kinds of discussions. I didn't want people to know my politics. Hell, I didn't even know what they were. And what could I say that would offer any help to these two? And here they were, looking at me expectantly for some answer or insight that would satisfy.

"I don't know, Ruth. The race thing looks to me like something we've been sitting on since the Civil War. For the most part this country's treated Negroes like shit from the beginning. North and South. Seems like they figured out we can't ask 'em to go off to fight and die like first class citizens, then treat 'em like second class, or worse, when they come home."

Ruth answered, "I do agree with that, Jack. Henry signed up for the Navy right after Roosevelt put in the draft. That was nineteen forty. Left Bessie with a baby and everything. He didn't come out until the war was over. Bessie's mother worked here for Daddy. Lucky she did because Daddy was able to get Henry his job at the mill. And this was when jobs were tough to come by. Especially for a black man."

Jo said, "Things are a little better now, I guess. At least they're not lynchin' like they used to do. But there is so much anger in this Black Power movement, it just makes me wonder if we're goin' to have another Civil War. But this time black against white."

I said, "I hope it doesn't come to that. But they've torn up so many of our cities. I wonder if some of those places will ever get back to what they were."

Ruth said, almost confessionally, "Bessie's younger boy is right smack dab in the middle of all that."

Jo responded, surprised, "You mean Willie McPherson is involved with Black Power? I haven't seen him in years. He used to come in the library *all* the time. He liked to read everything."

"Bessie doesn't like to talk about it because it stirs her up so. Here, she's got one son dodging bullets in Vietnam. And another one maybe dodging bullets from the police or who knows what."

"She has a son in Vietnam?" I asked. I wasn't really sure I wanted to get into this. I'd gotten kind of a bum rap a few years before when I'd gone off on the hippies and all the doping that was going on and burning flags and draft cards. But, truth be told, I was one angry s.o.b. then. Angry at things I didn't understand. Angry at all kinds of people pulling at me, wanting something from me. Wanting something I couldn't give. Mostly, I was angry at myself. Angry at being full of booze and empty of any ideas or ambition. Angry at getting old.

But Ruth and Jo didn't know that about me. I was just a travel writer to them. A travel writer who knew some of the people they'd known at a college that hadn't existed for fifteen years. A travel writer who was leaving the next day and would never see them again.

"Yes. Tom. The baby Henry left behind when he went into the Navy." Ruth sounded resigned to telling a story that didn't have a good ending. "Tom signed up for the Army right out of high school. He worked his way up to sergeant. It's been a good, stable life for him. Has a wife and two of his own. But he's over there for the second, or maybe a third, time. And of course Bessie worries every second he's gone."

She paused. We waited.

"Then having Willie—he calls himself 'A-mir-i' now—organizing protests and what not. She lets herself worry out loud for Henry. But her serious worrying about Tom and Willie she keeps to herself. The less I hear about them, the more I know she's scared to death about what could happen to either one."

Jo had a concerned look in her eye too. "I don't know what's more dangerous. That Vietnam. Or this black militance. If Willie—or whatever his name is now—is mixed up in that, that is dangerous stuff for a black man. I mean I thought Dr. King's marches were dangerous enough. And look what it got him!"

She paused, then asked, remembering something, "I thought he started college down there at Morehouse. I thought he was maybe going to be a teacher, or even a lawyer."

Ruth nodded. "He did. But he got involved in his radical politics. Jo, you wouldn't even know him now. Bessie showed me a picture. His hair is out to *here*!"

Ruth gestured with her hands about a foot from her head showing the size of his Afro.

I laughed because I thought about all the long hair I'd seen on the coasts starting four or five years ago. Men and women. White and black. And I laughed, too, at how angry that made me. Symbols of things changing that I didn't understand and therefore didn't like.

But I'd changed over the last six months and now those things didn't bother me like they did before. With my short hair and beard I looked like a real square. But that didn't bother me either.

Jo said, "Well, I can understand why Bessie'd be worried sick. All her men laid up or in danger of dyin'."

"April is the cruelest month, is it not, Jack?" Ruth was ready to change subjects.

"Breeding lilacs out of the dead land, mixing memory and desire, stirring dull roots with spring rain," I replied.

Ruth clapped her hands in delight that I could complete Eliot's opening lines to *The Waste Land.*

"Why, Jack, thank you! I hoped you would know a little of Mr. Eliot. Are you a fan of his?"

"Not a great one, Ruth, to be honest. But you can't ignore him either. I mean, like you said earlier, he and Pound were giants fifty years ago."

"I think they still may be, Jack. Mr. Eliot is only five years gone. And Mr. Pound is still with us."

"Ruth, I guess I'd have to say you're right. They're giants if for no other reason than a whole bunch of people have jumped on their ideas while trying to find their own."

"Are your friends, Mr. Creeley and...Duncan? Are they also lukewarm admirers?" Jo asked.

"Yeah. I think they'd probably see themselves that way. But, honestly, I haven't talked to them in years. So maybe they've changed their minds since I saw'em last."

"Are you...estranged?" Ruth really knew how to throw the zingers!

"No. Not really. Just they're out west and I've been stuck...well, not *stuck* exactly...I've been in Florida and just haven't had a chance to get out to see them. Until now."

"I do remember Mr. Creeley. He lost his eye, didn't he? The right one?"

"I think it's the left. But, yes. Childhood accident." I hoped they didn't press me for any of his lines. I would've drawn a blank.

"He seemed real nice. He was only here at the very end when things weren't very well...organized."

"As if they ever were, Jo!" Ruth added with a chuckle. "Lord, that was one long hand-to-mouth existence. Daddy used to say if he ran the bank that way, he and three quarters of the county's farmers would be on relief inside of a year."

"Is that why Black Mountain failed?" I asked.

Ruth waved her sherry at me a little testily.

"Jack, 'failed' would be an incorrect word! Black Mountain did not fail! It ran its course. It did what it set out to do. When it came time to close its doors forever, that's what Charles and the others did. But, my Lord, you look around at the artists and writers and musicians and others who came to this little college as teachers or students and then went on to really make names for themselves.

"Why, here it is almost fifteen years gone and you come poking around because of some long lost friends who said you needed to come here. So you come. Not knowing why exactly. But you come. And you are not alone! They may not have run the college in a businesslike way to satisfy Daddy, but they succeeded beyond wildest dreams in doing what a college is supposed to do...educate young people and inspire them to do things no one has ever done before."

Jo and I were both silent a moment, soaking in Ruth's defense of the college.

Finally Jo asked, "Ruth, who do you remember most fondly?"

The older woman's eyes softened as memories surfaced in response. Her voice did too.

"John Rice. I mentioned him to you earlier, Jack. Jo, I've mentioned him to you before too. As the

Jewish people like to say, he was a *mensch.* A real man. Without him there would never have been a Black Mountain. He knew what he wanted and he went out and got it. His wife, Nell, was a nice woman and a good mother to their boy Dan. But no way could she keep him corralled. John Rice was a force of *nature.*"

"Ruth, I do remember him from your photos. He was a nice-lookin' man."

"Oh, yes! And quite vain about that too!" Ruth laughed softly as she said this. "But, then, the college never seemed to lack for nice looking men during those times I visited."

"Who else?" I asked.

"Besides the Great Charles, himself?" Ruth asked back, good-naturedly. "Well, let's see, there was Merce Cunningham. A wonderful dancer! Have you heard of him?"

I had. But Jo hadn't.

"Oh he has choreographed some outstanding pieces! He is really one of the great ones of our times. I have not seen one of his shows in several years, but he formed his dance company here in the early fifties. And he danced with the great Martha Graham before that. A wonderful man.

"In New York, he paired up with another Black Mountain student, John Cage, who has composed much of the music that plays alongside Merce's dances. But, hoooo—eeeeeee! Do not ask me to understand what his music is about! I just know they are both very respected among the *avant-garde.*" Ruth said that last word with a mixture of amusement and awe.

"And I dare not forget the Albers. They were lucky to get away from the Nazis. And, truth be told, John was lucky to have them here. They were both from the Bauhaus, very accomplished artists. Josef brought a discipline and structure to the college I think John needed. They were a little of yin and yang, if you know what I mean. Anni was also the perfect companion for Josef. And a very good fabric artist in her own right.

"Of course, there were many others I never met but just heard about. Some stayed for a while, some just passed through. But it did seem like our little Black Mountain was quite a draw for the time it lasted. What did you say your friends' names were again, Jack?"

"Um. Two Roberts. Duncan. And Creeley. Writers. Poets, really."

"Yes, that Creeley name does sound familiar. Jo, I hate to be a bother, but could I ask you to retrieve another volume for me in the library? I believe you will find it on the fourth shelf under the B's. It should be my only edition of the *Black Mountain Review*."

Jo again moved between Ruth and me. And again I followed the easy sway of her hips. And again Ruth watched me watch Jo, smiling approvingly I think.

Of course I knew about the *Review*. Allen and I had been published in it back in the fifties. Creeley had edited it. Now I was trying to figure out quickly how much to say I knew about it.

"Found it!" Jo called from the library. She brought a crisp copy in and handed it to Ruth.

"No, no. Please give that to Jack. I think he might find it of interest."

Jo smiled as she handed it to me and settled back into the sofa. To be honest, she was of greater interest right now than the book in my hands. But I was here to get a better understanding of Black Mountain, so I had to show the proper amount of interest and respect for Ruth.

Ruth's *Review* issue was number seven. I knew about it because I was in and out of San Francisco when Creeley was there and rounding up work from Allen, Snyder, Whalen and some others to put into the *Review*. It also turned out to be the last one he or anybody else did. Thumbing the pages sure did bring back memories. But not ones I could share with these women.

"Does that publication look familiar to you, Jack?" Ruth asked with a smile.

"It does. I think Robert was putting this together about the time I first met him in San Francisco. I recognize some of these people. Allen Ginsberg. Gary Snyder. Phil Whalen. Ken Rexroth. Quite a lineup, really."

"Did you see the inside cover?"

There in a large, almost illegible scrawl, was this:

May 15, 1956

To Ruth,

For all your extraordinary generosity, artistic and financial, with this I bid adieu.

Still, what does not change is the will to change. These have sustained me and our little college to lengths far greater than you can ever know.

I remain always

Yr humble servant,

Charles

"He wanted to make sure I had at least this piece of the college before it all blew away."

Ruth said this wistfully, as though trying to push back Time's onslaught onto her own life. I was beginning to understand better why my visit was important to her in a far more personal way than she might ever be able to articulate to me or to Jo. Maybe to anyone.

She was in her own desperate fight to hold on. As we all are. I thought back to those San Francisco times. Crazy. Wild. Out of control. But something learned too.

"Looks like you must have been a big help to Charles and the college."

"Oh, more than you or anybody else can ever know, Jack!" Jo jumped in. "And not just the college. Ruth has helped all kinds of people all her life." I remembered what Jo had said yesterday about Ruth helping kids get to college.

"I have done what I could do. And I'm glad to have done it. And now you, Jack Moriarty, have to make sure that your friends and all those who made Black Mountain what it was—and still *is*—are never forgotten. So you write your articles for your travel magazines. But I know you have more than that in you. I could see that this morning. I think Jo saw it about the moment you walked into her library."

I shifted a little uncomfortably. Both women were really boring in on me now. Smiling, but serious. It had been a long time, a real long time, since someone took me or my writing seriously.

And here these two thought they were peeling back the veneer of some two-bit commercial writer to discover and encourage maybe something of a kindred spirit. Or someone who reminded them of the kind of people who made Black Mountain something magical. Now they wanted me to carry that torch forward. How? They were leaving that up to me. Was I supposed to give them an answer now? I hadn't a clue...

"Now, are you really up and leaving us tomorrow?"

"I...I...had planned on it. But it's Sunday, so I don't know."

"There's no place where you *have* to be, if I recall."

"Yes, that's right. My time is pretty much my own."

"Then why are you in such a fury to be gone?"

I tried to deflect her inquisition with a laugh. "Well, Ruth, I wouldn't say it was a fury. But I had no idea what to expect when I got here. Like I said this morning, I almost left town without seeing a thing.

But, thanks to Jo, and you, I've gotten to see a whole lot more than I could've imagined."

"I think what Ruth is tryin' to say is that there's a whole lot more that she could tell you...if you had the time, that is."

I looked at Ruth, who nodded slightly. "Sounds like you two want me to write a book or something!"

"Maybe we do!" Ruth jumped on that like she'd been thinking of it all day and was waiting for the moment to pop the question. "After all, you know Charles and Mr. Creeley and Mr....what was his name?"

"Duncan."

"Yes. Mr. Duncan."

Now I jumped in, pleading my case. "But believe me, Ruth, I don't know Olson anywhere close to how well you know him."

"Then maybe you should stay long enough to take some notes. So when you go to see him, you are prepared."

There was a line of logic to her argument that was hard to resist without just being rude, which I didn't want to be for either Ruth's sake or Jo's.

"Well, tomorrow is Sunday. Not likely to be a whole lot open on the road anyhow." I could feel my surrender becoming complete. How the hell did I get in this mess?

"So you will consider honoring our little town with your presence for perhaps another day, Mr. Moriarty?" Ruth asked, as though she were back on her New York stage forty years ago.

"Yeah. I'll give it some thought. I want to get some writing done anyway."

"I am delighted! I believe Jo might be as well."

"I think if you are serious about encouraging people to visit Black Mountain, we could add to your education a bit more. There is much to learn here, even if the doors to the college are closed." Jo smiled broadly saying this.

Then, almost as though a bell had rung, Ruth ended the evening. Standing up, she announced, "Children, it is much past my bedtime even if it is not yet yours. I am going to shoo you out of my house so you may continue your evening elsewhere."

She started towards the front door, wobbling a bit. I wasn't sure if she tottered from age or sherry. From what I could tell, she'd managed to get through most of a bottle during our three hours together. I'd have been tottering too, if I'd had that much.

We followed as she gave me orders for the next day. "Now Jack, if you would be so kind as to return at two o'clock tomorrow afternoon, perhaps we could entertain ourselves with a Sunday drive."

I got the feeling saying no wasn't an option.

"Sure, Ruth."

As she got to the door, she turned back and asked, "And, Jo, you will be joining us as well?"

"I believe I can, Ruth. That is, if Jack wouldn't mind."

"Me? Naw. That'd be great."

Ruth opened the door and a moist coolness swept in. She extended her hand to me.

"Jack, I am delighted that you would indulge an old woman and her memories this evening. I look forward to continuing our conversation tomorrow. And you may keep that *Review* until then, if you wish."

Her hand felt firm in mine. She looked almost luminous now. White hair, cheeks aglow, eyes intense, searching, knowing, her smile almost ever present yet ready to snap at foolish remarks (as she did with a couple of mine). She may have lost whatever steps she learned from Merce Cunningham, but she was not yet frail. She would not go gently into this or any other night, good or bad. I sensed she was still taking my measure, but I hadn't disappointed her yet.

"Ruth, these past couple days have been eye-openers, for sure. I might be able to spin two or three stories out of all you—and Jo—have shared with me."

"Well, you two get on now. I'll see you tomorrow afternoon. After I've had my conversation with the Man Upstairs and bribed my way into staying another week on this side of the Pearly Gates."

Jo gave Ruth a big hug, and with our good-nights, she closed the door behind us. The night and neighborhood were quiet. Beyond the porch light, a half moon cast enough light down so I could see the roof of Jo's car tucked in behind mine. A VW. We walked down the steps and over to the driveway in silence, Jo staying close enough that our shoulders brushed. We walked around to the driver's side.

"That Ruth is something! I think when she sat down with me this morning she had it in her head I was not leaving Black Mountain until she said so!"

Jo laughed. "Oh, Jack! You don't have to sound so conspiratorial! I'm sure she just found your company pleasant to be with. You should be flattered."

I ran my hand over the VW's roof. I flashed back to the wild parties we used to have in Mill Valley. "Used to see a lot of these on the West Coast. Not so many in Florida. You like it?"

"Yes I do. Except in the winter. Heater's not much good, I'm afraid."

I wanted to say hers was working pretty well. We stood close enough that I could feel and smell her warmth. It was intoxicating. I hadn't been close to a woman like this in a very long time.

My marriage to Stella hadn't been sexual. She understood this from the start. But I know that my drinking heavily had disappointed her in more ways than one. And I know I'd married her to be more nurse and companion to both me and Memere. Though unspoken, she knew this too. And accepted it as part of being close to me, her one true love from childhood to now. For that, Stella was, and is, a saint.

For my part, I hadn't been with anyone else since we married. Then again, I wouldn't have been much use if I had. My dick hadn't worked in years.

Because of the booze, I guessed. And that played on my mind. And then I drank to stop the worrying. And that just caused the whole thing to get worse. No wonder I was pissed off at the world.

But then yesterday at the restaurant I felt a twinge. Then this afternoon with Lissa, felt it again. And now I felt it one more time. I shifted to get more comfortable.

Jo put her hand on my left arm. "Jack, I don't want to sound like a woman who's lost her morals, I mean I hardly know you, but...if you'd prefer a soft bed to hard ground...you are welcome to stay with me tonight."

I didn't know what to say. So I reached for her hip with my hand and pulled her closer. She leaned into me for our kiss. Her lips and her body did not disappoint. I felt the softness of her breasts against my shirt. My long lost hardness pressed against a thigh.

We kissed like two people who had not felt the passion and touch of another for a long time. The way she kissed back at me said maybe I hadn't lost my way with women entirely. My hands greedily explored the back and sides of her body. Her heat and scent seemed to envelop us.

Twenty years ago, we'd never have made it back to her house. Twenty years ago, I'd have laid with her right there on the dampness of Ruth's grass. Twenty years ago, I'd have fallen so deep and far and fast in love that the only world that existed was ours, a tiny cocoon of fucking and drinking and wild plans and exhaustion. Then more of the same.

I broke our kiss and Jo came back at me for another. I wanted this woman. She was beautiful and strong and she wanted me. I pressed my crotch deep into hers, coaxing a whimper. Finally, we broke our bodies long enough to catch our breaths. I kissed her hair. I hated what I had to say. I wasn't even sure why I said it. But I knew I had to.

"Jo, I can't. Not tonight."

She pulled back, searching my face in the darkness.

"Is there...someone else?"

"No. And it's not that I don't want to. Twenty years ago you wouldn't have had time to ask. But...it's hard to explain."

She leaned into me for another kiss. Damn! I could tell hers would be exquisite woman flesh. She promised a night I would not forget.

"Jack, it's OK. I don't expect anything from you. Except you. For tonight." Her thigh moved across my groin. I was the one breathing hard now.

I ran my hands across her backside and pulled her close for more kisses. Then I separated us again. I tried again to explain.

"Jo, I haven't felt this way in a long time. But you hardly know me. I might come home with you tonight and not want to leave because being with you is too sweet. And then I wouldn't finish this trip and not get that book written you and Ruth want me to write."

"Maybe you don't need to go any farther than right here to write your book..."

I kissed her for that. A hand felt the underside of a full breast. I was lost. Almost.

"Jo, let me try the hard ground of my tent tonight. I'll see you tomorrow. Maybe you'll feel a whole lot different and happy you didn't have to wake up with me beside you. Maybe I'll wake up wishing I had."

She leaned in for one more kiss, then pulled away.

"Jack, you are one mysterious man for sure! I will let you get away for tonight. And make a miserable woman out of me because of it. But you had better show up here tomorrow promptly at two o'clock. Because if you are any kind of a serious writer, you will pay attention to what Ruth and I are going to show you. And then maybe you will think twice about havin' to run off to your New Yorks and your Bostons and what have yous!"

With that she gave me one more short, hard kiss. Then moved to open her door.

"Good night, Mr. Moriarty!"

I was still slightly stunned.

"Good night, Jo," I responded weakly. "I'll see you here tomorrow. At two."

Then I walked to my car, started it up and pulled out of the drive. Jo followed behind. And when I turned left to head back to the campground, she turned right towards her home. If Allen had seen this, he'd have called me a schmuck. And I'd have deserved it.

I drove slowly through Black Mountain's dark, quiet streets followed by the half moon all the way down the road. I almost missed the turnoff to Harrison's, then drove slowly and quietly to my site. One campfire still flickered in the distance.

I stumbled into the tent. Kicked off my shoes and pants. Tossed my shirt next to them. Crawled inside my sleeping bag. And, yes, wished I had followed Jo home instead.

Chapter 9 — Sabbath

"Mr. Moriarty!"

The voice pulled me out of a dreamless sleep. What the hell?

"Mr. Moriarty? You in there?"

"Yeah. Yeah. Just a sec." Who the hell was calling for me on a Sunday morning?

I pulled on my jeans and stepped into a dazzling morning. Outlined against the sun, I could barely see the man who'd woken me up. Beyond him I could hear a car motor running. As my eyes adjusted, I saw it was the campground owner, Harrison, a man in his mid-thirties in a dark suit that looked maybe a size too large. My height, but thinner. Wiry. Brown hair slicked back. White shirt buttoned to the neck. No tie. His smile was friendly but nervous, preoccupied. His teeth suffered from a lack of attention.

"I hate to bother you this early, bein' Sunday and all, but me and the missus and the young'uns are headed off to church and then to her family for supper. They's over in Asheville. Anyway we'll be gone the day and I jus' wanted to know if you were plannin' on stayin' another night."

"Yeah. Guess I am. This has turned into a longer stop than I'd planned."

"I trust that is a good thing." Pause. "Would it be too much askin' ya to pay now before we leave?"

"No, not at all. Let me get my wallet." I had the feeling he could use the three bucks for gas. Or maybe the donation plate. I ducked into the tent, pulled my wallet from the khakis. I came back out and handed him a five. He looked uneasy trying to fish for change.

"Don't worry about it. If I stay over tomorrow, I'll pay ya a buck then. If I don't, consider it thanks for letting me enjoy the quiet of your place."

"Thank you kindly. Glad you enjoyin' it. I think you'll be the only one again tonight. Others are just Saturday nighters. We're still a good month away from our busy season."

"I am! Have met some real nice people. Black Mountain seems to be a friendly town. Had a good breakfast at the Candy Kitchen yesterday, too."

"Yessuh, Kitchen's been feedin' folks 'bout long as I can remember. They have best grits 'round. Ham's good too."

He looked back over his shoulder at the old Woody station wagon. I could see his wife looking at him expectantly. Two or three kids were trying hard to stay seated in the back. I got the impression he'd rather spend time comparing menu items at the restaurant than doing what the rest of the day held.

"Best be goin'. Bein' late to the church door is not a path to a happy household, if'n ya know what I mean."

I smiled sympathetically. Then extended my hand. "Thanks so much for your hospitality, Mr. Harrison."

He took mine. "We've enjoyed havin' you, Mr. Moriarty. I hope the Lord sees you safely to your final destination."

Then he turned and walked quickly to the car and around to the driver's side. I watched him hand the five to his wife while saying something, probably about the extra two dollars. When he put the car in gear, she turned back and nodded slightly. A tow-headed boy stared at me, fingers hooked over a half-rolled window. I gave them a short wave as off they went.

It was a little after 9:30. Time to start a fire and get some coffee brewed. And figure out what the hell the rest of this day might bring for me.

I wrote a lot in my notebook that morning.

April 5 Sunday

Harrison's Campground—Black Mountain $3/ night.

Harrison stopped by. Young family. Wife. 2/3 kids. Joads?

Yesterday was women women women.

Ruth Parker Candy Kitchen.

Lissa Tawney studio/home.

Ruth and Jo at Ruth's house for supper.

Bessie McPherson housekeeper. Henry husband. Tom, Willie (Ameeri?) sons.

Ruth

Banker's daughter Vassar NY actress/model 20s/30s

Nobody's fool O'Keeffe?

Gave $$$ to keep BMC going at end

Knows Olson

Also John Rice guy who started BMC

Nell wife...son name?

Other BMC: Albers (paint) Cunningham (dance) Cage (music) Dryer?

Has BMC Review #7. Last one Olson note Let me borrow overnight

(Knew abt this in SF/Allen)

Told abt first campus Robt E. Lee Hall stopped huge place no one there

Wants to keep BMC flame alive

Wants me to help Don't know if I can

Lissa

30s A beauty Red hair freckles big smile STRONG

Part Cherokee?

Born NC Lived in Ohio/ Parents died young

Owns ceramics studio

BMC kiln (gift from Olson)

Self taught Classes at BMC NC State too
Bought mug $5

Jo

30s Beauty too black hair long dark eyes tall SMART
Part Cherokee also?
Librarian
Friend of Ruth's
Read Frost at dinner The Gift Outright "The land was ours before we were the land's"
Likes Plath
Knows who Creeley is
Wanted me last night / First goddam hardon in years
Wanted her
Turned her down
Why?

What is it about Black Mountain?

School only 20+ years. 30s-50s.
Rice opened. Olson closed.
Lots of experimentation
Two campuses: Lee Hall. Eden Lake.
Don't know enough history yet
Creeley: "Lovely place. Olson saved me."
Duncan: "Great energy. Olson crazy."
Ruth: "It did not fail. It did what it had to do."

Ruth got me going about Olson and Ishmael
"I take SPACE to be the central fact of man born in America from Folsom cave to now."
I dig that.
Olson writing same time I was hustling back and forth across this great big continent.
He gets it. Like Melville got it. Like I'm trying to get it.

Olson/Ishmael:

"no barriers to contain as restless a thing as Western man was becoming in Columbus' day"

"a harshness we still perpetuate, a sun like a tomahawk, small earthquakes but big tornadoes and hurrikans, a river north and south in the middle of the land running out the blood"

"We are the last 'first' people. We forget that. We act big, misuse our land, ourselves. We lose our own primary."

"He (Melville) had a pull to the origin of things, the first day, the first man, the unknown sea...From passive places his imagination sprang a harpoon."

This IS good stuff.

Me restless from the start. Esp. after Gerard died.
Football field/ Lowell not big enough.
Columbia not big enough.
Village not big enough.
Got out/ tested SPACE/ almost killed
Now this/ next voyage/ farther? deeper?/ make it back alive?
Neal/ Ahab. Or was. Primary. Grab space. Shake time. Down to Hell.
Me/ Ishmael? Survivor. Tell story. Courage to seek again?
Why I can't stay in BM. But maybe BM part of what I need.

List of last BM Review: Autumn '57

Creeley, editor (Allen on the side)
Cover art Ed Corbett

Writers:
Phil Whalen
Gary Snyder
Burroughs
Me
Art: Franz Kline, Aaron Suskind
Photos: Harry Callahan
Seems lifetime ago.
Some think 60s started about then.
If true, ended couple years ago. 1967-68
This decade starts with a different feel.

Leafing through the *Review* got me all anxious again. Itchy to get back out to San Francisco. Mill Valley. Mt. Tam. Sierras. I knew that's where I wanted to end up. If I could. But might be the worst place of all to stay underground.

I thought long and hard about just taking off. I knew going to Ruth's risked getting sucked into something that would derail my plans. At best. At worst she might make this whole thing unravel.

If I just hit the road, I could get up to the Cape, to Gloucester. Check in on Olson. Tell him Ruth said hi. (I wasn't thinking exactly clearly at this point, because he'd probably see the 'old' Jack Kerouac in a minute and not the 'new' Jack Moriarty.) Move on to Canada and start heading west. Back out into SPACE.

Then I heard Gerard talking to me again back at the hospital: *"Ti Jean, you always run away. Why, Ti Jean, why?"*

I knew leaving now was the easy way to go. Not give Ruth or Jo a second thought. Lissa either. I'd seen what I needed to see of Black Mountain and now it was time to get up East. Get out West. I was two days behind schedule!

"You always run away."

Damn you, Gerard!

"Possessed by what we now no more possessed."

Damn you, Ruth!

I knew just getting to Black Mountain somehow was part of this second chance I'd been given. And part of that second chance meant not running *away from*, but running *to* something. Like Ruth said Jo saw in me coming in the library. Maybe they're right.

But at the time I didn't have a real clue what I was running to, even if Jo thought I did. One thing I will say: I was glad the decisions were my own. I didn't have Neal or Allen or Henri or Joan or some chick tugging at me telling me to go this way and that. My path was my own. Always was. Or supposed to be.

OK, Gerard, you win. You too, Ruth. I decided not to run away. I'd see what else she, and Jo, had to show me about Black Mountain. At least I had a few hours before I had to be back at her house.

I took some time leafing through that last *Review*. I'd forgotten how big it was. 200 pages. Wonder how many copies ever got printed?

It sure brought back memories. Lots happened in '57. *On the Road* finally out. In its castrated, sanitized, lawsuit-free version. Bill Burroughs and *Naked Lunch* too. Its early form. The rest wouldn't come out for several more years. First bits in BM Review. Bill says I came up with the title. I don't really remember. But nice of him to say so.

It was the year of Allen's obscenity trial for *Howl*. Arrested for that crazy, crazy night. We had no idea what a firestorm was being lit on those Frisco streets, by those City Lights.

I saw the best minds of my generation destroyed by madness, starving hysterical, naked, dragging themselves through the negro streets at dawn looking for an angry fix, angelheaded hipsters burning for the ancient heavenly connection to the starry dynamo in the machinery of night...

Allen brought it down from Blake to Whitman/ Melville to Eliot/Pound to Williams to...Us.

1957 was the year the world "discovered" the Beats. The start of another kind of up-and-down, out-of-control ride that ended with me crashed and curled around that damn toilet bowl in St. Pete.

I guess "start" isn't quite fair. *The Town and The City* had been out for years. And we'd been raising hell from New York to San Francisco and all those places in between for a decade before the world decided we were "cool." But it was the start of those literary parties and interviews and speaking engagements. Where people looked at me like I was some kind of god. Hung on every word I uttered. And the pressure to write everything as good as *On The Road.* Believe it or not, it was tough. Really tough.

Here's the damnable thing: I spent years and years and years writing my ass off, trying to find new ways to put on paper what we were seeing, experiencing, feeling. I wanted to be recognized for my work. I wanted to be seen as a great writer. I wanted to say things no one had ever said before. Or say them in ways no one had ever thought to before.

And I did it. *On the Road* was good. Better than good! So were the others. Some, I liked better. Some, others liked better. But the really tough part was that a lot of the people who wanted me, who "loved" me didn't have a clue of who I was, what I was trying to say. They kind of fell in love with their idea of "Jack Kerouac." I became this "icon," whatever that was.

I know it made Allen and some of the others jealous as hell. But I didn't have anything to do with it! The country was changing. People were looking for different things. And they found some of it in what we were talking about. The Beats. We became "cool." But it ripped me up. And it pissed me off. And made it easier to run away. Run away into a bottle. I wanted the fame. But when I got it, I hated it. And I handled it by mostly flipping everybody off.

So it was trying to kind of come out of the other side of it all that made me decide to stay in Black Mountain a little longer. Maybe just to see what else Ruth had to say or show me about Black Mountain and myself.

It was coming on noon when I got cleaned up, waved to one of the "Saturday nighters" who'd packed up already and was headed out. I decided to get into town early enough so I could stop by Lissa's. Since I was staying another night at least, I thought it would be impolite not to say hello again. I set Ruth's *Review* on the seat and headed back into a town I'd expected to be a nice memory by now.

This time I parked in front of Lissa's house and knocked on the screen door. I was happy she was glad to see me, opening the door with a big smile. She looked really nice in a dress, which was unexpected. I guessed she'd just gotten home from church.

"Mr. Moriarty! This *is* a surprise! Please come in."

We shook, our hands lingering a second or two. She wore a modest blue dress that nonetheless showed off her figure nicely. That beautiful red hair was pulled back, held together with a slim bow.

I followed her into the living room I'd only seen a bit of from the kitchen the day before. It was decent sized and neat. Kind of had the artist's touch...a couple nice contemporary paintings on the walls...coffee table with some kind of sculpture on it...a tall vase that I guessed she'd made...a built-in bookcase with a couple shelves' worth of books along with what looked like family photos.

Lissa was all smiles. "To what do I owe this visit? I thought you'd be long gone by now."

"Yeah, well, plans got pushed back a little."

"Oh? Tell me more! But I just got home from church. Would you mind if I took a minute to change? Could I get you a cup of coffee?"

"No. Yes! That'd be great."

She laughed and asked, "So, that's yes to me changing *and* yes to coffee also?"

"Yes. To both. I mean, go ahead and change. I…uh… can wait for coffee."

"Ok. Be right back!" as she headed down the hall.

"You look nice," I called after her.

She stopped and turned back smiling, "Thank you! Make yourself at home."

I wandered over to the bookcase and scanned the titles. They included a fair number of art books reflecting a wide range of interests: Oldenburg. Raushenberg. O'Keeffe. Klee. Picasso. Modigliani. Monet. Also some books on Cherokee history.

The photos I guessed were various ones of her parents, the sister and her husband and children. None of her with a man or children that might have been her own. One black and white showed the family sitting on the porch of a small house. Lissa looked about 11 or 12. Even without color I could see she was all freckles with a big, toothy smile. Her father instantly reminded me of Harrison, a young man pushed too quickly into middle age by the demands of machines and family and bills. I wondered how long after this was taken had his own life had been pinched out by a machine gone mad. The mother looked strong, arms around both girls and smiling big.

I thought of Memere. Also strong, carrying my dad through his last years. But losing Gerard so long ago. Then Dad. And Nin…that was a surprise. And me. Almost. I never asked her about these deaths, how she felt about them, whether they made it easier for her to believe in God or tell Him off. If life is suffering and you learn by suffering, what did she learn from having almost her entire family taken from her? I could hardly bear to look at her in the last week before I left. She knew what I didn't want to know, but already knew myself: this would probably be the last she'd ever see of me. And that's pretty much how it happened. Even though I got to see her before she died, we didn't really talk, she being pretty much out of it by then.

"That was taken in Cleveland." Lissa jerked me back from my own faraway thoughts.

I turned around to see she'd changed into jeans and shirt, bow removed from her hair replaced by a barrette. She stood close enough for both of us to ponder the photo.

"I wondered. Early fifties?"

"Yes. I think fifty-one. I would have been eleven."

"You got your mother's smile."

"Thanks. She was always laughing about something, even through the hard times. But actually that picture was taken at a good time. They'd bought that house couple years before. First one either of them had lived in that wasn't a rental."

"My parents never had enough money to buy a house either. One my mom lives in down in Florida is the first one she's ever owned."

"Daddy made good money at Republic Steel. Must have been a lot of overtime because I don't remember seeing him much except Saturday afternoons and Sundays. Mama always had a head for numbers. She knew how to save. Good thing, 'cause Daddy'd like to have drunk half his paycheck away Saturday nights."

"Yeah, my mom's the same. And my dad sounds the same as yours. Took me to bars before I was tall enough to even see over 'em. She was never happy about that. But that's what the men did in Lowell."

"Lowell? Where's that?"

Another oops. Should've just said "Boston" and left it at that.

"Outside Boston."

"That's where you grew up?"

"Yeah. Used to be a mill town. But best days are behind her now."

"Steel mills? Like where Daddy worked?"

"Naw. Woolen. Clothes. But a lot a that work's down here now. People work cheaper here I guess."

There was a pause. I thought maybe she was going to say something about her dad getting killed. Or, worse, start asking me more questions about Lowell and then maybe I'd let something else slip.

"You still want that coffee?"

"Yeah, I would! Left my mug back at the campground though."

Lissa smiled. "I think I can find another. C'mon."

I followed her back into the kitchen and sat in the same chair I'd been in 24 hours before.

"So, what're you still doing here? More research?" she asked as she started the coffee.

I wanted to say "just to see you in jeans again," but I told her instead, "Yeah. Looks like I might be staying in town another day or two. I took a chance you might be home."

"Black Mountain's gettin' to ya, huh?" she said laughing.

"Yeah, that ol' black magic working its spell," I countered. "Actually, I met someone who might be able to help on the research."

"Oh? Who's that? Someone here in town, you mean?"

"Yeah. Her name is Ruth. Ruth Parker." I knew I was taking a chance dropping her name, but I also knew I couldn't keep up the charade much longer without telling at least some bit of truth.

Lissa stopped in mid scoop. "You know *Ruth Parker*?"

"Not really. Just met her. Like you." I smiled back. "You know her?"

"Well, not 'know' know her. But she's like the richest person in town. Think her daddy owned most of Black Mountain and then some. How did you meet her?"

Here I white lied. "By accident, really. At the restaurant yesterday. Right before I walked over here and met you. Must have been my lucky day."

"I guess so! Ruth Parker, huh? I heard stories she kept the college going its last few years. Friends with Charles. And the people who started it in the thirties."

"Yeah? I'm going over to her place at two. Guess maybe I'm going to learn couple more things about Black Mountain. Maybe help with the article."

"Oh, so maybe Tawney Ceramics won't be in your story anymore?" Lissa teased.

"I didn't say that! But I'm curious to see what she has to say. You said she's friends with Olson?"

"That's just what I heard from way back. I don't know if she still knows him. Or even if he's still alive!" She poured our coffees into matching mugs.

"Let's go sit in the living room. More comfy." I followed her to the sofa and sat.

"So, you and Ruth Parker? I guess if anybody can tell you what Black Mountain was all about, she's the one."

"Word must travel around here pretty quick because she seemed to know who I was and what I was looking for."

Lissa laughed at this. "Are you surprised? Stranger coming into a small town like ours? Even though we're getting used to tourists, you're early for the season. And if word got around you were askin' about the college, I could see where you might spark some interest from her."

"Anything I should ask her about in particular?"

"Boy, that's a tough one. What do you want to know that you haven't found out already?"

"Does the town miss the college?"

"Now that's a good writer's question, Jack! I think you ought to ask her."

"Do you?"

Here Lissa became pensive, remembering whatever details from her own life that dropped her here more than fifteen years ago.

"I was just a kid, remember. Like I said yesterday, felt like they adopted me. So my memories are mostly good ones."

"Mostly?"

She looked at me, seeing I'd caught that word. Then she looked away, remembering something else she'd rather not. "Oh, nothing. Kid stuff. It's over now."

I didn't press, but pretty clear she didn't want to talk about it, whatever "it" was.

I waited a second more. "So…you don't miss it?"

Now she looked back at me, eyes focused again. "Oh I do! It was a wonderful place! I learned so much! Maybe if it'd stayed open, I'd be teaching there now."

"You'd like to do that?"

She kept smiling broadly at me. Just like yesterday, we were settling in fast as friends.

"Yeah. I would! It's fun being with people who have a passion for the same things you do. And helping others pursue their dreams like I got to pursue mine. That's pretty cool I think." I could see she meant it.

"You thought about going back to the state college?"

"Not really. I got what I needed there. It never settled me like Black Mountain has. This is home. It's where I get my inspiration, if that doesn't sound too goofy."

"Not at all!"

Another pause.

"So, where's your home, Jack? Where do you get *your* inspiration?"

I looked at Lissa and took a deep sip of coffee trying to put together an answer that wouldn't give away another chunk of information about me, or the real me.

"Truthfully, since I left Massachusetts I've been on the road so much of my life I'm not sure I could call anyplace home. Maybe the road is my home. And my inspiration too. Maybe it's why I became a travel writer."

"That must get kinda lonely, doesn't it?"

"Yeah it does at times. My mother lives in St. Petersburg now. That's where I was before driving up here. But most of the time I'm on the road looking for stories."

"Is that all your family?"

"Almost," I white-lied. "Sister died a couple years ago. Father died many years ago. My brother died when he was nine."

Lissa looked long with very sympathetic eyes. "I'm sorry to hear that. It's tough to lose family."

"Yeah. I guess you know that as well as I do."

"No wife? Kids?"

"An ex. In Albany, I think. And a girl I've only seen a couple times. With her mother. Or maybe even on her own. Would be twenty now."

"You've only seen her a couple times?"

"Yeah," I said looking sadly at her. "Her mother and I split before she was born. We'd met in New York, had a crazy time there. Got married. Then split almost as fast. She headed back to family in Albany. They had money. I tried to work things out. But it was over." I took another sip.

"We were two lost souls who found each other for a brief time. And brought another into the world as a result." Then I repeated last night's line. "I just hope she's just half as beautiful as her mother. And twice as responsible as her father."

I could see Lissa was taking this in, now trying to figure out if I was legit or just another deadbeat.

"That's sad..."

"Yeah. I take no pride in my behavior. I mean, it's one thing if things don't work out between people. But when a kid's involved—or *kids* plural—it takes on a whole different slant. She deserved a father. And I wasn't there for her."

"Yeah..."

I wasn't sure if I should ask about her past so I decided not to. If she wanted to tell me, she would. I guessed there was more sadness in her life too. But maybe she'd put it way down inside where she didn't have to show it to anyone very easily. And I could understand that.

"So...what's your schedule now? Taking off after you interview Ruth Parker?"

"I guess. This was kind of unexpected. Hell, this whole stop's been unexpected!" I said trying to lighten the mood up again.

"Tomorrow, then?"

I could tell she was trying to figure out how much effort to invest in a guy she'd just met yesterday. I was smart enough to figure that out. Because maybe I was trying to do the very same thing.

"Yeah, I guess. Maybe depends on what all Ruth Parker has to say. Maybe she'll tell me some fantastic secret about Black Mountain that demands I stick around and do some more digging!"

Lissa brightened at this. "Would you? I mean, don't you have to get to Cape Cod or Massachusetts some place to see old Charles Olson?"

"Yeah, I do. Or at least I'd like to. But it's not like we have a lunch date set up for Tuesday, or anything like that."

"You have a deadline for your article?"

I white-lied again. "Yeah. They'd like it by end of the month. Think they want it for their fall vacations issue or something. Don't pay real close attention to their schedules. Just write what I have to. Get it in on time. And wait for the check."

She laughed. "Think I might go crazy working like that! I like working ahead, then selling off the inventory."

"Yours mostly a cash business?"

"Yeah! I like that too. I'll take a check if it's local. Or maybe an out-of-town one if the person's a dealer or a regular customer. But not too many of those. See more and more places around here taking credit cards, but I want to stay away from them if I can. Too much paperwork! How do you handle checks if you're traveling all the time?"

"I have 'em sent to my mother's house. She can sign them if I'm not there. Then she wires me cash when I need it."

"I guess that works. I've had a few galleries want my stuff on consignment. That's such a pain in the butt! But you almost have to do it because it's about the only way to get any exposure outside of here."

I remembered some of the art festivals I'd seen on the West Coast. "Do you have art festivals around here?"

"I heard of something like that over in Asheville. But mostly I rely on a kind of word of mouth. Somehow people seem to find me, just like you did."

There was a pause. I didn't want to leave. But I looked at the clock on one of the bookshelves: 1:45. Time to catch up with Ruth and Jo.

"You want more coffee? Or can I make you a sandwich? I'm usually starving when I get home from church."

"Yeah, I would. But looks like I gotta think about getting over to Ruth Parker's."

Lissa glanced at the clock and was definitely disappointed too. "Oh, right. You goin' to her house?"

"Yeah. I don't think it's too far from here."

"Nothing's too far from anything in Black Mountain," she said trying to put a good face on my leaving. Glancing again at the clock she continued, "But I see what ya mean. Don't want to be late for Miss Parker!"

We looked at each other over now empty coffee cups.

"Jack, I'm really glad you stopped by. I'd invite you to come back tomorrow if you're still around, but I'm leaving too, for a few days."

"Oh!" Now it was my turn to try and not sound disappointed. "Where're you off to?"

"Atlanta. Gallery wants to talk to me about doing a show maybe in the fall. They're looking at a Cherokee theme. Paintings and pottery. Maybe some fabrics. Indian stuff seems to be getting popular. It's a good time to go down there before things get too crazy around here."

"Sounds like a good opportunity. City looked really busy when I drove through on Thursday."

A brief pause again.

"I'll be back Wednesday night if you're still around. But I suppose you'll be on Cape Cod by then."

Smiling back, "Maybe. Maybe not. As I said, Ruth Parker might have a surprise or two waiting for me and I'll have to stick around."

"Well if she does, you'll definitely have to come back and tell me all about them! But now I'm going to push you out the door because I do not want you being late on my account."

We got up and walked to the door.

I turned back to her and said, "Hey, listen, if I'm still here when you get back maybe I could take you out to dinner someplace. I'm not into fancy places. Someplace easy. But not the Candy Kitchen!"

She stepped closer and said, "I'd like that. I really would. As long as I can make sure the only thing you write about Black Mountain is the famous potter you interviewed in her highly professional studio."

Her laugh and smiling eyes just lit up her room.

"You got it. And it wouldn't bend a single ethical rule I have!"

"OK. Then maybe I'll have something to look forward to on that long drive back from Atlanta. And now, goodbye again Mr. Jack Moriarty. Formerly of St. Petersburg. And Massachusetts! But always on the road."

I reached out and gave her a quick hug. "Yeah. Bye, Lissa. Thanks for the coffee. I'm glad you were home."

I opened the door and then turned. "Hey, if I do take off before you get back, I'll send a note. Let you know when I might be back. Don't forget, I have your card!"

"I think I'm expecting nothing less." She gave me a playful little shove.

Then I was out the door and on to Ruth's.

I pulled into her driveway a couple minutes after two and behind Jo's Bug. I could see them talking on the porch, sitting on that glider. Looked like both were wearing jeans, which seemed a surprise for Ruth. Then again, she seemed to be one surprise after another, as this entire stop was turning into.

After last night I expected things to be a little awkward with Jo. But she was here, so that was a good thing. Wondered if she told Ruth what happened. Or what didn't happen. Wondered if Ruth asked. Wouldn't be surprised if they were talking about me right now. That was one thing I'd learned. Women talked with women about the men in their lives a whole lot more than men talked to men about their women.

There wasn't anything I could do about that. Besides, I was just passing through town, wasn't I? No way I could let myself get tied down by them—Lissa included—and hope to get done what I wanted to do.

I waved as I got out and they waved back. I bounded up the steps, and they stood to greet me.

"Jack, so delighted you accepted my invitation to learn more about our small town." Ruth shook my hand vigorously. "Jo and I were speculating on that very thing when you pulled into the drive. As busy a man as you are, we were prepared for disappointment."

"After last night how could I say no, Ruth? I'm sure Charles isn't going to mind if I'm a day or two behind on an appointment he doesn't even know he has with me."

Jo also extended her hand. "Good to see you again, Jack. Did you sleep well?"

I took a hint in her question that maybe she hoped I had not. She looked every bit as beautiful today as she did last night, wearing a buttoned cotton shirt with the top two undone. Today, her hair was pulled back in a long ponytail. Between her and Lissa, I felt like I'd hit the women jackpot, even if it was one I hadn't cashed in yet.

"Yeah, guess I did. Overslept actually. Harrison—the campground owner—woke me up. Wanted paid before he and the family took off for the day." I know I added that so she wouldn't somehow think I'd left her to go off with someone else.

"Would you like a lemonade before we start our little exploration? Bessie was kind enough to put up another pitcher before she left last night."

"Yeah, I would! Sounds great." Between coffees and lemonade I also knew I'd have to pee before taking off on Ruth's "little exploration."

"I'll get it," Jo volunteered.

After she was inside, Ruth leaned closer and whispered conspiratorially, "I think you may have broken that young woman's heart last night, Jack. She is not used to putting herself forward as I understand she did with you. You seem to have entranced her in a way other men do not. Part of me applauds you for behaving like a gentleman. But I give you fair warning, when she is stirred up Jo is a very determined woman. And you have stirred her up some!"

I smiled back knowing now that I'd guessed right. "Ruth, I appreciate that. I just...ahh...I just didn't feel right...maybe taking advantage and then maybe taking off and never being heard from again."

"Ah! You are the gallant one, Mr. Moriarty! Maybe today will help you decide a bit more whether your imminent departure must also mean a permanent taking of your leave from our Black Mountain." She squeezed my hand again as she said this.

Just then, Jo's hip helped the screen door swing out. She carried a tray with a pitcher of lemonade and ice cubes, along with three glasses.

"Here we go!" Ruth said just a little too brightly, trying to cover her verbal tracks. She was loving her matchmaker role. If she'd known about Lissa, I imagined her scheming some way to get her out of the picture so Jo would be the only one in my field of view.

Jo set the tray on a small wicker table and poured our glasses. Her shirt draped open slightly, enough to make me guess she was braless again today. And yes, my cock stirred.

"Jack, if you'd allow me another toast on a Sunday afternoon..."

"Of course!"

"To a few hours indulging an old woman's trip down Memory Lane and to whatever harbingers of the future it may bring!"

"Here! Here!" Jo and I said together as our glasses clinked.

Ruth and Jo resumed their seats on the glider. I pulled up a large wicker chair with thick cushions.

"So, Jack," Ruth started in again clearly enjoying her ongoing role as mistress of ceremonies, "did you get a chance to look through my *Review*?"

"I did! Lots of really good writing. Guess I'd forgotten Creeley edited it. Saw some other names I'm familiar with. Probably met a time or two in San Francisco. It's in the car."

"I'm not sure I realized then that was going to be *finis*," Ruth said. "Although all the signs were certainly there. The college had collapsed for the last time. Charles was a mess. People were scattering. Yet somehow I thought the *Review* would prevail, carrying forward the spirit of the college between its covers."

"Yeah, imagine that must be pretty hard. Publishing's a tough business. Even when things are going good!" Boy, could I ever talk about that.

"I even offered to assist Charles financially again, much to Daddy's ongoing dismay! And Charles mumbled about doing Black Mountain seminars or some such around the country. But it was all a lot of talk that came to nothing."

Here, Jo jumped in. "I remember my Daddy sayin' good riddance to the college. But Mama told him hush. I think she could see some of the good things it had brought to Black Mountain."

"Yes, I think your Daddy probably spoke for a good many people, Jo. Sometimes they liked the money the college brought with it. But not some of the people…and their *ideas.* Then when they got into trouble and started owing money, well, that just became an easy excuse to criticize everything they were doing."

"Did you give them a lot of money, Ruth?"

"Oh, I don't know. Not a king's ransom. But I helped out from time to time. And, as I said, at the end maybe a little more than I usually did. It was the kind of thing one did quietly. For a number of very good reasons."

Ruth was ready to move on. She put her glass down with a thump and said, "Well! Are we all finished with our lemonades? We should start our exploration before Jack here changes his mind and decides to skedaddle despite the best of our intentions!"

"I'll take our glasses in," Jo volunteered again.

"Now, Jack, help me down these steps. I think your vehicle might provide a more comfortable alternative to Jo's, wouldn't you agree?"

I panicked a bit. Even with all my gear out, it was still crowded with a lot of my other stuff. Plus I kind of hoped we'd take Ruth's Caddy, assuming she'd let me drive, of course.

"Yeah, I guess. Got a bunch of my crap in the back."

"Oh, that's fine. I think we can all sit comfortably in front, don't you?"

Jo caught up to us and Ruth continued orchestrating. "Jo, we are going to take Jack's car and he tells me that the balance of his life is in the back seats, so why don't you sit up front in the middle and let me enjoy the sights from the window?" And that settled that.

After we got situated, and it was clear that Jo was just fine with this arrangement also, I asked, "OK, Ruth, where're we off to?"

"I thought we ought to pay a visit to the Robert E. Lee. As I understand it, you only had the briefest of acquaintances yesterday. And I believe it would do you both good to get to know each other a little better."

So I backed out of the drive and made my way down into town. Ruth chattered as I drove. Jo rested one hand between her leg and mine. The other held Ruth's *Review*. Our shoulders touched easily. She didn't seem to harbor any lingering disappointment from last night.

I easily found the same roads out of town leading to the huge structure that, if anything, seemed even more imposing on this silent Sunday afternoon. I wondered if anyone would be there to shoo us away, but then figured it wouldn't matter with Ruth along.

I pulled up to the tall white building. We got out and Ruth paused before walking up the steps. "Isn't it magnificent!!"

Jo and I stopped behind as the older woman seemed to slip back to when she was younger and the college was brand new. I had the feeling she hadn't been here for a long time, despite being just minutes away. Then she started walking up the steps without waiting for us.

"Jack, this is where it *all* started," she called out as though making an announcement to a crowd of hundreds. "All of it. Not just the college. But the *idea* of the college."

Ruth kind of pirouetted as she talked. And while I knew this was for my education, I also suspected she was talking as much to the ghosts and memories of Black Mountain.

"Seems a little ironic, doesn't it? That a college whose existence was founded on the *radical* idea of intellectual freedom was housed in this building...this symbol of the Old South and its dark ways? That here among our Bible-thumping and anti-Semitic brethren, a few Jews found a refuge from Hitler's madness?"

I jumped back in time to the best Jews I knew. Allen, of course...and his crazy mom. And friends from New York. And I remembered, too, my own prejudices. Then I thought back farther...to Sammy Sampas. Stella's brother. Killed at Anzio. An American Greek in Italy fighting Germans who were trying to kill all the Jews. And me...on the sidelines... a bum merchant seaman and a crappy, crazy, discharged sailor. Truthfully, I wasn't too proud of my war record. *"Ti Jean, you always run away..."*

Ruth walked over to one of the large windows and peered in. So did Jo. There was nothing to see. Nothing that meant anything to them. Or me. Talking to the glass, she continued, "Jack, I don't expect you to really understand why this building is important. But I remember coming up here Christmas of 1933—the school had just opened that fall, and meeting all these strange...creatures! I mean, for Black Mountain they were strange! For my father, they were strange! Of course I had met my share in New York and Paris and Berlin. But...right here...in Black Mountain! It was a wondrous thing, surely! John...and Ted...and the Albers—straight from Europe!—and women on the faculty too!

"Jack, I tell you, those were important years. I'm guessing you were just a boy in 1933 and probably couldn't fathom all that was happening. And, Jo, my goodness, you weren't even a sparkle in your daddy's eye yet! But those years between the wars were momentous. The world changed. And changed again. And changed *again*! Until we had to fight another war to sort things out.

"It seemed a lot of that played out right here in its own small way. A fight for ideas. And for rights. Not perfectly, of course. But the 'aliveness' of Black Mountain was a reflection of what was going on out there. The 'aliveness' here was electric at times."

Ruth turned away from the window and looked back across the drive. This was her stage. Jo and I were her audience.

"It wasn't just the Nazis. It was the Communists too. And the Fascists in Italy and Spain. Plus all the terrible destruction brought on by the Depression. You could just feel these great forces at work and you weren't sure where or how it was all going to end."

I kind of hoped this wasn't going to get into some big political talk. Thanks mostly to his mother, Allen was always going off the deep end. We'd have these arguments about the evils of capitalism and all that. I kind of saw all governments as evil. But if I had to choose between ours here in the U.S.A. and those gray, grumpy old men in Russia, I'd choose ours any day.

"...talked about academic freedom, but there was hardly any. Everything was so strict. What you would study. Who would teach it. How you would be tested. And if you had any different ideas—poof!—you were gone. That's what happened to John. Also to Ralph Lounsbury. Fred Georgia. And Ted Dreier too. All of them coming up from Rollins. All of them knowing that academic life...the life of *ideas*...could be better than what they had experienced with great disappointment."

Turning back, Ruth marched suddenly over to me, a teacher asking her hopefully attentive student, "Jack, what was your college experience like?"

"It sucked."

Ruth's eyes got wide at my profanity and then she laughed long and hard. "And may I ask where you matriculated into an environment that...*sucked*?"

Here I white-lied again. If I told her Columbia, it would be one more 'Kerouac' detail that I just didn't want to let out. I already felt like my cover was blown, if she or Jo ever tried piecing things together.

"Boston College."

Actually, this was almost true. I got leaned on hard by my father, who was getting leaned on hard by the archdiocese, to get me into BC so I could play football for them. But I didn't want BC because it was too close to home and already I had the itch to get away and see more of the world. When I chose Columbia, he got fired from his print job not too long after. I blamed myself for that and that sucked too. A lot.

"A Jesuit institution, is it not?"

"Yeah. They just wanted me because I could play football pretty well."

I glanced at Jo. She looked interested in this last bit of information. If I'd learned anything since high school, girls liked jocks. Seemed Jo was no different.

"And you did not adjust well to the discipline of Jesuit instruction?"

"Guess I didn't. They had this way of asking questions and it kind of seemed like there was real discussion going on. But the 'right answers' always led back to their way of thinking. Even on the football field. You did it their way. Or your butt sat on the bench. After a while, I said hell with this and struck out on my own."

Ruth smiled warmly, "An iconoclast through and through...that was John Rice too. Come! If you'll let me steady myself on your arm, I'd like to show you something if I can find it."

We walked down the steps and then past the south end of the building, across the grass and into a copse of trees. Neither Jo nor I had any idea where Ruth was headed, but her gait was firm, not betraying any infirmity due to age. She didn't really need my arm for support. I think she just liked being close to a man again. We stopped in front of a massive oak tree, one whose size was masked by the others surrounding.

"I believe this is the one," Ruth said letting go of my forearm and moving around the base of the tree. "It's been many years..." A pause and "Here it is! Come look, children!"

Ruth was on her knees having unearthed a fairly large, but otherwise ordinary-looking stone. "Give me your hand, Jack," she said trying to stand up, stone in hand. She couldn't quite manage both. I helped her up, then worked the stone out of the earth. It was about the size of a football, sandstone I think. Really ordinary though. Just as I was about to ask her what was the story, Ruth said quietly, "Turn it over, Jack. Now brush it off a little."

As I did, letters emerged. I brushed it clean so now complete words were visible. Hand scratched into the surface, they were weathered, but legible. The three of us huddled as Ruth read:

ARS LONGA EST. VITA BREVIS. SENECA
ET TEMPUS AMORAE. JRP

"Do you recognize this from your high school Latin, Jack?"

"Yeah. 'Art is long. Life is short.' From Seneca. But the 'And time of love?' And the 'JRP?' What're those?"

Ruth chuckled. "I guess I wouldn't expect you to understand those. John and I carved this in the summer of 1936. What we meant by the other words was that the time for love was both long and short. And that love could be love of art. And love of life. And love...of...another."

It was beginning to dawn on me. I looked at Jo, then Ruth. Both had tears starting at the corners of their eyes.

"You see, Jack, I fell in love with a man many years ago. A man who was married to another. And he fell in love with me. And the only permanence we could attach to our love was cut into this rock. At the place where we first confessed that love to each other."

"John Rice?" I asked, stupidly.

"Yes. I hope you'll forgive me if I act a bit schoolgirlish. I realize I am past the years when the mere mention of a boy's name should make my heart go thumpety-thump. And yet his does still."

"Hey, that's fine with me. Can I ask, who is 'JRP'?"

"Oh, that was our little conceit! If you look closely, you should see one 'R' written over another. Our initials...joined. We thought if anyone from the college should find this, their sleuthing probably would not be good enough to determine the authors of this bit of immortality."

Jo and I looked at each other and smiled. I'm not a sentimental guy, but even I choked up a little imagining the two of them conspiring to leave an obscure message of love for future generations.

"When did you fall in love?" I asked bending now to place the rock back in its spot JRP side up.

"Oh, I believe I was smitten that first Christmas in 1933! I had met many handsome men before. A few dashing ones even. How could you not in the places I had worked and visited? But John had something else. Something, frankly, I had not expected to find on a college campus, even one as wondrous as Black

Mountain turned out to be. He had purpose. Drive. He saw things others did not."

Ruth clearly relished bringing up these memories with people she could trust. It seemed as though she'd been waiting a long time to share them.

"Still, I was wise enough to keep my distance. He was married to a good, kind woman. I had made that mistake before. And, too, I was only in town sporadically, mostly on holiday.

"I thought at first it was the vitality of this brand new college that attracted me so. I looked forward to my trips home. And it seemed whenever I came up to visit, John would always be here. With others, of course. He would ask me about the latest in New York. What was O'Neill doing? Was there a new Odets play? Did I ever see Dorothy Parker holding court at The Algonquin? As though I happened to be close personal friends with these luminaries, which I was not."

Jo and I stood on either side of Ruth, the three of us looking down at the stone and its upturned message. It seemed she was ready now for it to be read by whoever should pass by this place.

Ruth continued talking, almost more with her memories than with us.

"It was the summer of 1936. The Fourth of July. I was home for an extended visit from New York. Daddy was having a problem with his health and I was needed here. John and a few others were getting ready for some summer play—it might have been Odets. Was it *Waiting For Lefty*? Anyway, they remembered my help from the year before with the O'Neill. So they asked if I would join the cast. And I said I would.

"Nell and the baby had left for a visit to her parents' and there John and I were. We were out here walking and I was just nervous as a fly! Children, I was thirty-six years old! I could see what was happening. I could have stopped it right then. But this man made me feel like I was a knock-kneed teenager again. We walked back here away from the others. And we stopped. And we faced each other in the darkness. And he reached for me. And I...I...felt like I was being lifted up into the heavens!

"I gave myself up to him. Completely. Right here. In the darkness. We could have been found out so easily. Yet I did not care. I had tried to be careful in love before. And I had been careless too. With John I tried to be careful, yet ended up more careless than ever.

"So here we were! That summer was a swirl unlike any other. The play went on. I was applauded for lending my talents to it. Even Daddy, through his illness, could see I was a changed woman and, of course, I could not tell him the truth for my disposition."

Jo asked, "Did anyone discover you and Mr. Rice?"

Here Ruth turned serious. "We tried *very* hard to be discreet. I had no desire to flaunt our affair. Nor did I want to cause Nell the hurt and embarrassment that inevitably comes when you learn of betrayal. I have always been an independent woman of mind and means and so I know there was a part of me that wanted John close, but perhaps not *too* close.

"But neither could I give him up as another summer fling! And so when I went back to New York in the fall, John would call on me. Of course, he had college business to conduct there from time to time, so I guess we had our cover. We did go to some college-related social events together. I as benefactor of sorts, he as its leader. I think we behaved ourselves... reasonably well!"

"So he was the love of your life, huh?" I knew as soon as I'd said it, I was in trouble. From both women. I'd said it a little too off-handedly. This was serious business.

Ruth turned and looked right at me. "Why, Jack, you surprise me with your cavalier attitude! I thought you were a gentleman with a more refined understanding of the complications and demands of love. Or have your interactions with the fairer sex been of the more...*casual*...variety?"

Jo, too, was looking at me intensely, thinking she might have misjudged this writer who had dropped into her life just a few days before.

Ruth continued, "Do you not believe in the possibilities of love to bond two souls together, even unto Eternity?"

Boy, how to answer that one? The easy answer should have been "Yes" and maybe hope the women would forgive my male slip of the tongue. But I had fallen in and out of love so many times that even if I believed it once and wanted to believe it now, I'd never been with a woman long enough to know if our souls had bonded beyond romps in the sack. Although Jo and Lissa seemed to be holding out the promise of another exploration if I decided I was up for it. Which, thankfully, my libido seemed to be urging me to do.

"Ruth," I started to answer as convincingly as I could to a question that maybe I'd tried to answer to myself many times but had never offered to anyone else, "I'd have to say you and John Rice had it about right. At least from my experience. I think love can be as long and lovely as art. Or as short and brutal as life itself. And I don't think we can know at the start where the love we have for another is going to finish. Nor do we know the quality of that love, except that it feels so damn good surrendering to it."

The women's looks were shifting from accusatory to something softer, maybe holding out hope that their Black Mountain hero hadn't disappointed them after all.

"It's been my experience that I always want love to be true and deep and everlasting. I think that's part of what love is. So, to answer your question, I *do* believe it's possible for love to bond two souls together, even unto Eternity. But I have not experienced that —yet—at least in the way you are telling us about your John Rice."

I could see that maybe I'd won them back over. So I added with my aw-shucks smile that I knew women loved, "But I'd have to say, too, I'd like to wait on finding out about the Eternity part, at least for a little while."

At this, Ruth clapped her hands in glee. "Now, Jack, you have shown us the heart of a poet! I knew it! And so to answer *your* question, yes, John Rice was the love of my life. There were men before him. But none after. Now he is gone forever. At least until Eternity comes calling for me."

Jo stepped over and grasped my hand, letting a breast again brush against the upper part of my arm. "Jack, I also believe love can be as elusive as it can be enduring. Ruth has told me about John Rice before, but not as...intimately...as just now. I knew she was strong in her convictions. But I did not know that she is as fierce in fighting for her heart as she is in fighting for the life of our little community."

At this she reached for Ruth's hand. The women looked at each other, Ruth's revelation adding another link of steel between them.

Then I reached for Ruth's hand. So the three of us stood in a small, tight circle of past and present. A silence settled over us as we stared down at the stone. I tried to imagine Ruth and John Rice locked together in the darkness. Both chasers of big ambitions, conceding little to the mortals around them, or to the bounds of morality that should have kept them apart. Delighting in their sublime pleasure. Thrilling at its secrecy. Reaching an understanding that exceeded words, defied years and miles.

This John Rice must have been a helluva guy to have gotten Ruth's attention back then. Then to have kept it all these years.

And Jo? What was her story? She was beautiful and smart enough to have had her pick of men. Had she been burned at love once and shut down her heart? Had I somehow awakened it? Maybe she saw me as her last chance at great love, in the same way John did for Ruth thirty years ago. There she was last night asking me to sleep with her. There was me wanting to and saying no. How crazy was that? Neal would've bedded and married her in the same night. Then be gone the next day. Only to show up two weeks later to bed and marry—and desert—her all over again. And somehow to leave her wanting more. Or maybe not.

LuAnne was easy. God, she was just a girl—fifteen!—when Neal took her. But Carolyn...she was more like Jo. Or I liked to think anyway. It took her a while, but she finally stood up to Neal and his bullshit. If I ever made it to San Francisco, it'd be hard for me to not want to look her up after all these years. I wondered how the kids were doing. She was strong enough to raise them by herself. What part of Neal would the kids have in them? The hustler-gangster Neal? Or the writer wannabe Neal?

And Joan? Somewhere in between. But maybe more towards LuAnne. She was young and hot and I was in love. She wanted to fit in with my New York crowd. But there was something else too. Something I couldn't quite put my finger on. She wanted to get married. I wanted to get married. Then she got pregnant. And I didn't want to be married. Then she went home to Albany. And I followed. Kind of. But it was over and she was done with the city. And me. Except for the support money which she and our child deserved.

Our child...not knowing more about her will haunt me to the end of my days. Not knowing what kind of father I could've been will haunt me too. Here we are talking about love and Eternity and what better expression of both than a child you've brought into the world and helped grow into a wonderful, loving adult...

"...it was time to move on. They had voted to send John on his way. And they had to get the new buildings up. Then the war came on and changed everything for everybody." I realized Ruth had been telling more of the school and their relationship and I had missed most of it, lost in my own thoughts. Our heads were bowed and it seemed she was talking more to the stone marker than to Jo and me.

"I was born the day the war started in Europe. September first, 1939. I'm glad I don't remember it! Mama lost her baby brother at D-Day..."

This comment seemed to shake Ruth from her reverie. "Children!" she said, letting go of our hands and clapping hers as a teacher would to get students' attention. "We need not tarry here any longer. Our business is done. We will leave our words for the wise here just as they are. But we need to go over to the other Black Mountain because there is more of the story to be told there."

And with that, Ruth started walking back to the Robert E. Lee and my car with a step and determination that belied her size and years. Jo and I looked at each other a moment, still holding hands.

"Jo, I..."

"Hush!" Putting a finger to my lips, as though knowing what the rest of my words were going to be. "We will have plenty of time to talk later. Ruth has you almost figured out, Mr. Moriarty, and I believe she is not going to let you just slip away. And neither am I!" With that she replaced her finger with her lips.

"Children!"

"Just a second, Ruth!" I called back to her. My dick was stirring again. But not just because of Jo. I looked back at her. She was smiling, almost expectantly. Did she want us to repeat that rush into love on the very spot where Ruth and John had united thirty-five years before? In broad daylight? With Ruth herself now almost out of sight, but maybe a willing co-conspirator to whatever plan Jo had in mind? If so, I was going to disappoint her again.

"I...uh...I have to...uh....pee."

At this Jo laughed out loud. "I never would have guessed *that* was the source of your discomfort! Would you like me to leave you alone with your... *penis*, then?"

Her directness was both a surprise and, surprisingly, a turn on.

"I'll be right back." Then I hustled twenty yards and ducked behind another large tree. I half expected Jo to follow. Instead she was waiting at Ruth's tree.

"Feel better now?" she said smiling when I returned.

"Yeah, sorry." Then I slipped my arm around her waist and gave her a kiss. "Much better!" Damn! She felt good.

"Children!" Ruth's voice was farther away. Now we rushed to catch up with this older woman who was proving to be one surprise after another. She had reached the porch, hands on hips as though ready to give us a final exam.

"Now, Jack, I want you to remember this place! When you write about Black Mountain do not forget this is where it all started. This is where John Rice realized his dream. Yes, you can write about the building and the grounds and the trees where you helped unearth a stone that had funny words on it.

"But Jack...*Jack*...it's more important that you write about the birth of an idea. Of *ideas*. I know it's hard. But, if you can, try to see the people who were here. Try to imagine what brought them together. Try to remember a time when all kinds of big ideas of what the world should be were bouncing around like protons and neutrons inside an atom bomb."

She took a step towards me, planting a firmer-than-expected hand on my chest. "Jack, it wasn't so long ago. You were growing into your manhood. We were trying to shake off the tomfoolery of the first war, which was supposed to be the last war. But then we had to also shake off the tomfoolery of the moneyed people and what they brought with the Depression.

"We were young. Yet we knew we had to dispose of the older generation if we were to have any chance at a life for ourselves. And the old people—including Daddy—they wanted to dismiss everything by calling it Communism or Socialism or what-have-you-ism. That was just their way of trying keep control, of trying to hold on. And never own up to the terrible mistakes they'd made."

Even though she'd said it was time to leave, it was clear Ruth wasn't ready to go just yet. I'd heard talk something like this from Allen. From him it always had a harder political edge. But from Ruth it sounded more like the kind of things I'd been chasing.

She stepped back now, but looked me straight in the eye. I felt like I was caught between one of my grade school nuns and Gerard himself. *Ti Jean, Ti Jean, you were given so much...*

"Jack, do you believe in ghosts?"

That was a question from way out in left field. I mean the easy thing to say is "No" because that's what people expect you to say. But after some of my experiences, especially with Gerard, I gave her the most honest answer I could instead.

"Sometimes."

Ruth clapped her hands and laughed out loud. Jo even gave me a little shove on the shoulder.

"Now, Jack, from about any other man I'd take that to be a smarty-pants answer. But from you, I think it is the verifiable truth. As for me, I am more inclined to agree with your 'sometimes.'

"I'd like to think John's ghost was right here with us now. And the ghosts of so many of the others who made Black Mountain sing and dance and write and paint and weld and weave, and shape it into what it became. But, to be honest, I don't think those ghosts are here. Maybe they're waiting for us on the other side with Eternity. I have tried and tried and tried to summon them up, but none have come forward.

"Yet when I come here, Jack, I can feel them. I can't come very often. But when I do, I close my eyes and I can see them again. They are young. And lithe. And free.

"I want to call out to them. And join them. And be free of this tired, old, worn out body! I want that Jack. And if I can't have it until I reach Eternity, then I want to tell people that here was a place where there was life. Life! Where women and men fought with their spirits against the death and destruction that others would bring unto this world."

As Ruth talked, she twirled again as though she were fifty years younger following instructions from Martha Graham. Jo and I were awed. Clearly this was not a woman who gave up easily. Who was not going gently into whatever good night waited for her.

She turned back to a full stop and looked at us, suddenly self-conscious. "You must think me an old fool!"

"No!" Jo and I cried together.

"Ruth, now how many years have I known you?"

"Too many!"

"You know that is not true! But I will tell you that through all the book clubs we have sat through and all the dinners Bessie's made for us and all the time we've just sat on your porch and talked, I knew you loved this ol' college more than just about anything else. But until today, I could never figure out exactly why. Then you brought us here. And showed us this wonderful place in a way I had never seen it before. And showed us that beautiful stone that means so much to you and your John Rice. And you talk about all the people who came here and made this so special.

"I'm not sure I believe in ghosts either. But I do believe in Eternity. And I believe you can reach out and bring little bits of Eternity right down here to our little ol' Earth. And I believe you are tryin' to show us how. And I also believe you are hopin' Mr. Jack here will help you do that!"

Both women bore in on me now for what seemed like the umpteenth time. And for the umpteenth time I tried to wriggle away.

"What're you lookin' at me that way for?"

"Because, Jack Moriarty, it is hoped you would accept the challenge of being more than just a travel writer."

That stung. Because I *was* more than a travel writer! But I knew that somehow these women also saw me for what I really was: someone who had more in him than he'd shown the world so far. Even though I'd tried and tried. And I'd already published a whole lot more than most of the sad sacks I'd met who said they wanted to be writers.

But now here with this college that had been little more than a myth a few days ago, they were pushing me to write something far deeper and more important than the little travelogue articles they imagined as my living.

They wanted me to find the others like Duncan and Creeley and Olson and get their stories about Black Mountain. And they wanted me to put it all together and tell *the* Black Mountain story—not the chronological and academic story. That could be told easily by even a mediocre historian. They wanted—needed?—me to tell the inspirational story...the mythological story...the story that would inspire another, younger generation. The story that would, ultimately, also be Ruth's story.

All this I could see in their searching, still smiling, eyes. And Jo was willing to trade me her body to get my OK. I could've told them all this and made them happy. Instead I tried to run. Again.

"But I make decent money as a travel writer."

Oops. Big mistake. Ruth's eyes flashed from seeking to derision.

"Why, of course, you do, Jack! I'm sure you do a *fine* job writing about beautiful mountains and sandy beaches and spacious restaurants. So people who can't afford to go can enjoy their escapes into the pages of your magazines from their dirtier, sorrier lives."

Her words were measured, dripping with a sarcasm that made each one feel like a little dagger. Jo took a half step back, folding her arms across her chest.

I looked from one to the other searching for some escape. There was none. Still, I tried.

"Look, I'm going to write a terrific article about Black Mountain. I'll even ask my editor if he'll take two thousand words instead the usual fifteen hundred. And I'll send some photos in too. This place will sell itself!"

What on God's green earth was I saying? I didn't have an editor! I didn't even have a story! I was lying through my teeth so these two women whom I barely knew would let me off the hook. And maybe give me another chance to get in Jo's pants...if that's what she wanted.

Ruth steadied her gaze. "Jack, we were hoping for something more...substantive. Although I'm sure our business community will appreciate your efforts on their behalf."

Ouch. Again.

"You want me to write a *book* about a college that lived for only twenty years and died fifteen years ago?"

"Yes."

"A college that few people remember, and fewer still care about?"

"Yes. Though I think you could be more charitable than that in your assessment."

"And do it for free?"

"I would compensate you for your time, if that's what you needed."

"But, Ruth, how would..."

"Now hush, Jack! You can do this. You can do it because you know it needs to be done. Because you have friends you can talk to. And because I can help you."

I looked at her, dumbfounded. How had I gotten myself into this mess? Not a week out of St. Pete and already I'm bogged down in a project that some old woman wants done and has her hooks into me so tight I can't get out.

Why did it seem so much easier with Neal? Or before him when I was on my own and just thumbing it around the country? When even I was at my most miserable and starving the land was still there? Open. Free. Taking life as it came at me. From beat down bus stations to rows and rows of grape vines, and a girl to pull me down between them. Why was that easier?

Was *that* what I hoped to find again when I pulled away from Memere and Stella with a wave, hiding my shit-eating grin until I was far enough down the road they couldn't possibly have seen?

If I'd just packed up this morning and headed East without a second thought, this would all be behind me. I'd be in Virginia now, thinking about Washington, D.C. Or maybe crossing that bridge into Delmarva and dreaming about crab cakes and a cold beer. Yeah! A cold beer. No Ruth. No Jo. No Lissa. Just me and the road. Always, always the road.

"Ruth, I honestly don't know what..."

"Oh please hush, Jack!" Ruth turned with a rush of disgust. "Let's get on over to Eden Lake. I think when we're through there, you will have come to your senses."

She was down the steps and halfway to the car when Jo gave me a gentle shove and shook me out of the shock of Ruth's words. Then she leaned in and said softly, "Come on. She needs you more than you know, Jack."

We rode in silence back through town and out again along the same roads Jo had guided me to a few days ago. I wondered if James Thomas would be there and guessed not on a Sunday.

The lake sparkled as we approached. And when we got out of the car, the grounds seemed even quieter than they had been a couple days ago. Again, Ruth started walking off by herself, this time towards the Studio Building. She approached it with a familiarity, but with a slower pace than she had the Robert E. Lee.

I looked at the building a little differently too. Lee Hall had been Rice's domain. This had been Olson's. At least in the final years.

The Black Mountain of Lee Hall had been born of revolution and passion. The spirit of the college infused a structure built in another century and for another purpose. And, if what Ruth tried to tell me was true, transformed it.

The Black Mountain of Lake Eden was the embodiment of those revolutionary ideas and those passions. The spirit of the college was built into these large, angled, sweeping buildings that literally seemed to be pointing into the future.

I didn't have these words then. But I started to feel them. Like the first notes of a beautifully long riff.

"They worked so hard." Ruth spoke almost as if we weren't there. Again, she had slipped away from 1970 back to 1940. She walked right up to the building and placed her hand on it, almost as if she were trying to summon ghosts from its walls.

"They worked so hard."

Jo and I walked up silently behind her.

"Some of them didn't know a hammer from a nail. Yet they tried. Everyone pitched in. Teachers and students. Did what they could. And they built this. *They. Built. This.* They took Walter's idea and made it real. Their college. Their home."

Now Ruth had both hands on the walls, moving them over the boards, fingers touching, even caressing nail heads. Still speaking to the wall and windows, she went on. Jo and I leaned in closer.

"I heard John speak once to a group of money people in New York. All men, mostly old. Lawyers, a few businessmen. And he started talking about philosophies of education. What it means when we say we want to educate young people. They listened politely, but if he'd gone another minute more that way, they'd all have been asleep, me included.

"Then he shifted gears. He started talking about Black Mountain. If he'd been a preacher, it was like he started selling that old time religion! Those old men looked like someone had just poked them in the ribs with a sharp stick!"

Ruth was getting wound up some herself. "John tried to explain how Black Mountain was different. He said sometimes we forget that philosophy books are written by old men. That kind of got their attention. We expect young people to follow every word—theirs and ours—as though these utterances are somehow sacred. We tell them to believe those truisms just because we say so.

"He said we approach education the same way. Old people handing down what we call 'knowledge' to young people until they have enough for us to decide *they* are now a whatever. A doctor. Lawyer. Teacher. Engineer. Banker.

"But we fail to show them *how* to become a doctor or a lawyer or an engineer. We fail to tell them that the only real way to find truth and know things is to go into the world and experience it."

Ruth's cheeks were becoming flush.

"Then he told them we should remember that there is the wisdom of youth, as well as the wisdom of old age. The wisdom to try new things. Not accept what *we* think is sacred as sacred.

"He finished by saying that at Black Mountain we do not treat young adults as empty vessels into which we pour our delicious 'wisdom.' At Black Mountain we share what we know. We admit what we do not. And we learn together how to think better. How to stretch old ideas until they break. And then how to create new ones. Black Mountain cherishes the wisdom of youth as well as the wisdom of old age."

Now Ruth turned around and her eyes were wide and a little wild.

"Children, he had these old men weeping from the memories of their own lost youth. John was spellbinding. I think no one had ever spoken to them like this before. They were leaders in their communities. Respected for what they said and thought.

"Yet, they knew this man was peeling away decades of stuffy thinking, proper rules, accepted behavior. He touched them at the core of their once-young hearts which had burned with energy and idealism and a mad desire to change the world. He brought them to a place they had been before. And wanted to be again. And they wrote large checks to those memories."

Ruth looked past us. She was still in another place.

I stared at her deep blue eyes, glittering with her own wisdom. I think I was beginning to get it. Beginning to get why this place was so damned important to her. Beginning to get why she seemingly had chosen *me* to find a way to tell its story. And in telling the story find a way to carry on what Black Mountain had been. And maybe what she had been.

I think I was beginning to get, too, what *I* was looking for. Maybe. But those thoughts were just forming. I needed my own space to understand all that better. Those words would come later.

We were silent for a long time.

"OK," I heard myself say finally.

That seemed to bring Ruth back to us. And me back to them.

Another long pause.

"OK, I'll do it." Even if I didn't know yet what "it" was.

The women stared at me for a couple of seconds, not quite sure what they just heard. Or if they heard, that they believed it.

Ruth and I looked at each other long and deep, each searching the other out. She was nobody's fool. Despite all the talk about Black Mountain ideals, she was also the banker's daughter. And her daddy had taught her how to measure people out, deciding if this farmer could make a crop from the loan for seed and fertilizer, or if the hardware store owner's drinking problem was going to force a call on his mortgage.

Just because I'd said I'd do whatever it was she was really looking for, she was trying to see if I was the writer's version of a deathbed convert, agreeing to do a project because maybe there was some money in it. Words, but no belief, no conviction. I knew that.

But my words kind of erupted from a deeper place than me calculating how the hell I could get out of here with the least amount of baggage. I kind of sensed they might actually be true...truer than maybe a lot of other things I'd been saying about my life and maybe the lives of others too. If Snyder were here, he would know, too.

Then the women rushed at me and wrapped me in a dual embrace. I loved Jo's softness against my left arm and her kiss on my cheek. I was surprised, but maybe I shouldn't have been, by the strength and ferocity in Ruth's embrace. I was in her grip now.

"Yes!" she cried. "Yes! Jack, you can *do* this! I knew it from the first minutes I met you. I knew it!"

I looked from Ruth's snow white hair to Jo's jet black and back again. They held on a few seconds longer and I started feeling a peace. I couldn't quite describe it then. And maybe peace isn't quite the right word. A direction?

Maybe by the time I finish this, I'll be able to explain it. But I was happy. Happy with a decision? But it felt like more. It was a feeling that carried me through the many years and miles ahead.

I smiled uncertainly. "So, Ruth, if I'm going to write this book, you're going to have to tell me more. Probably a lot more. I'm used to writing articles. Not anything as long as a whole book."

"Don't you worry, Mr. Jack Moriarty. I will help you every step of the way." And she gave my arm extra squeezes to make her point.

"And I can help you, too, Jack. With some of the research." Jo virtually cooed into my ear.

Ruth released me. There was no time to waste! She was about to set me on my mission. "Come, Jack! Let me tell you a little more about one of *the strangest* characters who has ever crossed my path." She didn't have to say his name. I knew. Charles Olson.

I looked back at Jo's dark, large, luminescent eyes. There was no mistaking what was going on now. Between either of us. She mouthed a quiet "Thank you."

If I was in over my head now, it was because I wanted to be.

Chapter 10 — Ruth's Story

For the next two hours Ruth talked almost non-stop through a detailed history of the Lake Eden Black Mountain. We walked around the lake to the Dining Hall, another long, sharply angled building that jutted towards the lake, pointing back to the Studies Building. The pair were modernist exclamation points to the antebellum home of the original campus.

She stopped us to tell us stories about some of the other buildings that had served as cottages or workshops. Odd names like Minimum House. Quiet House. Round House. Occasionally Jo or I would ask a question that would send Ruth on another ten or fifteen minutes of stories and history.

We paused at a large expanse of lawn. "This is where Bucky Fuller started playing with his domes. *Geodesic* domes. Laid out in a crazy quilt of aluminum sticks. Then he'd have the students start putting them together. They'd gather around the outside and lift it up and there it was! Oddest looking things you have ever seen. He was just one of the geniuses around here."

"I believe he remains among the living," Jo added.

"Yes, you are correct, Jo. One of the many who were here and have departed, yet are not altogether gone."

As she continued our tour, Ruth rattled off names that I'd heard back in New York, sometimes in San Francisco: Cage. Cunningham. Rauschenberg. Others that escape me now. All students at one time or another.

This was the early forties Black Mountain. These were the years when I left Lowell. Coming to

New York, first to Horace Mann then to Columbia. Later, I got my only taste of war as a merchant seaman on one run to Greenland and back. I flunked my try as a sailor.

Sammy was so disappointed because we didn't go in together like I said we would. And then him getting all shot up while I got myself stuck in a loony bin on my way to a general discharge. Was I really protesting all the killing, hating being ordered around like a slave? Or was I just a coward?

"Ti Jean, you always run away. Why?" I'd been trying to answer that question for so long now. Something about being here, with Ruth leading the way, maybe was going to help me figure that out. Maybe I was going to stop running. Maybe I was going to stop being a coward.

By the time Ruth was finished she'd taken us right up to the time the college closed for good in '56. It was late afternoon. I was real hungry. But I'd also gotten a taste for what had happened here twenty, thirty years before. We were back at the Studies Building. The view was spectacular in the spring light. The lake sparkled. Made me wish ghosts of faculty and students would show up for one of those big parties Ruth talked about.

I heard Ruth going on about Olson. But, honestly, I had other things on my mind. Then, with a clap of her hands, she said, "Children! That is enough for today! Let's go back to the house for something to eat...and a glass of sherry!" Clearly, she was happy that I'd eased her mind and agreed to take on this writing project.

So we hopped in the car and were at her house fifteen minutes later. None of us said much on the way back. But not much needed to be said. Ruth got what she wanted: me to write her book. And Jo was hoping to get what she wanted: me. That much was more than obvious by now.

Ruth pointed Jo to a ham that Bessie had done up and left in the refrigerator. Then to some beans and collards, and potatoes for boiling. Jo started pulling it all together for a meal while Ruth led me back to the library where she poured a glass of sherry for herself and a glass of red wine for Jo.

I took her the wine and again settled for something less, iced tea, in return. "You don't mind fixing dinner?"

Jo smiled another of her dazzling smiles and said, "No, Jack. I can do this. But now you need to spend some time with Ruth." Then she kissed me full on the lips. "And I will hold out just a drop of hope that you will consider spending some time with me later."

I have been very lucky with women, even as I disappointed virtually all of them. Yet here was one more inviting me into her life not knowing how long I'd stay there, if at all. And here I was married, kind of, and maybe I should've felt guilty. But I wasn't going to miss her invitation a second time. The hell with everything else!

"I'm definitely considering that invitation," I sighed, kissing her back.

"OK, now shoo! And pay attention to what Miss Ruth tells you. She is serious about what she wants. And she knows you are the one to tell the story. *Her* story, Jack. Do not miss that!" Then, just like Lissa, she gave me a gentle shove through the kitchen door and back to Ruth.

"Ah, there you are, Jack! I was beginning to wonder if perhaps you and Jolene were rearranging our dinner schedule."

Ruth had pulled out lots more of the photos I'd seen yesterday. She pointed to a large black and white photograph. "Now here...here is John Rice. Taken, I believe, in 1934 or perhaps '35."

The man was standing on the steps to Lee Hall with four other men. Dressed in a white shirt and slacks. He had a round face, glasses, mustache. Arms folded across his chest. Smiling a kind of relaxed smile. Like a guy in charge. Which he was at the time.

"And this is Ted Dreier. And Fred Georgia. Ralph Lounsbury. Bill Hinckley. These were the men who started it all. But it was John who led them." Her finger lingered on his image.

Then Ruth pushed through a stack of other images and pulled out another photo. It showed nine or ten young men and women lined up and smiling arm in arm. "This was taken at our curtain call of *Waiting For Lefty*. There I am on the left."

You couldn't miss Ruth. Her smile, her whole being radiated. Even dressed in trousers and a blouse, she should've been in the middle as the star. Sometimes people have said that about me even though I don't smile as much. I've been told in a crowd I can stand out even when I'm not trying to. Ruth was like that but even more so. I'd rather stand back and watch.

"Where's John?"

"Oh John never acted in any of the plays. That was not his forte. He liked to sit in the front row and take it all in. That night I knew I was acting for him. I really put on a performance even though mine was a very minor role."

"Ruth, somehow I can't imagine you ever having a minor role."

"Now, Jack, hush! I had my moments. But I was never destined to be a *star*." She paused. "That was quite an evening....quite an evening..."

Then she dug a little deeper and pulled out another photo. It too was of a performance. I could tell right away that it had been taken at a much later date than Ruth's. The photo was dominated by a huge man dressed in some outlandish costume. There were two others in the photo, but they were midgets playing to this giant. Ruth didn't have to say a word. I knew who it was. Olson.

"Jack, you cannot miss this man. This was taken in '50, or maybe '51." Again she paused, gathering her thoughts. Then she started in.

"Charles had come to dominate Black Mountain's stage. Figuratively and literally. He was a force. John, too, was a force. But his was a very controlled one. Like a big steam locomotive. Charles...Charles was like an atom bomb. He just exploded everywhere.

Not just his voice, which I swear echoed over and around our valley. But his ideas, his energy. When he was focused he could mesmerize every bit as much as John. Simply because of his size. My Lord, you just didn't expect this giant...this freak of *nature*...to talk so wondrously about language and myth and trying to find a poetry that tapped into the deepest parts of our ancient being."

This was the kind of stuff that got me excited too. The kind of stuff that I tried to get to in my books. But without a lot of the claptrap I think too many of the college guys get caught up in. Worrying too much about respectability and careers and getting comfortable, when the very things they searched for and wrote about were raw and unformed and uncomfortable.

"Was Olson the exact opposite of John Rice? Rice sounds like the kind of guy who had a clear idea of what he was after and wanted to get things done. Olson sounds like the kind of guy who pops off with a thousand ideas and hopes maybe somebody does something with a couple of them. Like they're a kind of yin and yang."

Ruth stared at me a long time, searching my face, thinking hard about what I'd just said.

"Now, Jack, that's a *very* interesting observation. And I agree with you. I had thought about them that way. For me John had been the beginning. Not just because he was the one who got everything started. John got the college going with a bang—at least in the way he envisioned Black Mountain apart from the rigidity of what he'd known. With Charles the college ended with a whimper. As big and loud and forceful as he was, Charles could not stop what was going to be."

"Did they ever meet?"

"No. Not ever. And, to be truthful, I think that was just as well. I am not sure they would have done well together. When it was time for John to go, it was time for John to go. I think meeting Charles would have been both a disappointment and a challenge. The truth is that the college changed a lot in that decade from when John left and Charles took over. Maybe John could have accepted that, but I doubt it.

"Because John, for all his talking about championing ideas and independence, still was a very strong-willed man. He liked people to agree with him."

"Sounds like those Jesuits I loved so much."

Ruth laughed. "Touché, my dear Jack! Touché!"

Jo walked in to announce that dinner would be ready in a few minutes. I noticed her glass was nearly empty. Made me wish for those times when I would match a woman glass for glass. And then some. But I knew, too, if I did I'd end up a big disappointment later. And now I'd figured out I didn't want to disappoint her again.

"Jolene," Ruth began waving her own glass a little, "I believe Mr. Moriarty is going to be our prize pupil after all. He shares my understanding of both John Rice and Charles Olson. And I believe he is getting prepared to apply his insights to the telling of our story forthrightly and comprehensively. Would you mind pouring me a little more sherry?"

"I am delighted to hear that! Jack, I hope you are beginning to understand what an opportunity is being extended to you. Here, Ruth, give me your glass. Jack, your tea is fine as it is?"

"Yeah, it's fine. Sorry I can't join you in the stronger stuff."

"You need not apologize. It's not an infirmity to acknowledge the limitations that our bodies impose upon us. It's our limitations that become the gateway to our liberation."

She said these words so sweetly, it was almost as if she was saying something else entirely. Jo's sexuality just radiated now. Maybe it was the wine. But my body was responding again in ways that it had not for years and years. And it was equally clear that Ruth was enjoying this interplay between her "children."

"Now, Jack, look here." Ruth again forced my attention to a photograph. This was of a couple taken thirty years before. Outdoors. Looked like the Lake Eden campus. "These are Josef and Anni Albers. Do you know them?"

I shook my head. Jo returned with Ruth's glass. We stood together, me wedged between the women. Again Jo rubbed her shoulder easily against my arm.

"They are, I think, every bit as important to the history and life of Black Mountain as John and Charles. We were very lucky to have them. Josef was a student and teacher at the Bauhaus school during the twenties. He is one of the most important painters of our century."

Ruth paused, again collecting memories. Not easy ones, it seemed. She continued with her voice lowered.

"Jack, they were Jews in Germany when the Nazis came to power. If they hadn't gotten out when they did, who knows what would have happened to them?"

Here Jo jumped in. "And they were very lucky to have us. Or, I should say, they were very lucky to have *her*."

Now I looked back to Ruth. She was running her fingers over the photo as though pulling details from their past into our present.

"Jack," she said slowly, "as you know that was a very dark time. As bad as the Depression was for us here, you know it was many, many, many times worse for the people in Europe—especially for the German people. The Nazis fed on their unhappiness. And also on their pride. They are a very prideful people, for better *and* for worse.

"The Nazis drew their power from the poverty and unhappiness and shame that losing the first war had brought. And when they seized the government, they were ready to pounce on the ones they blamed for all that unhappiness—the Jews. The intellectuals. And, yes, the Communists and the Socialists. And anyone else who they thought they could turn the people against for their own twisted, twisted goals.

"The Bauhaus was one of their easiest targets. Filled with great creativity with many intellectuals and leftists of different stripes. And Jews. I had met some of them a few years before on one of my trips. Including Josef and Anni. We became good friends. When they sent a letter telling what was starting to happen under Hitler, I knew I had to do something."

Jo interrupted gently, tugging on my arm at the same time. "Ruth, I believe our supper is ready. I hope you'll continue to tell Jack how you saved the Albers, and many more, at your table."

Ruth saving Jews from Hitler? How many more stories did this woman have stored inside her? It's too bad I didn't have a real writing assignment. She would've made the cover of whatever mag I would've been writing for.

But I did have a real writing assignment, didn't I? That's what I said yes to just an hour or two ago. Now it was my 'job' to find a way to somehow remember all these stories Ruth was sharing and pull them into something about Black Mountain worth reading.

We made our way to the dining room table. Ruth held my arm this time as though she really needed it, her sherry glass shaking perhaps a bit more in her other hand. We sat in the same seats we'd been in the night before.

We ate hungrily, or at least I did. Tried not to make a pig of myself. Truth was, I hadn't had a thing since the campsite, except coffee, lemonade and iced tea, and here it was after six. One thing about kicking the booze, my appetite was back up.

Jo and I exchanged glances a few times between bites. I was glad that I was doing for her whatever it was she needed doing. She was beautiful, no doubt. And deep. This was something kind of new for me. A different kind of challenge.

In the past I'd found it easy to be with women who were also beat, also down-and-outers. They were into life for life itself, even if their lives didn't have a whole lot going for them. And maybe they were easy to be with because they didn't ask a lot of me. Just treat 'em nice, buy 'em some beers and smokes, take 'em for a ride somewhere, anywhere.

I didn't go much for the girls who hung around my Columbia crowd. They were smart. Lot of 'em came from money. I guess they liked being at the edges of what we were getting into. The music. The writing. The whole scene.

But I always knew they would eventually end up out in the suburbs with an accountant for a husband and a big house and some kids to go along with it all. They liked hanging with us then because it would give them something to dream about later when they were bored with life and wondering if they'd missed out on something really big because they were too scared to plunge off into the madness where we were headed.

So I ended up with women who had none of that. Who maybe were scared of the madness, and the darkness too, but had nowhere else to go so they'd hang on for a while hoping maybe I could deliver them someplace that was safer and brighter and maybe had something of a future to offer. If they couldn't have the accountant and the house and the suburbs, maybe

I could give them at least something. Maybe they could have at least a house somewhere. A little house. Something they'd *own*. And a car too. Maybe *two* cars. And maybe there'd be kids too. And maybe those kids could grow up with more hope than they'd ever had. Maybe America would be kinder to them than it'd been to their parents and grandparents.

Maybe.

Because so far I hadn't seen much of that. Oh, I'd seen suburbs fill up with people escaping the cities. Or the blacks. Or both. And I'd seen advertisements upon advertisements selling America on this vision of itself as a land of endless prosperity, selling us on the idea that buying *things* would make us happy. The more we bought, the happier we'd be. And they started making it easier and easier for us to buy those things. Making it easier and easier for those women who had nothing to start thinking that maybe they had something. Making it easier to think that maybe America really was being kinder to them.

So as I sat across the table looking at Jo and wondering what kind of woman she was, America was becoming a place where if you didn't buy more and more, *on credit*, people began to question your patriotism. Maybe not out loud. But if you didn't have your house in the suburbs, your two cars, your outdoor gas grill, your riding lawn mower, then maybe something was wrong with you. Maybe you *were* a failure. Or, worse, a subversive, because you were not joining in the consumerism-equals-happiness America. And that made you a target for those who were.

America was not at peace. Not with itself or with a lot of the world either. We were at war with ourselves too. Mainly kids against their parents. The kids being sent by their parents to die in jungles for reasons that made no sense. Parents told their children to believe in the ideals of our Declaration of Independence, then got mad when the kids didn't want to fight others who thought they had their own rights to independence. By 1970 they'd forced them to fight and die over in Vietnam longer than we had during WWII. At least we won that war. These kids had nothing to show for it. No wonder everybody was pissed off.

So what did all of this have to do with Jo? I wasn't sure. But I was getting the feeling that maybe she wasn't like the Barnard girls who wanted to hang around, but never wanted to really get into it. Nor was she like the brown-skinned girls I had known who picked grapes and had babies. Or the junkies I'd seen in the Village trading their bodies for fixes. Or even girls like Lissa who had to grow up quick after their parents had been worn out fast and early—or even beaten to death—by machines.

Jo was looking for something else. That's why I think she and Ruth made fast friends. Ruth, too, was a seeker. I was getting that loud and clear now. In seventy years she had never settled down, even though she was living in the same house where her daddy had raised her in comfort. Ruth was after something else. So was Jo. They hoped I was too.

I had pretty much moved through that entire plate of ham and beans and collards before I had sense enough to ask about what Ruth had started to share back in the library about her being in Nazi Germany and rescuing her friends, the Albers.

"So, Ruth, what was that Jo was saying about your friends and getting them out of Germany? Did you really do that?"

Ruth stopped the slow pace of her eating and ran her fingers over the fine cut edges of her sherry glass. I looked at Jo. Her eyes said, "Be patient. There's a story here."

"Yes, I guess I did. It wasn't easy. I helped a few get out. But...but...there were so many more I wanted to help. But I could not. The Albers were lucky. All of it was just starting. They saw it and they knew. And they wrote me.

"At first I didn't know what to do. But then I talked Daddy into going with me to Washington, D.C., one time because he was friends with our senator. I took my letter and showed it to him. He just shook his head. Then he sent us over to the State Department. And they read it. And they shook their heads. And all of them said there was nothing they could do. Either they didn't think the Nazis were as bad as Josef and Anni said they were. Or they didn't want to have any more Jews in this country than we had already said we'd take. Or maybe both.

"I came home heartbroken. I will tell you, Jack," and here Ruth laughed a little wistfully, "even then I was a woman used to getting her way. And to be turned away like that. Well, at first I didn't know what to do with myself."

"I'm surprised your dad went with you. Wouldn't have guessed he was the kind of guy to stick his nose into politics like that."

Ruth didn't look at me. She continued fingering and talking to the glass.

"I kind of wondered about that too at first. When I first showed him the letter, he really wasn't too interested. 'The Germans have their problems. We have ours. Let's take care of ourselves before we start saving the world.' That's what he said.

"But I kept after him. Asking him what we should do. I went to New York and talked with friends there. They were also trying to get people out. I'd come back and tell him what others were doing.

"Finally, one night at supper, he just exploded on me. I was frightened! He said, 'Ruth, you just do not know what you are getting into here! It's not just the Nazis. The world has always had Nazis. Now they just have different names. Different faces. But they act just the same. Our people came to this country to get away from the same kind of Germans. They just wore different uniforms then.'

"And I looked at him, trying to understand. And I said, 'Daddy what do you mean 'our people.' I thought Great-grandfather Parker came here because he wanted to, because he wanted to have a bank in the United States.'

"I remember how Daddy looked at me then. He had always been a very confident man. But it was like something inside had broken. And I had done the breaking. And he said to me something that shook me to the very core of my being.

"'Ruth,' he said, 'you cannot tell a soul what I am about to tell you. If you do, it will mean the end of all that we have here. Do you understand me? But your mother, God rest her soul, raised you to be a fine and smart woman.' Here he paused, still maybe not quite sure if he should say what he was going to. But he took another deep breath and said, 'I guess it is time for you to know what you should know.'

"Then he looked at me with the most awful look. His eyes got red. I can see them still. And his nostrils flared as though breathing itself was hard. And his jaw muscles moved back and forth fighting to keep in the very words he was about to say to me.

"Finally, he said what could have brought down the bank, our house and everything in between if anybody else but me had heard them."

Now Ruth looked me square in the eyes almost as though she were conjuring up the ghost of her long-dead father.

"He said 'Ruth. We. Are Jews. Also.'"

I stared back trying to imagine the impact of those words on her. Her eyes flashed a sweep of emotions. Defeated. Defiant. Seeking.

"I said, 'Say that again, Daddy.'"

"And he looked at me so hard. Like he was as angry as could be. But also something else. Like forgiveness. But he repeated the words 'We. Are Jews. Also.'"

Ruth said them again with the same emphasis. Then she looked back at the glass and started her finger over it again. I looked at Jo. She knew.

"I am not easily shut up, as you have probably discovered by now. But that revelation shut me up for a good ten minutes. There was total silence in our house. We just looked and looked at each other."

I wasn't really sure what to say back. I guess I didn't get what made being a Jew in America so damning that it would have ruined Ruth's father and their lives if anyone had known. Allen tried talking to me at different times about anti-Semitism and how he'd experienced it growing up. But, shoot, everyone's got problems growing up. Even in Lowell. I knew the old, rich, Protestant types looked down on us French Canadians. "Canucks" they called us. Or "Frenchies." Made fun of us because we spoke a dialect, went to our own Catholic church.

I learned to get along with them because I ended up pretty smart and I could play football. But when I fell for one of "their" girls, I found out pretty quick that being a "Kerouac" meant staying on my side of town if I wanted sex.

We weren't alone in feeling like outsiders. The Irish. The Greeks. The Italians. The Portuguese. All of them had come to this country expecting to find a freedom that didn't exist in their home countries. And some of them found work and homes in Lowell. But that didn't mean they were welcomed with open arms by the English and Scots who had settled there long before them.

My friend Sammy Sampas was probably smarter than all of them. But that didn't keep him from getting called "Dirty Greek" and sometimes worse by the rich kids. Maybe it'd have been different if he'd made it back from the war and gone to medical school like he wanted.

So I asked, "Ruth, sorry for being dumb, but I guess I don't get it. Why would being a Jew be so awfully bad for your dad? He owned the bank. And sounds like most of the town too."

"Oh, Jack, that's just it. I know it's different in New York. Or maybe where you grew up in Boston. But here in North Carolina, Jews are not looked upon favorably. It may be a little better today, but not then. Not in 1933. And certainly not when Great-grandfather Parker, or should I say "Pachtenburg" arrived here in 1850."

"Jack," Jo tried to explain, "Ruth is right. People here were very isolated for a very, very long time. We knew our kind and trusted them. But outsiders—any outsiders—had a difficult time getting accepted. It would have been hard enough for her great-granddaddy to get accepted as a German. But to come here as a German and a Jew? No, he would have been shunned. He could have counted himself lucky if his house weren't burnt down too."

Ruth seemed to gather a second wind. Now that she'd started telling the story, she wanted to finish.

"So, Jack, he came to the United States because he had gotten in trouble politically. He'd been a successful merchant in Dusseldorf. But he sympathized with those who started a revolution in 1848 against the ridiculous patchwork of royal fiefdoms that Germany was then. When the revolution failed, he and a lot of other Germans had to leave or face jail or worse. He knew a Jewish family in Richmond and that's where he came first. But not before he changed his name to something more English sounding. That's how we became Parkers.

"He was able to bring most of his money with him. His friends in Richmond helped him get started with a mercantile store. He did quite well until the war came on. That would be the Civil War, Jack.

"He managed to survive through most of that as well, even though he was not a sympathizer to the politics of the Confederacy. He also had a growing family to think about. So he got out while he still could and found a quiet little place to restart his business and raise his family in peace."

"Let me guess. Black Mountain?"

"Yes. He had come through here on a trip with his family to see the Smoky Mountains. He knew this area was relatively unharmed by the war. But it was still good farm land and likely to prosper when the war was over. So in 1864 he opened Parker Mercantile and built a successful business for a third time. Plus, he had my granddaddy to help him.

"By the time Daddy was born in 1869, Parker Mercantile was well established. In 1890, Grandpa Parker and Daddy opened the Black Mountain Bank and Trust just in time for the Panic of '93."

I wasn't sure what the Panic of '93 was, but it didn't sound good. "Did they go under?"

"Almost! The other bank in town did. So when things got better, it was just Grandpa and Daddy. They had won a lot of friends, and business, because they could extend credit to farmers and businesses and tide them over until prices got better. If they hadn't done what they did, Black Mountain might have dried up and blown away."

"So why the fear about being found out...as Jews?"

"Because! Because even though they had settled into the community and it accepted them as 'good' Germans, if someone found out who we really were, then we would have been shunned as Shylocks or worse. Someone else would have opened another bank and all the money would have walked across the street just as quick as you could say...'Jew.'"

"It was that bad?"

"Was...and in some senses still is. That's why Daddy was so scared when I started making noises about saving the Albers and others. It was hard for me in a way to understand at the moment because by the time I came along Grandpa and Daddy were pretty much running the town.

"To tell you the truth, the news shook me up too. I had never given all that much thought to blood lines because I assumed ours were 'untainted.' But when he said who we really were, and that I'd been named for my great-grandmother, well that made me have to re-examine at a lot of things. I mean, I didn't *look* Jewish. But as I learned more about what the Jews in Europe had gone through...I began to feel a little guilty, for my extreme good fortune."

I thought about how my parents were sometimes a little ashamed of being "Frenchies" in WASPy Massachusetts. So they laid claim to our ancestral home in Brittany, thinking our continental pedigree would somehow elevate them in Lowell society.

Then when I went to France I learned how the Parisians looked down on all the other "country bumpkins" outside the city. Got me to thinking it's the same all over the world. Some people want to put it over on others just because they look a little different, or speak a little differently.

Of course, in the case of the Jews, it wasn't just looking down on them that made their situation different. The Germans—the Nazis—wanted to wipe them off the face of the Earth. I remembered Burroughs marrying that countess, or whatever she was, just so she could get away from them also.

It wasn't just the Nazis. The Russians and the Poles took their turns at driving Jews out of their countries decades before the Nazis came to power. And the French had reputations for being anti-Semites too. Hell, so did we!

"So, sounds like your family dropped its religion when it got here?" I asked.

"Yes. I never knew about it at all. Daddy told me that Great-Grandfather had never been highly observant even back in Europe. You know, the ones who wear the black hats and have long beards? I'm sure you've seen them in New York. But he was still proud of the family tradition. We'd managed to survive many years of acceptance and rejection.

"When Great-Grandfather came here, however, he was determined to become an American. So he dropped his German dress. And learned English very quickly. And insisted that his children lose all vestiges of their European background, including their—I guess I should say 'our'—religion."

"So, what happened to the Albers? I mean, how'd you get them out?"

"Jack maybe you've learned enough by now to know that money can seduce even the most vile of ideologies. And maybe you've learned, too, that sex is an international currency unto its own. With enough of both, the world will give you many things."

Now she stared straight at me, demanding full attention, conveying even more with her look than the words that had just stunned me. Somehow I knew not to ask more than she cared to reveal. Still, I was fascinated. I *wanted* to know more.

Oh Dean, oh Dean! This was a chick you could have really dug. But maybe a chick too gone even for the likes of you. At least when she was still a chick forty years ago.

Oh, Allen! This was a sad, deep doldrum playing out that would have kept you writing for weeks and weeks...*Black Mountain Doldrums*...you would have sung Ruth's song.

"I went back to Berlin. I got them out. And then they came to Black Mountain."

I thought that was the end of the story. But Ruth surprised me by going on a little more.

"One evening Daddy came home with his briefcase and put it right here on the table. He asked me to come over and then he opened it up. And there it was, full of cash. Twenty thousand dollars. He said, 'Take this. I think you will know how to use it to help your friends.'

"I was stunned. I had never seen so much money at one time. I hugged him so hard and we cried and cried. Then he told me, 'We are Americans. But you have reminded me what Grandpa and my father wanted us to forget, that they are our people too. I will talk to the senator again. You go and bring back as many as you can.' And...that is what I did."

"Ruth, that's one hell of a story. How many did you get out?" I was thinking hundreds, if not thousands.

Here, Ruth grew pensive again, remembering perhaps not those who escaped, but those who didn't.

"Not many. The Albers, maybe a dozen more. But Josef and Anni were the only ones who made it here. The United States, I mean. And that was only because Daddy leaned on his senator friend. I learned long before the war started that we Americans weren't much friendlier to the Jews than Hitler himself. I got the others as far as London. I did what I could. It wasn't enough."

"Oh, now, Ruth you shouldn't say that!" Jo jumped in now. "You risked your *life* for those people. I mean, you haven't told Jack a tenth of what you've told me."

"Jo, now stop! We'd be here all night and then some. I know you two would hardly stand for that!"

"At least tell him about meeting what's-his-name...that big fat Nazi."

Now Ruth looked back at me and decided I could be patient enough for one more story. Then she leaned forward and whispered loudly, but conspiratorially, "She means Goering."

My eyes got wide. I knew about Goering. I remembered him as the Number Two Nazi. How in the hell did Ruth meet this guy?

Ruth saw she still had her audience. That and the second glass of sherry had kicked in. She launched into one of her great stories. I swear she was a match for anything Neal or Allen or any of our bunch could've spun out!

"It was New Year's Eve 1933. I'd come over to London in November after the elections—I waited to make sure Roosevelt won—because some friends there had invited me to be in a play. We started rehearsals for a few weeks, then took a break for the holidays. Everything really was dreadful. The Depression, I think, was felt even more in England than here. In New York I saw people who were hungry. In London, I swear I saw some who were starving. Even though the government dole there was supposed to be much more generous than ours was here. Still, it was interesting being in another country for the holidays.

"I know Daddy hated me being away, but, as I said, we had never been a particularly religious family —it wasn't until the following spring that I found out why. But he always liked having me home for a month or two. And, truth be told, I always did enjoy coming home.

"One of our troupe did come from a wealthy family and so we did spend some days with them at their estate outside London. The weather was dreary. But huge fires and lots of gin were enough to make us all very merry! His family was glad to have us, too. I don't know if was them, or their money, but they seemed to be an isolated lot.

"I knew that we had more than most in Black Mountain. But we were always part of the town. Just like now. Bill's family—he was the young man whose father had the estate—they were all very nice people, but it seemed like they had so much money they didn't have to *do* anything. Be anywhere. Be with anyone. So they had their estate. It almost seemed like they waited for Bill to come back out from London and bring them news of the world. I think he brought us along to save him from the same loneliness. And his family enjoyed having us there for entertainment. A break from their wealthy loneliness! And entertain we did. We sang! We rehearsed. We told wonderful and horrible stories. I had to dodge his father's clutches more than once!

"Then Bill said the place to be for New Year's was Berlin. Big things were happening there. I remember his parents not being at all in favor of the idea. Germany was even more of a mess than England. When they saw Bill would not be dissuaded, his father said, I can hear him clear as day even now, 'Maybe things will get better when the "Nazis"—he said it like that, the British way—'start running the show. Maybe they'll scoop up all the Bolshies and toss 'em back to Stalin. Bring order to the bloody place!'

"I learned later, to my great surprise, that many of the wealthy in England were sympathetic to Hitler, even when it became apparent he was going to bring war on them. That was true even here! Roosevelt had a devil of a time trying to help Churchill when England was almost on its knees. But that's not the story you wanted to hear."

Ruth paused long enough to drain her glass. She held it and looked at Jo long enough for the message to get through. "Of course! And maybe I will refill my own."

Ruth reached out and put her hand across my arm. She leaned over again and whispered, this time so there was no way Jo would hear, "Now, Jack, you take good care of her! She is a keeper!"

Jesus! I'd just met both of these women a couple days before and here was Ruth practically marrying Jo off to me. I didn't know what to say. "I know she is."

"Jack, do not pass up your chances at happiness. Life is short. Love—true love—is the only real sweetness it offers. Remember that!" She squeezed my arm hard for emphasis.

Ruth leaned back when she heard Jo's steps in the living room. "Thank you, my dear!"

She reached for the glass and took a sip. Jo looked at me as she sipped hers as well. I felt like I was being seduced by *two* women!

"Now...where was I? Oh, yes! Berlin!

"So the day after Christmas we trained back into London. Then we sailed on to Hamburg. We got to Berlin on the 29th, I think it was. Bill paid for everything! Our tickets. Rooms. Meals. I could have paid my own way, of course. Maybe not as lavishly. But he had insisted. There were six of us altogether. And we just were having a mad time. A week in Berlin!

"Children, I know it is hard for you to appreciate the Berlin of today—split in two, a virtual war zone—with what it was then. But Berlin after the war, the *first* World War I mean, was full of ferment. It hadn't been ruined as it was during the second World War. But everything was changing. Everything."

Here Ruth paused for a minute. She stared down the table and into the living room. She was going away again. Back into her years. Back into memories that seemed as alive as the experiences themselves.

I could almost feel her go because the same thing happened to me back then. Still does. It's almost a séance-like feeling. You're here, but you're not here. You feel others come to you. You can talk without talking. See without seeing. And it's not ghosts. It's more real than that. Damnedest thing I ever felt.

"So we swirled into Berlin and Bill put us up in a very nice hotel. And just as fast he swirled us out into the town. He looked up some friends he'd met on his first trip to the continent right after the war and they took us along to a party that was getting started in some out-of-the-way place.

"Children, it felt like a madness was coming down all over us. But we wanted it. We wanted to feel it. To be taken up into it. The army and its uniforms. There was martial law. And the Nazis were all over the place too. Brown shirts. Black shirts. And yet their power didn't feel quite real. Not yet. It was more like they were in costume. Part of the partying madness. A German Halloween that would somehow end at the beginning of the New Year.

"I confess to this feeling myself. Even though I had always thought myself perhaps a bit more restrained than my theater mates. Yet something was happening. A beat. A throbbing. Something getting ready to explode all over. Here, almost forty years later, it is hard to capture quite what it was like.

"But Bill knew. I could feel him embracing it with all his soul. He raced through Berlin! And he was happy to drag us all along. He raced to escape the deadliness of his family. He knew he was racing into an abyss. And he hoped we would all hold hands as we plunged down together into a darkness from which we might never emerge.

"Children! I do not mean to sound so melodramatic. Yet, this is what I felt. What *we* felt. Far deeper, far more thrilling than what a child feels when he sees a thunderstorm approaching. The sounds. The lightning. The calm first, then the whirlwind. That was Berlin at New Year's.

"And so plunge we did. From one party into another. I saw and listened as just about every German I met mocked the Nazis. Even though they had just come into power, there was a very surrealistic sense about it all. As though it didn't really happen. Or if it did, surely they wouldn't last long. Spring at the latest. Then the Socialists—the *real* Socialists—would push them out. And they and their silly uniforms and ugly faces would be just a bad dream. The thunderstorm would be over.

"So that is it how it was on New Year's Eve when Bill's friends invited us to a party in a huge basement grotto. This party had a theme: everyone had to wear a costume, but everyone also had to cross-dress! Men must become women. And women must become men! Bill was thrilled! I found out later this was something he really embraced, as well as the men who came along with it.

"Of course, as theater people, we loved getting into costume. As the only American in the group, someone came up with the idea that I should become Charlie Chaplin. My hair was shorter then and black. We found a very respectable tuxedo. With enough room to conceal my bust! Added a top hat and cane. Plus, his funny little moustache! I practiced his famous little duck walk. My friends were amazed at the transformation.

"I was equally amazed at Bill's transformation. He changed from a five foot ten inch nicely muscled man into a six foot showgirl in heels, with cleavage! I'd only seen him as a slightly reserved minor character in our rehearsals. But he went at this role with real verve! I can still see him today, dressed in red from head to foot.

"So we six swirled through this end-of-the-year, end-of-the-world party...madness really...with all the energy and craziness we could summon. Oh, I was so glad Daddy was an ocean away! But the Germans loved my Chaplin! And I loved my Chaplin, too!

"I tittered and tottered and swirled and danced and did everything I could remember from his movies. Someone came dressed as Hitler himself! Which was *very* daring. And somewhere in the evening we started dancing together. We made a mad, mad couple! People gave us the dance floor and her Hitler led my Chaplin around and around.

"Then I turned the tables! And I twirled Herr Hitler around and around until the very end of the song when I tilted him way back and planted the biggest kiss on his lips. But then I wrinkled my nose and lips and wiggled my moustache suggesting perhaps it wasn't the nicest kiss in my life. The crowd went wild! Of course that gesture alone would have been Chaplin at his subversive best! It might have been my best role ever, Jack!

"That seemed to set everyone off. Men dancing with men and women dancing with women. Of course it looked just the opposite. Bill found himself a tall, distinguished-looking German to dance with. As tall as he was. In an electric blue dress. Wearing some sort of blondish wig as I recall. A red lipstick to match Bill's dress. They really made a striking pair.

"Bill's companion seemed quite smitten. I wasn't surprised when they slipped away sometime after we rang in the New Year. I *was* surprised when I found out later who it was he had slipped away with!"

I was thinking even in my craziest, gonest days in New York and Denver and San Francisco, even down in Mexico, nothing seemed to compare to this Berlin scene Ruth described. I thought of Neal in his madness rushing back and forth between Louanne and Allen, between LouAnn and Carolyn, between Diana and Carolyn, between anyone and anything that he needed. But this seemed to go beyond even him.

Maybe Allen could have dug it. Or old Bill Burroughs. But just looking at sweet, determined Ruth and then listening to her summon up forty-year-old memories...that was wild just in itself. She had me back in 1932 Berlin.

Ruth had paused to take a deep swallow of her sherry. I wondered how much more of her story there was because it seemed like we were moving deeper into an evening that I knew Jo and I wanted time for somewhere else.

"Well, children, that party carried on until dawn. To this day, I don't know how I managed it. The band played and played. I danced and danced. And drank more than I should have. And fended off more advances in one evening than I'd had in two years!

"Of course, I had been long separated from Bill and our other friends. But then it seemed I made at least a dozen new ones, even if they didn't speak a word of English! And every one of them lusted for a Chaplin kiss!

"I finally made it back to my room—*alone*—I think just before the sun was ready to come up. My suite shared a common living room with Bill's. But I do not remember a thing except a dying desire to fall into a comfortable bed, which I did, and there I slept until the middle of the afternoon.

"When I finally did get up I wandered out and there was Bill in a dressing gown along with his dancing companion from the night before, also in a dressing down but without his blonde wig! Bill was quite happy to see me in one piece, I think. He seemed equally comfortable introducing his companion, even though this was the first time I knew for a fact that Bill was—what's the word they use today?—gay? He certainly was!

"He introduced him as 'Wilhelm.' His English was very good. Certainly much better than my pidgin German. We had a delightful conversation. He complimented me on my Chaplin, saying he was one of his favorite actors. He even laughed at my reaction after kissing Hitler. He said, 'Der Fuhrer is not a very kissable man!' I remember then how he said it, as though he knew the man personally. Of course, it turned out that he did!"

Here she paused again. I just kind of stared back and forth between her and Jo, who kept looking at me with those "wait-there-is-more" eyes. Ruth charged on.

"I was curious about all the changes in Germany that I had been reading and talking about since we arrived in Berlin. 'Wilhelm', I must say, seemed eager to share his opinions. He talked bitterly about Germany's defeat in the World War for which he seemed to blame his own country's leadership more than any superiority on our part.

"When I asked if he had fought, he got very excited. 'Yes! I flew with Richthofen!' He went on for some time talking about various air battles he had been in. I confess that both Bill and I were rapt. Of course, we had no of idea what was to come in just a few years. Or that he would be in charge of trying to bomb England back to the Middle Ages.

"He then became very sarcastic speaking about the government that the Nazis were on the verge of replacing. Hitler was not yet the chancellor. That would not happen for a few weeks. But Bill's 'friend' talked about how weak it was. How the Communists had almost taken over.

"I remember him looking at us very seriously, almost pleadingly, and saying 'You English and you Americans should be very glad when we are fully in power. Then you will have someone to finally stand up to Stalin. And we will rid our country of those who would disgrace Germany with their red stain.'

"Of course, I was very surprised by this language because 'Wilhelm' had not said who he really was, which was, of course, Goering as I found out later. I remembered, too, how much he sounded like Bill's father. It was, I confess, frightening although I tried hard not to show the shudder I felt inside. It was frightening for reasons that I could not understand or express then. Maybe it was just the way he spoke about politics. Very cold blooded. Different from how we discussed culture or the theater."

Ruth paused again and sipped more sherry. I didn't know what to say or ask. I was totally absorbed by this woman's storytelling. She could've outtalked Neal and Allen together! Jo just looked back and forth between Ruth and me. She knew I was hooked. I knew it too. Ruth went on.

"Bill and 'Wilhelm' had not yet had their fill of each other. So after a while, they excused themselves to Bill's suite with the promise that they, or at least Bill, would catch up with me and our other friends later for supper and then another round of parties. I, too, was still somewhat exhausted from the night before and was glad I could retire before the wildness began again.

"So I retired as well for a few hours more. But then that night I caught up with Josef and Anni, quite by accident. I had rendezvoused with our friends at this lovely little restaurant and there we saw some of the people we had been celebrating with the night before. They had other friends with them, who turned out to be the Albers! So we all became one big party and the madness started swirling again!

"They seemed very glad to see me even though their English, especially Josef's, was as weak as my German. My friends begged me to reprise my Chaplin from the night before. I did my best, pantomiming for their entertainment, holding my finger across my lip to imitate the moustache. Everyone roared again. I was delighted, I must say.

"Then one of our German friends laughed to Josef and Anni, '*Und sie* Hitler *bussed*!' That means 'And she kissed Hitler!' The Albers looked as though they were about to faint. Then their friends explained the joke and we all roared. But I could see Josef and Anni were more relieved than amused. It was Anni who said '*Unmoglich,* Hitler *ist ein Scherz nicht.*' 'Hitler is not a joke, unfortunately.' That was something that stayed with me the rest of our time there. It was after I got home when they wrote and asked for my help in getting out."

"How did you do that? With the money?" Ruth looked at me like a high school teacher to a hopelessly ignorant student. It seemed all I could do was ask dumb questions.

"Yes. That and more. Bill helped immensely, as it turned out. Surprisingly so, I think. When we finally headed back to London, he said, 'Wilhelm was quite taken with you.' And I said, 'Oh? I thought *you* were the one he was taken with.' 'Do you know who he really is?' 'No. Who?' 'Goering!' 'Who's that?' And he looked at me as if I was a hopelessly naïve American, which wasn't far off actually. 'Herman Goering is the second most powerful man in Germany now. He and Hitler are like this.' And then he crossed his fingers. To which I responded wickedly 'Literally?' And Bill roared at my joke. 'No! At least I don't think so! If so, I shall be quite jealous!'

"So Bill proceeded to tell me all of his and Wilhelm's pillow talk. Apparently Wilhelm, or Herman, was quite boastful of their coming to power. No talk of war then. More about restoring Germany to her 'rightful place in the world' and that sort of thing. But he wanted to see more of Bill, and me apparently, and we had a standing invitation to return to Berlin in the spring or the summer."

Here Ruth paused again looking at me with a hard, searching stare trying to see if I was taking all this in. Without waiting for another dumb question, she went on.

"And so I did. After I had received the letter. After Daddy and I had gone to Washington. After he told me who we really were. And, then, after he brought home the money and told me to use it.

"I went back to Berlin with Bill that summer. We looked like a normal touring couple. I even wore a ring to appear as his wife! We stayed in an even more divine hotel than the one at New Year's. Soon after we were invited by Goering to his official quarters. He told us his wife had just gone to Bavaria to enjoy the mountains and cooler temperatures. And the evening wore on. We were having a grand time. Or at least Bill and Wilhelm were. Then it seemed it was later than maybe it should have been and ...well...he invited us to spend the night! Not just Bill. Both of us."

I really didn't want to know any more details than that. What people did in bed and with whom wasn't the kind of thing I was interested in hearing about. Not that I'm an old lady prude or anything. Seen and done plenty of things that I'm sure Memere and our Lowell priest would've said earned me a ticket straight to Hell. The way Allen and Neal went at it. With me right there in the room! Or LouAnn playing with my cock in the car with Neal sleeping right next to us. Or Bea and me doing it with her kid right there. Or Neal doing it with about anybody and anything at any time, night or day. Crazy what our need for love—or just plain old sex—will drive us to do.

Still, I wasn't anxious to hear about Ruth and Bill and Herman's own pillow talk. Thankfully, Ruth didn't feel a need to tell us. For me, it's always been hard to look at old people—even though Ruth hardly seemed to act her age and I'm ten years older now than she was then—and imagine them as young people doing all sorts of crazy things. But my understanding of her had certainly changed a lot in those few days from when I saw her pushing her way through the library doors. What a firecracker!

"The next day I felt brave enough to broach the question of getting Josef and Anni out. I expected to get a long lecture about the inferiority of Jews or the dangers to society posed by modern art. But, surprisingly, 'Wilhelm,' or Herman, as we were now allowed to call him, seemed to sense immediately a 'business opportunity' instead.

"It was all done in very coded language, of course. But once he realized that I was serious, and could back up my words with American cash, things moved along nicely. Of course, I couldn't tell Josef or Anni, or the others, exactly how they got their papers.

"Herman had to be discreet as well. It helped that the Nazis were still new to their power. They were just beginning to exercise their evil ways. I had negotiated a list of twenty with Goering. At the last minute only twelve got out. It took every last one of Daddy's twenty thousand dollars to get them. All the money went to Herman. But I am pretty sure he had to use some of it to pay others off down the line."

Ruth had said these last sentences very slowly, as though the telling itself was exhausting.

"What happened to the ones who got out?"

"We sailed with them back to London. Bill helped find lodging and jobs for some. He wasn't political, but he was a good soul. I guess it helped, too, that he and Herman got on so well. He went back a few more times after that to see him. I was conveniently left behind, of course, apparently to Herman's great disappointment, though certainly not to mine.

"I came back to New York in the fall. Then Daddy sent me a letter about the college starting up at the Robert E. Lee. For some reason I thought Josef and Anni might be a fit there. After what I saw in Berlin, I could sense that more bad times were coming to Europe. So did they. While I was still in London we talked about them maybe coming to America at some point. Of course, I had no idea it would be so soon!

"So I sent them a letter asking if they had any interest in coming to a brand new college as far from our cultural centers as Berlin is from New York. At the same time I sent a letter to John Rice, about whom of course I hadn't the foggiest idea, asking if there were room for Josef and Anni on his new faculty. To my surprise I got *telegrams* from both saying yes.

"That's when Daddy went to work with his political connections and arranged visas for them. It wasn't easy, he assured me. But I was so proud of him! He only asked one thing of me: that I would not breathe a word of what he did to *anyone*. He did not even go up to Lee Hall when the Albers arrived.

"Nor was I there. I'd signed on with another company for the fall and couldn't take the time to come back home. I did see them in New York as they were en route. It was...very emotional. Without any words being spoken, they knew and I knew, what it meant for them to reach our shores safely. Even when it meant leaving behind all they had known."

Here Ruth stopped. She *was* exhausted. She had great, memory-filled tears in her eyes. How much more did she see and experience that she hadn't told us yet? Or couldn't?

We sat with our silence. I looked again at Jo. With her great luminescent eyes she was gauging how well I was taking in Ruth's story. Maybe I could ask her later how much more there was that hadn't been revealed this evening.

Somehow what Ruth had been through made my life so far seem like a trifle. Especially when I thought again of my own "contributions" to the war. Evil was loose across the world and it had to be stopped. Innocents had to be protected. Perpetrators killed. Millions upon millions died fighting. Millions more slaughtered just for being Jews. Or just "different." But I ran away. I don't care what I called it then. I ran away. I ran away. I ran away. And now I must answer for my cowardice.

"Ti Jean, you were given so much."

I about jumped out of my skin! Gerard again! Sitting on the table looking at me. I jumped so much I shook all the dishes. I shook Ruth from her exhaustion. And Jo's eyes took on a different focus. Not at Gerard. Me.

"Jack, are you alright?" she asked. I could hear fear in her voice. Ruth just stared, now too tired for words.

I was shaken, too, back into the present. For that moment I had been staring right back at Gerard. Riveted to his eyes. Hearing his words. Ashamed at what my answer to him must be. I wanted to cry. I wanted to ask his forgiveness. How he got there, I do not know. How Ruth and Jo could not see him, could not hear him, I do not know. But he was *there*. Staring at me with his own great, sad, old wise man eyes. Telling me what I knew and was ashamed I knew.

I wanted to go and die with Sammy at Anzio. I wanted to lie comfortably in my grave knowing that I, too, had been brave and fought evil and lived and died as a man needs to live and die. I wanted Memere to come and cry over me, but for different reasons than she cried over me now. I *was* given so much. So much that I was a fool with riches, not knowing what I had and what I was wasting. Content to drown in my own blood curled around that toilet bowl.

I couldn't answer Jo right away. Didn't she see Gerard sitting there too? Didn't she hear him damn me? Didn't she see me for the fraud I was?

Ruth just stared at me differently. I was now almost afraid to meet her eyes. I felt like she knew. She *knew*. What? She didn't act like she too could see Gerard sitting there. But she knew I was there and not there. She knew that I was a fraud. But she was willing to take her chances on me. Why? Why? Why had she sat down at that restaurant, talking to me as though we had been friends all our lives? Why had she invited me to dinner that night? Me, a complete stranger? Why had she pushed me and touched me in places no one ever had before, not even Memere? What did she know about me that I didn't know, or didn't want to know?

"No. Yes. I'm OK. Sorry." I didn't want to say I'd just seen my brother sitting on Ruth's table and damning me in his own sweet way. "Ruth just got me thinking again about that good buddy of mine who died in the war. We were going to serve together. Then I ditched him and joined the Navy. He went into the Army and ended up getting shot on a beach in Italy. I guess in a way he died so your friends could have a life, Ruth."

That was probably more melodramatic than I needed it to be. But I wanted to show them I'd been really listening.

Now Jo jumped in, "Why now, Jack, I thought last night you said you had been in the Merchant

Marine. I don't recall you saying that you had been a Navy man also." She sounded like she wanted to be impressed.

"Yeah, I joined the Merchant Marine after the war started there, but before we got into it. Then after Pearl Harbor, I joined the Navy." But, jeez! I couldn't tell them I faked insanity so they'd throw me out. I couldn't tell them I was a coward!

"But my knee gave out again in training camp and they couldn't do anything but discharge me. Sammy'd joined the Army by that time and..." I stopped here thinking of Sammy always smiling, always pushing me to do better. I choked a little and cleared my throat. "...that was the last I saw of him."

The women looked at me sympathetically again. But Ruth knew more than she was willing to say right then. I felt completely exposed to her wise eyes.

"Those years were tough on all of us, Jack. You must not carry guilt for a sin that you did not commit," Ruth said.

"Yeah, I know what you mean, Ruth. What you did...what Sammy did...Well, when the kids ask 'What did you do during the war, Daddy?' I'll have to be honest and say 'Not much.'"

Now Ruth had an opportunity to switch topics and lighten the mood a little. "Oh! Are you planning to be a father again, Jack?"

She didn't have to add "with children who will know you," but I could feel it at the end of her question.

I laughed a little and said, "I've always dreamed of settling down with the right woman and raising a proper family. So, yeah. If I could make things work out, I'd like to be a father again. A *real* father." I looked right at Ruth as I said this, so she knew that I knew what she was thinking, but did not say. And, of course, I could feel Jo looking at me too, weighing my words and hoping.

"Well, Jack, let's see if we can make your dreams come true!" Ruth said slapping her hands down on the table and ending the evening. "Children, I apologize, but I am *exhausted*. If you would be so kind as to help clear the table, Bessie will wash them in the morning. I must get to bed!"

We did as we were told and a couple of minutes later we were hugging Ruth goodnight and stepping into the chill spring night.

Jo and I again walked in silence down the walk to our cars. Standing between them, she turned and kissed me.

"Jack, would you be so kind as to follow me home? It's a little bit of a drive out into the country."

"Right behind you."

Chapter 11 — Jo

The drive to Jo's house went miles south out of Black Mountain. I followed her little Beetle farther and farther into the night until we turned down a pitch black and bumpy lane that led to her equally pitch black house. Finally, our headlights danced across windows in a kind of ghostly welcome from a place that seemed content to be hidden away from all but the most familiar and accepting of eyes.

The lane curled behind the house and we stopped there. I got out and breathed deep. Soft earth, moist and rich as though it had just been turned over. A different smell from the campground or the grass at the campus. Fecund and ready for seed.

Jo called gently. Even though she was but feet away, I needed her voice to find her side. Then I felt warmth through the evening's coolness. More than warmth, a real heat. One hand found her waist. The other the tautness of her belly.

"Hold me here a minute, Jack. I love the quiet and the darkness." We stood silent for minutes, arms lightly around each other. We both knew what was coming, yet felt no need to rush. She was right to hold still and savor.

I kissed her hair lightly and took in her scent. Her hands traced my shoulders and down my arms. I pushed hair aside and kissed a cheek, feeling the high ridge of bone with my lips. She stepped closer, her leg then pelvis sliding along my thigh.

We kissed. Different from earlier kisses, a deep, searching kiss. A kiss from a woman who wanted to be kissed and in that kiss knew that the man kissing her wanted her as much as she wanted him.

Another followed. Then the welcome stiffening in my pants. She responded in kind, her breath quickening ever so slightly. My hand slid through the length of her hair, fingers vaguely remembering Bea's, also black, but finer than this mane. This one I could get lost in and wanted to. Jo moved up against me.

"Let's go inside. Hold my hand. My steps are a little uneven."

She led me toward the house, up two porch steps and through what might have been a screen door into a kitchen. But instead of turning on a light, she led me through darkness into another room, down a short hallway and into her bedroom. Then she let go, took a step away and turned on a small table lamp.

Now we moved together, embracing again and delighting in more hungry kisses. It had been years and years since I'd felt such pure, deep need. And from the way Jo was kissing and pressing against me, I guessed it was the same for her. We pushed and ground against each other, eager to explore and please. And yet doing so with more care than the straight on humping I did in my teens and twenties.

There is just something so beautiful about how a ripe, passionate, sexy woman feels. That feeling is the best thing on Earth, hands down. With her there were no questions, no wondering about intent. No worrying about too-fars and planned futures. There was just the now. The immediate. The desire to please and be pleased. God, it felt good to be alive again! Clothes yielding quickly to bare flesh. The incredible feel of breasts and belly, hips and thighs. Hard curves of buttocks. And kisses. Endless kisses across her body. And the soft sounds of a woman enjoying how she is being touched. Pure, deep, uninhibited sounds of pleasure.

Even though we were moving together for the first time, it felt like we'd been moving together for a hundred times, a thousand times! She was warm and willing. I was hot and ready. No second thoughts. Just the now. Knowing where to touch and how. Giving what she needed and wanted. Taking what I needed and wanted. A coming together. A deep, deep yearning that reached beyond spoken words, beyond commitments, beyond the past, beyond the future.

I knew I'd given her what she wanted. And she'd given me what I needed. And we lay together after in that easy, post-coital calm when the whole world is total and beautiful and all within easy reach. Nothing was said. Nothing needed to be said. More kisses. More caresses.

When I woke, it was with my arm around her waist, my body pushed up against her butt and back. It was still dark. I kissed her hair and listened to her breathing. Then my hand started caressing. The rest of my body woke up. And I wanted her again. And somehow, deep from her sleep, she responded. And so we wrestled again. More slowly this time. But with equal deliciousness. She spoke softly to me this time. But then pushed against me with an intensity I couldn't remember having felt before.

I was damned glad my body didn't betray my desires. I was glad for all the walks on the beach. All the weight I'd lost, the muscles that had found new youth. I was glad, too, that I hadn't taken that wine I'd wanted so bad yesterday and today. Because I knew myself well enough to know that I wouldn't have stopped at one. And it wouldn't have been long before my insides were torn up again and I would've ended up God knows where. And my dick wouldn't have worked.

I wasn't ready the night before. But tonight I was. What was the difference? Was it just Jo's persistence? Holding my hand? Pushing a breast against my shoulder? The quick kisses? The eyes that knew …and wanted? The confidence she showed? Even the little pushes Ruth started giving me? It was all that. And more.

We moved together and then we stopped. And we held each other again with an easy familiarity that belied our newness.

"Jack, if your writing is as good as your lovemaking I am prepared to be very jealous."

She caught me a little off guard with that one. "Why's that?"

"Because you are goin' to have all sorts of people grabbin' at you!" She tickled at the hair on my belly. Then lower. And laughed in the darkness at her joke, kissing me across cheeks and neck and collarbone.

It was weird she said those very words, because then I flashed back on that whole literary scene. The parties. The endless fights with my publisher. Playing cat and mouse with reporters and critics. The petty jealousies with other writers. The desperation of trying to write something better than what you just wrote. It was the women who wanted to hang on to you. The men too. It became a trip that started wonderfully. A swirl I loved. For a while. Then ended badly. One that I ultimately hated. And that almost killed me.

Then I put all that out of my mind. I leaned into Jo and kissed her, running my hand down her hip at the same time. A nipple brushed chest hair. I didn't say anything more. I was beat. But it was the best kind of beat. The kind I hadn't felt in years and years. I fell asleep again. A deep, dreamless, blessed, satiated sleep.

The next time I woke, sunlight was in my eyes and Jo was gone. I rolled away from the window and tried to get my bearings. I slid off the bed and saw the clock on her dresser. 8:20! Nothing like a soft woman and a firm mattress to guarantee a good night's sleep.

Hers was definitely a woman's bedroom. Not a hint of a man around anywhere. Decent sized. Room enough for the double bed and a cedar chest at the foot (our clothes piled there now). Plus a reading chair, foot stool and floor lamp. A big window that looked out to the barn and field beyond. Large chest of drawers next to it.

I had to piss badly and made my way to the bathroom. It had the same touches. Bathtub was a standalone with a shower head and curtain ring around it. Washing my face I took a good look in the mirror and liked what I saw, to be truthful. The beard was trim, showing a few flecks of gray. But hair still jet black. Good genes. Dad'd been the same way. Only showed a bit of gray right 'til' the end. I'd have liked to have shaved the beard, but then with the weight I'd lost someone would've recognized me for sure.

I stretched a little right there. Damn, I *did* feel good! I wasn't sure what the rest of the day held except it was Monday and I was pretty sure Jo would have to be at the library soon. That made me sad. I wanted more time with her. But I also didn't want to spend the day hanging around here. Or back out at Harrison's. I'd committed to the book. So I'd have to spend some time trying to figure out exactly what that meant. But maybe it was time to get to Massachusetts and see Olson. Of course, that meant figuring out how I was going to pull that off too. Maybe I could go up there for the week and come back here for the weekend. With Jo. With Jo? My plans were getting all messed up!

"Coffee?"

I about jumped out of my skin! Jo stood in the doorway with a nice mug of hot brew. Damn! She was beautiful. Smiling at me. Wearing my shirt. The look of a very happy woman.

"Good morning and thanks," I said smiling back, taking the mug and a big sip.

Then I put it down and pulled her close for a kiss. I think that was just what she was looking for. I'd been with enough women to know about that morning-after look when they're trying to figure out how you felt about the night before and what the day ahead—or *days* ahead—might hold, if anything, all at the same time. And they want to be held and loved as intensely in that bright morning light as you had held and loved them in the darkness just a few hours before.

Jo held me tightly. Seeing her beauty now was even more stunning than it had felt. She was physically strong. She was comfortable in her skin. Comfortable with *me*.

"Jack, I...I'm glad you came. And stayed." She kissed me again. "Why don't you let me fix you some breakfast? Before we get dressed and I have to get to work." Then she added, "And so do you!"

Actually, that got me thinking about my notebook and other stuff back at the campground. And wondering if Harrison would come poking around wondering where I was, but knowing I wouldn't leave without packing up.

Grabbing my mug, I followed her out to the kitchen passing stairs that I'd missed in the dark. Like Lissa's, Jo's house was orderly, with books and art in different places. I saw framed photos of two older people who I guessed must have been her parents. Next to them a young man in his high school graduation picture: clean cut, eyes focused on some horizon, the perfection of youth. The photos looked older also, but familiar in a way. I guessed from the late forties or maybe early fifties.

Her kitchen looked like a cook's kitchen. Utensils and pans everywhere, along with a couple shelves of books. It, too, was bright, facing east out to the barn and beyond. Stove, refrigerator, double sink and lots of block counter top. Something to *work* on.

This was an old house. Older than Lissa's. Maybe older than Ruth's. I wondered if the farm was hers, or if she was just a renter. By the way we were "dressed" she didn't seem to expect any company in the form of a farmer to come rumbling down the lane on his way to morning chores.

I sat at a round breakfast table tucked into a nook while she busied herself with eggs, grits, ham and toast from homemade bread. Guess she could tell from the meals at Ruth's I'd pack away a lot of food if it was put down in front of me.

"This feels like a real nice lived-in place, Jo. You been here long?"

"Long enough to have been born here and get through high school and off to college," she laughed as she said this. That answered the renter or owner question.

I watched the bottom of my shirt flutter as she made her away around the kitchen. Her smooth tan made more so as she stepped into streaks of sunlight.

"My daddy was raised here. And his daddy before him. My great-grandpa bought it from Ruth's granddaddy's bank after the Panic. It's been good to us."

"How many acres?"

"About two hundred. Forty of it's still in woods. My favorite part. We have some big ol' trees back there! Got a stream going through. We 'crop the rest."

I wondered if I needed to be worried about the 'we.' But, then, I'd just spent the night here and hadn't seen another soul.

"So, you've been here all your life then?"

"Well, not all of it. I went down to Durham for college. And stayed for a few years after I got my degree. But then I moved back ten years ago to help Mama here when Daddy got sick and then passed. Then I got the job at the library. Then Mama got sick and passed five years ago, so now it's just me." She said this slowly, but matter-of-factly.

"Brothers and sisters?"

"A brother." Now her voice took on a distinctly lonely tone. "But he lives in Los Angeles and I don't see him much. I send him his share from the farm, of course. Every year..."

She changed the subject, looking over while she stirred the grits. "Do you have any brothers or sisters?"

"One of each. But they're both...they've both passed." She looked at me, surprised.

"Oh, Jack, I am sorry to hear that! That must be awful...to lose a brother *and* a sister. And I remember you saying your father is already gone too."

"Yeah. I think it's been harder on my mom more than anyone. My brother was just nine. Had rheumatic fever of the heart." Took a deep sip of my coffee. "He was older. Really looked after me. Had the soul of a saint. Might've become a priest had he lived. Though I'm not sure I'd recommend that life for him. Or anyone!"

Jo had stopped stirring as I talked, looking at me intently.

"You miss him still?" she asked knowing the answer already.

"Yeah, I do." Then I plunged ahead not really knowing I should say what I did, looking back at Jo in all her morning loveliness. "You know, sometimes I think he's still around. I mean there have been times when I think I really hear him. Like he's talking to me. Or even...*see* him." Jo's eyes got wider as I spoke.

"You mean, like he's a spirit or something?"

"Yeah, kinda...I don't know what..."

The phone rang.

"Oh, Jack! Here, stir this while I get that!"

Jo bounded into the living room while the grits thickened up.

"Good morning, Ruth! "Yes! Fine, fine...You slept well, too?...Yes, at ten....I don't know. Yes, I'll tell him....See y'all later now. Bye bye!"

I tried to act like I hadn't been listening in on the conversation, so was bent full to my task when I heard Jo's feet behind me and then right after felt her hands on my butt and back. She kissed my shoulder.

"That was Miss Ruth. Checking up on us, I guess!" She said with a laugh and another kiss on the cheek.

"She'd like you to stop by at ten. Which gives both of us just about an hour!" We looked at each other smiling and thinking about how much we could get done in an hour. I didn't even bother to ask how Ruth knew I was here.

"Are those about ready?"

"Yeah, looks like."

"Good, I'll put a cover on them and we'll fry up the eggs and have ourselves a breakfast! Could you help with the toast?" She handed me a large knife and pointed to a brand new loaf on the counter. "Just cut off as many slices as you want. I'll take one. The toaster's right over there."

A few minutes later we had heaping plates of food and were sitting at the table with more sunlight pouring through the window. I surprised myself at how hungry I was, having eaten a lot the night before. Again, Jo loved my appetite, smiling a lot and saying little.

"Jo, this was a helluva lot better than I could ever have cooked up over my little campfire. And better even than what I had at the Candy Kitchen the other day."

"Well, Jack, thanks, and I'm glad you liked it. You looked like you were hungry enough to eat up a bear!"

We got up to put plates in the sink.

"You want me to wash them?"

"I think on another morning I might ask you to do that. But we both have places to be and...more important things to do." Arms around my neck and another kiss. "So, why don't we just set our priorities and leave those for later?"

She didn't have to say another word. I followed her back to the bedroom where the shirt came off and we made sweet love again. I'd like to have just rolled over and slept some more after, but time was running short. So then it was out of bed and into her bathtub and shower where I would have made her late to the library if she hadn't hustled me out of there.

As we dressed—quickly—she tried to understand what was going to happen now.

"Jack, after you see Ruth, what are your... plans?"

She tried to ask this matter-of-factly as she pulled on a skirt. But I could tell she was really asking about us—and whatever that meant now. I knew already she wasn't the clingy type. But at the same time, she'd just shared her bed with a man for the first time in how long and I knew that meant something. Actually more than something. A lot. She hadn't said the "L" word yet. But I could tell it was on her mind.

"Well, when I got here Thursday, I expected to be gone on Friday. But that was before I ran into you two...and got hooked into writing a book."

"Now, Jack...here, zip me up. You shouldn't feel *obligated* to anything you don't want to. But I expect Ruth will have some more to say about that when you see her."

"Yeah, and I want to talk to her more about that too. Jo, you were right. Ruth does have a lot of her life to talk about. And it's pretty interesting. Guess I gotta figure out how to get all that into one book."

Jo turned and kissed me. "I am sure you will. And I know you need to get up to Massachusetts to see your Mr. Olson and who knows who. But if you're not in an awful, awful hurry, maybe you could spend another day here and..."

She didn't have to say the rest.

"Jo, I'd like that. Very much. I mean I liked last night and..."

She touched my lips.

"Now, hush! You don't have to say anythin'. But the library closes at five o'clock. I guess I don't want people talkin' about nothin' they have no business knowin'. So meet me at the stoplight a few minutes after. And you can follow me back out here."

I smiled a big smile.

"That'd be great! I'd love that."

"Good! Now, we have to really hurry!"

With that she became a swirl. Minutes later we were out the door and in our cars. Again I followed her down the lane a bumpy couple hundred yards to the road. I wanted to learn more about this land.

Then we were in a mad dash across country roads, passing a farmer on an ancient Oliver, before running up behind a few cars that passed for morning traffic as we got close to town. She tooted as she veered off to the library and I turned to make my way over to 123 Sumter St. in what was already becoming a familiar drive.

Chapter 12 — A Fork in the Road

"Jack, I must say you are gaining a quick reputation for punctuality." The grandfather clock had just finished tolling its tenth bell.

Ruth was dressed in a nicely tailored skirt and a white blouse, as though she had important business ahead. I felt a little self-conscious wearing the same clothes as yesterday. But at least I'd showered and felt clean. And I had a feeling she understood why I hadn't changed.

Ruth grasped my hand and arm firmly as she greeted me in the sunroom where Bessie had led me. I'd missed this room on my previous visits. You got there by going through the kitchen and through another room for reading or something, then stepping down into this room that had large windows all round.

I could tell right away this was a room where Ruth spent a lot of time. There was a large wicker sofa with matching chairs at either end. A large coffee table was filled with magazines and books, and something that looked like a journal or a diary. I also noticed an oversized envelope that because of the large lettering I could read easily, even upside down: "JACK."

Then she gave me a verbal punch in the arm. "Although I believe firmly that you might not have been as nearly on time if the library didn't need opening at ten o'clock also."

"Aw, now Ruth. You said be here at ten. And here I am."

"And so you are. You rested comfortably, I presume?"

"Yeah. Got up once in the night. But slept well, thanks."

"And, Miss Jolene?" Zing.

I laughed a "gotcha" laugh. "Yeah, she slept well too."

"I am delighted to hear that. I really am. As I said, she is a *keeper*!" Again she fixed that really intense gaze on me, as though she could bend me to her will which, to be truthful, she was doing a pretty good job at. So far.

Bessie reappeared with a tray holding a coffee pot, a couple of cups and saucers and cream and sugar holders.

"Miss Ruth..."

"Oh, wonderful, Bessie! Here let's clear a space on the table. And Jack, you sit here." She pointed to the sofa and then began moving things aside. I sat and Ruth sat next to me.

"Bessie, after Jack and I have had our talk, I'll call Doctor Badgeley and see what we can do about Henry. How is he today?"

"He got hisself outta bed and dragged his sorry butt to the mill. But I know he ain't right. Even if he tells me he is."

"We'll get Badgeley to take a look at him. If he says rest, he will rest. And we will make sure that company doc doesn't turn him into a cripple!"

"I do 'preciate that, Miss Ruth. Backs're awfully tricky things. But Henry, he too proud to take anyone's money 'less he's worked for it. And he too dumb to know if he end up in a wheelchair rest of his life, we're done for anyhow." I could hear the fear in her voice.

"I understand, Bessie. Well, let us get on with Jack's little project. Then we'll talk to the doctor and do what's right," Ruth said with that confidence and finality that comes with having power and knowing how to use it.

"Yes'm. I'm gonna start on the laundry now." Bessie left. But I could hear her starting to hum a song, maybe already feeling better from the strength of Ruth's words.

"You take your coffee black, if I recall," Ruth said pouring. She'd already switched from Bessie's business to ours.

"Yes." She handed me my cup, then poured hers. Black also.

"Are you planning to leave today?" Once again, her directness caught me off-guard.

"No."

"Tomorrow?"

"Maybe."

"Good. I hoped we would have a little more time to discuss some of the particulars of the book. As well as our...financial arrangements." Ruth looked at me evenly. She had switched from teasing matchmaker to defense attorney to tough-minded publisher all in the space of a few minutes. I braced myself.

But instead of speaking, she paused and gazed at me. She was silent for a full minute, maybe longer. To the point where I was beginning to get a little uncomfortable, as though maybe she was waiting for me to say something first. Except I didn't know what to say. I sipped at my coffee a little nervously, though I tried not to show it.

Finally, she spoke.

"Well, Jack, we have certainly gotten to know quite a bit about each other in a very short period of time, haven't we?"

"Yeah, we have, Ruth. This has turned out to be quite an...assignment...so far." I clung to my cover as a travel writer.

She chuckled. "Yes, I imagine when your editor sent you over here, he had no idea what you might find. Of course, that's what every good writer does. Find things no one else has. Or at least repackage an old idea so everyone else thinks it's new!" She laughed again, pleased with her insight.

I realized now that, in addition to the book I agreed to write, I'd also have to produce at least a draft of the "article" to show her and Jo.

"Yeah, you're right about that, Ruth. But I've always been pretty good at sizing up a situation or a location. And then writing something that some people find at least tolerable."

"Oh, Jack, you are being far too modest, I am sure. Now, listen, I want to share with you my ideas about the book. Don't worry about notes, I've written them down here," she said patting the envelope.

Now she turned to face me squarely and took my hand at the same time.

"Jack, I want you to listen carefully. This book is very important—to *me*. Maybe it will be to others, too, in time. But as you write it, I want you to concentrate on me as your only audience.

"I know Black Mountain barely existed in the long history of our great colleges and universities. But it is my belief that the ideas born here and explored here and cast out into the world from here, have had their influence far beyond the confines of our little town. So, I want you to find out if that is true.

"I am so sorry John is no longer with us because you would have enjoyed meeting him, Jack. But perhaps you can find Dan, his son. He had many memorable years here. John could have told you what it was like teaching back in the twenties and thirties, when anyone who had 'different' ideas was shunned.

"I was delighted to hear you say that you plan to see Charles. Despite the chaos of those final years, he was a delight to be around. Even when he was, shall we say, troubled. I have a few notes for him that you may find helpful. When are you planning to see him?"

"I don't have a specific time, Ruth. But I'd planned to make Gloucester my next big stop after Black Mountain. So if I leave tomorrow, might be up there by Wednesday or Thursday. He shouldn't be hard to find!" I laughed at my little joke.

"No, you are right about that, Jack. You *are* right about that. But you're planning to leave... tomorrow?"

I knew what that meant, and so now it was time to talk about "it," meaning Jo and me.

"Yeah, I think so. I mean, I haven't talked about it with Jo yet. But..."

Ruth jumped in. "I don't think you have to worry about her, Jack. She's a big girl. Very strong. If what has developed between you is also good and strong, it will survive a separation...as long as you're not gone too long."

Here I jumped in. "What's her deal, Ruth? I mean she is smart and beautiful and..." Here I stopped, feeling a little embarrassed to talk about sex.

Now Ruth chuckled at my embarrassment. "Jack, I do believe you are blushing behind that beard of yours. That is such an interesting quality in a man."

Now she released my hand and poured herself, then me, more coffee.

"I guess you are asking why I keep insisting that she is a 'keeper.' Jo is a very particular woman. She does not give her heart—or the rest of her—easily. She knows her mind. She knows what she desires in a man. And she knows she doesn't need a man around just to have a man around. She is perfectly capable of going through this life as she pleases.

"Her parents were wonderful people. I do not mind saying they were terribly disappointed in her brother. So I also thought that Jo made her choices in ways to try and make up for what he did. And did not do."

"Yeah, she said something about moving back when her dad got sick."

"Yes, William passed almost ten years ago. He got cancer in the lung. And Marlene passed just a few years ago, three I think."

"I think she said five."

"Has it been that long? Lord..."

Ruth paused, sipped long on her coffee, as though trying to decide whether to say more and then plunged ahead.

"She was married to a professor at the university. At least, I think they were married. Then she caught him carrying on with one of his students and that ended that. Her daddy got sick about the same time, so moving back here became an easy thing to do. Miss Bergstrom passed away a year later and that opened up the library job for her.

"So now here she is. Educated. Beautiful. Kind as a soul can be. Yet, do not cross her. She is nobody's fool, that much I know. If I'd had a daughter..."

We sipped in silence. There was no more I could say about Jo. At least right now. We both understood where things were. I think.

Then Ruth was ready to move on with more talk about the book. She picked up the envelope and pulled out its contents, a few sheets of paper and another envelope.

"Now, Jack, I've made a few notes here that I hope will help you get started," she said picking up one sheet. "As I said yesterday, I do not want a *history* of Black Mountain College. I am sure others will do that, if they haven't already. I want something more. Something that explains...really explains...what this little college gave to our country. Just like how you came here because friends of yours had been here. Something happened to them while they were at Black Mountain that changed their lives. And now they are changing others'. What was that?

"There are many others like your friends. Most of them did not become famous artists. Most are off in their own small spaces of America. Doing whatever they're doing. Probably not even artists or writers. Maybe they're schoolteachers. Or doctors. Or... accountants!" We both laughed at that idea.

"But, you do see what I'm getting at, don't you?"

"Yeah, I do." And I did. "Won't be easy. I know it means getting out and talking to lots of people."

"Yes, that is true. But as a travel writer that's something you're used to doing?"

I chuckled. "Yeah. I suppose if I've gotten good at anything, it's learning how to talk to strangers." Which wasn't *exactly* true. I was good enough at talking with people, but it usually took me a good couple glasses of wine to get me going. But this was part of keeping up my cover, so I wasn't going to contradict her now.

She picked up a piece of paper. "Now here is Josef and Anni's address in New Haven. At least, I think it is still their address. I haven't heard from them in a few years. I don't have a phone number for them. But that would be a good start. Maybe you can try and see them on your way up to see Charles."

I tried not to look intimidated at the idea of knocking on the door of someone as famous—and ancient—as I imagined Albers to be. "Is he easy to talk to…about Black Mountain?"

"I have no idea! I imagine he's been asked about it many times over the years. But I also guess it's been the usual stuff. When did you arrive? When did you leave? What did you teach? Who were your best students? That kind of nonsense. I need you to try and dig deeper, Jack."

"Can I ask him about Berlin? And how you got them here?"

"Yes! Yes! By all means. Maybe he and Anni will tell how they felt being Jews there. And here. How they felt about Hitler's terror years before the rest of the world had an inkling of what was to come."

"Yeah, I'd like to know some of that stuff myself." I paused. Then another question popped into my head. "Were they discriminated against here?"

"You mean at the college? No, I don't think so. But then, it's not really for me to answer, is it? You'll have to ask them. You *should* ask them. When you are born on top of the mountain, as I was, sometimes it's hard to see things from the point of view of those who aren't."

I sure as hell wasn't born on top of the mountain. Yet I surely hadn't had it near as bad as the Jews in Europe. Or the blacks here. Or the Indians. Albers might turn out to be a good interview after all.

"Can they put me in touch with others?"

"I think so, Jack. At least I hope so. It would seem between Josef and Charles you ought to be able to get a pretty good start. Plus, all of your friends out West."

That was true. Although how exactly I was going to talk to my "friends out West" was going to be problematic.

Ruth pulled out the photo she showed me last night. "Now, Jack, I want you to take this with you. This will help with Josef. Maybe with Charles, too. Josef knew all of them. Worked with them. Maybe even argued with them a time or two. "

She jabbed a finger at the balding, blond-haired man. "Ted was the sweetest of them all. I think he and Barbara cared more for Black Mountain than anyone. They were here at the beginning and stayed almost to the end."

"Sounds like someone I should talk to also."

"Yes, you should! But I have lost track of them."

"They're still alive?"

"Yes, I believe they are. Or at least I hope they are. This is where I hope Josef will be of great help to you."

She pulled out another sheet of paper with her handwriting on it. "I've written all their names here and a sentence or two about them. That'll help you get started too when you see him and Anni."

"OK. Thanks." I scanned through her note. Her handwriting was very precise, almost elegant. "Yeah, this'll help."

"Now, let me just tell you that Josef is very strong-minded. He has his very definite ideas about art. About how to teach art. How a school should be organized to teach the best art. So, don't expect him to be all smiles and rose sunglasses when he talks about them and the college."

"Is he a crank?"

"No…I wouldn't say that. But, remember, he has seen an awful lot in his life. And a lot of what he has seen has been awful. So to talk with him about artistic principles and aesthetics in the abstract just doesn't mean much. Even though he practically invented abstract impressionism, Josef is very, very grounded in the realities—and horrors—of life. So you will get far with him if you ask him about how he tries to ground his students."

I wasn't going to betray my ignorance about "artistic principles and aesthetics." I just wrote and wrote and wrote about what felt real to me. Real people. Real experiences. In their words. What I saw. And heard. And smelled. And tasted. But then I hadn't really experienced the inhumanity that is common to far too of many of us as well. So Josef Albers might have some very different things to say about the world he experienced.

"What do you want Josef—and Anni—to tell you about Black Mountain that you don't already know?"

"Well, Jack, if I knew the answer to that question, I wouldn't really need your services, would I?" Ouch. Again.

She reached over and again grabbed my forearm with a strength that belied her size and age. "I want you to tell me things about Black Mountain that I could not in my wildest dreams and desires have ever known. I want to know where Black Mountain is now. And with whom. And why."

She'd been saying the same kinds of things from the first time, I'd met her just a couple days ago.

But she'd said it enough different ways that I was beginning to feel more confident that maybe I could actually pull this off. And, what the hell, maybe add some unexpected adventures to this road trip of mine.

"Maybe the book could be a series of interviews," I offered. "Starting with those who got the place going. Ted Dreier. Any of the others still living. Josef and Anni. Maybe they'll lead me to some of the faculty and maybe some students."

Ruth looked at me intently, as I was learning she always did whenever I tried to say something important. I could see she was evaluating my words carefully. "Yes, Jack, that would seem to be one obvious way of putting a book together. Do you have a tape recorder?"

"No. But I can pick up one of those new cassette type recorders. Not a lot to lug around. And probably a good idea to have one when I talk to the Albers."

"Yes, I would agree. I assume you have a camera?"

"Yes I do." But it wasn't much of one. Allen had been the photographer in our group. He always had that damn thing out! I was thinking already that I might need to buy a new one because I think she was expecting something approaching professional-quality photos from a 'travel writer.' I tried to cover my tracks a little. "The magazines usually send out a pro to get photos after I've sent my copy in. But they like it when I send along some pictures of the places I've been to so they can give their guy a little direction." I made a mental note to make sure I went back to the campuses and got some pictures.

That sounded good enough and Ruth seemed to accept my explanation. She reached for another business-size envelope. The one with my name on it.

"Now, Jack, I am asking a lot of you, I know it. I also think I am asking a lot of the right person." She ran her fingers along the flap, as though deciding whether to open it. Then she looked at me again.

"Are you sure this is something you can do? That you want to do?" She was giving me "The Look" again. "Is this going to interfere with your other ...obligations?"

The only way to be with Ruth, as I was learning, was to be straight and true. Otherwise, she'd smell the bullshit a mile away and be done with you.

"Ruth, look, I came here a few days ago on an assignment to write up something nice about Black Mountain, North Carolina. I was interested in the place because a couple of buddies on the West Coast said I ought to stop by and I talked my editors into letting me do a story. Not a big story. But something nice they could use as part of a sectional on North Carolina vacations or some such.

"Then I ran into you and Jo. And you've made this place a whole lot more interesting than even Creeley and Duncan made it sound. When you first started pushing this book on me, yeah, I was a little reluctant. Because I do have plans. Kind of! But I think I can make this work. Seeing the things I want to see and talking to the people who've taken what they experienced here and translated that into something bigger somewhere else."

Ruth was nodding as I finished up this little speech. Actually, it sounded pretty good.

"So, yeah, I want to do this. I can do this. And, no, it won't get in the way of what I'd already planned. In fact, it will add to it."

"Good!" Ruth was convinced, and happy, by what I'd said. "I believe you, Jack. And because I believe you, this is how I want our little arrangement to work."

Now she opened the flap and pulled out a small stack of fifty dollar bills.

"This is five hundred dollars. Not a lot. But it should help you some with whatever additional time and miles you have to put in over the next few weeks."

Might not have been a lot to her, but it was still a lot to me. My heart raced a little.

"You may consider this an advance or whatever. I know I take some risk in this because you could be on the road tomorrow and be gone forever. But I am willing to take my risk—as I believe Jo is taking hers—because we both think you have come into our lives at an extraordinary time. And I hope I do not sound too prideful in saying, Jack Moriarty, you have proven yourself worthy." She handed the bills to me.

I was taken aback. This was unexpected. And, truthfully, it thrust an unexpected layer of obligation on me. It *would* be hard now to drive off tomorrow and just leave all this behind. Obviously, I was not unfamiliar with advances. Had lived off them for years. But this felt different.

"Ruth, geez, I hadn't expected *this*. I mean with the magazines, you write, you get paid. Most times! I've gotten small advances once in a while, if I whined about it long enough. But nothing, nothing like this."

"Jack, I don't know your business. But, rest assured, I can afford to take what I believe to be a very reasonable risk on your account. Plus, I had to assume that since you were staying in a campground instead of a hotel, you must be on something of a budget. And so, since I was asking you to take on a rather large task above and beyond what you had already planned, it seemed that I should not strain you unduly."

"Thanks, I appreciate that. And, yeah, this will make it easier to take the time to find Josef and Anni, talk with them, and then move on to the others. I hadn't planned on spending all my time in campgrounds. But I can be a pretty frugal guy when I have to be."

"I'm delighted to hear that." She became pensive for a moment.

"Even though I grew up with much comfort, Daddy taught me how to be smart with money. We live in good times now. But it hasn't always been so, as you know. Lord, I hope we never fall back into the world of the thirties when millions died because of their leaders' stupidity. And then the forties when millions more died because of the evil they loosed upon us."

Then she was back with me. "Now, Jack, this is the arrangement I would like to make, if you are agreeable."

I nodded. She continued.

"I would like to pay you as you go along. And I would like to see your work as it progresses."

I'd never worked like that before. Always, it was get it done, send it in, get paid. Maybe.

She could see my hesitation.

"I know this is probably very different from how you are used to being compensated. But it would guarantee you an income stream, in addition to whatever else you are working on. Speaking selfishly, it would give me the satisfaction of seeing this book come to life...before I am too old to enjoy it."

I didn't want her to see that I really could use the money. Especially if it came in five hundred dollar chunks like this one. So I waited some seconds before saying anything.

"You're right. I've never really worked this way before. But it would give us a chance to kind of work together, if that's what you're looking for. I mean, you could see who I've talked to, what they've said and then you can kind of give me feedback. I'm sure I'm going to run into people you've never heard of. But maybe they'll know things that'll make it a better book. So this could work out better than the usual writer-editor thing."

Ruth seemed very pleased that I explained the arrangement this way. We understood each other. There'd be no contract. I was kind of on my honor to get this done. If I did, I'd get paid along the way. If I didn't, then she wasn't out a lot of money. But maybe, just maybe, we'd both end up with something we could both be proud of. It'd be a different kind of writing from what I'd done before, of course. But in some ways, maybe not so different. And, really, I'd spent a lot of my life listening to and watching people and trying to make sense of their lives, and mine.

So I'd head up to New Haven, then Gloucester. Or maybe Gloucester first. See what this guy Albers was all about. And Olson too. Except now I had this book as part of what I wanted to talk to him about in addition to the whole West Coast, Creeley, Duncan, and Patchen stuff. And I still hadn't figured out how to even approach him. Should I be "Jack Moriarty"? Would he recognize me? Should I just come clean on what I'm doing and why and hope he wouldn't blow my cover? I had to think about that. Later.

"Jack, I am glad to see that you are enthusiastic about helping an old woman's dream come true. Now, I have a meeting at the bank coming up." Here, she stood up and I followed. She stuck out her hand.

"So, let us shake hands on our agreement."

We did and again I was surprised by the strength in her grip. Then she scooped up the various pieces of paper, stuck them back in the envelope and handed it to me, minus the money which I pushed kind of self-consciously into my pocket.

"If you are leaving…tomorrow, then I shall not expect to see you for a while. But I hope it will not be a long while!" She laughed a little at this.

"Ruth, I really don't know right now how long this first part's gonna take. Maybe a week. Maybe two. Guess what I'd like to do is get up and see those guys, hear what they have to say and start writing it all down. When I come back I'd like to have a draft done. But you have to understand that just because Albers and Olson are the first guys I'm talking to, it doesn't mean they'll be the first guys in the book. I mean, obviously, Albers probably comes up pretty quick because he was here at the start, or close to. It'll just depend on how it all comes together. But when I come back you'll have something to read and respond to."

She clapped her hands and smiled big at my suggestion, almost like a kid waiting for Christmas. "That would be delightful!"

She led me out of the sun room and back through the kitchen, dining room and living room. In the foyer, she called out, "Bessie! Are you ready to go to town?"

"Yes'm! Be right down!"

She turned to me again and this time reached out with both arms for a quick embrace.

"Thank you, Jack. Thank you."

"Don't thank me just yet, Ruth! Let's see what Josef and Charles have to say and what I bring back to you."

"Oh, I have no doubt that if anyone can tell the real story of Black Mountain, it will be you, Jack Moriarty!" She gave both biceps a squeeze. Then turned me towards the door. "Now, shoo! The boys at the bank get nervous if I keep them waiting. Think I'm going to dump a truckload of bad news on them!"

And with that I was back outside and down the walk to the car. It was just coming up on eleven. Plenty of time to kill before following Jo and her Bug back out to the farm. First stop: Harrison's. Then to find a place to buy a portable typewriter and lots of paper. Then maybe another stop out at the two campuses for one more walk around. And some pictures. Absolutely, some pictures!

I was about to pull out of the drive when I saw Bessie hustling down the walk waving something and calling after me. I rolled down the window and between deep breaths she said, "Mistah Jack, Ruth wants you to have this. Says may help you a bit once you get goin'."

She handed me Ruth's *Black Mountain Review*.

"Bessie, thanks a lot. I think it will."

"Bye, now, Mister Jack. We'll see you when you get back."

"Yes, you will. And I hope the doctor can do something for your husband's back."

"Lord, yes! Ruth is talkin' to him right now. And thank you for thinkin' of him."

With a wave, I was gone and so headed to Harrison's place.

Chapter 13 — Making Plans

I drove up to Harrison's house which doubled as the campground's office, figuring I ought to pay him the dollar I owed for the night my tent stayed and I didn't. At the same time, I hoped he wouldn't try to draw me into conversation and poke around about where I'd been.

His wife answered the door. She smiled an all-business smile. Close up I could see a young woman already wearing quickly to middle age. She was thin, like her husband, despite having had two or three children close together. The lines at her eyes and mouth suggested worry instead of laughter. She pushed a strand of yellowish hair behind an ear.

"Good mornin', Mr. Moriarty. Can I help you?" I was surprised she knew my name, but maybe I shouldn't have been.

"Yes, good morning. I wanted to pay your husband the dollar I owed him."

"Mr. Moriarty, I believe you are paid up through last night. Are you plannin' to stay another night with us? If so, then yes, you will owe us another dollar."

I'd forgotten! I could've just come in and packed up and left them with a two dollar tip.

"You're right! Sorry, losing track of the days here. Uh....no...I won't be staying another night. Although I have appreciated your hospitality."

"We did wonder about you last night when we didn't see a campfire and all."

"Oh, I was fine. Some people I met invited me to dinner and then it got a little late, so they insisted I just sleep on their sofa."

I could feel her sizing me up as I told this story. My guess was they'd seen an awful lot of itinerants and maybe been stiffed by a few along the way. And maybe they were an extra pair of eyes and ears for the sheriff as well.

I felt a little nervous now because the last thing I needed was somebody deciding maybe I wasn't on the up and up and calling a cop to have me checked out. Not only would that have blown my cover, but could've ended up as a huge embarrassment for Ruth and God-knows-what for Jo. Maybe Lissa too.

"I'm doing a story about Black Mountain for a travel magazine. And a couple people who I interviewed were kind enough to see that I shouldn't be out driving the country roads at night. Guess they thought I could get lost easily."

She softened a little hearing this.

"My husband didn't say nothin' about you bein' a writer. Your friends were probably right in keeping you off our back roads when it's late. They can be awful twisty and turny. Easy to get lost, if you don't know your way around. So, you leavin' us now?"

"Yes, ma'am. I'm going to spend the day in town doing some more research. But then I have to get up to Massachusetts and interview some people there. People who'd been at the college here. When it was still open and all."

Her eyes got alert and dreamy at the same time. I'd seen this look many times before from people who'd lived their lives all in one place and wanted to go someplace else, but couldn't for one reason or another. The idea of travel made her suddenly chatty.

"I was born, raised over in Asheville. Been through the Smokies a few times, I guess. Clear over to Tennessee. We honeymooned down at Morehead City. Only time I've been to the ocean. Guess you've been all over, huh?"

"Been to quite a few places. Haven't seen it all, though!"

"What's the most beautiful place you ever been to?" She asked this not like she wanted a factual answer, but more like her mind was already taking her some place and just wanted an excuse to think about it.

I paused before answering, giving her question some weight and allowing her a few moments to dream some more.

"That's a tough question, Mrs. Harrison, because different places are beautiful for different reasons. But I'd have to say the one place I love going back to again and again is this mountain right outside San Francisco."

"San-Fran-*cis*-co!" She said like it was as magical and distant as Shangri-La, which maybe to her it was. "I've seen pictures of it in magazines. That funny little zig-zaggy street. And those cute little trolleys. What do they call them?"

"Cable cars?"

"Yes! Those are the ones! San-Fran-cis-co. So you been there?"

"Yeah. Quite a few times."

"Lord! I doubt I will ever get that far from here. Not with the little ones and this place to take care of."

"Well, you never know. Growing up, I never thought I'd ever get out of Boston."

"Yes, but look at you. Footloose and fancy free! And a writer! You musta been to college and everythin'. All's me and Bobby ever had was high school. We wouldn't even have this if'n Daddy hadn't helped out."

She was over asking me about beautiful places. She was back to thinking of the chores ahead for rest of the day. I heard a baby cry.

"Oh! He's awake! He'll want changed. And fed. I gotta go." She extended a hand.

"It was nice meetin' you, Mr. Moriarty. I hope the Lord sees you safely to your destination."

"The same, Mrs. Harrison." We shook and she was back inside.

I was a little relieved we didn't spend more time talking. Had plenty of things to do. But I've talked with thousands of Harrisons over the years. Hell, I'm a Harrison! It's just that I did get a chance to get out of my little town of Lowell. And I had some ability to write down what I saw and heard. And people liked what I wrote. But if I didn't have that—or if people hated what I wrote (some did!), then maybe I'd have ended up running a campground too. And asking people dreamy questions about the most beautiful places they'd ever been to. So I tried to remember that and take the time to listen to people talk about their dreams. Because they're worth having. It's what makes life what it is. Chasing dreams. Going for something bigger. Something more beautiful.

By the time I got everything packed up, it was after noon. Now I needed to find a place to buy a typewriter. A portable. I'd left my old Underwood back in St. Pete. I was going to take it, but then thought if I did Memere and Stella'd both figure out I was going for good and that would've changed the whole scene about why I was leaving and when I'd be back. So I left it behind, figuring I'd be doing my writing by hand anyhow.

I drove back into town and didn't see any likely candidates along Main Street. Figured my best chance was to head over to Asheville. Had to be an office supply store there. And I was right. Found one on what looked like the main business street. The guy wanted to sell me one of the new models he had up front. I asked if he had any used Underwoods. Don't ask me why. Just loved the feel of the one I left behind. But I really wanted a portable. He showed me a couple other brands that were almost new. Then I saw an old brown Undie sitting on a shelf. An Ace. In pretty good shape. Oiled up. Keys worked clean and easy. He wanted thirty bucks for it, but settled for twenty-five when I bought a half dozen ribbons and couple reams of paper along with it. Added a three-ring binder for good measure. Got out of there for about thirty-five bucks.

So now I had a new "old" typewriter and enough ribbons and paper to last me a good long while. Next I decided to stop out at the Lake Eden campus again. Walk around, try to remember all that Ruth tried to tell me. Make some notes. Take a couple pictures. I drove past the Studies Building to the Dining Hall. Looked for signs of James Thomas. But didn't see him, or anybody else for that matter. I walked out to the dock and snapped some photos of the Studies Building in the distance and the little peninsula-island out in the lake. Walked back into the grounds, seeing more of the smaller buildings.

It was hard imagining this place was once crazy with ideas and people from all over. Tried to imagine the Studies Building under construction with students and teachers crawling all over trying to get it built in time for school. They were here as war had broken out in Europe. They were probably nailing boards together when I was crossing the North Atlantic praying we wouldn't get nailed by a wolfpack of U-boats.

Where were they now? Why should I care? Truth is Ruth...and Jo...and even Lissa...made me start to care about this place a whole lot more than Creeley and Duncan did. It was easy to see this place still affected them long after it closed for good.

I thought about what kind of book Ruth was getting at. What would make it important beyond refreshing an old woman's memories? Who would read it besides her and maybe a couple hundred other people who'd gone to Black Mountain and now were scattered around the country? Who would even publish it? How could I make it her book *and* my book?

I knew I didn't want to write a history, and be stuck in some library room for God knows how many months reading old dead stuff. Thankfully, Ruth didn't want that either. She wanted something more. Now so did I. Something that caught the life of the place.

Something that also transcended the place. Maybe something that even said it was OK the place only lasted twenty-three years.

Too bad John Rice was dead. But Albers was still alive. And Olson. Maybe this Dreier guy too. And Fuller. Didn't Lissa say something about the professor who taught her pottery making? And I had the last copy of *Black Mountain Review.*

I also had to figure out how I was going to mix all this in with everything else I planned. And somehow still stay underground. Doing all the things I wanted when I started this trip less than a week ago. Had it only been that long? Seemed ages since I'd waved goodbye to Stella and Memere. And look what I'd gotten myself into.

I made some notes that day. Saw them maybe as the start of the book.

Monday
April 6
Black Mountain College
Lake Eden Campus

Black Mountain = Academic freedom
What's that?
Freedom to talk about, write about anything
Break mold, make new
Question rules Question authority Question Church
Push limits of understanding. Then push through.
Blake's Doors. New Jerusalem. Holy!

Easiest to see in push-pull between science-religion
50 years ago Universe only stars we could see
Now stars just small part of one Galaxy
Universe maybe millions of galaxies

2500 years ago gods ruled everything everywhere

Now God rules everything everywhere

But doesn't mix with everyday lives, far away (Heaven)

I don't think anyway

Man landed on Moon
That bring us closer to God?
Or push Him farther away?

What about Jewish God?
What about Muslim God?
What about Hindu gods?
What about Buddha?

Whose God is God of Gods?
Is there one?
Is science real God?

50 years ago many colleges religious—affiliated with a Christian church

Non-denominational Black Mountain born in middle of Baptist Bible Belt (!!)

Rice aiming for school without church ties, no church dictates on what can/cannot be taught

Also school run by faculty and students

Students learn by reading, writing, composing, performing, constructing, working

Albers saw freedoms taken away

Almost lost life because his Jewish God different from Nazi God

(Nazis believers? Check this)

Millions of others did

Millions more in Russia lost theirs because they didn't believe in Stalin-God

Or Old Joe didn't think so

U.S./Black Mountain safe haven for Albers, others
Ruth Jewish
She a believer? Don't know
Her father did helluva thing risking all to help get Jews out

So is Allen
He a believer? Don't think so
Mom's a Commie and crazy
So what?

Book will have many voices
My job pull together,
Make sing as one
We'll see

Not history but allegory
But not Nirvana or Shangri-La
Place where people explore own truth
And not be crucified for seeking it
Or gassed Or shot
Black Mountain place where 20th c. thinking stands on top of 19th etc
Like Fuller Domes moving from cubes to polyhedrons
Like Einstein tying space and time together
Moving from Universe created whole and beautiful and perfect by God
To Universe evolving every second rough and beautiful and imperfect
Go see Albers
Olson (more disguise?)
Others maybe
Then back to BM?
Back to Jo?

I felt a raindrop. Saw another hit the water in silence, turn silver, then send tiny silent ripples. I waited for another to hit. It did, disturbing the perfectly smooth surface, then just as silently losing itself in it. I thought of Snyder. How he could meditate for an hour around that single raindrop. How he helped me grow the patience to hear the silence. Another hit me. Then another hit me. Then another. Then I thought now wasn't the best time to get soaked and should move on.

I walked around a little more trying to see Black Mountain's ghosts again in this gray silent daylight. I tried to imagine Creeley, single eyed, teaching, writing, then editing that last *Review*.

I picked up a little book of his poetry a while ago. Here's a poem he wrote that could've been about the ghosts I was looking for.

"Place"

Faded mind,
fading colors,
old, dear clothes,
Hear

the ocean under
the road's edge,
down the side
of the hill.

It started raining harder and it really was time to say goodbye to this place—at least for a while—and head over to meet Jo.

I'd just pulled into a parking spot at the corner a couple minutes before when her red Bug came through the intersection. She didn't beep or wave. But she'd seen me—even in the rain that big old yellow Ford with Florida plates stuck out like a billboard on her North Carolina streets—and I pulled around the corner and followed her back out of town, back along rain slicked roads, back to the farm.

It was a downpour by the time we turned into the lane and made a muddy slidy slosh up to the house. We didn't even say hello until we'd hightailed it onto the porch and into the kitchen. Shaking off the wet, she turned and gave me a big kiss. "And how was your day?" she smiled. Clearly she was enjoying this fast-moving arrangement.

"It was…interesting," I answered as we continued wiping rain out of our hair and faces. I told her quickly about my meeting with Ruth. She smiled as though not surprised when I explained our financial arrangement. I told her about packing up and that I'd driven to Asheville to look around. Then about stopping back out at Lake Eden.

"I am sorry about the rain comin' on," she said. "I had hoped to show you more of the farm."

"Yeah, well, maybe when I get back. And how was *your* day?"

"Oh, the same silly old library stuff. Nothing ever changes there very much. Some days I like the quiet. Some days it seems the days just want to crawl by." Then she laughed. "That's why I was so excited when I saw you first comin' up the walk, although I tried not to show it. Somebody *new* to talk to!"

I gave her a hug when she said that. And I knew it was exactly the right thing to do exactly at that moment. How did I know? By looking at her beautiful face and really wanting to hear what she had to say. So much goes unspoken between a man and a woman. Or words said about one thing are really about something else altogether. It had taken me a long time to understand this. But when I finally did, I got a lot more successful with women. A lot happier, in a way. Even if the happiness didn't last more than a night or two. Because I think a lot of women will tell you that the hardest thing for them to find is a man who will listen, really listen to them. Because they do talk differently than we do. Say what they mean differently. Sometimes they say a lot. Sometimes they say a little.

Now Neal...well, he was different, for sure. He talked one helluva game so that lots of girls—I mean *lots*—believed he really got them. But hell...all he wanted was to get laid. Still, he had the words down right. And the look down right. And that cock down right. But Neal was all about Neal. There's just no other way to put it straight. With women or men. I saw him lay down line after line with all kinds of people. But in the end it was all about feeding something inside. Something kind of desperate, to tell you the truth. But, man! He could spend a lot of energy and get lots of people excited trying to feed that beast of his. Maybe he really did love Carolyn and the kids. Or LuAnne. Or shit, even Allen. Or even more shit...me. But I think, I really, really think, Neal was the gonest, loneliest guy I ever met. And maybe that's no surprise. No mom. A deadbeat for a dad. Fighting for anything he ever had from childhood. And then he went out almost same way he came in...alone and cold.

Now Jo, of course, had no idea when I hugged her it was because of all the other crazy shit I'd done with my life that got me to this place with this woman not even a week out from my "death." But it did feel damn good to hold her again. To run my hands down her back and across her firm thighs. Just like it had felt damn good to start the morning with her. And then, at the same time, knowing that this time tomorrow I'd be alone again. And so would she. Life is like that.

"Hungry?"

"Yeah!"

"I have a couple chops in the refrigerator. And some of last summer's corn in the icebox. And some sweet potatoes? How does that sound?" she asked with another kiss.

I hadn't eaten since the morning, except for Ruth's coffee. Just the words made my stomach growl. "Sounds great! How can I help?"

"How about doing up the dishes?"

There was so much I didn't know about this woman. And even more she didn't know about me. Yet here we were already settling into an easy domesticity. I'd been through this before...a kind of playing at house. It's fun. Maybe even a trial run for the real thing. She had no trouble asking me to wash dishes. Big difference from life in St. Pete where I had Stella and Memere to do everything and all I had to do was lie around and drink and watch TV and sometimes write and make long distance calls in the night to friends who'd maybe already given me up for dead.

Jo whisked her way around the kitchen, peeling and slicing the sweet potatoes, then getting them into some water. "Jack, keep an eye on those for a second. I'm going to get out of my library clothes."

I finished the dishes in the few minutes she was gone. She came back in jeans with a plaid flannel shirt worn loose. She'd also let her hair down and just looked lovely.

"So, tell me more about your arrangement with Miss Ruth." She said this as she again began moving effortlessly around the kitchen, pulling out the chops and corn and other things from the refrigerator and cupboard.

She offered me a Coke, which I took, and poured herself a glass of chianti without even asking this time.

"It's like I said, it's kind of a get-paid-as-I-go deal. She's smart enough not to give me a big advance like the New York people do. Because I could just take all that money and disappear." She looked at me quickly. "Which I'm not going to do anyway. But she also knows I can't just write her a book and maybe get paid at the end of it all."

Jo nodded while she breaded the chops.

"Plus, I think we both don't know exactly where all this is headed. She gave me Albers' address up in New Haven. And I already have Olson lined up. And there're my buddies out on the West Coast."

She shot me a look when I said this, and I knew what that meant too. She was trying to figure out if "West Coast" meant something like "gone for good." Of course, maybe she was trying to figure out if "West Coast" meant "Can I go, too?" and no way was I ready to answer that question.

"So, we'll take it a step at a time. Guess we're both hoping one person leads to another and another and when it's all done we'll have a book that tells Black Mountain's story as it lived and breathed." I could've been saying the same thing about her and me.

"Are you glad you took on this...assignment?" She asked this smiling, but again I knew she was really asking two questions.

"Yeah, I am." I tried to say this with as much honest enthusiasm as seemed right for the moment. "I mean, I have to finish this article and I'm waiting to hear about a couple others. But this should be nice, steady work. And Ruth does pay very well, if this first five hundred is any indication."

"Yes, she does," Jo agreed as she placed the chops in the frying pan and stirred the corn. "And, Jack, you should understand you are not the first writer she has tried to engage on this...project. This is something she has carried in her heart for many years."

This was a surprise. "Why didn't the others work out?" I'd worked with enough publishers and editors to know this was a dicey business, at best.

"Oh, I'm not totally sure. But I think maybe it was because they didn't understand really what Black Mountain was all about. I'm sure they were very good writers. But this is something that needs a writer's heart as well as his head.

"She is looking for something special, Jack. And she really hopes you are the one who can bring it to her. I mean, when she heard you came looking for Black Mountain that said something to her. Then she watched you very carefully through dinner. And again yesterday when we went to the campuses. And I'm sure she watched you again this morning before she decided to give you the money."

"Yeah, she was kind of giving me the full court press."

"Well, Jack, I am sure you can appreciate she can't afford to wait forever for someone to show up on her doorstep with the book she wants all done and ready for reading. She wants to leave something important behind. Something more than her money. And she is hoping you will be the one to help her do it.

"Well, I think this is all about done. Would you pull two plates down from the cupboard there? There are some nicer ones on the second shelf."

Couple of minutes later we were seated at her dining room table and I was wolfing down another delicious meal. Good cooking is something I've grown to love over the years. But have to say it really started that spring of 1970 right there in Black Mountain. Maybe it was just part of getting older. Maybe some of it had to do with quitting the booze. Some of it had to do with being around people—women mostly—who really knew how to cook. Like Bessie. And Jo. And who taught me a few tricks along the way.

After dinner we cleaned things up and headed into the living room. Before settling on her sofa, Jo put on a Bobby Darin album and then we got down to the business at hand—the future. We sat close and held hands. She wasted no time.

"So, Jack, what exactly are your plans? Or maybe I should ask, have they changed since this morning?"

"No, not exactly. I mean, I still want to get on the road. Head up east to see Albers and Olson. And then maybe they'll send me on to some others."

"And when are you...coming back?" She asked this quietly in the way women do when they're trying not to sound scared or clingy.

"To be honest Jo, I don't know exactly when. I mean, it could be a week. Maybe a couple weeks. Kind of depends on what I find when I get up there."

"I understand."

"I guess I hope to talk to enough people and get enough material that I can outline this book and maybe get a chapter or two written."

"Where are you going to do that?" I could feel where these questions were headed.

"To be honest, I don't know yet."

"Another campground? Won't it be awfully cold up there?"

"Yeah, might be. You never know this time of year."

She smiled, then asked, "And do you have anybody you can...stay with?" This was getting to the heart of the matter.

"Not really. I've been gone from there a long time. All my family's gone. Think all my school buddies are scattered. And their parents are old or dead. But if it's too cold to set up camp, I know places that'll rent rooms by the week. Or, worst case, just find some flea bag of a motel that won't charge me an arm and a leg for a bed and a shower."

I could feel Jo relax as I said this. I think she was smart enough to figure out that if I was going on to another woman, my words, or the way I said them, would've betrayed me. I know this because it's happened before.

She ran a hand along my bicep and down my wrist.

"Well, Mr. Jack Moriarty, I have already promised myself that I will worry about you only a little bit. You will come back to Black Mountain when you are good and ready. I will be here still. And waiting —if you want me to." She said those last words less like a question and more like a command. Because then she kissed me hard, with desire. And all the questions I wanted to ask her melted away with the rest of the night.

The morning came too fast. The clouds had moved on, replaced by a brilliant, dewy sunrise. To be truthful, if I could've made up an excuse for us to stay in bed all day, I would've done it. As it was, she remembered her tenant farmer was stopping by for an early coffee to talk about plans for spring plowing. That meant she had to kick me out even sooner than we wanted. But not before we'd had one more go of it. I promised her I'd be back before too long. I meant it.

Chapter 14 — Old Highways

To be honest, I had mixed emotions about leaving Black Mountain. Going there hadn't turned into the quick peek at somebody else's college campus I thought I'd do. Never expected to meet anyone like Ruth Parker with her story, and I certainly never counted on all that I'd fallen into with Jo, whatever it was or is, since we hadn't taken a lot of time to figure it out. Then there was Lissa too. All of them tied back to this college that'd been dead and gone for fifteen years. If Ruth was to be believed, it had planted seeds of creativity and ideas that had borne fruit across the country. Ruth had talked me into finding out if that was true, even as I was trying to find out other truths. As I headed east there was a part of me that wanted an excuse to turn around. But what would I turn around to? In one of the strange ways about roads, I had to leave Black Mountain in order to figure out what I'd found there.

Still, there was another part of me—honestly I'd say it was the stronger part—that wanted the freedom of the road again. The freedom to go where I wanted. Be where I wanted to be when I wanted to be there. Not answering to anything or anyone. Seeing new things. Meeting new people. Taking things as they came. It was the push that got me out of St. Pete. I could even say, deep down, it was the push that helped me kick the booze. Maybe the push, too, Gerard gave me in the hospital. The push that got me out of Lowell in the first place. Out of New York. On to the ocean. To Denver. San Francisco. The Sierras. Mexico City. Algiers. The push to see more. Always more.

> Afoot and light-hearted I take to the open road,
> Healthy, free, the world before me,

The long, brown path before me leading
  wherever I choose.
Henceforth I ask not good-fortune, I myself am
  good-fortune...

That's how Whitman starts "Song Of The Open Road." And that's just how I felt once I'd put a few miles of Black Mountain behind me. How I'd started so many roads. Gerard kept saying I was running away. Jo and Ruth saw something else.

When I headed out I didn't have an exact sense of where I was going except north—eventually. Route 70 was an old two-laner going up and down and curling around mountains, occasionally cutting through old valleys. After a while the country relaxed; woods giving way to fields, farmers disking up black earth.

I stopped in Statesville to gas up, take a piss, get some coffee and figure out how the hell I was going where I needed to be. I had to get up to New Haven and Gloucester sometime. And the Cape. Always the Cape. But I didn't have to get there right away. The warmth and brightness of this day, even after the rain, made me reluctant to leave the South and get into New England clouds and chill too quickly. A couple nights next to a woman can do that to you.

The truck stop was a hum of action. Trucks idling low patient growls while their tanks got filled. Drivers were walking around, stretching legs, unkinking backs, maybe thinking about a meal or calling back to whatever was home before climbing in for another four or five hours headed God knows where. They were young, old, big, small. Some looked like farm boys out for an afternoon drive with their girl. Others like beat down factory men putting in another day's work before that night's cold beer.

They were pulling all kinds of loads. A stake trailer filled with long, straight trunks of pine that might've been trees in the ground the day before. A flat bed with two massive coils of steel winched down tight. A caged car-hauler filled with brand new Camaros. A stainless steel tanker hauling orange juice. Their trucks were all shapes and sizes. Newer ones had cabs extending back that made room for a bed, small refrigerator, changes of clothes so all a man needed to drive coast to coast was the occasional stop to fill her up and drain him out.

These places replaced the bus stations and railroad stations I grew up with. There'd always been truck stops, but now most people had cars, and so truck stops, especially ones on interstates, became places where all kinds of people—not just drivers or wanderers like me—came together, maybe said a few words about the weather or road conditions, then in minutes went their own ways.

Even on a Tuesday morning, the place was so busy I had to wait for a urinal. A guy my age in a blue seersucker suit pissed to my left. An old guy in bright green Sansabelt pants was on my right. With luck I wouldn't get caught dead wearing either.

I followed the smell of bacon and coffee into the little restaurant. It had a dozen booths and a counter with as many seats. The counter was elbow to elbow. The booths were almost filled too. I was lucky enough to slide into one towards the back. Seconds later, a waitress with a pot of coffee was pouring.

I spread the map out and followed 70 across to where it ended at Morehead City, Beaufort and the ocean. It went through Greensboro, Durham and Raleigh, towns I knew a little about from my trips to see Nin and her family. At New Bern another road—US17—came up from South Carolina, cut through the Great Dismal Swamp and went on into Virginia. If I took that, I could cross the new bridge across the Chesapeake into Delmarva. Then run up past Baltimore, Philly and New York to New Haven. That it seemed like a plan. But first I wanted to see the ocean.

I sucked down enough coffee between a couple eggs, biscuits and sausage gravy, and I was ready for another piss before I left. In between bites I could catch bits of talk from drivers at the counter, sharing road news, but mostly playing with the waitresses. Their voices bounced up and down in a big hubbub.

"Y'all hear 'bout that driver fell 'sleep on seventy-seven? Down't Charlotte? Crossed over and wiped out a family headed for Flo'da. Damn!"

"I'm back through next Wednesday. I'll stop for the special, long as it's you, darlin'."

"Hell, I didn't know Loretta Lynn's twin sister worked here!"

I smiled. The bullshit was already thicker than the cigarette smoke and it was only 10:30. Time to get a move on.

The road first angled southeast out of Statesville before bending towards Salisbury. Then it was High Point, Greensboro and Burlington before curving again southeast at Durham and Raleigh. Like Atlanta, these two cities seemed to be *moving*. Not just traffic. But construction. Lots of it. Still this world of cement and asphalt, of real estate signs and big, glassy office buildings dulled the senses. It was a world cut off from the brown dirt and brown skins I mingled with and rolled with and smoked with in California and Texas and Mexico City. A world apart from fire tower-watched forests packed tight against granite mountains. A world alien to phosphorescent oceans and inky, starry nights. Even as I'd lived so much of my life in New York and San Francisco, it was these worlds that drew me again and again. Teased me. Taught me.

The country really flattened out east of Raleigh. At New Bern I thought I'd come to the ocean, but was fooled. Here the Neuse River met salt water and became Neuse Bay. It would be another twenty or thirty miles before it broadened into Pamlico Sound and the "real" ocean.

I stopped at the national forest near Croatan to stretch my legs before getting down to Morehead City and Beaufort, North Carolina. It was midafternoon and warm. I thought I could smell salt in the air. But right then I was more curious about these old piney woods. I followed a marked trail into the forest. Some of the trees were old alright. Originals, one sign said. The trail started broad and open, but then closed in after a while. Shadow replaced sunlight. It was quiet and humid. Closer to the water ancient cypress reminded me of those dreary swamps in Louisiana and Texas that scared the bejesus out of me, Neal and LuAnne. These trees were tougher than they might seem at first. They didn't have to worry about getting beaten down by snow and ice. But they had to make it in very poor soil. Fight off all kinds of bugs. Survive the occasional hurricane. They looked different from the waist-thick hardwoods of Nantahala. But very hardy in their own brackish, mucky way.

These pines were a continent removed from their redwood and sequoia cousins. Those trees grew huge in groves. They created a cathedral-like quiet. I whispered there. It was quiet here, too, but a different kind of quiet. Not the holy quiet I'd worshiped on the West Coast. Not the ghosts-of-Cherokee quiet I'd hiked in the week before. This seemed like a more alive quiet. A humming quiet. A things-lurking quiet. A buzzing-just-out-of-earshot quiet. I didn't walk relaxed like I had in Nantahala. Instead, I broke a good sweat keeping an eye out for wild animals, especially snakes. I hated snakes. The whole place made me jumpy. I'd had enough. I got out of there.

I finished the drive to Morehard City with the windows down, gulping the fresh, warm air, and loving the warm sunshine. Sitting at the end of a peninsula, Morehead reminded me of the Massachusetts fishing towns I'd grown up around. Lots of water, lots of boats, fish houses, and restaurants serving fresh catch. Its downtown also reminded me of those old upland towns I'd come through in the morning.

It took just a few minutes to find the kind of place I wanted to stay. The Gull Motel was just west of downtown and a block off the water on the Sound side, a single strip of a dozen rooms. Husband and wife owned it. I paid for three nights even though I thought I'd only stay one or maybe two. Harrison's wife had spooked me some. After all these years of traveling by my wits, thumbing rides, sleeping on benches, under trees, here I was at 48 worried about some nosy person thinking I was a vagrant, calling the cops and then blowing my cover.

I'd asked about places to eat and the couple recommended one a few blocks away. Captain Bill's on Evans Street. On the water. Perfect. I hauled my bag into the room along with the Undie and some paper. But for now I was hungry!

I headed for the restaurant and walked through the downtown past old storefronts. There was some traffic on the street. A few people walking around, enjoying the evening. The day had settled into a beautiful soft dusk. The sky held a few clouds and for a few minutes colors in the eastern sky jumped everywhere. Pink. Orange. Red-going-to-purple. There was sweetness everywhere. I breathed in two lungs full of salt sea air. Yes!

You couldn't miss Captain Bill's. It was big. A bar and restaurant together. Not exactly the small place I'd wanted. But it didn't look all that busy, so I walked in the restaurant side and got a table next to a window. Ordered up a bowl of clam chowder, then a flounder with hush puppies on the side. And gulped down glasses of Pepsi. Outside a bunch of fishing boats bobbed lazily on their lines, open water just beyond.

I'd be lying if I said I didn't think seriously about grabbing a stool instead of a table. I was tempted, really wanted to because that's where I'd have felt most at home. I'd already spent a good part of my life on bar stools, yakking it up with complete strangers who became best friends—at least for a night. But I also had a pretty good idea what'd happen there if I did and it wouldn't be good.

My insides were pretty much healed up. To be honest, I liked feeling good. Better than I had in years. Dying was doing wonders for my body! Still, I could feel the old tug. Just like at Ruth's. Maybe I always would. I liked that I was strong enough to resist it. For tonight anyway. Maybe I'd get to a point where I could say yes to one or two drinks. For now I steered clear. Instead I looked out at the boats and water and sky. Night had come on and now the restaurant's lights reflected off the harbor water. An evening star —Venus?—had risen brightly, waiting for others to appear.

I thought about all I'd seen and done since leaving. My first week—had it only been a week?—out of St. Pete had been a good one. A very good one. Maybe I'd have been on the Cape by now if I hadn't stopped at the Black Mountain library. But I'd have missed a lot. Like Yogi Berra says, "When you come to a fork in the road, take it" and Frost says, "Two roads diverged in a wood, and I—I took the one less traveled by." Maybe it was making a difference.

I ended up spending the next whole week in Morehead City. Three days wasn't enough. Like Black Mountain, there was more to see than I thought at first. And some things happened.

Next morning I got to talking with the Gull's owners, Elsie and Loyd. Told them my cover story of being a travel writer. They became really friendly after that. I think they hoped I might mention their motel in my article. They were also nice people. From the Cleveland area originally. A suburb. Rock River. Or maybe Rocky River. I didn't get it exact, to be honest.

They'd had a paint store, worked it together for decades, then sold it when neither of their sons wanted to take over the business. "They're both college boys. They had better things to do than spend sixty hours a week selling paint and brushes." Loyd and Elsie said those sentences together, Elsie starting, Loyd finishing. They'd been a couple so long they could talk like that and be comfortable doing it, completing thoughts not interrupting them. They told me how they'd vacationed down here for years, then bought the motel as part of their retirement plans.

Loyd picked up on my accent right away. When I told him I was from Lowell—I didn't worry about him putting two and two together—he got a big kick out of it. His people were from Pittsfield originally. His father had brought the family to Cleveland after World War I to take a machinist's job. He'd done the same after high school.

He and Elsie were married with two babies when the chance came to open the store after World War II. He took it and they'd made a decent living. Even though they'd hoped maybe one of the boys would take it over, "I'm glad we got out when we did." They talked about how the paint business was changing, "The big boys are really moving on it now." Sears. K-Mart. Montgomery Wards. They were opening lots of stores in big suburban shopping centers.

"People'll drive miles to save a buck a gallon. Makes no sense." So he and Elsie shrugged their shoulders, sold to someone who thought they could make a go of it and headed south. I got the feeling The Gull was more work than retirement.

I spent the next day poking around Morehead City. Took my journal down to the waterfront and started an outline for the book. Mostly I looked at the boats and the water. Men were working on them, repair work, painting, all the things you do to get ready for another season. This is a big sport fishing area. Lot of charters taking city guys out to the Gulf Stream for big fish. Marlin's the champ. I'd love to hook a marlin someday.

Thursday I sent postcards to Memere and Stella, Jo, Ruth and Lissa. Told them I was fine etc. Didn't say anything about how long I'd be in Morehead City or where I was headed next, although on Ruth's I mentioned looking forward to meeting the Albers soon. Wasn't sure how to sign Jo's—"love" didn't feel quite right—so I drew a little doodle of me fishing off a pier. Wasn't sure how to sign Memere's either—I didn't want the mailman getting any weird ideas—so I signed it "Sal." On Lissa's I mentioned the hotel owners were from Cleveland.

Then I drove down to Cape Carteret and over to Jacksonville and saw the signs for Camp Lejeune. I'd asked Loyd earlier why I was seeing Marines and sailors in Morehead City. He said because this was where the Marine Second Division left for duty —most for Vietnam. Judging from all the signs the camp must have been a very big place.

Friday I had a little scare. I was anxious to get real close to the ocean. Not just pier close. Surf close. I crossed over to Beaufort and followed 70 to its very end at Atlantic after passing through Bettie, Otway and Sealevel. I didn't ask for directions. I just pointed the car east to see where it took me. From there a narrow road led out to Cedar Island where I caught the ferry over to Ocracoke Island. Hadn't planned on it, but what the hell. It was another warm day, cooler on the water, with a high overcast. There were only two other cars besides mine, tourist season was still a ways off. The ride took more than two hours across Pamlico. I hung on the ferry's side and looked back at the coastline slipping away and disappearing, then tried to pick Ocracoke off the horizon. I felt better when I did. I drove up the island and caught the ferry to Hatteras. Spur of the moment. That was another forty-five minutes. It was well after noon when we docked and the high overcast had lowered into thicker clouds. I got to Buxton and parked the car.

These islands easily reminded me of the Cape, but more remote and fragile, sitting barely above sea level. In the summer they fill up with tourists, but in early April I was pretty much alone. I went out along the beach and headed for the lighthouse, maybe the most famous in America. The "Barber Pole." Even though it was only half a mile or so, I was glad for all the beach walking I'd done in St. Pete. You needed your legs to keep a decent pace against the wind which had picked up a little.

But the ocean seemed as laid back as the people who lived here. Each taking the other as they came and went. The rollers were long swells pounding the hard sand with a deep, familiar beat. Still, they were a constant reminder that some storm could rise up and swallow this land whole. That was different from Cape Cod where you could always move to higher ground. There I felt exposed, as though that same storm could rise up and swallow me whole as well.

Different birds worked ahead of me. Some scooting and poking bills into the sand. Others hovering, bobbing up and down just above the waves, occasionally dropping down for a fish. Usually missing. I thought what a crazy, hard way to live. Yet this was the only thing they knew. On this tiny strip where earth and sea met, they poked out shells, flew up into the air, ate, raised young, and died.

The lighthouse was on a point by itself. It seemed awfully close to the water, just a hundred feet or so from the surf. A jetty of some kind had been built to help slow erosion. I couldn't imagine letting something this big and important topple into the sea. A sign said its light could be seen 20 miles out. Hatteras, Ocracoke and the others were barrier islands. That made them sound safer and sturdier than they were. The ocean was stronger. It pushed them back and brought them forth. They helped protect the coastline, yes. But they were tiny, brittle fingers of land. The ocean could flick this lighthouse end-over-barber-pole-end wherever it wanted, whenever it wanted. It could do the same to me. Almost as if it was reading my thoughts, the wind picked up a little, becoming a steady breeze.

I was alone. I expected to see others, but in a way I was glad there was nobody here. Maybe there were park service people around somewhere. But for now it was me and the lighthouse and the surf. I stood between the two feeling small. A spit of rain started. I walked towards the jetty, closer to the hard, wet sand. Rollers hit the shore in a steady four-count beat. One-two-three-BOOM. One-two-three-BOOM. Even the sandpipers and seagulls had wandered off. I looked out as far as I could see. There was no horizon. I had wanted to come here. To see and feel the rawness of ocean. To stand at an easternmost point and know there was no land for thousands of miles. To remember what it was like to *want* to be on that ocean, challenging it and feeling it challenge you. To be master.

I thought about a book I'd read years ago, *The Outermost House.* In the middle twenties, the writer, Henry Beston, built a one-room house for himself far out on Cape Cod, near Eastham. He lived there a year, his only visitors the occasional Coast Guard watchman making his rounds up and down the beach, lantern in hand. He kept notes of what he saw, what he did, who he talked to. Those became his book. He was a close observer. He could see, like Blake, a world in a grain of sand. I liked how he recorded what happened there. He didn't try to make the Cape more or less than what it is—a place of great beauty where life and death are intimate neighbors.

Here are the opening paragraphs of his "Lanterns On The Beach" chapter:

"It is now the middle of March, cold winds stream between earth and the serene assurance of the sun, winter retreats, and for a little season the whole vast world here seems as empty as a shell.

"Winter is no mere negation, no mere absence of summer; it is another and positive presence, and between its ebbing and the slow, cautious inflow of our northern spring there is a phase of earth emptiness, half real, perhaps, and half subjective. A day of rain, another bright week, and all the earth will be filled with the tremor and the thrust of the new year's energies.

"There has just been a great wreck, the fifth this winter and the worst. On Monday morning last, shortly after five o'clock, the big three-masted schooner *Montclair* stranded at Orleans and went to pieces in an hour, drowning five of her crew...on her way from Halifax to New York, had had a hard passage, and sunrise found her off Orleans with her rigging iced up and her crew dog-weary. Helpless and unmanageable, she swung inshore and presently struck far out and began to break up. Lifted, rocked, and pounded by the morning's mountainous seas, her masts were seen to quiver at each crash..."

Beston's Cape was my Cape. Fullness next to emptiness. Kindness next to savagery. Commerce next to shipwreck. The living devouring the dead. All ebbing. All flowing.

This Atlantic coast has seen wrecks upon wrecks for hundreds of years. When I sailed that freighter during the war, torpedoes from German U-boats were dropping ships up and down the whole East Coast from Maine to Miami. Not just ours. One island near Hatteras has an all-British cemetery filled with bodies washed ashore after one sinking. Even when we had escort destroyers, you felt your whole life was just a crap shoot out there. You never really relaxed. You hid your fear with booze or card games or just bullshitting. All I could think about was the enemy out there unseen, lurking, ready to pounce and snuff my little life out as quickly and easily as if it had never been. The ocean was big and lonely and maybe angry at this war that added unwanted metal and bones to its depths. Crossing took forever. Every groan from the ship made me jump, thinking rivets were popping and soon we'd share the bottom alongside other nameless freighters filled with nameless sailors.

I tried to be Ishmael. I tried. I really tried. I wanted to write about the ocean, its beauty and its awfulness. I wanted to feel like I had conquered it. Had stared ol' Moby Dick right in the eye. I did write a half-ass little book that never got published. But I was no Melville. No Ishmael. I was just a chickenshit. Why had I failed? Why did I jump that ship soon as I could? Why did I duck the Navy by acting crazy? Why did I let Sammy die alone on that Anzio beach? Why? All these questions had haunted me through all these years. Sometimes I tried to answer them. But mostly I didn't. Mostly I did what Gerard sat there and accused me of in that damn old hospital: I ran away.

One-two-three-BOOM! One-two-three-BOOM! One-two-three-BOOM!

I didn't feel the water soak my shoes at first. I stared out at the waves. Those big, friendly rollers. Rolling their easy, endless beat. Coming out of the ocean-sky. They played one long, slow, easy riff. Long and easy. Long and easy. I fixed on one rising higher than the others coming in from far out. I watched it fall and rise, fall and rise, fall and rise, pushing to meet its fate on this lonely, lonely shore. And when it landed—BOOM!—it snuffed out the wave before it. BOOM! Another right behind pushed it even farther up the beach. I felt the wet now in my feet, up my legs. BOOM! Another one!

And then that Hatteras foghorn let loose. Eeeeeeawwwwwwwwwweeeeeeeeeawwwwwwwww! Like a big bass sax blowing counterpoint to the ocean's beat. Eeeeeeaaaaawwwwwwwww.

One-two-three-BOOM!
One-two-three-BOOM!
One-two-three-BOOM!
Eeeeeeawwwwwwwweeeeeeeeawwwwwwww!
BOOM!
BOOM!
BOOM!

I was caught in the middle of this great timeless riff. BoomBoomBOOM.

Eeeeeeeawwwwweeeeeeeeawwwwwwww. BoomBoomBOOM.

I wanted it to go on forever. BoomBoomBoom! I did a little jig. Dancing in the wet and cold. BoomBoomBOOM! I wasn't running away. I was there. BoomBoomBOOM! Come on, you waves! Come on, you wind! BoomBoomBOOM! Scream at me lighthouse! Tell me I'm not worth a shit!

Eeeeeeeawwwwweeeeeeeeawwwwwwww!! BoomBoomBOOM!

Come get me Gerard, if you dare! Come get me, Larry! Come get me, Allen! Come get me, Neal! Come all of you! Take me away, if you can! Boom BoomBOOM!

BoomBoomBOOM!

I shouted into the wind and rain. I took a step towards the water, the surf rising past my knees. I stumbled as one of the big ones almost took me down. I shouted some more. I only needed to take one more step. Just one more. Just one.

I can't tell you how or why, but somehow I made it to the car, carrying my shoes and socks. The rain started coming in sheets about halfway back and so the rest of me was soaked too. I needed to catch my breath. It almost felt like the wind had blown me off the beach and rolled me all the way back to town. I looked around to see if anybody was watching, but no one was out. My breath fogged the windshield. I didn't want to move.

I kinda knew, though, I had to hurry. Otherwise, I'd miss the Ocracoke ferry and the Cedar Island one too. I didn't want to be stranded out here. Not in this storm. What I really wanted was a smoke. And a bottle of dago red. Don't know why I was so jumpy. I found the landing despite wipers that barely moved the water off my windshield. I just made it, but the ride back was no picnic. The storm had kicked up these shallower waters into a good sea. I stayed in the car, found a towel and slowly dried off.

As I watched the ferry bow go up and down, I wondered if it might sink. Would we all get swept away, our bodies thrown up on some part of this coast, or maybe dragged out to the ocean itself never to be seen again, becoming a headline for the local paper, then quickly forgotten? That got me thinking about my other sinking. Out there. On the other coast. Where the surf and cold and fog of Big Sur cracked me wide open. What happened? Even now I'm not sure. But something...*something*...came howling through and laid me out. No Gerard to save me then. Or if he was there, he'd changed into something wild and ugly.

It'd happened about ten years before. I'd gone down from San Francisco at Ferlinghetti's suggestion, giving me his place to write in peace and quiet. Get away from all the grabby people who wanted pieces of me now that I'd been "discovered." Instead it felt like solitary confinement, even though I had nothing but the forest and mountain and ocean around me. The quiet was maddening. There was no peace. Until I lost it all. I couldn't smoke or drink enough to get back on balance. The big whale hit and I was left hanging for dear life to a piece of the *Pequod.*

The memories of that time chilled me more. Larry and Allen bailed me out. Got me back up to San Francisco. I wrote a book about it. That helped. But even though I never told anyone, I knew I was just hanging on. Maybe some people knew. Was I crazy? Was I just chasing something that had to end curled around that toilet bowl, except it didn't? Maybe I was just pushing it farther down the road. Maybe it was supposed to end back there. At the lighthouse. *Ti Jean, Ti Jean...*

I just made the Cedar Island ferry too. It was an even longer, darker trip. I found a blanket and curled up inside my Ford. I tried to sleep, but the bouncing and heaving made it impossible. The ferry fought for every yard across that sea. It was long after dark when it landed.

Then I had to crawl back down to Morehead City. My wipers were shot. I couldn't see a thing. I don't know what time it was when I finally got back to my room. But I was so beat it was all I could do just to make it under the covers. I shivered and shivered and wondered what the hell was going on. Maybe it was supposed to end on this coast. Not the wild and lonely Big Sur coast. Or the warm and maternal Gulf Coast. But here on this soft and deceptive bit of North Carolina Atlantic coast. I remembered smiling to myself glad I'd at least sent the postcards. I was out. Boomboomboom...

Chapter 15 — Glad Tidings

It was late morning when I finally woke up. The rain was still coming down hard. I was starving and sore. Like I'd wrestled through the night. The light next to the bed was on. I rolled over and right onto my journal. It was lying open face down. Why was that there? I flipped it and was amazed to see it filled with words. Four pages worth. When did I write that? I honestly had no memory of writing anything. This time I couldn't use booze or pills or pot or anything else an excuse. But there they were. In my hand, but unlike anything I'd written before. The letters thick and written large like I couldn't wait to get the words out, pushed across the paper almost in a scrawl. There are parts I still don't get, but here it is. All of it.

Hauled my ass to Hatteras
Big Sur's back side
Where once I danced in Pacific surf
Skipped under Bixby's bridge
High as a kite
Then fell from the sky when the wind died
Escaped doing a continental jig
Across rocky mountains and old man rivers.
Dust-deviled through Mormon deserts
Over great plains and great lakes

Til I landed on my Atlantic edge.
Here I hung with Montclair's crew
Far from cold Cod

Still I heard their iced rigging singing
They clung for life off Orleans

Beston could only watch from his outermost
house.
In deadly Petersburg
My mast cracked too

I swayed with the best of them
Backed against our light house
Pinched Aeneas-like
Between my rock and a damn hard place.
Now teetering at barber-poled Hatteras
I looked for you Gerard, my deliverance

I searched for you
Surfing with angels
Riding the biggest wave
All the way
To break point.
We're on a roll now!
I cried for you Sammy
Sprawled across Anzio sand
Torn to shreds by
Nazi bullets and Waspy slurs.
I called for you Neal
All blue-jeaned and smokes
You came once
Then hopped, skipped and
Jumped your Zephyr all the way
From Denver hustles
To frozen Mexican tracks.

I loved you Allen
Howling at your own madness
Singing your soft Berkeley sutras
Losing your hair
under hard city lights.
I wept for you Annie

Strawberry haired and morning lovely
And for you Joan
Wild in your pregnant New York streets
And you Edie
Running back to broken Midwestern homes
And you Carolyn
Caught in a brakeman's switch
And you Stella
Waiting for men who never came home
And Memere
Losing all but one who's most lost of all.
I wept for all of you
I wept for me
Running from you.
The light's out now
The tide's running away
Here on slopy sandy shifty shores
Here at bad ass Hatteras.

April 10-11
Gull Motel
Morehead City

I stared at the words wondering when and how I could have written them. Was this what booze-free madness looked like? Was this what I had to look forward to the rest of my trip to God-knows-where I was going to end up? Was this somehow a sign I should turn back? High tail it back to St. Pete? Call it quits? The beaten saint become prodigal son? Why now? Why after all that had happened in Black Mountain? How had this storm come on? I hadn't a clue. That scared me more than anything. Before, I could at least feel a squall in my head coming. Sometimes it happened at the end of the road. Or the end of a relationship. Or the end of a bottle. But this had come out of nowhere. Like some tsunami it rose out of the ocean and damn near pulled me under. Or so it seemed.

And then I cried. I bawled. Hunched over my journal, rocking back and forth on the bed. I wept and wept and wept. For what? For all the fucked up things I'd done with my sad life? For the legend of Duluoz that was really a sham? For trying to find more and more road again at the end of my earth? I didn't have any answers. Only questions upon questions upon questions. I rocked myself to sleep again.

When I woke next it was well after noon. I stared at the ceiling and listened to the rain still beating against the roof and window. I felt better. I didn't know why any more than I knew why I had plunged the day and night before. Now I drifted back to a warm afternoon when Henri, his girlfriend and I snuck onto an abandoned freighter anchored off Tiburon. Henri wanted to scrounge. His girlfriend wanted to sunbathe naked. I wanted to watch. And dream. And feel that sun warm my body through and through. And roll lazily with that old ship stuck on San Francisco Bay with nothing better to do than keep an eye on all the other ships going back and forth under that gleaming Golden Gate. How many times had I been back and forth across that bridge, diving into the city and its hip madness, then sliding back out to Marin and Mt. Tam, Stinson and Sausalito, Bodega Bay and Petaluma! How I loved that city, that Baghdad by the Bay, those redwoods and beaches and all the crazy, delicious people drawn to the same wondrous things as I! There'd been plenty of madness. But plenty of sweetness too. There you could live underground right in the middle of it all. There you could feel the ebb and flow of East and West, new and old, art and commerce. Right there on that deep, fault line where heaven and hell meet and kiss. I loved San Francisco! I ached to be there again!

I resolved right then in that little motel room on that rainy, beaty Saturday in April that San Francisco would be my destination, my end point. I'd find a way to hide out from Lawrence and Snyder and

Duncan and all the others. But I'd be there. Far from pillowy, maternal St. Pete. Far from these deadly capes. Far, even, from wild and fragile Big Sur.

I'd give Ruth her book, yes. Or as much of it as I could find. But Black Mountain would never be home. Just like St. Pete was never home. Or Ozone Park. Or any of the other dozen places I'd bedded down for stretches at a time. Hell, here I was at 48 and I didn't even own a stick of furniture!

When I left Lowell in 1940 I had no idea I was really leaving home for good. I mean a real home. A place where you know people and they know you. Where you live with the rhythms of the year. Where you have to fix a leaky pipe once in a while. Cut the grass. Where you can stick a book high up on a shelf and know where to get it when you remember it a year later.

Now thirty years later that's not how it's turned out. Even when I had dreams of a nice little house in a suburb snuggled down with Anne or Joan or maybe Edie, it never even got close to turning out that way. Not that I didn't try. Wanted to make it happen in Denver, but that move turned out to be a disaster. Nobody wanted to be there except me. It took a while, but then I understood that some people—maybe most—like to be just where they are. It's hard to get up and leave.

So even though I'd come to love Denver with the mountains close and the big open skies, it was pretty dumb of me to think Memere was going to love it too. Or Joan. Or Nin. They were Eastern people. Used to close-packed cities. Tall buildings. Trolleys. Lots of noise.

I should've known, too, that no way were they going to put up with the likes of Neal or Allen or Burroughs or Lucien Carr or any of my other crazy friends come busting through the door at all hours of the day or night to have beers and pull me out for God-knows-what. After that I didn't try. I'd just made sure Memere was someplace comfortable, like I'd promised my dad.

I wasn't sure what to make of what happened out there at Hatteras. But I did feel better, calmer. It shook me up how it'd come on without warning. I'd have to keep an eye out in the future. I know if I'd been with Neal or the other guys, I would've dealt with it the only way I've done before...diving inside a bottle. I still might.

The next day I did something else that surprised me: I found a little Catholic church—St. Egbert's— to go to. I hadn't been to church in years. But after what happened at Hatteras, and maybe what happened back at Black Mountain, I wanted to go. Just to sit and listen. Feel the rhythms of a service. Help my own thoughts. I'd asked Loyd if there was one around and he gave me directions. It wasn't far and it wasn't big. But it was full. I slipped into the rearmost pew next to a family with three young children. A girl about six swung her legs back and forth, occasionally hitting mine, despite the mother's best efforts to shush her. I didn't mind.

I could see right away there were a fair number of military men. Many with families, some just by themselves. The priest must have been used to having them come and go because his sermon was almost like talking to them personally. His accent was straight out of the Bronx. He looked to be in his forties. My height, maybe an inch shorter. Burly. Take off the frock and he might've been a longshoreman. He spoke of fear and sacrifice in a voice rough and tender at the same time. Another time, another place and we could've shared a beer. With his soft yet growly voice, he was easy to listen to.

"When we celebrate Easter, we celebrate hope. We celebrate His rising and the promise of life eternal. But imagine yourselves one of His disciples two weeks later, as we are now. Two weeks after the Crucifixion.

Two weeks after the Burial. Two weeks after the Miracle. Two weeks after all the hoopla has died down and people have returned to their normal lives. What hope have you? Yes, He is risen. But He is also dead and gone. Who leads you now? Who do you trust after one of your own betrayed Him? The man who denied Him three times? How do you face those who look to you for answers? How do you face those who want no answers and will eagerly do to you what they have done to Him? When confronted by others who have no faith, where is yours?"

The priest had my attention. He wasn't pushing out the usual crappy homilies like the priest and nuns did after Gerard died. When he died I think my faith in God died too. I never said so. I couldn't, or wouldn't. That would've broken Memere's heart again. (Of course, I was destined to break it many times over. But not for denying the one thing that she held onto more than anything, the one thing that maybe kept her sane through a lifetime of suffering.) And Gerard himself had so much faith. He saw God's hand at work in everything. And hadn't he been his own Miracle, coming to me after he died?

But what had God shown about this life that made it any more than one long path of suffering relieved only by death? What "lesson" was He teaching by taking my brother so young? What 'lesson' was there in having Sammy die at Anzio? Or baking millions in Hitler's ovens? Or leaving Neal to die alone out in the cold Mexican desert half out of his mind?

Yet here was this priest talking straight to these men and their young families. He was saying, "Yes, you may die before you want to. Yes, you may die in some faraway land. Yes, you may not even know for what or for whom you are dying. And, yes, those around you may help you die by betraying you with their own cowardice. Yet, you must have faith that what you do is right and just and will be rewarded in the next life, if not this one. And you must have faith in your fellow disciples. For without them, you too will perish." He didn't have to say the word "Vietnam" any more than he had to say "Gethsemane." Nor was he promising anything more than the power of faith to get them home alive. The question was: Would it be enough?

"Faith is hard. Each of you sitting here today has had moments of doubt, has wondered perhaps 'Where has my faith gone?' As hard as it may have been for you to hold onto your faith despite being surrounded here by all that is supportive and familiar and reassuring, think how much harder it was for those who had nothing. *Nothing.*

"Christ is my hero. But He is the Son of God. Despite all His suffering and doubts, His Father ultimately delivered him to the comforts and blessings of Heaven. What about His disciples? What did they have? Only their faith that what Jesus told them was true. To do what they did long after He was no longer with them, those disciples stand almost as big as He. They persevered and, in so doing, became heroes to humanity. Have faith and you, too, will be a hero."

As he finished, I saw tears streaming down the face of a young Marine, a lance corporal in uniform. He was there as I was, alone. I guessed his were tears of fear, of hope, maybe relief. I never cried those tears. Maybe if I'd had more faith I would've stayed in and done my duty. Maybe I wouldn't have jilted Sammy. Maybe we both would've made it back alive. Maybe I wouldn't have had to wait for Gerard to tell me I was getting a second chance six months ago.

Yet here I was sitting in this tiny church looking at young men getting ready to go off to a place from which they might never return. The priest offered them nothing more than faith. Here they were, leaning forward, anxious to have that faith sustain them through a hell they were about to enter. Where was mine? I had no answer today. Still I was glad someone at least pushed the question right in front of me. What *do* I believe in? Is this life all there is? Does all our suffering ever count for anything? What if I don't believe in Jesus? What if I believe in Buddha's path to perfection and Eternity? What if someone else believes as Mohammed does? Many faiths. Many paths. One destination.

I still had no clue. But I felt better knowing that priest had confidence in his.

I walked out of the cool darkness of St. Egbert's into bright sunlight and spent the better part of the day retracing the drive along the coast to Camp Lejeune. I took it easy. I was in no hurry. I also needed to kind of figure out what was going on inside. I'd like to say I had some kind of great revelation as a result of that near calamity at Hatteras, the night of mysterious writing and then the sermon, but I didn't. My life hasn't worked that way.

It's why I hated it when people grabbed at me as though I was already holding some big chunk of Truth, hoping I'd break off a piece and give it to them. I did want people to read me, to listen to me once in a while, and maybe figure out ways to find their own truths. But I could never be some kind of padre passing out pieces of Truth like communion wafers on Sundays.

What I did want to understand is how this God of love could tolerate so much suffering in His world. Or how the Jesus who urged us to turn the other cheek could accept so much war and atrocity. Or how our souls could be saved by faith alone after fingers had pulled triggers that killed others. Eternal questions. Temporary answers. I've seen how sometimes Death is cold and arbitrary. Sometimes Death is cold and calculating. But it is always cold. Somehow we hope that God is going to be there and deliver us into a safe and warm Eternity. We hope.

The next morning I decided to explore that Civil War fort across the water. There wasn't a whole lot to see there, but walking around it made me think how much of my life had been surrounded by war. I hated war. It seemed like my whole life had been fighting a war or getting ready to fight one. "Good" wars, "bad" wars, it didn't make a difference. People suffered. People died.

I came off that island in a foul mood. I'd made my mind up to leave the next day anyway. But visiting that fort cinched it. There wasn't anything else for me now in Morehead City. To try and shake off the clouds, I stopped in a little shell shop and bought another batch of postcards. The woman tending the store must've thought I was there for the fishing. She was big and friendly; her open smile showed someone used to laughing. As she rang up the cards, she asked, "Catch anything? I hear snapper're runnin' now."

I didn't care to set the record straight. "Naw. No luck."

"Well, there's always tomorrow, isn't there? You gots to just keep tryin'."

"You're right about that. Always tomorrow."

As she handed me my change, she said, "Yessir! Always tomorrow. You come back then, tell us what you caught."

"I'll do that."

I had to admit I liked her cheerfulness. Just what I needed after those feelings at the fort. Her optimism was genuine. Not the forced kind of empty talk some shopkeepers make while they're taking your money. If I were staying longer I might've made excuses to stop back in and talk with her some more. The world is full of interesting people with their own interesting stories. I bet she had hours full of them. Good bait for customers.

When I got back to the room I wrote up all the cards, told everyone I was leaving the next day and next stop would probably be somewhere on the Delmarva peninsula. To Memere and Stella I added something about going to church. To Ruth I added a "looking forward to meeting Josef and Anni." To Jo I added a silly drawing of a big fish holding a cane pole with me looking like a Tom Sawyer dangling at the other end.

Next morning I said goodbye to Loyd and Elsie and thanked them for their hospitality. It was midweek quiet, but they were happy. A group of ten businessmen were coming in Thursday from Columbus, Ohio, taking five rooms and staying a week. They'd chartered a boat from one of their friends who'd recommended The Gull to them. So almost half of their rooms would be sold for six nights, not counting drive-ups like me. Not bad for early April.

I got on the road back up to New Bern and headed north. The land stayed flat and got swampy at times. US 17 crossed the Pamlico River at Washington, made a beeline for Williamston where it met up with US 13 for a few miles then split off to the east. This felt like an old, old road that might've been an Indian trail once. It crossed a big expanse at the mouth of the Chowan River where it met Batchelor Bay which in turn pushed into Albemarle Sound.

At Elizabeth City, the road hooked due north and followed an old canal through the Great Dismal Swamp all the way to Chesapeake and Portsmouth. Then it was a straight shot into Norfolk, a true blue Navy town. It might've been where I'd ended up if I'd stayed on back in the war. Now with another war on the place was alive with white uniforms. The air had a different smell to it. I could smell the ocean. But it seemed layered over with the smell of metal and paint and diesel.

I was tempted to get over the new bridge across the Chesapeake right away and find a place to camp on the other side. But it was already late afternoon and I didn't want to go scrounging for a spot at nightfall. I knew I was getting soft. Dean would've scorned such thinking when an all-night drive into the heart of New York City was the only thing on his mind. Stopping anywhere short of his destination just never ever figured into down-to-the-minute calculations of his life. His obsession with time and schedules was just right for a railroad man. I found another little motel instead.

Then I drove out to Virginia Beach for a different look at the ocean. Along the way I saw this on a billboard and bumper stickers:

Virginia Is For Lovers.

I thought: OK, clever ad. But instead of thinking about Virginia, I thought about Jo. Then how New York and San Francisco are much better for lovers. At least from my experience.

I parked the car and headed for the boardwalk. Being April and midweek and late in the day, I had the place pretty much to myself. Shops were closed. A couple of others, like myself, were out for a walk. It seemed a quieter, safer place to see the Atlantic than from mad Hatteras and those bouncy, splashy, wind-furied ferries.

Maybe it was just the time of year, but the boardwalk had a scruffy down-on-its-luck air. In a couple months maybe it'd be different when the place would be filled with families, kids with faces full of cotton candy and melting ice cream. Sharpshooting teenage boys trying to score big stuffed animals for their girlfriends and maybe more later in the night. Grandmas and grandpas walking slowly, holding hands, looking at the kids running back and forth across the sand, squealing in the cold water, wondering how it all happened so fast. Here and there a con like Huncke moving out of the shadows bumming a cigarette, trying to make a mark. For now, all was closed, shuttered against a spring breeze that chilled just a little.

I decided to duck into a little oyster bar. I hoped to get some and maybe a big bowl of chowder and maybe some big fluffy biscuits. Inside was all dark wood and smoky with old time pictures of Atlantic City and fishing stuff on the walls. All the tables and all the seats at the small bar but two were filled. I sat down next to a sailor in shore uniform. Actually an officer, full lieutenant if I remembered my rankings right. A shudder went through me when the barkeep asked if I wanted a beer. I hoped he didn't see. Said no, a soda would be fine. Then I ordered up a dozen oysters and a bowl of chowder, couple of hard rolls and butter included.

The lieutenant was sipping a whiskey and smoking a Winston. I would've loved both. Think maybe I surprised myself that the pull wasn't stronger than I thought it would be. But it was there. It was there.

"Man, I'm sure going to miss this!" he said after his first to no one in particular.

"Yeah? Last ones for a while, huh?"

"Yep! No oysters' in the Delta."

I knew there was only one delta a military man could be talking about: the Mekong Delta.

"Headed to 'Nam?"

"Yes, sir. Shipping out first thing tomorrow."

My oysters arrived and we continued talking in between the slurping. Damn! They *were* good!

"First time over?"

"No, sir. My second. My wife isn't too happy about it, as you can imagine. But I told her this was my best chance to make lieutenant commander by 35. First hitch was cake. Destroyer support for the Enterprise. I need to show them some more."

"So you're career Navy?"

"Yes, sir. Or at least I hope to be. I'm Academy Class of '59. Things were pretty slow until Vietnam kicked off. A lot of opportunities now. But I still need to make lieutenant commander in the next couple of years. Otherwise, it's pretty much over for me."

We'd finished our oysters and now came the chowder. He ordered another whiskey. I got another Coke.

"Did you serve, sir?" It was not an unexpected question. There had to be thousands of retired military men around here.

"No, not really. I rode a freighter across the Atlantic during WWII before we really got into it. There were U-boats looking for us, but missed us that trip thank God. I signed up for the real thing after Pearl Harbor, but they bounced me on account of my knees."

"I see."

We both paused while we savored the chowder. I could tell he was disappointed that I didn't have any good war stories to pass along. Truth is, so was I. And no way I was going to spill the real truth to this earnest young officer.

"Where are you from?"

"Wilkes-Barre, Pennsylvania, sir. Yourself?"

"Near Boston. The name's Jack, by the way. Moriarty."

We shook hands. "Don. Don Michak. What brings you to Virginia Beach?"

"Just passing through. Came up from Morehead City today. Headed back to Massachusetts."

"Fishing trip?"

"No. Just traveling. I'm a writer. Left my mother's home in St. Petersburg couple of weeks ago. Stopped in western North Carolina for a bit. Near Asheville. Then headed over to the coast. I'd never been to Hatteras."

"Sounds great. Be able to travel like that. Of course, I get to travel a little bit too. You know what they say, 'Join the Navy. See the world!'"

I laughed politely.

"How'd you get from Wilkes-Barre to the Academy?"

"I come from a family of coal miners, sir. My grandfather came over from Czechoslovakia when it was still part of the Empire. He heard about mining jobs around Wilkes-Barre and worked until he was 60, then dropped over dead one day. My dad started mining when he was 16. They worked side by side for a long time. Dad was still at it until a couple years ago. But he got the black lung and had to quit. Coal's about gone anyway. He told me the only way out was to get an education. I was lucky enough to get recommended to the Academy."

As he talked I glanced his way a couple times. Lt. Michak was a good looking man. Short black hair. Strong face with blue eyes. Kind of like me in a way. Guessed he was several inches taller. Athletic build. Shirt and pants crisp and creased. A fit officer.

"You said you were a...writer?"

"Yeah."

"What kind of writing? Newspaperman?" He asked with a mixture of genuine curiosity and a little bit of wariness.

"No, I write travel stories for magazines. Have an assignment that's taking me back to New England." He seemed to relax a little with this.

"Sounds like a great job."

"Yeah, it's not too bad. You're on the road a lot. Hell on family life, though." I said this as a joke.

"Are you married?"

"Naw. Not anymore. The wife couldn't put up with me gone all the time. Maybe truth is I liked being out seeing things, meeting people more than I did holding down a 9-to-5er."

"Kids?"

"No." Pause. "None that I know of!" He laughed at this time-honored joke. He started warming to our conversation. I could tell he wanted to talk.

"Yeah, I kind of get where you're coming from. I married the sweetest girl I could imagine. Her dad's military also. Air Force. Got his first star two years ago. We have two little ones. They're back up in Bethesda. Miss 'em already. But, truth is, I like my tours. Already been to the Mediterranean. That was during the '67 war. Man, was that a hairy time! If I make lieutenant commander, then I can go for XO. Maybe on one of those nuclear frigates. Probably take me to North Atlantic tailing Ruskies." There was genuine enthusiasm here. He had a career planned out.

By this time we'd finished our chowder, and I was on my third Coke. Don pulled out his Winstons and offered me one. I took it. It'd been ages since I'd felt that sweet burning down through my throat and into my lungs. This was alright.

When the barkeep put the Coke down, Don asked, "You don't drink?"

"Not anymore."

"Must be tough to come into a bar and not have one."

"I like testing my willpower," I smiled.

"My destroyer skipper liked having a snort or two at the end of a day. He'd have a couple of us join him. Always kept my limit at two."

"Yeah, that's probably a good policy," I said, thinking back to the days when two was just getting warmed up.

Don was in a chatty mood now. "I saw some guys let that get the best of them. One of our sailors killed a man on shore leave in Australia. Dumb bar fight. Two punches and down. Other guy hit his head on the pavement and that was it. He'll spend the rest of his life in the brig."

I really don't like talking about drinking. It annoyed me when Ruth and Jo talked about my "infirmities." But, of course, I couldn't say anything. I thought I was doing pretty damn good just saying no thanks.

"So, what's it like over there? In 'Nam?" I wasn't sure why I asked this. I'd like to say it was just curiosity or making bar talk. But I didn't want to get political.

Don took a long slug finishing his whiskey then signaled for another.

"You want to know the truth?" Then answered, not waiting for me. "It sucks."

The barkeep put his third whiskey down.

Then Don looked at me long and hard as though wrestling with his words.

"You're a writer so I have to be careful with what I say. I don't want to screw things up."

"Yeah. Hey, if you can't talk about it, I get it."

He started into the whiskey. "Be a long time before I can do this again."

"Me too."

He chuckled.

"Reason wife's pissed off is because they're sending me up the Delta. Gonna command a gunboat squadron. Dicey stuff. Dirty fuckin' work. She was hoping I'd get to ride a desk at the Pentagon."

I didn't know how to answer, so I waited to see if he wanted to say more.

"You know anything about the Delta, Jack?"

"Not a thing, really."

"It's filled with VC. But you never know where. So you base from some shithole and then take a boat ride. Sometimes they ambush you. Sometimes they booby trap a village they know you're coming to 'pacify.'"

"Yeah, that sounds pretty shitty."

"It is. They never engage man-to-man. I hear talk that maybe the President is going to try and really go after 'em. It's like we're fighting with one arm tied behind our backs." Don was getting warmed up now. I could tell this is what he really wanted to talk about.

"The gooks just hit and run, hit and run. And when we try to really go after their asses, they slip into Cambodia and get safe haven."

I had to agree with Don. It was a shitty way to fight a war. In WWII and Korea you knew who the enemy was and where he was. Vietnam was all shadows.

"But you think maybe the President's going to try something different?"

"Yeah, it's what I heard during my command brief. I can't talk much about it. But I think Charlie's going to be surprised when we chase his ass where it's never been chased before."

"Is that part of your assignment?"

Don shot me a quick look with that one. I think he was trying to make sure I wasn't press who'd go and blab about something top secret and maybe screw up the whole mission.

"Hey, sorry. If that one's out of bounds, just forget it."

"No, that's OK. We just get warned all the time to watch out who we're talking to. 'Loose lips sink ships' and all that crap."

He sipped the whiskey a little more slowly now. My guess was he'd made up his mind this would be the last one. He stubbed out the last third of his cigarette, rubbing it in slow circles, before pulling the pack back out and lighting another. He offered me another and I turned it down. Not that maybe I didn't want it. But I've always been a little self-conscious about being a mooch.

When he started talking again, his voice sounded far away like maybe he was talking to someone else. Maybe his wife. Or maybe some high school buddy from Wilkes-Barre.

"I believe in what the President is doing. I know we can win this thing if they let us fight with both hands. The people are grateful. They really are. They can see we're there to help them. To do good."

I wasn't going to get into an argument with Don over this. He was leaving tomorrow for a shithole that he might never get out of. But I had my doubts. We'd been at this thing for five years and it was hard for me to see who was winning and who was losing. I was pretty sure some of the Vietnamese did see us doing good. I was also pretty sure some of them saw us as just another occupier like the French and the Japanese.

And I really didn't like how this war was tearing us apart here at home. I wasn't sure all the kids protesting was the right thing to do. But they were scared so they were yelling and trying to get this thing over with. The war was changing the country in ways I don't think we had a clue about.

"I think if we can really go after him, hit 'em with everything we've got, we can turn this thing around. Make people forget Tet. Bring 'em to the peace table and talk seriously! But that won't happen until Charlie believes he's got no chance in hell of winning."

I could sense the twists and turns Don had to be feeling. He knew he was going into the most dangerous assignment of his career. He knew he had to do it in order to earn the next promotion. And he wanted to believe in the president and the policy guys and his chain of command that were sending him into the darkness of the Mekong Delta. His faith was going to be sorely tested and he knew it. And here three whiskeys into his last night in the States he was talking bravely and saluting his orders to go into battle.

"Yeah, I feel for you guys. Our war was a lot simpler. Go overseas one way and beat the Germans. Go overseas the other way and beat the Japs."

"Yessir, it surely was. I've studied PT boat tactics and those Japanese were tricky, boy! Running in and around all those islands. You had to watch your ass! But that doesn't mean shit in 'Nam. Charlie doesn't have a damn thing on the water. Except booby trapped Saipans. They draw you up into tribs too narrow to turn around in. Ambush you like Indians did with the cavalry in ravines.

"Headquarters likes using gunboats to run the point. Keep going until you make contact. Best you can do is flush 'em out, then hope like hell you get air support real quick. Or maybe work a job with the grunts and squeeze 'em by the short hairs."

I tried to imagine what that operation would be like and I couldn't. Don kept going.

"You ever hear of noodling?" He laughed as he said this.

"No! What the hell's that?" thinking maybe he was going off into exotic Vietnamese sexual practices.

"One of my buddies from the Academy—Roger Ford—he's from Huntsville, Alabama. For fun on weekends folks down there go noodling. That's catching big ass catfish by sticking your arm into some muddy lake water and reaching for the underside of a log. That's where the big ones like to hang out."

Here Don rolled up his sleeve and stuck his right arm out and wiggled it.

"You reach right in there and hope that big fish just chomps down on it." Then he reached over with his left hand and grabbed his right wrist. "Then you yank your arm back quick and hope that cat's still hangin' on when you bring him up." He laughed as he mimicked the motion of landing a big fish with a bare arm.

"That's noodling! And you better damn well hope it's just a catfish on your arm and not a snapping turtle or a water moccasin."

I was sincerely impressed. "Have you ever... done that?"

"Naw! But Roger's showed me pictures of ones he's caught. Said he'd take me if I ever made it down there. And I just might someday."

Just as I was wondering why Don wanted to talk about noodling, he said in a slower voice as he rolled his sleeve back down, "I think going after Charlie in the Delta is going to be like noodling. You just reach down there in that dark stinky water and hope he decides to take a nibble on your hand. Then—

wham!—you yank him out and it's all over. And you damn well hope it's Charlie you got and not some cobra."

We paused at that. I looked over my shoulder and saw that most of the restaurant had emptied out. We were the only ones left at the bar. I was almost ready to go. Then I asked the question I probably shouldn't have. But I liked this young officer. And I didn't like the idea he was shipping out to an uncertain fate.

"Do you think we can win?"

The barkeep came over to see if we wanted another round. We both waved him off. I made a quick motion with my hand that meant bring my check.

Don looked at me long and hard. It was not an unfriendly stare. It was like I had read his mind. It was *the* question that hung over all the talk and laughing and bravado.

"Jack, if you were one of those long hairs I see hanging around the Lincoln Memorial and you'd asked me that I'd probably punch you in the nose and not regret it a second. Because they don't want us to win this war. They'd like it just fine if Charlie kicked our ass and let the whole country go over to the Commies. Then you can kiss Laos and Cambodia goodbye too. Then the line's back at Thailand. Or Malaysia. Or even back to Indonesia. Take your pick."

Here he paused and took a last look at what remained of the whiskey, then finished it off. Now he was ready to finish off this conversation.

"But I can see you're an honest guy and you deserve an honest answer. If we wanted to commit a million troops and maybe take another five or ten years and maybe organize a real campaign to take Hanoi, then, yeah, we can win this fuckin' war. But we've half-assed it from the beginning. So now President Nixon has to do his 'Peace With Honor' thing. Shit, we didn't do any peace-with-honor crap with Hitler or Hirohito. It was their unconditional *su-ren-der*. So there's your answer."

Don was off his stool, peeling a few bills from a small wad to pay his tab. Then he stuck his hand out.

"Jack, it was nice meetin' ya. In three days I'll be in Saigon. In five, I'll be leading my squad up some dirty ass part of the Mekong. With any luck by this time next year I'll be Lieutenant Commander Michak humpin' it at the Pentagon and home every night for my son's Little League games."

"Don, I enjoyed our talking too. I wish you luck. Or maybe good noodling."

We both laughed and then he was gone into the night. I sat a minute longer to crunch the last couple cubes in my Coke. Then I, too, was gone.

Chapter 16 — New Haven

I was up and out early the next day, but not before I'd scribbled a few notes about Lt. Michak. I didn't want to forget our little talk. Here's a haiku I wrote for him:

Lieutenant Michak
Sings soft Mekong songs into
His heart of darkness

Many years later I was in Washington, D.C. and visited the then-new Vietnam Memorial. I looked for his name and didn't see it. I smiled a little hoping that meant he made it back in one piece. And maybe he got to ride that Pentagon desk and watch his boy play baseball.

I'd decided to try and make New Haven. This was getting into the dicey part of the trip where I had to hope like hell no one recognized me. After Albers would be Olson and Gloucester. And I'd be close to all my old places in New York and Boston. Albers had never met me, but Olson had. I'd let the beard get a little thicker. And I'd get another haircut before I saw him. There wasn't anything I could do about my Lowell accent and roots. But with Ruth as a cover, I hoped Charles wouldn't be the wiser

The drive over and under Chesapeake Bay was spectacular. The bridge and tunnel system had opened up a few years before. Leading right out of Norfolk, it's 20 miles across, bisecting bay from ocean kind of like a big dashed line, before dropping you at Cape Charles. I've been across lots of bridges—the Golden Gate has been and always will be my favorite—but this was as pretty and awesome as anything. Then from the bottom of Delmarva it was a straight shot up US 13 through little old Virginia towns like Birdsnest and Accomac and Mappsville. I was into Maryland before noon. An hour later I made tiny Delaware. Stopping for gas in Dover, I plotted the next leg of the drive. Soon I'd be outside Philly and then on to New Jersey and New York with New Haven just beyond. Interstate 95 all the way.

I got through Philly OK, but the closer I got to New York I could feel the pull. Just jump off the Jersey Pike, cut through the Lincoln Tunnel and dive right back into the old places. If I did where would I go? Upper West Side? East Side? The Village? I thought about all those crazy apartments and crazier bars and clubs where we all met for the first times and started getting our heads around new ways of thinking and talking and writing. We *were* angel-headed hipsters. Bursting with ideas. Reading strange books and thinking they were wonderful and not wanting to waste a minute before talking about them with somebody. Not just somebody. Somebody who understood. Who could get it. Ideas that could overthrow all the old crap and start fresh with something new and big and wonderful.

I wondered who was still left there. Allen? For sure. Somewhere. I had the sense Allen would always be there. Burroughs? Maybe. Probably rubberbanding his arm and making new friends out of his hallucinations. Holmes? Yes. He'd never leave. Huncke? Probably still hustling a fix and trying to stay out of jail. But no Neal. Neal was dead. He was never for New York anyway. He was a shooting star that needed a big sky to burn across. Which he did. Now he was gone. The others were scattered. Some out on the West Coast. Hanging with Ferlinghetti. And with Snyder and Duncan and maybe Ken Patchen.

The women were all gone too. Scattered in their own women ways, most to families and kids and hopes for nice houses and not a lot of bills. There wasn't any surprise to this. We were a generation older now. Middle-aged. "Respectable." Supposed to be writing from the comfort of upper East Side apartments. Or teaching at leafy universities and getting invited to lecture at pretty campuses to kids who were bright and confused just like we had been, looking for answers—maybe—from old men like we were then. Even showing up on TV once in a while. Not out bumming around some Times Square bar in the middle of the day. Or limping into some alleyway deep in the night with a bottle of Thunderbird and maybe a girl. Or driving around from place to place, crashing coast to coast and not caring what the next day brought, if the next day came at all.

I thought about Memere's apartment in Queens where I did so much writing. It wasn't much of a place, but it was enough. And before then my great-aunt's place in Brooklyn where I landed fresh out of Lowell doing another year of prep before I could start at Columbia. I'm glad they were glad to have me, but I couldn't wait to get out. Wolfe's line about not going home again is cliché now, but that's because a large part of it is true. You can't go back to the place you were before. It's not there. Like the Greek guy said, you never step in the same river twice. New York used to be as close to home as anything after Lowell. Used to be. I kept going.

Crossing the George Washington bridge, I maneuvered through Harlem and the Bronx with more memories and more temptations, then hooked north into Westchester before sliding into suburban, wealthy Connecticut. Greenwich. Stamford. Darien. I thought of the Columbia and Barnard girls who'd come from those towns. Nice girls from nice families with hot shot lawyer and business executive dads who rode in comfortable train cars every day to Manhattan skyscrapers and fat paychecks. Raised by happy homemaker moms.

I used to think they had it made. School all paid for. Summers out on the Island. Or maybe upstate or even Europe. Then marriage right after that. With nice homes to move into just like the ones they grew up in. Making babies with safe, secure, prosperous husbands just like their fathers. Raising them into respectable kids just like they had been. Then going off to fine colleges just like they did. So the cycle repeats.

I could've had any number of them. Could've finished my degree. Married. Maybe been talked into trying out for grad school or even business school. Started teaching or join the firm. Kids. Had a big, nice house that would've made Memere cry for different reasons. Life would have been settled. And good in many ways. But I didn't. Couldn't. That's been one of the big mysteries. Why not? Was it just the running-away laziness Gerard was haunting me with? But I wasn't lazy! I'd worked my ass off at hard, hard jobs. Spent months on top of a mountain by myself watching for fires. Nearly starved to death trying to get out and see the country. Why had I been so fixed on becoming a writer? What was it about the Duluoz family that made it a "legend" anyway, one worth writing about? Why was it more important to thumb rides and jump boxcars and throw a rucksack over my shoulder than sit in commuter comfort reading the *New York Times* every day on my way to some plush office in Midtown? Why had I decided to roll in California dirt with a brown-skinned girl instead of in a Connecticut colonial with a beautiful blonde? Why was I a writer instead of an editor like Giroux, passing life-or-death judgments on poor slobs like me, then retiring to some club for martini lunches?

I was still searching for answers. Even after all the serious books and silly poems I'd written, I still wanted to know more. Maybe because Gerard had died so young, so innocent. So unworthy of death. Maybe because the world of business didn't interest me. Couldn't interest me. I'd watched it kill my dad. People making decisions about his life until they'd squeezed all the life out. Maybe it was because the world of *ideas*, of knowing first things, was much more important. But not ideas just for ideas. That's something that gets stuck in some university building and just dies there. I wanted to know how people *lived* with their ideas. What they believed in. Where they were headed with their lives. What moved them. Much more challenging. Much more about *life*. Because the more I could know about life—their lives—maybe then I could better understand my life—and my death. And if I could understand death, maybe I could find a way to cheat it. Maybe.

I jumped off 95 at the US 1 exit just past Milford and found another cheap place for the night where old Ford wagons sitting out front looked right at home. Even though it was just evening, I'd done a lot of driving and was ready to crash. If Neal'd been along we'd have hit the bars and craziness would've followed. Instead I bought a city map and found Albers' street. I'd look him up in the morning. I got a can of soda out of the motel machine, made myself a sandwich and watched a little TV. I kind of wondered what I'd find meeting him and his wife. I guessed they were older than Ruth. I'd use my journal for a notebook. I made a few notes about things to talk about.

But what if it turned into a dead end? What if Albers didn't give a hoot about old Black Mountain? What if his mind was gone? What should I write Ruth then? I knew how important this was to her. And she'd talked me into believing it was important for me too. I didn't want to disappoint her. But when the trail's gone cold...

I'd written into lots of dead ends over the years. Stories that turned out to be nothings. That's just the way it is. Not every idea you have is brilliant. Not every book you write's gonna win a Pulitzer. But then some of them turned into somethings. Writing can be like that. Sometimes you think you're onto something big and you go at it like hell on wheels. Then somewhere along the line...maybe ten pages in...maybe

20...maybe 50...you realize there's nothing there. So you have to stop and throw it all away.

But sometimes magic happens. Sometimes you go so far down into a story you have no idea where you are. But you keep sloshing and slopping around in the darkness. Then by some miracle you pop back up and you're at the end. And you look at it and say "Hey, that's pretty good." And maybe somebody else will agree with you. And maybe that somebody is a publisher who sees a way to make a buck off what you wrote. And maybe that's OK, because you need to make a buck too.

Writing this memoir has been different because a lot of my early writing came from what I experienced right then and there. Or I tried to get that down when I did write, even if it was months, even years, later. But I had my notes and a lot of them were written right when things were happening. And then I'd write like I was putting everything down on paper just as it happened right in front of me. Because that was what I was aiming for—to get people to feel things as I felt them right then. To feel the immediacy of life. The rawness of it. Sometimes the raw joy. Lots of times the raw sadness. But to be right there. "First thought, best thought."

Now I'm writing things down from over thirty years ago. Trying to remember. Trying to tell you what the country looked like and felt like then while I'm typing here looking out my little Marina District window. So much has changed. So much. My notebooks help. But I want you to feel 1970. And all the years after. 1970 was a dark time. A damn dark time. The beautiful, flowering sixties were over, at least by the calendar. But it was more than the calendar. Some say the sixties ended when Nixon got to be president. An innocence played with and lost. Now there was an ugliness all over. An anger that wouldn't let go. A war that would not end. Cities that burned and died. Children growing into adults but still fighting their parents and feeling all the anger and lostness of it all and diving into holes from which some never came out. Leaders dying. Leaders lying. A country wanting to fulfill the promise of its founding and having a damn hard time doing it. Maybe the promise was too big. Maybe the idea of America was too much. That's what 1970 felt like to me. That's why I was OK with a can of soda and a sandwich and watching some dumb TV show that first night in New Haven.

Actually, it wasn't so dumb. It was "The Johnny Cash Show." I don't remember the show being all that great. But I liked Johnny Cash. Loved his "Ring of Fire" song: "Love is a burning thing/And it makes a fiery ring/Bound by wild desire/I fell into a ring of fire." I knew all the words and would sing right along with Johnny when he came on the radio. Made me think of my firewatch times up on Desolation Peak when I could see real fires burning ten, fifteen miles away. Lightning strikes. Sometimes the boys would go fight 'em. More often rain from that or a following storm would put them out before they got close. Then I'd think of even hotter times with Anne and Joan and later Carolyn when I was bound by wild desire for their fiery bodies. Now I just watched Johnny talk to people and introduce other singing acts. To be honest, the show felt like Johnny had cashed in. He wasn't singing about or to cons and their hard lives at Folsom Prison anymore. Now he was hamming it up for middle class housewives who maybe wished they'd gone for a little danger when they were younger and instead were now going moonie over middle-aged Johnny. When it was over, I turned off the light and fell into a deep, dreamless sleep.

The next morning came early and overcast. But instead of jumping out of bed eager to find Albers, I just lay there. Why? Now I felt like a fool. I didn't feel like finding Albers. The whole Black Mountain thing felt foolish. I lay there thinking what could I do for Ruth really? I mean, I wasn't really going to travel all over the country running down this person or that person just because they'd gone to a now-dead college a lifetime ago and somehow would go all ga-ga because some strange writer shows up at their doorstep asking goofy questions. Now I felt like I'd just taken a woman's money as easily as ol' Huncke picked a wallet in a Times Square bar. I should make a run for it and just keep going. Skip New Haven. Skip Gloucester. Hell, skip Quebec too! Just drive. Drive and drive and drive. To hell with soft Black Mountain! Let's get back out to real mountains! Let's get out to wild Wyoming and titanic Tetons. And snow mountainous Montana. And the black Black Hills of South Dakota. And even wilder and crazier Alaska. To hell with Gerard! And Ruth! And Jo too! What do I need any of them for? I'm *Jack Kerouac*! King of the Beats! I've written more goddam books than anybody else I know. Why do I need to go off writing about some podunk college that crapped out a long time ago? I hate being made to do something I don't want to do.

I sat at the edge of the bed and wished I had a smoke. And a drink. Something—anything—that would let me hole up in this place for three or four days. Hell, maybe a week! Maybe I'd write something. Maybe I wouldn't. Who cares? I've done my job. They can read my books. I've said all I've got to say.

You've been given so much, Ti Jean. You've been given a second chance. Maybe a third even since the beach and the lighthouse.

I about hit the ceiling. There he was again! Jesus Christ, Gerard! Sitting cross-legged on top of the little black and white TV! Saying the same things since the hospital. I jumped back towards my pillows. He didn't even wait for me to say hello or anything.

And this man you are going to see. Maybe he knows a little more than you do!

I just stared back at my brother. He wore the same clothes as last time. The same sad look on his face. His eyes were fixed on mine. So big and soulful.

But a little pissed off too, to be honest. This was getting creepy, him showing up unannounced again and again.

"Gerard, I don't want to. I'm tired, Gerard."

Of course you don't want to. You never want to. He almost seemed to sigh with resignation. And he looked at me some more, like a parent trying to figure out what to do with a wayward child. Then he said, *Do you really think you are done? Then come! I will take you.*

I stared at him long and hard. His words sounded like a relief, an answer. Yes! Take me! I moved a little towards the end of the bed. He didn't move, staying right on top of the TV, just staring with a slight thin line of smile across his thin lips. He extended his thin right arm to me. His little fingers wiggled gently, inviting me to come. All I had to do was reach across that small space between the end of the bed and the dresser where the TV perched. I started to extend my still solid left arm, leaning forward a little. I wanted to touch him! Then he could take me and it would all be over. Here in New Haven. The end of the road. Inside a little motel. With an old Ford wagon parked outside. It would be so easy. So easy...

"Maybe...maybe I'm not ready yet, Gerard. I don't know. I was ready to go in the hospital. But you came and talked me out of it. Then you sat right in the middle of Ruth's table and talked me into this. I looked for you at Hatteras. If you'd come then, I'd have gone with you. Now you're here again. And you say come with you. And I want to. I *want* to. But maybe not just yet. Maybe...maybe I can go see Albers."

I waited for him to say "Come." I wanted my brother to make it easy for me. Our fingers nearly touched. Then Gerard pulled his arm back. Not fast. Very deliberately. Almost seductively. Like he was trying to pull me towards him. Like he wanted to make sure I reached—really reached—for him. But instead of reaching for him I just stared. Something held me back. Maybe if he'd reach for me again I would've let him take my hand in his little one. Instead he smiled a Cheshire Cat smile that I never remembered seeing before. Then he held up his translucent right hand and gave me a one motion wave. Without another word he was gone.

I continued staring into the space where he had been. Had he really been there? Why had he come at all? Or was my too-fucked-up mind playing more and more tricks with me? I didn't really know. I closed my eyes and shook my head, hoping when I opened them again he'd be there. But he wasn't. "Gerard!" Nothing. "Gerard?" Maybe I was losing it again just like I'd almost done days ago in North Carolina. I didn't *feel* bad. No boomboombooms. But I also knew that Gerard showing up like a little Buddha on top of the TV wasn't supposed to be part of the morning routine either.

I got into the shower, turned it up extra hot and stayed there a good long time. The pulsing of the water stinging my skin calmed me down. I still didn't know if Gerard was "real" or not. Part of me was really glad he showed up when he did. It was like he was giving me the choice to stay or go. If I stayed, maybe he'd be around to help me do whatever it is I wanted to do. If I went with him, maybe I'd find that peace I'd been looking for for so long. Now I felt a different peace and it felt good. My head was clearer now. Maybe I could go see Albers. Maybe he would have something to say that I could use for the book. I wondered if I could ask him about getting away from the Nazis. About Ruth and her English friend and Goering. I pulled myself together, put on some better clothes, stopped by the office to pay for another night, then drove towards downtown looking for a place to eat. An hour later I was ready to meet these people that Ruth adored.

I found the Albers house in West Haven pretty easily. It sat on a quiet street. Not big, but it looked comfortable from the road. When I knocked, a woman about my age answered the door. She was not who I expected, but then I thought maybe she's a housekeeper or something. She looked at me through the screen, a little bit wary.

"Mrs. Albers?"

"No."

"I'm sorry. I was looking for the Albers residence. This was the one given to me by a good friend of theirs."

"They moved."

That figured. Now that I'd finally gotten the balls to go find them and do what I'd promised Ruth, they were gone.

"Do you know, uh, where they went? Are they OK?"

"Who are you?" She'd taken half a step back from the screen as though ready to slam the door in my face. I figured I'd better spill it quick.

"My name's Jack Moriarty. I'm a writer. I'm doing a book on Black Mountain College where they taught a long time ago. A mutual friend said this is where I could find them."

She studied me a bit longer leaning now a little closer to the screen.

"You're a writer. And you say a friend of yours sent you to find them?"

"She's a mutual friend. Lives in Black Mountain. She's known Josef and Anni for years and years. She asked me to write a book about the college and said they should be the first ones I talk to."

I hoped that would be enough information to get her past the suspicious stage and maybe to helping me out.

"Look, the people who know them know they moved. You're not the first to pop out of nowhere looking for them. They're quite old now and want their privacy respected, especially from strangers dropping in from the Black Hills."

"Black *Mountain*. It's in North Carolina."

"OK. Whatever. They sold me the house with the understanding that I wouldn't bother them with stragglers."

Now I was getting steamed. I wasn't a "straggler." I didn't need to be treated like a jerk. I upped the ante.

"Look, this woman helped get them out of Nazi Germany and over to Black Mountain. They've been friends longer than you and I have been alive. They might not even be alive now if not for her. So I don't think they would mind very much if I stopped by and brought greetings."

She had her face almost pressing the screen now. She wasn't unpleasant to look at. But she also seemed to enjoy her role as the self-appointed Albers watchdog. Made me think again of Kesey's Ratched.

"What's her name?"

"Ruth Parker. Do you know her?"

"No." I could hear some weakening in her voice.

"Well, that's too bad. Because she's a helluva woman and done more in her life than you and I put together, and I've done a helluva lot myself."

"And you said your name was?"

"Jack Moriarty."

Now she seriously paused.

Finally she asked, "You know where Orange is?"

"Yes."

Then she gave me their address. I scribbled it into my notebook. Then I wrote down my name and Ruth's and "Black Mountain," tore it out and offered it to her.

"OK, thanks. Here's my name and hers again, if you want to remember who asked you next time you see them."

A hand slipped out from a now slightly opened door and took it quickly. "Can I tell them we talked?"

"Yes."

"And your name?"

"Sheila." I could tell that was all she was going to give me.

"OK. Thanks, Sheila. I'm sure they'll thank you too for putting us in touch."

I turned away towards the car, but I could feel she was watching every step. She was still standing at the door as I pulled away. Jeez! What a way to make a guy feel like a creep!

I found the other house pretty easily too. Orange was a little more country than West Haven. This time when I knocked, I was pretty sure it was Anni who answered.

"Mrs. Albers?"

"Ja."

"My name is Jack Moriarty."

"Ja?"

"I'm a writer. I'm doing a book on Black Mountain, the college, for Ruth Parker."

Her eyes got wide at the name.

"Ja?"

"And, well, she suggested that I come up and talk with you and Mr. Albers about it."

"Now?"

"Yes."

"How did you find us? She does not know we have moved."

"Yes, I know. I stopped at your old house and Sheila gave me the address."

"Sheila gave you the address?"

"Yes and I'm sorry for not calling ahead. I just got into town last night and..."

"You wait."

She walked away from the door a few paces.

"Josef!"

From deeper in the house I heard a muted "Ja?"

"Someone is here. About Black Mountain. He vants to talk."

"No! I am busy."

A pause.

"He comes from Ruth Parker." (With her accent, it came out sounding like "root".)

Another pause.

"Ruth?"

"Ja."

Another pause.

"What does he vant? Money?"

"No! He's a writer. *Sagt er ein buch uber* Black Mountain *schreibt.*"

Another pause.

"*Zehn minuten nur*. Then I must work."

Anni Albers turned back to me and the door. Then she held it open.

"Josef is very busy today. But he will talk a little while. Please, not too long. OK?" She smiled weakly as though she was used to being her husband's secretary.

I followed her into the living room. She pointed to a chair.

"Here you vait. May I get you some coffee?"

"Yes! That'd be great, thanks."

"Cream? Sugar?"

"No, black's fine. Thank you very much."

Then she disappeared with precise little steps into the kitchen. I could hear Josef rumbling about in another room, probably his studio.

The living room was a model of German orderliness. Shelves filled with books. Barely an inch of bare wall space, mostly paintings covering it, but also two moderately sized pieces of fabric art that I assumed were hers. Everything mounted precisely by size and perspective. The furniture was spare, but had the look of quality workmanship. A sofa. Two arm chairs flanking. A nice coffee table between. Another over-stuffed chair closer to the window with a reading table and lamp. The floor was solid wood mostly covered by an immense Persian rug showing wear at the ends.

In a second turn around the room, I saw a photo that I'd missed. It was smallish, maybe six inches by eight, almost overwhelmed by the paintings surrounding, some of which I guessed were Albers'. It was old, a black and white showing a group of six people crowded together and laughing or smiling at the camera. It looked like maybe it was in a restaurant or something. I leaned closer and recognized immediately a much younger Josef and Anni from the photos Ruth had shown me. On the far right was Ruth herself, looking even more glamorous and dazzling than in the old photos she'd shown me.

"Ah! I see you have found us already!"

Anni startled me, but her voice had a brightness that belied her years. She had slipped back in with a tray and a pot of coffee and three cups with saucers. Despite her age, she set it all on the table in one smooth motion.

"Yeah, guess I did. Ruth had shown me some pictures…from back then."

"Ja. That was a long time ago. Weimar Germany. The 20s. I think maybe that was her second visit to Berlin. When Josef was at Bauhaus. We were all so young then. And Ruth! She was beautiful."

"She still is, Mrs. Albers."

She smiled. "Oh! You may call me Anni. Please. Coffee?"

As she poured, I started telling her about meeting Ruth. Then I was interrupted with a simple, but authoritative, "Hello?"

I turned to meet a man about my height, thinner and shrunken some by age, but still very erect. The shock of white hair over his forehead was combed the same as it had been in all the pictures I'd seen of him stretching back 50 years. The eyes were very alert.

Intelligent, probing. Not unkind, but serious. He didn't look like a man in his eighties.

I extended my hand. "Mr. Albers. Hello, I'm Jack Moriarty. I'm a friend of Ruth Parker's. I'm writing a book for her about Black Mountain."

He shook it firmly, still taking his measure of me and trying to determine whether I was worth even "zehn minuten" of his time.

"Please, sit." He directed me to a high-backed chair; he and his wife took the sofa.

"And how is Ruth?" Anni jumped in as though she was long practiced in starting conversations for her husband.

"Oh, she's fine. I left her about a week and a half ago. But she's in very good health and was anxious to show me around both campuses."

Anni continued, "And now she wants you to write a book about the college?"

"Yes. But a different kind of book. She doesn't want a history. Or at least the boring, dried up old things that are usually written about places that are closed. She's asked me to talk to the people who taught there, who studied there, and come up with something that captures what they think the college was really all about...the spirit of Black Mountain. Something that says not just that it was different, but *how* it was different and why." Geez! I'd just met these people and already I was making speeches!

Now Josef seemed to engage. He leaned forward slightly and said more to Anni than to me, "*Der Geist des Schwartzbergs*!" and laughed at his joke. I didn't get quite get it.

She smiled back at him and interpreted for me. "He means, 'The Spirit of Black Mountain.'" I heard the "geist" and guessed maybe he meant "ghost."

"Yes! Exactly! She told me all about John Rice and his ideas for a college. Then about meeting you in Germany. During the Weimar. And then about... helping you...leave."

Their eyes widened at this.

Josef got serious. "She told you...all that?"

"Yes. Sounds like it was a pretty dicey business."

Both seemed confused with my choice of words.

"Dicey?" he asked.

"Sorry. Dangerous. She talked about her friend Bill and...Goering." I wasn't sure if this was territory I should get into or not. But I had the feeling with them as with Sheila that I'd better show my "credentials" pretty quick if this meeting was going to get anywhere.

"Oh! Ja! Goering! Goebbels! Hitler! All of dem! Mediocre men. Fools! But murderers. Blood thirsty murderers. And they had the people. So we were fools too."

After Josef said this, we were all silent for a moment, letting the words hang in the air.

Anni restarted the conversation. "Ruth was very, very good to us. And not only to us! To others too. Without her, I think Josef and I we would be...kaput." She kind of threw both hands into the air as she said this.

"She seemed angry that she couldn't get more out. Sounds like Goering reneged on some part of the deal."

Now Josef jumped in again, fueled by anger of the memories.

"Of course, he reneged! Who was he? A fat playboy who loved nothing as much as the money he could bribe. Or the art he could steal. Or...or...the boys he could play with." The words came out almost like spit with Goering's face as their target.

"How bad was it then, before the war I mean?"

Anni answered.

"Oh, it was so bad! And we all saw it coming! How many times we talked about the Nazis and their brown shirts and their stupid rallies. They could have been stopped. That is the worst thing! They could have been stopped!"

Josef turned to her with a calming reply. This looked like a conversation they'd had many, many times before.

"Anni, *die Leute schwach waren. Wissen wir das.*"

She nodded slowly, knowingly. Then he turned to me and translated.

"The people were weak. We were beaten by the first war. A war no one expected to lose. Even me! The Kaiser and his fool generals...ach! Then we were beaten into the ground by the terms of surrender. The reparations. The land. Then we were beaten by the collapse, the Depression. We were like chickens ready to be chopped." He gave a very precise movement of his hand to emphasize his point.

I didn't know what to say so I tried to lighten things up a bit. "Ruth told me about New Year's in Berlin with you and her Charlie Chaplin costume. Guess she made quite an impression."

At this both Albers laughed at the memory.

"Ja! Oh, she was so convincing!" Annie said. "But when they said she had kissed...Hitler. Ach!" Her nose wrinkled and she shook her head.

"They made much fun of us that night, Anni. Of course, even we didn't know how bad the Nazis truly were. Before the elections they were bullies. Afterward, they were...monsters."

Another pause. I hesitated, but out came this next question: "Did she tell you she was Jewish also?"

The question hit like a sledgehammer. Their silence spoke volumes.

Both Albers leaned towards me, shocked.

"NO!!" they said together. "How?"

"It was a story she told me at dinner the second night. She'd been talking to her father about the need to do something for the Jews in Europe. This must have been in the early thirties because I guess she'd already met you two."

The Albers nodded in agreement.

"But he had put her off and put her off until, I guess, he finally broke down and told her about their own heritage. His father and mother came over from Germany before our Civil War. I guess he got in some kind of political trouble. He'd been a merchant there and some friends helped him get set up in Virginia. Changed his name from Packenberg or something to Parker. Then he moved the family to Black Mountain to escape the worst of our war. He set up some kind of dry goods store and later on when Ruth's father was grown they started a bank."

The Albers were rapt.

"I guess he knew how people here felt about the Jews because one reason he didn't want Ruth running around trying to help them—you—was he feared that if Black Mountain people found out the Parkers were Jewish they'd pull all their money and he'd be ruined."

"Ja," Josef said slowly. "What he believed has truth to it. The Jews everywhere chased, kicked out, gassed. Things are much better for us today. But that does not mean the old feelings have gone away entirely. The Black Mountain people were polite to us. But that was all. We knew they said things behind our backs. But at least they didn't come to us with brown shirts and torches in the night.

"So, how did Ruth get the money to...to help us?" Here Josef again looked back at Anni both of them reliving the pain and horror of forty years before.

"She said he came home one night with a briefcase filled with cash. Twenty thousand dollars, I think. He gave it to her and said use it. Guess she carried it all the way from Black Mountain to Berlin."

Now the Albers were shaking their heads at the wonder of it. They'd known about the money that bought their freedom. But they'd never asked, or Ruth never said, where it came from. And then to learn that she and they were bound by more than a love of art or a defunct college.

I decided not to talk about the sexual part of the transaction. That was for her to share, not me. But I did add this, "She said the deal with Goering was for twenty to get visas, but he only delivered twelve. She was very sad and angry about that. Apparently these were friends of yours and she never learned what happened to them."

Anni's eyes filled with tears. Josef removed his glasses and wiped them carefully. Finally he said in a voice world weary, "Ja. We did not know either. Then after the war we learned. Auschwitz."

I didn't want to ask more. We sat in silence again. I stared at the table wondering if I'd worn them out with this talk and missed my chance to ask about the college. Finally, Anni stood up slowly and reaching for the pot asked, "Would you like some more coffee...Jack?"

I held my cup almost like a supplicant. She poured and sat down. It was Josef who broke the silence this time. "So, you did not come here to talk about old Jews. You want to know about Black Mountain College." Now he was looking directly at me. I had earned my spot in his living room. "Zehn minuten" had long passed.

"Yes. Do you mind if I take some notes?"

Albers nodded and I picked up my journal. Then he smiled and said, "I am a teacher, you know. Sometimes when we start talking it is very hard to stop."

I laughed at this and for the first time began to feel comfortable with them.

Anni stood up and said, "Josef, you talk. I am going to start *Mittagessen*—a lunch. Will you join us for that, Jack? I am going to cook some noodles and add a little chicken."

"Yes, thank you. I mean, if that's OK with you...Josef." A home cooked meal!

"Ja, ja! I am sorry only that Ruth is also not here to join us. Maybe she will come visit. You say she is well...Jack?"

"Yes, quite well. She has a housekeeper who helps with the cleaning and cooking. But she drives a nice, new Cadillac around town. And people know her and respect her. I got the idea she's very much involved in the business of the bank and other things."

Anni walked briskly into the kitchen. Now Josef and I got down to business as well.

"Gut! That is our Ruth. She and John were quite a pair..." Then realizing he was saying something maybe I didn't know about, he added, "...she would help raise money for us. She could be very...what is the word?...*persuasive*."

"She showed me the rock, Josef." I wanted to let him know I knew about her and Rice.

Now it was my turn to say something else that he didn't know about.

"The...rock?"

"The stone they buried by the tree, down the hill a bit from Lee Hall." I could see this was news, too, to Albers. "It's about this big." I held my hands out so he could understand that it was a stone, not a boulder. I definitely had the old man's attention with this one.

"They wrote a line of Seneca's on it. 'Ars longa est. Vita brevis.' Then added their initials. I guess it was their stab at immortality, although they figured by the time anyone found it they'd have no idea whose initials they were."

"Yes, I know the Seneca. But I did not know John and Ruth, they were...*Jungen*!" He laughed, then saw the confusion on my face. "Teenagers!" He laughed again and then continued more reflectively.

"His wife, Nell. She was a very, very good woman. And their son, Daniel, wonderful boy! But she could not compete with the likes of Ruth Parker. I could see from the start John was...*verliebt*...in love.

"They did very well in hiding it, unlike some of the others. And it helped that Ruth was in New York most of the time. Still, when they were together, it was *ein Blitz*...lightning...between them. I did not approve. I did not disapprove. It was what it was."

Another pause. Then refocusing.

"So, she took you to both campuses? And...how do they look? It has been a long time since we were there."

"I guess they look about the same. As you probably know they're used now by churches for camps. So not quite the same crowd as when the college was there."

Albers nodded.

"Do you know who designed the new buildings? At the lake...what is its name?"

"Lake Eden?"

"Yes, of course! How could I forget that! Is that little island still out there in the middle?"

"Yes it is."

"Ah, yes, sometimes we would make it a picnic."

"Ruth has a picture of you and Anni there along with some other people."

"Ah, yes, maybe I remember that one! It was taken soon after the war, I think. Walter was there. Gropius. He was the designer of those buildings. Beautiful! We were together at Bauhaus. And Ise his wife. And Dreier. Jean Varda. Maybe some others."

I couldn't help with the other names. But I wrote down the ones he said.

"You know Walter is dead now?"

"No."

Albers sighed.

"Yes. Last July. He was 85. I am 82. We are all old now."

"I think Ruth mentioned him designing the Studies Hall and the Dining Hall."

"Ja! But not only Walter. Breuer too. They worked together. Magnificent! But what they wanted to do, we only did a small part. We did not have the money to build what they thought we should have. And of course it was too much for John. He wanted to be modern in thought. But maybe not modern in action. He was not there when we built the buildings."

"What happened?" I kind of remembered Ruth saying something, but what it was escaped me.

"John, he was a dreamer. But sometimes his '*Arbeit*' did not match his '*Traumen*.'"

He saw my confusion with his German. "I am sorry. Arbeit. Work. Traumen. Dreams. He talked big. But his work not so much. So he was asked to leave."

Ruth hadn't told me this part of their story. "When was this?"

"1940. But…it had started years before. He liked being the Big Show. But we did not want Big Shows. We wanted everyone to be a show. *Ein tausend* little shows making even bigger Big Show. *Verstehen Sie*?" He sounded sad.

"Yes. I do. This was something Ruth did talk about. I mean trying to have a college that was a real democracy and where you tried to expose students to all kinds of learning and experiences. Sounds like the kind of place I wished I'd gone to."

"And where did you go?"

"Columbia." Oops. Big mistake. I'd told Ruth Boston College.

"Ah, yes, Columbia. A very good school. And you did not like it there?"

"Not really. Maybe I wasn't ready. Maybe it just wasn't a good fit."

"And what did you study?"

"Writing. English."

"Of course. And now, what kind of writing do you do?" I got the feeling he was asking more as a teacher than someone trying to zero in on my credentials.

"Travel writing. For magazines."

"Ahhhh...and this is how you met Ruth?" He was being polite, not impressed.

I laughed a little.

"Yeah, kinda. I got an assignment to write something about western North Carolina. I know a couple guys on the West Coast who'd always talked about the college. So I tried to find it and couldn't. Took a stop at the library to find out it'd closed. So happened the librarian's a good friend of Ruth's. She found me the next morning at a restaurant."

Albers seemed to enjoy hearing my story.

"So now she has—what is the word?—*side-tracked* you?"

"Yeah. Maybe. Not really. I'll finish my story. But we worked out a deal to get a book written too. As long as it's the right kind of book." Albers nodded slowly.

"Yes. I think I understand. Ruth would want something...different. Better. Well, she must think you are more than just a magazine writer if she picked you to write her book."

Ouch. I felt the same sting as I had with Ruth. She had pricked me with purpose. Albers just seemed to be making the passing observation of an intellectual. I tried not to take it personally. Of course, I couldn't tell him who I really was much as I would've liked.

Anni reappeared to announce lunch and we followed her to a sunny alcove off the kitchen where a third chair had been added to their small table. A steaming casserole of chicken and noodles sat in the center with a plate of thick sliced bread and another of butter off to the side. Three plates, three glasses of water.

For the next hour they shared happy stories —mostly—of the college they had helped start. Names started rolling off their tongues. Josef went on at length also about Black Mountain's philosophy of combining mental and physical labor. "This was not something on which all agreed, including John Rice.

But we could not have survived if we ourselves did not build the buildings and farm the land." I heard some of Josef's ideas about art and how it should be taught. I could tell right off he was a big believer in understanding how we see things and learning the rules of perspective and color and proportion. Work and work and work some more. "The rules are not rules to oppress. But you cannot build without a firm base of knowledge. How does what we do change all that surrounds? How can we expose the complex through the simple?" Clearly the teacher was enjoying teaching again.

He then asked who else I planned to talk to. When I mentioned Olson, he said something that surprised me, "I hear maybe he is not so well. Of course, that man was out of control! Everything in his life. Undisciplined! He was chaos. Everywhere! But he was not without his strengths also. Sometimes brilliant. His work on Melville. Marvelous! So American! His work on Mayans. He knew the power of reaching back to first causes. Drawing the line from them to the modern. Very good! But he was not a person to run a college! Maybe nobody could hold Black Mountain together. But Olson—pfft! Still, I hope he is well and he has not ruined his body with his drink."

I winced involuntarily at that last one.

We talked more about the war. Even though it'd been over for twenty-five years, it was very much with them still. "Very difficult for us. But it was for everyone. The Nazis and the Fascists, they had to be beaten totally and completely." He was cautious with his words here. "I am not for the politics now. I have seen too much politics. The Kaiser killed millions. Hitler killed millions and millions. Stalin killed millions and millions. Now we can kill *billions*. Just by pushing buttons! All I have seen of politics is murder. There must be better ways for human beings to live together. But we have to get rid of the madmen first. At this I throw up my hands! I am just an artist."

He asked about my service and I passed along the same lame story about the merchant marine and coming up with a bum knee when I tried out for the Navy. I don't think either of them was impressed. Of course, there's nothing impressive about it.

Even though he said he didn't want to talk any more about politics, he went on. "This Vietnam. Is madness. What is the United States doing? United States fights Hitlers. Not Ho Chi Minhs. It fights armies. Not little men in black pajamas. The students here they are protesting all the time.

"This man Nixon says he wants peace. But all he brings is more war. This is not good. The people were together fighting Hitler. But we are not together in this Vietnam."

Anni and I listened sympathetically. Then she added with a ferocity and a plea that surprised me. "We have seen so much evil and suffering! It is the curse of living a long life. How does one go on? The United States, we were blessed to be here and away from the war. But so many of our family and our friends were killed just for *being*...you ask why. You even ask God. Over and over...why? Why??"

If God had no answers, certainly I couldn't say anything that would mean anything to them. We fell silent. I thought of all the suffering I'd seen. All that I'd experienced. But somehow I felt inadequate to the level of suffering they were talking about. Yeah, I'd been hungry. Even to the point of starvation. But I'd never been starved to *death*.

Sure, I'd been scared about Nazi submarines and torpedoes in the night. But I'd never been marched into camps, gassed and stacked like cord wood to be burned by the next bunch to get the same treatment. Where was God in all that? Where was my happy Buddha? Where was fierce Mohammed? How does all the happy talk about turning other cheeks and waiting for rewards in heaven do anything to explain that kind of inhumanity? They were right. The madmen had to be eliminated. But how?

Josef added, weary now it seemed, "What does one do, but go on? What can one do, but create? My art is a protest against those who would destroy. We had that sense at Black Mountain! If we were not fighting Hitler with guns, we were fighting him with our ideas. Of course, not just Herr Hitler, but all the Hitlers. All the little Hitlers everywhere. Ach!"

I sensed maybe it was time to leave. I'd been there over two hours. When I said I should go, they both nodded. As we all stood he surprised me with, "You come tomorrow. Same time. I will have two students here. Two *Black Mountain* students. A little younger than you, I think. They maybe can help you with your story, yes?"

They both shook my hand warmly. Anni smiled, "We are glad Ruth sent you to us. We will talk more tomorrow, Jack."

With that I was off. It was still early afternoon. Lots of time to kill.

Chapter 17 — Progress

I stopped at a grocery store on the way back from Albers'. One of those little mom-and-pops run by an old Italian couple with a helper, maybe a grandson, working the shelves. You don't see much of them these days. I got more sodas, ice for the cooler, bologna, bread, chunk of cheese. The kind of stuff I'd been living off of ever since I left Lowell. And a pack of smokes. Camels. Maybe I shouldn't have. I'd promised the doc I'd quit. And I hadn't really missed them. But that one I had courtesy of Lieutenant Michak sure tasted good. Anyway, I got a pack. Just in case. But I passed on the Thunderbirds and Tokays racked up so prettily by the counter. Then I went back to the motel to write and think about the rest of the day and tomorrow.

As I opened the door to my room I peeked my head in first, just in case Gerard might be sitting on the TV again. Or maybe someplace else. But, nope, no Gerard. I was relieved and disappointed. I wasn't sure if his showing up was a sign I was losing my mind. Or if his not showing up was a sign I was losing my mind. I was no stranger to hallucinations, that's for sure. Those at least I knew came from some drug I'd swallowed or smoked. Or sometimes from being so hungry out on the road and having no idea where my next meal was coming from. But this was the third time he'd shown up since I'd gotten myself straightened out. I wasn't scared of him, or whatever madness he might represent. But I'd sure like to know who or what he was. And if he's there to help me end my folly, so be it. I'm ready. He's there for some reason. I'd sure like to know what it was or is.

After a couple hours, I decided to drive into New Haven and walk around. I didn't want to get close to campus, there was a decent chance somebody'd recognize me even with a jacket and cap and my beard. Walking a lot was something I was really glad I'd gotten into back in St. Pete. My legs felt better than they had in years. Between losing weight and cutting out the booze and smokes, felt like maybe I'd beaten that phlebitis. But also knew I had to keep it up or those old blood problems would creep back in and lay me low.

New Haven was the first northern city I'd been to in a while. I never went into St. Pete. Wasn't much to see there even though it was one of the oldest cities on the continent. But it just wasn't like New York or San Francisco or Mexico City. Or the fiery muscular cities of the Midwest—Cleveland, Detroit, Chicago, St, Louis. And I'd avoided the emerging cities of the South—Tampa, Atlanta, Charlotte. Maybe I should've gone to see Miami and its great Cuban population. Or back to jumpin' New Orleans and all its Burroughs memories. But before I landed in the hospital and dried out, I didn't have much desire to see or do much of anything. For a long time I'd just hidden out at Memere's and drank and sometimes made long, lonely calls into my dark, unholy nights.

So here I am walking the old, dirty, Negro streets of New Haven. It wasn't a big city, but it was a city. There was life on the streets. But it was a beat life. It didn't take long for me to feel it as a mad, angry city whose famous campus felt far, far away. I took my time. I've found if you hustle through a town, the town will hustle you away. If you want to get a good look at the people, you have to let them get a good look at you first. And I could feel dark, angry, Negro eyes on me. Just like I'd felt the narrow hipster eyes on me in New York. And the slitty, crazy, Oriental eyes on me in San Francisco. And the wide open, hemped up brown eyes of Mexico City. You learned to accept it. Learned to walk in a way that said "Hey, look at me all you want. I'm on these streets for the same reasons you are." And those eyes could see that. And those eyes left you alone.

I turned a corner and walked away from the main street to a block that looked even dirtier and sadder. I walked another block and looked down a street with more storefronts boarded and abandoned. Had American cities always been this way and I missed it or didn't care? Or did something change and I missed that too? There was a group of men gathered about halfway down this block that got my curiosity. A bar? Night club? Maybe there was something going on. I headed towards them.

I approached slowly. The group was small, maybe ten. Mostly young white guys, long hair, wearing Army surplus and jeans. One black guy was dressed the same way, but also had an enormous Afro. I wondered if maybe they were vets. They eyed me up as I got closer. But I didn't feel the fear you get when you know you're gonna get jumped for no reason at all. They parted a little for me thinking I was just passing through. Then one said, "You lookin' for the debate?" That stopped me. Given my age, maybe they were surprised by me too.

"No, don't think so. What debate?"

"Direction for the Movement, man." This came from a short, intense man I hadn't even seen until he spoke up. I didn't have to guess which "Movement" he was talking about.

"Oh. No. Just out for a walk, that's all. Saw you guys. Thought maybe this was a place to eat."

Another guy asked, "You from around here?"

Same kind of small-minded questions just like the ones Jimmy asked me down in Georgia.

"Nope. Just passin' through."

The short guy said, "Watch it, Dean. Could be a narc." Everyone tensed with that last word, including me.

The one he called Dean replied, "Might be, Dom. But I don't think so. I can smell narcs a mile away. He doesn't smell like a narc. Besides, he's too old."

"I don't know, man. Narcs're gettin' good at lookin' like they ain't narcs, you know?"

While they debated my legitimacy I looked past them to the storefront.

The Militant Bookstore

In the window was a large poster announcing an anti-Vietnam War protest in a couple of weeks. Next to it and smaller was a crudely made poster for the night's event: a debate between lefties about the war and how to end it. I'd been through countless "debates" all over the country with everyone from Allen to my brother-in-law. They tired me out and bored me beyond recognition. I hated politics. I hated war. I hated politics that brought war. I hated protests that did everything to get people pissed off and nothing to stop war.

I was about to move on when the tall one—Dean—asked in a surprisingly gentle voice, "You a vet?"

He caught me off guard with that one. Should've just moved on, but instead I turned to him and gave him the answer I gave everybody, "Not really. Did a year in the Merchant Marine during World War II before we got into it."

Then for some crazy reason I asked him, "You?"

He looked young enough to be my son. That made me wonder for a second how I would've felt if I did have a son and he'd gotten drafted into this crazy war.

"Yeah." And in one word that twenty-something sounded older than me.

Before he could say anything more this mountain of a man appeared in the doorway. And everyone kind of moved a step towards the street to make room for him.

"Anyone got a cigarette?" he growled in a slow, deep way that suggested more weariness than threat. To me anyway.

"Yeah, I got one Fred," said the little guy stepping forward with a pack of Kools. The big guy had to bend over far to get the offering and the light. "Thanks."

As he exhaled, we caught each other's eye. Maybe I stood out because I was older than the rest. Closer to his age, maybe even older. The others were now fixed on him. Standing on the stoop, plus his natural size, made him a foot taller than the rest. And twice as heavy. "Fred" was a *Big* man. He filled the entire opening. Could've been a bouncer in his younger days. Now he was a graying guy. Just his size reminded me of what Ruth and Lissa had said about Olson.

"You from the Labor Council?" he asked me in a friendly way, almost hopefully.

The others looked at me again, this time a little differently as though they hadn't thought I might be somebody legit in their eyes. Even the little guy seemed to drop his suspicions, for a moment anyway.

"No, I'm not. I was just saying that I'm only passing through."

Soon as I said no, the little guy's suspicions came roaring back and he repeated what he'd said a minute ago, obviously kissing the big man's ass, "I told Dean I thought he might be a narc." He took a step towards me as though he was ready to take me on right then if Fred just said the word.

Fred seemed amused. "And what makes you think he's a narc, Dominic?"

Now the man lost his courage again, shuffling those feet but trying to keep an eye on me.

"I dunno, Fred, he just didn't look like one of us, y'know? Just walked up like he knew what was goin' on, then actin' like he's cool and not wantin' to mess, y'know?"

Then the big man stepped off the entrance to the bookstore and extended a huge hand, "I'm Fred Halstead. I'm one of the speakers tonight."

I felt my hand encased in his. "Jack Moriarty. And I was just passing through."

The rest kind of formed a semicircle around us. I didn't feel threatened. But this was definitely more than I'd bargained for when I turned the corner.

"Oh, so you're not here for the meeting?"

"Naw, politics isn't really my thing."

He chuckled. "Yeah it can be pretty boring."

"Was telling them I was just out for a walk. I thought maybe this was a bar or a place to eat."

"Sorry I mistook you from the Council. We've been working hard to get their support. But Building Trades've been slow to come around. You just look like a working guy."

"I come from working class people. But I do other stuff now."

"What do you do for a living, if you don't mind my asking?"

"Well, I'm a writer."

"Yeah? A writer? Never would've guessed that. I write a little bit too. You make any money at it?"

"Yeah. A little." I smiled weakly. "It's about the only thing I'm any good at." He laughed again.

This guy had a way of making you feel comfortable even as big as he was. It was clear he had the total respect of the group around us. He took a deep drag on the cigarette. Then he tossed what was left and rubbed it out on the pavement.

"What kind of writing you do?"

"I'm a travel writer."

"Oh! A *travel* writer!" Now I could tell he wasn't impressed. Just like Ruth and maybe the Albers. "You go around and write about beautiful places people should spend lots of money at? *If* they have any to spend?"

This time I laughed. "Yeah, that's about it."

A pause. Then I asked, "What do you do, when you're not giving speeches?" I smiled so he'd know I wasn't being the smartass I can be sometimes.

"Well, sometimes I work in the city. In the Garment District."

That struck a chord. There was only one Garment District as far as I was concerned. Lower East Side. Meant he probably knew some of the same places I did.

"You a supervisor or something?"

I felt the rest of the guys crowding a little closer as we got into a conversation I didn't plan on having. Like I said there was something about this huge man that got my attention more than sheer size. A keen intelligence. But also something else...I couldn't quite put my finger on it. I decided he was worth a few more minutes of my time. While we were talking a couple more people walked up, nodded to the others and slipped around Fred into the bookstore. Someone behind me whispered, "Sparts." I wondered what the hell that meant.

"Naw...I'm a cutter. Union man."

That surprised me. Hard to imagine him with a pair of scissors in his hand cutting bolts of cloth. I liked that he was a working man and a writer, kind of like me. Most of the college kids I'd met after I became "famous" came from professional families, fathers who were well-paid company lawyers or insurance executives or third-generation running a family business. They were growing up in wealth and destined for even more wealth. Except for this war, there wasn't much they had to worry about except getting that degree, maybe going on to law or business school, then sliding right back into the same upper middle class lives they came from. Think it's why I got so pissy with them coming after me, pretending to be beatniks or hippies or what have you.

They weren't all phonies. Some really wanted something. Something real. Like that nurse's kid maybe. But then they wanted me or Allen or maybe

Lawrence or someone else to show them how to get it. Or have us just *give* it to them. They weren't strong enough to go out and grab it themselves.

So when this big stranger said he'd worked in the Garment District, I could see he meant it. He was telling the truth. If he'd sweated through ten hour days and nights in 100 degree heat, then he knew. If he'd felt the tongue lash to hurry up, then he knew. If he'd stared down some corporate lackey for an extra nickel an hour, then he knew. And in that split second I figured if he knew, then maybe I wanted to know more about him too.

"Hard work."

"Yeah. It's a ballbuster."

"I've picked cotton."

"Yeah? That's ballbustin' too. Where? Down South?"

"Nope. Out west. Near L.A."

His eyes got wide when I said that.

"I'm from L.A. I know those fields! Out in the Valley. Bakersfield."

"Yeah, the same!"

"When'd you do that? I thought only Mexicans did that work."

"Late forties. Met up with a Mexican girl on a bus headed to L.A. We kinda fell for each other. She talked me into workin' the fields with her family."

"I'll be damned!" Then he talked over my head to the crowd around us. "You guys hear this? This man picked cotton! That's *real* work!"

Then a woman appeared in the doorway. I guessed she was in her late twenties/early thirties. Brown curly hair, blue eyes. Big smile. Altogether lovely.

"Hey, Fred, they said come get you. It's time."

He turned and smiled weakly, "OK, Lynda. We're comin' in."

Then he turned back to me. "Hey, you said you don't care much for politics. But it sounds like you care a little bit for the workin' man. Why don't you come on in, listen a little bit? I'd like to hear more about your times in California. Unless you got something better to do?"

I guessed I had nothing better to do. But this guy sounded kind of interesting too. I know Allen would've talked with him. When he turned to go in, I felt a slight push from the crowd behind me, so I followed. There were a few more kids mingling inside who I could tell wondered who the old guy was who'd just made friends with Fred. I didn't care. I wasn't sure exactly what I'd gotten myself into, but figured if I was OK with the big guy, then the rest of'em weren't going to hassle me.

Back at Columbia we'd get into these terrific arguments over who was worse, Hitler or Stalin. And some of the Commies couldn't stand it if you said one bad word about Stalin even though everyone knew about the Show Trials and heard stories about the intellectuals and leaders of the Communist Party in Russia getting rounded up and shot or sent to Siberia and the gulags. Then the same thing happening to their peasants, only instead of thousands it was millions. And this was in the thirties before the war really got going and Hitler unleashed his madness. But I couldn't stand a politics that tried to defend one kind of tyranny against another. And I thought the people who tried to say the USA was the root of all evil hadn't ever really seen evil up close and personal like the old Bolsheviks did or the *kulaks* did or the Jews did.

I took a seat in the back. The tall guy, Dean, sat next to me. The others who came in behind sat together towards the front. Except Dominic, who paced nervously along the sides of the room. The room itself was mostly full, I'd say 40 or more. Virtually all student types, early twenties. Talking low, looking around. Fred and I were definitely the oldest there, except for one really old guy who sat in the front row.

Fred sat up front at a table with two others. The woman who'd called us in ran the show.

The debate itself bored me. Everybody talked about these demonstrations that were going to happen in Washington and San Francisco. By 1970 it seemed there were demonstrations all the time, and it was hard to tell how much good they were doing. Yeah, Johnson hadn't run again because the war was going so badly. But then Nixon got elected and you couldn't tell things were any better. He said he was going to end the war, but it was still going strong despite all the protests. It seemed all the kids could do was yell and scream. But it didn't seem to make any difference.

Maybe because Fred was older or because he was bigger or something, but anyway he really ran the show. The way he talked about the group he represented—something called the National Peace Action Coalition—and what they were doing to organize the demonstrations and why. Somehow he made a lot of sense. Some people can talk politics in a way that ordinary people understand and like. Fred talked that way.

Fred said he belonged to the Socialist Workers Party—that's whose bookstore and offices we were in—and had been its candidate for president in '68. I didn't know a lot about them or any of the other little left parties running around then. Mostly all I'd ever heard about was the Communist Party. But it was pretty much worthless from WWII on. They took orders from Moscow and no way was any group that took orders from Moscow going to make it in America.

Another speaker, a Yale law student earnest and ready for a government career, talked about supporting this Senator or that Congressman and how Democrats were going to cut off funding for the war and force Nixon to make peace and bring the troops home. But if that was such a great idea why didn't they do that to Johnson? That's why it was so hard to get too excited about politics. Just seemed like one big bullshit game.

He got me thinking of when I went on Buckley's TV show a couple years before and got ambushed by him. I thought I was going on to have a real intellectual discussion about writing and maybe some politics with the guy. Turns out he'd invited two others on and all he wanted was to talk about hippies and make us look like fools. Good thing I'd had a little to drink and couldn't care less, except getting off that stage as fast as I could.

The third speaker, an intense New York type who reminded me of some of the Columbia crowd, got going about imperialism and racism and how we needed to show "solidarity" with the Viet Cong. He was with some People's Coalition for Peace and Justice. I had no idea what that was. There were a lot of those type of groups running around in those days. He talked about the "people's struggle" and tossed out little sayings from Mao's Little Red Book that a lot of kids used to pack around like a commie Bible. You don't see them as much anymore and I don't know why.

Fred talked about trying to get the most amount of people united around one simple idea: Get out of Vietnam. Now. Like I said, even though I didn't want to get all political, I agreed with that. It made sense because that war was going nowhere except to rip up the country…theirs and ours. And Laos and Cambodia and probably Thailand too.

It's not that I didn't care what Fred and the others were talking about. I did. How could you not care about another people suffering through bombings and napalm and babies being killed and wondering what the hell for? But it sure felt different from WWII. Even worse, it's like all we'd known was war since then. Like this country *had* to be at war for one reason or another in some godforsaken part of the world.

I remembered what Eisenhower had said about watching out for the military-industrial complex. That they'd get so big and strong that the country would need them just to keep the economy rolling along. Or they'd have so many plants and bases in so many states they'd have the Congress bought off and protect them from making any really big cutbacks and sell them on the next missile system or aircraft carrier or bazooka or what have you. I liked Ike even if Allen didn't.

That's what Vietnam felt like. We were fighting a war we didn't need to fight, for reasons that had nothing to do with the safety of our country, but had a lot to do with keeping the economy rolling along even if it meant killing thousands of our young men and hundreds of thousands of a people about whom we knew little and cared less. Along with keeping us scared to death about the Russians or Chinese spending every breathing moment trying to wipe us out. Things got a little lively after the three of 'em talked and the audience started asking questions or making little speeches. I guessed maybe half of the room were Fred supporters. But the other half seemed to be made up of a bunch of other groups. Each one tried to stand up and make a little speech. They'd be tolerated for a few minutes then the girl Lynda would step in and try to tell them time's up. Most sat down.

But this one girl, a very tall blonde—kinda nice looking—started going off on Fred and the rest of the others for betraying the working class and not "taking a harder line and being a true vanguardist." When Lynda tried to shut her up, she just got louder. And the guy next to her jumped up too shouting back at Lynda. That's when Dominic and Dean and maybe a half dozen other men sprung into action. They grabbed her and the other guy who really started yelling and wrestling with the "guards" as they were hustled out the front door. Then we heard it slam, but could still hear muffled yelling outside. Couple minutes later some of the others walked back in and sat down, but not Dean and Dominic. The whole thing wound down after that, with Lynda pitching sales of the newspaper and Fred encouraging people to sign up for buses down to Washington. But it seemed like everyone left already had a paper and was signed up. Except me. And I wasn't going in that direction.

I wasn't sure what to do as the rest either milled around or drifted out. Somebody tried to sell me a newspaper but I said no. Then Fred caught my eye and gave a quick nod like he wanted me to hang around, so I did.

I wandered out front and there were Dean and Dominic standing outside guarding the door. I could see and hear the tall blonde and her companion still yelling. And then also trying to sell copies of their newspaper to people as they came out. From what I could see they had no takers, although someone did try to argue with them.

The bookstore itself seemed to have a lot of books by or about Trotsky. I'd always thought he was kind of an interesting guy from the little I'd heard. He'd been a bigshot in the Russian Revolution. Allen talked about him from time to time. But then he'd been murdered in Mexico—a hatchet in the head from one of his guards. This happened in 1940 at the artist Diego Rivera's house after Trotsky had been on the run from Stalin and his goons for years.

I wandered around as the place emptied out slowly. Glancing out the window, I saw that even the tall blonde and her friend had gotten tired and left. Dean and Dominic kept their watch, but now they chatted with a couple of their "comrades" including the pretty brunette Lynda.

"Well, whadja think?"

I jumped hearing Fred's voice behind me. I hadn't even heard him rumble out from the meeting room.

"Not much." It was hard not to be intimidated by his sheer size. Seemed like he was a foot taller than me, although I knew it wasn't that much.

"Yeah. Some of the kids get excited. They're still learning."

"Learning what?"

We got interrupted by one of the others. "Hey, Fred, you comin'?"

"Yeah."

Then he turned back to me.

"We're goin' out for a beer. Why don't you come along? I'd like to hear more about your days out in the Valley."

"Well, I got my car parked a couple blocks over. Not sure I want to leave it out there where I can't see it."

"Yeah, yeah." Then he shouted out the doorway, "Hey, Dean! Come here a sec."

Dean stepped inside, flicking an ash on the sidewalk before he did.

"What's up?"

"Jack says he's got his car parked couple blocks from here. Whyn't you walk over with him and show him where the bar is." Turning back to me, "It's not far."

"Sure. No problem, Fred."

Dean looked at me. "Ready to go?"

"OK, I guess."

We stepped out the door. Then heard Fred saying, "We'll see you at the Rooster." I waved.

It was totally dark now. We started walking back the way I came, turning right at the end of the block and heading back downtown. I was thinking how this Dean looked nothing like the other Dean.

"Where did you say you were from?" I think he was trying to be friendly.

"I didn't." Pause. "Originally from Boston. Now I live in Florida."

"Yeah, you got the accent. I think I heard you say you're a writer?"

"Yeah."

"What kind?"

"Travel."

"Right. You said."

"What do you do?"

"Right now I'm on assignment for the party. We're trying to make this demonstration a really big one."

He pulled out another cigarette. Marlboro. I decided to do the same. We paused to light. Damn! That Camel tasted good! Now we were two little red dots in the night. When we started walking again I asked, "What's that mean, 'on assignment for the party'?"

I sounded just like a narc. Good thing Dominic wasn't with us. "Sorry, but this kind of politics is something I don't get into every day."

"Hey, that's cool. When you join Socialist Workers it means you take your politics real serious. It means you're willing to do things for the party when asked. I got asked to come here to help build the demonstration, so I did."

We walked some more just smoking. A breeze had kicked up into our faces so we walked heads bowed into the chill air. It was a lot cooler than when I left the car. I was glad for the warmth of the cigarette.

"So, if you're a travel writer why'd you come by the bookstore?"

Uh-oh. The narc thing again.

"Hadn't planned to. Didn't know what it was. Just out for a walk and saw you guys hanging out and thought I'd see what was going on. I thought maybe it was a bar or restaurant where I might hang a while."

We'd turned back onto the main street. The car was a hundred yards ahead. I was glad for Dean's company, even though the street didn't seem too ready for trouble at nine o'clock this night. A couple blacks hung outside the door to a bar, maybe waiting for their angry fixes. Twenty years before I'd been looking for those fixes myself. Twenty years? Hell...five years! I never thought of myself as a junkie. Burroughs and

Huncke, they were junkies, looking to shoot up whenever and wherever they could. But I was content with wine and beer and weed and pills once in a while. Content—shit! That was enough to almost do me in.

When we got to the car, Dean seemed a little surprised that this is what I'd be driving.

"Ford wagon, huh? That's what my mom and dad drove when I was growing up. First car I remember was an old Woody. You remember those?"

"Yeah. Used to see quite a few of'em out West. Good cars. Where'd you grow up?"

"Indiana. Near Fort Wayne."

"Never been there. Been to Toledo. Rode the bus a couple times across the state."

We stubbed our cigarettes out and climbed in.

"Where we headed?"

"Place called The Green Rooster. It's about a mile."

Dean gave me directions, and five minutes later we were there. We parked across the street and went into a little place that had a rooster in neon green lit up in the window. Man, I felt right at home! It was a small, friendly little bar like thousands of others I'd been in. Couple small tables near the door. Also by the door, a wheelbarrow filled with bottles of booze and a rough, handwritten sign: **"50/50 Raffle Every Friday Erin Go Bragh!"** Then the long bar on the right with three or four taps and lines of beautiful bottles stacked up on the wall behind. Smoky, but not too smoky. Just enough to make you feel comfortable. The stools had metal legs and leather coverings, the kind you slid onto and then rested your feet along the rail. There were more tables in the back.

It looked like a slow night. Just a few of those seats filled. At the far end of the bar was a huge glass jar almost two feet high, half filled with money, coins and bills. Was that for tips?

Fred was already holding court in the back. There were maybe half a dozen sitting with him. He saw us and waved us on. I followed Dean. Fred pointed me to a seat next to him. Looked like he was already into his second cigarette and maybe second beer too. Dean got stuck at the other end of the table, next to Lynda. I didn't recognize the others. I wondered why the intense little Dominic hadn't joined us.

As I sat down, I realized the old guy who'd been in the front row was now next to Fred. The "kids" around us were talking among themselves, but definitely leaning in our direction trying to listen in on Fred's and the old man's conversation and wanting to catch whatever ours was going to be.

"You want a beer?" Fred asked in a way that didn't allow "No." There was already an empty glass waiting for me.

Truth was, I did. It'd been a good six months since I'd any booze of any kind. I thought a glass of beer wouldn't kill my insides. It was that other cheap stuff I'd been drinking that really did me in. Still, the memory of nearly dying around that damned toilet at Memere's and the pain of drying out was enough to make me think twice before I did. But I lit another cigarette and nodded. Something made me want this night, whatever it was going to be.

"Jack, this is Farrell Dobbs." Fred introduced us as he poured me one out of the pitcher. "He's the National Secretary of our party." We shook hands.

Now that I got a closer look at him, he didn't look so old. Sixties maybe. His hair was gray and combed back straight. He had piercing blue eyes, the kind people said I had. As with Fred, right away I sensed a keen intelligence. This guy was nobody's fool.

"Nice to meet ya. Forgive me if I sound stupid, but what's a 'national secretary'?"

He laughed gently. "Guess it means I'm in charge." Then he nodded towards Fred and the rest of the table. "As long as Fred and the rest think I ought to be." The whole table laughed, including Fred. But this guy really was in charge. He seemed to command attention without pushing his weight around.

I took a long sip on the cold beer.

Fred jumped in. "Farrell, Jack didn't think a whole lot of our debate tonight."

God, I hoped he wasn't baiting me. At least the car was close if I wanted to get out of there quick.

"I didn't either, Fred, to be honest with you. I thought two weeks out we'd have twice that many." Then he seemed to catch himself, maybe mindful of the others at the table. "But it's hard to predict with great accuracy how these things are going to turn out. The best you can do is keep organizing, keep pushing, knowing you're doing the right thing and changing people's minds even if they don't say so at the moment you want them to."

Dobbs spoke with a flat Midwestern accent that was music to my ears when I heard it on my first trips across the country. It was an accent that brought with it wide open spaces and huge starry skies, the very things I'd longed for and looked for when I hit the road back then.

"Where ya from, Farrell?" I asked, then took another long draw on the beer, almost emptying the glass. Fred filled it for me again, then signaled for another pitcher. I pulled a ten out and laid it on the table. If we were getting into serious drinking, I'd do my part.

"I was born in Missouri. But my father moved the family to Minneapolis for work when I was a kid. Yourself?"

"Boston. Just outside, actually. But family's moved all over. And I've moved even more. My dad's dead now. Along with a brother who died young and a sister who died just a couple years ago. But my mother lives in Florida. St. Petersburg."

Fred jumped in again. "He's been to California too, Farrell. Said he picked cotton outside Bakersfield."

Dobbs' eyes widened a little, maybe taking me a little more seriously.

"My dad was a coal miner. I drove truck for a while."

It was my turn now.

"Yeah, I've done my share of physical labor. Even when all I wanted to do was write."

I paused. Fred and Farrell and the rest of the table waited. They wanted to hear my story. Or at least the part of it that connected with their politics. Truth was, the beer was starting to work its magic and I got to thinking about Bea and our beautiful, brown and rosy days working those white puffy fields of southern California.

"My time there goes back to the forties, right after the war. I'd been in San Francisco visiting friends and then it was time to head back to New York where I'd been living. But first I wanted to take a peek at Los Angeles, so I hopped a bus that took me down the San Joaquin. That's how I met the cutest little Mexican girl. We rode together into L.A. and spent some time together. Then she said why don't we catch up with her family in the Valley and pick cotton and make some money and live good close to the ground? Sounded like an adventure, so I did."

Fred jumped in, excited, I think, at having met someone who knew part of the world where he was from.

"Damn! I know that bus. I've taken it to Frisco and back a dozen times. And I know those fields! I've seen families out there picking in hundred degree heat. Man, I don't know how you did it."

"It was about the toughest work I've ever done, Fred. You got paid by the pound. First couple days I hardly made anything. If my girl hadn't been next to me, we'd both have starved I think."

"How long were you at it?"

"Only a few weeks. I met her brothers, but never met her dad. They had to hide me out in a barn that had these big spiders in the rafters that half-scared me to death. She also had a kid and was married, I guess. But she was on the bus to L.A. because he'd been beating her. Still, her old man didn't think what she was doing was right. I did have some wild times with her brothers though. They took me right in. Seemed like all they wanted to do was pick and drink. Pick and drink." I smiled with the memories. Fred and Farrell smiled too. The kids just leaned in.

"Did she go with you?" Farrell asked.

"No. She wanted to. But she couldn't just leave her kid behind. And I told her once I got to New York, I'd send for them. But, well, things happen and...you know."

"Yeah. All that's mechanized now. You probably know that."

I didn't, but pretended I did.

Fred continued, "But the Latinos, they're still picking tomatoes and lettuce and grapes. Chavez is trying to get them organized. He's got a grape boycott going on. Trying to make it nationwide."

Dean shot from the other end of the table, "I hear A&P might go with him on that, Fred."

Fred took another drag on his cigarette, then stubbed it out. "Yeah, that'd be good. But we've been hearing that for a year now."

"Farmworkers have it the worst of all," Dobbs said calmly. "They get their work through individual farms. But the real power's with the corporations that buy their produce. They won't recognize a farmworkers union, saying their contracts are with the farmers. And the farmers, even the big ones, are so numerous that there's no way a union can negotiate a contract to cover them all. Plus, the farmers will play one working family off against another."

"Yeah," I said. "Saw some of that myself. And Steinbeck wrote all about it."

Dobbs smiled at the name. "Yes he did. He's one of my favorite writers. But, that's not the kind of writing you do, is it?"

"No. I wish I was as good as Steinbeck." And I wasn't lying saying that. But my books were pretty good too. "So, you think this guy—Chavez—is going to get them organized?"

Dobbs sipped his beer slowly. "I don't know. We're trying to help him where we can. But he's gotten so dependent on his Democratic friends that he pulls his punches sometimes when they ask him to. He doesn't see—or doesn't want to see—that they're as tied to agribusiness and the big corporations as the Republicans."

"Why do you say that? I thought Democrats were the party of labor?"

Fred smiled, glanced at Farrell, then asked me, "When you were picking cotton, what was the most important thing for you to do?"

"Pick enough so I could buy food for dinner that night. Maybe have enough left over for a beer."

"Exactly." Fred poured me a third. "Now that girl of yours had to pick enough for her and her kid. No work, no money. No money, no food. Pretty simple life equation. So when someone comes around and says, 'Walk out of that field and I'll get you more money,' what are the chances she or you or her brothers are going to do that?"

"Not very high."

"Exactly. And the farm bosses know that. That's why they run off people like Chavez with clubs and worse. Or get their lackeys in the government or the courts to do it for them. The Democrats play along because they're *supposed* to be the 'party of labor.' But that's only true when it suits them. The sad fact is Latinos count for very little in their world."

I had to agree with him on that. The Mexicans I'd known were about the beatest people I know.

Except for maybe the blacks. But I'd known a lot more Latinos than blacks.

Then Dobbs added, "But it wasn't so long ago men and women who worked in factories or in the mines or drove trucks had the exact same problem. They got beat over the head when they tried to organize. And they got beat at the ballot box when the people they trusted with their votes didn't do squat once they got to office."

I nodded, not so much in agreement, but kinda like I'd taken the bait. It was probably the beer, but I decided to mix it up a little. "So you guys are Communists, huh? I mean, the real thing? I never dug politics all that much. People still get screwed over in their lives and it doesn't seem to make much difference if it's a Stalin or a Roosevelt or a Mao or a Nixon who's in power."

Dobbs answered. "Yes, we're Communists. But not the Stalin brand. Or the Mao brand. And we're not the Norman Thomas brand. Or even the Willy Brandt brand. We're revolutionaries who follow the political teachings of Marx, Lenin and Trotsky."

"So what're you trying to do? Make a revolution here in the good ol' U.S. of A.?" I knew I was baiting them a little, but what the hell. "How're you going to help my little Beatrice and her boy out there in those cotton fields? How are Marx and Lenin and... Trostky...going to put bread on their table or a roof over their heads or give them something of pleasure in life?"

I felt the kids next to us lean away a little. Maybe they'd never heard someone talk to their leaders like that. I didn't want to be rude, not when someone's buying your beer and it tastes good. Besides, I was liking really being in a bar and drinking again. The place with Michak had been more restaurant with a bar on the side. The Green Rooster was all bar. I lit another cigarette.

Fred took the lead. "That's a fair question, Jack. Believe it or not, it's one we ask ourselves every day. We're serious about what we do. And we want to be better at it than anybody else."

Fred had a way of talking to you that commanded your attention. I liked that he didn't jump down your throat if you asked a question or challenged something he said.

"You say you're not much interested in politics and that's OK. Except this. You wanted your girlfriend and her boy to have a better life, right?"

"Yeah."

"OK. How was she going to get that? One way was to make more money picking cotton. And how was that going to happen? Was the guy or the company that owned those fields just going to give it to her? Of course not. It's in their interest to pay those workers the very least they can possibly get away with. Maybe the farmer's not even a bad guy. Maybe he'd pay them more if he could. But his main job is to maximize the profits coming out of those fields. If he doesn't, then he's probably out of a job, or a farm, too. And that means paying the least amount for labor. So there you have it: your girlfriend's desire to make a better life running right into her boss's need to pay her as little as possible. That's politics. That's *real* politics."

"Yeah, I see where you're going. But if her boss can't make a buck, like you say, he's out of business *and* she's out of a job. And worse off than before." For a moment I thought of my dad and how he got screwed in the printing business.

"In a capitalist society, that's true." Fred continued, "But that's also a false dichotomy. By that logic, we shouldn't question the capitalist's right to do anything with his business as he pleases. So if he wants to treat 'em like serfs, that's his right. If he wants to make 'em work ten, twelve hour days, that's his right. If he wants to make 'em run machinery that cuts off fingers and arms, that's his right too."

"I hear what you're saying, Fred. But you trying to tell me the Ruskies and the Chinese don't make their people work like slaves? Or they don't have machines that cut off fingers and arms too?"

Dobbs stepped in there. Again with that calm voice that wasn't taking the bait I'd just thrown back at him and Fred.

"Jack, you're absolutely right. Workers in those countries don't have it good. And that's not the kind of socialism we think is best for workers here, or there."

"Is there any other kind?" I could hear my voice getting louder. Three quick beers after a six-month layoff can do that. Actually, I was kind of enjoying myself. Fred and Farrell didn't strike me as the dark, dour, conspiratorial commies I'd met from time to time in New York. This was good ol' bar talk. Beers and cigarettes talk.

"Yeah, actually there is," Farrell continued. "Just like all capitalist societies aren't the same, the same can be said for socialist societies. The economies of western Europe are sometimes called socialist by American politicians. They're not. At least in the strictest sense. But I'd say workers are treated, on the whole, a lot better there than they are here.

"I know darn well that if the American people chose to make ours a socialist society it would look very different from the ones in the Soviet Union and the People's Republic of China. Or the ones in Europe. We think we could do it better."

"How can you be so sure of that, Farrell? The Russians have been at it for over fifty years and it seems like those people are as sad as ever. And from some of the commies I've met in New York, I sure as hell wouldn't want any of them running my government. I doubt if they smile even when they're getting laid...*if* they ever get laid."

This crack actually got a laugh from around the table. I realized now that the kids were all listening closely to our "debate." I drained the last of the pitcher into Fred's glass and held it up for our waitress to bring another.

"Jack, you won't get much of an argument from me on that, like I said. But let me ask you, did you think it was fair the way your girlfriend and her family got treated in those cotton fields?"

"Nah, not really."

"OK, but the only way those people can even think of changing things is sticking together and demanding something different."

"You're talking union again, right?"

"Yes, I am."

I took a long drag on another cigarette.

"Yeah, well, I kinda get the union thing. Except when the big shots start acting more like crooks or thugs. Or like the business guys they're supposed to be working against."

Dobbs answered again. "Fair enough. I don't care for that either. You ever been in a union, Jack?"

"Yeah. Seaman's union. Not very long though. But enough to see how things worked in the hiring halls. You?"

Fred chuckled when I asked that. "I'd say you have a little experience in that arena, wouldn't you, Farrell?"

Dobbs smiled. I could see his eyes going back to some place when he was a younger man. I knew that look. I found myself doing that too. Memories from a quarter century ago when I was new to New York streets, itching to get to someplace big and wide and equally new.

"Yes, yes I have. Jack, when were you born, if you don't mind my asking?"

"1922."

"Well, I've got about fifteen years on you then. You remember much about the Depression?"

"Yeah. Some. Not much. I was in school. We were all poor."

Fred chuckled. "You got that right."

"Ever hear of the Teamsters Union?"

"Sure. Hoffa's outfit."

"It was. Maybe still is. But...he's in prison now."

"Yeah, I remember reading about that. Pretty big deal when it happened."

"It was." Now it seemed Dobbs turned really serious, like some kind of power was filling up inside. The nice old man became something more. "But it never would've happened if Jimmy hadn't built it into the single most powerful union in the country. And Jimmy wouldn't have done that if he hadn't been such a good student of what we did in Minneapolis back in '34."

"What happened then?"

"I won't bore you with details. But I'll say that before 1934 the Teamsters Union was weak. It was a bunch of tiny little locals scattered across the country. Strikes, if they ever happened, were broken easily by the companies and their muscle.

"But up in Minneapolis we figured out a way to organize over-the-road drivers. We talked to them about how to stick together with the warehouse guys and what they could get if they did. When we struck, we went for the whole city. And we got it."

I was beginning to be impressed. Something about Farrell *was* impressive. Like I felt with Fred, there was intelligence and toughness. Idealism and practicality. Not what I'd run into when I'd met other union guys who knew how to fight in the workplace but knew little about larger issues of politics and economics.

"You guys shut down the whole city? That's usually an invitation to get your heads bashed in."

"You're right. They tried. Even got the governor to bring in National Guard. Some people got hurt. It got pretty wild up there for a while.

"Even the International president, Dan Tobin, tried to give us the boot. He didn't like things he couldn't control. But once people saw results from sticking together, the tide turned. From there we organized locals across the Midwest. Packing plants in Nebraska and Iowa. Drivers and warehousemen sticking together."

"And Jimmy Hoffa? Where'd he fit in?"

"He came up and saw what we were doing and how we were doing it. Took our lessons back to Detroit. Organized car-haulers and other drivers just as the UAW was getting off the ground. It was quite a time!"

"Pretty rough too," Fred added, looking at Farrell. Dobbs nodded slowly.

"It was."

I glanced at the rest of the table. The college kids were rapturous, as though listening to tales from the Wild West or the Revolution.

Dobbs took a long drag on his cigarette, stuffed it out. I lit another, but he was done. I loved the warm fire I'd started in my lungs. The way smoke hung in the air, changing the bar's light.

"You can never underestimate the determination of the ruling class to protect its interests. I don't care if it's trucking company owners in Minneapolis, or bankers in New York. They all act the same. They have money and property to protect. And they'll go to war to protect them. Primarily against workers in their own country. But against each other when they have to."

"What do you mean?" I wasn't trying to be smart. But I'd heard some of this stuff from Allen and others and lots of times it sounded like a bunch of malarkey.

"Jack, they act the same because they have the same interests to protect. They protect their wealth. Their position in society. Their right to make the rules. And their right to break 'em too, when it suits their needs." His eyes drilled right into me. This guy was deadly serious. He'd been in his share of fights. And he knew which side he was on.

"OK," I said, not quite sure if I agreed. I did kind of sympathize with the problems he pointed out. But it was usually at this point the other commies I'd met went off the deep end. Lots of talk about solidarity and government run by workers. All of which sounded glorious, but didn't mean a hill of beans to me as to how it actually got done.

"What makes you think things can get any better? Seems to me suffering is what life's all about. You're born. You suffer. You die. Maybe things are a little better for some people than others, but that's the way it is. Maybe we go on to a heaven where everything's fixed up fine. Or maybe we come back through and take another shot at life again and try to make ourselves better. Or maybe there's nothing at all!

"But all this talk about a workers' paradise, or whatever it's called, just sounds like pie in the sky. No offense, but how can you sell American workers that the Soviet system's better than what they have now, shitty as it may be?"

I was getting wound up now. Another glass of beer. Losing count. I'd also kind of figured out now that Fred and Farrell wanted this "debate" for the kids. And that was OK too. I was enjoying this. These guys were smart.

"You like to write?" Farrell asked. That was a curve ball.

"Yeah, I do. Especially when I get paid."

Laughs.

"Why do you write? I assume it's because you want something more than just a chance to visit nice places and tell people they ought to spend their vacation money where you tell them." Farrell was as tough as Ruth. Maybe tougher. What could I tell him that would keep my cover?

"I dunno. I like it. Sometimes I meet interesting people. Sometimes I learn things about a place. Sometimes I even learn something about myself."

"So it's safe to say that maybe you write to alleviate your 'suffering'?" Farrell smiled as he asked me this. I smiled back. I knew he'd got me.

"Yeah. That's not to say writing can't be a pain in the ass."

Dobbs laughed. "I think I can agree with you about that!"

"Me too!" Fred added.

"I'm not sure why you're trying to sound so cynical, Jack. You don't strike me as the cynical type."

"Look, Farrell, you've been around a bit. You've seen what the world's like. How many millions got killed in World War II? How many millions before that in World War I? How many millions did Stalin kill in his gulags? Or Hitler in his gas chambers? Or how many kids die even today before they have a chance at life because of disease or starvation? Or because they're getting napalmed right now in some God-forsaken part of a Vietnamese jungle? And for what? Some crappy idea about what a perfect human society should look like? Or worse, to keep us scared to shit about being infiltrated by creepy people who want to take away our freedom?

"I'm not saying I don't maybe admire you—and the rest of you—for doing whatever it is you're doing. But life is pain. I don't see how you escape it. Yeah, you try to maybe find a little pleasure somewhere in it. Like with this beer right now. Or maybe with a girl later on. But sooner or later you're gonna come face to face with good ol' Death and then it's over. And what do most of us have to show for it? Who will know we've ever really been here? And who will care if we have?"

My little speech kind of put a pause to all the talk. Farrell gave me a look that was both stern and kind. Fred sucked at his beer. Maybe they'd figured I was hopeless and asking me out to a bar had been a mistake. God knows I'd been in so many bar talks that turned out hopeless. Or worse. I sounded like the

Existentialists I'd met in Paris. They really were cynical sons-a-bitches. Then I remembered this sounded like me not too many years before when I was so far down the alcohol hole I couldn't tell up from down. I heard an echo of the Hatteras surf coming from somewhere. I shuddered and hoped no one saw me do it.

Farrell started at me again. "Jack, I've run through that very drill myself countless times. And, fundamentally, who can disagree with what you're saying? Life is a mystery. Death is an even greater mystery. Fair enough. But don't you want to do something with the time you have here, however much or little that might be? I can't believe all you do, or want to do, is bounce around the country writing stories about pretty places. Or maybe you do. But, pardon my French, what you said sounded pretty damn stupid. In a way, it's remarkable most people want to make things better. Most people want to live in peace. And provide for their families. Leave things a little better off than they found them. And find some happiness maybe along the way. Not everybody. I know that. But enough that as a species we seem to make something called progress. So it's not all suffering. And it's not all for nothing.

"At the biological level you could say it's for our survival as a race. But I think it's more than that. We organize ourselves into societies because we like it that way. We are very social animals. We recognize there's something intrinsically human about our desire for life...liberty...the pursuit of happiness. I really believe in those words. I don't want to make a speech about them. But I will say that my politics is rooted much more in the ideals of our own revolution than they are in anybody else's."

I hated sounding like some pruny, foot-in-the-grave tired old man. I hated it at Ruth's. And I hated it here. Why was I saying these things? Sounding like a beat up bum when I wasn't really. Was I? Why did I let myself get cornered by someone who could speak a bigger truth than I did? Yet that's exactly how I felt now after half a dozen beers.

Fred said quietly, "Tell him about the Old Man, Farrell." The kids scooted even closer when he said this. More beers. Another cigarette. A group of guys had come in, gathered at another table. A couple looked like me in my younger days. Jukebox playing rock and roll.

Dobbs nodded, then looked back at me. "You've heard of Trotsky?" he asked, this time quietly.

"Yeah. Of course."

"Know much about him?"

"Not a lot. A Bolshie. Run out by Stalin. Killed in Mexico. I met a couple Mexicans who knew Rivera. The artist. That's where he was killed, right?"

"That's right. In 1940. By an agent of Stalin's. Also Mexican. Trotsky was maybe the smartest person I've ever met. And I've had the chance to meet a lot of smart people."

"So, you knew him?"

"That's right."

"In Mexico? At Rivera's?"

"That's right."

"OK. That's pretty impressive." And it was. No bullshit.

Fred explained, "Farrell got asked to come down and be a bodyguard and a secretary for him. He was there when the Old Man got attacked."

"You couldn't stop it?"

"I would have if I could have. But I was in the hospital with a stomach problem. They took advantage of my absence."

"It wasn't your fault, Farrell!" Lynda shot this back up to our end of the table.

Dobbs smiled a thin smile.

"No, strictly speaking, it wasn't I guess. But my going to the hospital caused a security breakdown. And that's when Mercador struck."

"Did you know this guy was working for Stalin?" I had to admit I was drawn into this. Of course, I'd been to Mexico City many times and had heard about Trotsky's murder more than once. But I'd never met anyone who'd been this close to a major world event.

"No. Of course not. None of us did. He infiltrated, became trusted, and did his deed when our guard was down. We wanted to kill him on the spot, but the Old Man, weakened as he was, said no. He wanted us to learn more about how and who engineered this."

"So Trotsky wasn't killed right away?"

"No. But the wound was mortal. That he lived for even a day after it showed how tough he was. Still, his death was a big setback for revolutionary socialism around the world."

I wasn't sure I wanted to get into a big discussion about the merits of "revolutionary socialism" so instead I asked, "What kind of guy was Trotsky?"

"Tough. Just really tough. He'd been through it all. You didn't have to agree with his politics to still be amazed at all he'd seen and done in his sixty years. Of course, I did agree with his politics, or the vast majority of it anyways. But he'd seen the poverty and the pogroms of Czarist Russia.

"Then he saw the destruction of World War I. It's hard for these young people here to appreciate, or for even us old guys, but sixty years ago all of Europe—plus colonies in Africa and Asia—was run by a few families. Anybody who got in their way got sent to prison or worse. It's also hard to appreciate how exciting the ideas of Marx and Engels were to the young people of that time. Not just them. Others too. They provided an explanation for all the misery and chaos that capitalism had unleashed. But more than that, they showed a way forward. A way for humanity to put all the injustices of royalism behind us. Lenin, along with Trotsky, provided a political theory and organization on how to oppose capitalism.

And replace it with a system that would be more humane and really reward people for the hard, terrible work they did."

Dobbs paused and smiled kind of sheepishly.

"Sorry, Jack, I know you didn't want to hear another speech."

"Naw...that's OK, Farrell. I get a lot of what you and Fred have been talking about. I come from a family of working stiffs. But we just don't get involved in crazy politics. Still, I remember my dad getting screwed over by people with money. And I've had friends of mine—other writers—get screwed by their publishers.

"But to be honest with you, the radicals I've met seemed a lot more interested in *talking* about revolution than dealing with the day-to-day problems of people like my mom and dad. And when Stalin made peace with Hitler right before the war and the communists here tried to convince us that was a good thing, well they just lost everybody with that."

Now it was my turn to stop making speeches. "So Trotsky was a Bolshie from the beginning, huh?"

"Yes and no. He didn't storm the Winter Palace with the Bolsheviks in November of 1917. But he was in Petrograd—Leningrad—for the Revolution. After they took over, he was part of the inner circle that made peace with the Germans and got Russia out of the war. Pretty ballsy what they did, really."

"Then he led the Red Army in its fight against the Whites during their civil war. Like I said the capitalists knew what a danger this revolution represented to their order. By the time it was over in 1920, the country was totally exhausted. He argued with Lenin against the fast, forced collectivization and expropriation of property. Eventually Lenin came around to Trotsky's way of thinking, but he was also very ill and unable to resist Stalin's growing control of the government. When Lenin died, the fight between Stalin and Trotsky burst into the open and, well, we know what history tells us. Trotsky was exiled. Then the purges and Show Trials began."

His talking took me back to my first years in New York. The first time I met real lefties. Students at Columbia mostly. We drank and talked a lot of politics. But that talk had a different feel to it than this one. This wasn't academic bullshit. This was real life stuff.

"I'm glad I had a few months with the Old Man. He was the most extraordinary person I have ever met. Not only for what he did. But how he viewed all the tragedies around him. A daughter committed suicide. A son was murdered by Stalin's agents. He spent the last years of his life a hunted man, a threat to his eventual murderer even half a world away. You want to talk about suffering? That man suffered to his deepest core. Yet he maintained this most wonderful and generous view of humanity to the very end. Among his final written words were these simple ones: 'Life is beautiful.' I believe that too."

With that Farrell sat back and waited for me to say something. Even Fred and the rest of the table seemed awed by this unassuming man who'd apparently seen much too. Not as much as Trotsky. But a lot.

"I've talked to a lot of lefties over the years, Farrell, but I've never heard anyone explain some of these things like you have. Like I said, I'm not real big into politics because it seems like a business where people use people. But your man Trotsky, sounds like he saw it all. And to be able to say that at the end..."

"You see, Jack," Farrell continued, having warmed to his story now, "in a way it's too easy to look at the Soviet Union today with all its repression and paranoia in the leadership and say that's the way it's always been, or that's what happens when you put the working class in charge, or whatever it is that makes them the bad guys and us the good guys.

"But back when they had their revolution things really were in awful shape. They'd lost hundreds of thousands—maybe millions—in the war against Germany. Russia was also the last major European country to industrialize. Instead it was a country overwhelmingly of poor farmers—serfs—who, just like your Mexican girlfriend, were virtually powerless. So they were kind of behind the eight ball politically. Even the Bolsheviks were amazed they succeeded where so many others had failed."

"But when they did, they showed the world that a whole other way of organizing society was possible. They became a major threat to the capitalists! Have you seen that movie *Dr. Zhivago*?"

"Nope. Buddy of mine said I should've. Why?"

"Because for a Hollywood movie it did a pretty good job showing what the war and the Revolution and the civil war after were like. Really brutal times for the Russian people. I didn't like what Stalin did either. But when you see how those people suffered ...*really suffered*...it's easier to understand how some-one like Stalin could come to power."

"I think I've always been suspicious of power, Farrell. Because the ones who want it always seem to use it against the ones who gave it to them."

"So you're right, Russia is no socialist paradise. In some ways it's remarkable the Soviet Union exists at all. There are so many centrifugal forces at work and just barely contained by the state and all its machinery. I wouldn't be surprised if in 20-25 years, after this generation of leaders is dead and gone, it all falls apart. Unless they find ways to reform the state, end the grayness of it all."

As he spoke, I drifted into thoughts of Dostoevsky. Allen and me and the other guys used to talk about him a lot. How I loved his writing! The passion. The wretchedness of life. The reverence for life. His undying faith in the Innocent! The pain. The humiliation. The living who are already dead and don't even know it. Salvation from suffering. It was all there. It was all here. Inside. Me.

Farrell went on talking and I kind of looked like I was listening, but already my mind was racing to other places. I wanted to write something down about the Russians and us and suffering and how it was there and what it's like here and why this country keeps holding this great big myth about itself as protector of all that is good and kind and beatific when it's not.

We like the Western myth about ourselves, wearing the white cowboy hat and riding into towns to shoot up the bad guys just before they rob and rape all the townspeople. But this John Wayne America is just something up on a movie screen. The reality of America is what I've seen. What I almost lost down there in Florida. What I set out to find again.

I liked this guy across the table. I really did. He seemed like a no-bullshit kind of guy. I could never do what he's done. And he'd worked with someone who did something big in his life too. I wondered how they would look to Dostoevsky. Or how Dostoevsky would look to them. Was there ever a holier piece of literature written than "The Grand Inquisitor"? Was there ever a holier person to be found on the written page than the Idiot? Was there ever someone more like me than Raskolnikov? Was there anyone more for me to be like than the poor, wretched sonofabitch from "Notes From The Underground"?

I kind of listened on as Dobbs talked about other things. How Stalin's rise caused a split among American communists. How he, Dobbs, got tossed out of the Teamsters. Something about a trial for his not supporting the war and going to prison for it.

I paid enough attention to ask a question from time to time. But my mind was, like I said, racing ahead to other things. Maybe it was the beer. Maybe the cigarettes. Maybe it was the Irish songs that started up over the jukebox.

Maybe just the exhilaration of feeling like I was cutting loose for the first time in a long time and all was good right now. No insides being pulled apart. No breaking down in uncontrollable tears. No loathing of myself and all I'd become. No...I just felt the need to write. Write even more. Reach up there where Dostoevsky was. And Melville. And Blake. And Whitman. Reach. Reach!

"Well, Jack, I've really dug meeting you. But time for this old timer to hit the road and find a warm bed." Farrell's words kind of pulled me back into the room. I looked around the table. The kids were disappointed it seemed. Like they wanted this talk to go late into the late, just like I did when I was their age. Things to learn! Things to discuss, debate, figure out! Meaning to decipher.

"Hey, Farrell, before we go, answer me this. Why are you still a revolutionary? I mean, what keeps you going? Why not slow down, take it easy? Sounds like you've earned it."

He nodded his head slowly, thinking about his answer. Then he folded his hands and leaned into the table, close to me.

"Fair question, Jack. Good question. Here's what I have to say about that. There is nothing that makes you feel more alive than being out front, on the edge. You feel it intensely like these young people do at their age. That's part of being young. And that's good. They *are* going to move the world forward. But I feel it too. I'm now three years older than the Old Man was when he was murdered. But like I said, he was fighting right up to the end. Even after all that had happened to him.

"Not just Trotsky. Think about our American revolutionaries. Ben Franklin was an old man, older than me, when he signed the Declaration of Independence. He kept pushing right up to the end...in his *eighties*. So did Jefferson. I think Lincoln got more radical as the war went on. More radical and more visionary. More *human*, if that's possible."

Farrell paused and looked around the table. He knew what this moment was. He knew he was saying things the kids would remember and carry forward. He relished it and was careful.

"When you're young, you want to change the world because you can see all its wrongs so clearly. And you have that unbounded energy to step into the fray, take on the enemy no matter the odds. That is good. Really good. Revolutions are not fought by old men.

"But change doesn't happen quick. Sometimes you get beat. If you know the history of our own Revolution, then you know how many times Washington and his army were on the ropes.

"Now we're in a war that is tearing this country apart. It is an imperialist war. It is a war to propagate the interests of a class of people who want to keep the vast majority in chains economically and politically. If we can defeat the tiny minority of those who wage it by mobilizing the millions of others who are opposed, then we will have set the stage for something even larger. And that is when the class who creates wealth takes power from those who exploit that labor and appropriate that wealth."

Farrell's words hung in the air. Then he wrote something on a piece of paper and stood up as did I along with everybody else. We shook hands. Farrell handed me the paper. "Jack, feel free to look me up. Here's my address down in the city. You know the Lower West Side, don't you? And below it is my daughter's place in Oakland. That's where I'll be later on this year. So if your travel writing ever gets you to the West Coast, feel free to stop by and we can talk some more if you'd like."

"Farrell, thanks, man. Fred, you too. I'd give you my address but I don't think it'd do much good. I'm going to be on the road a good bit the next several months. But, listen, thanks a lot. Been a long, long time since I've talked leftie politics with anyone worth a damn. Seriously."

I saw Fred drop a couple bucks in the jar. Then so did the kids. I pulled out a five. "Here, wanted to leave this for a tip. Is that where it goes?"

Fred gave a booming laugh. "No! That money's headed to Ireland. Help free the North from the Brits. You can leave a tip. But on the table. Or, better yet, give it right to Maggie. She'll appreciate it."

So that's what I did. Five bucks was enough to bring a big smile to her beautiful Irish face wreathed with flaming red hair.

We moved towards the door just as the table of men joined the jukebox singing, "The Rising Of The Moon."

At the rising of the moon, at the rising of the moon
For the pikes must be together at the rising of the moon.

The fresh spring breeze hit me full in the face and sobered me up a bit as I said last goodbyes and crossed the street to my faithful old Ford. I was ready to drive and drive and drive! And damn if the good ol' moon didn't move out from behind a cloud! Good ol' moon! Rising!

Chapter 18 — Green Rooster Sutra

I made it back to the motel OK without getting lost or, worse, "finding" a cop along the way. I was very drunk. It was a feel-good drunk! A dive-into-a-dive drunk. A best-friends-with-strangers drunk. A double-lines-in-the-road drunk. A speeding-into-the-curve drunk. A bursting-through-the-doors-throw-off-your-clothes-with-a-brand-new-woman drunk.

It felt a little like the old days when I'd get all jazzed up and come home and write 'til morning. Sometimes I'd get into a groove and beautiful words and sentences really flowed. Sometimes it was just silly, goofy stuff that shouldn't have gone any farther than the paper it was on, like some of my poems that Allen and Ferlinghetti published years after I "died." Called them "Pomes." I thought a lot of what they published was pretty crappy. But if you've been "famous," even after you're dead, the crappy stuff can sell as though crap in life becomes holy in death. Like Indian cow turds.

I woke up late, almost noon, and hung over. Not as bad as I've been before, but sure didn't feel like moving fast any time soon. Glad I didn't have to be at the Albers' right away. I shifted a little as I lay looking at the ceiling expecting my insides to pitchfork me like they did when I was drying out in the hospital. But they didn't, so I considered myself lucky. I got up slowly to piss then came back and just lay there wanting something in my stomach but not wanting to get up again to get it. My head hurt, but not like some I've had where it feels like it's stuck inside a garbage can and someone's beating on the outside with a baseball bat.

Hangovers suck. And they sucked worse the older I got. So why'd I drink so much last night? Why'd I drink at all? With people I didn't even know? The whole evening became a weird kind of blur. Why'd I go into that political meeting? Then the bar after? You want to know the truth? Because I was lonely. Because I wanted a drink. Bad. Because I wanted to feel that old feeling again. That good feeling of being with people who might be interesting in their own little ways. That cut-loose, what-the-hell feeling. That talk-all-night, jack-to-music-all-night, fuck-all-night feeling. And for a while maybe it was there. I liked that Green Rooster. My kind of place. Even if we were just talking commie politics. But hell! It was over before we really got into the crazy, deep shit I used to get into with Dean and Allen and some of that old New York crowd. That Denver crowd. That San Francisco crowd. That Mexico City crowd.

Instead, when Farrell called it a night, so did everyone else. Maybe the kids went someplace else. But that was it for the old men—Farrell, Fred...and me. Damn! That was a hard thing, thinking of me as an old man. But I was. At least compared to the kids who seemed to really respect Fred and revered Farrell. Maybe it was a good thing they did, because those guys had really done some things. They were trying to make a difference. They'd given up some things, a lot of things, to do it. You gotta respect that. Something of the Buddha in both of them, I thought. Still do.

But now I had to get into some reasonable shape to meet these former Black Mountain students. They wouldn't be kids like the ones from last night. Even if they were the last students there when it closed in '56, they'd be mid-thirties at their youngest. Probably closer to my age. I wanted to call Jo, but she was at the library by now. I'd send her another postcard. To Ruth and Memere and Stella too. Women in my life. All these women.

Instead of finding another place to finish off the night, like I said, I dove into my journal. And did it without drinking any more. It'd been a helluva day.

Between the Alberses and that chance meeting with Fred and Farrell and the kids, I had some stuff to write about.

Here's some of it.

New Haven. April 16/17. Melrose Motel. 12:30 AM
After Albers drove into NH. Walked around to see what's up. Felt eyes on me. Didn't care. Walked into crowd outside antiwar meeting by accident. Invited me in. What the hell. All kinds of lefties talking about Vietnam, how to end it, mixing in every other issue they could think of. Farrell Dobbs, Fred Halstead. Others. Socialist Workers Party. Trots. Organizing another demo in DC. Hope it does some good. Not sure it will.
Won't keep Lt Michak from his Delta duty.
Won't protect that well-churched, teary Marine from whatever hell awaits him.
Won't ground B-52s from making moon-sized craters out of rice paddies or jets from spitting flesh-burning napalm onto little girls.
Won't stop corrupt Saigon cops from popping pajamaed peasants in the temple.
Won't keep Nixon and Kissinger from plotting more monstrosities
Most of country sick and tired of war. War war war. War without end. Orwellian war. Friends today, enemies tomorrow. Enemies today, friends tomorrow. But keep us at war. Keep the boot heel on our necks. Make us love Big Brother. But lefties lose a lot of us when they talk about "imperialism" and "solidarity with the NLF." That's just BS to most people. Me included. Foreign, crazy words that don't mean anything. So country's sick of war and just wants out. Now. But they ain't going to sign on to the commie shit either.
I hate war. I hate politics. I hate chicken hawk old men even more who never packed a rifle or

had the shit scared out of them, but have no problem sending kids off to die for their own crazy ideas. Johnson is a chicken hawk. Nixon is a chicken hawk. Lt Michak is not a chicken hawk. That young Marine is not a chicken hawk. But both may die because of two chicken hawk and chicken shit presidents. Country changing and not for better and it sucks.
Irish bar after. Green Rooster. Drank beer. Lots. Smoked half pack of Camels too. Feeling good! Rising of the moon. 20-gallon tip jar. Half filled. Wheelbarrow of booze for raffle. All $$$ goes to IRA. Irish trying to throw Brits out of the North. Finish the Rising Yeats sang about.
"Now and in time to be,
Wherever green is worn,
Are changed, changed utterly:
A terrible beauty is born."
Maggie got my tip.
So much depends
On a green wheelbarrow!
Dobbs, Halstead good men. Union men. Honest (I think).
Dobbs worked for Trotsky in Mexico. There when he got hatchet in the head. 1940. Still feels guilty being in hospital with the trots instead of guarding The Trot.
Told things about Russians and their Revolution I hadn't heard before. All the suffering. Decades! Promise to paranoia. Red to gray. Romanovs to Bolsheviks. Czar to Lenin. Lenin to Stalin. Any better if Trotsky had beat Stalin? Who knows? Dostoevsky. First Existentialist? Notes From The Underground! The Idiot. Prince Myshkin. Suffering to enlightenment. Brothers Karamazov. Grand Inquisitor.
All this suffering! All this writing about suffering! Suffering brings enlightenment.

Spirit. After life. Better ways of explaining craziness of human condition. Better songs.
MAYBE.
Dostoevsky:
Q: If Christ came back would anybody believe him? Would the Church crucify its own Savior?
A: Yes. Because Church has too much invested in The Story as is. People have too much invested in The Story as is. The world couldn't stand to have the Savior return.
Christ revolutionary. Inquisitor reactionary.
Trotsky revolutionary. Stalin reactionary.
Jefferson revolutionary. DAR reactionary.
Orc revolutionary. Nobodaddy reactionary. (Blake)
Whitman revolutionary...Pound reactionary
The moon was hiding
When the Green Rooster crowed
Erin Go Bragh!
And the moon is now arising!
The moon was glowing
When the Red Rooster crowed
Arise, ye prisoners of starvation
But now the moon is sadly waning
The moon was breaking
When the Blue Rooster crowed
And Delaware's ice.

I dozed off. When I woke up, I felt better, but had to hustle to make it to the Albers' by two. One other car already there. Nothing to eat had me hoping Anni would have something for us. I wasn't disappointed.

The Black Mountain students I met had been there at different times. Jane graduated in '46. Just a few years younger than me. Tall, slender, dark. Nice eyes. Single. Very New York chic. She was from Ohio. Shaker Heights. Cleveland suburb. She was now an artist. She smoked cigarettes with long, expressive hands.

Tom graduated in '53, from New Jersey originally. Reminded me of an aging football player. Lineman. He had a family, now lived in Westchester and rode the train to a Manhattan job in the insurance industry. He looked like the kind of guy the girls who hung around us at Columbia would end up marrying and having kids with. But he'd been writing on the side, hoping to break free of the corporate world. It was his car out front. Jane had trained up and cabbed over. They didn't know each other before meeting at the Albers'.

Jane had taken classes from both Josef and Anni. Tom started at Black Mountain in '48. Then got drafted for Korea. He'd come back on the G.I. Bill, met the Albers through his Black Mountain girlfriend and had stayed in touch with them even as he and the girlfriend went separate ways. He'd also known Olson. Neither knew Ruth. And Rice was long gone.

I told them what kind of book I was after. Explained a little who Ruth was. Then Josef and Anni jumped in with their own stories about Ruth and the college and we laughed again when they asked me to tell the "Chaplin-Hitler" *pas-de-deux* story. The war years also brought more painful memories. Jane lost a brother at D-Day. I talked about losing my best friend in Italy. Tom had an older brother who had an arm shot off in the Battle of the Bulge. He'd been a Marine and seen some awful stuff himself in Korea, but counted himself lucky for coming home whole. Almost. "I think I write to keep myself from going crazy." He said it as a joke, but we all knew better.

It took Jane to get us off the war shit. She started talking about how wonderful it was to take classes with the Albers. They beamed as she explained how much she appreciated the "rules" they taught. "It took me a little while to understand, but they didn't have rules for rules' sake. There was a discipline being taught about what and how the eye saw, the hand moved."

Josef nodded vigorously as she talked. "*Ja! Und sie versteht*!"

Jane laughed at this. "I think what Professor Albers means is I paid more attention to his instructions than some of my classmates."

"Like who?" I asked. At this her eyes grew mischievous and looked at Albers.

"Oh....maybe Rob...Rauschenburg!" And she laughed knowing the mere mention would get a rise out of the old art teacher.

"*Ja! Ja! Er war kein* Student!" Albers really got worked up at the mention of his name. "He did...not... listen...to...ANYTHING! Instead he does this..."

Here Albers held his right hand up and wiggled his fingers downward.

"...drip...drip...drip...and this he calls ART!"

Jane howled at the old man's anger. Even Anni allowed herself a thin smile, acting as though she had seen and heard this act many times before.

I knew about Rauschenburg. A little. But Jane had to explain why Joe was so upset.

"Rob paints these wild, crazy abstractions. Totally flowing with colors. Seemingly without any rhyme or reason. But they are beautiful. *Energetic*!"

"Ja! No reason! He plays! A big canvas with drips...this is not art!"

I heard an echo of little Capote lisping about *On the Road*: "That's not writing, that's typing." I sympathized with Rauschenburg.

"Oh, now, Josef, you know that's not true. Just because you like to play with squares and he likes to...how did you say it...dripdripdrip?...and you know there's a lot more to what he does than just splatter!" She laughed some more to show her amusement and also so he knew she also respected and loved her old professor.

Albers was mollified. But only a little.

"So much talent! This Rauschenburg. And you too, *liebe* Jane. But you...you worked hard! You learned! And now look! Big success, yes?"

I noticed how Jane, even in her forties and a little bit New York 'hard,' blushed under her teacher's praise.

"Thank you, professor. My art is appreciated, yes. I'm good technically. And sometimes, yes, I'm even inspired. But Robert...Robert sees different things entirely. Just because he has no use for our rules, doesn't mean he's without rules entirely. Or that he doesn't know what he's doing. He's well liked in the avant-garde circles, *liebe* professor."

She reached over and patted the old man's hand. He harrumphed and decided to change the conversation. Even though the purpose of this get together was for me to interview these former students for the book, Albers still held court. This was his domain.

"And you, Tom, the writing you are doing. It is getting published, ja?"

"Yes. Once in a while. I keep writing. I keep sending things in. I'm getting close to having enough for a book."

"Ja, this is good. *Schreiben*. The writing. You keep doing it. Over and over. It is like the stroke of a brush, no? Over and over. And then the line of syllables and words and stanzas, they grow. Like leaves and flowers. One growing out of the other. Strong! A poem is born."

"That's a wonderful way of putting it, professor. I try and try. I'm afraid I'm not good enough to match the kind of things Olson tried to teach us, though."

"Ach! Do not worry about Olson! Worry about what is here! *Die Geist*!" Albers pointed to his heart.

"You don't think much of Olson as a writer, Josef?" I asked.

"I do not know him well, so who I am to say? We are together because of the college. But in many ways the college I came to when it was new and the one he closed, they were two very different places."

Tom seemed to agree. "I could feel a difference after I came back from Korea. It was there. But it seemed like the teachers were looking to move on, like they knew it was the end. I didn't really see Olson much. Not sure he was ever there a lot of the time."

Albers nodded slowly, "Ja, that is what I heard. Too much of this," gesturing with his fingers as if lifting crumbs to his mouth. "A college lives. It must be strong. Not enough to eat and—pfft!—it dies. Such is life."

Jane jumped in again. "I have to say my years were wonderful! Even though the war made many things scarce, I loved that we could grow our own food. And that we students could help make decisions about how the college should be run. Wouldn't you agree with that, professor?" She seemed eager to keep him from getting grumpy.

The old man softened a bit with his former student's coaxing. "Ja. We tried." Then he added, laughing, "We had no choice! Work. Or starve! Very simple!"

"Like the lines that make your squares! Simple, but strong!" Jane added laughing.

He smiled now as he heard one of his lessons played back by the student.

"You always paid attention, Jane. Simple and strong. Ja. That is why I draw the squares. It is about perspective! What is it that you see? And why do you see it? And how do you tell others what it is that you see? And what do they see when you tell them? Perspective!"

We settled into an afternoon of reminiscences. I scribbled notes as the four of them talked about the school, the faculty, other students. I could see details coming together that would help flesh out a book. I tried not to interrupt, just listen. If I heard a name whose spelling I was unsure of, I put a (?) next to it. I'd confirm those later on. Maybe even with a trip over to the University of North Carolina, where Black Mountain's records were kept.

What emerged in those couple of hours was a picture of a college that had high ideals, was radical for its time, fostered genuine affection and loyalty among its students and teachers and had some of the best and brightest of America's artists and writers cross both of its campuses. Black Mountain was also not immune to the petty jealousies, love affairs and financial turmoil that beset other communities, academic and otherwise. And of Ruth's affair with John Rice—it's clear that Josef and Anni knew all about it, too, and decided they felt no need to bring it up. They didn't talk much about Olson either, which was a bit of a disappointment. Nor did they mention Duncan or Creeley. My heart jumped a little when Tom said he had copies of the *Black Mountain Review*. But not the final copy with my stuff in it.

By the time we left, I had enough notes to get going on an opening chapter and felt anxious to get back to the motel and start typing. I also had contact information for five other Black Mountaineers, three students and two teachers, that the four of them thought I should seek out. I was going to offer Jane a ride back to the train station, but Tom stepped in before I could, and maybe that made more sense anyway.

I thanked the Albers and left with a promise I'd make Ruth come up and see them soon. They invited me to come back the next day if I wanted to talk some more. I said I'd love to, but I had to see Olson in Gloucester. They also asked how they could reach me and I said I'd be on the road for several more weeks, but they could write in care of my mother in St. Petersburg if they wanted to. I was relieved when they said that was OK, but they wouldn't bother and that I was welcome to come back and see them anytime.

I went back to the room and typed out a couple pages of an opening. It was a start and something I could write to Ruth and so say her book was underway.

Writing is a bitch. It's hard. Even in the best of times when you're hopped up on an idea or a person and you can feel the words just pouring out of your head and through your fingers and onto a page. By the time I'd finished two and a half pages of Ruth's book, I was whipped. And hungry. I wanted a beer. I headed back to the Green Rooster.

Chapter 19 — Maximus Gloucester

I only stayed long enough at the Green Rooster for a hamburger and a couple beers. The place was packed with after-work stiffs, guys looking for a quick drink maybe before heading home to wives and kids. I sat at the bar and tried to make small talk with the same waitress—Maggie—from the night before. She remembered me, but was so busy drawing drafts and getting food orders in she didn't have time to bullshit.

I drank slow, wanting an excuse to hang around for a few more minutes. I needed to think about this Olson visit for real now. How was I going to pull it off? Like I said, we'd met a few years before at his place in Gloucester. From what Allen told me after we were both so out of it, the visit was a total waste. So there was a good chance that with my beard and having lost that bunch of weight and not being blown out of my mind, Olson wouldn't recognize me. Still, I rehearsed my story. I'd put all the focus on Ruth and been careful not to mention Creeley and Duncan. I figured it'd help to add some of the stuff I'd learned from the Albers and Joan and Tom.

I wouldn't mention *Call Me Ishmael,* at least right away. I didn't want to come across as some hack writer looking to kiss some hot shit literary ass (although from what I'd heard he wouldn't have minded). I'd get up to Gloucester around noon, figuring it was three hours' drive from New Haven without pushing it. I didn't have his address, but hoped maybe I'd recognize it from the last time. I figured even if I didn't, people would know where he lived. Gloucester was a small town and he was a big man. A *very* big man.

Next morning I was up early and in good shape. But the drive ended up tougher than I'd imagined. Not the drive itself. I knew the way like the back of my hand. But once I crossed into Massachusetts, I started feeling the tug of Lowell, and home. Of all the old places I couldn't go to anymore.

Not that I'd been back much since I left for New York and Columbia thirty years before. But Lowell *was* home, the center of the Duluoz Universe! It was where I'd had some of my most joyous days (and nights). And where I'd had some of my deepest, weepiest sorrows. Sorrows that have never really left me. Most of my parents' generation was gone. Some of the guys I grew up with were still around. Truth was, they had nowhere else to go. They'd recognize me for sure. I'd like to see them too. Except I'd gone off and done so much, seen so much, written so much, what would we have in common anymore? There's truth in Wolfe's line that you can't go home again.

Maybe if Gerard were still alive and living there, I could've gone. If he'd lived, maybe I wouldn't have run off like I did. Maybe by now he'd be the priest at our old church blessing all the little boys and girls like he got blessed before his heart failed him and the angels took him away. Born in 1916, five years before me, he'd be 53. He would've been a great priest, the kind of padre a whole community leans on for everything that holds them together. That was the kind of faith he had.

It's why the nuns cried so when he died. He believed deeply, actively, in God, saw God in every living thing, giving grace to even the tiniest animal. The nuns felt closer to God through him than they did through the leathery old priests. Religion can be a hard business. But in his innocence and his joy, and in his fearlessness before death, he was like an angel on earth. A Gabriel angel. Or a Michael angel. Fierce in his love for all that lives.

For Gerard life was holy. And because of him I saw life as holy too. Not church holy. Not rules and catechisms and cardinal and venal sins holy. *Life* holy. All life. All were expressions of God's love. Later on,

I learned how Blake saw it too. I felt a bond with him because his brother also died when he was young. And together they saw the holy and shared the holy and it drove Blake crazy. Good crazy. Imagination crazy. Jump-out-ahead-of-the-rest-of-the-world crazy. He saw the Divine in the Everyday. Not just saw, but lived. That's why his poetry and his visions are so much more alive than anything his contemporaries wrote or painted. He got it. Like Milton before him got it. (Even if he didn't think he got it in the way Blake said he got it.) In the way Allen and I tried to get it. Gary Snyder too. He got it through Buddhism, which may be the holiest way to be in life, although I tried it and I was never as good a believer as Gary was. (And *is,* he's still around!)

Gerard was the same, especially when he talked about the joys and sorrows of life in ways that my three and four year-old mind could understand. He was patient that way. Showing me the way. The wisdom. The divinity of life even as life was seeping away from him, his poor little heart beating fainter and fainter until it stopped.

And yet as I saw his small lifeless body lying in that casket, released finally from the pain that wracked him from birth, I knew he was with the angels. I knew it. I knew it deeper and holier than any of the nuns and the priests and all their wailing. And that was why I wrote. Because of Gerard. Because through him I could find salvation. Or peace. Or joy. Or some damn thing that gave this life some semblance of meaning through all the suffering. Meaning beyond the joy rides and the girls and the bars and the drinks and the smokes. It's why I believed in him and talked to him when he showed up at the hospital. And on top of Ruth's table. And in that godforsaken motel room. And why I really thought he'd come riding in on a wave with angels at Hatteras. Gerard was my guardian angel, my Buddha. And it was something I couldn't talk about easily when I was "alive"—except through that book I wrote about him and that was the purest, most beautiful expression of love I could write. But now that I'm "dead," I can say it all. Gerard. My angel. My Buddha. My link to the divine.

How I wanted to drive into Lowell and see our house and see our church and see all the places he used to walk with me! How he held my hand. How he talked to me. Cooing about birds and mice and even flies. But I couldn't. I just couldn't. Just like I couldn't drive up to Nashua and see his grave. I was a ghost. Dead to the living. Moving in a netherworld of my own creation.

I bent the Ford around Boston, away from Lowell, headed for the North Shore. It was early afternoon when I reached Gloucester ...the tough, old fishing town. At the very end of old route 128. I drove slowly down to Rogers Street and the harbor, rolling down the window to smell the sea. There was a briskness to this ocean air different from balmy Morehead City. North Atlantic air. More alive. Less seductive. More dangerous. Closer in spirit to the cold, foggy waters of San Francisco Bay and the colder, craggier, deadlier waters of Big Sur. The boats were back in from their early morning runs, bobbing lazily now at anchor, their catches iced and headed to Boston and other cities south and west.

I'd like to say it looked familiar from the last time I was there to see Olsen with Allen and the rest, but it didn't. And even though I was just a tourist, I felt at home here. I drove along the few streets lined with fading mansions thinking maybe a house would jump out at me and all the memories of that not-too-distant day would come flooding back. But none did. I did kind of remember he lived in a big place. Olson had to have a big place to live. At 6' 8" and 300+ pounds, he'd have wrecked anything small.

I headed downtown for something I'd missed for years—a deep bowl of lobster chowder. I found a cozy little place, the Cape Ann, and slipped into a booth towards the back lined with windows facing out to the harbor. The place was afternoon busy, but not crowded. The walls were plastered with news clippings, photos of boats with catches, some tools of the trade. One section of wall was bare except for several large plaques carrying the names of Gloucestermen lost at sea. Names going back more than three centuries.

It was good to be among "my" people again. I knew them. They were like my mom and dad and the people I grew up with. They had to work hard to provide. But they did and they did. Mostly Irish. But lots of Italians. Some Portuguese too. People who drew their living from the seas.

My people were French Canadian. We came from Quebec to work in the woolen mills. But before Canada we were Breton. Linked across the English Channel by blood to the Black Irish and the Celts of Wales. Maybe even to the Basques of northern Spain. We, too, were people of the sea. Fishermen. Mariners. Explorers. So, even though in Lowell we were put right down there with the Irish and the Greeks and the blacks, we were proud of our roots.

I relaxed, listened to the bar chatter. The afternoon drinking was starting up and would crescendo right into evening and late into another Saturday night. I knew this pattern well. The talk would rise and fall and rise again, like swells coming in with the tide. I loved how it felt a world away from dark New Haven. Far from politics and incessant talk of war. Here it was all about life and lives. Who was marrying who and whose boy maybe was going to be a sports star. What the latest catches had been and where. Whose boat needed a new engine. Whose wife had a kid. Whose dad just died.

I remembered those Lowell Saturdays when it'd be my dad at the bar and talking up the latest victory his son had won on the football field the night before. When the talk had been about how fast the

Kerouac kid was. Boy, did he know how to make a cut! And smart enough for college too. Full ride! Boston College! The Eagles! Pride of Lowell! Pride of the Catholics! Pride of all the working stiffs secretly envious because their boys weren't smart enough or fast enough to escape the hard lives they were in.

Other men bought my dad drinks because of what his kid did. And my dad basked in the attention that came to him because of me. "Leo! Your Jean-Louis, he's the best Lowell's ever had." "Leo! The Kerouacs, they are tough, no?" "Leo! Your boy he runs like the wind. An All-American, for sure!" Things were promised. A wink here. A nod there. I would be his way to a better life. A better life for him and Memere. A life that would help heal over the huge hole torn open by Gerard's death. A real house for Leo and Gabrielle! With a yard and a fence and a garage full of tools and a car all paid for! All I had to do was go to Boston, go to college and, most importantly, do on the football field Saturday afternoons what I'd done on Friday nights at Lowell.

Except I didn't.

I didn't go to Boston. I didn't play for BC. I didn't do the things that might've set up my old man for the rest of his life. Instead I ran away to New York City. I went to Columbia, the "Jewish School," instead of Catholic Boston College. And then I broke my leg. I refused to play hurt and risk becoming a cripple the rest of my life. And I mouthed off to the coach and quit the team. Then I quit the college. And all the winks and nods and drinks for my dad stopped. And instead of prospering at his own print place again after the Flood of '36, he stayed a working stiff the rest of his life. And instead of maybe enjoying a few years of this hard life where he'd already buried his oldest boy, he died. Young. And left me with the guilt of having screwed him out of a little bit of joy and pride. And burdened with a promise that I'd take care of Memere until she, too, died. Some kind of "holy" I turned out to be!

Why'd I do this? Why'd I do this to my father? Why'd I do this to my mother? I loved them both. They did everything they could for me. The honest answer is: I don't know. *I don't know.* ***I don't know!*** I didn't want to hurt them. I didn't want to screw my dad out of the business that was promised as long as I played ball at BC. I didn't plan to turn into this 48-year-old heartache for my mother. Or be more of a patient than a husband to Stella. Or a father who never was to Jan. That wasn't my way. Yet that's what happened. So now I'm a ghost sitting in a restaurant spooning chowder and with some cockamamie plan to meet a guy who may know me from when I was alive. And me hoping like hell he doesn't.

Voices at the end of the bar got louder. A bunch of guys my age were huddled around someone else I couldn't see. They were five or six large, muscular men in jeans and coveralls. I thought there was going to be a fight. Which seemed unusual. Most of the fights I'd been in were at two in the morning, not two in the afternoon. Then one voice rose above the others. And an arm shot up in the air holding something. Then the arguing was drowned out by a wail. A pitiful, grown man wail. And the hand that was holding something turned my way and it was a piece of paper. A photo. Black and white. I couldn't make out any more. Then it disappeared below the huddle just as I heard the words "My boy!" When a grown man cries those words, it can only mean one thing: death. Then there were no more words. Just a muffled sobbing. And the sound of empty glasses hitting the bar. Hard. The sound of solidarity. Then "Danny!" wailed above them and sank. The corner grew quiet as the other men tried to comfort their friend. The rest of the place grew quiet too, tense, not knowing if the man's grief would erupt again. And not knowing what to do if it did. For a minute I thought maybe the boy had been lost at sea, the grave of too many Gloucestermen, another name to be added to the newest plaque. Then another, deeper voice shouted "fuckin' war!" into the air and I knew. As did everyone else. The swamp of Vietnam had swallowed another working man's son.

A few minutes later the group left, five huddled around their sobbing, and very drunk, friend. The barmaid watched them with sad, weary eyes. She'd seen this before. They'd get him home to his wife and help him to bed. Then hope he slept it off until morning when it was time for church when maybe a priest could say something that would push back the grief and disbelief and anger at a young life picked off by a Viet Cong sniper or detonated by a land mine or booby-trapped doll. Fuckin' war.

I didn't feel like finding Mr. Charles Olson now. But I didn't feel like drinking the day away either. I could've, if my guys had been around. But now it was just me. I got out of there and decided to walk around, hoping maybe this ocean air would clear my head and shake off these dark thoughts. Seemed like ever since I'd left St. Pete, Vietnam was every place I turned. And it was a bummer war. No evil to defeat. No big victories to lift the spirits. Nothing to say all the sacrifice was worth it. Nothing that would convince that father his son hadn't died in vain. It was a dangerous thing for a government to do to its people.

I started walking, not really paying attention to where I was going. Just wanting to walk. And breathe. And walk. And breathe. I loved being close to the ocean again, even though that trip out to Hatteras got me a bit too close. And now I was here in Gloucester. *Gloucester!* Heart of America's whaling industry. Where, during Melville's time, brave and crazy men set out for years-long trips around the world, through the roughest oceans, braving the deadliest storms, all in pursuit of the world's largest mammals. Then taking them with nothing but long metal spears flung from the bow of a rowboat. Spears attached to hundreds of yards of thick rope that would, once the metal found its mark, begin feeding out feet per second as the whale tried to escape. Rope that could also coil around a man's leg and drag him into the water and down to his final pursuit of a wounded animal plunging into the cold, lightless depths. In boats that became matchsticks, splintered by this same animal shooting up from those same depths, wreaking bloody revenge. Moby Dick.

Whaling on eternal Pacific waters was the most elemental of contests. Olson said in *Call Me Ishmael* that it was the most American of contests. "I take SPACE to be the central fact to man born in America, from Folsom cave to now. I spell it large because it comes large here. Large, and without mercy."

The walking made me feel better about why I was here. Olson was worth the effort. I'd been too drunk to talk before, but now I wanted to meet this mountain of a man. Even if I had to come under false pretenses. I'd heard through the grapevine years before that he'd become jealous of the celebrity bullshit that came with my being "discovered" as the so-called King of the Beat Generation. Supposedly he'd written out pages of *On the Road* so he could try and feel the beat of the book. I didn't give a shit for that. I wanted to get into the man's mind. I sensed we were chasing some of the same things. Ruth's book became a good excuse.

A few paragraphs further, he wrote:

"We are the last 'first' people. We forget that. We act big, misuse our land, ourselves. We lose our own primary...Melville went back, to discover us, to come forward. He got as far as *Moby-Dick*...Whitman appears, because of his notation of the features of American life and his conscious identification of himself with the people, to be the more poet. But Melville had the will. He was homeless in his land, his society, his self...Logic and classification had led civilization toward man, away from space. Melville went to space to probe and find man. Whitman we have called our greatest voice because he gave us hope. Melville is the truer man. He lived intensely his people's wrong, their guilt. But he remembered the first dream. The *White Whale* is more accurate than *Leaves of Grass*. Because it is America, all of her space, the malice, the root."

As I walked the harbor and stared out to the water and the ever-present gulls bobbing and shrieking and stealing, and to the innocent rocks exposed now at low tide and the little islands and the sheltering crook of land here protecting us from the wild sea beyond, that line came back again and again: "I take SPACE to be the central fact to man born in America..."

We love the land. Like old Frost said, "The land was ours before we were the land's." We love its bigness. Like when I hit those open western lands and skies for the first time. But something in us makes us want to escape it too. Like wanting to get away from home. Running across the land to new lands. Or over the water. Hopping a ship for the hell of it. And further out now, into the skies, into space, maybe to new worlds. We're grateful for having been born into the warmth and comfort of snug harbors, of great cities and small towns and tidy farms. But something longs for that unknown beyond too.

We all came from somewhere else. We came to a land as big and open and welcoming and dangerous as the seas we crossed to get here. Like Josef and Anni Albers, uprooted, thrown out of their birthplace, threatened with death if they did not leave. Coming here and finding new life. First at a tiny, fetal college. And later at a great university.

I'd been thinking about these things a lot for a long time. Feeling them before I could know about them. Experiencing them before I could write about them. But it was more than mere restlessness. Something more. I knew that. More than a longing to see things I hadn't seen before. More than a desire to run away. I was beginning to feel that maybe this meeting with Olson would be more than just reminiscences of Black Mountain. Without tipping my hand—or resurrecting the dead!—maybe we'd have some things to talk about, some real things. Things that would help me write.

I thought about that connected line: "We are the last first people." With the Americas settled there are no more first peoples. Of course the Indians, all of 'em up and down both continents were the *first* first peoples. We got here last and made ourselves first. Then, as Melville and Whitman and later Olson and Allen and Burroughs and I did, we went back around looking for the first stories from the first peoples, looking in them for answers to who we are today. We searched them out in different places. Deep in viney, Mayan forests, long overgrown and forgotten cultures that had conquered their bloody worlds, raised high their gods, then fell into a long, long sleep. Wide across flat, flat lands. Lands as open and dangerous as the seas themselves where the only guide was a big, bloody sun tracking long across universal skies. And high up in cloudy, snowy, lonely, desolate mountains where the only soul in the world belonged to you. And then maybe not even to you. We searched them out everywhere.

We ran away from civilization to find what was really civilized in our souls. And what was truly animal. And what was truly divine. We ran away from priests and merchants and officers and the rich and the greedy and the greasy hands of commerce. We looked for things bigger—and smaller—than ourselves. We became devils so we could consort with angels. We shattered the squares of our lives and let our imaginations dripdripdrip onto other canvases.

I was back at the car having walked almost two hours. I felt better. My head was cleared. I felt that kind of good exhaustion that reminded me of my Dharma Bums hike with Snyder up in the Sierras.

After a quiet, dreamless Saturday night, I was up the next day, ready this time to go see Olson and see what he'd share about his time at Black Mountain. I had another full breakfast at a place packed with Catholics after their nine o'clock Mass. Families with bunches of little kids squirming in their chairs, spilling glasses, Sunday clothes soiled with butter and syrup, milk and juice. But now it was time to find Charles. I was ready. I decided to ask the waitress if she knew where "Olson, the writer" lived.

"Who?" she asked.

"Charles Olson. He's a pretty famous writer. Big guy. Lives here in town somewhere."

Her eyes widened and mouth spread into a broad smile.

"Oh, *him*! The Jolly Green Giant!" She laughed, then paused, remembering. "You know, I haven't seen him in a *long* time, now that you mention it. But I think he lives over on Fort Square. Or used to at any rate. Yeah, haven't seen him in like forever."

I got directions. It wasn't far. Fort Square was a loop of a street that came down to the water. Had some old houses on it. Fish houses too. The smell of fish guts hung in the air. I drove by a small park where a mother pushed her child gently on a swing.

I drove the loop a couple times again hoping I'd see the house I'd passed out in couple years ago. But nothing looked familiar. I passed an older Italian-looking guy scratching up dirt in a little flower bed carved out in front of his house. I stopped and got out.

"Morning. Hoping you can help me. I'm looking for Charles Olson. Understand he lives around here. You know which house might be his?"

He straightened up and gave me a good looking over.

"You're looking for Charlie, eh? And why might that be?"

He wasn't being rude, but I could tell right away he wasn't going to take any bullshit from me. I was right about his nationality; I could hear traces of an Italian accent lingering. And he may have been old, 70s, but he still had the build of a strong man. Shorter than me, but broader across the chest. His arms were muscled. A full head of white hair and a beard too. I guessed him for a fisherman in an instant.

"Well, I'm working on a book. About the college he used to be in charge of. A long time ago. I was hoping I could ask him some questions about it."

"Uh-huh." Then he turned back to his little hoe and the hard ground. Chunks sprayed up with each bite into the earth.

"A very good friend of his, who helped him a lot with the college, wanted me to make sure I got up here to talk to him."

"Uh-huh." He kept digging at the ground trying to decide if I was worth his—or Olson's—time. Then he stopped, leaned on the hoe and looked right at me.

"OK. First off, you're on the wrong side of the day to have any chance of seeing Charlie. He don't get up much before four or five in the afternoon. Or at least he used to.

"And, second, you're too late anyhow." Here he paused just a second. "Charlie, he died. Back in January."

"He's…he's…*dead*?"

"Yop. The drink and the smoke. And then the cancer. Got him good. But that was his house, right there. Rented the second floor." The old man gestured to a large three-story building two down from his.

I was stunned. The man I'd hoped to see alive by pretending I was dead, was really dead while I remained very much alive.

"Yop. Thought everybody'd heard of it by now. Guess I was wrong." He turned back to his hoe. Then stopped and looked at me again. "What'd you say your name was?"

"I didn't. But it's Jack. Moriarty. I'm a writer."

"Yop. So you said. Never heard of you. Charlie, he used to have quite a crew around here taking care of him. A'course, there was a *lot* to take care of!"

I smiled at the weak joke.

"That's terrible! Olson's dead...unbelievable. I just came from people who knew him well and they didn't say a thing about him even being sick. When did he die?"

"I told you. January. In New York. Cancer of the liver. But he hadn't looked good for a long time. He took terrible care of himself. A big man like that, he gotta be careful. But Charlie, he just seemed like he was out of control...all the time."

I shuddered. Not because of Olson. Because of me. It was the "out of control...all the time" that reminded me of my "last" years. Except I had a wife and a doctor and a nurse who refused to let me die. Sounded like maybe Olson hadn't been so lucky.

"Is there anybody there now? Anybody...you know...I could talk to?"

"Nope. His stuff is still there. His daughter she comes up once in a while, but haven't seen her in weeks. She's at school anyways. More important things to do than clean up after her dead father."

"No wife? Friends?"

"Yop. Around. Scattered. But nobody here. Nobody really liked Gloucester, except Charlie himself. And he loved being here. He talked about it almost like it was some sort of...magical place, ya know what I mean?"

I didn't, but I agreed with him anyway.

"Did you know him well? Were you friends?"

"Oh, sometimes in the summer we'd sit outside and talk. And he liked to come down to the docks and bullshit. Man, could he talk! But half the time you couldna make out a thing he was saying. I mean between the smokes and the arms waving around and talkin' about things I never heard about. The guys they didna know what to make of him. They just thought he was crazy.

"I think he meant well. Like he wanted to be one of the guys. He and I, we'd talk. But always out here. Never went inside. I don't think he really wanted people inside. Unless they were bringing him food or drink. I don't know. He was all right, I guess."

Olson dead. I wondered why Ruth or Albers hadn't heard yet. Had Allen? Surely Creeley had. And Duncan. And all the other guys. Of course, maybe no wonder I hadn't heard since they all thought I was dead too. But didn't sound like Charles was faking his.

"Yeah, from what I heard, that sounds about right. I've read some things he wrote. He had big ideas, that's for sure."

The old man chuckled. "He said he was writing a big book about Gloucester. Started calling himself a silly name. 'Maximus'...like he was some Roman Caesar or something! Then he talked like he wanted to go out on a run to the Banks. But no way could I see that man do anything but be in the way, even on a big boat like my Alex's." Then he paused and asked, "Was he from around here? I mean, originally? He never talked too much about himself."

I tried to add a little. "I think he was born up in Worcester. Came here as a kid in summers. Don't know a whole lot more about him. Except that college down south. He ran it until it closed. That was in the 50s. But the people I met said he was quite a guy."

He looked at me, nodding once, appreciating the information. "You from around here too? You sound like it."

"Nah, Boston originally. I live in Florida now. Help take care of my mother. Got asked to do this book about the college. Why I'm here."

"So you said. Well, I been a fishin' alla my life. My papa, he taught me. Now my two sons, they try. They gotta go farther and they don't bring back as much. But they do OK. It's a hard life."

"Yeah, can imagine. Only been out there a couple times. During the war." I knew he knew from my age which war I was talking about.

"You in the Navy then?"

"Nah. Merchant Marine. Supply ship. Ran to Greenland and back couple times is all."

"Still, that is dangerous work! I know! There was a couple Gloucester boys went down North Atlantic. Nazi subs."

"Yeah. That was rough stuff. I was lucky. Missed most of it."

"My boys. They were both Navy too. One, he was Atlantic and Mediterranean. Not so bad. The other, he was Pacific. Hoo boy! Did he see a lot! But they came home not a scratch on them. Thanks be to God."

"I'm glad for them. And you."

"The one who was in the Pacific, he don' like to talk about it. Even though he wasn't Marines and landing on all those islands, he saw lot of 'em chopped up. And the kamikazes. Hoo boy! That wassa rough stuff."

"Yeah. Sure was."

We paused. He picked at the dirt a bit more. This was hard ground. If he was lucky, by July a few flowers, some petunias, some snapdragons maybe, would fill the small space.

I was about to go, disappointed and trying to figure out what's next when he stopped his hoe again and said, "Would you like to share a cup of tea with an old man? We talk. Maybe there's more about Charlie I can remember."

This guy seemed friendly. And he had a way of looking you in the eye that made you look back. With Olson good and dead it wasn't like I had a whole helluva lot to fill up the rest of my Sunday.

"Yeah. That'd be OK. I'd planned to spend the day with Olson anyway. So I got nothin' else going on."

He leaned the hoe against the saltbox. I followed him up three concrete steps onto a window-enclosed porch crowded with old wicker furniture. He jimmied the main door open and we walked into a small living room that was big enough for a sofa, a couple of reclining chairs, a small table between and a small TV set perched on another small table. There was also a little Franklin stove tucked into one corner.

Various family photos were on the walls and table, and on an inset of shelves. A large framed one of him and a woman I guessed was his wife dominated the middle shelf. The other shelves were packed with books, which was something I wasn't expecting in a fisherman's house. A set of stairs on the right led up to bedrooms, I supposed. I followed him back into his kitchen where—just like at Lissa's, I sat at a small wooden table while he boiled water and got the tea and two large mugs.

"So, Jack Moriarty, I am forgetting my manners. I should tell you my name also!" He had started slicing some bread and pulled a butter dish out of an ancient refrigerator. Even though I'd stuffed myself at breakfast, it was clear he'd decided we'd have more than a "cup of tea."

He stopped slicing, moved efficiently around the kitchen to pull out plates, knives, a jar of jam, like a man used to boats and small spaces. Placing all on the table, he stood erect and extended his hand, with a large, friendly smile.

"My full name is Prospero Giovanetti." He said it with pride, the syllables rolling off his tongue in a way only the Italians can say them. "That was too much for my friends, so they just called me 'Pross.'" He could see my surprise at the name, maybe pleased I recognized it.

"How did I get a name like Prospero? My father! He was a man of the sea, but also of books.

And he said, 'If my son is going to live his life on the water like me, then I give him the name of one who can rule the waves and disperse the storms.' So, he named me after his favorite person in all of Shakespeare."

He delighted in telling this story, one he'd probably told all his life. Still, looking at him I could see how the name fit. "Yeah, that's pretty cool. *The Tempest* is one of my favorites too."

"I know it by heart!" He drew himself up, remembering a favorite line. "'I'll deliver all; and promise you calm seas, auspicious gales, and sail so expeditious that shall catch your royal fleet far off.' This I used to say as we set off for every trip to the Banks."

"Not a bad way to wish yourselves good luck."

"Oh, it was more than a wish for luck! When you're out there and a storm's full in your face, you better have more than luck to keep you." He said this in a kind way, his voice full of experience.

He poured steaming water into our mugs, the tea steeping. "You take some milk with that?"

"No, thanks. I like it just this way."

"Me too."

The old man sat. We shared bread, butter, jam. "I bake it myself!" Then he took a long, thoughtful sip from his mug.

"So, Jack, tell me more about this book and why it was so important to see Charles."

I told him about stopping in Black Mountain, about the chance meeting with Ruth, how one thing led to another, then meeting with Josef and Anni, Don and Jean, and the hope of seeing Olson to get his take on the college in its last years.

Prospero nodded as I talked, looking at me full on just as he had outside. When I finished he said, "Yes. This Black Mountain. I remember him talking about it. I didn't ask him many questions. With Charles, you didn't ask. You listened. He talked and talked and talked! And smoked when he wasn't talking. Inhale the smoke and exhale the words. Or maybe some of the other things I heard about. I heard you mention a name at the beginning. A Creeley?"

"Yeah. Robert Creeley."

"Is he the one-eyed poet?"

"Yeah! Someone I met a long time ago. One of the guys who said I oughtta stop by Black Mountain."

"Yes! I know him. Or, I have met him. Here."

This was a surprise! Maybe Prospero knew more than he was letting on.

"Did you talk with him?"

"Yes. Oh just a little. He and Charles, they both wanted to know more about the fishing life. They were like schoolboys. Asking what it was like to go out every day and come back maybe with a full boat, maybe with nothing. That was about the only time I could talk with Charles, when he was asking about the ocean! Then he would listen. This Creeley, he did too."

I didn't feel like tipping my hand and letting him know that maybe I knew more about both Creeley and Olson than I'd let on so far. Still, I was enjoying his company and, it seemed, he was enjoying mine.

"Did Olson know you loved Shakespeare?"

"Oh, yes, that too! He thought it wonderful that a simple man as myself could know someone as great as Shakespeare!"

"Did he have a favorite? *The Tempest* also?"

"He never said a favorite. But, you know, I think he liked *King Lear*. He liked to say its lines and show me he knew Shakespeare too." Here, Prospero drew himself as big as he could make himself, trying to imitate a man twice or three times his size. "'Blow, winds, and crack your cheeks. Rage, blow, you cataracts and hurricanoes…' And he would roar when he said them. Like he was on a stage. The men at the docks, they would just shake their heads." The old man laughed as he recalled the memories.

"Sounds like you guys talked quite a bit."

"Oh, well, you know. Some maybe. He liked to go down to the boats. We would talk there. But he was not in good shape. Not good shape at all. And someone who had so much. And he was much younger than me, almost as a son! My boys, they thought he was just a big, old crazy man."

"Did you?"

"Me? No. Or maybe not crazy in the way my boys did. They...they...are much more the business-men. Or at least my Alex is. They don't have time for ideas, especially crazy ones! The fishing...they have to go farther. And there are more and more boats. And they have to send the fish farther and farther to markets. The whole business...it's not the same. I wish maybe they didn't have to do it. But...the sea...if it's in your blood, it's in your blood."

"Yeah. I think Olson kind of got that. The way he wrote about Melville. And the way Melville wrote about the sea. The way he actually experienced it. Did you ever see whales when you were out?"

"See whales?" The old man roared at this one. "Yes! All the time. They are out there. The small ones mostly. Baleens. Meinkes. And humpbacks too! Have you ever seen a humpback breach? Magnificent! But no Moby Dicks, if that's what you were asking!"

"You think that really happened? A whale ramming a ship? Destroying it?"

"Do I? Yes! Of course! We think we are masters of the sea. But it is the sea who is the master! And if the sea decides you are to stay with it forever, then you stay. If you come to murder a whale, why should you be surprised if he decides to murder you right back?"

"When I was on that old freighter headed to England, I tried to imagine what it was like for Melville. Going away for years on a whaler. Sailing through places like Cape Horn. Then being in the Pacific where water goes on and on like the universe itself. And going through the chase and killing of a whale. Then living to come home and tell the tale."

"But...you did not stay on the water? You came home." I could see he was looking for me to tell more of my story.

"Yeah. I did sign up for the Navy. But I'd hurt my knee playing football and they decided they didn't want me. So maybe I got lucky and sat out the war." I hoped like I'd hoped at Ruth's that he couldn't tell I was lying through my teeth.

"Yes. Maybe you did. I am a great reader of history. War is much of our history. The Civil War general Robert E. Lee said something that I have always thought carried much wisdom. He said, 'It is good that war is hell, lest we grow too fond of it.'"

"Yeah. That's a good way of putting it. Did you ever have to go to war?"

"I am seventy-five years old! I have seen too much war. But I am lucky too. I was a young man, too, at the Great War. When time came I also signed for the Navy. Gloucestermen didn't need to be in trenches. We were needed where we knew best—the ocean! I served on a troop ship and we also made those runs dodging German U-boats and their torpedoes. They hunted us in groups. Wolf packs, they called them. We were lucky. Others not so much.

"My papa, he came to America to get away from all the silly wars. Poor men dying for rich men. He did not want me to go back over. But, sometimes war comes to you and then you must fight, no? War came to America and I am an American, so I fight. Just like you and my boys."

"What part of Italy was he from?" I really wanted to change the subject off of war. Enough of that crap! Even though he hadn't told me, I decided to guess at his nationality.

"Italy? No! We are *Sicilian*! We are *Syracusa*! Our first blood is Greek. We followed the great Aeneas. From the beginning we are of the water. The sea gives us life. Poseidon is our father! We were

Romans long before those two boys suckled on wolves' titties. He-he."

"I've never been to Sicily. Been close. Algiers. Marseille."

"Ah! That is good! Then you know a little the beauty of the Mediterranean! *Most* of the time! When Poseidon he gets angry—whoomph!—you better watch out!"

"Yeah, it was beautiful. The water is so blue. I met a girl a couple weeks ago. Her family is from the island of Rhodes." Prospero nodded he knew where the island was. "Now they live in Florida and have a restaurant. Have you been back to visit?"

"Yes! A few times. The first in 1920's. With my father and mother. We had saved enough and we went back to visit their families. Most of it was very good. But some not so good. The *fascisti.* Thugs! Italy wanted the black boot. And they got it!

"Then we go again in 1951. My wife and I took our boys. Boys! They were men already! Things were OK. Many places they were still broken from the second war. My cousins, they were getting by. But they thought we were princes! Rich!"

Prospero paused and looked away. His eyes darkened, just for a moment, then he focused on me again.

"I went one more time. Seven years ago. Just before my Maria died. Everyone there was old now! Things were better, yes. But I am thankful my papa he wanted to come to America. He worked hard. I worked hard. My boys, they work hard. Sometimes I wish maybe not so hard. But, that is life, no?"

"Yeah, I think you're right about that. What is life, but work? You stop working, you die. Seems that's how it is for all living creatures." I was really warming up to Prospero. We'd only been talking for maybe an hour, but something about him made me comfortable sitting there and talking some more. I still couldn't believe Olson was dead. But maybe here was someone that could help me add to the Black Mountain story in other ways.

"I'm sorry. I guessed that was her in the picture?" I nodded towards the living room.

"Yes! Yes." His face sunk now, pulled down by memories. "She got the female cancer. Here." He spread his hands across his groin. "She was sick when we went to Sicily. But I tell you, I didn't know how sick. She was so strong that way. Never let me know when she was hurting. Even when I knew! She didn't want to put her pain on me or her boys. Then we were back three months and—poof!—she was gone."

Prospero and I looked at each other without saying a word, me taking on the sadness in his eyes and in his voice. It was a sadness that I knew and yet would never know. The sadness of Gerard dying. But not the sadness of losing a life's mate. That was a sadness I could not allow myself.

Then he stood. I thought our talk was over, the grief of the memory having overshadowed whatever enjoyment he'd been getting from our conversation.

"Would you mind if I show you something? An indulgence for an old man?" he asked as he started moving towards the living room. "Maybe we'll make some more tea in a few minutes."

"Sure. I've got time."

"Here, sit." He gestured towards the sofa. Then he walked over to the book shelves and pulled something large from the bottom. It was an old photo album. He sat in the reclining chair next to the sofa and put the book on the coffee table. He opened to the first page, an 8 x10 black and white photo of him and a woman I guessed to be his wife, Maria. They were in formal wear, a suit for him, a flowing dress for her. It was an old photo. But Prospero's look was unmistakable. His hair was thick and black. No beard. But eyes that looked happy and confident. And a smile that reflected the same. As though he was the proudest man on earth.

"This was taken fifty-five years ago, the day of our wedding, to this very day."

"Today's your anniversary?"

"Yes."

"She's really pretty."

"Maria Contessa Consolo." He said her name slowly, each syllable coming out full of memories and love. He ran his fingers over the photo in much the same way Ruth did with John Rice's.

"I knew her from the very first. In school I say to her 'Someday we are going to marry.' But first, I have to work and help my father get a bigger boat. So we can find enough fish to support two families." He paused. "Fifty-five years. It's a long time, no?"

"Yes, a very long time."

"She was the only woman I have been with. The only woman I wanted to be with. She was strong. She had to be. Being a fisherman's wife is not easy! Papa and I would leave for days. Each time she didn't know if we would come back or not. So many Gloucestermen lost.

"Each time I would leave, she would walk with me down to the dock and I would say my little *Tempest* line. But soon, I would start with 'I'll deliver all' and she would finish with 'and I promise you calm seas, auspicious gales, and sail so expeditious that shall catch your royal fleet far off.' You see, it was our pledge, and our prayer, to each other."

"That's a beautiful story. I can see why you miss her so much."

He nodded again, memories filling the space between us. "Are you married, Jack? Or, have you ever been?"

This was a little more personal than I cared to get, but he had opened up so much it was hard not to share some. Still, I didn't tell all.

"I was. But it didn't last long. I was young, she was young..."

Prospero was looking hard at me. I wasn't quite sure why. Disapproval for a divorce? Sensing I was holding back?

"Did you love her?" That's a question that's haunted me all my life. Not just Edie or Joan or now Stella. And what about my daughter, Jan? What is love, not in the general, academic or even poetic sense, but in my life? What has love meant to me? What has my love meant to others? I am haunted.

"Yes! Of course. But then things changed. And then the love changed. And then it wasn't love. And then...then...I left."

"You are a man who likes to be on the road a lot?" He asked it as an honest question, not judgmentally.

"Yeah, guess I am. Being a writer, it can take you all kinds of places."

"Yes. A writer on the road maybe is a lot like being a fisherman on the sea. You go out, cast your line into the dark and hope you hook something big, no?" He chuckled as he said this.

I laughed along with him. "Yeah, that's not a bad way of looking at it." I heard Olson's "I take SPACE..." echoing in my head. "A lot of times I do feel like I'm casting into the dark. Sometimes I pull up something big. Other times...nothing!"

"For me, I had no choice. I was born to be a fisherman. My boys, maybe they had choices. But they chose the sea also. Alex, he is my oldest, the Atlantic one, he is divorced now too. His wife, she did not have the patience—or the courage!—to be a fisherman's wife. Now, she is in Lowell. With an insurance salesman!"

Prospero spit out those last words, making "insurance salesman" sound like the lowest form of life on earth. Which maybe they are. And I jumped a little hearing "Lowell." A reminder of how close, and how far, I was from home.

"Johnny, my youngest, he never married. I don't know. Sometimes I wish he could still find a nice girl and settle down. But it's fish and drink for him. Fish and drink. He works as hard as his brother. But then it's down to the bar. And Florida. He likes to go to Florida. The Keys. Maybe the war never left him. I don' ask him about it no more. It's his life."

"I will tell you," he continued, "that there is nothing sweeter in this life than the love of a woman. I have spent my life on the sea. It has given me life. Given life to my family. I love it. And I fear it. Yet nothing was so good as when I saw her waiting for me at the dock when we came in with a boat full of fish. And I knew she was so happy that I came back again safe and whole. And I was proud that I had done what I said for her.

"I would jump off the boat into her arms and smile with a big kiss and tell her 'You gave me calm seas and now I deliver all!'" Then he chuckled again at the memories. "Even when the seas were not so calm, I did not tell her. And even if she knew we had been in storms, she did not ask. It was enough that I was home." He tapped at the photo again. Then turned page after page in the album, looking at the years moving along.

"Did you ever have bad times, when you came home with little or nothing?" He nodded his head slowly without looking at me, staring down at the pictures.

"Yes...yes. Many times. That is a fisherman's fate, no? Even when you knew the fish were there, sometimes they would not come. And you stay longer. And you fish harder. But sometimes, you have to give up and come home. But Maria, she never said a word. Not a word! Our home was always calm seas and bright skies. Such was her love."

He paused again, now looking at me. I could see tears starting at the corners of his eyes. But they stayed there.

"Her love was deep and abiding. Unchanging."

"Like Miranda's for Prospero?" thinking he'd like my reference to Shakespeare.

"No! That was the love of a daughter for her father. It was a good love, no? Maria's love was of a wife for her husband. It was trusting. Hopeful. She believed in me." Now his voice was somewhere else, but he continued distantly, "That love, it sustained me through hard storms and heavy seas...through nights so dark, I wondered if I would ever see the light again. Her love was there whether my nets were full or empty. I tell you, Jack, it was a love that wound two into one. Truly. Truly."

As he spoke, my mind raced through all the women in my life maybe hoping to settle on one who could have been my Maria. Maybe there was one. Maybe...maybe...

"Well, Jack!" now Prospero thundered again, as if putting the past back in its place. "I am not being a good host. You did not come into my house to listen to an old man weep through his memories! May I get you more tea?"

"Yeah. But, if you don't mind, gotta empty the ol' bladder."

He laughed and said, "Yes, of course! Upstairs and at the end of the hall."

When I went downstairs, the old man was back in the kitchen. The kettle was starting to whistle for the second time. On the table was another album.

"Do you mind if I look at the pictures? In this other one?" I raised my voice into the kitchen.

"No! These I want you to see! Look at them, please!"

The first photo was a brilliant sunset at sea. (At least I think it was sunset. The evening colors were so different from morning.) Just the final crescent of sun was above the watery horizon. A moment before the green flash. The sea was flat, ready to go from blue to black. It was a beautiful photograph. Taken by an experienced hand.

Prospero came back in with two mugs steaming.

"That was taken about fifteen years ago. We were on our way back from the Stellwagen Bank. Me and the boys. We had a nice load of cod. But it had been a rough day. A storm, she came up before dawn and stayed with us most of the day. Then she broke in the afternoon and by sunset the seas were as pretty as you hope for. My boys had the wheel. So I took some pictures. It seemed like a blessing was laid down for us."

"It's a beautiful photo. I thought a professional had taken it."

Prospero laughed, appreciating the compliment. "No, no! Just me. Something I started doing because you see so much out there and it's hard to tell people who've never been what there is.

"That catch...that was the catch that let us get the second boat. We'd been working and saving for years. I knew and the boys knew we'd need a second boat if we were going to feed all the mouths we thought were coming."

"You still have two boats?"

"Yes. But I don't go out anymore. Or not every day like they do. They run their own crews. Alex, he got the newer one. And Johnny, he likes my old one. They are good boats. Now when they ask me to go, it is for luck only. I know this."

I turned more pages. Lots of pictures of catches. Of his boys. Their crews. But then some others of sea life. A tern perched on a spar rigging. A flock of pelicans swooped low just above the water. A pod of porpoises leaping in unison. With each Prospero told a story of where and when. I got the feeling he knew North Atlantic waters as intimately as that little patch of ground he'd been hoeing.

And then the final one, a magnificent photo of a humpback breaching. It couldn't have been more than thirty feet from the boat. You could see the whale's skin all barnacled. Even its eye. About twenty feet of it was out of the water, almost as if trying to leave it altogether.

"That's outstanding, Prospero! He's really close!"

"Yes, yes. And it's not a he, it's a she. You can't see, but there was a calf with her just below the surface. She was teaching him how to do this." He gestured the breaching with his arms. "Then she came right up to the side of the boat, so close I could almost reach out and touch her."

"You weren't worried she might turn into a Moby Dick?"

"Oh, no no no. This was a very smart whale. She—I could look right in the eye and see intelligence. Yes, intelligence! Their songs, it is a language, no?"

I had to plead ignorance on this one.

"I do not pretend to understand all. But after a life at sea, I have come to understand we know so little. We pretend we understand. But what we know of the ocean life barely touches the surface. We are plankton! These creatures," he said tapping the photo, "they travel the world, they know the currents and the ridges and the valleys like we know the roads from Gloucester to Boston. We can drown in a few feet of water; they go down a mile and back up like it is nothing! And their songs, their language, they speak it over hundreds of miles. We think we are the masters! But, no, it is they."

"I'd love to see one of those sometime."

"You would?" My statement stirred him again. "What about tomorrow?"

"Tomorrow?" I was hesitant, not sure what he was driving at.

"Tomorrow, yes! We take my boat. Johnny's now, but he is in Florida again this week. We take it to Stellwagen. A short run. I can't promise you whales. But I know where to look."

He was looking at me with that I-won't-take-no-for-an-answer look. I'd seen that before—from Ruth.

"Tomorrow?" I asked again, trying to buy a moment's time to consider, thinking maybe the old man's enthusiasm would wane as quickly as it waxed.

"What is tomorrow? You have no Charles Olson to talk to. And I do not like to go out alone anymore. The weather, it is supposed to be good. We go. Maybe we catch a cod. Maybe we see a whale. Maybe you find something else to write about. Casting into dark waters, no? The fisherman and the writer!" He laughed at his little joke.

I looked at him. I didn't know what to say. It sounded like an adventure, no doubt. And the chance to see a whale!

"OK. OK. Yes. I can do that. Maybe get a taste of what Olson and his Melville were after."

Prospero clapped his hands. "Good! I know everything to make ready. All you have to do is be here. Six a.m. sharp. Earlier if you can."

I kind of got a kick out of making this old man happy. Something else for his anniversary besides thinking of his dead wife.

It was time for me to leave anyway. Most of the afternoon was already gone.

We stood and Prospero extended his hand.

"Jack, thank you. I am sorry your Charles Olson was not here. But maybe you discover something more. Tomorrow!"

"Prospero, thanks a lot. Maybe you will be right. You don't have to deliver all. But I'd appreciate calm seas and auspicious gales."

"Yes! Yes, of course! We will have a fine time! I promise!"

With that I was out the door.

"Six a.m.!" he called after me.

"Six a.m.!" I called back.

Chapter 20 — Stellwagen Bank

The next morning came quicker than I expected. I'd set the alarm for five thirty and damn near slept through it. Even after kicking the booze and getting back on the road, I wasn't used to getting up this early. It hadn't been so long ago when five in the morning meant crashing into bed instead of getting up. I dragged my ass out of bed, got dressed and cleared some things out of the car, thinking maybe Prospero might have some gear to load. There was just a touch of dawn coming on when I pulled up to his place again, a spring nip in the air. I was already glad I'd dressed warm, remembering it'd be cooler yet, even cold, on the water. The old guy was ready for me, coming down the steps and giving me a big handshake.

"Jack! You are right on time! This is good! Come inside! I have everything ready. But first we have a good cup of coffee."

Back in the kitchen he had an old depth chart spread out, wrinkled, marked and a corner torn. He poured us mugs and started again talking excitedly, "Look here! This is my favorite map. I have used it more than thirty years! Do you know where Stellwagen Bank is?"

I had no idea what he was talking about, which was OK because it gave Prospero a chance to do something I'd already learned he loved to do: Tell stories.

"Stellwagen is where we fish today. OK. We are here." He pointed to Cape Ann and Gloucester. Then he moved his finger along the shoreline. "And here is your Boston. And, of course, you know Cape Cod. Falmouth. Wellfleet. Provincetown—where the Mayflower and the Pilgrims really landed first. You knew that, yes?" Not pausing for an answer, he then moved his finger into Massachusetts Bay and slowly to the east. "Now, you see how shallow it is here? Five fathoms. Then deeper a little. 10. 15. And then, see how fast it gets deep? 35 fathoms. 40 fathoms. And out here, shallow again! 15 fathoms. 20 fathoms. That is Stellwagen Bank. See how quick it rises? A wonderful plateau under the sea." He used his hands to show how the ocean bottom went down, then moved up and flattened out. "I have been reading how much lower the ocean was at the last Ice Age. I think Stellwagen was above the sea! Dry land! Yes!" Then he swept his hand over ocean back to land. "I think dry land to the Cape and maybe most of the Bay. Imagine! Could people have been here? Perhaps!"

"The Bank is named for Henry Stellwagen. He mapped it first for the United States government. 1854. They needed to know how to help all the ships avoid shoals and reefs. He was a Lieutenant Commander in the Navy. I read about him."

He ran his fingers again over this part of the North Atlantic bordering New England and the Canadian Maritime Provinces like he was reading a favorite passage from an old book. He continued talking about how the deep, cold, nutrient-rich waters from the Arctic north come down and hit the steep upswell of land to feed the fish and mammals who preferred the warmer waters on top. He rattled off so many kinds of fish that I lost count. Cod. Flounder. Tuna. Bass. Along with lobster, scallops and squid. And then he finished with sharks.

"The Great White?" I asked naively.

"Yes! The Great White! We do not want to catch one of those! Let me tell you! They will catch you! Ha-ha!! They are a great, great animal. Magnificent! But, like the Moby Dick whale, you respect this fierce fish."

The mention of Moby Dick made me ask again about whether we'd see any whales.

"Yes! Yes! We will look for the humpback! But we may see others too! Minkes. Fins. And the Right Whale. Very rare. But, I have seen it!

"Yes, Jack, we will fish for cod and tuna. Maybe some nice haddock. But we will also look for the whales. Maybe we will see a breach. If we are very lucky and get close, I will photograph. Maybe you can put that in your book, a substitute for our big, dead friend."

He put his finger on a pencil dot a fraction of an inch to the east of where he said the Stellwagen Bank started.

"We will go here first. Northwest Corner. It is close. I know this water. We will find fish! Yes! Other boats may be there already. The fish, they are waiting for us!"

"How long will it take to get there?"

"Not long. An hour and a half. Two hours most. A good day for a boat ride, no?"

Then Prospero rolled up the map and bound it. We'd take it with us. He'd also filled a cooler with sandwiches and drinks. Plus a large thermos of coffee. And an old Olympus camera.

"Prospero, I'm impressed. Looks like you've got everything ready."

"I have been up since four o'clock! This I used to do every day. It is the fisherman's life! Because, as they say today, 'you snooze, you lose!' Ha-ha! But my sons, they do not want me to fish anymore. They say I have earned my rest. Rest! What is that? Plenty of that in the next life. But I am too old to take the boat by myself. So, you are here. And now you go with me. Come! We are already late. Let's get all we have to take into your car."

With that, we loaded the food and other gear into the Ford. Dawn was coming on strong now, a blazing red, thinly clouded eastern sky. A light breeze came from the ocean, just enough to accent the morning's crispness. Now I was fully awake and excited. A day at sea! Then it was just a couple minutes down to the docks. Some men were getting ready to go out. Many moorings were empty, their boats having left way before dawn. Maybe the day before if they were headed to the Grand Bank, like truckers leaving their homes Sunday afternoons to get headstarts toward delivering Monday morning loads.

Prospero was greeted with warmth and respect and some good-natured ribbing as we made our way down to his boat.

"Hey, Pross! Good to see you! Breaking in a new man, I see!"

"Prospero! You gonna steal Johnny's boat while he's playing in Florida? Ha-ha!"

"Prossie, if you're lookin' for Alex, he beat you out of the harbor. First one out! Before four!"

The old man laughed and loved being among his pals. Or his sons' pals. Men my age and younger. To each he said good morning, asked about their families, where they expected to fish. When they asked the same, he said "My usual. We will try Northwest Corner. But maybe we move a little further out, closer to the Murray. My friend here, he wants to see whales!"

All smiled, acknowledging Prospero's experience and wisdom of the same waters they made their livings from. One man said something about weather moving in by evening. "They're sayin' maybe a nor'easter, Prossie," in a tone that also said "Be careful, old man." This caused me to look at the eastern sky a bit anxiously. "Yes. We will be back much before then." Prospero said cheerfully. "I am hoping beginner's luck for him!"

He introduced me as someone who'd come to see Olson, not knowing he was four months dead. To a man, they nodded in recognition, but said nothing more as though not wanting to speak ill of those already passed.

When we got to his boat, his son Johnny's, Prospero made me stop to admire it and to tell another story. It was a beauty, made of wood, more than thirty feet long. It wasn't the biggest one left at the docks, but it looked plenty big enough for Prospero and me. Freshly painted, white with a distinctive bright orange band painted along the outside top rail, it was deep hulled like other seafaring boats with a glass-enclosed wheelhouse topped with a radio antenna. It had a broad, open deck and an iced hold for landing and storing a catch. Lines and buoys and nets were all neatly racked, along with life preservers and an inflatable raft.

Prospero beamed as he waved his arms "You see! This is it! A beautiful boat! Not too big. But big enough to bring back a catch that can support a man and his family. And, look! The name!"

In large, blue, neatly painted letters was

Mariel III

"You like?"

"Yeah. Nice name. Where'd it come from?"

"A boat of Prospero's had to be named 'Ariel,' no? But, I also wanted to name it for my Maria. So, the first boat I tried 'Maria Ariel.' And then she said, why not combine the two? And it became 'Mariel.' Perfect! A marriage of flesh and spirit. That was in 1920. My second I buy in 1941. Mariel II. And this I buy in 1958 and give to Johnny five years ago when they say I am too old to go out every day.

"This has been a very, very good boat. The best! And Johnny, he takes very good care of it. I am proud of him for this. Like his brother, they know this is their lives. Alex, he is out with his crew now. Grand Banks. Big trip! His boat is large, forty-five feet! He takes with him a crew of three. My Johnny he can work with just one."

Then he paused. His eyes twinkled. He spread his arms like an actor addressing his audience and bellowed, "I'll deliver all!" Then he lowered his voice with equally dramatic effect: "And promise you calm seas, auspicious gales, and sail so expeditious that shall catch your royal fleet far off." What a ham!

I laughed. "Well said, Prospero! Let us seize the day, O Captain, My Captain!"

He clapped his hands in delight. "Yes! Yes! Seize the day! We shall seize the day!"

We loaded the boat quickly. Prospero stepped below to check on the engine and the hold. For 75, the man moved nimbly. In the meantime, I scanned the harbor, watching one boat, then another, head out into the sunrise.

He climbed back up. "Everything looks good, Jack. I start her up. You grab the lines when I give you the signal." I jumped to, feeling like it was 1943 again and our ship, the *Dorchester*, was leaving New York loaded with war materiel, headed for Greenland and beyond. But this time I felt the excitement of meeting the sea on better terms than 30 years before. This time we were the hunters and not the hunted. There would be no cold sweats in a rusty hold, no thoughts of torpedoes and watery graves.

Mariel's diesels started up easily, her engines gurgling that deep, comforting rumble of a boat ready to go. Prospero gave me the word and I slipped the ropes off our hooks and we backed away from the dock, one of the other fishermen giving us a quick wave. I stood on the port side of the bow looking at the low wake in the dark water. Then it was into the channel, headed southwest, passing Five Pound Island. In five minutes we passed Fort Square with Prospero gesturing and I nodding. In ten minutes we passed Ten Pound Island, turning left and pointed due south out around the end of Cape Ann.

The sun had already pushed up out of the water, a brilliant red disk. I was a little sorry we'd missed the sunrise. I loved that action, seeing the first curve of red, brilliant and uneven, then more, then a partial disc, the sun coming on bolder and bolder and you wondering if it might pause—just for half a minute

—so you could admire it, but it never does, coming and coming and coming until birthed out of the ocean, full red and beaming and taking the day. Of all the sunrises I'd seen from canyoned streets to mountain-tops, nothing inspired—even awed—like those at sea. Those were full, honest, pure. Fire out of water. The only thing that might beat those would be the ones Armstrong and the other astronauts saw when coming around the moon. But that's for them to say. For me, it's the sun and the sea.

Prospero gunned the engines and the boat moved eagerly through short swells. Seagulls swooped and bobbed in our wake, chasing fish, screaming for their bits of watery territory. I joined him in the wheelhouse, where he was gingerly pouring our second cups of coffee. Ahead we could see two boats in the distance headed to their own special spots, vectors to unknown destinations. The blood-red sunrise was already fading now into a soft, gray overcast.

"Jack! This is good, yes? I go to sea a happy man. You think about your wife and your little ones. And making sure your men they are safe too. I never took more than one. That is all I need! Sometimes not even one, if he is hung over from drink or a woman.

"But here it is you and the sea. Matching wits with her nature, her beauty and sometimes, her uglies, too. Yes! Sometimes the sea is my mother. Sometimes it is my brother. Sometimes it gives me all I could ever want. Sometimes it wants to take all from me. It *is* all."

He pointed behind us to the fast receding shoreline.

"Look! Soon it will just be us and the sea. But remember what the land looks like. You see where it breaks? You see the light? There is the harbor. Remember, you come to it from the south. We will be back much before dark. But many times I was not. I learned how to read the land and to find the harbor at night or in storm. Maps, they are good. And now radio. But my papa taught me to know the water and the land like it was ours. Every bit! It was easy when skies were fair and the sea was still. But if we become caught in a storm...then you had to know!"

As we headed east towards Stellwagen Bank's northwest corner, Prospero told stories from decades fishing his part of the North Atlantic. How he learned from his father to sail farther out, to the Georges Bank and the Grand Bank. How they still fished in the first decades of the century from sailing ships and dories. Then how they made enough money to buy boats with motors. How they were lucky to avoid the tragedies that touched so many Gloucester families. How that luck made the Giovanettis one of the village's most respected families.

He talked about how he taught his sons to fish. How the elder son, Alex, started fishing for himself while still in high school. How the younger son, John, was good at school, a star football player recruited to a college in Pennsylvania. How he might have been destined for bigger things. But then how he quit after two years to stay home and fish.

"My Alex, he is the hard worker! Always working! But sometimes I wonder if he is happy with the fishing life. He is always worried about something. The money! The boat. The men. He has done well. But sometimes, I feel sad for him. My papa, he loved the sea! And I love the sea. Alex, I don't know if he loves it. He respects it, yes! He takes from the sea. But it seems like he is always mad at it, as though it hasn't given him enough. I don't know. I try to talk to him, but he does not want to talk about this.

"My Johnny, the sea for him is like a woman. He takes what it gives, but he leaves it when he wants. But he is a *good* fisherman! Yes! He can *feel* where the fish are. Like he is swimming with them! I have gone with him many times. And he has headed to places I have never gone. And, of course, I do not say anything. A father, he must know when to talk and when to be silent. I watch and learn. Johnny will lay down his nets and in a few hours, he has his catch! So many times I have seen him leave after Alex and come back before. With *more* fish!

"But he only takes what he needs. He works. He saves. He takes care of his boat. Then he leaves. Like now. He is in Florida enjoying himself. Who am I to say he is wrong? He even gives me some money now and then. Not that I need it. But he says it is what a son does for a father after all the father has done for the son."

I winced with these words. Not that Prospero could see. But he'd struck a nerve, memories of Lowell and after.

"My Alex, I think this makes him a little mad too. Why? I don't know. He is a leader among the men. He is on the Fisherman's Council. He can fight with the politicians. But I think he wishes the fishing was as easy for him as it is for his brother. Sometimes they talk. But whenever Johnny tries to explain how he fishes, Alex he just gets mad. I don't know. Two men from the same mother and father. Yet so different." He paused, then asked quietly, "Do you have a brother, Jack?"

The question jarred me out of the semi-reverie I'd slipped into amid the hum of the engines, the easy bounce of the gentle swells and listening to Prospero. As he spoke his hands and arms would move around as well. And his voice was loud then. Not annoyingly loud. But as though he were speaking to a room of people instead of just me.

"I did, Prospero. But he died when I was very young."

"Ah! So sad, so sad." I could tell he was moved. "Do you remember him much?"

He looked at me with wise, searching eyes. Eyes that knew death.

"I do. He taught me a lot in the short time I knew him."

"And, how did he come to die?"

"A fever in the heart. He had it from very young. It never got better. He was in almost constant pain. All over. His legs swelled up like balloons. He just got weaker and weaker, until he died."

I almost cried now telling a story I'd told dozens of times before.

"Ah, that is very, very sad. Between our Alex and our Johnny, Maria and me we lost one also. A girl. She lost her before birth, at seven months. We called her Angela. I tell you a parent losing a child is hundreds times worse than when a child loses the parent."

We both fell silent and looked out at the gently rolling sea in front of us. All hint of the sun had gone away, the morning settling into a monotonous gray, almost obscuring the horizon. But Prospero steered the boat with a familiar assurance.

"Do you remember much about him?" This time Prospero asked so gently that I almost didn't hear him.

"Yeah, I do. Some. He was the kindest, gentlest, most perceptive soul I've ever known. Even though he knew he was dying, he never said a word in despair about it. Instead, he taught me about the little, innocent things in the world. About birds. And even insects."

I wanted to tell him I'd even written a book about him, which, of course, I couldn't. I wanted to tell him that he'd visited me three times since I'd left St. Petersburg. But of course I couldn't do that without Prospero thinking me mad.

"How old was he when he died?" Again, Prospero probed gently.

"Nine. I was four."

"Yes, so young. Did he go to school? Or did his illness keep him at home?"

"No. He went to school some. The nuns loved him. They really did. He could read the catechism better than anybody. So I was told. But it was more than that, Prospero. He had the faith. Yes, the faith! He told them at school one day he had seen the Virgin in Heaven. Right there at the church school! And that he was being pulled in a white wagon by two lambs. And they crossed themselves and asked him to tell one nun, then another and another. And he did, and told them so matter-of-factly they believed him all the more. He died less than a year later. But those nuns loved him because he showed a faith so innocent and pure and strong."

I stopped. Here I was spilling my guts out to a stranger. But rather than be embarrassed by my outburst, Prospero seemed to nod knowingly and sympathetically.

"Yes. Yes. The wisdom of the young. In their innocence they can see farther than we whose eyes have been blurred by too many tears. You loved him very much, Jack."

He patted my shoulder as he said this. And I felt a strange kind of relief, almost as though I were back in the confessional when I still thought confessing was good for my godforsaken soul.

"Yeah, I did, Prospero. He was so sweet and tender he could get little birds to land on his hand and he would feed them. And if our mother swatted a fly he would cringe. He would pick flowers for me and we would look at each petal, following the little veins from bottom to top."

"It must have been very hard on all of you to lose him." He paused for a moment, then asked quietly, "Did you have any other brothers or sisters?"

"Yes. A sister. Nin. Short for Caroline. She was also sweet, but for some reason we were never as close as my brother and I were. She married and moved to North Carolina, then Florida. And I saw her there a few times. But she died six years ago. And my father, he died twenty years ago. So now it's just my mother and me."

"That's much dying for your mother to endure."

"Yeah, it is. And I haven't made it any easier, gone as much as I am."

"You are gone a lot?"

"Yeah. It's the life of a travel writer. We get to see the world. But we don't have much of a place to really call home. The world's our home, I guess. Or as much of one as we care to make it."

"Yes. 'Home' can mean a lot of different things. Sometimes it means a lot. Sometimes it is nothing, but maybe a memory."

We fell silent into our thoughts. Prospero focused on the horizon, aiming us closer to whatever destination he had in mind. Me thinking more about Nin and her sad life. Her bum of a husband running out on her. Her dying of a heart attack not long after at forty-five. And me too drunk or whatever to even go to her funeral in Orlando, leaving Memere to go by herself. Another stellar moment in my star-filled life.

I'd gone through all of life telling my story and hearing countless life stories from men and women all over the country. Each one of us was talking to the other as though we'd been friends since kinder-garten. Lots of times it was bar talk. But other times it was a genuine reaching out of lonely souls trying to make connections in this big, dark world. We did this over and over again. And why?

Then I thought about the hours and hours and hours Allen and Neal, or Allen and somebody, would sit up and talk and talk and talk, trying to talk their ways to eternal truths about themselves, about each other, about the Universe and the Eternal. Emptying their minds and their souls one into another and hoping to be renewed with the other doing the same to them.

And for what? Did they know more about the darkness than they did before? Did they get a little peek behind the Eternal Curtain? I think they thought they did. We all think we do. Else why bother? Why make the effort? One step. Then another. The dance up the mountain. We go. We go.

I noticed the boat was bouncing a little more now. It seemed the swells were a little deeper. In the distance I could see little whitecaps starting. Prospero saw and explained.

"The wind. She has picked up. Not too bad. Maybe a little rain later. But we will have our fish before then and be home for supper!" Prospero's confidence and cheerfulness swept away any worries that might've started to gather. I took comfort and warmth from his words. But it was as though he changed subjects, maybe to be polite and avoid poking further into the sadness that had already leaked from my life.

He began to tell me how we'd fish first for tuna, casting four lines with squid for bait. When one hit, I'd be the "muscle" to reel it in. He would steer the boat slowly in its direction. He used his hands to show how the fish would run to try and break the line, even go under the boat. But then it would tire and I would slowly get it closer and closer. Then he would be the one to harpoon it at the boat. He saw the look on my face. "Yes! Harpoon! Just like your Moby Dick! Ha-ha!! We catch a big one and it pays for the whole trip and more! Yes!"

"How big are these tuna?" I tried not to sound like a complete naïf, but, in fact, I pretty much was. The thought of having to harpoon something to get it into the boat was a little bit more than I'd bargained for yesterday.

"The ones we might see, maybe four feet and a couple hundred pounds. But, I tell you, I have seen much larger! Five, six feet. And three, four, even five hundred pounds! We used to see many more of those when I started with my papa than we see today. But now, so many boats and not so many fish.

"That is why my Alex and my Johnny, they have to go farther and farther to make their catch. The Stellwagen Bank it is not what it used to be. But today, it is good enough for us. Yes! We will get our tuna!" So we continued our trip east.

The wheelhouse was tight, but it was easy to see we were headed into a stiffening breeze. The swells grew deeper, capped now with a slight froth. But the boat took them easily, befitting one familiar with these waters. I was glad again I'd dressed warmly. Shirt, sweater, jacket. Jeans, wool socks and good boots. Stuff I'd packed for cold nights outdoors. I didn't bring a hat and wished I had. Prospero was dressed similarly with a pair of Woolriches over his sweater. He had brought an old pea coat, now on a hook in the cabin, and a stocking cap that sat cocked on top of his head.

At about eight thirty, he said, "We are getting close! Here, you take the wheel. I have to check below." I'd never done anything like that before, not that there was much to it. He told me to just keep it steady, pointed in the line we were on, showing me the needle on the compass. I nodded, grabbed the wheel and tried to look as though I'd been helming for twenty years.

He was gone maybe ten or fifteen minutes, time enough for me to get a feel for the wheel and the boat. All I could see was water, Gloucester and Cape Ann now long behind. At the horizon it seemed clouds and sea had merged into one, the normal line between earth and sky smudged beyond distinction. I scanned the waters, looking for whales blowing or breaching, pretending I was a modern day Ishmael perched on my mast.

When Prospero returned he had two pairs of gloves and another stocking cap. "Here! You will need these."

"Everything OK?"

"Oh yes, yes. Just making sure everything is all right. I turn on the ice-making machine. We start to fish soon! You like handling the wheel?" he asked nodding.

"Yeah, I do! I can feel the boat better. When I was in the Merchant Marine, closest I got to the wheelhouse was seeing the captain about a hundred feet away."

Prospero chuckled. "And what job did you have on your boat?"

"The lowest. I served meals in the mess."

"Ah, yes. We must start at the bottom and work our way up, yes?"

I nodded and added, "Good thing to have the compass though. With the clouds it's hard for me to tell which way we're headed."

"Yes. We use the compass. But also our eyes. I know these waters. And this boat, she is a good one. She knows how to move through the waves." Prospero made his arms into a V thrusting forward like the boat's bow. "Not so bumpy."

Then he unfurled his old map. "Look, we are about here," stabbing a finger to a penciled point a few inches from land. "In a few minutes, we will be at northwest corner and then we will find fish!"

"How do you know when we're there?"

"That is a good question. But I just know. The water, she changes color a little as it gets shallower. And the waves, they change a little too. But I also kept the time from when we left the harbor and our speed, and then I know how long it takes to get us here." He pointed to his watch—8:55.

Ten minutes later, Prospero cut the engine. We climbed down to the deck and baited our poles with squid. He showed me how to cast the long poles and after a few tries we had four poles cast and lodged in their holds along the railing.

Prospero smiled and said, "Now we wait! Would you go back up and get the coffee?"

As we sipped, the boat bobbed in the water, maybe three foot swells pushed now by the breeze.

Prospero explained where the current was and how we were being carried in a south-southwest direction. He waved off the end of the boat. "Cape Cod, she is out there!"

"How far?"

"Oh, many, many miles. More than 30. We will not see her today."

I nodded and tried to imagine a different landscape from thousands of years ago with a mountain range of ice piled a mile high to the west and maybe dry land where we were sitting over sixty feet of water. Would the first Americans have hunted mammoths here? Or would they, too, have been fishermen, the first Gloucestermen? What would Olson have had to say about such an America at the time Folsom Cave was being explored and lived in at the same time humans were hacking through the jungles of the Yucatan? Then these southern Americans, maybe just a dozen generations split from their cold-living cousins, learning to worship an ever-present sun, blood-red in life and in death. Their North American cousins hunted mammoths—their own Moby Dicks—with crude spears. What in their lives had been passed down to us? What part of our consciousness, or subconsciousness, belongs to them?

The old man interrupted with more instructions on how we'd fish the day.

"So, Jack, we wait. If we do not find here, then we will move someplace else. If my Johnny were with us, we would have the nets out and move through the water to get our catch. But now we move with the water and let the catch find us! Remember, when we get a strike, let it go for a little while. That sets the hook good. Then we start to bring him in. Slow. Let him fight himself out. We respect the fish, yes! But keep the tension on the line. Let him know he cannot get away. And do not let him run under the boat. No! The fish they are smart. He will try to break the line. I will work the boat. You, my friend, will be the fisherman. You will be the one who says 'I am master here!'"

"I'll do my best, Prospero. Been a long time since I fished anywhere. And never out here like this. But as long as you can captain, I'll be your mate."

"Yes, yes! That is fine, Jack. You will know what to do. Do not worry." He paused, then ventured, "Tell me, your father, he never took you fishing?"

"Awww, no. Not really. I mean, maybe we half-assed it a couple times. On a river. And later in high school I went with a couple buddies. But small stuff. Nothing like this, Prospero."

"And what kind of work did he do? A busy man, yes?"

These were simple, friendly questions. But they were making me think and try not to give back an answer more complicated than asked.

"He was a printer most of his life. So, yeah, seemed like he was pretty busy. At least that's how I remembered him growing up."

"A printer! A noble profession, yes? Like a Benjamin Franklin!"

I wouldn't have put my father and old Ben Franklin in the same sentence, but it was nice that Prospero did. I'd thought of him more as a screw-up and business failure than someone engaged in a "noble profession." I remembered him more as being best at drinking than anything else. And me…the apple that didn't fall far from the tree.

"Yeah, I guess so. Although he didn't do quite the same quality of work as ol' Franklin."

"No *Poor Richard's Almanac*? No newspapers? No Declaration of Independence?" He asked gently, not mockingly, which I appreciated. He said something then about the Revolution that I read as a schoolboy and always remembered. "'We must all hang together. Or, surely, we shall all hang separately.' A wise man, yes?"

"He had his own shop for a while. But he got wiped out by a flood in 1936. Then he worked for others. At the end he had to really depend on my mother to make enough to pay the bills."

"Yes, it is not easy having a business for yourself. I know! My papa, he came here with nothing. But he worked and worked and he made a family and he got himself a boat of his own. And he showed me how to make money from the sea. And this I have showed my sons also. But it was my Maria who really knew how to make the money work. So even when the fish were not there, we did not starve or have to give up the boats."

"That's good, Prospero. I think sometimes my dad wanted me to work with him. I helped a little through high school. But then I went away to college. These were the Depression years. It was tough all over, so I don't blame him too much."

"Ah, yes, the Depression. The times, they are good now. My boys, they forget. They think times were always good. A fisherman's life is always hard. But people they need to eat! So we always have something for them to buy. When they cannot afford the meat, they will eat fish. But the Depression, sometimes prices were so low you almost could not afford to go out. Still, this is what you do. You catch. They buy. We eat. It is simple, no?"

I smiled back at Prospero, but my thoughts were far away, back with my old man. I didn't want him to be a screw-up. I didn't want Leo to be known as a good guy to drink with, but someone you joked at behind his back. He was liked. But I always felt he wasn't respected. At least by people beyond his small circle of drinking buddies. I wanted more from him and he couldn't do it. Then he wanted more from me and I couldn't do it. The apple didn't fall far.

He was one reason Susan's parents tried to keep her away from me, despite being a big shot in high school. I was proud of being a Kerouac. A

Quebecois. A Breton! A proud and ancient race! But to her Scottish Highland parents we were just Catholic lowlifes. We lived in the same town, but our people were their *employees.* We filled their factories, cleaned their houses. Our sweat made their money, eased their lives. But those were to be the only exchanges between them and us. No dalliances between owners' daughters and workers' sons.

Prospero caught me. "You thinking of him, no?"

"Yeah, sorry."

"No, no! It is good to remember your father. We honor them for what they gave us. And we give to our children so that we may earn their honor."

I winced and he caught that too, but not for the reason he thought.

"You loved him, yes? You miss him?" He asked honestly, not judgmentally, for which—again—I was appreciative.

"Yeah, I loved him. All in all, he was a good guy. He loved my mother. He tried to provide. But losing my brother so young...I think that changed all of us, Prospero. I didn't understand it at the time. Or at least I didn't understand what had changed. But something did. When Death comes at you so unfairly, it makes you think. Sometimes it makes you want to forget."

I didn't want to say my dad had disappointed me. I didn't want to admit I had disappointed him.

"Yes. I understand this, what you are saying. Is it Death that gives us faith? If we did not fear Death, would we love God as much as we do? Or as much as we say we do? You, Jack, are a Believer, too, raised in the Church?"

Boy, I had no idea how to answer that one. I wasn't expecting a catechism, especially on a fishing trip! If I said yes, would that be an end to the questions, an end to all questions? If I said no, would that prompt more questions? Had I been captured by my own Grand Inquisitor? Of course not! No one would ever mistake *me* for the Second Coming! Still, the question rattled. If we'd been on land, I'd have found an excuse to walk away. But none of that here. I was stuck. I unloaded.

"Believe in what? Sometimes I think, yeah, I believe in Something. I mean, most people believe in Something, don't they? Or want to. But what is that Something? I spent my whole life trying to find out. Gerard...he knew. He had it. The Faith. And I've tried to get it from him. But I've never had it like he did. I'm more like my dad, I guess. If God is really out there, He's too far away to really give a crap about us. We're on our own to make the best of what we have.

"But my mom, she prays every day. God is close to her, or at least she believes He is. And sometimes, Prospero, sometimes I can feel that too. But it's never stayed long enough for me to get it like Gerard got it. Or maybe my mom has it. But as for me, I'm still looking."

We were eye to eye as I delivered my little speech. I wanted to say something that would mean something to him—and me. That was as honest as I could be. He nodded slowly as I talked, almost as if in rhythm with the waves that were pushing our boat towards some kind of fishing payday.

"Yes, it is a great mystery, Jack. Even though my Maria she is gone seven years now, I can feel her close. Not all the time. But enough that I don't feel like a lonely old man just waiting for Him to take me."

Prospero was starting to say something more when a loud, high-pitched, unmistakable whirring interrupted. We looked aft to see one of our poles nearly doubled over, its reel unwinding ferociously.

"A strike! A big one, Jack! Quick! Grab!" I was already out of my chair before he finished. I grabbed the base and the rod and held tight before whatever it was yanked it out altogether.

"Let it play! Let it play, Jack! We will give him a minute more of freedom, yes!" Prospero was jumping around excited as a kid.

I had no idea what took our bait, but I could feel all its strength through the line and rod into my hands, shoulders and chest. It was a strong sure pull, full of confidence, not the panicked thrashing of a pan fish.

"He is taking the bait deeper and the hook will be set good when you start to pull him back to us. But for a little bit we let him pull us." I tried pulling back a little just to get his measure, but the reel was still feeding out. No way I was going to land this monster, Prospero's confidence and encouragement aside. "Careful, Jack! You pull too much when he is running hard and the line will go snap. I go up now and we start coming at him. Slow. You help me when he starts to change direction. Just keep the line tight."

He scrambled up and turned the engines on low, making a gradual turn in the direction of the line. Our fish was still trying to move away, but now with the boat headed in his direction I was able to reel in a bit of slack one slow turn at a time. Damn! This was work! Ten minutes into this catch and I was sweating and could feel the burn starting to build in my arms. Prospero handled the boat expertly, taking a slow, steady course towards our catch. I had no idea how much line had fed out, but it seemed like he was a quarter mile away and still headed in whatever direction he wanted to go. I reeled in slowly, slowly as Prospero gave me some slack. One turn after another, each one feeling like I was doing curls with too much weight.

Then—just like that—the line went limp! Limp! I started reeling in feet at a time. Had I lost him? I yelled up to Prospero so he knew what had happened. He nodded and slowed the boat while I reeled and reeled like crazy now trying to find the tension again. How could I have lost him? I knew it happened a lot.

Lines break. But one moment it was taking every ounce of strength to keep the pole from being pulled out of its holder and into the sea, the next nothing. Except the line didn't snap. It just sagged.

"Jack! Watch it!" Prospero called down from the wheelhouse. "I think he has turned and is running at us now!"

"What do you think it is?" I shouted. I imagined some leviathan totally pissed off at being tricked into biting on squid—instead finding a hook deep in its mouth—and looking to wreak holy hell on whoever was dumb enough to mess with him. What could it be? A mad as hell Great White? The mythical giant squid? Moby Dick himself??

"I don't know! But he is big! Very big! I turn the boat and make him come with us. I will go slow. Watch your line and make sure he doesn't turn again. Then it will snap!" I nodded as he ducked inside again and turned *Mariel* to the north. I shifted aft and tried to imagine how deep and far the line was now. We'd definitely made progress, he was in closer than ever. In a minute the line was again taut, and it felt like we were pulling him again. I didn't try to reel any more.

Another ten minutes and Prospero yelled he was bringing the boat around again to the east and I should try to pull him closer. "Let us see if he is tiring of the fight, yes!"

I kind of felt like I was getting the hang of this and gotten a second wind of sorts. My arms didn't burn like before and I could feel strength in my chest. I reeled twenty feet of line when I felt the pull and it started feeding again. "He's running again, Prospero!" The old man nodded and turned the boat towards him and shifted into neutral. Then he clambered down next to me and watched the line carefully.

"Jack, you are doing good! He is a big one for sure! Watch now! I think he will run at us again! Fool us into thinking he is giving up."

I tried giving it a reel or two, but he wasn't budging. "That's all right, Jack. He is stronger than both of us together. But we must convince him there is no getting away. He is ours!" He saw the sweat streaming down my face. "This is work, yes! But you are young and strong, still. This is why you and me we work as a team. When you get him to the side, I will harpoon. Then we will get the net under and winch him onto the deck. But watch the tail! One hit, he can break your leg."

I nodded. While Prospero climbed back to the wheelhouse, I almost wished Neal and Allen were here to see me. Allen would be yelling encouragement. He'd probably compose a poem on the spot turning the adventure into a happening! "The Tuna Sutra." He'd dance and sing around me in some sort of Buddhist blessing. But Neal, he'd try to pull the pole away and show how he could do it himself, bragging all along, no help needed from me or Prospero or anybody else. I flashed on the eternal image of him in shirtsleeves, pole in hand, leaning back, biceps rock hard and pulling against the deep, cigarette cocked out of the corner of his mouth, talking a mile a minute. Demanding to be the center of attention. Showing how he could outfish, outdance, outfuck anyone. That was Neal. That would always be Neal.

My daydream was interrupted with another shout from Prospero. "Jack! Now is the time! I am coming at him! Reel hard! Reel hard!" He brought the boat into a near tack to the line and closed slowly, giving me a decent pace to shorten the distance between us and our still unknown catch. I pulled foot after foot of line back onto the reel.

"Prospero!" I yelled, "What do I do if it's a Great White?" I shouted more out of nerves than noise. I didn't want to think about anything larger than could swallow us whole, Jonah-like. Or smash us to bits.

He nodded and climbed back down.

"Here!" He unsheathed a no-nonsense, eight-inch knife, thick-bladed and serrated. "If it is a Great White, you do this." And with a quick motion he showed how to draw the blade under the line. I was relieved the old man didn't want to press our luck. "But do it quick and watch the water. He could jump at you and take your arm."

"OK! Will I see it before it gets too close?" I hated sounding like a scared schoolboy, but all of a sudden the prospect of being face to face with something more than I could handle seemed very real.

"Yes. Probably. You know the fin? He should show himself out there somewhere." He waved his arm at a spot maybe thirty feet from the boat. "But make sure he is a shark before you cut! And do not let him jump into the boat! No, we do not want a Great White on our deck! I did not bring a pistol. But if he is tuna, we want him! Yes! He will bring us money!" Prospero shoved the knife into its sheath and both into my back pocket, then bounded back up to the wheelhouse. I nodded my thanks. I didn't thank him for putting into my head the idea of a huge, pissed-off shark leaping out of the water, jaws monstrously open, razor teeth aimed at my jugular, ready to feed on us instead of the other way around.

We were definitely closing now. Less than fifty yards away, I could see where the line disappeared into the water to our starboard aft. I reeled some more. One turn. Two. A third. I was pumped and scared. I wanted this fish too. I knew he would make Prospero's day and more. A triumphant return to Gloucester docks. A show to his sons and their friends that he could still master the seas. *His* seas.

I reeled steady. It felt like whatever it was, was giving in, yielding grudgingly to our collective will. Our progress was certain. I stared into lightly white-capped swells for some sign of him, maybe fearful of the telltale fin more than anything else. The world itself felt like it was closing in, the clouds lowered now and threatening rain, the breeze steady with little gusts. It was just our boat and the pole and the line extending into darkness attached to some thing, some live thing that definitely did not want to be connected to our alien world.

I reeled another turn. My arms were beyond aching. It seemed the pole and my body were one. Another turn. Twenty yards. The angle sharp now, as though he were just below the surface. Yet I couldn't see a thing. Another turn of the reel. Another. Another. Come on, you bastard!

"Steady, Jack." I about jumped overboard! I'd become so focused on trying to see into the water, I hadn't heard Prospero climb back down. His voice was deadly serious now, his hand firmly on my shoulder. "Do not fight it. You will lose and he will win. Take a deep breath. Good. Now another. Good. Just hold steady. I think he is about to show himself. Keep your hold while I get the harpoon ready."

I relaxed a little, but steeled myself for the big moment. I could see Prospero out of the corner of my eye removing the long spear from its hold. I was still amazed at how purposefully and calmly he moved. Undoubtedly he'd done this thousands of times, but I was awed being with a pro. Someone who would've been at home equally on the *Dorchester,* the *Essex* or even the *Pequod*!

Then movement! I think! Something darker just under the surface? A shadow? The line into the water was less than twenty yards away. The weight was firm, still moving, maybe unsure of what to do next. Did it know the spear was coming? Would it fight to the very end? Could I hold on long enough for Prospero to swing the net out and under and finally relieve the pain shooting through my arms deep into my shoulders? I didn't want to lose it now, not after all this, the better part of an hour.

Then, there it was! Huge! A fish, not a shark! But mammoth! At the surface for a moment, then a dive, but not so vigorous. I hung on, letting line slowly now.

"Jack, it is tuna! A big one! He is almost ready! Stay with him, Jack! Stay with him!"

Prospero stood poised next to me, harpoon at his side. We hung for what seemed like another eternity as the fish circled and dove again. Another jolt of adrenaline kicked in at the sighting. Now I felt I could get him close. Close enough for Prospero to finish him off. A trophy for our efforts. Beginner's luck for me! Bragging rights for Prospero back at the dock and in the bar, no doubt! Boat, pole, line, me and fish were one. He was mine!

Prospero saw what was happening before I did. He tried to shout and pushed me aft as the line went slack again. The tuna was making a hard run under the boat. Line whizzed and cut a sloppy finger. My pole nearly doubled over and I could barely hang on. Prospero grabbed the back of my jeans to keep me in the boat. Then...a snap and all was limp...and quiet ...and over. Just that fast.

I panted, trying to catch my breath and stared at my pole and the line dangling now in the water. I turned around to look at Prospero who looked back with profound disappointment, eyes still wide from the fight. Neither said anything for a full minute. I scanned the water thinking, fantasizing really, that somehow this fish was going to surface and give us a final salute before heading off to safer depths to heal its wounds and relish its triumph over death.

"You gave it all, Jack." He was trying to console, but the loss was palpable. He wanted it. He really wanted it. And because he did, I did. Finally, I reeled in the remaining yards of line. We both fingered the cut end as though somehow we'd find an answer there for what had just happened, a drop of my blood sliding along it, a stinging reminder there'd be no bragging back at the dock today.

"It happens, Jack. It happens. A fish that big is old and wise. He does not give up easily."

"How big was it, Prospero?" I asked, now weary and still catching my breath.

"He must be six feet. Four or five hundred pounds. He was a big fish, Jack. A trophy for sure!"

"Could we have gotten him in the boat?"

"I think so, yes. If I hit him good with the harpoon." Now he lay the spear on the deck. "I have seen tuna that big before. But rare." Already he sounded wistful, refraining that old man's lament, wondering if he had just seen something for the very last time.

"I'm sorry, Prospero. He moved faster than I expected. I...I...didn't know what to do."

"Jack, it is not your fault. You fought him good. Even my Alex or my Johnny, I do not think they could have kept him from going under. That was a very big fish! Maybe if we had one more man..." I appreciated that he was trying to make me feel better. "Come. Let us go below and rest a little. Maybe there will be another. I will get the sandwiches."

When I slumped onto a cushion, all my energy drained out and I was bone tired. I could barely extend my right arm to take one of Prospero's sandwiches. I knew I'd be sore for days. Prospero sat on the boat's only bunk opposite me. We ate slowly, quietly, and sipped sodas. I was almost asleep when Prospero seemed to get his second wind.

"Jack, you see how the fishing life it is good and it is bad, no? I feel I am lucky to see 75 years. So many I have known did not even see 20!"

I thought of the man in the bar and his wail for a son lost to war instead of sea.

"When I was young and sailing with my papa, I did not think of death. No! All I wanted was to bring home the biggest catch. I wanted the Giovanetti name to be talked abput in the town! I was strong! My papa, he was strong! Together, we go to the waters no one goes and we bring back the fish. And the people they talk of the Giovanetti luck. Men, they want to fish with us. Yes! Their boats follow ours. We do not mind. The sea, she belongs to all, no? Sometimes I feel like we are leading a fleet! And then one time, we make for the Grand Bank where Alex is now. It is spring. There are maybe twenty boats all wanting to go where Papa and I know where the fish are. The big fish! And we fish for three days.

"Everybody has boats full! Cod! Haddock! We are ready to come home and the Sortino boat is behind everybody. It is smaller and Jimmy is full and low in the water. But he wanted one more catch. This will give him money to buy a bigger boat. And then we are caught! A storm from the north we did not expect. I almost lost Papa over the side! We get wind fierce! And rain. Then snow too! We are an extra day and night getting home. But we make it and I thank our God we are safe.

"Then someone says, 'There are only 19!' A boat is missing and it is Sortino. Somewhere in the night Jimmy he must have gone down and no one saw. And no one knew he was down until we are all home and he is not. Papa and me we unload our catch and go back out looking. So do others. But the sea is still angry and cold. And we know what is done. Jimmy and his son Jimmy and George Ruda's son Angelo. Three. Gone."

"Not a sign of them at all?"

"No. And we did not expect to see a sign. A boat goes down and the sea takes all. But still, you go. Out of respect for the men. Out of respect for the families."

We sat silent for a minute. I finished my sandwich. Prospero finished his story.

"From that day, Papa says 'We take only what we need, not what we want.' We will never take more than what our *Mariel* she can handle. This Papa and I agree to. Even when we could on calm seas. We say no. Sometimes the others they say we are foolish not to take more. But why? And this I teach to Alex and Johnny. Johnny he does this. Alex, he always wants more. So far he is lucky, so maybe who am I to say?"

"Was that the only boat you've ever been with that sunk?"

"Yes. Other boats they have been lost. But never with a Giovanetti. It is why the others they like to sail with us. Maybe we are good luck! But Papa he always knew when to go out and when to stay in. And he knew when to come home, even when maybe we weren't ready. He would say 'Tomorrow there will be fish. But we must be there to catch them!'"

"What happened to the rest of the Sortino family?"

"Everyone, they try to help a little. That is our way. But she had two small ones to take care of. Eventually she moved to a sister. In Michigan, I think."

Again, we sat in silence for a minute, Prospero reliving the memory, I trying to imagine a boat going down and then not wanting to. Despite Prospero's experience and cheerful nature, *Mariel* felt small and lonely. I wouldn't have minded if he'd said it was time to head back. I wanted to feel dry land. Wanted to taste hot chowder and cold beer. But then he had something else in mind. He slapped my knee, almost like a foreman signaling break was over and time to get back to it.

"Come! Let us go up and see if there are more Moby Dicks out there for us. We do not go back empty. No! I am Giovanetti! And today, you are Giovanetti's son! We catch! We catch!"

With that he was up and stepping up to the deck with me in tow.

Chapter 21 — Call Me Ishmael

While Prospero tied another hook, I reeled in the other three rods, re-baited them and cast again into a now very choppy sea. The wind had picked up and I wondered if the weather was moving in faster than forecast. Prospero didn't seem worried, chattering away on how we would catch fish and be home before dark. It was afternoon and felt like we'd been at this all day. If Prospero could make a full day of it, then I guessed his "son" could as well. In fact, it seemed the clouds had lifted a little and I'd gotten my second wind. I kept watch on the deck while Prospero went back up to the wheelhouse and kept *Mariel* turned into the breeze so we wouldn't bounce quite so much. Then, just fifteen minutes later, a strike! I shouted to Prospero and he shouted back "Yes!" and turned the boat towards the line but kept a little broader tack than with the first one so we wouldn't get smacked too hard by the waves.

More comfortable with the drill now, I let the line play out, then began the slow dance of getting him close to the boat. I also didn't feel the weight and strength of that first huge tuna, so maybe we had something smaller, a cod or a haddock. Fifteen minutes more I had my answer. Another tuna! Nicely sized, but smaller than the morning giant. Prospero scrambled down just in time to get his harpoon ready and after one miss—my fault—he speared it. We swung the net under and boomed it aboard. His harpoon had struck straight and true, the fish was dead within a couple minutes on the deck.

"Well done, Jack! Well done! We have a very nice yellowfin!"

It was over three feet long and Prospero thought a couple hundred pounds. I was proud landing one, although I had no idea how I'd have gotten that into the boat if I'd been out here by myself. Maybe Prospero could've in his younger days. Or maybe his boys do now. He moved efficiently around the fish, removing the hook and opening the ice hold. Together we slid it down and closed the hold.

While I caught my breath, Prospero extended his hand and we shook. "Jack, my friend, that was excellent! You learned from this morning, yes! You did not fight it. You let him come to us. And by the time he was here, he was too tired to try a run under. This is a hundred-dollar fish! We make money today!"

I was pleased because he was pleased. And, yeah, I felt good that I'd done my job when it mattered. Now we'd head back and the Gloucestermen would have one more story about the Giovanettis and the "beginner's luck" of the writer who came looking for that whale of a man Olson and got a hundred-dollar tuna instead!

The building waves smacked us broadside a couple times and staggered me when I hadn't anticipated the rise and fall of the boat. Prospero's sea legs steadied him like he was on dry land. I felt a small relief when he said, "Jack, we have done our work. Now we go home. You will eat with me tonight, yes? We celebrate at the Cape Ann!"

Now I really wanted to get back to harbor and close out what had turned into a helluva day. "Pross, that'd be great! I'm ready to go."

"Let's get the rest of our lines in. Then we turn for home."

We'd just settled in and Prospero had the engines revved up and was ready to swing west when he leaned hard towards the window and shouted, "Jack! Look!"

I looked out towards where he was leaning, but didn't see a thing.

"What Pross? I missed it."

"A humpback! She breached! About half a mile. We go!"

He kicked the boat into gear and we set off across the waves faster than I thought *Mariel* was able.

"Are you sure?" Given the building sea I wasn't sure we'd see anything breaking the surface unless it was right next to us.

"Yes! Yes!! We run up on her and get our pictures too. Then we have a full day on Stellwagen!" Who was I to argue with a man so clearly in his element and having the fun of a kid?

Prospero gunned *Mariel's* engine to get us up on plane and cut down the bounce some. But it was still a damn bumpy ride and I hung on tight to a hand rail while Pross steadied himself at the helm. He could've sat in the captain's seat, but chose to stand instead, eyes fixed on some destination. We were headed north by east, which was the opposite direction I kind of wished we were headed. But Pross was all excited, for both of us.

"Jack, we are almost where she breached. Keep an eye out to your left. She is heading north to the Arctic for summer."

"How close are we gonna get?"

"If we are lucky, she will be right there," he gestured out the window to just off the bow.

"Will she...uh...try to hit us?" I know I sounded like a goddam scared little kid, but I wanted to know.

He laughed at the innocence of my question, then answered it seriously.

"No...no. This is not the White Whale! We do not hunt them anymore, except to get pictures. And look!" Pointing just off the port bow a couple hundred yards ahead, a huge humpback was now sliding back into the water. "Thar she blows!" I stared at empty space where the huge animal had just been. Now Prospero throttled back the engines. "Jack, she is a beauty! We slow and see how close we can be. My camera! It is below. Would you please get?"

I tried to hustle down the steps, but had to steady myself all the way. As he throttled back, *Mariel* was really rocking now in what looked like four and five foot swells. I had no idea if the boat was going to be steady enough to get pictures, even something as big as a whale. And I was really nervous now about how close we were going to get to an animal that could flip even a boat as seaworthy as ours.

He came down from the wheelhouse as I got back to the deck. "OK, Jack! Now I need your help. I think she is going to come up about there." He pointed to a spot about fifty yards to our port side. "This is getting pretty choppy, so I am going to steady myself here against the side. But when I am ready to shoot, I need you to hold me behind, OK?" I nodded. "Then, if I am good enough, I can get a couple pictures."

"You think there's only one?" My mind was wild now with thoughts of a pod of Moby Dicks all breaching at once and we in the middle tossed like matchsticks into the air, fools caught on a photographic errand.

"Yes, I think so. Although, possible she may have a calf with her. We must watch close! That would be something to see!"

"How do you know it's female?"

"Oh, I don't! But my chances are fifty-fifty, no?" And he laughed again with childlike glee. We watched and watched, long minutes playing out longer than I thought we'd have to wait. Then as *Mariel* crested a wave, Prospero saw it in the water a couple hundred yards ahead surfacing not breaching. "Ah, Jack, we must wait a little longer. Come, we go back up and try to get closer." So our pursuit began anew.

"How does it know we're not hunting?" I asked back in the wheelhouse.

"Oh, it may not, Jack. I cannot read the animal's mind. But I have been out when we have been this close to them!" He held his arms six feet apart. "I have looked them in the eye. Yes! This I have done. There is intelligence. I think maybe they know the difference between hunting with a gun or harpoon, and hunting with a camera. Maybe when they get to Eskimo waters, they act different."

Prospero revved up *Mariel* once more to try and get closer. We continued north by east. The clouds lowered again. The horizon now looked darker still as we'd passed the middle of the afternoon. There was no mistaking that some kind of weather moving in, but he seemed comfortable with us getting our pictures and still beating it to port ahead of whatever was coming. I just wanted to get back.

"There! Jack, do you see her?" Again, Prospero pointed off our port bow between fifty and a hundred yards ahead where I could barely see the back of a whale and its blowhole spray breaking the surface. It was moving at what seemed a leisurely pace. I looked for a calf, but didn't see one.

"OK, I go back down. Here, you take the wheel. Keep it slow. When I call, you put in neutral and come down to steady me. This time we get pictures, yes!"

"OK, Pross. We'll get it this time." I tried to at least *sound* like I knew what I was doing. The old man again scrambled down to the deck with his camera, leaning against the side, waiting for the whale to surface again. I kept the boat slow, moving up and down with the waves. The windows looked like they were picking up sprinkles from the sky. I looked back at Pross; he was totally focused on his "prey," holding the camera up and adjusting the lens for where he thought it might appear.

Then, there she was again! Closer than ever!! Maybe only twenty, twenty-five yards away! It looked huge! Prospero didn't have to call me. I tried to nudge us a little closer, then shifted *Mariel* into neutral and jumped down to steady him.

"Ah, magnificent, Jack! Magnificent! Hold me now!"

I gripped the old man's solid shoulders, trying to steady his arms as he aimed the camera at the huge gray, barnacled mass. It seemed almost close enough to reach out and touch. Finally, I felt the thrill of the chase and the "catch" too. The whale was beautiful! It was easily as long as our boat, even though I couldn't see its head or its tail. And just as wide or wider. So it could have been even bigger. Prospero was in his element. Clearly, he felt a comfort, almost an intimacy, with this animal and this environment. I'd felt that at different times too. But for me it'd been at the top of a mountain, or deep in a redwood forest, or on a rock wetted by Pacific spray. This was a different kind of space. More open. More alien. More...dangerous? Maybe for me. But for Prospero, no. For him this was as much home as Fort Square. I could see it in his delight. His desire to be close to this whale. He wanted to connect. He was the anti-Ahab.

"Yes! Got it!" he cried. "Jack, I think it will be a good one! We will frame! Now! Hold me again and I think we can get a couple more. She is a beauty, yes?"

Again, he held the camera up. And I gripped his left shoulder while steadying his right arm. And there we were locked together alongside our Moby Dick, which seemed the calmest, least fazed creature I'd ever been this close to. I think I heard a click and then our world turned upside down. One moment I was looking over Prospero's shoulder at whale and sea. The next all I saw was sky. And I was falling back and back. The boat had reared up like a wild stallion. For a moment I could even see the wheelhouse pointing heavenward. We were almost vertical and then a crash! Pain shot like a harpoon through my arm and shoulder. I blacked out. When I came to I was gasping for breath, staring up at clouds that spit now contemptuously in my face. The boat rocked uneasily. I sat up slowly, trying to get my bearings. I heard a groan.

I looked to my right and there was Prospero sprawled awkwardly against the boat. He looked as though someone had just picked him up and flung him aside like so much used bait. And he wasn't moving. Jesus Christ!

"Prospero! Prospero!" I got to my knees and crawled over to him. He was semi-conscious. "Prospero!" Silence. Then, another groan. Weaker.

"Oh…Jack. My leg...hurts..." At first I wasn't sure what he meant. Then I looked down at his right leg and ankle and saw a dark spot soaking through his coveralls. And I knew.

"Here, Pross, roll this way. Slow! Let's get you flat."

I reached for him and tried to untangle the old man's body, careful not to move the leg too much. When I got his face turned to me, I saw more blood and a huge welt already turning an ugly black and blue above his right eye. Both eyes were closed. He was conscious, but barely.

I looked again at the leg. Slowly, I pulled pants cloth up, exposing skin. I didn't see any bone coming through, one good sign. But I knew I had to get that leg set with some kind of a splint. And make sure he stayed warm so he didn't go into shock. And I had to do it pretty fast.

The old man groaned. A little louder now. I still couldn't tell if he was fully conscious or not. I was, as the pain in my arm and shoulder reminded me whenever I moved them. "I'll be right back, Pross. Gotta find something to steady that leg."

Nothing of use on the deck, I went below and rummaged through his son's gear. Then, a bit of luck. I found a tool box in a storage bin and next to it a couple of 1x2s about two feet long and maybe four or five inches wide. Not perfect, but they'd have to do. The tool box also had a roll of electrical tape. That'd have to do, too.

I went back up, trying to stay on my feet with the boat rolling and my left arm hurting like hell and carrying boards and tape with my right. I knelt next to Prospero who was quiet and maybe passed out. I didn't worry about that just yet. As long as he was breathing, that was enough for now.

I took the knife he'd given me and cut his Woolriches up to his knee. I cut a dozen lengths of tape and strung them above me. Then I positioned the boards on either side from ankle to knee. In a few minutes I had them taped tight, the leg immobilized. First job done. Then I remembered his foot would probably swell and so I loosened his boot. I was glad he was out of it. I might have panicked if he'd been making a lot of noise.

I still had no idea what the hell had happened. Except I knew now we were in a jam. Sprinkles had turned into a steady drizzle. The way the wind was blowing I figured this was only going to get worse. And if it was a nor'easter bearing down, no way we'd last long if we didn't get our asses back to Gloucester before nightfall.

I moved up to the old man's head, looking at the welt and blood. If he had a concussion, not much I could do except find a way to make him as comfortable as possible.

"Prospero?" I almost whispered. "Pross?"

A groan.

"Pross. We got to get you down below. Can you sit up?"

Another groan. "Come on."

I reached under his shoulder with my good arm and tried lifting him gently.

"Jack."

"I'm here, buddy. Try to sit up."

Another groan. Louder. He was feeling the pain, no doubt. Slowly I was able to get him into a sitting position. For 75 the man was solid.

"Pross, listen to me. I think your right leg is broken. But not bad, OK? I got a splint on it. But we gotta get below so you can lie down again. I'm going to try and help you stand, OK? Don't put any weight on it. Just lean on me."

He grunted. I got into a crouch and tried to get both of us standing. But the boat was rocking pretty good and I almost dropped him. After a couple tries, it worked and he had enough of his wits to hold onto the side while we shuffled slowly to the steps in between crests and falls with the waves. I couldn't worry too much about the pain, his or mine.

It took us a good five minutes, but when we reached the steps I got in front of him and went down first, putting his weight on me and half carrying him into the cabin. He was slowly coming back into consciousness, groaning louder with each step down. Then I was able to lay him down on the bunk, his right leg against the bulkhead so it couldn't jostle too much. I found a couple old blankets, one I folded to elevate the leg, the other I covered him with. Then I removed his boots. Finally, I sat down myself. It was only then I realized I was almost sweated through and shaking.

Pross was really out of it. He looked like he'd come out on the losing end of an alley fight. The welt on his forehead had turned into an ugly knot, and the corner of his right eye was black and blue too. I realized maybe I should get some ice on the welt at least. I found a small towel and went back up to the deck and opened the ice hold where our hundred-dollar tuna lay. I was about to head back down when I saw Prossie's camera pitched into the corner where he'd been thrown. I picked it up, glad that it hadn't gone overboard. Glad *we* hadn't gone overboard!

Down below, he groaned louder as I set the towel and ice over his forehead. This was good. I told him again what happened.

"Pross, listen to me. I got you as comfortable as I can. Your leg's busted, but I don't think too bad. And I got your camera. But now I gotta leave you for a while and try to get us home. You got that?"

Grunt.

That was enough for me. I'd done the best I could. Now I had to figure out how the hell to get home.

Back in the wheelhouse I poured more coffee, lukewarm now, thankful there was some left. It was a shaky job, holding the mug with my left hand—barely—and pouring the thermos with my good right while the boat rocked and probably wondered what the hell was going on.

Wind and rain were coming on and the waves were turning ugly. No longer white-tipped swells, now they were a mad rough sea, one wave wanting to push on another. *Mariel* had been idling the whole time, so I knew we hadn't gone any further north or east. If anything maybe we'd been pushed back south and west. I kicked her into a half throttle and turned slowly to the west taking care with both the boat and Prospero below. I had no idea how far we were from land. But we'd been about two hours getting out. So I knew it'd be longer getting back because of the whale and fighting the weather. We needed to make Gloucester by six or six-thirty to beat whatever was going to pass for sunset today. It was now after four.

I didn't know anything more about how to handle the boat. But common sense and the pain in my shoulder, as well as Pross, told me I shouldn't try to hightail it over these waves. Still, I had to go fast enough to keep spray and waves off the aft end. When I looked back, it seemed like the sea was building more, and more and when we dipped into troughs, we lost the horizon altogether with the deck picking up sheets of spray.

The pain in my shoulder had settled down to a dull throb. I kept my elbow tucked against my ribs as best I could, steering with my right hand. I'd hurt something, but I didn't think anything was broken. Or at least broken enough to cause more problems than I already had. I could move my arm some, but whenever I did the pain in my shoulder was sharp.

After a half hour laboring in these seas, I wanted to check on Prospero. I didn't dare slow the boat any more for fear of being swamped from behind.

Yet I needed to see how he was and if he'd awakened could he tell me what to do? The day was darkening fast. Could we make it back before dark? And if we couldn't...well, I didn't want to think about that yet.

I turned on *Mariel*'s running lights just in case someone else was also in a jam and might see us. Already it felt very lonely out there. There was nothing to see but wave after wave. Even when we crested, there was no relief, feeling more like we were scraping the bottom of the sky. Cloud and rain and spray and wave were one. And even though I knew a whole continent's beginnings were out there, just fifteen or twenty miles away, this felt more like the ends of the earth.

I figured out if I brought the boat around and faced into the waves, then we wouldn't swamp. I also figured out how to lock the wheel so we wouldn't get turned while I was below. Then I throttled back, so we wouldn't retrace too much of what we covered. The boat steadied into the wind and waves and I made my way below.

Prospero was awake, but still very groggy. He tried to sit up, the ice bag sliding to the floor, and I pushed back gently on his chest. "Easy, Pross. You got a bum leg right now. And that knot on your head's about the size of a golf ball." He eased back down, realizing now he was in no shape to move around. The cabin was almost dark now, a reminder that we had to find a way to make port soon. But I could see his eyes focused on my left arm tucked against me.

"Jack, are you...alright?" nodding ever so slightly.

"My arm's banged up. But it's not broken I don't think."

"And my leg, you think it is?"

"Yeah. But it didn't break the skin. I got you splinted up best I could."

"What time?"

"Quarter to five."

He closed his eyes and groaned again. "We won't make it."

I was glad it was dark because he didn't see me shudder at those words.

"What do you mean, Pross? We've been headed west almost half an hour. "

"How much fuel?"

"Half a tank."

"Um-hmm. And the weather?"

"Getting worse. Rain and wind picking up. The storm's catching up to us."

"The sea?"

"Waves are building. I'd say five footers easy now. Some bigger. I tried to go fast enough so we wouldn't get swamped."

Pross was silent, which terrified me more than his words. Meanwhile the boat pitched with an uneasy back and forth.

Finally he said in a tone I could barely hear. "Jack, we cannot outrun."

"What do you mean, Pross?"

"The storm. She will catch us. Soon. This is just the start."

"So, what do we do? I mean, shouldn't we keep going?"

"Jack, there is a light at the end. A switch on it below, I think."

I felt the wall at the end of the bunk and found the light. It cast a harsh shadow across the top half of Pross's face. But I could see his eyes now wide and deadly serious.

"Jack, you have never handled a boat before, yes?" He spoke slowly and deliberately.

"No, Pross, I haven't."

"In calm seas, it is easy. In storm, it is most tricky. In storm at night, impossible."

We were both silent, studying each other's faces for some hint of truth and maybe salvation.

"You feel how the waves carry us now?"

"Yes."

"Later, they will not want to carry. Later, they will want to bury, take us down. To the bottom."

"But this boat feels pretty solid, Pross. You said that yourself."

"Yes. And if my Johnny were here, maybe he could get us through. But..."

He didn't have to finish. I felt like Prospero had just uttered our death sentences. How could a day that began so well end like this? Was this it, then? Was he saying to stay below with him until the last big wave came over the transom, filled *Mariel* with cold Atlantic water and put a silent, total end to us like it'd done to the Sortinos and countless others foolish enough to tempt the capriciousness of storm and ocean all the way back to Odysseus and Aeneas?

I looked back at Pross, his eyes closed, as though he, too, were contemplating the end. Maybe he always thought his end would be at sea too. Maybe not. But it seemed all his years at sea, all his Giovanetti luck, was coming to naught simply because he indulged his own desires and too eagerly took a greenhorn onto a sea that was already forecast for change. He had dared the gods and now he was going to die because of his rashness. An old story. An old, old story.

"Isn't there anything we...I...can do?"

Pross opened his eyes again and looked right at me.

"Give me your hand." He gripped my right forearm tightly. I tried to do the same. His was stronger than mine.

"Jack, I am sorry. This is all my fault. If we turn after we catch our tuna, we beat the storm and are home. But, no, we chase our whale. I want too much. And now we are caught."

"But Prospero, we aren't simply going to give up, are we? This is a good boat. I may not be your Johnny, but I can be your Ishmael!" His eyes got wide at that. Mine did too. Where did that come from? I just blurted it out. And then, the most improbable thing happened. We both started laughing. Deep, belly laughter. Laughter at the absurd. Laughter in the face of death men share with each other only. He drew me to him and we embraced awkwardly, but genuinely. I didn't even let on that our embrace included more pain from my left arm and shoulder.

"Jack, yes. Yes, you can. You be my Ishmael. But I am only Prospero Giovanetti, not Father Abraham." We paused, wondering what the hell that meant exactly. Then Prospero got an idea, his eyes brightening.

"OK. Now listen. Maybe we have a chance. You are right, *Mariel* is a good boat. She cares about us. Here is what you do. We are going to ride this out. It will take all night. And it will take every bit of your strength. Yes. But what you must do is keep *Mariel* pointed into the storm. Stay on a very low idle. But just enough to face the waves. Feel it ride up and down. Up and down. Do not panic or we are lost. Understand?"

I squeezed his arm for an answer. "Yes. I can do that, Prospero."

"The sea and the wind they will carry us. We will ride the storm. We are too far away to hit land. But we must watch our fuel and our batteries. Lose them and we are really done."

"I understand. Into the wind, low throttle. Ride it out."

"*Mariel* will do her best to take care of us. But you must help her do that."

It was totally dark now, except for the feeble light at the end of the bunk.

"Pross, I will do that. And you, you must try to rest easy."

"OK. Now you must go. Watch the compass. North and east. Feel the waves. Keep her right into them. If there is another blanket, take it. You will need. And turn out the light. We save on the batteries."

"Are you going to be OK, Pross? You need anything?"

"Jack, go! Tonight, you are Ishmael!"

I took heart from his bounce of courage and hugged him quickly again. "I'll check on you in a couple hours." He nodded. I found a small blanket, then flicked off the light and staggered out of the cabin, into the storm and back up into the wheelhouse. That effort alone cost me my breath. It was going to be one long night. With luck, lots of it, it wouldn't be our last.

Chapter 22 — Darkest Night of My Soul

Consider the subtleness of the sea; how its most dreaded creatures glide under the water, unapparent for the most part, and treacherously hidden beneath the loveliest tints of azure. Consider the most devilish brilliance and beauty of many of its most remorseless tribes, as the dainty embellished shape of many species of sharks. Consider, once more, the universal cannibalism of the sea; all whose creatures prey upon each other, carrying on eternal war since the world began.

Consider all this; and then turn to this green, gentle, and most docile earth; consider them both, the sea and the land; and do you not find a strange analogy to something in yourself? For as this appalling ocean surrounds the verdant land, so in the soul of man there lies one insular Tahiti, full of peace and joy, but encompassed by all the horrors of the half-known life. God keep thee! Push not off from that isle, thou canst never return!" ~Moby-Dick; Or, The Whale Chapter 57

An early dusk had come with the storm. In half an hour, probably less, it'd be totally dark. We'd have to ride this out at least twelve hours before a hint of the next day's light. It was up to me to help *Mariel* get us through. But I really didn't know what to do other than what he'd told me: keep her pointed into the storm. The rest was on her. We'd ride the waves and they'd take us where they would. Maybe being stuck out here was the best thing. There was nothing we could bump into. If we'd been closer to land, I'd have had no way of knowing if we were getting pushed onto a reef or even the shore until too late.

I took the blanket, really a beach towel, and made a half-assed sling that slid under my arm and over my neck. That bit of support kept my arm from bouncing around and stopped the spears of pain shooting from the back of my shoulder. It still ached, but whatever it was didn't feel like a break, so maybe I'd torn some cartilage and separated something. But it sure hurt like a bitch!

The wind and sea continued to build. Rain beat with an intense *rat-a-tap-tap* against the wheelhouse windows. It seemed to be coming at us harder and harder. With the last light all I could see were the frothy tips of wave after wave. There was nothing to suggest this world had anything to it but water. No land. No sky. No life. Just two sad suckers now bobbing up and down on a lonely boat.

I kept the engine in gear, giving it just enough juice to meet each wave without getting pushed around too much. I still had to keep a firm hold on the wheel, squeezed between my right hand and left knee. I kept the running lights on, even though I was tempted to turn them off to save the batteries. The tiny lights, Christmas green and red, provided a small comfort in my now pitch black world.

I turned the wheelhouse lights on to check my watch and snatch a moment of comfort, then kicked myself for not looking for a flashlight below. I was filled with a nervous energy not knowing if the next wave would be our last or not. Prospero and his sons would've handled the whole thing a whole lot better, having been through many storms. I had no idea what to expect. These little shots of terror didn't come when we were cresting. They came at the bottom when it was all water and felt like forever before we rose up to meet the next wave. They were rough for sure. But gradually I got their rhythm. First, the thump of bow against wave. Then up up up. And down down down. Pause. Thump. Up up up. Down down down. Pause. Thump. One after the other. On and on and on. Time soon meant nothing.

Once in a while, one came along that felt out of synch. I couldn't see it, of course, but it felt bigger, madder than the rest. THUMP. Up up up up UP.

Pause. Down down DOWN! Pause. Pause. Thump. Up up up. Down down down. On and on and on it went. I tried counting to see if I could figure out when the next "monster" would come along. But I couldn't. All I could do was hold my breath and hope we'd make it over to the back side. I knew water was splashing across our bow and washing down to the stern. I just hoped our hold was locked tight and nothing was working its way below. Same with the cabin. That would be the surest way to get swamped and dragged to the bottom.

Then there was the wind. What had started midmorning gentle and wispy became a steady breeze through the afternoon that grew stronger and louder until now in the dark it was an unrelenting roar that drowned out even the sound of waves hitting our boat. It just blew and blew and blew, so much so that after a while its howl almost settled into a kind of background noise, a constant that would not stop and so the mind tries to put it aside to keep from going mad. We'd ride up one of those really big waves and at the crest get an even stiffer, high-pitched blast. I tried tuning it out. Its howling got on my nerves like some wild animal clawing and scratching to get at me and rip me to shreds.

Getting washed or blown off the deck became a real fear. I knew I was stuck in the wheelhouse for the duration. I'd been lonely before, but nothing like this. I felt like the only person left in the world. Even though we were only feet apart, I wondered if Prospero felt the same. If anything, it was worse for him because his *Mariel* was in the hands of a hopeless incompetent. There wasn't a damn thing he could do. I only hoped he was comfortable. Or maybe so groggy from the knock on the head, he didn't care.

After a while the rush of nerves and adrenaline wore off. Then I realized how tired I was. Bone tired. Dead on my feet tired. Our slim hopes depended on me staying awake. If I fell asleep, I'd be just like some trucker dozing off with his eighteen-wheeler barreling down the highway. It'd only take seconds for him to be off the highway and on his way to another world. Same for us. This storm would turn *Mariel* just as quickly and swamp her for sure. I could lock down the wheel and rudder like before. But now I was too scared to even do that. I didn't trust it to hold if I fell asleep! Any thoughts of checking on Pross would have to wait. In a way, it didn't make any difference if I got to see him or not. There wasn't anything I could do except try to keep us pointed into the storm. And hope my fears were enough to keep from falling into one last eternal sleep.

To stay awake I played little mind games like I did in the fire tower keeping watch during a long night of storms. Counts between thunder and lightning strikes. Or think back to women I'd known, especially the one I'd dated in New York, Anne, one of the Barnard girls. Sometimes I'd do little poems in my head. Short, silly things that usually meant nothing in the morning. But here's one I remembered:

The waters see
The waters saw
So this is eternity

I wrote that in the fifties. But I could've made it up this night while I waited for eternity to find us bobbing over Stellwagen Bank like a bottle with its cork about to pop. I played it over and over in my head, trying to make a little song and keep the horror at bay.

Another game I played was to focus on five a.m. when I imagined daylight would bring salvation. I whispered "Stay alive to five" over and over like a little mantra. If we made it then Pross and I both would have something to brag about back in Gloucester. We survived the Nor'easter of 1970! Hurricane winds! Monster waves! And Moby Dicks too! But when I flicked on the flashlight and saw it was only seven thirty, I felt the wearies seep into my bones again. I yawned. Shook my head. Sipped now-cool coffee from a thermos. And tried to hold on. Our little boat must think it queer that we are stuck on oceans deep with hours to go before I sleep.

What silly, stupid, crazy turns life takes sometimes. If Ruth or Josef had known Olson was three months dead, I probably never would've gone out to Gloucester. Then I'd never have met Prospero and neither of us would be in this fix. But I was glad I'd met this old man. He certainly knew more about this world than how to fill a hold with cod. Now I could only pray I might get a chance to know him better.

If we were to die out here where no one would see us again, what of it? I was already "dead" to my former world as "King of the Beats"—so called. Prospero already had 75 very good years it sounded like. The Giovanetti luck others called it. But his Marie was already seven years dead. And it was clear he missed her every day. Their boys were grown. He'd done his bit for this world. Maybe he was ready for the next. Maybe that's why he didn't fear the storm, choosing to chase the whale instead. Maybe he knew the only chance he had to chase the whale again was to get someone like me to go with him. And maybe he figured that was a decent trade off, instead of spending the rest of his days coaxing scraggly petunias from rocky soil. Maybe I'd get a chance to ask him about that, if we were lucky enough to see one more sunrise. Maybe.

I tried to think about contingencies. If the boat did swamp what would we do? We'd never bothered with life jackets earlier in the day. Maybe that was stupid then. There were a couple hanging right there in the wheelhouse and I'd seen more below. But not now. What use would they be? If *Mariel* swamped and went down, having jackets would only prolong our agony. In these waters, hypothermia would set in fast. So our life-jacketed deaths would be numb and watery instead of just watery. Same with the raft. Even if somehow I could get it inflated, how would I get Prospero out from below and into it? And with my bum wing and his broken leg, neither of us could paddle anyway. No, that would just give us a few minutes more to contemplate our stupidity and our sad, stormy end to this life.

The only "contingency" that made any sense was just to hold on for dear life. Dear life. Ha! Now that was a thought. Six months ago, holding on for dear life meant grabbing the base of a toilet as hard as I could and spilling my guts—literally—into the bowl. Life wasn't so dear then. Hadn't been for quite a while. I knew it. Memere knew it. Stella knew it. And my pals knew it. What nobody could figure out —me included—was why. Why had I wasted away so much of my life? I mean, I was *Jack Kerouac*. I'd captured the voice of a generation, some said. And turned on another. Like that nurse cooed, "Mister Kerouac, you're too young and good lookin' to leave us now." Maybe she was right. Drying out in that hospital, I wasn't so sure. Gerard had sure chewed my ass. And I deserved it.

I wasn't one of those one-and-done guys. I'd written fifteen novels. Books of poems. *On the Road* had become a big hit. Made me world famous! And I didn't even think it was my best work. At least the way my pansy publisher insisted it had to be to see the light of day. The way I wrote it, the way I felt it, was pretty good. But Giroux sucked all the life out of it so he wouldn't get his ass sued. Even at that it was still pretty good. Not my best, but pretty good. And I hadn't run out of things to say. The Duluoz Legend was incomplete. But then it was like I'd given up. Run away. Couldn't do it anymore. Instead I was left holding on for what was left of my not-so-dear life in a tiny bathroom inside a cinderblock house in a godforsaken St. Petersburg neighborhood.

But for some reason I'd been saved, given a second chance. Given more time to figure things out. More time to write about whatever it was that really made this life dear. And I'd hit the road again to do just that. I knew I couldn't do it sitting around St. Pete. There had always been something in me that needed to be out. Out of doors. Out of town. Sometimes, even, out of my mind. And I knew I couldn't do it dragging Stella and Memere around with me. Not that they would've wanted to. I tried that once with the whole Denver fiasco. No. They wanted quiet, soft Florida lives. Stella would've been perfectly happy watching over me while I mended up and started writing again even if I was a husband in name only. She deserved better. She really did. For some crazy reason she seemed content to be Mrs. Jack Kerouac. Maybe in a weird way it helped her stay close to her brother Sammy too.

Sammy. Maybe if I'd been a better buddy, we'd have stuck together. Instead I dumped him for the New York crowd. I'd would've made it in the Army if I'd been with him instead of washing out in the Navy. He wouldn't have let me walk away. He wouldn't have let me coward my way out, playing crazy for the Navy docs. Maybe we would've hit the Anzio beach together. Maybe we'd both have died there. Or maybe I could've saved his life. Or maybe he would've saved mine. And maybe we'd have come home heroes. Then he would've had a shot at saving lives back here, becoming the doctor he dreamed of. But instead of him getting a chance to have a life, I, who chickenshit my way out of war and death, get not one, but two, chances at life. And just when I think maybe I'm going to do something with that, here I am stuck in the middle of the ocean in the middle of the night in the middle of a killer storm.

You think about things like that and wonder where is God and all His justice.

Sammy and Gerard, they were the ones who deserved to live. They were the ones who deserved a chance to have a life and make it a little better for the rest of us. They were the ones who lived for others. The soldier and the saint. The doctor and the priest who might have been. Instead, it was me. A coward and beat saint rolled into one. The one who lived for me only. The one who ran away from relationships and commitments. The one who abandoned his only child. I was the one who lived. What justice was there in that? I was the one who got to go forward, do the things they couldn't do. And forward I went. Fast. And far away. Until I couldn't get any farther. And then I was ready to go with them. Except I couldn't. They wouldn't let me. I had to stay here. And my "reward" for six more months of life was the very real chance of dying out here where no one would miss me. Had it just been a week before at Hatteras when I looked for Gerard to ride in on a wave with angels and take me away? Had it been just two weeks when I'd met Jo and Ruth and somehow got talked into writing a book about a college that'd been dead and gone for fifteen years? Had it been just three weeks when I'd waved goodbyes and given big, happy smiles to Stella and Memere, saying I'd be back soon when I knew damn well I wouldn't? All these seemed lifetimes ago now as I hung on for dear life. Again.

Just as I was sorting through all these thoughts, another monster wave hit us. WHAM! I didn't even feel it coming like I was beginning to with the others. It reared *Mariel* up to a point where I thought "This is it. We're going over." I hung on to the wheel tight as I could, but felt that sick, sick feeling when Death is upon you and there is nothing you can do but wait for It to finish the job. Our whole watery world went vertical. Up up up up up UP! Just like in the afternoon when we got tossed like a couple of caught mackerel across the deck. Except now I was in total pitch darkness. I couldn't orient myself. I couldn't feel up from down, only like I was about to get tossed out of the wheelhouse and out onto the deck and from there into the water and oblivion. I felt like Jonah about to be swallowed whole into the maw of a leviathan. It happened fast and in slow motion at the same time and not a damn thing I could do about it.

Somehow *Mariel* refused to tip. She fought over the top of that wave and started sliding down the other side. But the big one had turned us and now we were caught sideways in the trough. If the next one got her broadside, *Mariel* might not hold and we'd be rolled sure as hell. By instinct, or ignorance, I turned the wheel hard right and gunned the engine. All I could hope was she wouldn't let us go down without a fight. We caught the next wave at what felt like a 45 degree angle. It tried to push us around, but *Mariel* wouldn't let it. I kept the wheel turned and yelled "Fuck you!" at whatever was out there that sought to destroy and devour. *Mariel* fought back. She really did. I could feel it. She refused to surrender. I could feel her determination to hold on. To fight back. To...survive.

When the one after that hit we were close to back on point. We got up and down OK. And then met the one after that straight on. And the one after that. Then things seemed to settle down a little. Not a lot, but enough so I didn't think the next minute was our last. But my heart damn near jumped out of my chest and I was breathing like I'd just run a mile. I checked the compass; the needle was back to N-NE. Still, the waves beat at us. And the rain pelted the windows like little fingers of Death rat-a-tap-tapping rat-a-tap-tapping rat-a-tap-tapping. And the wind howled and howled.

As hard as the wind blew and the waves and rain beat at us, I had the sense we'd just taken the worst of it. I could only hope like hell Prospero had managed to hang on to his bunk. I throttled back to the slow ahead we'd been doing before. But there'd be no way of knowing if the next one was also going to be a monster and try to roll us straight to the bottom. All this doughty boat and I could do was fight back when it came. And she was a helluva fighter. And because of her, maybe I'd become a fighter too.

I checked my watch: 11:30. Only five and a half hours to go. "Make it to five, we stay alive." But we had less than a half tank of gas. If we ran out, that'd be it for us as sure as that monster wave should've been. Now I hoped the storm would at least blow us within sight of land by morning, so we could make a run for it.

I closed my eyes and tried to collect my thoughts. I've been lonely and miserable before, but nothing, nothing like this. Yet fighting off those monster waves somehow made me feel better, like maybe we had more than a pissant's chance of making it as long as that was the worst this storm could throw at us. As long as I kept my wits about me. And as long as *Mariel* continued to show she was tougher than the seas trying to bring us down. Pross was depending on us for sure. Maybe he was content dying out here. Maybe he wasn't. Maybe I was too. Maybe I wasn't. But there was no running away. No road to hit. No truck to thumb down. No woman to sneak away from. No bottle to crawl into.

What happened next was real simple now: it was all on me whether we lived or died. If I gave up, we'd be gone, and pretty quick too. But if I hung on, *Mariel* would do her part. Prospero had told me what to do, that was simple too. But it was more than just keeping the boat pointed in the right direction, it was wanting to keep the boat pointed in the right direction. It wasn't just the desire to live, it was the will to live. Even in my saddest, beatest days, times where I'd had little or nothing to eat for days on end, where I'd shivered sick and alone, where I felt so lost I didn't know where I was or who I was, I'd never been to the point where the choice to live or die was made so simple, so stark. Yet, here it was. Here I was. At this moment when the sea just wanted to snuff us out, I felt new life. I could feel it. What it meant to want to live. Mariel refused to go down. And now I was right there with her. Jack Kerouac would fight as I had never fought before.

I'd seen just the opposite many times. As Mariel fought up one wave and pushed down to another, my thoughts drifted to guys I'd known just waiting to die. On the streets. In bars. Or lots of times just parked in front of living room TV sets. Maybe they never said it that way, hardly anyone ever did, but you could tell. How else to account for endless hours inside a bar when the rest of the world's at work, trying like hell to make a buck? What do you make of all the empty hours of bar talk when a few beers solved all the world's problems, but none of your own? Hours and hours, and days and days, and months and months, and years and years of talk talk talk?

After a while, you knew. You knew when talk turned from soul-baring to pure bullshit even before yours became an incoherent ramble. And you knew the only reason you were there, head pitched toward the bar, a drink shy of passing out altogether, was because this was as good a place as any to hide away from your own problems. At the bottom, and I'd been there many times, the bar was the last stop before the funeral home, where the final chapters of their wasted lives played out. The question wasn't what did he do, but why he did it? What moves a man, and sometimes a woman, to want to up and quit life? And do it the slow way with a drink, instead of quick and fast with a gun or maybe pills or some other way to suicide? When life itself may be all there is, why give it away so easily? I'm so glad Gerard never saw me the countless times when I was falling down drunk at a Skid Row bar or some uptown soiree.

All these thoughts of Death! But how could I escape it? We were in a killer storm and already dodged Death twice. How many more times would we again before morning and, hopefully, land or rescue? *Mariel* continued to climb wave after wave, refusing to go down. Rain and wind beat us all around. A true fury! Made worse because I couldn't see a thing. Just feeling and hearing water and water and water. *Rat-a-tap-tap, rat-a-tap-tap, rat-a-tap-tap, rat-a-tap-tap, rat-a-tap-tap.* Enough to drive a guy mad if you let it. It was very simple now. Hands on for Life. Or hands up for Death. That's all there was. I, who'd danced Death's tune time after time not caring whether I finished or not, was now fighting for my life—and Prospero's. Maybe I didn't deserve to live, but Prospero did. Even if he was resigned to end his 75 years here where he'd made his life, I owed it to him to give it my all, to get him back to land and home and his sons and his friends. And so I hung on tight to the wheel, ignoring the throbbing in my shoulder, wanting to see another day. Together, Mariel and I fought through the rage and the wet. It felt as though she and I became one, protecting our worthy passenger below. I could only guess where the storm was pushing us, but the compass pointed a steady N-NE, which meant we were being pushed south. How far and how fast was anybody's guess. I think I was doing a good job not wasting fuel, the gauge still holding just a bit below 3/8ths. But there was nothing I could do to make sure we had enough 'til morning. We had to keep our heading. If we ran out, we ran out, and with it went our luck and our lives.

Then, after a while, it seemed like the storm let up just a little. Or maybe, finally, I'd gotten used to it. After that monster wave almost tipped us, none of the others that came after seemed as bad. I could almost feel them coming and would give *Mariel* a little more gas to get up and over. I knew we were far from making it through, it was only one o'clock. But at least we'd gotten to another day. "Alive to five" played on in my head. The waters see. The waters saw.

I was in the middle of a monster storm with a broken shoulder trying my damnedest to hold on for just a little longer. And for what? A chance to go back? A chance to write more? A chance to say out loud "JACK KEROUAC IS ALIVE! YES, ALIVE!" Is this what I was holding on to here? A chance to say I am still in this world? To say I want to be in this world? Even as a subterranean of my own making? To say I am not yet ready to quit and step through Death's Door?

The storm beat on and on. It had tried *Mariel* and me and we did not roll for it. Still, it beat and beat and beat at us trying to find a way in. *Rat-a-tat-tapping* at our windows, at our souls. But I kept our bearings. And *Mariel* kept us upright. The storm raged at our refusal to go down. We held fast. Another hour into the new day. Just three more and it would be five. "Five and alive. Five and alive."

As I held tight, I imagined our *Mariel* as the *Pequod* rounding Cape Horn fighting colliding seas from two oceans. Then I pictured myself as Ishmael astride its crow's nest on the lookout for Pacific whale spouts. Ishmael, that most mysterious of sailors. Why did Melville choose that name above all others? Who was his Ishmael? Someone crazy to get away from civilized society. Anxious to try the far more dangerous whaling life. Wanting to push out to the limits of life. An outcast. But of his own choosing. He says: "I am tormented with an everlasting itch for things remote. I love to sail forbidden seas, and land on barbarous coasts." Isn't that what I've been doing all my life? Isn't that what drew me west into open skies and onto desolate peaks? Isn't that how I imagined the sea as my brother? Haven't I landed on barbarous coasts too many times to count?

What about his crazy Ahab? Who was he? Ahab wants his revenge. But he wants more than that and that's what I think Melville, and later Olson, were trying to get at. Ahab, too, is tormented by an everlasting itch for things remote. He and Ishmael are two chicks in a shell.

And who did I know who'd been as tormented as Ahab? As driven? Seduced into doing things—or seducing them!—by women and men and spanning a continent in the doing? Who was as blinded by his desire and then could, by the sheer force of his being, pull the innocent and guilty alike for rides that seemed aimless but were in fact single minded? Who ate up life in great gulps and tried to dig the deepest depths of souls, his own and others? Who? Who, but Neal Cassady? The Great Mystery and Force of my life. Neal Cassady the driver, taking his own revenge out on the great American landscape. Captain of his ship, a shiny new Hudson or Cadillac, or beat up Ford or junkyard truck, didn't matter. Neal. Dead Neal. Yet who burned as bright as any god or star across our American skies. Neal running scared from the horrors of his absent mother and father, deep into Denver pool halls and darkened alleys. Scarred by the long cut running the length of his soul. A huge prick of a scar touched by the likes of Justin Brierly and Allen Ginsberg. And JoAnn and Carolyn. And countless others. But not by me. Not by me.

Ahab the driver and Ishmael along for the ride. Wasn't that Neal and me? Wasn't that it? Neal driven to find his biggest, wildest kicks somewhere out there on the great ocean of America. Me riding along to write it all down and pass it along, as sure as Ishmael lived to tell the tale of Ahab's wild hunt for Moby Dick? All of us wild in the SPACE that was America, is America, an America stretching soul-searching sea to soul-searching sea. America two seas bonded by one land. An America that was as much water as it was land. An America whose spirit was the world's spirit. Wasn't that it? Wasn't that why I blurted out Melville's line not knowing why, but now maybe I did? Something pulled from the depths of my own twisted, yearning subconscious?

"Call me Ishmael! Yes! Ishmael! I am outcast. And though the whale has dragged my friend to his deadly, eternal depths, I will bring him back to life! Ahab lives! Cassady lives! Ishmael lives! Kerouac lives!" I roared this into the storm now, meaning those words more than anything I'd yelled in years. Loud enough that even Prospero had a chance of hearing me, if he were still conscious, if he were still alive.

I am Ishmael, wild ass of a man, more dangerous even than magical Prospero and his Tempest. More primitive. From Folsom Cave to now. Tormented with an everlasting itch for things remote. I will subdue the storm. I will conquer the depths and calm the waters. I am Ishmael. I rage and I write. And my rage will be holy. And I will write the pure and the true. Yin. And yang. Satori. Light out of dark. Creation out of chaos.

I leaned hard into the wheel, pressing towards the glass, feeling fully awake and alive. Mariel and I were one, rode her like she was the wildest mustang on the Great Plains. If I'd had my typewriter I could've written through the night to tell this tale. "Three o'clock! Alive to five!" I was about to flick off the cabin light when I glanced to my left and there he was. Gerard! Jesus! I about jumped through the wheelhouse window! How long had he been there? Did he hear me? Maybe I shouldn't have been surprised, given how he seemed to be making a habit of showing up when I least expected him. Or when I didn't expect him at all. Maybe under ordinary circumstances I wouldn't have been. But nothing was ordinary now. Hadn't been for some time.

Gerard. In deep shadow, I could barely see his face and the top of his shirt. It looked like the same one from each time before. The rest of his body was dark as this night, so dark I couldn't really be sure if he was all there or not. He stared with his same full, sad, Cheshire Cat eyes. But also with a little half smile, something I hadn't seen before. Hadn't he worn a little frown the other times, a sad, disappointed look at how his Ti Jean had turned out? And while I still was holding fast to the wheel, moving with *Mariel* through the fearful pounding of waves and wind and rain, it seemed Gerard was able to stand as calmly as if we were in our bedroom back home.

He seemed in no hurry to speak, just standing there, looking. I was alarmed, yet strangely comforted by his presence. In the hospital I'd been too beat up to care. At Ruth's he was all hallucination, making me question my sanity. In the motel room, he was ready to be my deliverance. And now? Why was he here? Because I'd called to him? I didn't remember doing that. Because I needed him? Had he helped Mariel push over that monster wave and keep us afloat? I doubted that. I think she did that all on her own. So why now? Why here? Was he really taking me away? Was he the sign that this was it, that we'd dodged Death once, twice, but not this third time? Was it time to let go? Not fight it anymore? Take the next step wherever that might lead?

"What are you doing here?" I didn't ask in anger or even disbelief. It felt more like resignation, like maybe this was it.

Do you want me to go? As before, his voice was gentle and patient. Even when he'd scolded me, it was done with a patience of the wise older brother trying to help the younger screw-up.

"No." I stared at him some more. He looked back with that same expression. Yet something felt different, but I couldn't yet figure out what it was. *Mariel* continued to take on the storm wave for wave.

"Is this it, Gerard?"

What do you mean?

"Are you here to take me away, once and for all?"

Do you want to go?

"Hell no. Maybe once I did. Not anymore."

He continued to stare at me, but his lips stayed bent into a knowing smile. He waited.

"I can't go now Gerard! I got this old man down below and he's got this broken leg and maybe a concussion and this is his boat and I got to get him back to his sons, if we ever get through this storm, which was kind of his fault anyway."

I was babbling and it felt like I was arguing or negotiating with Gerard and I didn't care. It'd been ten hours since I'd seen Pross. Ten hours of hell. With nothing to do but hold on for dear life. Yes, dear life! Ten hours of fighting and thinking it was already over and being hungry and having a shoulder that hurt like hell.

He didn't say a thing, just nodded slightly along with his small, cat-like grin.

"I just met this guy yesterday, his name is Prospero Giovanetti, and the only reason I did was because the guy I was really looking for is dead and he was his neighbor and we started talking and you know what Gerard? He reminded me of Papa, or maybe what I wished Papa had been. He's a good man, Gerard, a real Gloucester fisherman and he knows Shakespeare and was married to the same woman for almost fifty years. Fifty years, Gerard! Imagine that! And he asked me to go fishing with him and I said OK. And we got one, a nice tuna. I got it, Gerard! Even after I lost an even bigger one, that one was a monster let me tell you!

"And then he saw a whale jumping out of the water, so we chased it until we could get close enough to take a couple pictures, then—WHAM! Out of nowhere something hit the boat and almost turned us over and we got tossed and he broke his leg and I did something to my shoulder, that's why I got this sling on. And then...and then the storm caught us. And it's been a bitch, let me tell you. More than once I thought we were going down. But we fought through it, Gerard. We fought through it. And...and...I think we're going to make it. Yep. I do. I think we're going to make it. Just a couple hours more. I can hang on.

I'm so damn tired, though. So damn tired. But, no, I'm not going to let her go down. I'm not going to let her. She's too good a boat. And he's too good a man. I'm not going down. No!"

And when I finished my chest was heaving like I'd swam a mile. And I stared back at my smiling brother who looked at me with his arms crossed like he did when I was trying to maybe build something with blocks and he waited for the right moment to show me how to do it. Always the big brother. Always the big and kind brother. And God! I missed him!

Poor Ti Jean. There is no more running away. No more. He didn't say this judgmentally, more like a statement of fact.

I stared back at him wild eyed, trying to understand the meaning of what he said. Then he did something that scared the bejesus out of me. Just like in the motel room, he extended his right hand inviting me to take it. But I couldn't reach him with my left arm in the sling. And if I took my right hand off the wheel, *Mariel* would be rudderless and we'd get turned around and swamped in no time. Is that what he was offering? Is that what he wanted me to do? Let go? Hands on for Life. Hands off for Death. Was that it? In the hospital he'd been my angel savior. But…here…Gerard…my Angel of…Death? Oh no. No! Not here! Not now!

"No, Gerard. I can't take your hand. Not now. Can't you see? If I take your hand, then I'd lose the boat and we'd be swamped and…it'd all be over Gerard. And I can't do that. Not now. No!" To make my point, I leaned away from him almost like I worried he was going to touch me and take me anyhow.

"Why, Ti Jean? Papa, he is waiting. Nin, she is waiting. Memere, she will come. We can be together again and happy." Gerard didn't move, but he kept his arm extended. His hand was a foot away, maybe less. All I had to do was turn and let go. Turn and let go.

"Oh, Gerard, I want to see them so bad! I do! I want to tell Papa how sorry I am. I messed up everything for him. He was counting on me and I let him down. I know it Gerard. I know it. But he doesn't know why. Why I couldn't be his football hero forever. He doesn't know why I had to go. What I needed to see." I was about to cry. If our father had stood next to Gerard right then, I probably would've let go. I probably would've bawled myself right into his arms and asked for forgiveness. And he would have forgiven. And there would be peace. But not now. How could I explain Ishmael and Ahab to Gerard?

"Ti Jean, you have fought for so long. Yes, you were given another chance at life. But here you are. Fighting this storm that wants to bring you back to us. Can't you see? It is easy now. You do not have to fight."

Why was he talking like this? Maybe he was testing me! Maybe that's all this was. Just to see how much I wanted to live. By making it easy to die. That had to be it! Why would he say these things now after the scolding he'd given me in the hospital? I was being given a second chance! I was healthy again! I had a book to write for Ruth. For me! I wanted to see America again. I wanted to get to San Francisco! Maybe I'd even ask Jo to join me there. Or Lissa. Or maybe I'd just stay on my own, doing what I needed when I needed.

I just needed to get through this night. Just needed to save Pross and myself. Get back to dry land and hit the road. Drink life like Whitman. Dare life like Melville. But be me. ME. JACK KEROUAC!

I looked down at Gerard's tiny translucent hand. Such a beautiful hand. It had held little birds and tiny bugs with the gentlest of care. A saint's hand. It had held my hand, guiding me to school, to church. It had brushed my hair. And shown me how to make things. And pointed to the sky, to the very spot where he knew he was going and I couldn't follow. At least right away. And now that hand offered to take me again.

"No, Gerard. I can't go. Not now. I want to be with all of you so bad. But not now. I really do have more to do. I am going to get this boat through the night. And we are going to find a harbor. And I am going to get Prospero to a hospital. And we are going to live. Live! You told me at the hospital I was getting a second chance and you are right. I've met a lot of people since then and they are good people and they want me to live also. Dying is easy. Whether you get it from a bottle or a gun. We come, we go. Poof! I am not going easy, Gerard. Not now. No."

Then another monster hit us and I turned towards the windows and gunned *Mariel's* engines and we fought through it. This time when we topped out I thought I saw some little change in the sky. But then we were down again and I had to keep her steady and on point. And it was dark. "See, Gerard? See how I had to fight that bastard! If I took your hand, it'd all be over for me and Pross and this damn blessed boat. It's called *Mariel*, Gerard. You know why? It's a cross between Pross's wife's name. She was Maria. And Ariel, the beautiful spirit in *The Tempest*. You never got a chance to read *The Tempest*, I know. It's a great story, Gerard. By Shakespeare. Maria and Ariel. Mariel! Get it, Gerard? This is *Mariel III*. If she goes down, which she isn't, I don't know if there'd be a fourth. Maybe. Who knows? But we're gonna make it, Gerard. We're gonna make it. Tell Papa and Nin I love them. I will see them later. But not now, Gerard. Not now. Nope. I gotta get this baby to safe harbor."

I turned back to see his reaction, but he was gone. And instead of being sad, I was relieved! We were going to make it, dammit. And I didn't need Gerard holding out his hand and having me betray my friend below. No!

Chapter 23 — Provincetown

After Gerard left, I felt a kind of crazed energetic renewal that fought off my dead bone weariness of trying to just stay alive. I started to think maybe we'd made it through the worst of the storm. The ocean was still plenty rough. We were still getting whacked pretty good. Maybe I'd just gotten used to it, but I didn't feel the *menace* of a few hours before. The rain kept rat-a-tapping at us, but the wind seemed more of a howl than a scream. And maybe there was a band of lighter sky at the horizon off to my right. Could it be? I checked my watch. 5:05! We made it to five and still alive! Or at least I was and could only hope for Pross. But our gas was below the quarter mark, and even the dawn couldn't save us if we ran out. I throttled back and checked for more hints of dawn.

What a night! Twelve hours on my own. No help from Prospero below. And Gerard hadn't brought any help from above either. But I'm dead certain if I'd taken his little hand that would've been the end of me in this world for sure, as well as for Pross and *Mariel*. Maybe he'd have taken me to Papa and Nin and happiness, but I wasn't ready to find out. Not just yet. Ol' Ti-Jean has more miles to go before he's ready to check out for good. That's one thing I've figured out. Even if I wasn't so sure down there at Hatteras. I'm up and I'm down. But I'm not ready to stay down. No, not yet.

By 5:30 I could see dawn coming on. There was a thin grayness that separated the blackness of sky and ocean. Just a crack. But enough. My spirits soared. I would get us home! I looked all around for some hint of land. I still couldn't see anything west and south. But now I somehow had the feeling that this storm, instead of taking us to the bottom, would deliver us to safe harbor just as Shakespeare's tempest delivered the Duke of Milan and others to Prospero's magical island.

The crack at the horizon widened. Only a brighter band of gray. No hint of a sunrise. Still it was enough. I looked back over my right shoulder and thought maybe I saw something different. A darker band along that horizon? Not sure. I kept *Mariel* headed into the waves and wind, but now I kept looking back hoping, hoping maybe it was what we needed—land.

Ten minutes more and yes! Light in the east! The storm was moving on. I looked back once more and now I could definitely see a thin slice of land — LAND!—when we crested the waves. Now I had to help *Mariel* finish her task and get us into some kind of safe harbor. I brought her around slowly and throttled up to ride the waves as we made for whatever it was out there.

The shoreline kept cutting to the south and then it bent back to the east! I tried and tried to get a picture of where we were. There were no other boats out. Then ten minutes more and land starting coming up in front of me. A shoreline rising in the east and running south as far as I could see. Now at least I knew we were safe from any more storm and monster waves and the morning was here and I'd get us home somehow.

Finally the curl of beach on my left fell away and there it was…harbor lights and a town! I brought *Mariel* around to the north and could see a bunch of docks to aim for. Just then she gave her first sputter. The first sign of weariness after a long day and deadly night. "Come on, baby, just a little more." I played with the throttle and she caught again. I gave her the last little bit of gas which she took and got us to shouting distance of a dock.

I opened the window and shouted to some guy standing on one. "Help! Help! Out of gas."

He yelled back and ran over to the dock where *Mariel* got us within fifty feet before she gave it up for good. We bounced close enough for me to get out of the wheelhouse and onto the bow where I threw him a line and he pulled us in. He saw my bum arm and helped me tie her up before we said a word.

I tried to extend my hand but just managed, "Thank God! Where am I?"

His eyes got wide as though maybe he'd wrapped up a lunatic. "Are ya serious? Ya don't know Provincetown when ya see it?" He thumbed to a big sign that read "Welcome to Provincetown."

"Hey! I've been out all night."

"Whacha say? Out all night?! In that noreastah? Jesus, man! That storm was a killer!" He bent in for a closer look at my face, then my slinged arm.

"Ya look like hell, if ya ask me."

The last of my adrenaline was draining fast. I just wanted to sit. Then I remembered.

"Oh, God! I got a guy below. He's the owner of this boat. He might be dead. Hit his head, broke his leg when we got tossed. Come on!"

We clambered back on board and went below. I feared the worst: finding Prospero dead or on the way there. I wasn't wrong. He was lying face up unconscious in a heap on the floor. I tried to wake him and got a grunt, but that was all.

"We need to get him to a hospital!"

"Hospital? Nearest one's in Barnstable."

"Don't you have an ambulance or something?"

"Not here. Listen, I'll run up and find the chief. He'll know what to do." Then he looked back over at Prospero's slumped body. "Do ya think he's....ya know ...alive?"

I leaned close to his chest, then his face. I felt a breath come out.

"Yeah, he is. But I think barely. Listen, hurry won'tcha?"

"Yeah, yeah."

"Hurry! I can't let him die!"

I turned back to Prospero, looking for more signs of life. "Pross, we made it," I half whispered, but could feel the panic rising in my throat. He couldn't die now! Not after all this! "We got help on the way. Just hang in there a little longer. Pross. Pross...don't leave me!"

I looked back down at his leg and almost threw up when I saw the splint all turned and the leg itself swollen black and blue. I tried twisting the splint back around, but only half-assed it. I took a life preserver and propped it underneath to try and help with the swelling. Then it was lights out.

I woke to white. Sort of. My eyes opened half way, and all they saw was white. Beautiful white. Beautiful peaceful white. Where the hell was I? Had Gerard come back and finally taken me with him? I tried moving my right hand to see if it would touch his. But my body felt like it wasn't there. Strange. I was vaguely aware of movement and murmurings, punctuated by an occasional far-off voice. Then another. And another.

These voices were close yet distant, almost like I had traveled outside my body and was taking it all in but from far away. Taking what in? I didn't know. It was all whiteness. Just whiteness. A good whiteness. Comforting. Maybe this is what death feels like. Some sort of super awareness but outside the "real" world. Not good or bad, just different. Like a trance. Sweet, murmurings, so soothing after the night I'd been through. Had it been just a night? How long ago?

The next time I opened my eyes the whiteness seemed different. More subdued. My thoughts seemed out of place, out of time, an eternity between one moment of consciousness and the next. But I *was* conscious. And that meant I was alive. I hadn't crossed over. Yet. Or maybe I'd crossed and came back. Too confusing right now. But the whiteness and voices around me weren't heaven, they were something else. Another drift.

When my eyes opened again, it was because I felt something in my arm. Warm. Then a face. A smile. And a "There you are!"

"Where...I?"

"Lucky to be alive, from what I've heard! You're in Barnstable Hospital, Mr....Mr. Moriarty? Is that correct?"

I nodded weakly to the voice, still not quite focusing on the face floating above me.

Fade to black.

When I woke next, it felt like a brand new morning. Back in my body. Mind alert. I tried to move and now felt my left arm taped to my side. And there was an IV in my right.

How long had I been here? No idea. Except for the soreness in my shoulder, I felt like a brand new man. Sort of. I tried to sit up. Not yet.

I found out it was Thursday which meant we'd been here three days. Also learned that I'd separated my shoulder, kind of like I thought I did. But I'd also gotten a concussion. That was kind of funny because I didn't remember hitting my head on anything. And I didn't remember having a headache or anything. Other than that and a few bruises I'd gotten through OK, although the nurses and docs were still amazed we survived at all.

The nurse told me that Prospero did get the worst of it. His concussion was bad. And, of course, his leg was broken. He'd also gone into shock sometime during the night. One of the docs said if we'd gotten in any later, Pross might not have made it at all. I wanted to see him right away, but they said he was still knocked out pretty good. A nurse did help me walk the hall down towards his room and I looked in. Part of me was relieved that he was all right. And part of me was sick that he was so out of it. Especially the part about his going into shock and almost dying.

The other thing I learned was that I had no ID on me! Keys, yes. Some change, yes. ID, no. Just what you'd expect from a drifter! That's when I remembered sticking my wallet in the glove box of the car. Don't ask me why. Maybe I figured I wouldn't be spending any money out on the ocean! Or maybe I was just being super cautious about losing it overboard for some stupid reason. Anyway, that meant they didn't find the driver's license with my Kerouac name and address on it. So I could keep my Moriarty story going a little longer.

When the doc checked me out late that day, he said I was good enough to go home the next day. Home being the motel, of course. How exactly I was going to get there was still a problem left to be solved. And solved it was the next morning. I walked down to Pross's room again to check on him and there was another guy watching him. He motioned me in.

"You the guy Pop went fishing with?" He asked quietly, but seriously. I knew already this was Alex, the older son. We were about the same age and height, but he was thicker from a life spent hauling tons of fish out of the ocean. A bigger, younger version of Pross. Black hair flecked with gray. Dark, brooding eyes. Couple days without a shave. A hard smile.

"Yeah. Name's Jack. Moriarty." I thought about extending my good hand to shake, but something held me back. We both nodded.

"Yeah, I know. Pop was awake some yesterday. Told me about your little adventure. Nice to meetcha, I guess. I'm Alex. His son."

I didn't like the "I guess."

"Yeah, I figured. He talked a lot about you too. How's he doing?"

"Aw, he'll be OK. Might take a couple more days. Least that's what the docs say. Pop's tough. But way too old to be taking on killer storms."

"Good. They said it was close. If we hadn't gotten in when we did..."

"Yeah..."

We both looked at the old man sleeping soundly, his broken leg in a cast and elevated.

"When they lettin' you out?" he asked, still looking at his father.

"Today. Soon as I figure out how to pay the bill and get a ride back."

"Yeah, well, don't worry about the bill. Pop's already taken care of that."

"He has?" I was stunned to learn this bit of news.

"Yep...and I can give you a ride back when you're ready."

Another surprise. But sometimes the best rides come when they're least expected.

"Hey, that'd be great. Let me check with the nurse. If they're ready to let me go, I'm ready to get out of here if you are."

"Yeah, I gotta get back and check on some things. Pop'll be good until tomorrow."

Forty-five minutes later, I was riding shotgun in Alex's pickup headed off the Cape and back up to Gloucester. And I was ready for the questions. They weren't long in coming.

"So, what I hear, you're a writer or something?"

"Yeah. Came up here to talk to a guy about a book I'm writing. Your dad's neighbor. Former neighbor now."

"Charlie? Yeah, he died...when? January?"

"Yeah. What your dad told me. Complete surprise. I came up from North Carolina, stopped in New Haven and the people in both places knew him pretty good and thought he was still crankin' away up here."

"You from down there? Sound like you're from around here."

"Boston originally. Been livin' in Florida when I'm not on the road."

"So that's how you met Pop, huh?" I knew Alex wasn't interested in books or Olson or anything of the like. He was trying to figure out how this guy next to him almost got his father killed.

"Yep. He was outside working on his garden. I told him I was looking for Olson. He said I was too late. We started talking. Invited me in. I think he really wanted to talk to someone more than anything." I knew this was kind of a push-back at Alex, suggesting maybe he had been ignoring his father. "I was getting ready to leave and he said 'You want to go fishing tomorrow?' That was Monday. Had nothing better to do, so I said sure. Showed up at six and he had everything ready to go."

"That's Pop. Of course, he never bothered to tell me he was goin' out. Told him right after Mama died he was too old to go alone. That was seven goddam years ago! Told him every year since. But he knew I was headed to the Banks. And my fag brother was already in Florida. You came along and— bam!— he's got his 'crew' for a day on the water!"

I was surprised, and maybe I shouldn't have been, at how Alex spit out his words. He was tense and mad. Mad at me? Maybe. But, in truth, maybe really mad at his father for disobeying his orders, though I got the sense nobody really ordered Prospero to do anything he didn't want to do. And scared because he'd almost died. Maybe even more mad at his "faggot brother"—what was that all about?—for being away and playing in Florida. Some of what Prospero had said about his sons was beginning to come together.

When Alex spoke next, it seemed he'd calmed down some.

"So, where'd ya go?"

"Stellwagen Bank. Northwest corner, I think he called it."

"Figures. Been his favorite spot for 50 years. Didn't he know about the storm?"

"Somebody said something about it. But Pross —your dad—said we'd be back way before it hit."

"So why weren't you?" Alex had turned prosecutor again. And I was in the box pleading my innocence. The words spilled out like a confession.

"We got our tuna. Your dad said it was a hundred-dollar one. We'd almost caught an even bigger one before. Your dad said it might've been three or four hundred pounds. But it ran under the boat and cut the line. But he was happy with the one we got.

"We were about to turn back when he saw a humpback breach. He'd been talking about whales the day before and even said we might see one that day. So he got really excited and said he wanted some pictures, so well, we...chased it." I knew how stupid that was going to sound even before I said it. But it was truth.

More silence.

"Yeah, I got that fish off," he said finally. I felt a little relieved Alex knew I wasn't lying about our catch. "It might've been a hundred-dollar tuna when you caught it. But wasn't worth shit when we got it. Sold it for chum. So where'd you chase this humper? All the way to Iceland or something? Right into the teeth of that storm?" He asked like I should've known better.

"I don't know how far we went. But we were headed east by northeast. Didn't seem to take us all that long. Maybe twenty, thirty minutes."

"What time was it?" Damn! He was drilling me like he already knew the story. Felt like if I didn't get every last detail right maybe he was going to drive me straight to the Gloucester police station.

"By the time we were close enough for the picture maybe four o'clock."

"Four o'clock?! Jesus H. Christ! No way you could've made it back in time if you were that far out. What in God's name was he thinkin'?"

"I think he thought we had enough time. And we might've if the boat hadn't almost flipped."

"The boat almost flipped? He never said anything about that. What the hell were ya doin'?"

"Honestly, Alex, I don't know what happened. One minute I was standing behind your dad, holding him steady while he tried to get another picture. The next we were ass over heels at the aft. I don't know if it was the whale. Or another whale. Or maybe even a wave."

"How rough was the water?"

"Waves'd been picking up with the wind. Whitecaps. But they weren't that bad. Maybe four or five footers. But I'm telling you that boat went vertical. And when it came down we were messed up!"

"No shit! I'd say you both were. An old man on seventy-five-year-old legs. And a guy who likes to chase whales because of some book he read as a kid." I got a little hot with that crack.

"Hey! It wasn't me who wanted the pictures. It was your dad. I didn't think it was such a terrific idea because even I could see the weather coming on. But your dad, he didn't seem the least bit worried. And he'd been out there all his life, so I figured he knew what he was doing. Who was I to say, 'Pross, we better turn back now?'"

That brought more silence.

The next time he talked, Alex had a little softer tone to his voice.

"So, what happened after you got tossed?"

"I saw right away he was hurt. I didn't know how bad, except I figured the leg was broke. I got him down below and stretched out. He was pretty groggy, but he told me what to do with the boat, which wasn't much except keep her pointed into the storm."

"So he knew the storm was coming?"

"Yeah. And I think he knew we'd fucked up. That we couldn't outrun it. So he just told me to ride it out and hope for the best. I kept her throttled enough so we wouldn't get turned and swamped. But that almost happened a couple times. Once I thought we were going down for sure. There were some monster waves out there. We went vertical a couple times, but the boat always fought through them."

Alex's tone changed a little now. Maybe my story was checking out.

"Damn! I still can't believe you made it. Trawler went down about fifty miles east. Crew of twenty-two. Lost eight of 'em."

"Yeah, think I heard one of the docs say something. I've never seen a storm like that. Hope I never do again."

Alex seemed to be settling down, so I relaxed a little too. We'd made our way past Plymouth and were closing on Weymouth. We talked about our lives. He liked that I was a Sox fan. The early hardness in his voice softened into a sadness when he mentioned his failed marriage and the child he only rarely saw now.

Our talking had taken us through Salem and Beverly and the turn onto 128 to Gloucester. Seemed almost a lifetime ago I'd driven this very road looking for Olson. In a way, it was. Now, not only was Olson not there, but so many other things had changed too. Ol' Heraclitus was sure right about never stepping into the same river twice. I was itching to get to my journal and write as much stuff as I could get down about Prospero and the boat trip and Gerard and almost dying and that crossing over and back thing. I was even trying to figure out if any of this could be worked into the Black Mountain book.

"Whaddaya say?" Alex's question woke me out of my daydream.

"Sorry. Missed that."

"I was just sayin' you can join me and the guys at the Cape Ann later if ya want. We usually get there around five. Beers are cheap on Fridays."

"Hey, thanks. Might do that. Let me see how I do driving with one arm first."

"Heh-heh. Yeah. Hadn't thought of that. But, hell, you handled the *Mariel* OK with one arm didn't ya?" I appreciated the compliment.

"Guess I did, thanks. But that boat is special. Tough. Refused to go down."

We were now in town and headed for the docks. I worried for a second if the Ford would still be there. Then realized the Giovanettis probably kept a close watch on this town. Or this end of it anyhow. A minute later we pulled up to the station wagon and I was glad to see it again, like finding a long lost horse.

Told Alex I wanted to see his dad one more time before I left town and that I might see him in a few hours at the Cape Ann. With that I fished out my keys, got in the car and headed back to the motel. Driving with the one arm was OK, but a little tricky making turns. I was glad I only had a couple miles to go.

I stopped in the office, worried they might've tossed my stuff out since I hadn't been around in almost a week. But the old man running the place with his wife seemed happy to see me.

"We wondered when you might show up again," he said teasingly. "Heard about you and old Pross gettin' caught in the storm." He nodded at my arm. "You don't look too worse for the wear. Could've gone down with that trawler."

"Yeah, you're right." I'd forgotten how fast word travels in small towns. "It was something I don't ever want to do again."

"So, are you here to check out?"

"No. I'd like to stay through the weekend. Make sure my shoulder's healed up OK."

"That's fine. We didn't touch your room. Figured either you'd show up again or someone else would to...you know." I knew.

I pulled out my wallet expecting to pay him for a week's worth of nights, plus three more through Monday.

"Let's see. That'll be twenty-five dollars."

"Twenty-five? But what about..."

"Naw. Not gonna charge you for the nights you weren't here. Besides, sounds like you been through enough. Just glad you got Pross and his boat back safe and sound. We lose too many out there."

I thanked him for the "free" nights, but gave him thirty anyway. He didn't push back on that. It was still off-season. It felt good to be back in my little room. I gave myself a few minutes, then opened my journal and tried to write a little. But words weren't coming just then. So I just stretched out and tried to think about this blur of a week.

I was awake after six and hungry. I remembered Alex's invite to the Cape Ann. Even with my bum wing, a cold beer and steaming chowder sounded good. So I got cleaned up and made my way back down to the water.

The place was Friday night crowded. I made my way through until I spotted Alex down at the same corner of the bar where I'd seen and heard the father crying for his son. He motioned me over and quickly introduced me to four of his buddies, all fishing captains and boat owners like him. It seemed pretty clear this was their spot for Friday nights. And probably more than a few Saturday nights as well.

I was still slinged up, so the guys gave me a little extra room at the bar. Alex signaled for another pitcher and another glass. Then I realized he'd invited me down so I could tell them all what happened. In detail.

But after a couple hours and a few beers, I was bushed. I used my arm as an excuse and said I had to go. It was still early for them. And would've been for me too in my younger days. But something in me wanted to be fresh for the next day when I would start to write again.

Alex walked me outside. I sensed he wanted to say something.

"Listen, Pop told me you had a lot of guts. I wasn't too sure until we had our little talk today. Then coming here tonight. I could tell the guys agreed. Anyway, Pop wanted me to make sure to give you this."

With that he pulled out something white and about four or five inches long from of his jacket.

"He said Olson gave it to him last year when he thought he was dying. Pop said you deserved to have it."

He handed it to me and it felt heavy, but I couldn't really tell what it was in the dark.

"Thanks a lot, Alex." I turned it over in my hand. It felt smooth, but I could also feel something else, little marks or something. "Your dad is quite a guy. But you know that already."

"Yeah. Pop's tough. But he's also seventy-five. And they're not gonna let him go while his noggin's still scrambled."

"I'm gonna lie low for the weekend. But I'll drive back down to the hospital Monday before heading out."

"Yeah. We got a trip to the Banks planned again. So I won't see ya. But Johnny's supposed to be back tomorrow or Sunday. You might see him down there."

"OK. Well, it was good meeting you. Thanks for the ride. And the beers! And this!" I held up in the night the object which I had to stuff in my pockets before shaking hands for maybe the last time.

Back in my room, I pulled the object out and held it under the little desk lamp. It looked like a tooth. A whale's tooth? I felt the marks in it and then looked more closely. They were letters! I turned it in the light for a better look and there in a kind of ragged scrawl were letters that quite literally sent a chill up my spine:

Ishmael

Chapter 24 — The Boatswain

I spent the rest of the weekend recouping. With my left arm still in a sling, I couldn't use the typewriter. I found even writing in my journal a pain in the ass. I scribbled some notes that I hoped would help me remember more details later. And I sent out another round of postcards, not mentioning anything about my latest brush with death. Mostly I just took it easy. I walked through town, but then began to feel weird because I could've sworn people seemed to look at me knowing who I was and why my arm was tied up. I never saw Alex or his friends again. Maybe they were working their boats, getting them ready for the next trip out. And despite my imagined celebrity, Gloucester now felt distant with Olson dead and Prospero recuperating. I knew this feeling well. Plus having people look at me, and then maybe "mistaking" me for who I really was, was not something I'd planned on when I decided to go underground. It was time to move on.

I looked over the tooth again and again. I had no idea what kind of whale it was from or why it had passed from Olson to Prospero through Alex to me. Given how beat up Pross was, there's no way he could've heard me shouting through the storm. So, why me? I'd have to ask when I saw him.

Prospero had his older son figured right; Alex was a hard-working, driven man. I sensed his real home was either on the *Caliban* or at the corner of the Cape Ann bar with his buddies. I could see how a lonely wife might end up in the arms of her insurance man. And how Alex would be murderously enraged and uncomprehending of what he'd done to contribute to the betrayal. He did not give easily, reflecting a life on the sea where he took what he could wrest from its depths. Where a man was measured by the size of his catch. No fish, no money. No money, no eat. Life—and death—were simple and transactional. Even though it probably wasn't worth much, the whale tooth was hard currency to Alex. It came from his father, the one man he respected on land and on the water. If I hadn't brought home a fish that even paid the gas to catch him, at least I'd saved his father's life. That was enough. I got the tooth.

I moved my index finger slowly over the letters, wondering who put them there. I assumed it was Olson, but still I stared at them wondering if an even older hand might have scratched into that hard bone. Someone who saw in Melville all the things Olson did. Someone even closer in time and space than the century that separated Melville's great book from Olson's imaginative essay. Some unknown who might've been the temporal and creative bridge between the two.

Maybe this had come from Melville himself to that unknown hand, and from that to Olson! Of course, I had no way of knowing. Regardless, it felt special. Already I was thinking of how to put a chain through and wear it around my neck.

The letters were a scrawl, maybe an eighth of an inch high. But of all the words one might have found on an old tooth, none could have matched this one. It spooked me as much as Gerard offering to relieve me of my duties—permanently. One thing was for sure, I had to see Prospero before I left. I *wanted* to see him. Lots to talk about. Not just the tooth. Everything. I just hoped he'd be recovered enough to do it.

This got me thinking about next steps. Where to? Not a month into my journey and I felt as if I'd left Florida years ago. I'd promised Memere I'd go to Quebec and look up family roots. But I didn't feel that pull as much anymore. I was feeling something I couldn't quite put a finger on.

I also had to figure out what to do with Ruth's book, now that the one person we'd hoped would help us was gone. I had to stop back at the Albers and give them the news. And I had to go back to Black Mountain and tell Ruth and Jo the news as well. And Jo...what the hell to do about her? I don't think she was looking for commitment from me. But then she wasn't the kind of woman to sleep with a man just for the hell of it. Truth was I didn't want to get derailed. But she was special. Still, there was Memere and Stella and my dying and all that. No way I could put Jo through the crap of all that unraveling. I had to keep going.

But then what to do? More than the money, this book had grown on me too. I'd have to write it on the road. This was not something I could do cooped up in some room. Especially some room in Black Mountain. Or worse, Florida. I had to go find the people who'd been there. That was the only way to tell the Black Mountain story. Because, as Ruth said, Black Mountain was much less of a place and much more an idea. The kind of idea that gave birth to thousands of other ideas, to make old men weep for their youth and give money to an evangelist like John Rice.

I had the list of names. Seeing them would give me a route to follow west. Something of a "purpose" to get me to San Francisco. I'd meet these people and talk to them and start writing. And finish when I got holed up in the city. Then I'd send it all back to Ruth and she could decide how and where she'd want to get it published. Hell, she could put her own name on it, if she wanted to. I didn't care. I just wanted to get the story down on paper. Before I headed back to New Haven and Black Mountain, I needed to see Prospero.

Monday morning I tested my arm. It was still sore, but mending. The concussion headaches had gone away too. Those were what the doc had said would be the "go" signs. It was time to go. I figured I could drive OK without the sling. So I packed up and did one last turn through Gloucester, driving slow by Prospero's and Olson's houses, figuring I'd probably never see them again. Then I headed for the Cape. Once again, I was at one end of the continent with the other end my destination. I found another old motel in Barnstable to stay for the night. That's all I figured this stay would be, no more unplanned fishing expeditions. Then I went over to the hospital.

I found Prospero propped up and reading *The Globe*. He looked comfortable, even with the cast up to his knee and a larger bandage covering half of his forehead.

"Jack! Come in! Come in! I was beginning to worry maybe you leave without saying goodbye to an old man!"

"Prospero, no way I was going anywhere without seeing how you were. I had to make sure you were OK."

"I am getting better every day! Come!"

He stretched his right arm for a warm and surprisingly strong handshake for someone who'd just been through hell.

"I'm sorry I cannot stand, Jack. But, as you see, they have me tied down pretty good."

I pulled a chair up close. I was glad to see him.

"How're you feeling?"

"Oh! Better and better! They say they will send me home in a couple days." I sensed a little bravado in his voice, but I didn't want to say anything to dim the old man's cheerfulness.

"And how are you, my friend? I see your arm is free. It is healed now?"

"Yeah. Still a little sore. But the doc said to expect that. As long as I don't feel any real sharp pain, I should be OK."

"This is good. And now you are ready to leave us? Off on your next grand adventure? Maybe a skydive without a parachute?" His eyes twinkled. He seemed in command of his room as easily as he'd skippered the *Mariel*.

"I'm staying here tonight. But tomorrow I'm heading back to touch base with the people helping me on the book. Let them know Charles died. Try to figure out what to do next. I'd counted on him for a lot of information."

"Do you think maybe you will not write the book?"

"No, I'm still going to write it if I find enough other people to talk to. Especially ones who would've been at the college with Charles."

"Yes. He was quite a talker. He knew a lot. When he talked of this Black Mountain, I could tell this means a lot to him. But I tell you, I think it also made him sad."

"Why do you say that?"

"He could not keep it open! He was not a good manager of money, Jack. But then maybe you know that already. Maybe he was not the best person to run a college. A talker, yes! But not a manager of things."

Now was as good a time as any and I had to ask.

"Pross, what happened? Out...there?"

He knew exactly what I meant.

"Jack, I have thought about it and thought about it. I have talked it over with Alex many times now. If you ask me if I think we got too close and the whale tried to flip us, I will say no. If you ask me if there was another whale that came up under us, I will also say no. This was a humpback not a Moby Dick. I have been close to many, many whales. All kinds! In all my years I have never seen a whale attack a boat. Never! And who were we? Two tuna fishermen! With a camera! Not harpoons! So, no, I do not believe that we were caught by some mad whale. I am not Ahab! And you...you are not Ishmael, no? Or maybe you are!"

I was caught totally off-guard by that last comment. Of course, Prospero was not monomaniac

Ahab. But me and Ishmael? How would he even know to say that? And what about the tooth in my pocket?

"Then what the hell happened?"

"There is only thing that could have done to us like that out there."

"Giant squid?"

"No, no, Jack! No more of sea monsters! No, I think we get hit by a big wave. A rogue."

"That's what Alex and his friends said. Is that possible?"

"Yes! I have seen these! Rare! But real!" Pross moved his hands to make like waves and then made a big curve to suggest the rogue.

I'd heard about these before too. Coming out of nowhere. Nothing before it. Nothing after. A rogue.

"I thought about that too, Pross. Then how come we didn't see it coming?"

"I have only seen one in my whole life. Now, I think, two. Maybe if we were not so close to the whale and watching maybe we would have seen."

"How big was it, you think?"

"I do not know for sure. But our seas were what? Five feet? Maybe six? This rogue must have been twenty or twenty-five to lift us that high."

"Sure as hell caught me by surprise, Pross."

"I was thinking more about pictures than our lives. That is not a good captain!"

"You can't blame yourself, Pross. Yeah, the weather was getting bad. But nothing that said a monster wave was on its way."

"This is true. But what do I get for my foolishness? A knock on the head and a break in the leg. And leaving you to face something no man should have to face alone. Even with a *Mariel*."

"You did your best. You told me what to do."

"What did I say?"

"Not much. But you said we couldn't outrun the storm. That the best I could do was keep *Mariel* just headed into it and hope we'd make it." I paused a second, then added, "But you didn't sound very confident I could pull it off. To be honest, Pross, neither was I."

"Ah! I really do not remember."

"It was a helluva storm, let me tell you. More than once I really thought this is it, we're going over. Some monster waves that took us almost vertical. But *Mariel*, she was fighting right with us."

Pross brightened at that. "She is a very, very good boat, Jack. More than once I have been caught in storms with her and the only woman more faithful to me than she was my Maria!"

"Well, Pross, I don't know how she did it—or how we did it—because it seemed like it was wave after wave and boomboomboom! And the wind and the rain. They were like banshees! Screaming and pounding on the windows, trying to reach in and rip me out. I thought the glass would break any minute. I couldn't see a damn thing! Total, complete blackness. I tried to keep her headed the best I could, just like you said I should. But minute after minute, hour after hour…it seemed to go on forever. Almost enough to drive me a little nutso."

Pross watched me closely as I talked. When he spoke, he surprised me with what he said and how he said it. Deep. From his heart.

"Jack, you were not 'nutso.' You did what you had to do. And you did it very, very well. You showed tremendous courage. More than courage! It was not luck that we survived. Nor even faithful *Mariel* could have done it without you. *You* saved us. This I know! Yes!

"When I heard from Alex how bad that storm was, I knew we should have been at the bottom if not for you. I am not sure even my Alex could have made it through. This is truth! That was a storm to take men from here to there." He raised his arm up to suggest the surface of the sea and then lowered it to suggest its bottom.

"Men, when they come face to face with Death, each acts differently. Then we know what kind of man is he. Many hide. They draw the blanket over them and hope Death does not know where they are. They cling to life like a baby. They cry for God to save them. Then are surprised when He does not. Instead, they drown in their fear. They are not bad men for this. This is just who they are.

"Jack, you could have taken to your blanket. Or you could have let us been swept away. The pain, it would not have been long. Then, pfft!" He snapped his fingers. "But, no! You stared into that storm and bared your soul, and you fought with Death and you did not give up. It was very much impressive, my friend." He smiled warmly, but seriously, at me.

I was stunned by his words. No one had ever talked to me that way. Not my dad. Not Neal. Not Allen. Not Gary. Maybe because most of the time they saw me, they saw a fuck-up. Tears do not come easily to me. But they were ready now. I fought to hold them back.

"My Alex, I have seen him in storms. He, too, is weak with fear, I am sorry to say. This he tries to hide by yelling and shouting at the men. But Alex, he is also smart. He covers himself with a blanket of words. He fights the storm. But all his yelling and cursing, what is it but the cry of a man who does not want his soul bared to Nature and his God? The men, they know. But they cover for him.

"My Johnny, he, too, is smart. He can smell a storm days away. Yes, this is true Jack. I am good with the weather, but Johnny he is better. Like his mother. Maria would tell me do not go when skies were blue. Then I would. And then the storm would come. And I would come home exhausted and she would look but she would not speak. We both know.

"Johnny, he knows. That is why he likes to fish close. And he is good enough to do that. He can to go places no one else knows and bring home a full boat.

And so he does not get caught by the storms. But he is tested...in other ways." He stopped here, looking out the window.

I was shocked at how Prospero talked of his own sons. I think I knew what he was talking about with Johnny, but it was not something I wanted to bring up. Then he looked back at me with a smile, like he'd gotten a second wind.

"Do you remember how *The Tempest* starts with that terrible storm? All the men feared for their lives? The king. The duke. Everyone! Yes! Who was the real man among them? The boatswain! He tries to save them. But his passengers, they did not take orders!

"What does he say? 'If you can command these elements to silence, we will not hand a rope more. If you cannot, give thanks you have lived so long and make yourself ready for the mischance of the hour.' The boatswain knows the feeble power of men before God. And this makes him more powerful than those who would strut the deck at their peril."

I smiled big back at Pross.

"That boatswain knew Death was upon them. And he knew his only chance of beating it was to take it on full. Do his best and see where things come out. My Alex is a king and duke kind of leader. Men follow him because he has money and power. Maybe they fear him. But they do not love him. And when he comes into a storm, he will rage to hide his fear. He will shout to command the elements to silence. But it is others who handle the ropes and deliver them safely back to land. I wish it were not so, but such is he. He has been lucky so far his boat has not followed so many others to the bottom."

"But, you, Jack...you kept your wits about you. You were our boatswain and you brought us through the storm to a safe shore. They will talk about you in Gloucester for a long time.

I was dumbfounded. What could I say? What is it about a man that he can have reached his maturity, yet feel as though he had not yet found his manhood? What is it when a man finds it when he least expects? I let the tears come.

I tried to explain. "Pross, I...I don't know what to say. I'm sorry I'm crying. Maybe it's after all that's happened. I'm sorry."

"Why are you ashamed of your tears? You come by them honestly! Do you think because we are safe and dry now that what happened to us out there is just a memory? A wisp to blow away in the breeze? No! Never! What was out there is in here now! Forever!" Prospero pounded on his chest and then pointed at mine.

"Prospero, there is so much I would like to tell you. I don't know what I did or why I did it, but I will tell you this: I could not let you die out there. I don't know if you wanted to or not. But you are too good a man to go down like that. *Mariel* and me, well, we decided we had to make it through somehow. I'm just a writer. It's all I ever wanted to be. I was lousy at sea before. But...but...something did happen out there and I'll be damned if I can find words for it now."

"Jack, you will find your words later. They will come to you, I know. Now is not the time. Now is the time for knowing you are more than a writer. You are a man. A man without fear. I do not know many. But you...you are one. Come, hold my hand one more time."

I stood and leaned over the old man and we embraced. God, his arms felt good around me! We had spoken a little and left unsaid much. But what he said meant more to me than all the crap my dad and I had talked about through the years. More than all the even more crap Neal and Allen and I had talked about. Something had changed. Something that would take me a while to understand. And even longer to write down. I stood and looked down at him, wiping the tears away.

There was a slight rap behind us. "Mr. Giovanetti?" A young nurse interrupted. "Oh, I'm sorry! I didn't mean to interrupt. But it's time for your bath."

"Of course! My favorite time of the day! Jack, they treat me like a baby here and I love it!"

The nurse brought a wheelchair over and helped Prospero off the bed. "And is this your son?" she asked smiling politely at me.

"Yes, this is my son. My son, Jack. He has come a long way."

"Very nice to meet you, Jack. You may wait here if you want. We will be about forty-five minutes, I think."

"I...I have to get going."

"Yes. Yes, I know. You go, now, Jack. But you come back, yes?" Now his eyes smiled too, but there was something more.

"Of course! If they ever let you out of this place, I'll see you at home." We shook hands again and held our grasp an extra moment or two.

"Yes, at home."

The nurse started to wheel him out of the room when I remembered something.

"Hey, Pro...Wait!" I fished the tooth out of my pocket. "I wanted to ask you about this."

Prospero smiled his big grin.

"Ah, good! Alex gave it to you. I wanted to make sure you have it."

"He said this came from...Charles?"

Pross nodded and said, "Yes. He gave it to me last year when I think he knew for sure he was dying. It is a tooth from a sperm whale. Beautiful, yes? And now it should be yours."

I handed it to him so he could feel it one more time.

"What did he say about it? I mean, what does this 'Ishmael' mean?"

"Ah, Jack, I was hoping maybe you would be the one to tell me."

"Well, yeah, I gave it some thought and I have some ideas. But, did he tell you if he scratched the letters? Or if someone else did?"

"He did not say. But Ishmael...the one of the Bible...he was a wild ass of a man, no? And Herman Melville told his story through the voice of Ishmael. No Ishmael, no Ahab. No Ahab, no Moby Dick. This is it, no? You will tell me more next time. At home."

He extended his hand one more time. "OK, Jack, you go! I go! I am so glad you came, son."

"Thanks. I'm glad you're OK. I'll see you again soon. At home."

And with that Prospero's nurse whisked him out of the room and down the hall. I turned and made my way to the exit.

It was only when I was back out on Route 6 that something Prospero said sent a shiver through me and I started bawling. "He gave it to me last year when he knew for sure he was dying..." Jesus Christ! Did Prospero know something even his doctors hadn't yet figured out? Who knew when I'd be back this way again?

Chapter 25 — Wellfleet

Leaving Barnstable and headed to Provincetown, I stopped at Orleans to stretch my legs. I followed a path towards the ocean and looked beyond the dunes to a point where I imagined Henry Beston built his "outermost house" in 1925. Where he befriended Coast Guard men walking the beach at night, large lamps swinging to warn ships away from shore. Where he'd watched the three-masted *Montclair* founder and five men drown during a winter storm and found people combing the beach the next day claiming for their own what had been the ship's.

It was also where one scavenger hadn't counted on a hand reaching up through the sand, one's man's misfortune greeting another's opportunism. Who'd it belong to? The captain? The mate? The cook? One of the two deckhands? Who could blame the newcomer if he wasn't quite ready for this sandy grave, thrusting his hand skyward instead, wanting one more chance to see the sun rise, to feel the breeze, even to taste the salt snow?

I didn't hear *Montclair's* iced rigging singing that day as I had at Hatteras. Would I again? I hoped not. Between Hatteras and Cod, these two capes had tested and shaken me deeper than I had ever been tested and shaken before.

I wondered now how those men behaved when that winter storm laid bare their souls one last time. Had they faced Death with the courage of Shakespeare's boatswain? Or had they bawled like Prospero said his son Alex did? Or had they succumbed to their fate quietly, going over and down without a fight? I wondered when they knew Death was upon them? When do any of us?

Had Death become Gerard's companion long before he drew his last breath?

Did Neal know he'd been invited through Death's door as he stumbled into that freezing Mexican night?

Did Death have its arm curled around my shoulder while I hunched over that toilet bowl, spilling out my guts along with the last of my miserable life?

Death had come for me six months ago. Memere and Stella had pushed him away.

Death had come for me again a week ago. This time I had pushed him away.

When he came again, as I knew he must, would we embrace? Or would I again push him away, my own hand thrusting up through the sand demanding a little more of life?

With one of our last live talks, Gerard taught me a lesson I never forgot. A little kitten had become his last bedside companion. As he held it he said to me, "See? The little face, the little head, look, I could break his head by squeezing my hand—it's only a little thing with no strength—God put these little things on earth to see if we want to hurt them—those who don't do it who *can*, are for his Heaven—those who see they can hurt, and *do* hurt, they're not for his Heaven."

He was nine. I was four. He died soon after. Those words convinced me he was in Heaven. He was there; he had to be. He spoke quietly and easily with more wisdom than a thousand old sermons could have done. He had more strength than a bar full of Alexes. He had more love in his little heart than Neal and me and all our women put together. I put his words into the book I wrote about him. I wanted others to know who my big little brother was. And now I wanted to know why he kept coming back for me.

I began to cry soft, slow tears. They stung from the breeze blowing over the dunes, across a cattailed marsh to where I stood on a lonely sandy pathway that wound between tall, still-brown grasses and led back to the town and everything beyond. This day was turning weepy, but I didn't care. The wind dried the tears; my salt mixed with the ocean's. I saw with Beston. I hung with *Montclair*. I floated with Gerard. I was air.

There was a lot going on. I'd known it for some time. But, like Prospero said, now wasn't the time for words. I'd tried them after Hatteras. I'd try them again. They would come. They always did. I spoke for myself. I spoke for others. Whitman in my veins. Melville in my dark nights. Blake where there was light. And Gerard. Always Gerard.

But not just these. Others. My ghost along the Susquehanna. The happy-go-lucky truck-driving brothers with their flatbed full of whiskey-sipping seekers all rolling together under starry Plains nights. Soft, brown Bea and her brothers too, mixing picking and beer and sex and calling it life. And winos in dark Detroit movie houses curled against hard seats for a little bit of warmth and sleep and not wanting to call that life, but it was.

And thousands of others *not* just like them. Thousands of others with their own stories. Their own truths. Their own loves. Thousands who'd passed in and out of my life and left their stories behind. I could feel them all. Hear them all. Make their words come out of my throat, through my fingers. And now I would do the same with Prospero. There was a lot going on. A lot.

I could feel a nervousness in my leg like I needed to get to Provincetown. *Now*. When I'd left Gloucester I was easy about getting through Boston, onto the Cape and over to Barnstable. And I felt OK when I left Barnstable, even though my stop to see Prospero had shaken me up some. I wasn't used to being talked to the way he talked to me, seeing something in me maybe even I wasn't sure about. But that stop at Orleans really got me jumpy and now I just wanted to see Provincetown quick, look at MacMillan Pier one more time and start heading west. All the way.

So that's what I did. A quick stop. Just long enough to see where I'd somehow managed to dock *Mariel* and passed out next to Prospero. Maybe another day, different circumstances, I'd've hung around longer. But it was time to go. I'd touched my tag-back and now I started my run to the other side of the continent.

The day was getting on. I got only as far as Wellfleet and decided to stop. It was dinnertime and I was dying for one more bowl of chowder and maybe scallops along with a cold beer. Just one. It seemed like my insides were holding up OK if I watched the drinking. But once I started west, I knew I wouldn't taste this seafood again for a long, long time.

The restaurant—"Southfleet"—looked like the kinds of place I'd been enjoying ever since I left St. Pete. Cozy. Family run. Good food. Cheap. Friendly waitresses. I settled into a booth, glad the place was weekday quiet.

I was making a good dent on my chowder and the cold beer was going down slow and easy when I felt someone walk up and stop close to me. I didn't know a soul out here, so I ignored whoever it was. I was lost in my thoughts of Prospero and what he'd said and Orleans and what I'd felt and the Provincetown tag-and-go and where to head after seeing the Albers tomorrow. Probably Black Mountain. Probably. I'd see how it went. More postcards. Gotta send more postcards.

"Jack?"

I took another spoonful. I heard the voice. But it couldn't have been for me. That voice came out of a dream. Steady, Jack. It's been a long day.

"Jack? Is...that you?"

Now I looked up to see female legs in nice, flared slacks next to me. The question was definitely meant for me. And it was a voice I knew. A voice from long ago and far away. A voice that shouldn't have been in Wellfleet, Massachusetts, on an April night in 1970. A voice that meant the person knew me. And not "Jack *Moriarty*." Jack *Kerouac*. Jesus Christ! My cover was blown!! In this tiny little place far away from all the other places I figured I had to stay away from for this very reason! I knew this voice and this person and if it was who I thought it was my underground world had just been blown wide open. I raised my head slowly, not wanting to know. But our eyes met and, my God, of all the people to see me out here, of all the people from my past who could rip up the present.

Anne.

She was smiling uncertainly, maybe thinking she had the wrong person. Or maybe she had the right person, but the wrong time and place. But it was her and I was me. Anne. No mistaking her beauty even twenty-five years later. Her long strawberry blonde hair had gone over to an early white, but with a fashionable, well-tamed, above-the-shoulders cut. Her skin as smooth and freckled as I remembered it. Her eyes hazel and large. Her teeth perfect.

Her blouse looked expensive. The kind of well-made, comfortable clothes Barnard girls bought off the rack at Saks or Bergdorf's on their daddy's account. And that's who she was...one of the Barnard girls. For me, she was *the* Barnard girl. But for her hair, it didn't look as though she'd changed a bit.

I was stunned. And just stared for what must have been an uncomfortably long time.

"Jack, is it you? I mean, do you remember me? Anne?" My silence had made her even more nervous.

"My God. It really is you," I finally managed. I just couldn't comprehend. *Her.*

"May I sit down? Or, are you...waiting...for someone else?" She was still smiling, but I could tell she was really nervous.

I was so stunned I'd forgotten my manners. Then I just babbled.

"No, no! Please! Anne! My God! Sit! I'm here by myself. What a surprise!"

She did and we just looked at each other for a long moment, peeling away years, pulling up memories. I was dumbstruck, quickly trying to figure out how to deal with *this*. Finally, she spoke first.

"I saw you when I walked in. But almost didn't recognize you with *that*." She laughed lightly and pointed at the beard. "But then I thought, 'No, it has to be!'"

"You don't approve?" I smiled back, pulling my hand across my growth.

"I guess it's something I never expected to see you wearing. You never had one in any of the pictures I've seen."

"Yeah, well, I tried it on for size a few months ago. Decided I liked it and well...here it is."

The waitress brought a menu. Anne looked at me. "Am I intruding? Is this OK?"

"No, no! This is fine. Do you want a drink?"

She asked for a Manhattan, her favorite from our college days. Damn! Then she ordered a cup of chowder and scallops, same as me. The memories were coming fast and furious now. We'd done that twenty-five years ago too. And a lot more.

The drink came. She raised the glass, I my half-empty bottle of beer.

"Well...I guess we should toast something," she said. I could tell she was still nervous as a colt.

"How about...to a wonderful accident and damned glad to see ya after—how long?—twenty-five years?"

"Longer, I think, Jack. But, yes, a wonderful accident. And it's awfully nice to see you, too."

We clinked and sipped. I was already thinking I might need a second beer.

"So, what br..." We both started the same question at the same time and laughed.

I answered first.

"I'm researching another book. Been between here and Gloucester for a week."

Anne smiled, "I'm not surprised. You've written an awful lot, Jack."

"Yeah, guess I have. I think it's the only thing I know how to do."

"I haven't read all of your books. But I've read most of them."

"Thanks. That's nice to hear. Most people say they've read *On the Road*. Sometimes I'll meet someone who's actually read them all. You kinda have to watch out for those. They like to ask questions as though you've been best buddies since high school." That got a laugh from her. "Maybe I shouldn't ask, but...did you like them?"

"Oh yes! Well, some more than others. I did like *On The Road*. I guess a lot of people did."

"Yeah, that was the big one. But what I wrote and what they published, it was like two different books."

"Really? I didn't know that."

"I wouldn't expect you to. Hardly anybody does. The publisher and my editor, they cut out so much and made me change names and everything that even I had a hard time believing it was the same book!"

"What happened? Why did they do that?"

The waitress brought the chowder. Anne dove in with a relish that belied her refined looks.

"Oh! This is delicious! I've had a craving for really good clam chowder for so long."

"Yeah, when I'm up here can't get enough of it myself." We looked at each other and smiled. This was going so easy. It was like we were both back at the Columbia fountain or across the street at the Hungarian bakery again horsing around with our crowd.

Then I remembered her question. "They said there was too much in it. They said they'd get sued if they kept everything and all the people and told it like I said it was."

"I'm sorry to hear that. Some of that makes sense now. I had guessed a lot of it was from your life. But I didn't like some of the goofy names you put in there. Still, it was quite a book."

"Thanks. Took forever for it to hit. I sweated for years wondering if it ever would. But when it did ...bingo!"

"I guess I shouldn't ask this either, but I've wanted to know for a long time. I didn't see...us...in the book. Was I...were *we*...in the part that got cut?"

"To be honest, I thought about it. Writing about us, I mean. I really did. But the 'road' story started after..."

We both knew what "after" meant...after I dumped her for a girl in the Village. The silence was awkward. Then she smiled again and got me off the hook.

"Actually, I'm glad to know that. I'm not sure I'd want my life splattered all over a book, even one of best ones written in the twentieth century. Even if you would've had to change my name!"

We kept on smiling. And finished our chowder.

The waitress brought our scallops.

"Oh! I didn't know you'd ordered the same thing! Isn't that a funny one!"

"As I recall, we did that a lot back...then. You introduced me to a lot of new things."

"Did I? That's nice of you to say so."

"You did! I mean, I was just a dumb Canuck from the bad side of Lowell, Mass. What did I know about the finer things in life? You showed me quite a few." I smiled back at her, our eyes meeting and more and more said without words, memory peeling back years, peeling back emotions.

"Oh, Jack, you weren't a 'dumb Canuck!' You were the handsomest, sexiest man on that campus. A football player! And a writer and a poet, too. All the girls wanted you!"

"Well, if they did, someone forgot to tell me. Besides, you were all so...When my Columbia guys met

Barnard girls and I met you, you just like knocked me out. I'd never, ever met anyone like you."

I could see her eyes moisten. Then she worked on a scallop.

This was the God's honest truth. Anne Tyler was a beauty. She had class. She wasn't all giggly and googly like a lot of her friends were. She'd come from Westchester. Her father was a big shot doctor up there. Her mother had been a nurse, then settled in to raise three kids. She was refined like her classmates, but wasn't stuck up like they were. We'd hit it off right away. I was kind of shy, but she had a way of getting me to talk. And talk. And talk. She was the one I first confessed my dreams to, about wanting to see this big, wide world and drink deep of life. About wanting to write about it in ways that would be fresh and new and make others see it that way too.

She helped me dream those dreams. And in the course of all that talking and all that dreaming, we fell in love. And all that was a dream too. The most intense, pleasurable, sinful, delicious dreaming I'd ever done. We'd lie in her bed after and I felt like I had it all. I would make this world mine. She had that effect on me. She was beauty and light and had taken this poor, wrong-side-of-the-tracks boy and turned him into a man with power and strength and the confidence to chase his dreams half way around the world. Which is exactly what I did. Except I left her behind to do it.

"So, what brings you out here out of season? Last I recall, Wellfleet's not exactly on the rail line from Westchester."

"My singing group had a conference and competition in Boston over the weekend. So I planned to take a few extra days out here for myself."

"Singing group? I remember your lovely voice. What kind of group? Jazz?"

"Oh, it's a silly thing. Barbershop singing." She could see I hadn't a clue what she was talking about.

"Barbershop singing is old time singing. Men's groups are the barbershoppers. Women's groups are called Sweet Adelines. We sing in quartets. I sing baritone, the low part. And we get to put on glitzy dresses for these gatherings and competitions. That's what I was doing in Boston. It's fun. Gives me something to do."

"Did you do that when we were in college?"

"Noooo...I actually had dreams about trying show business. Maybe you don't remember. But Daddy wasn't for that at all. It was something I picked up after I got married and the kids were in school."

Subconsciously, I glanced at her left hand and noticed the large, well-cut diamond ring.

The waitress interrupted and we both ordered another drink, now wine for her and another beer for me. Just like old times.

"Sounds like the singing is a lot of fun for you." I wanted to keep things loose. "So, tell me about your life. You're married. Kids. Where're you living? How are things?"

She smiled again. Hers had always been a beautiful smile. And she did have a great voice. You wouldn't have expected a baritone coming from a trim person on the shorter side, but her saying that recalled other memories of us and friends singing in bars late at night. She had a quiet side, but then something else came out, especially at night, especially after a couple drinks. This time the smile failed to hide something else in her eyes. Not quite sadness, but something...

"Well, I guess there's a lot to catch up on, isn't there? I married Jay Lennon, he was a couple years ahead of you at Columbia, about two years after we graduated. I don't think you knew him. He's an accountant. Well, more than that now. He's been at Price Waterhouse since he graduated and he's been a partner for almost ten years."

I nodded politely. She was right; I had no idea who the guy was. But it fit the pattern.

"We live in Westfield, New Jersey, about an hour out of the city. We have three children. The first two—boys—are in college. The last one, my girl, is a sophomore in high school. And I'm proud of them all!"

"Sounds like you're doing well. How're your parents?" I'd met them a couple times when she took me up to Westchester on weekends. Nice people. Her mother was from the South and spoke in a delicious drawl. I remembered her hair was just like Anne's now. She'd been a fabulous cook. I could still taste a crab casserole we'd had one night. I made a pig of myself going for seconds, then thirds. But they didn't seem to mind, even if her father was wary about this working class kid who talked of wanting to be a writer. He was much more interested in my football days and why I wasn't playing anymore.

"My dad's retired. They sold their home and moved into a new development just north of Myrtle Beach, South Carolina. They get to play a lot of golf. They're happy. They miss being close to us. But they don't miss our winters!"

"I always liked your folks."

"They liked you too."

"Well, I thought maybe your dad wasn't that impressed with me." We laughed at that.

"Oh, Jack, maybe he wasn't sure where you were headed with your life. But my mom liked you a lot. She could see why we were…together."

"I always liked your mom. Boy, could she cook!"

We paused to keep working our way through our scallops. This was becoming easier than I'd thought.

"I showed them your books, Jack…"

"You did?" This was a surprise.

"Yes. When I'd go up to visit. Not with Jay and the kids. But when *On the Road* came out I showed it to my mom."

"Did she read it?"

"Oh, no! I'm not sure she would have enjoyed it that much, to be honest. It's a young person's book. Maybe even a young *man's* book."

"Yeah, that's true. Thanks for showing them. That's nice you did that."

"I think Dad was impressed that you got published. And when I showed them the others, they would mention that they'd heard something or other about you. Or maybe read it in *The Times* or *The New Yorker*."

"Which ones did you show them?"

"Oh, the one about you going off on that mountain hike with your friends."

"*Dharma Bums*?"

"Yes! That's it. And the other one where you were all alone at that...firetower? Was that it?"

"Yeah. *Desolation Angels*."

"Yes. If all that's true, you have done some wild things with your life. The trips to Mexico sounded dangerous! You've seen and done a lot. Hitchhiking all over. I don't know how anyone could've kept up with you!"

"I guess I have. I didn't plan on it turning out the way it did, but it's all true. That's what I decided I would write about. My life. And the people who've passed through it. Try to tell others what I've seen and done and maybe learned."

Anne was really focused now. I'd seen that look before. It was when she wanted to tell me something *really important*.

"Jack, can I tell you my favorite?"

"Sure!"

"It's the one about your brother. I loved it. I...I didn't know..."

"Yeah. *Visions of Gerard*. That was a tough one to write, Annie. But I had to do it."

"I thought it was...beautiful. Very spiritual. But so sad. I thought it helped me know you better also, even though I hadn't seen you in years. Of all your books, it was the one that made me feel close to you ...again."

"Really? That's nice of you to say."

"It showed how much you loved him. That was sweet. How much you missed him. How much you lost. And maybe why later you became such a...seeker."

She smiled really warmly as she said this. Of all the women I'd been with, including my wives, Anne might've known me best. She was the one I spilled my dreams to when they were just dreams and before a lot of my talk became just bar talk. She was quiet and accepting in many ways and it was easy to underestimate her, which is just what I did. Especially once our campus crowd started heading down to the Village and other places for kicks.

"Yeah, not many people talk to me about *Gerard*. But what you said is interesting. Because his dying like that was such a blow...to all of us. A tough, tough blow."

"How did he...die?" She asked uncertainly, afraid maybe the memory was still too painful to talk about. It wasn't. But neither was I ready to tell her about how Gerard'd been making appearances throughout my life, including most recently out on the *Mariel*.

"It was a heart problem. Might've been rheumatic fever. Or congestive failure. I guess I don't really remember for sure. It's so ironic, or just plain cruel, Anne, that he'd die because his heart gave out. Because he had the biggest heart of anybody I've ever known."

"Jack, I cried when I read it. Not only because of him, but because I then knew how much you hurt. And how much of that hurt you carried around inside and nobody ever knew about. But it helped explain why I would see sadness in your eyes and couldn't tell where it came from. Sometimes you would just, like, go away, right in front of me. I know you didn't mean to abandon me, but there'd be that look in your eyes and I knew you were someplace else. After I read about your brother, I had a better idea of where you might have gone."

Her words triggered a memory of a Saturday afternoon in her room, she propped up against her bed, I lying face up with my head in her lap. She ran her fingers through my hair and I'm not sure if we were saying much or not. But I remember how tears came silently because the very act of her fingers through my hair recalled the many times Memere would do that for Gerard, cooing at him to try and ease his pain. I'd stood silently in the doorway watching, not really understanding but knowing it was sad. And as I felt the warmth of her body and the soothing of her fingers, I was back in Lowell again not understanding why it had to be my brother who was so sick and everyone else who was so sad.

When Anne had asked why I was crying, I couldn't say why. Or I could, but I didn't want to. Of course, she thought she'd done something wrong and nothing was farther from the truth. But I wasn't ready to share with her, or anybody else, the depths of the sadness I felt then and lugged around all those years after. But she continued to stroke my hair and bent over to kiss my forehead and for that moment I felt blessed and closed my eyes and went to sleep.

"Anne, to be honest, I think it might be my favorite too. I don't talk about it too much. But then hardly anyone ever asks. And you're right. As easy as it was for me to talk with you and tell you things I'd never shared with anyone else, there were some things I couldn't talk about then. Couldn't talk about for a long time. It was hard writing about my brother. But I felt a lot better after I did."

We'd finished our meals and the waitress brought our check. I reached to pick it up and Anne took it instead, her fingers covering mine and I jumped a little at the touch. "Jack, if you don't mind, I'd like to pay for this." I was going to insist, but she had this determination in her voice that I'd forgotten about.

"Well, OK. That's really nice of you. Next one's on me then." We laughed. It was time to go, but I sensed she wanted to keep talking. Plus, I had to figure out how to tell her what was really going on and somehow bank on our past to protect my future.

"Are you staying here in town?" she asked, looking at me and then down at her fingers feeling the side of her glass.

"No. I'm over in Barnstable."

"Oh."

"You said you're here?"

"Yes. I rented a little cottage just a bit out of town. It's nice."

The waitress brought her change.

"Anne, there's..."

"Jack, wou..." Once again our words bumped into each other.

I smiled and said, "You first."

The nerves were there again. "Would you like to...see it?" Even though the drinks had relaxed us both, we were still edging around the heart of the matter—us—and all that had happened from the 40's to now. She carried the added "burden" of being married with children. But it was something she wanted. And so did I.

"Yeah. I would." I smiled back with a mix of nerves and relief.

Our waitress smiled as we walked out. Even though she was much younger, the thought crossed my mind that maybe she'd already seen more than her share of similar rendezvous. Even if ours wasn't, it sure as hell looked like one from her end of things. And the woman paid! Turns out she'd parked right next to my old Ford with what looked like a brand-new Volvo station wagon. At dusk it looked dark blue or maybe just black.

"This yours?"

"Yes."

"Nice car."

"Thanks. It was a birthday present last fall from Jay. He's a very practical guy. I'd been hinting at something a little sportier, but this is what I got. It's a good car."

"Well, this is my trusty Ford. A '66. Bought it for the trip. Been good so far. Big enough to haul all my crap."

"We had one kind of like this a few years ago when the kids were little. We needed lots of space then."

"So...guess I'll follow you?"

"Sure. It's not far. Maybe five minutes."

We headed north out of town, then turned east on a sandy road that led out to the bay side of the Cape. A left into a drive and our lights shined on a lonely little cottage that, for a second, reminded me of what Beston's might've looked like. Nothing else around. When I got out, I could feel the ocean breeze and wondered if her place had a view of the water. It was a moonless night.

I followed Anne with a "watch your step" onto a small porch, and then inside. She flicked on a couple of table lamps and it was what it was, a simple saltbox. Living room, small, leading to a dining table and chairs and an even smaller kitchen at the back. A small hallway led to two tiny bedrooms and a bath-room just big enough for a sink and a toilet. "The shower's outside," she explained. "I'm their first customer of the season!"

The living room had a small sofa, two easy chairs, and some folding chairs stacked against a wall. A couple of shelves were filled with typical summer fare, paperback romances alongside ocean tales. I wondered if *Moby Dick* was among them. The wooden floor was partially covered with an oval rag rug, the kind that would take lots of wear and tear from all kinds of feet, big and small.

"As you can see, pretty simple. But it's just what I wanted."

"Yeah, it's nice. You been here before?"

"Oh, no! When the kids were small, we'd take them to the Jersey shore. Jay really likes Cape May. Then, when they got older and vacations with Mom and Dad weren't 'cool' they'd go off to camps in the Adirondacks and we'd maybe get away someplace fun. We went to Europe a few years ago. Hawaii last year. We look for places with lots of golf courses."

She could see my surprise and laughed. "Yes, it's something I've taken up in the last few years. But Jay really likes to play and so I do it mostly for him."

"Are you good?"

"Oh, no! I mean, I guess I can do OK. But Jay gets short with me sometimes because he's a really good golfer and I slow him down a bit."

"I remember you as a really good swimmer." I really did. She'd belonged to a swim club in high school, but quit swimming competitively when she grew into her woman's body.

"Yes! I still love to swim. We belong to a club in Westfield. When the kids were little I swear we were there almost every day in the summer. The boys lettered in high school and Sallie, my girl, made the varsity this year as a sophomore."

Another pregnant pause, kind of looking at each other wondering what next.

"Well! I'm not being a very good hostess! I have a bottle of wine chilling. But no beer, I'm afraid. Or some Pepsi."

"Pepsi'd be great, thanks."

"You sure? I remember when you started drinking you could be very funny, if you didn't drink too much and just pass out."

Ouch. Her memories were both accurate and a little painful to recall.

"Yeah, I've cut back quite a bit the last six months or so. To be honest, Anne, I'd gotten to the point where I had to. Or bad things, really bad things, were going to happen."

"I'm glad to hear that, Jack. That you've cut back, I mean. I'd hate to think of you as a beat up alcoholic like some I know. You look terrific! Except for that!" She laughed, again pointing to the beard.

I followed her back into the little kitchen where she pulled a couple bottles out of a six-pack and some ice from the refrigerator and filled two glasses—converted grape jelly containers with a Flintstones theme. Typical cottage fare.

"It's the best I can offer, I'm afraid," she said a little apologetically.

"That's fine." I didn't add that I'd spent a lot of hours watching *The Flintstones* when I was drunk or stoned in Florida. Back in the living room we sat at opposite ends of the small sofa.

"So, where were we?"

"I think I'd just finished filling you in on my life since Columbia."

She laughed and then bore in, "Now, Jack, you can't get off that easily! You don't have to tell me everything, but, you know, I'd like to know a little. You had big dreams. And now you're a big, famous author. And you're driving around the country, fancy free, *as always*, just finding more things to write about. Sounds pretty exciting, Mr. Kerouac."

It was clear she found her idea of whatever it was I was doing exciting and she'd been keeping some kind of tabs on me through the years. But it was a jolt to hear my real name out loud again. And a reminder that I had to explain what was going on and hope like hell she could keep a secret.

"I know it looks exciting from just reading the books. I've had a lot of good times, Anne. And some not so good times. But writing is hard work. Finding something to write about, or taking what happened to me and writing it in ways that's interesting to others, that's work."

"I know it must be. I sweated just having to write a five or ten page paper. Do you remember how you helped me with Shakespeare?"

I did. It was our falling-in-love paper. *King Lear*. She wrote about why two of Lear's daughters had been so awful to him.

"Yeah. As I recall, I didn't do a whole lot except maybe give you some confidence that you could write it just fine."

"That professor was just a windbag! But I always felt a little—intimidated—hanging with you and what was the skinny little Jewish guy's name?"

"Allen?"

"Yes! Allen! Whatever happened to him?"

I guess I wasn't too surprised she might ask this. She might've read my books, but with all the names changed she'd have no idea who was who. And unless she'd followed the whole Beat thing, she probably would've never seen or heard of him.

"He's become a pretty well-known poet. His publisher got arrested for one of his poems about fifteen years ago. Somebody said it was pornographic. All the publicity around the trial got him known across the country. He's had a lot published. And he helped me a lot getting published. And then doing all the promotional bullshit you gotta do if you're actually going to sell books. Interviews, college visits, that sort of thing. He's been a good friend for a lot of years."

"So you've stayed in touch?"

"Oh, yeah."

"Is he in your books?"

"Yep. Not all of them. But *On The Road* and *The Dharma Bums*. Some others."

"A lot of your friends, they were pretty serious about writing and always talking big ideas. Whew! Jack, so much of that just went right over my head." I was thinking right then I'm glad she didn't meet Neal because he would've tried to make her and I'd've gotten really sore, but then maybe didn't do anything about it because that just seemed to be the way it was with him and me.

"Yeah, a lot of it was pure bullshit. But some of it wasn't. Some of us, maybe just a few, worked hard to become writers. *Good* writers. We were trying out different ideas seeing what worked, what didn't."

"I kind of remember sitting in while you guys talked and argued and feeling too dumb to even try to say anything. Someone was always quoting somebody or another. Whitman this. Or Shakespeare that."

"Yeah, I remember that. I think some of it was the insecurity of being young and not really knowing a whole lot, but trying to show off to hide that. It wasn't nice and it wasn't fair. I think you tried asking me stuff after and you'd let me talk and talk and talk. But I was kind of a jerk about it too."

She laughed. "Welll...I guess there were times when I got frustrated with you. I knew you were chasing something, even if I had a hard time figuring out exactly what it was. But it also made you seem more...dashing!"

"But, Anne, I loved that you seemed pretty serious too. I mean, some of your girlfriends, well, they wanted to have a good time—we all did!—but you were different. I liked that."

"That's awfully nice of you to say. But there were some real brains at Barnard too. I remember Becky Jakeman became a lawyer. Then she got elected judge. In Pittsburgh, I think."

The name was a blank to me. But I really did remember Anne that way. She had a quiet intelligence. Perceptive. Didn't have to say a lot. But then she'd say something that blew me away totally.

"Whatever happened to all those guys, Jack? Do you still stay in touch?"

"A couple. Allen's been a good friend—maybe my best friend—from then to now. But I've lost track of a lot of 'em too. How about you?"

"Like you, a few. Sorority sisters. Patty Stiller. Do you remember her?" I didn't. "She lives outside Philadelphia. Her husband is a banker. They have two children, both in college. And Suzanne Rawlings? Remember her?" Boy, did I! A vivacious platinum blonde, she got everybody's attention. "She went back home to Florida after graduation. She met and married a stock broker from Miami. Then he got in trouble. I heard it was some kind of Ponzi scheme. So he went to prison and she divorced him. She remarried a few years ago. An older guy. His second also. Or maybe third! Anyway, they live now in West Palm Beach. So, she's happy. Or at least rich again! Sometimes, I don't know about her. She never wanted to start a family. She just wanted to be...free, I guess!" She laughed again, this time more to herself.

"And you're living in north Jersey and have three great kids and a wonderful husband and life has been good for you..." There was a part of me who could envy her stability and comfort and all the things that said a life well led. She'd been born into comfort, raised in comfort, and now was providing the same for her children. It was the life she deserved. And the life I could have never provided, even if I was now a famous author.

There was a pause. We looked at each other. Then away. Then back to each other. I was happy for her. Truly happy. And I was happy that we could have this moment to catch up. Even as I knew that soon I'd be headed back to Barnstable and tomorrow off to the West Coast via New Haven and Black Mountain. She was on the verge of saying something, pulled back, then plunged ahead.

"Jack...I haven't talked to Jay about this. But I always felt like I could talk about anything to you. About anything! It was one of the things that made you...special. And here you are! Almost like you were sent here."

She shifted to a different tone of voice, something confessional, almost conspiratorial, intimate. It took me back again to those spring Saturdays in her room when the world was just us. I had no idea what could be on her mind, but she wanted to talk, to share something. And here I was, a surprise ready-made audience for getting something off her chest.

"About a year ago, a friend of mine invited me to a meeting, a coffee really. Just women. Most around our age. In Westfield. And it was just to talk. I guess it'd started about a year before with a few of them because one of them—Betty—was having a terrible time with her husband. He was hitting her, Jack. A lot. And she didn't know what to do. He's a very successful builder. A lot of important people know him. A 'pillar of our community.'

"Yet behind closed doors he was treating her terribly. Especially when he drank. He just turned into a monster. She finally got it out to one of her girlfriends. Then another. And another. I guess they started talking about what they could do. And these meetings started because we all had something wrong with our lives and we kind of put up with it because we didn't know what it was. Then when we got together and started sharing, we found out some things that helped."

Anne stopped to sip the Pepsi.

"So, what happened to...Betty?" I didn't want to think about all the crappy ways I'd been with women. Or the even crappier ways Neal had been. Or old Bill Burroughs shooting his wife and killing her—by accident!—but still.

"She ended up leaving him. But at first she and the kids had to hide at one of her friends' cabins in the Catskills, because he came looking for them and I think something really bad could have happened if he'd found her. Eventually, they moved back to her parents' place in Cherry Hill. But it was very scary for a while. I don't think she would've had the courage to leave if it hadn't been for all the support we gave her. One in our group is an attorney and she helped Betty with the legal aspects, including getting a restraining order against Frank. So now they're divorced and life goes on for Frank like nothing happened. He still has his business. He pays her some alimony, but I don't think much in child support. She's had to get a job. From what I've seen, the divorce hasn't put a crimp in his lifestyle. Still belongs to the country club. Has some bimbo for a girlfriend. And no one knows who he really is." There was a righteous anger now in Anne's voice. Something I couldn't recall ever hearing before.

"Jack, I wouldn't expect you to know but it takes a lot—*a lot*—of courage to leave a man who beats you. You're afraid. You feel guilty. You feel ashamed. You feel like a terrible mom. It's awful!"

God! The way she was talking made me wonder if this had happened to her, but I didn't have the guts to ask. And of course it regurgitated all the guilt and other shitty feelings I'd been carrying around in me for Joan and Jan and all the bullshit I'd put them through because of my own irresponsibility. Would Anne turn that righteous anger on me if I spilled my guts about this part of my past? Would she suddenly have a much different "appreciation" of her former-boyfriend-turned-famous-author?

"Is she OK now?" trying my best to sound sympathetic.

"I guess. She got a small house in Cherry Hill from her settlement money. So she's still close to her parents who can help. She had to get a job. Marcia tried hard to get more out of Frank, but he was really sly in hiding it. His attorney made it sound like he was totally broke and the judge bought it. Betty's still too scared to go after him for more."

When Anne sat down this time it was in the middle of the couch, our knees nearly touching.

"So then we started talking about other things. Marcia joined this new group, the National Organization for Women. And somebody else suggested we read something together, a book written a few years ago. *The Feminine Mystique*. And that got us going about who we were as women and what we thought was unfair about the rules men made for us. We weren't trying to be political, Jack. But something about it made me think of you and all the political talks I'd hear from your friends when we were in a bar or something."

"Yeah, I remember those. Allen was the one who'd get most excited. Of course, he grew up with a Commie mother. Me? I don't know. Sometimes politics interested me. Sometimes it was just boring, guys making speeches and not knowing what the hell they were talking about, I thought." I also thought about Fred Halstead and Farrell Dobbs, two guys who were serious and informed about their politics even if I didn't agree with a lot of what they talked about that night.

Anne laughed. "Jack, I remember! These guys would get into these big arguments and then you would say something just outrageous and everybody would stop and look at you. Then we'd all laugh because you'd kind of burst the bubble and we could get back to drinking and having a good time."

"Yeah. Some of those guys took themselves too seriously at times. So, your group. Have you done anything, I mean besides helping your friend get away from her SOB of a husband?"

"I guess nothing specific yet. But it's one of the reasons I wanted to come out here for a few days. I needed to think about things. Jay was not too happy when he found out I was going to the meetings. He thinks Marcia is just a 'loud mouthed broad.' That's what he calls her! And, of course, he and Frank are golfing buddies. So, a few weeks ago he put his foot down and said I wasn't to go to the meetings anymore.

And we had a little bit of a fight. Thankfully, Sallie wasn't home to hear it."

Now Anne was into it. It wasn't because of me. She just needed to talk. And, of all people, I happened to be in the same restaurant she'd wandered into. And because of our "history" I became a trusted listening buddy. Of course, as I write this and look back, I realize she and her friends were part of the new Women's Movement, even if they didn't realize it or necessarily wanted to be if they did.

"Jack, why would he do that? I mean we are all, or just about all, college-educated women. We can think. We can write and we can talk. We know how to do more things than just change diapers or put a Band-Aid over a bloody knee. I don't want him to be upset with me. But I don't think he has the right to tell me I can't go to a meeting, do you?"

"No, that sounds extreme. It's not like you're plotting a revolution or anything crazy like some of the kids are these days."

"We're not! But we do have some radicals in our group!" Anne laughed as she said this. I knew she wouldn't be among them. But, like I said, she had this inner strength that showed itself only rarely. When it did, she could prove tougher than any union guy I'd met. "Marcia's one. But we all knew that. Then last month, Carol, she's one of our younger members, came and she wasn't wearing a bra! And you could tell she wasn't! Ha-ha! She said she was making a statement that she didn't feel bound by men's rules any longer and she wouldn't be bound by the clothes they make us wear either. That was one of our best meetings!"

As she talked, I thought of Carolyn Cassady. In many ways, she might be the strongest woman I know. Except maybe Memere. She was the only one I knew who was able to keep Neal in line. Sort of. And even though he treated her like shit most of the time, somehow she was able to keep that family together, or at least get the kids raised to a decent point, despite often having no money and no one to help her, least of all Neal.

"Jay didn't like that I was coming out here either. *By myself*. Like I was going to turn myself into some floozy." She paused, something else getting her attention, almost to the point of tears. "Jack..." she paused again. "Jack, one of the women has a lovely girl. Wonderful student. She's going to be near the top of her high school class. Or was. I'm not sure now. She got pregnant. And a friend of a friend sent her to a doctor in the city." Anne struggled here, talking more to herself and not to me. "To terminate. And he made a...mistake. And...she almost bled to death."

She fell silent. I didn't know what to say, so I said nothing. I knew about abortion doctors. Joan had considered it when she got pregnant with Jan. But she was still hoping for the best between us, and maybe I was too, and besides I didn't know if I would've let her go off someplace to have that done.

Anne let out a big sigh and continued, "She's home now. But she won't finish with her class. And I guess there's a real question about whether she'll ever be able to have children. It's all...so sad!

"It's really shaken us up. For so many reasons. Some of us are wondering why sex education and birth control can't be more in the open. Talked about more honestly in the schools. I don't want Sallie on the Pill yet. But I don't want her getting in trouble and then sneaking off to have something like that done that maybe kills her!"

Anne looked at me with a pleading for an understanding that I wasn't sure I could give. But I tried. Then she just plowed ahead.

"Abortions happen. They're a sad fact of life. And the bad ones that happen happen more with women who are poor and alone. More and more we're thinking—*I'm* thinking–that a woman has a right to choose what happens to her body. And if there are going to be abortions, they ought to be managed like any other medical procedure. Something that is discussed openly and legally between a woman and her doctor. In licensed medical offices that are safe and clean.

"But until things change, Jack, women will put their own lives at risk because of an unwanted pregnancy. Sometimes that pregnancy happens out of love. Sometimes it doesn't." She looked at me again, now a bit of righteous anger replacing the pleading. This was not a new subject to her. I wondered if it had been the source of another argument with her husband.

"Have you talked about this with...Jay?"

"Oh, yes! And he's just as pig-headed and chauvinistic as his drinking and golfing buddies!"

She mimicked him, "'If she didn't want to get pregnant, she wouldn't have.' 'When a boy gets all heated up, he can't control himself. The girl has to be responsible.' Ooohhh!! He makes me so mad sometimes!"

Wow, *that* hit a nerve. Then the storm passed. Kind of.

"Jack, I'm sorry. I didn't mean to hit you with all this. We should be spending the evening catching up on old times and here I am laying out all my troubles. I'm sorry for being selfish."

"That's OK. There's a lot of stuff going on now. People are getting caught up in all sorts of things."

Another pause.

It's strange when two people get together who used to be real close and then haven't seen each other for a long time. You're not quite sure how close to get again. Or even if you want to. I went long stretches of time without seeing Neal. Then–boom!—he'd be in my room, or I'd be in his room, and it was like no time had passed at all. We'd be into it and off we'd go. It's why Carolyn hated to see me even when she loved to see me. Because whatever bit of stability and sanity she'd fought to bring to their household in the months from the last time I'd seen Neal would be destroyed in minutes after I showed up. Not that I wanted that to happen. It just did. It's how we were.

So there I was with Anne and we're both feeling a zillion different feelings. But we're not sure how to get into them. So we talked about other stuff. Plus, it sounded like she'd been dealing with on her own. And I was still trying to figure out how in the hell I was going to talk to her about my "dying."

"So, Jack, why don't I just shut up and you tell me what your life's been like that maybe didn't make it into your books? What's this book you're writing? You're living where? Is there a special someone in your life? Are you a dad? Just talk to me and I won't bother you anymore with my troubles from home."

What she was really saying is that she didn't want to have to think any more about her husband or her group or these big existential questions that weren't supposed to sprout crabgrass ugly when you have a comfortable leafy life in the suburbs. And now it was on me to share as much, or as little, as I wanted about life since I left her and the rest of a promising future behind on that Columbia campus and started digging for something more. It was almost like she was asking me to tell the rest of the story I'd started all those Saturdays ago lying on her bed, head in her lap, staring at a white ceiling and seeing much more somewhere out there. Much more…

"OK. Where do I start? You've already read some of the books, so maybe I don't have to tell you *everything* that's happened. But, like I wrote, since I left New York, I've been all over. I've been back and forth across this country too many times to count. I've seen it hitchhiking, on buses, in pickup trucks, on the backs of flatbeds. I've seen it riding in jalopies and driving brand new Cadillacs. I've seen swamps and mountains, jam-packed cities and places so remote that it'd be weeks between seeing another person. I've lived in Colorado and California and now Florida. I've had times when I had a lot of money and the parties were non-stop. And other times when I've been so broke I couldn't eat for days."

For some reason I was wound up and Anne was leaning forward wanting to hear my stories. She wanted to hear me talk. She wanted to hear stories about places and people that would take her away from this place and this time. And I was in a mood to oblige. Normally, I wasn't the story-telling type, at least in conversation. It was easier for me to tell my stories through the typewriter, onto paper, into books. But because it was her, and because we were here, and because of all that'd happened since I left her in New York and Memere and Stella in St. Petersburg, especially what'd happened in the last week, I felt like talking. I wouldn't tell her everything, couldn't tell her everything, but I'd tell her a lot. And when I was done, maybe she'd be grateful that I'd lifted some of her sadness for a while. And maybe I'd be grateful that I'd had someone to talk to who'd help me fit things together.

"I've been to Mexico and seen some of the beatest places on this earth there. I've seen a little bit of Africa and a little bit of Europe too. I've worked on freighters and pulled cotton and hauled crates of fruit. I've worked on trains and watched for fires on lonely mountains. But you already know a lot of that.

"I've been married and divorced twice. You know about Joan. She left New York and went back to Albany to have our daughter, Jan. Then I married another woman and that only lasted a little bit too. Then I was single for a long, long time. Finally, a few years ago I married the sister of my best hometown buddy. We live with my mother down in St. Petersburg."

I could feel Anne judging me, even if she wanted to give me the benefit of the doubt. But I think I figured out if I had to trust her with the one big secret to come, I'd trust her with most the other stuff too. She had to believe in me all the way down to now, or she wouldn't believe why I had to ask her to trust me with this last one.

"Tell me about your daughter. Do you see her much?"

She about broke my heart with those simple questions. And when I looked at her she could see my answer before I said a word.

"There's not much to tell. After we split, I only saw her twice. Very briefly. And mostly it's my fault. Joan even had to hound me for support because I was so broke and on the move that she could never depend on me for even that little bit of fatherly responsibility. Jan should be graduating from high school right now. But I have no idea if she is. Or where. It's probably the saddest thing that's happened in my life, Anne."

We were both silent for a moment. Just as with Ruth and Jo and Lissa, I felt like I was completely at the mercy of this woman as she judged whether I was worth continuing the conversation or if she should just ask me to leave now. Here she was raising three kids the responsible way and giving them a decent chance at making it in the world. And here I was with one kid and no idea how she was doing, if she was doing at all.

Finally she spoke with a sigh.

"Oh, Jack, you don't have to say any more. I can see from your eyes this is hard to talk about. I'm sorry for you. And I'm sorry for her. I think you could've been a good dad, if you'd gotten a chance to."

I was getting forgiveness from her and it felt good. Of all the dumbshit things I'd done in my life, this had been the dumbest and shittiest.

"That's nice of you to say. If I could, I would. Maybe someday we'll find a way to connect."

More silence. Again she broke it with a question that was easy to ask and hard to answer.

"Your wife, now. Is she nice? You said she was your friend's sister?"

"Yes. She's a saint, really. I haven't been too well the last couple years and she's had to be more nurse than wife. But she took good care of me, even through times when I didn't care if anyone cared for me or not."

"What's her name?"

"Stella. Stella Sampas. Her brother, Sammy, was my best friend growing up in Lowell. But he got killed during World War II."

"How sad. Was she your girlfriend back home?"

"Oh, no! She was Sammy's kid sister. That was all. We didn't get married until a few years ago. Like I said, I've been more patient than husband to her. But we get along OK. And she and my mom get along OK too. Mom likes having her around. Helps make up for losing my sister a couple years ago."

"That's sad, Jack! Losing your brother so little. And your sister, too. Did she have the same problem?"

"Funny you ask it that way. No, she didn't have Gerard's problem. But both died from heart problems. Gerard's just gave out when it couldn't work anymore. Nin had a heart attack. But what really killed her I think was the heartbreak from her husband leaving her. It was just sad, sad, sad."

"And your father, I haven't heard you mention him."

"He's dead, too, quite a few years ago now. Made me promise to take care of Mom no matter what. So now it's just Mom and me. And Stella. And they're down in Florida. And I'm up here in Massachusetts and doing what I usually do, traveling and writing."

"Yes. You said something about another book. What are you writing about now?" Anne sensed I wanted to move off the family stuff. There wasn't much good news or easy chatter there.

"It's about a college in North Carolina. It's not there anymore. Opened in the thirties and closed in the fifties. Name was Black Mountain. It's an assignment I kind of fell into a few weeks ago."

"Sounds like a different kind of book for you."

"Yeah, it is. But it's not going to be the kind of dead history that gets written by equally dead academic types and then promptly forgotten by the rest of the world. The college was a special place and deserves a special telling of its story."

"What kind of place was it? What was the name again?"

"Black Mountain College. It was founded by education radicals who'd gotten the boot at another place. Couple guys I know taught there."

"You said you kind of fell into it. An assignment. That's not how you usually do things, is it? You like to go out and *do* stuff and then write about it after!" She shoved my knee and laughed a little at this. I had to admit that talking about a writing assignment wasn't the way I wrote. Then again, she didn't know Ruth Parker.

"Yeah, you're right. But I met this woman who was there at the beginning and tried to keep it open at the end. I'd known a little bit about it. They had a review that published a thing of mine. But she really talked me into taking this on as a special project. It's why I'm up here now."

"She must be very persuasive. I don't recall me or anyone else having such a hold on you!" Anne laughed again. Damn! She was loving this tease. And I loved how she was making it so easy to remember how good we used to be together.

"In her own way, she is, I guess. But this kind of fits into the other things I wanted to be doing anyway. Like I said, the kind of book she wants is the kind I can write. And she's paying me good money to do it, so what the hell?" I sounded like I was apologizing all over myself for this book, but I wasn't. I wanted to do it, Olson or no Olson.

"So if the college is in North Carolina, why are you up here doing...research?"

"Because the guy who ran it at the end lives here. Or, rather in Gloucester. Or *lived.* I just found out he died a few months ago."

"So, does that change your plans? Sounds like he was important to what you wanted to do."

"Yeah. Changes things a little. But I'm going to talk to lots of people who were there. Teachers and students. I met one of the founders in New Haven a week ago. He's a pretty famous artist. His wife is too. They introduced me to a couple former students. They gave me names and addresses of some more. So I think if I keep at it, I'll have enough interviews to get the story and kind of tell it through their words."

"And then we'll have a book by 'Jack Kerouac, historian'?" She really was teasing and enjoying. But these were the kind of questions she'd ask when we were together. I called it her Bullshit Barometer, checking me out to see if I really knew what I was talking about. And sometimes she'd have me completely. And when she did, all she'd say is "Uh huh" and I knew I was busted.

"Naw. Actually, my plan is to turn the manuscript over to her and she can do with it what she wants. Even put her own name on it. Like I said, she's paying me good money to write it so it should be hers when it's done. Plus, I have this sense if people see my name on it, they'll think it's something it's not. I'd rather just help tell the story and let it stand on its own. If I do my job, it will."

She was nodding now. "I can see that. It makes some sense." Shifting gears again. "It must be wonderful to have that freedom, Jack. To go where you want, when you want. Write things that just come out of your head and have people pay you money to read them."

"Yeah. It seems glamorous in a way. But there were long, empty years when I had no clue about what was coming next. I wanted success. Then I got it and it about ate me alive. I'm not kidding! First, it was just getting a book written. Then it was finding a publisher. Then it was fighting with an editor who thought he was a better writer than I was, even when the only trains he's ridden are between Manhattan and the Hamptons.

"Then it was all the proofing and little changes and you think this damn thing is never going to see the light of day. Death by a thousand cuts! Then, it does! And you think, 'My God, I've made it!'

"Then another reality sinks in. Once it's published, you have to go out and sell it. The publisher pushes you out there to cocktail parties where people hang all over you because you're 'the author.' And then you sweat it out hoping like hell one of them writes something nice about you and the book in a review. Then there's the book signings where you have to be nice to people who don't give a rat's ass who you are as long as you sign their books like you've known them all their life. Then there's the TV and radio interviews. And on and on.

"It's a racket. Just like any business is a racket. And after a while, you realize you're just a piece of meat to them. As long as you have another book coming out, they love you. But if you say you want to take a break or maybe skip this cocktail party or that book signing, they drop you quicker than a warm piece of dog crap. And all I wanted to do was write. Just write. And, yeah, make a little money. But all the people and all the booze and the fakery, it eats you up. It ate me up, Anne! It's why I had to get away!"

This whole thing had to come out. I had to explain. To someone. And now, maybe it was best that someone was her. Someone who knew me better than anyone before all this other life happened. I wanted her to reach out and hold me like she had before. But that was something I couldn't ask for.

We were silent a while. Maybe she was disappointed I didn't paint her the big life glamorous picture she'd imagined sitting next to a famous author.

"Oh, Jack. I...I don't know what to say. Except you sound so sad. I'm sorry." And she reached over and touched my arm.

"Yeah, sorry I dumped on you. But it's another reason I grew the beard. I kinda hoped to travel around in a way so no one would recognize me. And it worked. Until I got here." I smiled back at her as I said it, so she'd know it was OK.

"And then I went and spoiled it all!"

"Yeah! But you didn't really. Still it was a shock seeing you there at that tiny restaurant of all places! I felt like Rick in *Casablanca*. 'Out of all gin joints in all the world...'"

Anne laughed. "Not half as surprised as I was seeing *you*, Mr. Kerouac!"

Silence again. But with looks and smiles now.

"So, how long are you here for?"

"I'm leaving tomorrow. Think I've learned all I can up here. You?"

"I'm booked until Wednesday. Then I have to get back. Sallie has a part in the spring play and their dress rehearsal's Thursday. I told her I'd be there."

More silence. That awkward time when two people are making calculations, but afraid to say the wrong thing at the wrong time. Then Anne broke it.

"Listen, Jack, it's getting awfully late and..."

"Yeah, I know. I should be going." But I still had to tell her the *real* story!

"I know. But Barnstable's quite a few miles, isn't it?"

"Yeah, I don't know. Maybe forty, forty-five minutes. But there won't be any traffic."

"Listen, I don't want you to take this the wrong way, but...you could stay here if you want."

Wow. We hadn't even gotten into 'our stuff' and she's asking me to spend the night?

"But, Jack, I'm just offering you the extra bed. That's *all*, OK?"

I nodded. "Yeah. Um. That's fine. You sure? I mean, your husband..."

"Jack! He's not here! And there's no one out here to spy on us. And we are adults. And you are going to stay in your room. Or, you can drive back..."

Here's the thing. I wanted to stay. I felt she wanted me to stay, but wasn't really sure she wanted to take the sex step. To be honest, neither was I, even though she looked damned good. But both of us were remembering how good it had been once. And both of us wanted to hang onto that memory a while longer. And whatever this thing was with her husband and that group, maybe she was trying to say something for herself in a way she never had before. And we really hadn't finished catching up. There was more. And I still had to get her to hold tight to my secret.

"Anne, OK. I get it. Yeah, I'd like to stay. Feel like we haven't caught up on everything. And there's something else I want to talk to you about that I'm going to need your help on. But I'm bushed. So, yeah, show me which room is mine."

She smiled again, relieved. She showed me the one at the other end of the short hallway from hers, a small bathroom in between. And the room was tiny. Even though the bed was a little bigger than a twin, a chair at the foot took up enough room that you had to step over it to get to the bed's far side where it was pushed up against a wall with a small window. A nightstand and an ancient lamp completed the furnishings, such as they were. Any family trying to stay would surely go mad within twenty-four hours. Maybe Beston could stay in a place like this for a year, and, God knows, I've stayed in much worse, but if I really were a travel writer I'd have a damned hard time recommending this for anyone but the hermit crowd.

We lingered for a minute in the doorway. "OK, Jack, well there you are. There's already a blanket on the bed, so you should be comfy enough. Good night and see you in the morning." Then she gave me a quick hug and a peck on the cheek and turned towards her room.

I watched until she closed her door, in case she changed her mind, then closed mine slowly and undressed. I eased onto the bed, sending old springs into a riot of complaint, and then lay there wondering if she was pulling up the same memories as I of our youth and our passion and how she did all the things "good" girls weren't supposed to and how she drove me wild when she did. How I learned to be a man with her. How I grew up in her bed. And did so inside a love that was true and good and pure. And how that love was strong enough to let me forget, for a little while at least, what it meant to be poor and a Canuck and trying to shut out my father's pleas to go to BC and maybe bring some money and a little happiness into our sad, miserable lives.

I was tempted to go to her and bring those memories alive again for one night. But something else held me back. Not wanting to put her in a spot. Not wanting to take one step without knowing where the next one would go. So for now I was content with the memories and what she had meant to me then and what seeing her now had done to tie the past to today.

Then I slept. And somewhere in my sleep, I dreamt. And in my dream she came to me. And once again we were skin to skin. And my arm found her waist. And my lips found her shoulder. And as she settled against me, I heard the words that once had fired even bigger dreams: "I love you, Jack." And then I fell into the deep, contented sleep that has come to me too rarely in this life. A sleep that comes only with a woman. A woman who loves you. And you love back. Deeply, truly, purely.

Chapter 26 — Sand and Sunflowers

I woke rested and happy. I reached for Anne's breast and felt the disappointment of my pillow. Yet when I rolled into it I swore I could smell her. I inhaled deeply, trying to get dragged back into my dream and wanting to confuse my mind even more. Had she really been there? I felt the intensity of a dream that felt more real than reality. I stroked the pillowcase for strands of hair and found none. I touched the sheet for some bit of her heat left behind and felt nothing. I had a hard-on brought on by a night of desire and now left with a morning of tease.

I rolled out of bed, threw on my shorts, then added my jeans. When I opened the door, I saw hers was open too. I took a piss and then followed the warm smell of coffee brewing. Anne had her back to me, slicing something at the counter. Her floor length flannel nightgown surely wasn't sexy, but stirred memories. I wanted to wrap my arms around her as I had so many years ago and maybe had again last night. Then a floorboard creaked and she turned and smiled a beautiful smile.

"Good morning!"

She looked at my chest and that made me suddenly conscious of the boundaries we'd set last night. But she didn't act embarrassed or disapproving so I stayed in the small opening between living room and kitchen.

"Morning!"

"Sleep well?"

"Yeah! The springs were a little noisy. But they settled down. I was really tired. Thanks for letting me stay. Looks like it's going to be a beautiful day."

"Yes it is! Lots of sunshine and warm already! I love it! Coffee's ready. Want some?"

"Yeah. Black, thanks."

"I remember! You always liked your coffee black and very strong."

"Yeah. You're right. Good memory!"

"I remember lots of things, Jack..."

She handed me a mug and then poured one for herself.

"Let's go outside. I love walking the beach in the morning."

Out a screen door in the kitchen I saw that the saltbox had a short wraparound porch with steps on this side leading to a sandy path that wound between grasses. It led to a dune that we scaled and ran then down and up to another dune which opened to a broad beach. The deadly ocean glittered calmly.

I followed her down the second dune to the upper beach. She stopped in the coolness of soft sand, soaking in the morning's beauty and warmth. We watched seagulls and the play of morning light on gentle swells, shoulders touching easily.

"So rare that I have any time like this for myself." Again, it seemed she was talking more to herself than to me.

"I needed this. Yesterday I was up for the sunrise and stood here for half an hour, just watching the sun and the water. And I thought, 'Oh my God, how lucky I am to have this moment.'" She paused, then continued, "We used to be up early at Cape May with the kids. But they'd need breakfast or want to swim or maybe there was some spat I had to settle. I loved being there for them and with them, but it was hardly vacation in the sense of just lying back and relaxing and being alone with your thoughts."

I don't know why I did it, but I put my arm around her shoulder and she settled against me as though she'd been waiting for just that. That simple act felt so comfortable and familiar! It was something I'd done countless times years ago. Once we were in Morning-side Park on a bench just watching people and pigeons and feeling the oneness of being young and in love. Then we were in my room looking out the window from my bed at nothing in particular, but holding on to that peace that lingers after making love. And there I was with her again not knowing if my dream from last night had been real or not and not wanting to ask, but feeling her warmth again and somehow all of it feeling right without a word having been spoken.

"Come, let's walk." She slipped from under my grasp, setting her empty mug in the sand and starting for the water's edge. I followed quickly and soon we were walking on the beach just above where a lazy surf lapped at our feet.

We walked in silence. The beach was ours alone and I was thankful for our solitude. I guessed Anne had more on her mind. What it was exactly I had no clue. One thing I remembered from those long-ago times was patience; she'd speak when she was ready to and not before. Any prompting from me would only annoy, as I'd learned from too many "What's wrong?" and "What're you thinking?" So I waited, enjoying the sunshine, glad it was warm enough that I didn't miss my shirt and she felt comfortable being here in her nightgown.

She waded into our next conversation with "So, you're leaving today?"

"Yeah, guess so."

More silence.

"And where was it you said you had to be?"

I answered more crankily than I intended. "I don't *have* to be anywhere. But I'm going to stop back in New Haven and tell the Albers that Olson's dead. Then I'm driving down to Black Mountain to tell Ruth the same thing and maybe take a few days to write up my notes. Then I'm headed west. To San Francisco. With a few stops along the way, I figure, to talk to students and teachers from the college."

More silence. I didn't add that I had to tell her *the* story and swear her silence.

Then...

"Is there any chance you could stay an extra day?"

I stopped. She stopped. We looked at each other.

"Seriously?"

"Yes."

"Yeah, I guess I could."

"Do you want to?"

My turn to pause here. What was she really asking?

"Sure, I guess. But, why? I thought you came out here for just yourself. Then you run into me—of all people! I thought you'd want me on my way as soon as I finished that cup of coffee, which was pretty good by the way."

"Oh, Jack! Don't be that way!" She turned away, then back. "That was always so frustrating about you! Putting yourself down when you didn't need to!"

That was something else I'd forgotten about her. She could be quiet one moment, but if I'd say something stupid, at least in her mind, and wham! she'd knock me flat with a sharp slap of her tongue.

"Look, I'm sorry! I didn't want to be in the way."

"Jack, if I really wanted to be all alone I wouldn't have asked you back to the cottage. Or I'd have shooed you out the door last night when I was tired."

"OK! OK! I can stay!"

"OK. Good." A pause, then a softer tone back in her voice. "It just felt like we started talking about things last night and we didn't finish. And I didn't want to wait another twenty-five years to get through it all."

So that was it.

When I'd dropped her for the dancer in the Village, there'd been no real goodbyes, no real fights or tears. No letters. No phone calls. Nothing that said "The End." It was just over. At least for me. Or at least I thought it was at the time, even though I'd thought of her many times over the years, remembering how good our times had been. But now it seemed it hadn't been over for her. And even though her life had gone on merrily since then—mostly, it seemed—her stumbling on me last night had unleashed all those memories, good and bad.

So here we were, middle-aged and married to others, standing on a big wide beach on a big sunlit morning, bare chested and flannel covered, with one more day to maybe put to rest ghosts that had haunted her, and maybe me too, for all those years. Because, truth be told, I'd tried to figure out why all my relationships had started so wonderfully and ended so miserably. And why I'd been unable to keep any of them going even when I thought the woman of the moment was the most perfect of all women, and our love the most perfect of all loves, and the moment of our love one that embraced all eternity.

"Have you really thought about me all these years?"

"No. Please, Jack, don't flatter yourself either! But from time to time, I've wondered how you were. And...well...I look back at our time together very ...fondly." She was smiling again, if a little uncertainly.

"I do too."

"What do you remember?" This was definitely a woman's test to see if the guy really meant what he said, or if he was just shooting some bullshit so he could get in her pants.

"Well, like I said last night, I remember how you just stood out from your crowd. You were fun to be with. But you had your serious side. I always felt like you didn't care for people saying stupid things, or talking like they knew what they were talking about when they were really just full of it. I remember when I met your dad, I knew where you got that from. He was a no-nonsense kind of guy."

A little breeze started up, just enough to tickle up goose bumps. I flashed back again to our time and how a spring breeze coming down the Hudson had been enough for me to hold her and holding her had been enough to want her and wanting her had been enough to find a quiet place where we could make our own warmth and did.

Now I just said, "Getting a little chilly. Mind if we start back?"

"Sure."

After a little while I added, "I remember being with you and feeling like I was the luckiest guy in the world. Like I couldn't believe you had picked me of all the guys to be with."

"Like who?" She acted surprised, but I could tell she felt flattered as well. This was going better.

"Like Hal Chase for one. Good looking guy. Family loaded with money. Didn't have to work a day in his life, but he did anyway. Tried to become a decent writer. I know he had a thing for you."

"He did? I barely remember him, Jack. Was he one of the ones who talked all the time?"

"Yeah, couple a beers and some smokes and he'd be off on some of his crazy ideas."

"Well, if he's the one I'm thinking of, he did nothing for me."

"I just kind of remember he was jealous as hell because you and I were together. He wanted to be my best friend, but as long as I was with you, it just drove him nuts."

Anne laughed at that, enjoying the memory and the flattery. Somewhere on that walk back her hand found mine and it was easy. And I kept talking. Just like old times. "I also remember Allen talking about you, but in a different way. He's queer, you know, so no chance you were going to be a crush of his."

"No! I didn't. But I'm not sure I remember him well."

"Yep. I think he tried to like girls. For a while anyway. But then found he liked being with guys a whole lot better."

"I always thought he was a little funny. But never in *that* way!"

"Anyway, Allen thought you were really smart. And coming from Allen that meant a lot because overall he didn't think girls were all that smart. Fun to be with, yeah. But not to talk with. Really talk with."

"That's nice to hear, I guess."

"When we were talking and making plans of maybe getting to San Francisco, he asked me more than once, 'Are you gonna marry her?'"

"He *did*?"

"Yeah. I think he was worried that if I married you, then that would screw up all our other plans. Which it probably would have."

After a pause, she laid me out with what she said next.

"I would've said yes...if you'd asked." She said it quietly, but was deadly serious. I stopped us and looked at her.

"Seriously?"

"Yes."

"Wow." Now it was my turn to pause. "I almost did. At least three times I can think of."

"Really?"

"Yeah, really."

"That's...that's nice to know, too, Jack. Even if you're twenty-five years too late." Another pause. "So, umm, why didn't you?"

"Oh, lots of reasons I think. One, I was scared. I didn't know what I wanted or what I didn't. Two, I felt sure you'd say no. I mean, what could I offer you besides craziness and poverty? Three, there was all that talk about San Francisco and maybe a chance to become a big writer. And something in me really wanted that."

Now I stopped and looked at her again. This was one of those Moments of Truth when words come out that maybe you didn't intend at first and once you've said them maybe wished you hadn't, but they are good words because they speak a deep truth.

"But, Anne, I want you to know you were the best thing that ever happened to me and maybe we should've been together, or maybe we shouldn't have. But through all the years and all the good times and bad when I thought of you, I'd smile and think of what you'd meant to me then and how I was a better guy—a much better guy—because of you. It's like the love you gave me set me on a course that has shown me things I could never have seen without it. It's like you gave me the courage to do all those things I thought about doing and talked about doing all those times we were together and you let me dream and believe those dreams could come true. And even though you weren't with me physically, you were always with me here." I pointed to my chest. "That's the God's honest truth." And it was.

All those words. All those memories. All that truth. Spilled out there on that sunny beach right next to the very same water that had tried to kill me a week ago. With someone I'd never ever expected to see again in my life, but now I was damn glad I had.

Then I pulled her into a hug. Surprisingly, or maybe not, she hung onto me like she had all those years ago. And I did mean every word I said. It was like our time was an innocence, our Paradise, which I then lost, and have been trying to find again ever since. It's why I'd wondered over the years why I'd never been able to recapture that feeling with anyone else, even when I thought I was in love, even with the women I married, even when I thought I felt that way only to discover I didn't.

"I've never forgotten you, Jack," she said into my shoulder. I felt a small heave in her chest as though maybe she was going to cry. I ran a hand down her back, feeling the rise of her hip.

I kissed her hair and wasn't sure where all this was supposed to lead right now. Twenty years ago I'd have known. But now? We just had twenty-four hours. And then the tides in our lives would sweep us apart again, probably forever. So what did this moment mean?

With Jo it'd been different. I think we both knew that ours was one of those relationships that come together for a brief time, enjoy and learn from each other, and leave pleasant memories behind but never settle into anything resembling permanence. I wanted to see her again. But no way was I asking her to go with me to San Francisco. Truthfully, it felt like her life was set in Black Mountain. Maybe not the way she'd imagined it. And maybe when someone like me popped into town it got her thinking of how her life could be different. But I also sensed she liked being close to her land. It was something I'd ask her when I got back.

And Stella, my wife? All she wanted was to be with me. And the time I gave her just sucked. I was an angry, broken down drunk who needed her to take care of me and Memere. It wasn't fair. If Sammy were looking down from heaven, I knew he'd be mightily pissed at me for treating his sister this way. But the fact is, I never would've and never should've married her except I needed the nursing and caring she seemed more than willing to give. She saved my life. She gave me a second chance. She is a saint. But for me our marriage was just damned selfishness. I knew it. Maybe she did too.

"Selfishness." That's an interesting word. Maybe that's been just what I've been most of my life—selfish. Doing what I wanted when I wanted with whom I wanted and calling that life. And even though I was headed back out on my everlasting road, something had changed inside. Something that started with meeting Ruth Parker, then continued with looking for Olson and finding Prospero instead, and now coming back full circle with Anne.

The joy I remembered with her was that joy of selflessness. Of wanting to give myself up for her. Of that wonderful feeling of losing yourself totally in the love and embrace of another. I held onto Anne tightly too. I wanted that feeling again. I kissed her hair again. Then she lifted away from me slightly to look at me. There were tears. Soft tears. Hers. Then mine. Then a soft, silent kiss. Earnest, serious, reaching. And a kindling of desire. But of what? From where?

When we broke again, she smiled this time. A rueful smile maybe, thinking of what had been and what might have been.

"That was nice." Then, "Let's go back."

I nodded and we started again. Back to what I wasn't sure. We had both said things that needed to be said. And there was more we both wanted to say, I'm sure. But the easy friendship that we'd had long ago had returned, a friendship that bloomed into love. The kind of friendship that makes love easier to find and grow than the passion that calls itself love until it's spent and there is no more of either. I *liked* being with her then. And I liked being with her now.

We picked up our cups, scaled the dunes and were almost back to the cottage before another word was said.

"Ja..."

"An..." Nervous laughter.

"You first," I begged.

"No, you first."

"OK," I said. "Well, if I'm staying another night I need to do two things. One, I'd love a shower if this place really has one. And, two, I need to drive back to Barnstable, get my things and check out. It'd be great if you wanted to come along, although I'd understand if you want to just stay here and relax."

"Well, there is a shower. It's outdoors on the other side. Not the best, but it works. And, yes, I'd love to go with you. But let me fix us some breakfast first. I'm starving!"

"Me too! Sounds great!" I moved in for another kiss. She pulled back this time. "Jack, I'm..."

"It's OK. I understand. I think."

"I'm sorry. But everything...it's all so...I don't know."

"Hey, Anne, it's OK. I understand. I do. Didn't mean to get out of line. But...God, I'm happy I'm here!"

She smiled and relaxed a little. We were up on the deck and around the back side.

"I am too, Jack. But..." She stopped and held open the door revealing inside an ancient shower head and equally ancient wood bench with a bar of last season's soap stuck to it. A big spider scurried up into a damp corner. "Ok, here's the shower. I tried it yesterday. The warm water takes a little while. And it never gets really hot. There's the washcloth and a bar of soap, I don't know how old. I'll get you a towel."

I stepped in, stripped, turned the ancient knobs and yelped at the cold water that half spit, half trickled out of the shower head. I stepped as far back as I could and waited for ice cold to become temperate. In a couple minutes it did and I stepped under to wash off yesterday's grunge. I also made up my mind to behave myself and just let today and tomorrow be easy for us both. We had a lot more to talk about.

"Here's your towel!" Anne lapped it over the top of the door. I was disappointed she didn't open it and hand it to me.

"Thanks!"

Minutes later I felt like a new man as I walked through the back door into the kitchen where Anne was spooning out a pile of scrambled eggs onto our plates.

"Just in time. Would you butter those last pieces of toast? There's some jam on the table. I'll pour us more coffee if you'll take the plates out. Here."

We ate quickly and didn't talk much. But it was a very comfortable meal between old friends. We still had the whole day, and night, ahead of us and I wondered how it would all play out. Right now it felt like a gift.

After, I washed dishes and cleaned up the kitchen while she showered. And, yeah, I was tempted to slip out and surprise her. She still looked fantastic. But then I remembered how she'd backed away from that second kiss, and I realized I'd mess up the entire day if I said or did something stupid. By the time I'd gotten things straightened up, she'd finished dressing in chinos and a nice, casual blouse along with sneakers.

Then it was off to Barnstable in the Ford. Along the way, we talked more about our lives. Hers had been pretty much all in Westfield. When she married they moved right away to New Jersey and then to a bigger home when they started the family. She'd settled into the suburban housewife routine, while he took the train every day to his Manhattan job. This had gone on for more than twenty years now. She'd done the PTA and bake sales, and attended the concerts and baseball games and all the other things the moms did for their kids and their schools.

I told her more about life in St. Pete. How we'd all arrived there after various stops along the way in Queens, North Carolina, and Denver. I talked about my trips to San Francisco and living out there and how I got the job as fire watch in Washington, then later working the railroad. How I kept notes on all these experiences and why I decided to use them in my books. I didn't talk much about Mexico, but did tell her about Tangiers and France.

She asked a little more about my marriages and I told her. Why things hadn't worked out with Joan. Why I hadn't been much of a husband or a father. Somehow, it was easier talking to her about these things while I was driving. She was good about it all and listened without being judgmental.

After I got my stuff, we talked about where to go next. We'd come down through East Dennis and Dennis, so we decided to cut over to and take a look at Falmouth before heading back up through the

Yarmouths and the Chathams. We made no plans beyond taking the day as it came.

We had lunch at a pizza joint in Falmouth. We walked around town after, not really looking for anything, but just enjoying being together. It reminded me of the long walks we took during that first New York spring. We stopped in a gift shop and she bought a little knick-knack she thought her daughter would like.

On the drive back out, Anne fell asleep and I looked at her still youthful face. She *was* different from many of the other Barnard girls I'd known. She was a lot smarter than some of the ditzes that got into that school with their old man's money. But she didn't have some of the neuroses and insecurities that came along with some of the other really smart girls. Yet, no way she could've been happy following me around the country and all the crazy stuff I'd gotten into. Even if I'd "settled down" as a railroad brakeman in San Francisco, she would've been unhappy as a working man's wife when she'd been raised with so much more.

And no way could I have been happy with a life wearing a suit, carrying a briefcase and taking the train to some nondescript office in midtown. So going our separate ways was probably inevitable. Still, I could have handled the whole thing better. Anne deserved better. But ours was the beginning of fabulous starts and lousy ends to a whole bunch of relationships with women who deserved better.

Anne woke as we got to West Yarmouth. I looked at her and smiled and she smiled back. "This is so relaxing, Jack. I don't think I could've asked for a better day." She reached over and ran her hand along my arm.

"Yeah. I was thinking how crazy right life can be. Running into each other like this. Having this time with you. To think, a week ago I was almost dead."

"What?!" She was wide awake now.

That slipped out. I'd been thinking about it while she slept. But hadn't intended to say anything about the storm and Prospero until maybe later, if at all. Too late now, so I told her the whole story, including Gerard, as we drove on through South Yarmouth and crossed over to West Dennis. I didn't finish until we were coming into South Chatham.

Anne was moved.

"Sounds like you were very lucky. But maybe something more than that, too. You had to be very brave. And strong! Even though you were hurt badly. I wonder how you did it. That's almost spooky about your brother, especially after reading your book." She reached for my arm again, taking a moment to rub my bicep and forearm.

"Yeah. I'm not a big believer in ghosts. But, Annie, I tell you he was *right there*."

"Do you think he saved you and...your friend?"

"I don't know. Well, maybe I do. I mean, I was at the wheel the whole time. So there was nothing he could have done to steer the boat. If anything, it seemed like he was telling me it was OK to give up, let it all go right then."

"You mean...die?" She sounded a little scared saying those words. Understandable, considering.

"Yeah. Like I said, it certainly felt like we were going over a couple times at least. So, if he was there for real, or even in my mind, just saying it's OK to let go, it would've made sense. Except I wasn't ready to let go."

"Did you touch him?"

"No! But he kind of reached out to me, almost like inviting me to take his hand. But I had this feeling if I did, that'd be it. We'd go over and..."

"I think I know what you mean." She paused, then plowed ahead wanting to talk more. "I don't know what I believe about those things. Spirits, I mean. And an afterlife. But your story about Gerard is so interesting! You may remember, I was raised with very strict instructions of what Heaven is and who it's for, and what Hell is and who it's for. Our family was Presbyterian and so was Jay's." Another pause, then a laugh. "Daddy wasn't happy when I had to tell him you were a *Catholic*, Jack! But Jay and I made sure the kids went to Sunday school even if we weren't the best at getting to church ourselves. Now, it seems a lot of that is getting kind of mixed up. The kids don't seem to think the different denominations are all that important anymore.

"David, my eldest, is dating a Jewish girl at college and she's very nice. It's caused a little discussion between Jay and me. And he's also had words with David. If they get married, I don't think Jay will be very happy about that, but if she's good for David and he's good for her what's the difference?"

It was easy for me to agree with that. I'd long ago come to the conclusion that the differences between Catholics and Protestants didn't amount to a hill of beans, even though Europeans had been killing each other for centuries over them. Same with Christians and Jews and Muslims. Or between Muslims and Hindus and Buddhists. Not that people who believed strongly one way didn't stop hating and killing people who believed another way. All in the name of God and love. Peace.

We fell silent again for a few minutes until we got to Chatham. Then Anne said, "Let's stop here and walk some more."

When we did, she took my hand and walked without saying too much. I knew she was thinking about what I'd said about the trip and the storm and Gerard and surviving. This was kind of weird, too, because, until yesterday, I'd been as good as dead to her for more than twenty years, except for whatever she learned about me through my books. Now, she'd been horrified by the fact that I'd narrowly escaped death for real just a week ago. I could only wonder how she'd react when I told about my "dying" in St. Petersburg and why I was really on the road again. And after tomorrow, I'd slip again into memory for her and we'd probably never see each other again.

Amidst all this talk of death, I was feeling a sort of rebirth, both from what happened last week and now here with her. It was a good feeling, a really good feeling, especially after all the weeks and months and years of lousy feelings. Some have said I could be really depressed at times and I guess that's true. Why, I don't know. Well, that's not true. I do. But it's not like I *want* to be depressed. I don't enjoy feeling bad. But sometimes the blues are the blues. And you can't help it. When you see all the sadness in the world and wonder why it's so, why so many have to suffer, why *you* have to suffer, for no reason, it is enough to make you depressed.

But then, there, that day with Anne, I wasn't. As far as anybody could tell, we were just a middle-aged couple walking slowly and contentedly down an old sidewalk in this old Cape town almost at its eastern-most edge. We walked by the Railroad Museum and it prompted Anne to ask more about my railroad days. So I told her of what it was like, that it could be dangerous work, told her about Neal almost losing his thumb working the cars and how he taught me how to jump on a moving car.

When she asked, "Did you like it?" I had to stop and think. The honest answer is yes and no. I liked some of the work, being out with the guys, learning a trade, hearing stories and of course, the pay. It was good pay. Union pay.

But her question also just triggered another flood of memories from San Francisco and some of them both my best and my beatest times ever. Allen may have written the best poem of that time, however, next to his most famous *Howl*. It's pretty famous now, at least among the poetry crowd: "Sunflower Sutra." I told Anne about it and even remembered some of the lines which I recited for her right on the sidewalk there in dear, old Chatham in the sharp sunlight of late afternoon.

I walked on the banks of the tincan banana dock and sat down under the huge shade of a Southern Pacific locomotive to look at the sunset over the box house hills and cry.

Kerouac sat beside me on a busted rusty iron pole, companion, we thought the same thoughts of the soul, bleak and blue and sad-eyed, surrounded by the gnarled steel roots of machinery.

The oily water on the river mirrored the red sky, sun sank on top of final Frisco peaks, no fish in that stream, no hermit in those mounts, just ourselves, rheumy-eyed and hung-over like old bums on the riverbank, tired and wily.

Look at the Sunflower, he said, there was a dead gray shadow against the sky, big as a man, sitting dry on top of a pile of ancient sawdust—I rushed up enchanted—it was my first sunflower, memories of Blake—my visions—Harlem.

She listened politely, but didn't really get it. Not that I expected her too. And I don't think she would have gotten it if I'd recited the whole thing, which I didn't because I couldn't remember it all, and even if I had, I wouldn't have because Allen throws in some pretty rough words as only Allen can. But the poem captures pretty well the yes-and-no answer to her question. The things we did and saw and wrote about were the kind of rough edges of life that are hard to experience if you have a relationship tagging along because it's the kind of thing women just don't want to see if they don't have to. Certainly not the Barnard women I knew. Or their grown up versions I met later in life in the Manhattan salons. And the women I met who did experience all that wanted to get away from it as fast as they could. They saw me as a ticket out. Until they didn't. And maybe that's why my relation-ships busted up.

Anne took my hand again and we continued our walk through Chatham. She talked about taking the train on cross-country vacations with her family to see relatives in Los Angeles and San Diego. She remembered the Pullman porters who served meals and pulled down beds at night. "I'm glad Daddy made those trips. It helped me appreciate how big this country is!" The way she said it had that kind of well-bred, naïve tone I'd heard a lot from the Barnard girls. Riding the rails in comfort with other people doing every last little thing for you wasn't quite the same as hopping a box car in the middle of a winter night and sharing it with half a dozen other guys all headed somewhere and nowhere and trying to figure it all out between swigs of really cheap whiskey that was still better than nothing because it gave you a few miles of fire in the belly.

It wasn't her fault either. Her father was a success, had money and did the things in America you did when you had both. I wonder if she could have even understood any of Allen's "Sunflower Sutra." Could she have looked at a couple of bums like we were in that Frisco railyard and believed what he wrote, "we're all golden sunflowers inside, blessed by our seed & hairy naked accomplishment-bodies growing into mad black formal sunflowers in the sunset"? I didn't think she could and that's why our lives had taken the directions they had.

Like I said, it wasn't her fault. If anything, the fault's mine, because that success was there for me too. Not a doctor success like her old man—and he was a good guy, raised himself up and made good for himself and his family—but a respectable career writing and teaching, maybe publishing; a Manhattan cocktail party success sitting in judgment of other poor slobs like me. But then I could never have written about train rides and bus rides and bummed rides and no rides, and through them all, seen an America that looked and smelled and sounded and tasted like the rough and tumble and wild and crazy place it is, peeled back from the veneer we call society.

A long time ago I wrote a poem, "Bus East." And I wrote it on the buses that took me all the way from San Fran to New York. I wrote it when I was 32 years old, after all the crazy stuff with Neal and our back-and-forths across the country. I'm not saying it's the greatest poem in the world. But the only way I could've written it was to be out there on it, seeing the country in all its ups and downs.

Here's just a part of it:

Then Chicago
Spitters in the spotty street
Cheap beans, loop,
Girls made eyes at me
And I had 35
Cents in my jeans—

Then Toledo
Springtime starry
Lover night
Of hot rod boys
And cool girls
A wandering
A wandering
In search of April pain
A plash of rain
Will not dispel
This fumigatin hell
Of lover lane
This park of roses
Blue as bees

So how do you tell a girl you love her with all your heart and really mean it—really, truly mean it —but then you have this other part of you that's pulling you off into something so poor and sad and blue there's no way to know how to tell her what it is that's sending you away and sending her into a heartbreak that you never intended, but still there it is and it was all forgotten until somehow, some way, you stumbled across each other after dozens of years and tens of thousands of miles and the old feelings feel as fresh as those big red roses you sniffed together and laughed with and hugged until the only universe was you two? How?

I never answered that question. Instead, I just ran away. From Anne. Joan. Edie. My daughter, Jan. How many others? And now it's come full circle and now I have to answer. Whether Anne asks or not. Now I have to figure out how to explain what the hell I've been doing all this time with all this love and all this talk of big things and all these books and everything and still trying to answer that Big Question. For myself. For Anne. For all those whose lives I've touched and left.

Can I still believe in that One True Love that seemed so real with her all those years ago? Or is the only one I truly love—and truly hate—myself and all the selfish, dumbass things that I've done in my name in one way or the other?

All these thoughts were playing in my head even as I talked with Anne as we finished up in Chatham and decided to look for a cozy restaurant in Orleans. Others have seen me go into these funks and think I'm really depressed or something. But that's not it exactly. It's more than that. It's these thoughts. One gets started, then another comes off that, then another and pretty soon I'm wrapped up in my head and kind of forget what's going on around me. It's almost like a meditation, except it can happen right in the middle of a bunch of people.

So when Anne asked if I was alright, I apologized and said sorry, I was thinking a little more about the boat and the storm and how maybe I was lucky we made it through.

"One of things that really attracted me was that I could tell you were serious when you said you wanted to be a writer, even if you weren't quite sure what that would mean or where it would take you. Of course, it helped that you were so darned handsome my heart fluttered the first time I saw you." She laughed her deep, throaty laugh.

I then said something else I'd waited a very long time to say. "Anne, I might've become a writer even if I'd never met you. But you helped me get started. All those hours when I just talked and talked, you were patient and listened and asked me good questions. You made me a better writer and I've never forgotten that."

She rubbed my shoulder lightly and said, "I did that, Jack, because you wanted to see things that I never could. You opened up my world. When I read your books, I felt like I was traveling with you. I felt close to you again, even if there were a couple places I don't think I'd ever want to go!" She laughed again and I knew what she meant.

"Looking back, there were a couple places I probably shouldn't have gone!" I said smiling back at her.

Actually, more than a couple. But the thing is, if you really want to know what the world's all about, you have to go where it's dirty and smelly and you see both the best and worst parts of humanity exposed raw. Where love and hate sleep side by side. Where disease and pestilence are neighbors. Where men strong and beautiful in their youth are broken and bent before they're forty. Where women who've never had a thing in their lives must still give the world as many children as they can before they too break down and die. That's the world. That's America. That's the truth.

And that's why I had to go and see and be far from Columbia's protective walls, far from tweedy publishers, far from, even, Anne. Of course, I couldn't tell her that, or at least not in those words, but maybe she knew that too. But seeing me again gave her a chance to think about all those things in ways she never could with her CPA husband and never would with her well-bred children. She was looking for something more, too, with her women meetings and that singing. Not the same things I went off in search of, but something. Something that would say her life was more than being a devoted wife and good mother, something that was for herself too.

We made our way up to Orleans and got there as the sun was thinking about setting. We found a tiny seafood place overlooking Rock Harbor. It was their first week of the season, so we had the place almost to ourselves. They didn't have a liquor license, but we could bring our own if we wanted. So while Anne got a table that looked out to the water, I scooted down the block and bought a chardonnay—a couple steps up from what I used to drink—and hurried back to watch a glorious end to what had really been one helluva nice day.

Through dinner I told her more stories about my life since Columbia. I talked about how I traveled from one end of the country to the other with just a few bucks in my pocket, how I'd buy a loaf of bread and a slab of bologna and make enough sandwiches to last a bus trip from San Francisco to New York. Or, worse, when I didn't have any money and wouldn't eat for days on end, living on packs of LifeSavers and chewing gum.

Then the wine got us in a pretty chatty, cheery mood and eventually we started laughing over some of the dumb stuff we'd done with our friends in New York. I told her how the opening chapters of my first book that never got published, *The Sea Is My Brother*, included some of our bar scenes. They showed how a couple of my friends got really drunk and pretty obnoxious and I did too, and we made big speeches about this and that and the girls tried to follow and act like they were impressed. And it was a reminder again of how good things had been between us. How much I'd truly loved her and all the good things that came from being with her.

The idea for that first book came from talking about those bar nights and the war and whether we should go and fight or not or if any of us were brave enough to go off and fight. And how that got us talking about fascism and communism and how the Spanish republicans got screwed by England and France and the U.S. during the civil war when Hitler and Mussolini turned the tide for Franco. And how that led to brave, stupid speeches, but it also led me to thinking more about breaking out from this tight little New York circle. And that led to those first, furtive trips downtown, down into the jazz joints where whites and blacks mixed, where hustlers met businessmen, where a different language was being spoken because different things were being experienced. I liked it. And it liked me.

I emptied the bottle, splitting the last half glass between hers and mine. And the look between us was full of memories and love, and I know I was touching her in places that her husband never had, and maybe hadn't been since the world was just the two of us. And it wasn't like I was trying to seduce or make her or anything like that. I wasn't.

Then she asked finally what had to be asked, "Jack, this has been so nice, but I just have to know…I mean this is something I've wanted to ask for years and thought there'd never be a chance. I mean, who thought we'd ever see each other again? Life goes on. But from time to time when I've thought of you, where you might be, how you were doing, did you *really* do all those things you wrote about, I couldn't help asking myself where did we go wrong? I know maybe I shouldn't ask and bring up bad old stuff. But here you are and maybe you've asked yourself the same question from time to time."

There it was. She asked the question I hoped I wouldn't have to answer, but knew eventually I would. No way we could leave tomorrow and not touch on this part of our past. She'd been carrying this around all those years, through marriage and motherhood, and maybe even into her singing and these meetings her husband didn't want her going to. It sure was nice to be remembered that way. And truth was I had thought of her through the years because our time together had been so good and because I'd screwed it up and then went on to screw up a whole bunch more. So I did my best to answer her honestly and completely.

"Anne, we didn't go wrong. And you didn't go wrong. I went wrong, even if I didn't know it at the time. But when I started going down to the Village and meeting these different people, it was like a taste of something I thought I'd been hungering for for a long time. There was jazz and wild parties and new, wild talk. It all felt like something was trying to be born and I was there helping it along because I wanted to be born too. I wanted to find a new way of talking and writing that felt close to what people were doing and saying.

"I figured out that I didn't want tweedy Columbia with its constipated professors and neurotic, insecure students. I wanted to be out on the streets watching pickpockets hustle cashmere overcoated businessmen. I wanted to watch whores work their bars and their corners, and learn what they knew of the world and why they had to sell their bodies and why they stayed with their pimps. I wanted to smoke dope in seedy little tenement apartments and watch little kids play stickball between piles of garbage. Maybe that's a dark side of me I didn't know about until I got to New York. Maybe there's a dark side to everyone that I wanted to see and write about. And while I was out doing this stuff, I found out women liked me. And in my craziness and vanity and selfishness, I forgot about you. That's the God's honest truth, Anne."

I paused and Anne had stopped smiling. Her eyes were filling a little, remembering the pain of the time and added to it with what I was telling her now.

"Was there someone in particular? Or were you just with all the...whores...or whoever?" Her Presbyterian sensibilities were really hurt, a righteous anger bubbling. She'd had sex with me before marriage in violation of the strict morals she'd been raised with. And she'd done it because she loved me more than anyone else she'd ever met. And she'd done it probably expecting we'd get married and have kids and repeat the same, sane, stable life she'd been raised with. And then I'd taken off and was gone from her life and wrecked it all and she'd been left to pick up pieces and figure things out and work through her shame.

"She wasn't a whore. She was a dancer. Modern dance. The Martha Graham stuff."

I paused. She waited.

"She was serving drinks at a jazz joint in the Village. Taking classes with the money she earned. Then she also got a part in a chorus line for a show that never made it to Broadway."

"Did you move in with her?"

"No. I mean, yeah, I spent nights at her place, but she shared it with a couple other girls so it was crowded sometimes. But, no, we didn't shack up if that's what you're asking."

We finished our wine and while waiting for the check, she asked the zinger.

"Did you love her?"

"Yes. No. I don't know. I was attracted to her because she had the same kind of craziness inside that I was feeling. And for some reason she was mad for me. She'd come to New York from Texas looking for something different, something bigger. But if you're asking if I loved her the same way I loved you, the answer is no. That, too, is the God's truth."

"I cried a lot for you, Jack," she said quietly to her memory.

I didn't know what to say. In my selfishness and craziness I hadn't thought a lot about what I did to her when I was off getting into the stuff I did. I just went. With some of the women in my life the breakups had been loud and angry. But I'd never been angry with Anne and, as far as I knew, she'd never been angry with me. We never fought when we were together and it was one of the things that I really loved about our relationship. We were friends. We cared for each other. But then I went and pissed it all away.

"It was like you disappeared. You weren't on campus. You didn't come around. You didn't write or call. I even kind of wondered if you'd been hurt or worse."

"Yeah, I was pretty shitty through the whole thing. When it comes right down to it, Anne, I was a coward. It's taken me a long time to figure things out, a lonnnnng time, but Columbia was the start of me running away from things, from problems, from things I didn't like. I did it to you. I did it to my football coach and the team. Later on, I did it to a whole bunch of other people. And I did it, in part, because I could get away with it. People liked me."

Anne smiled a little at that. Her eyes were still sad. I was sorry for her pain, then and now.

I'd gone to Columbia with everything going for me. The looks. The smarts. The moves. But then part of me wanted something else, something more. And another part of me was scared shitless about what all that meant. Even with Anne's help, I didn't have the balls to go and grab the professional success that was laying out there for me. Instead, I slipped downtown and dove into a hole. Then another. And another.

"Anne, there's a lot more to tell you, and I think I put a lot of it in my books, although maybe you'd have to read between the lines to figure out what else I was saying. But what happened last week told me something. Something about myself, I think. Like I said, when Gerard held his hand out it was like an invitation to give it all up. To *die*. At the time, it seemed almost like the easiest thing to do. Die. And maybe see what's on the other side—if there is another side. But then I thought of all the people who lose life so easily, so carelessly, sometimes so murderously. And I decided I didn't want to throw away my life anymore. I didn't want to run away. I didn't take Gerard's hand."

I stared at my wine glass as I said these words, running my finger around the edge. I looked back at her, hoping she might understand. Her eyes filled with tears. Silent, holy tears. I reached across to hold her hand and she let me. Then she burbled an "I'm sorry." Then "Let's go home." I paid this time and, when we walked to the car, she put her arm around my waist and said nothing.

The drive back was slow and pretty quiet. But not a bad quiet. A things settled quiet. A good, good friends quiet. When we got inside the cottage, we hugged again. And she said into my shoulder, "I'm glad you're here."

"Me too." And a few more minutes of quiet. A quiet reminder of just how special she'd been once.

Then it was a "Come, sit." And we sat close on the sofa, Anne still quiet, running her finger over the top of my hand and up my forearm. We hadn't said all that needed to be said, but we'd said a lot. And maybe a lot would have to be left unsaid. But for now, it was enough.

I also knew it was time.

It was time to tell her the real reason I'd left Memere and Stella in St. Pete, why I'd grown the beard and what I expected when I finally got to San Francisco. I started slowly.

"Anne, I need to tell you more about my life." She kept her hand on my arm.

"You remembered how much fun I was after a few beers. I guess that's true. But after I left college ....left you...I drank more and more. Maybe not every day. Sometimes not for weeks or even months. But it seemed like when I drank, I drank hard. Smoked too much. And then there'd be more. Weed. Bennies."

I paused and Anne asked somberly, almost clinically, "Jack, did you become an addict?" She still held me.

"Not on drugs. But when I wrote *On the Road* I tried to do it in a straight shot, pouring it out on one long scroll of paper so it read and sounded and *felt* like the crazy time it was. I used speed to help me get it out. But I was wrecked by the time I got it done. What I wrote was beautiful. But I don't think the real book will ever get published.

"Anne, I did become an alcoholic. A bad one. Of course, I didn't think I was. At least not for a very long time. But there became so many times Allen or someone else would have to tell me the next day what'd happened the night before because I'd blacked out. Days on end when it would begin with booze and end with booze and one day floated into the next and the next."

"Well, how did you get so much written then?"

"Because I still had enough desire and discipline to sit down and pound out the words. And I was blessed with a good, strong body…almost the opposite of my poor, little brother."

Another pause. Then I kept going.

"It got worse after I became famous. Like I told you, the publishing world is a racket. Everybody's out for themselves. Writers are just meat. But it's the game you gotta play if you ever want to have a prayer of having someone read your stuff. The press just loved the whole Beat idea. They really played it up. And they crowned me King of the Beats. After years and years of obscurity and starving and wondering what the hell all my writing was going to amount to, all of a sudden I was a celebrity. And my publisher figured six ways to Sunday how to pump my books with interviews and parties and appearances on TV shows. I gotta admit, at first it felt great! But then after a while I realized that most people, even the high brow literary types, didn't give a flip about what

I was trying to say. They just wanted to meet Jack Kerouac—King Of The Beats, like I was some monkey in a traveling circus. They just wanted to hear how crazy the parties really were. They even tried to find sly ways to ask how big Neal's dong really was, for Chrissake!"

Anne never let go of my arm. And I was damn glad she didn't. I was finally getting it out. All the stuff I'd never been able to tell anyone. All the reasons why seven months before I'd ended up curled around that goddam toilet. She didn't ask any more questions. She knew I needed to talk. And she wanted to listen and take it all in. I was back in her New York apartment, head on her lap, her fingers through my hair, spilling my guts. Except now it felt like the end of the story, not the beginning. Or the end of something.

"So it seemed as the years went on, I stayed drunk more and more often. And it seemed I got angrier and angrier. At who? The two-faced publishers and editors and press relations types. The fakes. And the academic types who wanted to dissect every last sentence like I was some lab rat. And the kids who started looking at me like I was their Buddha. Most of all, I was angry at me. At something deep inside I couldn't even put words to.

"But I kept on writing. I had in my head that all my books would be part of one big story with our family at the center of it. I called it the Duluoz Legend. That was the name I made up for Kerouac. Then in 1962 I had kind of a nervous breakdown out in California. At a friend's cabin in Big Sur, right on the coast. I just went a little wacko with some people there and then I crashed. But I was still strong enough to write a book about it all.

"What should've been a wake-up call wasn't. There I was forty years old and already starting to feel ten years older. I should've figured out it was time to quit doing all the crazy stuff I'd been doing for the past twenty years. Instead, I became a train wreck in slow motion."

"It's funny you would say that. Bill, my middle one, said something about reading *On the Road* for one of his college classes. He doesn't know I know you! But it was a reminder that I hadn't heard about you or read about you for a while. Made me wonder if something had happened..."

"Anne, the last few years have been almost a total waste. We got that little place in St. Pete and I was just drinking and watching TV and just going downhill. And what was worse, it was like I didn't care. Like I was just waiting for Death to take me by the hand to a place where I'd meet my dad and Nin, my sister, and of course, Gerard. And then it almost happened. Last fall, I got sick. Or sicker. And I was literally spilling my guts out in the bathroom when Stella and my mom called the ambulance and got me to the hospital.

"Turns out, they got me there just in time. I was hemorrhaging. Doc said later if they'd waited another twenty minutes or so, it would've been too late. I'd've been dead."

"That's amazing. Because you look so good now. Except for *that*." And she laughed as she reached to stroke my beard.

"Yeah, they brought me back from the brink. I was in there for a month. But the doc said he'd only really be able to help me if I kicked the booze. That was the hardest part. Goddam that hurt. The drying out. The shakes. I didn't know how deep into it I was until they had to pull me out."

"But, Jack, you drank tonight and last night. Are you supposed to do that?"

"No. And my doc would kill me if he knew. But I hadn't had a drop until a week and a half ago. My insides didn't tear up then. And I'm OK now. But, you're right. It can't be a regular thing anymore. Maybe it can't even be a sometimes thing and that's what I'm figuring out. But I'm never going to drink like I used to. Because it won't be for long, one way or the other."

"So what happened after you got out? Your mother and wife must have been relieved."

"Yeah, they were. And I was too. I really felt better than I had in years. I started going down to the beach and taking long walks. I dropped forty pounds, Anne!" Her eyes widened and gave me a quick once over.

"About a month after I got home—this was around Christmastime—I started getting the itch again. No! Not to drink. I wanted to get out. See the world again. To keep writing.

"But I couldn't do it as the old Jack Kerouac. I knew I'd get pulled back into the old way of doing things. Being suckered into interviews and that whole King Of The Beats thing again. And then I'd get pissed. And I knew I'd start drinking again to stop being mad. Or to make it easier to be mad. Or whatever it is that I'd use as an excuse to go down the rabbit hole again.

"I figured out I wanted to see the world again as I did when I first hit the road twenty-five years ago. I wanted to see its beauty, feel the wonder of being in it. I wanted to do it as an unknown. Just a wanderer. Or a pilgrim. A Siddartha. But to do that, Anne, I had to lose the old Jack Kerouac. I had to go underground. So I figured out a plan and talked it over with Memere and Stella and here's what I came up with..."

I then told her about the plans I made to "die" and the obituary I wrote and some sort of quiet announcement from Stella and Memere and maybe some kind of memorial service later. I explained how I'd made arrangements with my lawyer to have my will all set so that they'd receive whatever monies still came in from the books. I also wrote a letter for Allen explaining all this for him alone to know, that Stella would send later when I told her to and that I'd contact him later on.

Then I explained how I'd bought the Ford, made my plans to hit the road around April 1 and decided to drive north to look for this college in North Carolina that Creeley and Duncan and some others had told me about, but was now closed. How I met Ruth Parker and how she talked me—"Jack Moriarty," into writing this book about Black Mountain. How then I'd traveled this way to look for Olson only to find out he was really dead. How I'd met Prospero instead and all that had happened last week.

"So that's why I may have looked double shocked seeing you last night. I worried a little that Olson might've recognized me from a long time ago. But not you!" I smiled as I said this.

"Whew! That's quite a story, Mr. Kerouac. Or Mr. Moriarty! Or whoever you are!" And she laughed a little at this too. "So, now that I've exposed your little secret, what are you going to do? Come back from the dead?" She paused and added, "Actually, that might be kind of nice."

"Anne, I can't go back to being the old Jack Kerouac. I just can't. What I know of myself now, it would kill me. It really would. No, I have to try and do it this way for as long as I can."

We were both silent, Anne trying to understand all of what I'd just said. Finally, we looked at each other and she spoke up.

"I think I've figured this out. You need me to keep a secret."

"Yes." I know I sounded worried. More silence.

"OK. I think I can do it."

"You can?"

"Yes. I think so. I mean, really, who am I going to tell that I ran into my old boyfriend, you know, the famous writer Jack Kerouac and we spent two lovely nights together at this fabulous little cottage outside Wellfleet, Massachusetts?"

I laughed. A relieved laugh. But I knew my secret was safe with her.

"Since you put it that way, I guess it would be hard to explain. Especially to your husband."

"Oh, I'm not worried about him! He's just a stale, old accountant!"

Another pause.

"Well, I'm very happy, and kinda relieved to be honest, that you understand and don't mind keeping a secret."

"Oh, Jack, I'll just add it to the other secret I've been carrying around for a long time."

"Guess I'm supposed to ask 'What's that?' But then it wouldn't be a secret anymore, would it?"

"No, it wouldn't." She smiled saying this and I kind of knew what it was without any more needing to be said.

"So, tell me again exactly what you're up to and how you're going to be 'Jack Moriarty' for…for the rest of your days?" This was practical Anne speaking, the one who'd rein me in whenever I got talking really crazy stuff.

"I guess I don't have every last detail thought through, but I want to travel and write. There's still a lot of the country I haven't seen. And it seems like we're going through a lot of big changes and the country's not right. People are thinking new things. The kids are out there protesting the war and the environment and what have you. The blacks are still pushing for their rights. And, like you said, women are looking around and thinking maybe things could be better for them too."

I held back on what I'd really been thinking about…all the Ishmael stuff and the whale's tooth and wanting a deeper, even more spiritual understanding of the world. Maybe it was because I hadn't really put it into words for myself yet. I didn't want to come off sounding a little nuts, even with someone who'd listened to me when I was sounding pretty nutty a long time ago.

Then, I added with a smile, "Besides, like I said yesterday, writing is all I really know how to do."

The Scottish doctor's daughter kept after me. "How are you going to make money? How are you going to survive under an alias? I hope you're not planning to live on the streets!" There was a scolding, even maternal, tone now. But also something that expressed her genuine concern.

"Fair enough. And it's not like I haven't thought about that. A lot, in fact. But I don't mind saying I don't have it all figured out. But here's the best I can do right now. One, I've got enough cash to get me to the coast and settled for a few months at least. Two, writing the Black Mountain book actually is going to help. Looks like Ruth is willing to pay a lot for it. She gave me five hundred bucks to get started. When I get back to Black Mountain, we'll talk more about who I talked to up here and I'll give her a good outline of how I think it can come together. Three, I've still got royalties coming in from my books and, though I've set things for that to take care of Memere and Stella, they can wire me money if I get in a pinch.

"Four, my letter to Allen explains what I'm doing and why, minus the Black Mountain thing, and asks him to be 'Jack Moriarty's agent.' That'll be my nom de plume! Allen was always the best at helping to get my stuff out before I became the darling to the rest of the goddam publishing world. Five, if worse comes to worst, I'll 'come back from the dead' and that'll probably become a literary sensation all its own!"

I finally had Anne nodding—slowly—by the time I finished. I think she was impressed I'd thought this through far enough to make it seem like I just wasn't running away, although, like I said, all this was happening because I did have to run away...from the old, drunk, beat up Jack Kerouac.

"When will you get to San Francisco?"

"Don't have an exact date. But I'm kind of figuring between the time I spend in Black Mountain roughing out the book, maybe making arrangements to see some more former students and teachers on the way out and seeing a few other things along the way, maybe a month, six weeks."

"Aren't you worried you'll run into people who know you out there...like here?" She smiled, her skepticism not entirely dispelled.

"Yeah. That'll be something I have to worry about a lot, especially when I first get there. But word'll eventually filter out I've died and, after a while, people will forget about me. So even if someone I know out there thinks they've seen me, they'll remember I'm dead and just chalk it up to a lookalike. And if someone asks, I can shrug it off with 'Yeah, I get that a lot. Who is this guy?' Besides, I know some pretty good places to hang out in the city where it's doubtful I'll run into people like Ferlinghetti." At least that's what I hope will happen.

"I don't know, Jack. I hope it works out for you." A pause, and then another question that I think really got to the heart of what was on her mind. "So, after tomorrow, are you just going to vanish from my life again? Or am I going to have to start looking for books by 'Jack Moriarty' to keep tabs on you?" She said it as kind of a tease, but I knew she was really serious in a way maybe I hadn't quite expected. Just like the last twenty-four hours had been quite unexpected. Just like this entire trip from St. Pete had been entirely unexpected.

"I don't know. I really don't. I mean, if you're asking if I'd like to stay in touch, yeah I would. But you're gonna have to tell me how to do that. I mean, I can send you postcards or letters when I'm traveling, if you want me to. Hell, I'll even send you my address when I find a place out there!"

"I'd like you to stay in touch, if you can. I get the mail first most days, but I guess I do worry if Sallie or Jay might see something from you and they start asking questions. I have a feeling Jay really wouldn't like it very much."

"Hey, not a surprise there."

Then she leaned against my shoulder. "Put your arm around me, please." I did and we were quiet. I felt good. She felt good.

Finally she said, "My friend Suzanne is always traveling someplace. You could send me postcards and sign her name."

"Yeah, I could do that." I gave her, kissing her hair gently. "In fact, I'd like to, Anne. It'd be nice to let you know how I'm doing."

"Her new husband's name is Jerry, with a 'J.' And she signs her Christmas cards as 'Suze.' So if you said something about a long vacation or something, they'd think it was her and I'd know it was you. Just don't write anything too silly." She was liking this little plan she'd just made up.

"I'll do that. 'Greetings from Suze and Jerry!' 'Hello, from Long Stink, South Dakota!' 'Wish you were here in Busted Flats, Nevada!' How's that sound?"

She laughed. "Suzanne likes to travel very first class. But I think if anyone asks I can cover for her." Pause and a hand over my chest. "Thank you, Jack."

"Hey, it'll be fun. Just don't expect a postcard every other day."

"Oh, no no. I won't. But maybe when you get to San Francisco and find a place, you could call me? Then I'll know you're safe and sound."

"Yeah, I'll do that too."

"OK. Good." Another pause that settled into gentle minutes of quiet. Then, "Jack, I think it's time for bed." And she sat up.

"OK."

We looked at each other and she was wrestling with something. Then she said something that both surprised me and didn't.

"Jack, would you sleep with me tonight? I mean...*sleep*...I can't break my vows with...but it would be nice to have you close one more time. Do you understand?"

She asked, both pleading and with desire. And I knew. Because I felt it too. And even though we could easily do "the other," I knew she had to go home to husband and family and this would be a secret she'd have to keep, not as a joy but a burden.

"Yeah. I know what you're saying. And, yeah, I want to be with you too." And now I leaned across and gave her a long, deep kiss. And she came back with another.

So with that we went to her slightly larger bedroom and bed. I could see she had this sort of middle-aged shyness about showing a body no longer as young and beautiful as once remembered. And I didn't care, just wanting her closeness. She'd reached for her nightgown and I stayed her hand asking if she'd at least let me see her as I had. "But, Jack, I've had three children..." But I kissed away her resistance, however slight, and, after telling her how beautiful she was with each item of clothing removed, we settled under the covers—me holding her as I once had so many years ago, she settling against me with a surprising familiarity.

With my arm around her waist and my hand cupping her breast, I got aroused and was glad for it.

"Jack, you promised..."

"I can't help it if being like this makes me feel as I did way back when."

"I know, but..."

I kissed her hair and squeezed gently. "I'll behave. But, damn, you feel good Anne."

"That's nice. You feel good too, Jack. Just hold me. And be nice."

"OK." I relaxed and then, just before drifting off to sleep, I said softly, "I dreamt last night you came to my bed. I was so disappointed this morning when I reached for you and you weren't there."

"Ummm." She pushed against me slightly and was asleep. Then I was too.

We woke to an early dawn drizzle. A gray morning perfect for staying in bed and snuggling. I woke first and had to untangle myself from her to take a piss. When I came back she was awake and lying on her back and for one more time looking morning lovely. She smiled, giving me an approving once over as I slipped under the covers and against her. We kissed and she smiled a contented, memory-filled smile. I caressed her, each stroke calling up mornings from long ago. I again rose to the occasion and slid over her to show my appreciation for last night's invitation. And I kissed her hair. Her cheeks. Her lips. Her neck. And with each I could feel desire and more for her building an wanting.

Then I did what I learned and loved doing when we were young: I kissed her body slowly from head to foot and back again. She had clearly stayed in wonderful shape and made me glad I'd exercised as much as I had after I got out of the hospital. I kissed freckles on her breasts. Then I kissed her appendectomy scar the same way I had before. Then I kissed lower.

"Oh, Jack..."

Then she wanted me and I wanted her and we forgot last night's good faith pledges and broke open a love that I had kicked away and she'd gathered up and kept sealed all these years. And in that middle-aged morning, tucked away in a little cottage far from the world, we gave each other the gift of a moment of happiness. And it was holy.

After, she curled against me, her hand running through fast-graying chest hair. We were quiet now, the only sound the dull thuds of raindrops against cedar shingles. It was bliss. Neither of us wanted to speak and break the spell. Neither of us wanted to crack this little egg of solitude, this universe of two. And so we drifted.

When we awoke, the morning had moved on. The rain had slackened. We stretched against each other and then she said the words that had to be said and neither wanted to say or hear: "Jack, I have to think about getting back."

"I know."

She kissed me and said, "This…this has been wonderful." A pause. Another kiss. Then, "I don't know what else to say."

I propped myself up on my elbow and looking down at her loveliness, I said, "Let's just say, 'What we had was special. What we discovered here was special too. Because of that let's make sure our lives stay connected whatever the future brings to us. I don't want to lose you again.'"

They were the right words. She loved them. And I meant every one of them. I had no illusions we'd ever be together (I don't think she did either), or even that I'd ever see her again. But I'd send her postcards from my trips and let her know where I'd settled. And of course she could keep track of the success of this 'emerging' writer Jack Moriarty.

Then the day accelerated as she realized she was now behind schedule; she'd promised her daughter and husband to be home before supper and to have something ready for them. It was part of the negotiation in getting these few days of freedom. We breakfasted, made love again under a warm shower and cool drizzle, and packed quickly. She gave me her address and phone number. I gave her my St. Pete address, but I think we both knew that was one she couldn't use unless it was a dire emergency, whatever that would be.

There was an embrace and some tears in the living room before we had to hustle through the rain to our cars.

"Jack, I love you. I think you know now there's always been a special place in my heart for you, for us. I can't believe that I found you—out here! I know we have to go our separate ways. But it would make me very happy if you'd think to send a postcard from 'Suze' once in a while."

"Anne, I love you too. And I'll make sure she sends you greetings from around the country. Somehow, some way, I'll try to share with you what I'm seeing out there."

One more embrace and out the door. I followed her Volvo through the rain into town, then through all the Cape towns until we got to the Route 6 bridge. There I got caught by a light so that the last I saw of her was the new station wagon disappearing with traffic across that familiar rain-slicked bridge.

Chapter 27 — Pacific Man

After watching Anne's Volvo disappear over the bridge, I kept thinking I'd catch up to her again in one of the towns on the other side. Then I'd wave and smile and maybe she'd remember something she meant to tell me and she'd pull off into a gas station or little restaurant and we'd talk and kiss one more time. But I never saw her. So something that had started with unexpected surprise and anxiety, then turned into unexpected happiness and another sort of rebirth, now came to its quick, inevitable end.

By mid-afternoon I found the same New Haven motel I'd stayed at before and was remembered. I then called the Albers and spoke to Anni, who sounded very happy to see me. I agreed to stop by at 11 the next day. I also called Ruth and got Bessie. She, too, sounded very happy to hear from me, especially when I said I'd be back in Black Mountain Friday evening. "We'll put a big supper on for you, Mr. Moriarty! I know Miss Ruth will be very happy to hear this news. I suspect Miss Jolene will as well. You travel safe!" She lightened this drizzly day.

I tried writing, but couldn't do it. I pulled the tooth out of my jacket, running my fingers over the letters, wanting to write something about it and Prospero and all we'd been through. But everything that happened at Gloucester and the Cape with Prospero and Anne hit me like a ton of bricks, like I'd been running on some reservoir of energy that hit empty in that motel room. I collapsed on the bed and slept. No dreams. No Gerard. Just sweet sweet sleep. I woke up starving and found a family-run Italian place and got my fill of bread and antipasto and ravioli. Then it was back to the motel and more sleep. More dreamless, Gerard-less sleep.

I felt recharged in the morning, and Josef and Anni were truly happy to see me. Turns out they had a list of a dozen or so former students and teachers with addresses and some phone numbers to hand over to me. Jane and Tom, the former students I'd met at their place, mailed them information and they added a couple more they knew as well. As expected, they were spread all over the country, from New York to LA, so I had to figure out a route to the coast that would get to as many of them as possible. But Ruth would be happy knowing I could continue my work beyond the Albers and Olson.

Of course, they wanted to know about Olson and were shocked at the news of his death. "*Er ist Tot? Wirklich*?" Josef asked with both surprise and sadness. Even if he and Charles might have been artistic and personal opposites, Albers still respected him. "*Er war ein Jungen, nicht war*?" He and Anni figured Olson couldn't have been more than 60, young by their standards. Still, the way he said it I could tell Josef couldn't resist a little jab at Charles' appetites.

I told them about meeting Prospero, but skipped *Mariel*, the Storm and Anne. I even showed them the whale tooth. They were impressed by the size, of course, but even more by the inscription.

"What does this mean? 'Eesh-may-el'?" Anni asked. "He is first-born of Abraham, no?"

"I don't know exactly. But you know Charles' book, *Call Me Ishmael*, he was trying to say a lot in there about Melville. Very modern. Big stuff."

Josef nodded.

"These letters...are they from Charles?" she continued.

"I don't know and Prospero didn't know. I think Olson gave it to him as a sign that he was dying and he wanted his friend to have something that would bond them forever. Taking a guess from the stuff he's written, but maybe Charles saw a certain connection that came down from the Biblical Ishmael to Melville and his Ishmael, and their bonds to Ahab and the White Whale, to Olson himself and his fisherman friend."

Josef nodded even more vigorously. "Ja, that is good. That is very good. And now that line is drawn to you, my friend! The line it is important. Strong. Clear. Your Prospero, he knew what he was doing."

"I hope so! It means a lot that he wanted me to have it when he could have given it to one of his sons." I didn't add my fear that maybe he was dying too and this was his way of saying so without saying the words.

I stayed through lunch. As I was leaving, Anni handed me the list in an envelope and Josef surprised me with a small, framed package wrapped in brown paper. "This is for Ruth. Mit our love," he said smiling. "Tell her we would like to see her again. Soon."

I didn't feel like retracing my tracks up from Delaware and Virginia. So when I recrossed the George Washington Bridge, that high, beautiful, familiar old highway that led to so many adventures with Neal and Allen and all the others, I headed west.

I played with the fantasy of curling south on the Jersey Parkway and driving to Westfield. I imagined seeing Anne again, maybe coming out of a grocery store, and being glad to see me. But I already knew what Westfield was. Suburban, comfortable, full of kids and Volvos. What would going there do except make her crazy? We'd had our time and maybe would again, but going to Westfield was not it. Instead, I stayed on I-80 across New Jersey and spent the night in a nice little motel on the Pennsylvania side of the Delaware Water Gap. It was dark and quiet and old and reminded me of earlier trips without a car or a room. Next morning, I continued on through the ups and downs of eastern Pennsylvania. I thought of Lt. Michak and his grandfather and father joining tens of thousands of others coming into these old Allegheny mountains to hack hard coal from deep mines and call that a better living than ones they'd left in Europe. And if it wasn't for them, it was for their children and grandchildren, or at least the lucky ones like Michak who got a college education and the chance—maybe—at a desk job if he got back from Vietnam alive.

When I crossed the Susquehanna River, I turned south on US15, stopping for gas and a sandwich in Lewisburg. Two road signs said the town was home to a university—Bucknell—and a federal penitentiary. The latter called up a fuzzy memory that Jimmy Hoffa, the former Teamster president, might be there. Didn't Farrell Dobbs say something about Hoffa? How long ago had that been? Couple weeks?

South of Lewisburg, at Sunbury, the west and north branches of the Susquehanna merged and the river broadened out to become the beautiful waterway I remembered from long ago and the ghost of a man I met alongside it outside of Harrisburg. After Harrisburg, US15 cut away from the river and made a beeline for Gettysburg. I wanted to see the battlefield, but also said I'd be in Black Mountain by nightfall and still had plenty of driving to do. I kept going.

I stopped again for gas in Danville, Virginia. The guy who filled me up was a kid. Tall and lanky. Polite. Clean cut. Wore a Senators ball cap. As he washed my windshield he said, "Did you hear the news?"

"No."

"We invaded Cambodia."

"What?"

"Yessir. Heard it on the radio."

"That's really something. *Cambodia*?"

"Yessir." He finished wiping then leaned in towards the window, wanting to spill what was on his mind. "I graduate next month. Got my birthday in June. If my number's low enough, I'll be going in the Army sure 'nuff. I was hopin' to go to college. But looks like this war'll go on forever now."

"Yeah. I hope it doesn't."

"Yessir. We've already lost three from my high school and there's quite a few over there now. That'll be seven fifty."

I gave him a ten.

"Be right back with your change."

Cambodia! Jesus Christ. I thought again of Dobbs and Halstead and the kids at that bar. There'd be more trouble for sure.

"Here you are, sir."

"Thanks. And good luck."

"Thank you. I'd feel a whole lot better if I knew what we was fightin' for. Thought I had this here Vietnam figured out, but maybe I don't. Have a good day, sir."

I drove off shocked back into a different reality than the one I'd left up in Massachusetts. Prospero and I never talked about the war. Neither did Anne and I, and she had two boys of prime age. What in the hell was Nixon doing invading Cambodia?

By the time I got to Greensboro, I knew it'd be way after dark before I got to Black Mountain. So I stopped and called Ruth's house again. This time she answered.

"Well, Jack, how nice of you to call! We've been waiting supper on you and wondered when you might appear."

"Ruth, sorry, I should've called earlier. But I didn't do a very good job figuring how long it'd take to drive down from Pennsylvania."

"And where are you now?"

"Greensboro."

"Oh, well, you've got a couple hours left to go! We are going to go ahead and eat because we are *famished*. But we'll save something for you when you get here."

"Great! I appreciate that Ruth. I'll try to get there between 8 and 9."

"Now you drive carefully! We are all very much anticipating your return!"

It was good to see the porch lights on and the house lit up when I finally pulled in behind Jo's Beetle. I was greeted as some kind of returning hero with hugs and kisses by both women, on the cheek from Ruth, the lips from Jo. I must've looked pretty beat because they dragged me to the dining room table and made me sit while Jo warmed up supper. Even though it was late and I'd just finished a long day's drive, Ruth was full of energy and peppered me with questions as soon as they had a glass of lemonade in front of me.

"We were pleased with your postcards, but they hardly said a word about your travels. You were in Morehead City for a while. Then you saw Josef and Anni. And how are they?"

"They're doing great. They were a big help and told me many stories. I think they're easier now remembering how you danced with 'Hitler' way back then."

Ruth chortled. "They send their love and want you to visit soon." I'd forgotten their gift in the car.

"Well, yes. I believe that could be arranged and I should see them again."

"Then you finally made it out to Gloucester to see Charles! You must have had a grand time. And how is our gentle giant?"

I paused for a second and then broke the news, "He's dead, Ruth. He died in January."

Ruth's shock was palpable. The color that had rushed to her cheeks as we talked about the Albers rushed away just as fast.

"Oh! Do not tell me that! He is too young a man to have departed this earth so soon." She looked at me long and hard, eyes brimming, hoping maybe I hadn't just said those words.

"It was a shock to me, too. I might've never known what happened if I hadn't met his neighbor who just happened to be out when I drove up looking for him."

Jo brought supper. Pork chops. Yam baked and buttered. A pile of corn. I dove right in. She sat opposite just as she had weeks ago, our eyes meeting. I was glad to see her, even after the unexpected time with Anne.

"And what did he say of Charles' demise?"

"Cancer. Sounded like they'd been pretty good friends. But once Olson left for the hospital end of last year, he never saw him again."

"I am never one to comment on one's habits, but I would have to say what I remember of Charles' would not lend confidence to an extended life. Still, I cannot believe this. He is too good a man to be taken this early!"

"How old was he?" Jo asked.

"Anni and Josef figured he couldn't have been more than 60."

"Yes, I think that is correct," Ruth replied, still absorbing the news. "I distinctly remember a fortieth birthday celebration for him when he was rector. That was 1950. Good Lord! It seems but a few years ago and here it is twenty!"

Recovering, she insisted on a toast to his memory, which she made with us standing, our glasses touching.

"To Charles Olson, a great poet, writer and rector of Black Mountain College to its final days. He lived life large in his physical person and even larger in his spiritual being. We salute you as your journey continues."

We clinked a "To Charles!" and sat.

I finished my supper in a hurry and answered more of Ruth's questions. We moved on to talk more about Josef and Anni and their list of names and Ruth was delighted with that. Then she could see I was fading rapidly, so she shooed us out the door with a command to return tomorrow at 2 o'clock. Clearly, she wanted to talk more about the book, her college and her friends, living and dead.

I followed Jo back out to her farm. I loved the smell of her ground, it becoming familiar even after just a couple days.

Inside, she pulled me into a tight hug and kiss. "I'm so glad you are back with us, safe and sound."

"Me too."

"Come to bed. We can talk in the morning."

And so I did. And she did. And I held her lithe, smooth body and fell into a deep, contented sleep.

In the morning she reached for me and I for her and without a word spoken we made the kind of delicious love that feels like that first welcoming kiss and embrace. I love the feel of a strong woman under you, wanting, responding, moving in surprising ways. Jo was all that and more.

After, I told her more of what I'd done. I left out the really big stuff like crashing at Cape Hatteras and what I wrote at the motel in Morehead City and later with the Storm and the whole business with Gerard.

She curled into me with another kiss and said, "Mr. Moriarty, it sounds as though you have had an adventurous time. We certainly enjoyed your post-cards, even if they were somewhat stingy with details!" I liked that she didn't press me for more. I liked, too, that she accepted and enjoyed our reunion for what it was, for however long it might be. I liked it so much, in fact, that I rolled over on top of her again and extended our good morning kiss. Then, too soon, it became rushabout time again, so she wouldn't be late to the library and her work.

I was left alone until it was time to see Ruth. I did feel like writing, getting thoughts together for later. I looked over the list. Fourteen names and addresses, eight phone numbers also. Three were in New York, so I crossed them off for visits, at least for now. Two in Ohio. One in a town called Yellow Springs. The other in the same town Jane was from, Shaker Heights. Two more in Chicago. One in Madison, Wisconsin. Another in Boulder, Colorado. Another in Albuquerque. Then one in Seattle, another in Bend, Oregon. And two in the San Francisco Bay area. So I could see a trip working itself out from Black Mountain north to Ohio then west.

I was finally able to write some about Prospero and Alex and Gloucester and Cape Cod. I wanted to write about the Storm, but all I felt like saying right then was that we went fishing, saw a whale and ran into some weather. I also traced the tooth and copied the letters as exactly as I could. I'd probably never know who inscribed it, but I wanted a record in case the worst happened and I fucked up and lost it. I also made a note about the Cambodia thing. But I was too weary of war to write much. I made a note next to Lt. Michak's haiku as a reminder that maybe he already knew something big was going to happen. Maybe he was already in the thick of it.

I got to Ruth's right at 2 and this made her happy, giving me another hug and kiss. Bessie was there and she, too, gave me a hug. For only having known these people a few days, I was sure getting a lot of love. I remembered the Albers' gift, which was one of Josef's latest paintings. She was thrilled and a little teary, saying again she had to go up to see them. I also passed the news of Walter Gropius' passing the year before and this, too, was news she hadn't heard.

We sat outside on her stone patio. A large oak tree shaded us from the warm sun while the yard was ringed with color. Azaleas. Daffodils. Tulips. Redbud. A large magnolia dominated the back end of the yard. Spring was just coming on at the Cape. Here, even though we were in the foothills of the old Appalachians, it was full season and already thinking of summer.

We spent the next couple of hours talking about my travels. She surprised me a little by asking if I'd finished my article about Black Mountain. I lied and said I had. She then asked if I had any more assignments imminent. I told the truth and said I didn't. Then she pumped me for more information about Josef and Anni. I described their new house, how both seemed to be in excellent health and good spirits. She was glad I'd had a chance to meet Tom and Jane.

I showed her my outline. Since I'd never written anything like this, I was flying by the seat of my old pants. She asked how many I thought I'd need to talk to. I made up a number and said 30-50. She nodded in agreement.

When she asked how long I thought it'd take to do that, I said I hoped to talk to most everyone on the list when I left for San Francisco. From those I expected to get more names to write or visit. Between the time to contact, travel and talk to everyone, I guessed at least a year. She considered that and then startled me with this: "Do you think you could finish before this year is out?"

I paused. I really wasn't sure if I could do what she wanted in that short time. At the same time, I knew she wanted, and needed, this done. And she didn't want to, or couldn't, wait.

"I know you are a very busy man, Jack. But if somehow you were able to make this a priority, I would be willing to make it worth your while. I would like to offer you a retainer of two thousand dollars a month, plus your expenses of course." Two thousand a month! I tried not to jump up out of my seat and do a little dance.

"Ruth, if I told my editors not to give me anything for the rest of the year, I could probably make that work." Probably make that work? I'd never had a deal like that before. It'd set me up easily in San Francisco and give me a base to work from.

She smiled and clapped her hands, then extended her hand and we shook. "Good, then it's settled. I am delighted with what you have done so far."

A pause, then leaning in a little conspiratorially. "Now, it is not my prerogative to ask about your personal business, Jack. But how long do you expect to be with us before you set off again?"

"I was thinking a week. Or maybe two, depending."

"Well, I can tell you that Miss Harris was very much looking forward to your return. She did not say as much, but I believe she was hoping you might remain with us for a little while."

"Yeah. She didn't say as much last night either, or this morning, but she seemed really glad to see me again."

"And may I presume the feeling was mutual?" Uh-oh. Ruth playing matchmaker again.

"Yeah. Like you said, Jo's pretty special." And I meant that. She was.

"I am delighted to hear that from you. I confess my first impression was that you were a man who could win and break a woman's heart too easily. And that you probably had already—many times!" She said this less as an accusation, more like a flirt.

"Jolene was quite taken with you from the start. She deserves to be in a larger city where there are more men of her...caliber...where she might find a suitable mate. Unfortunately, Black Mountain does not offer many. And so, on the rare occasion that one makes his presence known, she responds as a healthy woman of her age would do. Although, please understand she is extremely selective with her affections."

I had to give Ruth her due; she knew how to sink her hooks in before you even knew you were caught.

"Ruth, I was lucky I ran into her. When I drove into town I expected to see lots of buildings and a campus and everything. When I didn't, I was ready to move on. Then, on a hunch, I stopped at the library and everything else happened."

"Yes, that was a fortunate detour you took, Mr. Moriarty. We are so glad you decided to do so."

We talked more about the book, Ruth telling stories, including a couple more about her and John Rice. Then, right at four and somewhat abruptly, she ended it but with an invitation for Jo and me to return the next day for supper.

I had an hour to kill before Jo was done, so I drove out to Lake Eden and walked the grounds again. The campus was quiet, I had it all to myself. I walked around the lake studying the silent, angular buildings, trying to see ghosts from the forties and fifties, imagining men and women the same age I was then coming here to study art or dance or weaving or literature or science and then also learning how to cut boards, nail joists, lay wire. I heard sharp Brooklyn voices mixing with broad Midwestern twangs becoming a soft cacophony of laughter and song. I saw a faculty with rolled up sleeves, working for almost nothing, delighted to be liberated from the confines and mores and politics of traditional university life. I smiled thinking of Olson straddling over all, a Colossus of Black Mountain, a jolly, chain-smoking, root-searching whale of a man.

I could tell this story. And I would if I continued to get help from the ones who'd lived it. I'd tell it in their words and maybe through them the college could live and breathe again not just for those who went there, but those who might dream that another place like it could exist someplace else. Black Mountain was, as Ruth said, like a seed pod cast to the winds. It was a sunflower pushing and growing and blossoming in gravelly, rule-ridden soil between ivy-covered tracks of rigid rules and iron fists.

I crossed over the wooden bridge to the little island in the middle of the lake, just a hump of land with a tree big enough for shade. I fished the whale tooth out of my pocket and sat on the grass, turning it slowly over and over, pausing each time to run my fingers across the letters, trying to divine whatever meaning it might hold.

I wondered if Olson carried it here, and if he did, did he sit on this same grass, thinking about Melville and Ishmael and the White Whale? Melville had faced his Storm, managed to keep his grip on the wheel and made it safely back to land. Had he brought this tooth with him, hard won evidence that he'd survived? Had he then passed it on to another who'd faced the Storm and survived? Olson had also gone out. Had he held on, too, made it back to port and received this from that unknown someone?

The tooth had weight, as though it were some sea-borne talisman. I closed my eyes and again followed each letter with my finger trying to imagine the original keeper carving them and wondering why. I imagined Olson's excitement as he dove deep into Melville and came up with something to match his own appetites.

And there was Prospero, master of his own sea, taming his tempests. He was the real deal and Olson knew it. Prospero was *his* Melville. Olson knew the tooth had to go to him. Just as Prospero knew it could not go to his own sons for reasons he would not, or could not, share with them.

So it came to me. Because Prospero knew what I didn't know, what I couldn't know until we had traveled into the teeth of the Storm together, until I had survived my own tempest.

"I *am* Ishmael."

Those words again. Quietly and simply they came. But when I heard them, I knew they were true. I had thought about them much since the Storm. But they spoke a truth about all that had happened from last fall until now. And all that I'd been looking for since I left Lowell and broke my father's heart.

I am son of Abraham. I am a wild ass of a man. I am son of Ahab. I am cast onto wild seas. I, too, have battled the White Whale and lived. I am Ishmael, survivor and teller of tales.

I never tried to explain this to anyone else, not even Allen, except through my writing. And I'm not going to explain it all here because I can't. But there on that little manmade island in the middle of little manmade Lake Eden in the middle of that little, almost forgotten college campus on the first day of May, 1970, those words came to me again. Not in stormy defiance. More like revelation. And with those words came a great sense of peace. And genuine, at-rest-with-your-soul-and-beyond happiness. Satori.

I meditated on those words. I almost wished Snyder had been there with me. He might have helped me understand better. One thing I was sure of, I didn't expect to turn into some kind of monk or Siddhartha or even some kind of street preacher. No. What I wrote to that boy months ago was even truer now. Try to see my path. Then make your own. I could see my path a little clearer now. I didn't need Gerard's help anymore. I didn't want to go with him. I'd see him and Dad and Nin when I was ready. But I wasn't ready now. I had things to do.

Now it was time to go. Something unexpected had clearly happened here. Something good. I'd leave again soon. But like Creeley and Duncan before me, something about Black Mountain had gotten under my skin and would stay. Maybe I didn't see Henry Miller's Asian mountains, and it wouldn't be right to call this a Shangri-La, but after Ruth and the Albers and Tom and Jane, and then especially after Prospero and the Storm, I knew I was bound to this place.

Jo was already home and changed into jeans and a shirt and hiking boots when I got back. She truly was a beautiful woman and I liked being with her. She didn't have the history with me that Anne had, but she was very easy to be with and we really were friends. I guess she could tell the day had gone well, because when she kissed me she smiled big and said, "You look happy. Your time with Ruth must have been good."

I said it had, then added I'd gone out to Lake Eden and that's why I was late getting back.

The evening was warm and clear so when she suggested we walk the fields, I was ready. The ground had been plowed and disked while I was gone. It was black and moist. Jo said her farmer would start planting next week. Corn mostly. Some soybeans. We held hands and she explained how this land had been in her family for four generations.

"I can tell you like it here."

"I do. I mean, I grew up here. And while I was at the university, I thought maybe I'd go on to a city and see what I could find there. Like Ruth did! But then Daddy got sick and they needed me. My brother was already in Raleigh with his own family. So it kind of fell to me to keep the place going. I don't mind, I guess..."

"What's your brother do?"

"Oh, he's a lawyer. He started in Raleigh, but now he works for the state of California. He's been out there for a while now. He's done very well. Daddy was proud he didn't have to be a farmer like he was. But when I came home and got the job at the library, we contracted with Frank Stubbs to crop our land. A few years ago his boy, Frank Jr., took over. They're good people. It's worked out well. We don't make a lot of money, but we've kept the land."

We'd been walking a lane that split fields and had almost reached the end where the woods began. I asked how much farther her property ran.

"A few hundred yards. Through the woods. Then there's Hickory Run. That splits our property from the Minshalls'."

The lane ended at the woods, but a well-worn path continued into this forest. A few steps in was already dark and cool and feeling old, reminding me of the Natahala woods. We stopped next to a huge tree, easily four feet or more across. She walked me to the side and pointed to an 'X' hacked into the bark, barely visible but unmistakable.

"When my great-granddaddy bought this land, he thought this had been an Indian trail and someone marked it. Of course, he was a quarter Indian so he must have known what he was talking about!" She laughed as she said this.

"He was?" I asked, although from the first time I saw her it seemed like Jo had Indian blood in her, her high cheekbones and beautiful skin tone lasting gifts from some ancestor.

"Yes. His grandmother was Cherokee. His grandfather fell in love with her when he first came to North Carolina. Then her family and the rest got forced out of their homes and moved to Oklahoma. She stayed behind with him."

"It looks like you inherited a lot of her beauty."

"Thank you, Jack. I wish I knew more about her. For a long time people were ashamed to say they were part Indian. But that's changing, I think."

We finished our walk at Hickory Run, a beautiful little stream running full and clear. It was about four or five feet wide with stepping stones to more woods on the other side. They were almost covered now, the spring water running high.

"When it's really hot I like to come here and just dip. It's very peaceful. The best way to stay cool!"

I smiled at the vision of her doing that. Maybe I'd do the same someday.

We turned and walked back to the house. It was almost dusk, but I could see better why Jo had stayed around. The way she talked about the farm, her family, this earth, those woods, this town. This was her blood. Even though her brother had left and made a good life elsewhere, and as much as she might have a longing to see more of the world as Ruth and I had, this was her home, her roots, where she gained both energy and comfort. Where she felt planted and part of a community. One that she would share with the right man. And I knew she was thinking she hoped it might be me. And I know Ruth was too. But she also knew I had to go other places. Maybe I'd come back to her. Maybe.

Jo and I spent Saturday afternoon and evening with Ruth. At 70 she had lived through two world wars, a worldwide depression, the birth of movies, radio and TV, as well as the atom bomb and Cold War, the end of Jim Crow, and landing men on the moon. As she said that night, "Children, sometimes I feel as though I have lived three lives! How much can a body take?" She laughed as she said it, but there was something else in her voice I couldn't quite put my finger on. I told Jo about the deal she made with me on the book and I asked if there was any reason, like a medical one, that would move Ruth to push me to have it written by year's end. Jo then confided that she knew Ruth had been going to the doctor fairly regularly, but she didn't know what for.

By Monday, I'd made up my mind: I'd leave for San Francisco in two weeks. That meant sending letters right away to all the people I wanted to see on the way out. Wanted them to know I was coming and why and hoped they'd send me something saying OK before I left. I also wrote Memere and Stella a letter telling them a little more of what I'd been doing, where

I'd been. I didn't say anything about when I'd be back in St. Pete.

Then I figured I'd better make copies for myself and extra sets for Ruth and Jo in case they heard from someone after I left. So I drove to the library in the afternoon to use their copying machine. When I walked in it seemed the place was even quieter than normal. No one was at the front desk. I heard a little noise coming from the office area and wandered back there looking for Jo. I peeked in and saw her and a few other women huddled around a small TV set. I knocked lightly on the door and when they turned, all had tears in their eyes.

What the...?

No one said a word, but Jo motioned me over to the TV. There a newsman was reporting on something big, but I didn't quite catch it at first. The screen showed students protesting, nothing new about that. Then tear gas canisters in a crowd. I heard "Kent State" and "Ohio" and "students killed." Jesus Christ! What the hell was going on?

I leaned in closer and started to get the story. There had been protests against Nixon's invasion of Cambodia that started the previous week and built up over the weekend. The protests didn't surprise me. They'd been going on for years. But what could they've done to provoke shootings? And who shot them? Where was Kent State?

At the commercial break everyone started talking through their tears asking the same questions. Jo looked at me wanting a hug, but kept her distance. Instead, she asked if I needed help and I mumbled something about copies and held out my folder. But then I asked what happened, pointing to the TV set, and everyone started talking again.

"They shot them!"

"The National Guard killed four students!"

"At Kent State University."

"Ohio. Near Cleveland."

"They were protesting the invasion, and the National Guard was on this hill. Then they shot right into the crowd!"

"Nine wounded. Four dead!"

"They killed the kids. They were unarmed. They just turned and shot. In *cold blood.* Why?"

The last question hung, suspended like smoke on the TV screen. The women looked at me as though I might have an answer, and of course I did not. I just felt sick.

The rest of the afternoon blurred. I got my copies, mailed the letters and went back to the farm to wait for Jo. Earlier I'd thought about swinging by Lissa's shop to see if she was around. But now I just wanted to go someplace and sit and think and not try to explain what seemed inexplicable. What had the protesters been doing that would've provoked gunfire? Had someone in the crowd fired first? Had they attacked the Guardsmen? Why Kent State, a quiet university in the Midwest that I'd barely heard of?

When she got home a couple hours later, I could see she was exhausted by the news and the tears and the fears. I just held her for a long time, both of us silent. Finally, she spoke.

"Jack, this is so awful, I don't know what to say. A couple of our high school kids came and they looked scared. I just wanted to hug them."

I didn't know what to say. I thought back again to that New Haven meeting I'd stumbled on and all the talk about how to organize their demonstrations. Then the Cambodia invasion. Then the protests escalating fast to a crescendo all across the country. And now this. I wondered if this would scare the anti-war movement into silence. Would this mean the government would shoot again, if necessary, to end the protests? Had the United States dropped the veil of democracy and bared the fangs of fascism?

For the first time in a long time, I wished I were with Allen. He might not have any better answers than I did, but he'd give vent to our shared emotions.

All these thoughts had run through my mind while we sat on Jo's porch looking out at black fields. But I didn't want to upset her any more so I just kept silent. For now, it was enough to just let Jo talk. And she did, not having any more information really, but asking the same question echoed around the country that night: Why?

We turned to the TV and Walter Cronkite for answers. He didn't have any. But we saw the footage again. The crowd. The tear gas. The Guardsmen. The shots. Chaos. Quiet. Just as he had at JFK's assassination, then King's, then Robert Kennedy's, he too struggled for understanding, his calm, Uncle Walter way of talking not hiding well the grief and anger in his voice and eyes.

What was the country coming to? What was I going to find in a week or so when I set out to Ohio? Were we going to be under martial law? Would there be open rebellion? Was Nixon savage enough to suppress dissent even as he risked nuclear war with his crazy talk of "peace through honor"? Jo and I tried talking through questions and it didn't do anything but make us crazier. Exhausted, she realized she'd forgotten someone.

"I should call Ruth. I can't believe I didn't think to do that earlier."

While they talked I opened my journal and made some half-assed notes about what happened that day. Crazy things not making a whole lot of sense, some way to get down on paper the anger and despair I felt. It made my book project feel silly and important at the same time. What were Black Mountain's lofty ideals when the government could shoot them down at will? I wondered if Josef and Anni were shuddering again, dark memories of Berlin resurrected.

The next day brought news of students striking across the country. It also brought reports of many people saying what the National Guard did was right. I stopped at Jump's clothing store for a few things. The guy at the counter, might've been Jump himself for all I know, very pleasant, smiley, porcine, made small talk as he rang me up.

"Quite a thing happened up in O-hi-o yesterday."

"Yeah."

"Them kids got themselves a lesson, I 'spect."

"Yeah."

"You don't mess with the National Guard. You go about tryin' to tear the country down, don't be surprised if someone might take a shot at you."

"Yeah."

"Reckon that'll quiet things down a bit. Heh-heh."

"Yeah."

"That'll be six dollars and thirty-seven cents."

That was the last time I was in Jump's.

We had dinner with Ruth that night. The events seemed to have sucked the energy out of her too. It was a quiet evening. We tried talking about the book, but kept turning back to the shootings and wondering what it all meant. When we left, Ruth gave me a hug like she was hanging on. Her eyes were weary. Maybe mine were too.

"Jack, if you feel like you have some other writing to do, don't feel obligated to me or this book."

"Ruth, I know what you're saying. Truth is, who knows what I'll find when I get to Cleveland. But I've gotta try."

And that's what I did. A week later I left Black Mountain, letters from eight of the college's former students in hand.

The day before I left I met with Ruth and showed her the letters I'd gotten back and how I'd travel to San Francisco. She surprised with me an envelope that contained the first two-thousand-dollar payment on the book. I hadn't even spent close to the first five hundred she'd given me. I'd be traveling with more money in my pocket than I ever had. She also said something I've never forgotten.

"Jack, there is something different about you. Since you came back, I can't quite put my finger on it, but I do believe you are a changed man. For the better, I might add." With that and a hug and kiss on the cheek she sent me on my way with a promise to write regularly and come back soon.

Jo and I also said our goodbyes. We had become real friends, liking each other's company as much as we enjoyed the sex. Yet not once did we talk of being together in San Francisco. Her home was Black Mountain. Mine was there. Or would be, hopefully, once I got settled. But we'd talked enough of the book that she knew I'd be back. I had no idea of how the women part of my life was going to settle out. But because of Jo and Anne, I felt I could be a better partner.

I got to Cleveland a couple days after that and met with my first Black Mountain alum, a woman who'd been there in the late forties and early fifties. She now lived in Shaker Heights and taught art at Cleveland Heights High School. She remembered her years at the college with a big smile and stories. She also gave me two more names and addresses of former students with whom she'd made lifelong friendships. Then we talked about the unavoidable...the shootings. There was sadness and anger in her voice. "I have never been one for politics. It's just a waste. But this war is so wrong. And what they did to those kids is so wrong. Maybe it's time I did something. This is my country too."

The next day I drove down to Kent to see for myself. Stores were boarded up where windows had been smashed the weekend before the shootings. The campus was closed, as were many across the country. There were a few people like myself wandering around looking at the hill where the Guardsmen fired and the buildings below where students gathered as though it were a Gettysburg-like battlefield. There was nothing unusual about the rest of the campus or the town. It was ordinary Middle America. Where working-class kids came for education and business degrees and then moved on into middle class jobs. It was eerily quiet, still shocked by the war that came to its streets and blasted holes through its small town doors.

I went back to Cleveland and its steel mills and auto plants and narrow frame houses covered with the soot of sweaty industry. One morning I drove down to the lakefront and the Cuyahoga River. The year before, choked with debris and pushed to the banks by freighters and tug boats, it had caught fire on its own, and the city became the butt of Johnny Carson jokes. That same year race riots set fire to another part of town. This was an even darker time. I stood in the dawn light looking out at the blank lake a long while, gulls squawking overhead, and then I got the hell out.

Epilogue

I write here for those who've shared this journey so far and care about all the great people.

Despite the darkness that Nixon and Vietnam brought into my life and the lives of millions of others, the light from Jo and Anne and Ruth and Prospero and even Gerard outshone all the other crap. I made it to San Francisco after several stops along the way to talk to the former Black Mountain students. And, as expected, they gave me more names and places to go. I didn't finish the book by the end of the year as Ruth and I had hoped. But I finally delivered her a finished manuscript in the Fall of 1971. It was good and I watched as tears came to her eyes as we went through the stories I had collected. I left it to her to find a publisher.

Jo and I continued our bonding and that too was good. But I only saw her during the times when I came to Black Mountain to show Ruth where I was with the book. She seemed content to see me on that limited basis. Although she asked many questions about San Francisco, she never asked to come out for a visit. It was as though that was an unspoken part of our relationship. She was rooted in her Black Mountain and would never move. I was living in San Francisco, but always on the move. And so we accepted the physical and geographical limits on our relationship as just what they were.

I sent Anne postcards from "Suze and Jerry" as I traveled around. When I chanced a visit to New York City to see Black Mountain students, I was tempted to give her a call or even drive down to Westfield. But just as it was when I left New Haven and the Albers that day, it seemed like dropping into her world unannounced like that would be a dumb thing to do. And, of course, I couldn't put my address on a postcard for her to write back.

I wrote Memere and Stella regularly to let them know I was all right and had found a place to stay "temporarily" in San Francisco. I never told them about Black Mountain or Ruth or the book. I had to be content with their knowing I hadn't gone off the deep end again. Stella wrote me back, and so it seemed like they had adjusted to my being gone, if not for good, at least for a long while.

As it turned out, I didn't have to worry about being recognized in San Francisco as much as I thought I would. I found a nice little apartment in the Castro district. It was quiet and nobody bothered me. Once, maybe two times, someone would stop me and say "Hey, aren't you that writer...Jack Kerouac?" I would just back away blankly and ask "Who?" And that was enough to put an end to that. Of course, I had to stay away from City Lights Books and the jazz places we loved to go to. But that turned out to be OK too. I was plenty busy.

All through the rest of 1970 and 1971 I wasn't in town for long stretches of time. I traveled a lot. Mostly to find and interview Black Mountain folks and an occasional teacher. So I got to see great parts of this country which I'd never seen before. The growing miles of interstates made that easier. America had grown, yet I took time to get off the highways onto the slower roads through the smaller towns.

I don't want to dwell too much on the politics of that time. The Kent State shootings were bad and followed by others at Jackson State. It seemed like the gap between young and old just grew wider and wider. The music grew angrier. Drugs had always been around. But now they seemed to be in a lot more places. I'll just say that war and that president were taking the country to places it had never been before.

Then in the spring of 1972 my world started to change again. I got a call from Jo asking me to hurry back to Black Mountain. Ruth was very sick. This time I flew back, Jo making the drive to Atlanta to pick me up. It turns out Ruth had been fighting a cancer when we first met, although at the time only Bessie knew.

At Christmas Ruth had confided in Jo that what had been in remission had returned and was aggressive. Ruth was getting things in order and she was leaving her a good sum of money. By the time Jo called, Ruth was in the hospital and not expected to leave. We got there in time for a last visit. She smiled when she saw me, squeezed my hand and whispered, "Jack. You did well. The book. Find a home for it."

She died the next day. I stayed through the funeral, shared with the whole town. And I hung around a few more weeks with Jo. When she drove me to the airport she asked me when I was coming back, and I said, "I don't know for sure. Whenever you want me, I guess." And while that was not the end of our relationship, it turned out to be the beginning of the end.

That fall I got another surprise. A letter from Anne. Somehow she had found my address. It was a short letter with bits of news about her children, her singing, and how she'd been back to the Cape. And then at the very end she wrote that she and Jay were divorcing. No more than that. But it was enough. And that is a big part of what I have to write about next.

Notes:

Under the publishers' "fair practice" agreement, we acknowledge use of short quotations from the following publications in this book:

Robert Frost, "The Gift Outright," in *Robert Frost's Poems* (Washington Square Press 1969); Charles Olson from *Call Me Ishmael* (Reynal & Hitchcock 1947); Allen Ginsberg, "Howl" and "Sunflower Sutra," in *Collected Poems 1947-1980* (Harper & Row 1984); Robert Creeley, "Place," in *Thirty Things* (Black Sparrow Press 1976); Walt Whitman, from "Song of the Open Road," in *Leaves of Grass* (Paddington Press Ltd 1976); Henry Beston, from *The Outermost House* (Holt, Henry & Company 2013); W. B. Yeats, from "The Rising of the Moon" in *The Collected Poems of W.B. Yeats* (MacMillan 1989); Herman Melville, from "Ch. 57" *Moby-Dick; or, The Whale* (1851); Jack Kerouac, "Beginning with a Few Haikus" and "Bus East," in *Pomes All Sizes* (City Lights Books 1992).

56T

About the Author

Kurt Landefeld was born in San Francisco and moved next to Rocky River, Ohio, where he attended high school. He considers San Francisco his second home. Prior to becoming an award-winning writer and creative director in the advertising industry, he spent several post-college years working as a machinist in and around Toledo.

At Bucknell University he was introduced to Jack Kerouac's writing, as well as the poetry of Allen Ginsberg, Charles Olson, Robert Creeley and others, and has declared, "They changed the way America saw itself in the last half of the 20th century." Of this novel, he has said, "As with millions of others, the lyricism and wildness of *On the Road* fired my imagination decades ago and continued to do so through my life. As I read more of Jack's novels and poetry, the question of 'What if he hadn't died so young?' has both intrigued and haunted. I decided to try and answer the question myself. What has resulted is an American story about second chances and the possibility of redemption."

In addition to his own writing, Landefeld has helped launch a children's book publishing company, VanitaBooks, in 2006. He has edited a debut novel from Newburn Drive Press and a volume of poetry. Active in political and community affairs, as well as the local writing scene, he lives with his wife Carol and dog Jack on the shores of Lake Erie in Huron, Ohio.

Bottom Dog Press

Books in the Harmony Series

Jack's Memoirs: Off the Road
By Kurt Landefeld, 590 pgs. $19.95
Daughters of the Grasslands: A Memoir
By Mary Woster Haug, 200 pgs. $18
Lake Winds: Poems
By Larry Smith, 218 pgs. $18
An Act of Courage: Selected Poems of Mort Krahling
Eds. Judy Platz & Brooke Horvath, 104 pgs. $16
On the Flyleaf: Poems
By Herbert Woodward Martin, 104 pgs. $16
The Stolen Child: A Novel
By Suzanne Kelly, 350 pgs. $18
The Harmonist at Nightfall: Poems of Indiana
By Shari Wagner, 114 pgs. $16
Painting Bridges: A Novel
By Patricia Averbach, 234 pgs. $18
Ariadne & Other Poems
By Ingrid Swanberg, 120 pgs. $16
Kenneth Patchen: Rebel Poet in America
By Larry Smith, Revised 2nd Edition, 326 pgs. Cloth $28
Selected Correspondence of Kenneth Patchen,
Edited with introduction by Allen Frost,
312 pgs. Paper $18/ Cloth $28
Awash with Roses: Collected Love Poems of Kenneth Patchen
Eds. Laura Smith and Larry Smith
Introduction by Larry Smith, 200 pgs. $16

* * * *

Harmony Collections and Anthologies

Come Together: Imagine Peace
Eds. Ann Smith, Larry Smith, Philip Metres, 204 pgs. $16
Evensong: Contemporary American Poets on Spirituality
Eds. Gerry LaFemina and Chad Prevost, 240 pgs. $16
America Zen: A Gathering of Poets
Eds. Ray McNiece and Larry Smith, 224 pgs. $16
Family Matters: Poems of Our Families
Eds. Ann Smith and Larry Smith, 232 pgs. $16

Bottom Dog Press, Inc.
PO Box 425/ Huron, Ohio 44839
http://smithdocs.net

CPSIA information can be obtained
at www.ICGtesting.com
Printed in the USA
FFOW01n1730171214
9552FF

9 781933 964911